The Dan Roy Series

Books 1-3
Dan Roy Series Boxed Set

Mick Bose

I would love to hear from you, so please feel free to visit my FB author page - https://www.facebook.com/WriterMickBose

My website - https://www.mickbose.com

or write to me at mick@mickbose.com.

If you want advance notice of a new title and other offers, then Join the readers' group. It's spam free and I will only contact you when I have a new release.

Join here - https://www.subscribepage.com/p6f4a1

Contents

Hellfire 1

Hidden Agenda 73

Dark Water 253

The Tonkin Protocol 411

HELLFIRE

A Novella

For ABx2 and MA

USS BASTION
ARABIAN SEA
FIFTY NAUTICAL MILES NORTH OF SOMALIA
PRESENT DAY

Dan Roy, ex-Sergeant of Squadron A, SFOD-D or Delta Force, jerked awake as his head hit something hard.

Instantly, he was awake. Out of reflex his right hand slid under his pillow, and his fingers curled around the grained butt of his trusted Sig P226. In a flash, his elbow was ramrod straight, the gun pointing out. His arm moved around, scanning.

A few human beings have full awareness when their eyes open from deep slumber. Dan was one of them. It was one of the reasons why he was chosen to do the job he did.

Even then, awareness consisted of sights, sounds, and the signals the brain received and processed in microseconds. The reality might not sink in, but just like a ball player who connects at the mere hint of a speeding shape, Dan recognized an alien atmosphere almost by instinct.

He did not know where he was, but he knew he was somewhere different to the night before. And that could be dangerous. Lethal. The risk could be right in front of him, and he had survived this long by neutralizing those risks.

He felt bright light on his eyes, and cold steel against his forehead. A bunk bed. His body moved again, forwards, then back. A rolling motion. He smelled clean cotton sheets. The sense of olfaction is the oldest one. It reminded him of another life. As a child in Bethesda, West Virginia, rolling around in his comfy bed at home.

He lowered the gun and squinted. Sunlight poured in through the round hole of the cabin window. He rubbed his eyes. The cord-like muscles on his neck rippled as he flexed his neck. He yawned and swung his legs out of the bunk.

He was in a ship's cabin. He could see that much. Dan rested his massive shoulders by putting his elbows on his knees. His large, paw-like hands, the skin on them gnarled and thick from holding an assortment of light and heavy weapons, drooped towards the floor. He stared in the same direction.

Last night's memory started to come back to him. He had been flown from Djibouti in the Horn of Africa to a town on the coast of Somalia. A place called Bosaso. Not far from the tip of the Horn, and overlooking the Gulf of Aden. The channel of international pirates.

5

In Bosaso, he had neutralized the chief bomb maker of the local chapter of Al-Shabaab. It had been a long-range shot from nine hundred meters away. The extraction had been tricky, as the boat waiting for him had come under sustained fire from a pirate dhow loyal to the terrorists.

Once the 0.50-caliber Browning machine gun on the boat had started chattering, the dhow had ceased to be an issue.

And here he was. Nudging off the coast of Somalia, in the Arabian Sea, just one hundred nautical miles away from the Gulf of Aden. Aboard the latest edition of an American aircraft carrier. All eight billion dollars' worth of it.

Dan stood up. He felt slightly nauseous. The roll in the cabin, mild as it was, did not help. He went out the door and walked down the narrow hallway, stopping to say hello to a blue-uniformed US Navy serviceman. In the bathroom, he splashed water on his face and looked in the mirror. A square-jawed, brown-eyed face looked back at him. Not handsome. Not ugly. But one that had won admirers from the opposite sex. He rubbed water in his hair.

At thirty-four, he did not feel old. Served with Delta for last five years, then tapped on the shoulder to join a new outfit. An outfit so secret that even his own Delta brethren did not know about it. And those that did were sworn to secrecy.

Intercept. An organization with an executive arm that went straight to the highest echelons of power in Capitol Hill. An organization that was used when all else had failed, and a mission needed to be accomplished with the minimum of fuss.

That meant not getting caught. If he did get caught, then being captured and questioned was not an option. Silence was forever guaranteed. If that guarantee was not kept by Intercept operatives, then it would be enforced.

Dan looked away from the mirror. He didn't like looking at himself when that question bubbled up to the surface of his mind.

Why?

Why did he leave the Army to join Intercept? To undertake the most dangerous missions of his life, separated from his brethren?

He missed the banter of Army life. The comradery. But he did not miss the bureaucracy of the Army. The endless infighting. The often deplorable way that soldiers were treated.

In his new role, he was given a problem, and he had to eliminate it. No questions asked, no answers given. He had to admit it. The thrill of the fight was the reason why he had become a warfighter. With Intercept, he was able to take that life to a new level.

It was an answer he found strange. Of why he felt so calm with the enemy's head in the cross hairs of his rifle sight. Why he relished CQB, close quarters battle, to the extent that he did. Especially with his kukri knife, the curved, 16-inch blade beloved of the Gurkha warrior.

Dan shook his head once and toweled his face dry. Introspection was not always useful, and often frustrating. He was who he was.

A warrior. Most days, that was enough.

Dan walked back to his small cabin. He had to search for it, inside the labyrinthine deck levels of the massive ship, it was easy to get lost.

He found new cams on the bed. They were dusty yellow, not much different from the ones they had before. He struggled into them, as usual. At six feet, he clocked in at two hundred and twenty pounds. The width of his shoulders and chest accounted for that.

There was a chirp from the desk next to the wardrobe. Dan stepped to it, and saw a small cellphone with a green light flashing on it. He picked it up and answered.

"Who's this?"

"My name is Tom Slater, Dan. I work for Intercept." He did not recognize the voice. Another faceless official. He didn't care. The person obviously knew who he was. Dan waited for the person to speak.

"Briefing in ten minutes, CO's office," Slater said.

The Commanding Officer was Gary "Gaz" Peterson, US Navy Strike Force Six. There was a good chance the CO would not be there, and the room had been taken over by Intercept for the briefing. Intercept had enough clout to do that, but Dan surmised the US Navy would be happier with their own Special Ops guys, the DEVGRU and Navy SEALs.

Once again, he could not help wondering why he was there.

CHAPTER 1

The two men descended into the depths of the massive floating citadel. Tom Slater led the way. He looked middle-aged, and tired. Another CIA agent pulled in from his day job to provide intel on a clandestine mission, Dan thought.

The steel door of the CO's office was shut, and Tom rapped on it. An officer opened the door, nodded to them and stepped aside. Dan saw the bank of monitors against one wall, and the three big screens on the other.

On two of the monitors he could see a grainy image of a mud-walled compound. The monitor next to it had a map of Southeast Asia. One of the three large screens on the wall held a live image of a man in desert combat uniform. He was in his late-fifties, with pinched, sallow cheeks, sharp blue eyes and buzz cut silvery hair. Dan would have known Major John Guptill's face anywhere in the world.

He had been Dan's first mentor when Dan joined the Delta Force, from the 75th US Rangers Battalion. And he had been Dan's trainer when Dan had been the first one in his team to complete the last stage of Delta selection. That involved a forty-mile hike with full kit through the highest mountains of the Appalachian range. When Dan collapsed at the final station, he had asked Major Guptill for a drink. Guptill had eyed him coldly.

"Get it yourself," he said. "First operation begins in forty-eight hours." With that, he had turned and left his protégé on the floor, dying of thirst. Dan had to hike another two miles to get a jug of water from the nearest canteen.

An AV technician appeared and fitted the men with microphones, and showed them their seats in front of a camera. Guy Peterson stepped out of the shadows. He nodded stiffly at Dan, then stared at Guptill on the screen. The screen next to Guptill flickered to life. A clear image came on, of a shorter man in combat uniform, with salt-and-pepper hair.

Peterson appeared to know him. He turned to the screen and said, "Is it time to start the brief, Colonel McBride?"

Dan had heard of Lieutenant Colonel Jim "Fighter" McBride, one of the men who led the JSOC. It was the first time he was seeing the man.

"Hey, Gaz," McBride said in an even voice. "Hey, Guppy." Guptill nodded at them from the screen.

"You guys all set?" McBride asked the team. They all nodded and exchanged greetings. All knew one another from recent operations.

Then there was a silence. McBride cleared his throat and looked at Guy Peterson. So did Guptill.

"I am sorry, Gaz," McBride said quietly.

Peterson looked irritated. "What?" he demanded in a rough voice.

"This is for USSOCOM- and CIA-cleared personnel only."

"You are on-board my ship, Lieutenant. Have you forgotten that? I have a right to know."

McBride shook his head slightly. "I am sorry, Gaz. This comes from O'Toole in MacDill."

Dan sat up straighter. MacDill Air Force Base in Florida was the HQ of USSOCOM. O'Toole was the Command Sergeant Major and a National Security Advisor.

Dan stayed quiet. Gary Peterson stood up. He looked at Dan, then at his commanders on the screen. His eyes were scathing.

"I can promise you one thing, Lieutenant," Peterson said. "If my men or this ship is compromised in any way, then O'Toole will get a direct call from the President. Do you understand?"

McBride kept his face impassive. Dan knew from the man's reputation that he did not take threats casually. But he had a job to do. Not much space to do it in.

"I got that, Gaz," McBride said, keeping his eyes level with Peterson. The CO turned and stormed out of the room. His officer and the technician followed.

"We all alone?" Guptill asked from the screen.

"Yes," Dan said.

"Right," McBride took over. "We have a situation near a town in Afghanistan called Surobi. It's located along the Kabul-Jalalabad Highway, on the banks of the Kabul River. This is northern 'Stan, gentlemen." Many soldiers called Afghanistan by this nickname. McBride continued.

"Twenty klicks outside Surobi, in a village called Mumtaz, we have three CIA SOG men holed up with an Iranian national. This person is defecting to the West. They made it from Herat, up north near the Iranian border in the east, down to here, but then their luck ran out. An Afghan contingent was helping them. They came down by road. They were supposed to take the highway through into Pakistan, and travel to the nearest city in Pakistan, called Peshawar. There is a US Consulate office there. But they woke up one morning and found their compound surrounded by the Taliban."

Guptill said, "The compound is a former police station. It was taken over by Para 1 Company of the British Army. They held it till the CIA guys arrived, then they exfiltrated." Dan knew of the elite Parachute Regiment, which had three Companies.

"Why don't the Para 1 guys go back?" Dan asked.

"Operational reasons," Guptill said. "The enemy have launched a major offensive in the small towns around Surobi. Para 1 need to relieve two Infantry Regiments who have taken heavy casualties."

"You don't have any special forces in northern 'Stan already?"

"Yes, we do," McBride said. "But none with the experience you have of northern 'Stan. You have worked in tough situations up there. Remember the Delta push into Tora Bora? That's why you are here."

Dan did remember the mission into Tora Bora mountains, looking for bin Laden. Intel got it wrong that time. The terrorist had already fled. Dan and his unit had chased after them. Dan was part of Delta Squadron B then, and his actions had won him a Bronze Star.

Not being able to find bin Laden that time had weighed heavily on his mind. For him, it had been a failed mission. Now, his pulse quickened at McBride's words. Would he be able to make amends on this occasion?

McBride clicked some buttons on the desk in front of him, and pointed to the bank of monitors. The map of Southeast Asia focused on the Arabian Sea and the Pakistan sea port of Karachi, then zoomed further up towards the border with Afghanistan. On the other screen, satellite images of the compound flashed up.

McBride said, "You will be dropped off at the Landing Zone ten klicks outside the compound under cover of night. Mission is to storm the compound, retrieve the CIA guys and the Iranian, then escape to the LZ. Exfil by Close Air Support from Bagram Air Base."

Dan pointed to the screen. "This is a large compound, sir. Seventy meters wide, going by the scale."

Guptill said, "You will have two CIA operatives in there, who are assets, I am told. Plus you have the Afghan National Police to help you."

Help is not what Dan would call it himself. His experience of the ANP had never been a positive one. But he kept his thoughts to himself.

"One thing, son," McBride said. Something in his voice made Dan look up at the screen. "It is mission critical to have the Iranian alive. For reasons I cannot go into. Roger that?"

Dan nodded in silence.

Guptill said, "Pack your bags. Your ride is waiting on deck."

CHAPTER 2

The flight desk was noisy even with his headphones on.

It was 1000 hours. The sun off the coast of Somalia was blinding.

Dan heard some shouts and looked up. Yellow-jacketed flight support staff were lined up in the distance along the runway. They wore red helmets and face wrap goggles. Dan could hear the F/A-18E Super Hornet jet gearing up for take-off, the swarm of men around it and the buzz of the engine getting louder by the minute.

The F/A-18E was one of four strike fighter squadrons that made their sea home on-board the massive aircraft carrier. Each squadron had eleven planes, which made forty-four anti-air and land strike fighter jets the ship carried.

On top of that, it had five EA-18G "Growler" electronic fighter jets designed to jam enemy radio, radar and GPS, and three whole squadrons of MH-60, Sea Knight and Raptor helicopters.

Together with the transport planes, more than seventy aircraft made a nest in this giant, floating city. No less than 6,000 men and women worked round-the-clock to keep it functioning.

The F/A-18E boomed and ran down the runway. The ground shook beneath Dan's feet, rattling every bone in his body. Everyone on deck flinched as the jet's rear emissions hit them, even from a distance. The plane rose up in the sky, doing a salute around the ship. The yellow jackets cheered and waved at it. Then the jet zoomed off, becoming a speck on the endless horizon within seconds.

Dan felt the salty mist of the Arabian Sea on his face. His sixty-pound bag was on his shoulders already. The helmet was on his head, with the NVGs attached on top. The sides of the helmet were cut off to make room for his earphones. A mic hung over his lower lip. An M4 carbine was attached by the belt to his waist, the same belt he would use to clip himself to the safety lanyard on the plane. Strapped to the Kevlar vest on his chest he had his trusted Sig P226 handgun. Three flashbangs and three frags on the belt line.

On the back, in a black leather scabbard, his trusted 16-inch kukri knife. Designed to chop limbs and tree branches with equal ease. Apart from the firearms, it was his weapon of choice.

Dan looked around at the mad rush of men. There was a rumbling sound behind him. Their transport had arrived. The C-2A twin jet Greyhound cargo aircraft was definitely the most pedestrian of all the aircraft the USS *Bastion* carried. As usual, flight support men gathered round the plane, getting it ready for flight.

Tom Slater, the intelligence guy, gave Dan a thumbs-up as he walked past. Dan barely acknowledged him. He worked alone. He did not have time for small talk, especially with someone who looked like they could faint at the sight of blood.

Slater got his ears close to Dan's, the only way to have a conversation on the flight deck.

"When we boarding?"

Dan held up five fingers, then moved away.

With their luggage, extra kit and ammo safely stashed on the C-2A, Dan strapped himself to the safety lanyard and sat back on the hard bench of the aircraft. They had a three-hour flight to the US Air Force Support Base in Muscat, capital of Oman. From there another flight would take them to Bagram Air Base near Kabul. Reflexively, Dan's fingers went to his radio for the comms check. Then he relaxed. They would not be operational till they got to Bagram. He closed his eyes.

Although getting back into north Afghanistan would give him a chance to lay old ghosts to rest, something about the mission bothered him. His eyes opened.

Someone had dropped the CIA guys and their asset into this mess. No way they could wake up the day after and see Taliban crawling around. They were expected.

In any case, he thought to himself, what the hell was an Iranian doing in Afghanistan with the CIA? Far from home, wasn't she?

The plane rumbled down the ship's runway. The ground crew waved at him, and he waved back.

*****

Mariam Panahi looked around the mud walls of her room, and the brittle wooden sticks that served as the grills for the square window.

The window was merely a hole in the wall, and it looked out into the moonlit compound. The air was dry and bright, what she had expected here. It was not far from her home town of Mashhad in Iran. She had been working in the Iranian town of Arak before that. There, too, the weather was now dry and cold.

13

The compound was large, and it formed a perimeter around the huts scattered at its edges. The Afghan policemen and the two white men had been kind to her so far. She had received the largest room in the enclave where they made their home. The compound was rectangular in shape. The mud walls were two meters thick and three meters high. A massive wooden door, three meters high, guarded the main entrance.

They had entered in the middle of the night, and she had not seen the village outside the gates. She had heard the gunfire the next day, and then the blast of the grenades as they had been lobbed into the compound. The older CIA guy in charge, Roderick Sparks, had told her to stay in her room. The fighting had not let up, and she knew at least two of the six Afghans traveling with them had died.

Her thoughts went back to the mad dash in the middle of the night from Mashhad to Islām Qala, the border town between Mashhad in Iran and Herat in Afghanistan.

At the guest house in Islām Qala, the heavily armed policemen had taken money from Roderick, the senior CIA agent.

Mariam had boarded one of the three Range Rovers with the two CIA men and the Afghans, and the convoy had left for Herat. She had always wanted to see Herat. It was an ancient town, part of the Silk Route, and known in the Middle Ages for its wine. All they did in Herat was change to another Range Rover. Then they drove through the night again. Her car was always the middle one of the convoy. Checkpost after checkpost followed. The leader of the Afghan policemen traveling with them was a man called Faisal Ahmed.

When they were stopped, Ahmed gave the checkpost guards money, and they were waved through.

As she stared at the compound, silvery in the moonlight, Mariam wondered idly if she would ever see Mashhad again. The clerics there had got on her nerves. Islam was not her religion. But, like all women in Iran, she had to wear a headscarf. It was a pain in the neck for her. At least here she did not have to worry about that. She got up to make for the door, and take a stroll while she had the chance.

The sudden explosion knocked her off her feet, and she fell backwards.

CHAPTER 3

Dan lifted his rucksack onto the trembling floor of the Chinook and got on it. The tailgate was down and the rotors where whining, gathering up speed. He switched on the comms system, located the channel and spoke into his mic.

"Desert One, this is Zero," Dan said.

Zero was his call sign for this mission. After a brief crackle of static, the pilot fed back to him.

"Receiving, Zero. Strap in, we are due to take off."

"Roger that, Desert One." Dan said.

The whining of the rotor blades gathered steam, then became a blur as the sound rose to deafening. With a jolt, the bird rose in the air vertically. Then it dipped its nose like it was nodding to someone and speeded up, gaining height rapidly.

As they approached the LZ, Dan heard the Chinook flight maintenance crew on his earphone.

"Alpha, this is Desert One. Requesting confirmation of green light. Repeat, requesting confirmation of green light."

The flight crew was seeking last-minute confirmation from the secret Intercept base in Jalalabad Air Base, which had live satellite connections to the Intercept HQ in Virginia. After a pause, a familiar voice crackled in Dan's earpiece. It was Major Guptill.

"You are a Go, Desert One. I repeat, you are a Go. Good luck. Over and out."

Dan could see a panoply of stars studded like diamonds in the black sky overhead. In the distance, he could see the faint outline of mountain ranges.

In just over half an hour they had arrived.

"5 minutes to LZ," the flight attendant's voice came over on the mic. Dan checked his lanyard and equipment. As the ground rushed up, a vision of his last fight in the Tora Bora mountains flashed before his eyes. Then it was gone.

The bird banked steeply down, then turned left and right. Dan and the flight support crew wobbled in their seats. The maneuvering was to confuse any enemy waiting with their RPGs (rocket-propelled grenades) or any type of surface-to-air missile. No one forgot the somber story of the SEAL team whose Chinook had been brought down by a Taliban RPG.

A crew member waited near the tailgate. In a blaze of dust and sound the Chinook got closer to the ground. Dan flipped on his NVGs. These new NVGs gave him excellent peripheral vision. Everything around was instantly bathed in a green glow. The tailgate swung open to reveal a blizzard of dust, seen as a brown haze through the NVGs.

"Go, go!" the pilot shouted into his mic.

Dan scrambled out and disappeared into the cloud of dust as it swirled up around him. Not much of a cover, but one of the flight crew doubled up as a gunner with the 50-cal machine gun on-board. That would silence any small arms within an eight hundred-meter range. Dan wiped the dust from his goggles and ran to the side of the Chinook. A technician was at the other end, doing the same thing as him. Together, they unstrapped the quad bike that was fixed to the side of the Chinook.

Dan checked the quad's ignition, and the small carrier load on two wheels that was attached to it. Then he heard the other sound.

TAKTAKTAKTAKTAK.

Staccato burst of rifle fire.

The pilot screamed in his mic. "Contact!"

Dan left the quad bike and dived for the floor. His M4 was out in firing position, and he was scanning for the source of fire through the target sight mounted on the rail. The telescoping butt was firm against his right shoulder. Blood was pounding in his ears, and his breath came in gasps. Two rounds pinged against the body of the Chinook, their ricochet whining against his ears.

DAMDAMDAMDAMDAM

Dan swore as rounds whined over his head. The sound had changed from small arms to heavy machine gun fire. This was the worst situation imaginable. They were out in the open and taking fire from a hidden enemy.

Dan ran round to the other side, bullets kicking the dust around him. Then he saw it. He said to the pilot, "Two o'clock! Two o'clock! Muzzle flash in the bushes."

Dan knew the two-man crew on-board would be getting the 50-cal ready, to lay down suppressive fire. But that wouldn't be much good if the Chinook got hit in the fuselage. He knew that's what the enemy bullets were searching for.

He also knew they were in a semi-arid desert valley, surrounded by hills. He needed to get out of there, that's why he had the quad bike. But now his main worry was the Chinook getting hit.

Even if the flight crew escaped, the last thing he wanted was a fireball that lit them up perfectly.

He located the source, and returned fire. The SOPMOD or Special Operations Peculiar Modification M4 carbine roared in his ear. The muzzle flash from his rifle blinded Dan as he was wearing his NVGs. It could not be avoided. Clips of 5.56mm NATO ordnance flew out of the breech as he squeezed the trigger.

"I'm gonna paint this fucker," Dan growled on the mic. "Then take him out with the UGL. Before they spread out." UGL-underarm grenade launcher.

Dan saw the infrared targeting beam from his rifle point to a clump of trees to their right. The beam was only visible in the NVGs.

Dan scrambled around the back of the Chinook and ran forward. Bullets whined around him, inches from his feet.

Thirty meters out he threw himself on the ground again. Through his night sight he could now see them. Four insurgents in the trees. He could see their dark keffiyehs rolled up on their heads, and the chain of ammunition crossed on their chest. Two of them were leaning over a machine gun on a tripod. From experience, he guessed the machine gun was a DShK or Dushka, a Russian artillery gun. It was a heavy gun, much heavier than the 50-cal. If they got hit by this they were finished.

He breathed out and focused. His right index finger caressed the trigger.

BOP.

One insurgent's head exploded into a red mist.

BOP.

Another down. That took care of the two over the DShK. Dan took aim and fired liberally now, as the other two insurgents had taken cover. The presence of the DShK machine gun bothered him. They needed transport to get this here. This was a planned event. Not good.

Not good at all.

Dan reached down the barrel of his rifle, and used the UGL, or Underslung Grenade Launcher. The tree clump exploded in an orange glow. Two more grenades followed.

"Evacuate, evacuate," Dan screamed ion his mic. "I am covering."

The radio buzzed in his ear. The pilot sounded scared. "Zero, are you sure?

There could be more Tangos out there. I could stay."

Dan spoke fast, keeping his eyes on the burning trees. "Negative, Desert One. Right now, you are too big a target. The sooner you go, the better."

Dan switched to automatic mode and sprayed out a long burst of ordnance in the direction of the trees. There was no return fire.

The pilot said, "Roger that, Zero. See you soon, and take care."

"Amen to that, Desert One."

Dan looked behind him. In the green glow he could see the quad, powered up. He looked because he wanted to be sure of their position, because in a second everything would be invisible in a storm of dust.

The rotor wash from the Chinook pressed him down further as the big bird took off. The ground shook underneath him, and the dust storm felt like a blizzard. Within a minute the huge machine was airborne, and then rose swiftly up into the desert night sky.

Silence returned, save the crackle from the burning of the trees. It seemed as if he had got them all, Dan thought with satisfaction. But there would be more behind. He did not wait any longer. He ran to the quad, jumped on the seat, and pulled out into the cold night.

He had a GPS unit strapped to his wrist, showing him the map. He was twenty klicks out, and with the speed of the quad, and the bumpy terrain, Dan knew he had a one-hour ride ahead of him.

If the Taliban had bought the DShK in a pick-up truck, there could be a convoy of vehicles behind it. They came with headlights switched off, hence the Chinook flight crew had not seen it from above. They must have been setting up while they landed. If the Chinook had gone down, the Taliban would take photos in the morning, and Al Jazeera would beam them around the world.

But they had not counted on Dan being on-board.

Now, they could be following him. Eager for revenge.

Be grateful for what you receive, Dan thought grimly as his bike speeded in the icy night air. He could feel the radio antenna bobbing up and down on his back, along with the Semtex breach explosive attached below it. His nose and lips below the NVG were freezing.

It was just the start of a long night.

CHAPTER 4

Dan glanced briefly at the GPS. He was still headed in the right direction – southwest. Surobi was fifteen klicks away.

Dan strained his ears, his senses on overdrive. The desert night was silent apart from the groan of the quad. Any minute now, he expected to hear something else. The rattle of gun fire, or the roar of engines.

For now, all he had was the whistle of cold night air. The road ahead narrowed between two hills and the ground got softer. It slowed the bikes down. Dan realized where he was. A dry riverbed. A wadi, in Pashto. Sparse vegetation grew around them. Dan slowed down and killed his engine.

A desolate silence flowed in around him. Dan got off his bike, and ran backwards. He checked the trolley, and took off its tarpaulin cover. It contained the heavier weapons.

Minimi was the name for the Light Machine Gun, primed for 7.62mm NATO ordnance. The gun, with its adjustable bipod, was strapped down on the floor of the trolley, along with two ILAWs or Anti-Tank Light Armor Weapons.

Ideally, Dan would like the Minimi to be set up on top of a Weapon-Mounted Installation Kit, or WMIK, as the machine gun-armed Range Rovers were known. Intel had told him there was a WMIK inside the compound.

Dan was considering what to do when his thoughts were interrupted by the chirp of radio in his ears.

"Zero, this is Alpha, do you copy?" Major Guptill's voice, from HQ in Jalalabad Air Base.

"Roger that, Alpha," Dan said.

"You better get a move on. The compound is under attack. I repeat, the compound is under attack."

*****

Mariam lay still for a while, wondering if she was injured. The sound of gunfire and screams filled the air, shattering the silence of the night. All her limbs were moving. She sat up, then raised herself quickly. She saw the flash

19

of gunfire from her window, and another scream. She saw a figure fall from the compound wall, and land with a thud on the floor. Bullets streamed from one of the windows, and the body jerked around like a puppy on a string.

Mariam realized what was happening. The Taliban had launched an offensive. They were climbing over the walls. Fear turned her into cold ice. Including her, they were seven. Against how many? The door to her room opened suddenly. Mariam recoiled as a dark figure filled the doorway.

"It's me, Derek."

She sighed in relief. Derek Jones was the younger CIA agent. He reached forward, a black figure against a moonlit background, lit up sporadically by gunfire. Derek raised his voice.

"You fired a gun before?"

"No," Mariam said.

"Ok, look here." Derek stood beside her, pulled out a handgun and showed her how to use it.

"Anyone comes in that does not identify themselves, you fire at the chest. Not the head or legs, aim for the chest. Got that?"

Mariam held the gun in her hand, the warm butt snug against her palm. A Glock 22.

"Yes," she said. Derek took the Heckler & Koch 416 rifle off his back and started out the door again. He stopped and looked back at her. "And whatever you do, make sure you stay here."

A stream of gunfire swallowed up his words. Mariam watched as Derek slunk in the shadows, heading for one of the sangars, or raised wooden outposts on top of the compound wall. There was one in each corner, and one in the middle of the long walls. There was a sudden flash of yellow light, and an explosion rocked the compound. Mariam stumbled back inside her room. Her door had been flung open, and dust was pouring in, choking her.

*****

Five klicks out from the compound, Dan could hear the faint sound of explosions in the still night air. He speeded up. The sound of gunfire got louder as he approached. One klick out, Dan came to a stop. He had approached a small screen of trees. Behind it, Dan could see the dim outline of a single-story structure. It appeared deserted. He got out quickly, and used the night sight on his M4 to see. No movement around the structure, which looked like a concrete bunker. The sloping roof was broken in. In 'Stan, most of the buildings were made of mud. He had never seen a concrete structure like this before. He aimed further, and saw the clump of huts that signified the village of Mumtaz. The occasional flash of gunfire made the location even more obvious.

Directly in front of him, and further away, he could see the south wall of the compound. Through the night sight, he could see the wall had a sangar. But the sangar seemed empty. The fighting seemed to be concentrated at the north end. Dan could see why. That was where the village lay. Where the insurgents had most of their weapons.

The few huts to his left were like an outpost. But he could not be sure if they were occupied. If they were, then he could be in trouble. He had to cross almost seven hundred meters of open terrain, carrying the heavy weapons on his back. He wanted to hide the quad inside the bunker ahead of him. He could not get the quad inside, and leaving it by the wall meant it would fall into enemy hands.

The quad was also part of his route back to the LZ, if things went badly wrong, or if there weren't any WMIKs in the compound.

Dan settled down in the dust, and observed the concrete bunker for a while with his NVG. He saw a cat coming out, but nothing else. He rolled the quad bike down to the bunker. It was covered by weeds and bushes. The entrance had a small tree growing in front. He hacked away with his kukri and cleared some space.

He shone a light inside, finger on the trigger of his M4. An odd structure. Large windows at the rear, like they were made for sightseeing. On either side, concrete slabs like desks. Below them, he could see rusting old machines. They looked like old radios. Plants had grown between them.

He put the quad bike in one corner, and spent fifteen minutes covering it with branches and leaves.

Then he picked up the Minimi, and strapped it to his front. On his back went the ILAWs, twenty-five pounds each. He was now carrying almost eighty pounds in extra weight. It was going to slow him down. And it would make climbing up the ladder harder.

He adjusted his radio, and located the channel of the CIA team inside the compound. The buzz and static cleared, and he heard a humming sound.

CHAPTER 5

"Bravo, this is Zero, do you copy?" Dan repeated the message twice. Nothing but silence greeted his ears. He tried again after two minutes. Radio channels could be listened to easily. Anyone with a scanner and a set of microphones could hear what he was saying. It had always been a problem in 'Stan.

But the radio silence was a bigger problem for him now.

The CIA guys, with their asset, could be dead. In the fighting that was going on now. Dan had arrived too late.

His mission was over before it had started. But it also presented the possibility that he had to enter the compound and check for himself. Without it, he could never be sure. If the asset was alive, he had to bring her back.

Dan spoke again on the radio, and heard nothing but silence. He swore, then, with the weapons on his back, came out of the bunker.

Then he started to run on open ground. Directly ahead of him, he could see the walls of the compound. As the satellite images had shown, it was a large structure, about seventy-five meters wide.

Everything around him was bathed in a green hue. To the left of the compound he could make out several single-story mud huts. A few of them were on an elevation. Dan caught the sound of fire, and briefly saw a muzzle flash. It came again, and he knew with certainty he had found the source of the machine gun fire that was aimed at the compound.

The whine of the bullet caught him off guard.

More rounds followed and he threw himself to the ground. Breath left his chest as the heavy weapons pressed on his back. He heard a round go into something metallic above him and ping off. The round must have hit one of the ILAW covers.

Dan turned around. Another round whistled over his head, way above. Someone was shooting at him, but they had got lucky. Maybe they had seen something move in the dark. That was the danger with open ground.

Dan could set the bipod up, aim the Minimi and be blasting away in a couple of minutes. But that would give his position away. In this open terrain, he could be pinned down with heavy fire.

A few more rounds came his way. He used the ILAW as his shield and watched, staying motionless. He located it eventually. The clump of huts next to the compound. The ones he had noticed before setting off. As he had feared, they were guard outposts.

Now the scumbags had seen him. They could not see much more, as he was lying still now. They did not have NVGs, or IR night sights on their AK-47s. Dan put the seventeen-pound steel case that held the Light Machine Gun, Minimi, on his back, and slithered along the ground, leaving the heavy weapons out in the open. It was the best he could do for now. He could not take them and run. They would weigh him down. But neither could he leave the threat as it was.

Like every threat, it had to be neutralized. That was the way he operated.

Dan got up and ran, heading for the shape of a single-story building to the left of the main residential huts of the village. It was close to him. Less than a hundred meters. He ran tactically. Crouched for one minute. Run. Drop and assess. Repeat.

He had already clocked the building as empty. Unusually for a building out in the open in 'Stan, it seemed to be made of concrete. Like the bunker where he had stored his bike.

He could not detect any movement in his NVGs. But he could not take any chances. He unhooked a frag grenade from his belt. Twenty meters out, he went flat on the cold ground. He gave himself five seconds. The sound of more fire, directed to the spot he had just run from. He needed to get into this building, and see if he could use it as a lying-up point.

Getting in through the heavy main doors of the compound was out of the question – the heavy machine gun fire was aimed at it.

Five seconds gone.

Grenade in hand, Dan approached the building cautiously.

The square concrete structure seemed more like a bunker with windows that faced him, and the compound. The door was open. Dan's breath was a ragged whisper. If he was walking into an ambush, he would throw the frag, make sure he took them with him. Rifle pointed towards the dark door, and frag in the other, he nudged the door with his foot. Heavy metal door. It creaked open.

Dan flinched at the noise, and there was a sudden flurry of movement in the darkness beyond. He fired automatically, falling backwards as he did so. He landed with a thud, just in time to see a small, dark shape scurry out of the bunker and run away. A cat, or small dog. Dan did not relax. He got up and poked his rifle into the darkness. He lifted up his NVG, and flicked a switch on the M4 muzzle. A flashlight lit up the interior. He kept the beam pointed downwards. The smell of animal waste hit his nostrils. The floor was dusty with some leaves and weeds growing in the cracks. Next to the windows, to his right, there was a row of console desks. Old, rusting machines underneath them. Old TV screens and computers.

Dan only had a few seconds to process it. He ensured the room was empty, then crouched under one of the windows, and set off a volley of fire towards the huts. He guessed it might be the reception committee who had now caught up with them. It did not matter. He had to do something, and fast. Dan ran out of ammo, reclipped a new mag, and kept up the fire. As he had hoped, the insurgents fired back at him. Dan ducked as the heavy rounds knocked plaster off the walls. He unhooked the Minimi, and lay it on the ground.

He unchained the hundred-round ammo belt he was going to feed into the machine, and took up position on the window. The source of fire was at ten o'clock to him. In a minute, he had set up the bipod, had the butt against his shoulder, and let off a barrage of suppressive fire. The enemy firing stopped almost instantly, as the heavy rounds found their mark three hundred meters away with ease.

Dan emptied two-thirds of his ammo on the clump of huts that were firing at him. As soon as he took a break the return fire increased.

Dan scrambled away from the window, hearing the bullets whine above his head. He picked up his M4, and used the NVG's only visible infrared pointer to beam at the group of huts. There were about three of them, set apart from the main street.

He knew what they were trying to do. Their plan would be to keep up the fire, then send a patrol up around the back to the bunker to finish him off.

Dan would not let that happen.

He pushed the heavy metallic door open and stepped outside. There was still the chatter of guns aimed at the bunker, and further up front, at the compound. Dan went around the back and got his bearings.

To his left, three hundred meters away lay the beginnings of the village, and the mud huts. Dead straight lay the south wall of the compound. To his right, empty land with sparse tree cover. Where he had to leave the two ILAWs.

Dan stayed low, and ran towards the huts. The small huts were probably built as a sentry post before the main streets of the village began. The Taliban had obviously taken control of the village. Given the amount of fighting going on, he doubted any of the Afghan villagers still lived there.

Dan's feet slipped on something and he fell flat on his front. He shook his head, and put his palms on the ground to lift himself up. The ground was icy, and movement was not easy. He felt a hardness under his palms and took a closer look at the ground. It felt different. He brushed away some loose earth. He frowned, and used the butt of his rifle to dislodge more of the ground around him.

Black. Hard. Concrete. Dan skirted around quickly, keeping an eye ahead, kicking the ground around him. He was on a concrete road.

TAKTAKTAKTAK

He went to ground again as the bullets flew, but they went to his right, towards the bunker. Dan quickly calculated the arcs of fire. He was outside it, but a stray bullet was always possible. He would have to take that risk. Soon, the friends of the Taliban firing at them would join them, and probably bring another heavy weapon.

Dan ran fast. He circled behind the huts. The sporadic firing continued, clearly identifying the huts. Dan could now clearly see the main road that led into the village. A mud road, like in most Afghan villages. Huts were spread in a straight line on either side of the road. Dan had been in many villages like these. Normally, lights glowed from windows and smoke rose from the chimneys. But not these huts. They were dark and silent. The entire village was deserted. The moon broke free from the clouds above, bathing the scene in a silvery glow. It illuminated the large compound about four hundred meters in front. Dan looked away from the flash on his NVG with the natural light. He focused on the three huts ahead of him.

The central hut was the biggest, and seemed to be the source of fire. The two smaller huts on either side appeared deserted. Dan waited ten seconds. No movement from the two huts on either side, but plenty from the central hut. No animals in the backyard. He could make out the muzzle of a gun poking out the front window. Dan rose up. There was a rickety, waist-high fence, and he climbed over it easily. He watched his footstep.

Silent as a ghost, he approached the hut in the middle.

CHAPTER 6

Six feet away, he sank to the ground. He could hear whispered voices inside. They fired out the front window suddenly, a loud sound in the relative silence. The men in the hut fired again, a volley of shots that again went without reply.

Dan sidled up to the side of the hut. It was raised on a wooden platform, with three steps going up to it. Dan raised his head, rifle pointed up. With the NVG, he could see three men. Bent over their weapons at the window. Leaning against the mud wall, Dan pointed his rifle to the figure nearest to him.

Three in a row, like ducks. His first shot exploded the head, and the figure slumped to the ground. Before the figure had dropped, Dan had aimed and taken out the man next to him. But the third guy turned around. Fast.

Even as Dan squeezed the trigger, the man let off a flurry of rounds from his AK-47. Bullets splattered the door frame and Dan fell to the ground. The man kept up a wall of fire, bullets pumping out the doorway of the hut. Not good. These bullets made a big bang, which would alert his friends, if they were around. Dan checked himself, but he was unhurt. He stayed beneath the platform. The man stopped firing eventually, and Dan heard a sound. He was approaching the door. Silently, Dan unsheathed his kukri. He flattened himself against the mud wall.

Dan saw the snout of the AK-47 first, poking out the doorway. He grabbed it and pulled, pointing it upwards. Rounds flew harmlessly into the night sky. In the same movement, Dan dragged the Taliban into his body. The man was tall and strong. He wrestled for control of the rifle with one hand, and with the other clawed Dan's face. He was shouting gibberish in Pashto, probably trying to get some help. He did not shout for long.

The kukri sparkled in the moonlight as Dan lifted it high, then plunged the eleven-inch blade into the man's neck. It cut through the tight knots of the sternocleidomastoid neck muscles, and ripped out the trachea. Dan took the kukri out and thrust it in again, this time feeling the spine snap at the back. He put pressure and moved the long, curved knife sideways, and the head separated from the muscles, nerves and blood vessels of the neck. The head fell to the floor, and Dan let go of the limp body.

He spun around quickly, muzzle up, expecting more fire. There was none. Sporadic fire came from the front, where a gun battle still raged. But around him there was silence.

Dan looked down the village path. It went straight, then curved around the front of the compound. He could not see beyond that, but he knew the gunfire was coming from there. He thought quickly. He could go further into the village, but he could well be surrounded by the enemy. Each dark hut presented a threat. Besides, he had to assume the headless Taliban at his feet had fired enough rounds to attract attention already. Dan decided. He would have to pick up the weapons he had left and somehow get inside the compound.

Rifle up at his shoulder, Dan stepped out. He looked around him, jerking his weapon left and right. Once he had reached the bunker again, he used his radio.

"Bravo, this is Zero. Do you copy?"

He got silence again. Dan was getting a sinking feeling. If the compound was swarming with Taliban now, what happened to the CIA guys? He didn't like the answer. Death would be the easiest way out for them. As for the woman…Dan clenched his jaws. He would get into that compound, just to find out, if nothing else.

Suddenly his mic chirped. "Zero, this is Bravo One. Over and out."

Dan breathed a sigh of relief. "Loud and clear, Bravo One. I was starting to get worried."

The male voice said, "We need help here, Zero. How many of you are there?"

"Just me. But my mission is to evacuate you now."

"Negative, Zero. They have us surrounded. Getting out now would be suicidal."

Dan said, "The south wall is quiet. Throw down a hook ladder. ETA eight minutes."

"Roger that, Zero. Out."

Dan packed the Minimi up. He ran out into the open ground, ready to fling himself down at the first sound of gunfire.

None came. Dan put the two rocket launchers on his back, a total weight of fifty pounds. With his thirty-pound rucksack, weapons and ammo, he stood up effortlessly, and ran like a hare for the south wall.

The ladder was thrown down quickly when he arrived. A rope was sent down, too, and Dan tied the ILAWs and Minimi and sent them up. Then he climbed himself, as fast as he could.

There was a sangar at the top. Sangars were a common feature of compounds in 'Stan, and used to defend compounds. Before Dan went down the stairs, he stole a look around from the platform. It was a strange place to have a sangar. All he could see around him, with his NVGs, was dark and bleak countryside suffused in green. Anyone coming would be spotted miles out, and picked up easily. Opposite, almost seven hundred meters away, he could see the bunker where he had fired the Minimi from.

Roderick and Jones, the two CIA guys, were waiting for him at the bottom. They shook hands with Dan and introduced themselves. Dan put the weapons from his back down with a thud.

Roderick, the older guy, said, "Did HQ just send you? Seriously?"

Dan looked at him evenly. "I don't know which HQ you mean."

Roderick frowned. "Bagram HQ. Isn't that where you are from?"

"No. I am from Intercept."

Roderick's face cleared. "Ah. Heard of you guys." He looked at Dan curiously. "What are you, ex-Delta?"

Dan didn't like the questions. He had many of his own, but he was keeping them to himself. Why the hell couldn't this guy do the same?

He remained silent. Eventually, Roderick looked away.

Dan looked around him. It was chaotic. They were standing under the shade of a building. The courtyard was pock-marked with excoriations, and several of the buildings had their doors blasted in. The sound of gunfire increased even as they spoke.

"You been hit by mortars?" Dan asked.

Roderick shook his head. The tiredness was apparent on his face. "No, only grenades so far. But I figure it's coming."

Dan nodded. Exploding mortar shells in this closed compound would be a disaster.

"You got the woman?" Dan asked.

Roderick and Jones stood up straighter. "Yes, we do," Jones said shortly. Dan turned towards the younger man.

"Who is she?" Dan knew what answer he would get. But he had to ask it anyway.

"That information is classified. You know that," Roderick said.

"We need to exfil," Dan said.

"How?" Roderick asked.

"We go to an LZ about ten klicks from here. That should be enough distance. HQ will look at sat images and find a secluded spot."

"How do we get there?"

"Do you have a WMIK?"

"A what?"

"An armored car. A technical. Preferably with a central or rear-mounted gun."

Roderick nodded. "I think there is one here. We also have three armored Range Rovers."

Dan nodded. That should be ample transport, as long as they did not get ambushed.

"Talk about it tomorrow," Dan said. He pointed to the sangars. "Are they all occupied?"

Roderick shook his head. "No. One insurgent climbed over. We shot him down. We are down to four ANPs, and two of us. Six in total."

Dan asked, "Your call sign is Bravo One, what about Jones?"

"Bravo Two," Jones said.

"Ok. Show me the sangars looking at the village. That's where the fire is coming from, right?"

Jones led them across to the north wall that faced the main block of the village. "This used to be the police station. Before that, it was an operating base for the Russians."

"This is sangar 1." Dan turned to Jones who pointed out the sangars to them. They were standing in the middle of the compound. A small building, three by two meters stood in the center. A grenade must have hit it, as its roof was caved in. Sangars 1 and 2 took up the two corners of the north wall. Sangar 3 was on the side wall facing the village.

Dan said to Jones, "Take the Minimi and set up in Sangar 2. Don't start firing till I give the word. We need to locate the source." Jones looked at Roderick, who nodded. He jogged off without a word. Dan put his rucksack and both of the ILAWs down in a hut that Jones pointed out to him. Then with his M4, he strode out towards sangar 3. The stairs going up were wooden, and the sides were covered with hessian cloth to hide anyone going up and down.

"Hello," Dan called as he got to the top. He did not want to stay on the stairs for long. There was still a firefight going on. He could make out two figures on the floor of the sangar.

One of them turned around, and suddenly a round screamed in from outside and hit Dan.

CHAPTER 7

Dan was stooping low already, but he could not avoid the bullet. A roar erupted from his throat as he was flung back against the wooden slats of the sangar. He collapsed in a heap, on top of one of the men on the floor. They moved swiftly, pulling him to one side. One of them raised himself up on one knee and returned fire. Dan lay on the floor gasping. There was a pain on the right side of his chest. With an effort, he pulled his right arm out, and felt his body. On the bulletproof Kevlar suit he found a hot depression. An embedded round, still smoking. Dan grunted and reached underneath his Kevlar. It was dry. He felt further, his hands exploring all around his chest. No slick of blood. It was all dry. The pain in his chest remained, but he ignored it. He was still alive.

Gasping, he sat up against the sangar wall. The Kevlar had saved his life. He should not have waited on the steps. Dan tore the Kevlar vest off him and explored the rest of his body. No further wounds.

Both of the men in the sangar were now firing back.

"Hey!" Dan shouted. One of them looked back. He tapped his friend and they both turned to look at Dan. They were Afghanis, and one wore the blue uniform of the Afghan National Police. They looked Dan up and down, fear and curiosity mixed in their eyes.

"Do you know what you are firing at?" Dan asked.

The two men looked at each other. The one in the blue uniform answered. "Yes," he said.

"Show me." Dan nudged between them. "What's your name?"

"Ahmed."

Dan looked in the direction Ahmed was pointing. It was not easy to see in the dark, and the moon had scudded behind clouds. With his NVGs Dan could only see dark undulations of the mud huts. A few rounds suddenly splattered against the wood and the sandbags, and they ducked down low.

"Where was that from?" Dan asked.

"Same place," Ahmed said.

"No, it's not," Dan said. "If you fire without locating the source you waste ammo and also give away your location. They are sniping at us from multiple locations."

"So, what do we do?" Ahmed asked.

The main trajectory of the bullets, Dan knew, pointed to their two and three o'clock. He was about to say something but, right on cue, he heard the sound of more fire headed their way. Dan raised his head and took a quick peek.

"There's a hill facing us," he told Ahmed in an urgent voice. "To my eleven o'clock. It's on an elevation to us, so anyone up there can fire directly in."

"Yes," Ahmed nodded. Dan could not make out the young man's face properly, but his eyes shone in the dark. "It's called Butcher's Hill. The butchers slaughtered their sheep there. We have seen gunfire from there before."

Dan stole another glance. The hill rose at the back of the village. About seven hundred meters, but he could not be sure in the dark. It was too far away for the ILAWs, but a General-Purpose Machine Gun or Gimpy, as it was called, in sustained fire mode would be useful. He doubted they had such a weapon here, but it was worth asking. More rounds came in, pecking at the wood and sandbags, flying over their heads.

Dan waited for a lull in the fire. He told Ahmed, "Don't fire back. Wait for my signal. We have three sangars facing the village, and three arcs of fire. Let's use them."

Dan took a deep breath, then crawled out to the edge. He could see the stairs, covered by the hessian cloth. How had they seen him?

He took a deep breath, and ran down the stairs. He flinched as some more bullets hit the sandbags at the base of the sangar. Then he was below the wall of the compound, and on the ground.

He ran to sangar 2 at the far end of the north wall. Roderick was there with an ANP. Dan hunkered down beside them. It was a tight fit with all three of them.

"Where is it coming from?" Dan asked.

"Multiple places," Roderick said. "But mainly from the village center. There's a two-story house there." Dan tried to look, but they had to duck as bullets splattered against the wood decking.

"Shit," Roderick said, crouching. "They're coming on heavy tonight."

Dan shouted above the din of the rounds. "I'm going back to sangar 1. When I give the word, increase your fire. Understand?"

Roderick gave him a thumbs-up. Dan got up and flung himself down the stairs. He ran to the hut by the wall where he had stashed the weapons. He took one of the ILAWs out. He carried it back up to sangar 1. Ahmed and the other ANP were firing intermittently.

He pressed on his ear mic, calling Roderick.

Roderick answered straight away. The staccato beat of rounds interrupted the transmission but Dan could make out the words. "Still the same. Two-story building…center of village….my one o'clock."

Dan leaned out the back of the sangar and looked at the arcs of fire. He was at the corner, with Roderick opposite him. In the middle, Jones was in place. He did not want a blue on blue. Never, and certainly not with what he had planned.

Dan tapped Ahmed on the back. "Hold your fire," he said. The Afghan nodded, curiosity in his eyes.

"Bravo One," Dan instructed, "draw their fire. Both of you." He relayed the same message to Jones. The two CIA SOG men, along with the ANP, laid down heavy fire towards their right. Soon enough, rounds pinged back at them.

"Keep going!" Dan shouted. He bent over the ILAW and took it out of its case.

The rocket-launched missile was very effective at ranges of four or five hundred meters. It would go through a tank, and definitely blast the hell out of a house. Dan lifted his head briefly again, and this time he spotted the two-story house, whose upper floor was the source of fire. They were firing indiscriminately now. The sound of bullets and smell of cordite hung like a mist in the air. Dan could also see what he had suspected – the heavy ordnance came from that two-story house in the center, beyond the village square. Inside the square, and from either side, smaller fire from AK-74s came in, supporting the big gun.

Probably a DShK, RPK, or some other Russian heavy-artillery gun. Old but brutal. At eight hundred meters it would stop any infantry battalion dead in their tracks. That's why they had it placed further back, out of the range of small arms fire.

But they had not taken Dan's weapon into account.

Dan got the launcher out and prepared it. Then he put the twenty-pound rocket on his right shoulder. He would have to expose himself for this, but it was a risk worth taking. This guy needed to be silenced.

"Cover me," Dan said on his mic to Roderick and Jones. Then he tapped Ahmed on the back and nodded. If their sangar was quiet for too long, the Taliban would suspect something was amiss. Ahmed looked back, nodded, and got back to work.

Dan flipped his NVGs down, and taking a deep breath, clambered out onto the stairs where, a few minutes ago, he had been hit. There was a platform below it, adjacent to the sangar. The wooden base shook with the sound of gunfire.

Dan made sure the weapon was stable on his shoulder. He had earplugs on. He flipped up the night vision finder on the ILAW. He would have three to five seconds when he was down there. Out in the open. He knew where the target was: they kept firing. He would have to aim, fire, then dive back in. Hoping he did not get shot himself.

The firing continued, the cackle of machine gun exploding in the night. The bullets were smashing against the sangar above. Dan crouched and turned. He got out onto the wooden platform. Bent over, he looked into the night sight. Yellow traces of bullets, like LED lights, were pouring into the compound. He found the target quickly, and pressed the trigger.

BOOOM!

The rocket hissed loudly in his ear, almost deafening him, even with the earplugs on. He stumbled backwards. The missile thundered out and, in two seconds, the night sky was lit up in an orange-red fire glow. The double-story house was hit with a loud explosion, smack bang in the middle where the heavy gun was poking its barrel out. Dan heard Roderick cheering on his mic.

"Bullseye! Fuckin A, man!!"

Dan went out swiftly, and climbed back on the sangar. He was breathing fast. He wiped the sweat off his forehead. The two Afghans looked at him, wonder on their faces.

"What was that?" Ahmed asked.

"Anti-tank weapon," Dan said.

"Like an RPG?"

"Better." Dan said shortly.

"Who are you?" Ahmed asked.

"Helper," Dan said. He took a closer look at Ahmed. The man dropped his gaze and looked away.

The gunfire had stopped. The sudden silence was unnerving. Dan strained his ears, as he knew everyone else was. The moon broke free from the clouds again. Dan peeked above the sangar wall. Moonlight splashed above the domed huts of the villages. Some had flat roofs. The minaret of a mosque rose in the distance. Farther away, a black knot of mountains. To his right, moonlight made visible the destruction the ILAW had wrought. The building had been approximately five hundred meters away, and the entire top floor had been blown away by the missile.

Dan nodded at the Afghans, and made his way down the stairs. He was met by the CIA agents.

"Did you fire that weapon?" Jones asked. Dan nodded.

"Good work." There was a hint of respect in his voice.

Dan checked his watch. 0230 hours. Less than three hours till daylight. He suddenly realized how tired he was. And hungry.

"Time for an MRE?" Jones asked, reading Dan's thoughts. Dan nodded. Meals Ready-to-Eat would have to be all the food they had in this place. Dan turned to Roderick.

"Where do we sleep?"

Roderick pointed to a row of huts by the south wall. "The last one has been cleared for you. We keep a sentry duty, by the way. Two hours on and four hours off."

"Sure thing," Dan said. "Where do you guys sleep?"

Roderick said, "Next to you. The ANP sleep there." He jerked his thumb towards a group of huts by the north wall, directly opposite.

Dan headed out for his quarters. The wooden door was shut, and he opened it to find darkness inside. He shone his torch. Four beds were placed in four corners of the floor. They looked threadbare and uncomfortable, but to his exhausted body, they looked like a slice of Heaven. Groaning, he rested his body on one of them.

He took out one of the packets of MRE from his rucksack. He got the lamb stew and dumpling. He squeezed the contents down his throat. They all tasted the same. He chugged down some much-needed water from his can.

The CIA guys were in the hut next to him. He wondered where the woman was. She probably had the last hut, the one in the corner.

Dan decided to get some shut-eye before Roderick came to call him for sentry duty.

CHAPTER 8

It was dark inside the room. The night was cold outside, and Dan was wearing his life-saving Kevlar vest as he slept. Despite the door being shut, the cold night air seeped in. He listened to the snoring from the adjacent room. The rhythmic sound was like a gentle lullaby, and soon his eyelids dropped. He did not know how long he had slept for. But a sound awoke him.

A creaking sound.

It came from the doorway. Dan's hand curled around the butt of the Sig P226 at his belt. No safety catch. Round chambered. Point and shoot. Best thing about the P226. He lifted the gun, pointing it at the door.

The door creaked again.

Dan's finger caressed the trigger. He sat up in the bed without making a sound. One of the two door frames opened. A figure was silhouetted in the soft white moonlight. Dan gripped the butt tightly, but for some reason, his hands trembled. That was a first for him.

The figure was smaller than a man. It was slightly hunched as well. Dan swallowed hard as the dark figure came inside the room. Dan pointed the gun at the figure and stood up slowly.

"Who is it?"

"Dan, is that you?"

"Mother?" Dan lowered the gun. He stepped forward. Rita Roy's face was looking up at him in the darkness. She gripped his shoulders.

"Son, I had to come and see you. It's been so long. Didn't know if you were alive or dead."

Dan was bewildered. But this was real. No mistaking it. "Mom, what are you doing here?"

"I came to warn you."

Dan frowned. "About what?"

Dan heard a noise by the doorway and he looked up. He froze. Ahmed, the ANP, was standing there, AK-47 in his hand. His eyes were burning with hate. They glowed like coals in the dark. He looked at Dan, then at Rita.

Before Dan could do anything, Ahmed had pointed the gun at Rita and fired. She crumpled to the floor.

"No!" Dan screamed. "No, no, no!"

Dan was sitting up in bed, sweat pouring down his face, and he was screaming. He heard guns being uncocked, and a flashlight suddenly stung his face, blinding him. The light left him and jerked around the room.

"What the hell?" It was Roderick, and he was standing at the open door. Out of instinct Dan turned his Sig on him.

"Whoa!" Roderick said, and pointed his weapon down. "What was that?"

"Nothing," Dan said sheepishly. "I reckon I had a dream. Sorry, just get back to bed."

Roderick gave Dan a look, then went off.

Dan did not sleep well. He tossed and turned in the rickety, creaking bed till he felt a hand shaking him awake.

"It's morning, pal." It was Jones. Dan saw a bright light coming in through the window. He was awake instantly. Jones looked tired. It was silent outside. 0630 hours. Dan got up, took his water bottle outside into the compound, and splashed water on his face.

He turned to head back to his hut and stopped in his tracks.

A woman was facing him. Six feet away, standing on the slightly raised mud verandah outside the huts. Her jet-black hair fell around her shoulders. Her skin was the color of milk, and her eyes were green. Her large eyes were expressive, with a curious twinkle in them. But they were also worried and watchful. She had a long, slender neck, a small nose and high cheekbones. Even in her bedraggled state, she looked beautiful. She was about his age, early thirties. She wore the same shapeless gown that women were made to wear in this part of the world. But it seemed tighter, and she wore it differently. Her figure was not shapeless.

Dan broke off eye contact, and walked back. Which happened to be towards her. When he was facing her, in front of the doors of his hut, he lowered his head and rolled his massive shoulders.

"I am Dan Roy. I was sent to help you get to safety." Dan did not know if the woman spoke English. He felt like an idiot after he opened his mouth. He should have just ignored her, and gone back inside. He did not owe her an explanation. But something about her held him there.

"I am Mariam Panahi," the woman said after a pause. "Thank you for coming." Her English was perfect, without any trace of an accent. Her voice was light. A faint trace of a smile appeared at the corner of her ruby-red lips, then vanished. She turned and went back inside the hut.

Dan stood there for a second. "Pleasure was all mine," he said. He spoke to empty air. The door was already shut.

Three ANPs were standing in one corner of the perimeter wall. Their weapons were out, with fingers on triggers. They gazed at Dan, sizing him up. Dan returned the favor. In his past contacts with the ANP, Dan had never been sure if he could trust them. What he had seen of the ANP so far was different. These guys seemed more agile, on the ball.

Another ANP strode out of the hut at the far end. Dan was close enough to make out Ahmed's features. He spoke sharply to the three ANPs and they brushed the dust off their hips and stood to attention. Ahmed looked at the guns and checked they were loaded. He turned around to see Dan.

"Hello," Ahmed said in English. "Good morning."

"Morning," Dan nodded. "Are you setting up for sentry duty?"

"Yes, as usual." Dan watched as Ahmed strode towards him. In the bright morning light, he could see the man's features clearly. He was much younger than Dan. He looked at Dan curiously.

"Which army do you work for?"

"I don't."

Dan stared at the man with a stony expression. It did not invite further comment, and Ahmed dropped his gaze after a few seconds.

Ahmed said, "You will help us exfiltrate."

"Maybe." Dan looked around but he could not see any Roderick or Jones. "Do you know if there is a WMI....I mean an armored car here?"

Ahmed smiled. "There is a WMIK here. Left by the previous platoon."

"You know what a WMIK is?"

"Yes. A weapon-mounted installation kit. I was trained by soldiers from the 1st Battalion, the Royal Welsh."

Dan did not reply. Ahmed said, "Would you like to see the WMIK?"

"Yes."

Dan walked with Ahmed to the long wall that faced the village. A row of mud huts, all with a domed roof and a flight of stairs going up their side, stood against the wall. Behind them, Ahmed pointed out the sand-colored open top, weapon-mounted, converted Range Rover. Dan noticed the GPMG, or Gimpy, that was still present. He checked the car over. It looked to be in reasonable condition. The fuel tank was still half-full.

Dan heard his name being called, and saw Roderick heading for him. The CIA man pointed to sangar 1.

"Seen something interesting up there. Care to have a look?"

"Yes," Dan said. "Thanks," he said to Ahmed.

CHAPTER 9

Dan crouched on the floor of the sangar with Roderick. He handed Dan a pair of binoculars. Dan looked out at the village in front of him. Typical rows of mud huts that seemed out of a biblical landscape. Yellow-gray, sandy, dusty streets. He had seen them a hundred times before in 'Stan – on foot patrol, on operations, and from a helicopter. But never had they been this empty. He was looking out at a derelict ghost village. Not one soul stirred in the quietness.

Dan heard a noise behind him, and looked around to see Ahmed squatting on the floor. With the three of them it was a tight fit.

"It might look empty," Ahmed said, "but they are out there. They dig tunnels to move from house to house. They use pulleys for their guns and ammo in the tunnels."

Roderick said, "And they wait till we get bored of watching. Then suddenly they attack. At high noon, when the sun is strongest. Or late at night, when we are tired."

Dan nodded. "You got their radio channels?"

Roderick said, "Ahmed has been using the Icom scanner to check the radio waves. Any news, Ahmed?"

Ahmed said, "We located one frequency. Their code for attacking seems to be *The harvest is gathered*. We heard that last night before you turned up." He indicated Dan.

"Good work, Ahmed," Roderick said.

Dan looked behind them at the rooftop of one of the huts at the north-west corner of the compound. He could see long antennas and a satellite radio dish pointing to the sky. He pointed. "That your comms tower?"

"Yes," said Roderick.

Dan scanned the area outside. He saw the building that he had decapitated with the ILAW that morning. It looked worse in daylight. But dotted around them, Dan could see double-story buildings, most of them level with the compound wall, and some higher. He pointed to those buildings.

"These are dangerous. They negate our height advantage." He swept around with the binoculars in the distance. He stopped when he saw the convoy of pickup trucks approaching. They were loaded with men. He could see their turbans, and some rifles poking up in the air.

Roderick said, "Have you seen them?"

Dan realized this is what Roderick had asked him to come up for. He counted five pickup trucks with men and ammunition. They were far, more than one klick away. He looked further, and saw a trail of dust rising in the air. More reinforcements were on their way.

"Shit," Dan said, lowering the binoculars. He asked Roderick, "Why all the interest?"

Roderick shrugged and avoided Dan's eyes. "Damned if I know."

Dan checked his watch. 0900 hours. He went down from the sangar, and walked towards his hut. The others were out already. They had their mics on. Jones chirped in his ear.

"Looks dead from sangar 1."

"Look again. A boatload of Tangos just arrived at the edge of town. Reckon there's going to be a big party soon."

Dan went into his hut and took his satellite phone out. He needed to speak to Guptill. There was too much going on here that he could not make sense of, and speaking to the CIA guys would not help. He was about to punch the number in when he saw something that made him stop.

The woman. Mariam.

She was poking her head out from one of the buildings in the north-west corner, where the ANPs lived. The building was made of concrete, and had blue and white stripes on it. Mariam looked around, then slipped out of the building. She stood by the doorway for five seconds, watching the compound. It was empty. All the men were up in the sangars. She could not see Dan as he was inside the hut. Mariam crossed the compound quickly, head bent low. Dan shrank back against the wall. He watched as Mariam went into her room and he heard the door shut.

His reverie did not last long. In the blink of an eye, all hell broke loose. There was a loud explosion, followed by shouts, and the sudden chatter of gunfire.

"RPG!" Several voices shouted at once. Dan ran out into the courtyard. He still had his radio on and called Roderick.

"Bravo One, do you copy?" Gunfire drowned his voice.

"Roger that." Roderick's voice was calm. Dan knew he was scanning around him from the sangar, looking for a possible source. An RPG would be fired from within two hundred meters, and smoke would be visible, especially through binoculars.

"What did it hit?"

"The wall to my right," Roderick said. "They were aiming for the sangar."

Dan clenched his jaws. A direct hit from an RPG would damage the sangar. Definitely wound anyone inside it. A second hit would be fatal.

Jones' excited voice from the north-west sangar, number 3, interrupted Dan. "Got him!"

"Where?" Dan asked.

"Smoke to the west, my nine o'clock."

Dan informed Roderick. The Minimi started blasting, rising stridently above the sound of small arms fire. Dan looked up. It was Roderick from sangar 1, letting rip at the position of the RPG. While commotion reigned, he caught sight of something that moved in the corner of his eye.

Mariam. She slunk across the perimeter wall, in the shadow of the huts. She went to the far end, by the ANP block, where she had been before. Dan saw her open the door, enter and shut it.

Dan made a mental note of the building she had gone into. Then he ran across and climbed into the sangar he had just vacated. Roderick and Ahmed were still in there. Both were hunched over, firing intensely. Rounds came at them thick and fast. Bullets splattered against the wood, pinged above their heads, thudded into sandbags.

The ear-splitting sound of heavy ordnance from the Minimi thundered again, making Dan cover his ears. Dan patted Rod on the back. He sprung around.

"Easy," Dan said.

"We got RPGs, too," Rod said.

"We need to move the GPMG you have mounted on the WMIK. I mean the armored car. We need the Gimpy up here, blasting away. Rusty has got the north. We need to hit the west of the village." Dan pointed. "And the bazaar area."

"Ok," said Roderick, "I'll get one of the ANP to help you."

After the prolonged burst from the Minimi, the guns were silent. They heard screams in the silence, coming from the village. Rod raised his head.

"100 meters ahead, one of the houses we fired on last night. We hit some of them."

Dan nodded, satisfied. "I need to have a talk with you. Can we do it now?"

Rod raised his eyebrows. He spoke to Ahmed briefly, then walked down with Dan. They walked to the CIA agents' hut. Dan shut the door.

"You need to level with me," Dan said.

Roderick wiped the sweat off his brows, and leaned the Heckler & Koch rifle against the wall. "Hey, you came here to help extract us. The rest is classified, I told you."

"The hell it is. Did you know about the ambush we landed in?"

The surprise on Roderick's face was genuine. "You were ambushed?"

Dan told him what happened when the Chinook had dropped him off.

"Jesus," Roderick said.

Dan said, "The way I see it, there are two options. There's a mole here, or in HQ."

"You suspect anyone?"

"I have some ideas. But nothing definite yet."

Roderick smiled. "Jones or me in any of your ideas?"

Dan ignored him. "Who is the woman?"

Roderick did not say anything. Dan said, "You either tell me, or I pick up the satphone and call HQ. Tell them there is a mole here. HQ can inform Langley right now."

"I cannot let you do that."

"Do you think you can stop me?"

CHAPTER 10

Roderick and Dan stared at each other for a few seconds. Roderick was the first to look away.

"She's Iranian."

"I know that."

"A nuclear scientist at the IR-40 heavy water plant in Arak."

"Defecting to the West?"

"Yes."

"The Taliban know," Dan said. He was not asking a question. Roderick did not say anything.

Dan said, "The Taliban know, and you can't figure out how. Informed by the same person who told them about us. You have had a mole right from the beginning."

"She knows a lot, Dan. This will be a game-changer. We have to take the chance, even if we have a mole."

"Maybe. But you are missing something here."

"What?"

"The Taliban let you get into this place. They followed you here, and then surrounded you. I don't think they have any intention of letting you leave."

Roderick was silent again. Dan said, "What's in those buildings next to the ANP quarter?"

"What building?"

"Don't play games with me, Rod. There is something here that the Taliban want. I'm not talking about the woman. What is it?"

Roderick said, "You are right. There's more to this. But right now, I've told you all I can."

"I have worked with you guys before."

"You should know, then."

"I know this is a suicide mission. There's seven of us fighting hundreds. We need a platoon-strength force here."

"What are you saying?"

"I am saying someone messed up pretty bad here. Either you were not expecting to land in this shithole, or..."

"Or what?"

Dan said quietly, "Or you are the mole."

Roderick narrowed his eyes. "You are barking up the wrong tree here, my friend."

"I hope so," Dan said.

He left Rod standing there, and walked out. He strode over to sangar 2 on the north wall. Jones and one of the ANP were watching the huts and alleyways.

"Gone very quiet," Jones murmured. "Why did they fire that one RPG?"

"Probably testing their range. They stopped because we got their position, and fired back," Dan said.

"So?"

"So they will come under cover of night."

"We have to be ready," Dan said.

"How many ILAWs we got left?" Jones asked.

"Only one now. But we can get the Gimpy out of the WMIK and bring it up to sangar 1. That sangar is best positioned for all arcs of fire."

"Shit," Jones said. He was looking through the scope on his M4.

"What?"

"Movement. 100 meters away. About ten Tangos."

Dan grabbed the binoculars. He focused them in the right direction. Sure enough, he saw about ten Taliban, wearing their distinctive headgear, covering their faces as well. The men slipped behind a house, and more appeared, before vanishing inside another house.

"They're getting into position," Dan said. He flicked the switch of his radio to get Roderick's channel.

"Bravo One, this is Zero."

"Roger that, Zero."

"Enemy seen on north-west village section. Be on high alert. Contact imminent."

"Roger, out."

Dan spoke to Rod again briefly and came down from the sangar. He was walking over to the WMIK when he saw Ahmed climb down from sangar 3 and join him.

"Agent Roderick told me to help you with the Gimpy."

Dan nodded. They crossed the compound together. They unhooked the Gimpy from its base and put it on the compound. Dan lifted the twenty-six-pound machine, while Ahmed helped him. Together, they carried the weapon up to sangar 1 and positioned it between the sandbags.

"You ever fired a machine gun before?" Dan asked Ahmed, wiping the sweat and dust off his face.

Ahmed looked awed as he gazed at the gun. "No."

Dan showed him. "You need to get some oil," he explained. "The machine needs it after a long firing spell to help it cool down. About four hundred rounds."

He held up the ammo chain. "Straighten this out. Any chinks in the chain could stop the gun, and that could be the difference between life and death."

Ahmed nodded vigorously, his face a mask of concentration.

Roderick was watching outside. He had turned around when they came up, but had not said a word since. He spoke now.

"Sangars 2 and 4 have also reported enemy movement. But none with guns. We are getting ready for a contact."

"Make sure all sangars have enough ammo and drinking water. We don't want to be running up and down these stairs, getting shot at by snipers."

Dan went down into the compound. He looked up at the satellite dishes. They were a big worry. If the enemy hit that, they would be out of contact with HQ. They had their own radios. But it was better to have a direct satellite link.

He watched across the courtyard as Mariam came out of her hut.

She looked around, and Dan pressed himself against the shadow of the stairs. She went inside the blue and white striped building at the northern end, and disappeared inside. Dan gave her five minutes, then followed.

The door had a padlock chain, but it was unlocked. He opened it and stepped inside. He let his eyes adjust to the sudden dark. Inside was cool, and silent. Dan blinked. The walls were of concrete, and the floor had a timber frame. Shafts of sunlight came in through the ceiling.

The room was empty. Completely. It did not have any windows, and no doors apart from the one he had just opened. Mariam had disappeared. Dan looked at the walls carefully. He went over and ran his hands along them. Smooth, no breaks.

Then he stared at the floor. He got down on his knees. Felt every inch of the floor with his hands. He found it at the far corner. A section of timber that looked like the rest of the floor. But this section moved. He pushed it, and it slid back to reveal a black space. A hole. Dan flashed his torchlight inside. Looked like a concrete slab.

Dan pushed the floor again, and another section slid back. He could see more of the concrete. But something else as well. Two hinges, and a heavy, round copper ring. A trapdoor, built on a concrete slab. He grabbed the ring and pulled. It was heavy, and made a rusty, groaning sound, but came up easily. He used his flashlight again. Concrete steps going down. He got his shoulders inside with some difficulty, and put his feet on the stairs. Then he shut the trapdoor over his head. Flashlight on, he could see below him. He was in a dark, cold, silent place. The stairs descended below him. The flashlight's beam got swallowed into a black hole.

Dan climbed down slowly. He counted the stairs as he went down in a straight line. No curves or rolls. The stairs were broad and flat, designed for big shoes like his. After one hundred and fifty stairs, he touched flat ground. Concrete again. He shone his light up. Steel beams criss-crossed the ceiling. He was in an underground bunker. He was in the atrium, and corridors branched off all around him. The corridors were narrow, and seemed to have shelves on them. Like a storage vault. The ceiling was tall enough for a man to stand.

"So, you found me at last," Mariam said from behind him.

CHAPTER 11

Mariam flicked a switch and lights came on. Dan squeezed his eyes shut and opened them. Bulbs hung on naked wires from the ceiling. Mariam came and stood in front of Dan. Her hair was tied back in a ponytail, throwing her features into sharper relief. Her large, green eyes flicked over Dan's face. Serious. Her elegant, thin neck was straight and her chin was raised. She looked slimmer and after a while Dan realized why. She had tied the silken black gown at the waist with a tie. The hem was raised, exposing her ankles.

They stared at each other for a moment without speaking.

"What's going on here?" Dan finally found his voice.

Mariam's expression did not change. "Whatever the CIA guys told you."

"Not much."

Mariam said, "They told you about me."

"Yes."

"What?"

"You are a nuclear scientist. You work in Akra."

"And?"

"You are leaving Iran. Going to America."

"Is that it?"

"That's all I know."

Dan pointed to the now lit corridors behind them. "What is this?"

"Come. I will show you."

Mariam led the way. As they walked into the first row, Dan looked up at the sign. It said something in Russian. Mariam spoke without turning around.

"That says *Ostorozhno*. It means danger in Russian."

Dan gazed at the floor-to-ceiling rows of black mortar shells, arranged by size. They took up both sides of the corridor, leaving them with a narrow space to walk in the middle. They walked for a minute and came onto a clearing. From this space, more corridors branched out. Like spokes radiating out from a hub. Mariam flicked another light switch, then pointed down another corridor.

"This way."

Dan craned his neck up to see rockets nested within their launch pads.

They had sharply tapered noses, and went up in size. He stood close to a black rocket, more than two meters high, taller than him. He could not read the Cyrillic writing on the side, and the numbers did not mean anything to him.

"The CR-2," Mariam said, coming closer. "One of the first surface-to-air missiles that the Soviets made in the 1950s. Range and speed are both limited, and they are not nuclear warhead capable."

Dan looked at the other rockets lined up in the corridor. A flight of steps went down to another level. He took a deep breath, and followed Mariam as she went slowly down the stairs. When he came to the bottom of the stairs, the breath got stuck in his chest. His heart hammered against his ribs.

"Oh my God," he said.

"You recognize these?" Mariam asked.

She looked up at the long, tall missile that towered over them. Dan was gazing, too. He guessed the height was more than ten meters. About one meter thick. He saw the fixed broad fins on the base. Steps on the side for engineers to climb up. It was dark gray in color, and its nose narrowed to a cap of a white circle, then narrowed again to a sharp tip with an antenna.

Mariam said, "The *R-17 Zemlya* ballistic missile. Capable of conventional, including chemical, and nuclear warheads up to fifty kilotons. Maximum range of two hundred miles, and capable of a speed of Mach 5. A game-changer in the SAM field."

Dan blinked once. "A goddamn Scud missile."

"Yes, that is the name NATO gave them."

"They need command vehicles to launch them, and erector trucks to transport."

"Yes, and no. The early Scuds did require TEL or transport erector launch vehicles. These can be wheeled on rail tracks, and can be erected by cranes. But yes, they need a command and control station, which can be portable, in a truck."

"That is why there is a runway outside. Control towers. This is a missile silo."

Mariam sounded surprised. "You saw the runway?"

"I stumbled upon it while trying not to get shot. There are control rooms in there as well. Those concrete bunkers. Five hundred meters from the south wall."

"Yes."

Dan touched the Scud missile. Cold, metallic. He had seen wrecks of them in the second Gulf War. Saddam Hussein had been an enthusiastic collector. Russia had been a generous donor.

He felt unreal. He said, "What the hell are Scud missiles doing here?"

"More Scud missiles were fired in Afghanistan between 1989 and 1992 than in any other war. Including the Iran-Iraq War, which saw the greatest deployment of these ballistic missiles."

"Really?"

Mariam nodded. "After the Russians left in 1989, civil war broke out here. The Russians backed the Afghan government. Delivered more than five hundred Scuds to them, with advisors to help them launch them."

"Jesus."

"Afghanistan, in fact, has seen more missile launches than the Second World War. Most of the five hundred plus got fired. But when the advisors left, some missiles were left behind. That's what you have left here."

"How many are in here?"

"Twenty-five."

"How do you know about them?" Dan asked.

She replied after a pause. "My professor in Iran trained in Russia. He was approached to help."

"Approached by who?"

"That is classified."

Dan stared at her, then looked back at the missiles.

Dan said, "The Taliban are a Pakistani construct. They were formed out of Afghan refugees during the Russian war. The CIA helped fund them directly, and through the Pakistani Army. The Taliban movement grew out of madrassas in border towns between Pakistan and 'Stan."

"You know your history."

"That is why the Taliban are concentrated in the south of Afghanistan. Close to Pakistan. The north is ruled by the Northern Alliance, but the Taliban is still strong in pockets."

"What is your point?"

"I think the people who approached your Professor were agents of the ISI, the Inter-Services Intelligence Agency. The Pakistan Army's secret service. They heard rumors about this site from the Taliban. But they did not know the precise location. You did. Hence they let you in here."

Mariam folded her arms in a gesture that was both delicate and thoughtful. Her white hands showed against her black gown.

"How do you know any of this is true?"

"Because you agreed to help the CIA in tracking this place down. You don't want this to fall into Pakistan's hands."

"Why not?"

"They are Sunni, and Iranians are Shia."

"That's true. But I am Assyrian Christian."

"You are?"

"We are a substantial minority in Iran now. Many of us have fled from neighboring Iraq and Syria. Some of my cousins have been killed in Iraq." She looked down at the floor.

Dan said, "I am sorry. So your parents are Assyrian Christians from Iran?"

"Yes. From Shiraz, a city in the south."

"Iran took a huge battering from these Scud missiles during the Iran-Iraq War. You don't want that to happen again."

"Yes."

"But there is another reason why you are helping the CIA."

"What is that?"

"You are not Iranian."

Something changed in Mariam's eyes. A sudden lack of composure, then she corrected herself. A half-smile played on her lips.

"What am I, then?"

"You are American."

CHAPTER 12

Mariam stood very still, her eyes not leaving Dan's face. The mirth in her face slowly disappeared.

"What makes you say that?" she asked.

Dan said, "You cannot take the West Coast out of your voice. I am thinking Los Angeles, or somewhere in Orange County."

"Do you?"

"Yes. You thought I would not recognize your accent. But I am American, too. I am guessing you don't speak to Rod or Jones much, just to hide your accent."

"You guessed right," Mariam said softly.

"I thought so. Your parents immigrated to America. You were born there."

"Yes. But how could I be American, and also an Iranian nuclear scientist?"

"Everyone knows the CIA have assets inside Iran. The Persian-American community is based around LA. It's where the Shah's son lives, and thinks he leads a government in exile."

"You did not answer my question, Dan."

It was the first time she had said his name. She had given up hiding her accent, it was obvious now.

Dan said, "A number of ways. Did you go to college in the USA?"

"Yes."

"I'm thinking UCLA, Berkeley or Stanford. Maybe you came to Iran after that to work. Help the fledgling atomic industry. Then went back to do your PhD in USA. That's when you got recruited by the CIA. Or maybe as an undergrad. Less likely, as you did not have much direct Iran experience as an undergrad."

"Carry on."

"Something happened recently. In Arak, your cover was blown. Maybe one of your contacts got caught. The Republican Guards tortured the truth out of him. You had to escape. The land route was easier as no checks at the borders. You were doubly important to us. You know about the nuclear industry in Iran, and you knew about this missile silo, too."

Mariam regarded Dan thoughtfully. "How did you know?"

"Your accent. You carry a weapon. It's under the sleeve of your right arm. You exposed it briefly when you lifted your arm to point at the Scud."

Mariam peeled back the sleeve of her gown. The black Glock 22 was taped to her wrist.

She said, "You work for the CIA."

"No."

"Some other government agency."

Dan did not answer. She was right, but he could not admit it. He would *never* be able to admit it.

Silence. They stared at each other, eyes searching. Dan's eyes moved to her neck and below, then jerked back up quickly.

Mariam said, "You are very good. You should work in intelligence."

"I prefer dealing with the enemy directly."

Dan said, "Do the two agents know?"

"Roderick does. Derek does not. He's subordinate to Rod."

Dan nodded. No need to tell Jones what he did not need to know. Speaking of which, he had to get back upstairs. The outline of a plan was forming in his mind.

He pointed to the ceiling above the Scud missiles. "How are these raised to ground level?"

"The ceiling is bifolding. It separates into two. Opens out into the compound floor."

"Does the mechanism still work?"

"Not been tried, but I'm willing to bet it does. The cables are still connected. Electricity works here."

"Alright. I have to go back up. The enemy is coming for a big push tonight. You would be better off either in your hut, or down here."

"Thanks."

Dan walked backed to the first corridor he had entered. He squatted on his haunches and looked at the mortar shells. He left the heavier shells alone and focused on what looked like 82mm mortars. He found a number of base plates and launchers for the 82mm. Mariam had come up behind him.

"That's the 2B14 Podnos range," she said, reading off the side of the base plate.

"82mm, aren't they?" Dan asked.

"Yes."

Dan tried to lift the base plate. He could move it, but lifting it alone was difficult. One man could not take it up that flight of stairs. He would have to come back with help.

"What are you trying to do?" Mariam asked.

Dan picked up a mortar shell in each hand. "Trying to survive tonight," he said.

He jogged up the stairs. He went up to sangar 1 and got hold of Roderick. Jones came down from sangar 3 and they went down into the missile silo. Mariam was still there.

"I figured you would need to know where the lights are," she said.

"Good thinking," Dan said.

Roderick gaped at her. "You American?"

"Yes," Mariam said. The three men followed her into the corridor.

"Holy shit," Jones said. He walked around with wonder in his eyes. He disappeared down a corridor, and Dan heard him yelp. Jones poked his head in at the far end.

"You gotta come and see this."

Roderick rolled his eyes, and Dan followed. Jones was gazing at a hallway with row upon row of rockets. About one and a half meters tall. White in color, with black fins and black warheads.

Mariam said, "Katyusha rockets. First deployed in the Second World War, but these are the 1980s models."

"This place is like a museum," Jones said.

"You ain't seen the Scuds yet," Dan said.

"No way." Jones' eyes were big.

The tour ended in a half-hour. It took two of them to lift each one of the ninety-six-pound base plates and tubes up to the surface, and several more trips to get the mortars. Roderick and Jones were waiting for them in the room by the time they finished unloading. Dan did not want them out in the compound. He explained to Roderick why. The CIA veteran nodded and went to work.

*****

Dan climbed into sangar 3. Ahmed was keeping watch.

"I don't like it," he told Dan.

"They are organizing weapons for which they need a light source at night. Easier to set them up now," Dan said.

"How do you know?" Ahmed asked.

"Because that is what I would do."

Ahmed's handheld radio crackled. He spoke into it and listened.

"Agent Roderick wants me downstairs."

52

"I'll stay here and keep watch," Dan said. He took the position vacated by Ahmed.

He was looking at the bazaar, and a collection of one- and two-story buildings beyond it, including the one he had hit. About one hundred meters distant. About three hundred meters away the mud huts became less numerous, and there was a clump of trees.

Dan unhooked his M4 from his back. He used the weapon's image magnifier to focus on the screen of trees. Their base was obscure. He was in a straight line to the trees, and he looked harder. He swung his rifle around, searching. Then he saw it.

A row of three black, linear, tube-like nozzles sticking up at forty-five degrees. Attached to metal base plates. Similar to the mortar base plate they had just unloaded. Only these seemed larger. For 120mm mortar shells, he guessed.

Cursing, he took out the grid reference map from the shoulder pocket of his vest. He marked the rough coordinates on the map.

Dan aimed the Gimpy at the clump of trees dead ahead, four hundred meters away. He fired a long burst, feeling the machine shake in his hands, and watched the shots raise puffs of small dust in the distance. He kept firing for thirty seconds.

Then he watched with his weapon's scope again. He had hit all of them. The nozzles were on the floor, and he could see where the springs had burst from the base plates. He fired another round to be sure, then told Jones to keep an eye out from their ends for more base plates or rocket launchers. The RPGs they could not do anything about. Those things were portable, and it was just a matter of luck when and where they hit.

Dan spoke briefly to Jones again and went down from the sangar. He headed towards the communication room, from whose square roof the satellite dish and antenna sprouted. Ahmed was inside, listening intently in front of a radio receiver, headphones over his ears.

"Are you on their channel?" Dan asked.

Ahmed nodded. Dan took a seat opposite him.

He said, "Sangar 1 took a hit last night. We need more sandbags up there."

Ahmed glanced at Dan and nodded again. He took his headphones off.

"There is some chatter about mortar base plates."

Dan said, "I know. I just hit some of them. We need to keep an eye out for more. Are your men ready?"

"To be honest," Ahmed said, "their training is basic. They can fire an

SA80 rifle and lob grenades, that's about it."

"That will do," Dan said. "Looks like we will be holed up here for another night, at least. Try your best to find out what they are planning."

Ahmed gave him a thumbs-up. "I will."

Dan went outside and spoke to his team. He went to Roderick's hut and spoke to the two CIA agents. Then he spent some time chatting to Guptill on the satellite phone. When he finished his conversation, it was time to wolf down an unappetizing MRE. Dan got up on the south wall sangar, designated as sangar 4. The ANP who had been on duty had gone for his lunch.

He poked his head above the wooden slats and piled up sandbags. Barren land stretching out for miles greeted his eyes.

Directly below him, underneath the sandbags, he could see the wall they had scaled the first night with their hook ladders. With his binoculars, Dan located the concrete bunker where he had taken refuge. To his extreme right lay the beginning of the village. Straight ahead, he could make out the dim, small shape of the other bunker where he had hidden his quad.

The Taliban were experts in guerrilla warfare. They knew their terrain. They would be easy pickings for a sniper out in this zone, bereft of any cover. Hence they never attacked from here. The tree cover was more than eight hundred meters away. Most of their weapons would be out of range. Their cover was the village. Dan searched the south side with his binoculars and rifle sight for a while longer, then started down the stairs.

He flinched as the loud sound of machine gun fire shattered the silence of the afternoon.

CHAPTER 13

"Contact!" It was Roderick's voice, sharp and excited. He said something else but it was drowned out by gunfire.

Roderick was back in sangar 1. Dan knew he could not go up to it while the firing was this heavy.

"Where is it coming from?" Dan asked on his radio.

"Damned if I know. But it's heavy!" Roderick yelled.

Dan ran up the steps to sangar 3. He had barely hit the wooden floor when rounds began to pop around him. They hit the sandbags with a dull *thwack*, and pinged off the wooden arches. Dan lifted his head momentarily and looked. More rounds greeted him. He tried to look for the source, but it was difficult. The firing was accurate. More than five guns had to be aimed at the sangar. Heavier for Roderick, Dan felt.

"I got a sighter," Jones said in his mic.

"Where?" Dan asked.

"Three-story house, behind the bazaar, dead straight to me, north-west."

"Roger that."

Dan knelt on the floor and got the Gimpy ready. He could not aim well with the rounds flying above him, and hitting the protection, but he could fire in the desired direction. He took a quick peek, and then checked his grid reference map, sweat pouring down his forehead.

BAMBAMBAMBAMBAM

The heavy gun shook in his hands. The magazine was full, and he squeezed the trigger remorselessly. He saw his rounds hitting the house, mud splattering off the walls. The incoming fire lessened, and he saw a weapon appear at a window on the first floor. The snout of an RPG was unmistakable.

"RPG! Take cover!" Dan shouted into his mic and fired straight at the weapon.

He snarled with glee as his bullets hit the mark. The weapon fell from the window, out of sight, and he realized he must have hit the insurgent holding the RPG.

The firing towards sangar 1 lessened, but Dan was now taking heavy fire. Sangar 3 shook with the reverberation of heavy ordnance. Dan tried to see the direction but the firing was too heavy. Dimly he heard something in his mic. He could not understand it, but he heard the Minimi on sangar 1 open up. It was joined by small arms fire, and he knew Jones was firing back.

Dan looked through a gap in the sandbags. Streaking flashes of light were flying out from sangar 1 towards the tree line. The tree line where he had hit the mortar plates. Dan took the Gimpy and fired at the trees. The sangar was filled with gun smoke, and the smell of dust, sweat and anxiety. Dan switched radio channels, his heart hammering against his ribs. It was 1400 hours. They did not have much time.

"Bravo One, this is Zero."

"Are you ok up there, Zero?" Roderick sounded concerned.

"Yes. Time to get set up."

"Roger that."

Dan fired for another minute with the Gimpy, joined by sangar 1. He stopped when he realized there was no return fire.

Slowly, the eerie, creepy silence returned. Only the dusty breeze rustled and moved in the air. An empty, cloudless blue sky stretched overhead. It seemed as if they were at the edges of the known human world.

Nothing moved or happened here. Apart from sudden and deadly gunfire.

*****

Roderick was in the communication room, standing next to Ahmed. The Afghan was hunched over the radio again, headphones on.

Dan said, "We need to start getting the mortars ready."

Ahmed looked up. Roderick said, "Do we have coordinates?"

"Not specific, but we can use the grid map. We have enough base plates to set up a barrage, so missing by a meter won't make any difference."

Dan asked Ahmed, "How many Taliban are out there now?"

Ahmed said, "More than a hundred and fifty. They have gathered from surrounding villages."

Dan said, "We need to get the rockets as well?"

Ahmed sounded surprised. "We have rockets, too?"

"A whole lot," Dan said. "There are masses of weapons stored underneath this compound. Tonight we have to launch a major assault. It's the only way we will survive."

Roderick said, "Ahmed, keep scanning their channels to make sure we know what their plans are."

"We wait till nightfall. The fireworks begin at 2100 hours," Dan said.

Dan headed down to the missile silo. Jones had climbed up the steps of a Scud missile and removed the warhead cover. Mariam was on the floor, directing him. Dan stood next to Mariam, looking up at the men.

"Any news?" he asked.

Mariam said, "Ten are loaded so far. Conventional nitrate-compound explosives. The rest are empty."

"What's the payload?"

"Five hundred pounds in each, approximately."

Dan whistled. "That's a lot. Should be interesting."

Dan went upstairs, crossed the compound and entered his hut in the south end. He jabbed numbers into his satellite phone and had a quick chat with Major Guptill. He listened, hung up, waited for ten minutes, then rang Guptill back. He listened again, his head bent.

He called Roderick, and went into the communication room, where Ahmed was on his own, glued to the radio. Dan went and sat in front of him, on the opposite side of the table.

"Any news?"

"No." Ahmed's eyebrows were furrowed in concentration. Dan saw Roderick enter the room from the back, shutting the door without a sound.

"Did you tell them about the rockets?" Dan asked conversationally.

Ahmed looked up, confused. "What?"

CHAPTER 14

"The rockets. You used a code word for them. Hailstones. You were just on the Taliban channel. Your exact message to them was: *Hailstones* will fall tonight, and a *Toofan* is coming. *Toofan* means storm in Farsi and Dari."

Ahmed's face had lost all color. He opened his mouth and licked dry lips. "I am a captain in the Afghan National Police. Why would I tell the Taliban our secrets?"

"Because you have been doing it all along. They knew you were coming here because you told them. You told them about us coming as well, hence we had a welcome party."

Ahmed took the headphones off his head. "This is ridiculous. Why would I do this when I know you can catch me easily?"

"You speak to them in Pashto and Dari. We don't understand that. But you forgot about Mariam. She overheard you one day when she was going down to the missile silo. Then I spoke to HQ, and they hooked onto the channels you were surfing. We know it's you, Ahmed."

Ahmed tried to stand up but he could not. Roderick's hands clamped down on his shoulders and pushed him down on the chair. Ahmed wriggled to get free, without success. Dan stood up and walked around the table.

"Shortly after I told you about sangar 1 needing protection, it was hit by heavy fire. You knew about their mortar base plates, because you told us about them. The Taliban would use a code word for mortars in their radio transmissions. How did you know the code word?"

Silence. Ahmed looked at Dan with baleful eyes. Dan watched them, and his jaws clenched.

It was only a dream. But you appeared in the doorway, when my dead mother, God bless her soul, had come to warn me.

It was only a dream, but you pulled the trigger.

My subconscious was trying to tell me something.

Aloud, Dan said, "You are the mole who has been in this operation from when Mariam escaped from Iran. Who do you work for?"

Ahmed stared at Dan, hatred burning in his eyes. "I don't know what you are talking about."

"What else have you told them, Ahmed?"

Silence again. Dan glanced at Roderick, who nodded.

Dan reached for his belt and with a flourish pulled out his kukri.

Ahmed's eyes widened at the sight of the hooked, eleven-inch, serrated blade. The five-inch handle was made of wood and black leather, making the entire knife sixteen inches in length.

With his other hand, Dan took out a Zippo lighter from his pants pocket. He flicked the cap off and lit the flame. Roderick pressed down on Ahmed's shoulders, grabbing him with a neck hold. He pulled Ahmed's hair back, thrusting his face forward.

Dan ignored them while he used the flame to make the tip of the kukri glow to a red-hot point. Then he squatted on his haunches, and got closer to Ahmed. The man struggled under Roderick's grip, and his breathing was fast and loose. He looked at Dan with wild eyes.

"I hate to do this, Ahmed," Dan said. "These are standard field interrogation techniques. You tell us what I asked you, and I promise, you die quickly. If you don't tell us, we have a long way to go. And you won't like what happens."

"Are you doing the eyelids first?" Roderick asked. Dan liked it. He was improvising.

"Yes," Dan said. "Becomes easier to take the eyes out. The heat from the knife will melt the eyeballs."

"Last time we did the fingers first. I got the hammer."

"We can do that after the eyes."

Roderick did his best to shrug while holding Ahmed down. "Whatever. Just hurry up."

"No," Ahmed whispered.

Dan pressed down on Ahmed with his knee, holding the chin steady with one hand.

Dan lifted the red tip of the kukri, and reached it just under Ahmed's eyebrows. Ahmed jerked and twisted, but Roderick pulled his hair back tightly. Dan paused. "Last chance, Ahmed. I know you told them about the rockets. What else?"

Ahmed spat something out in Pashto. Dan shrugged, and touched the tip of the knife to Ahmed's right upper eyelid. The flesh singed and burned, turning black.

Ahmed screamed, stomped his legs, and tried to slide down the chair. Dan removed the knife. The touch had been enough to scare the man out of his wits. Dan lifted his knee and stood up. He still had his hand on the man's chin, while Rusty pulled back on the hair.

"This is only the beginning, Ahmed," Dan whispered. "Shall I carry on?"

Blood poured down Ahmed's right eye, trickling onto his chin. He was gasping. "I told them…I told them about the woman."

"What else?"

"The rockets, the mortars, everything you told me."

"Have you told them what time we are launching the rockets?"

"You said 2100."

"How many did you say we had?"

"Hundreds. Thousands even. I told them the missile silo was here. It was all here."

"Good man."

Dan removed a pair of plastic handcuffs from his vest, while Roderick took out a black head mask. He pulled it over Ahmed's head and stood him up. Dan tied his hands.

They both looked up as Jones came in through the door.

"We got their weapons," Jones said. "They surrendered without a word." He was talking about the other ANP guards.

"Probably innocent," Dan said. "They might not have known what this guy was doing. But we can't take that chance."

Dan turned his radio on. "Let's go outside and set the base plates set up. Fixed on the coordinates from the grid map."

"Divide the Afghans up, and lock them in the hut," Dan said. "Keep Ahmed in the compound, out in the open where we can see him."

*****

At sunset, pink and golden light played on the shoulders of the far granite mountains. Dan kept watch from the south-facing sangar. The skies were soon shadowed in dark blue and indigo, and the mountains disappeared into folds of black.

1800 hours. Dan pressed on his mic. "Bravo One, this is Zero. Steel rain."

"Roger that, Zero. Wait out."

Dan checked with Jones in sangar 2. He was all set with the Minimi, and Dan had the Gimpy.

There was a sudden boom from the compound, followed by a loud whoosh as the first mortar flew out of the launcher. Dan heard the whoosh become fainter, then a whine as the shell flew through the air. A dull thud and a mild tremor followed as the shell hit its target six hundred meters away.

That was the signal.

Immediately, the loud staccato burst from the machine guns started. Roderick kept loading the mortar shells and firing. As an SOG operative, Roderick had received paramilitary training, and knew how to operate most field artillery guns.

Smoke and the smell of cordite filled the compound. The ground shook with the sound of explosions. Dan did not have any earplugs, but he had picked up two spent cases of the 5.56mm ordnance from one of the rifles. They worked perfectly as earplugs. While the bombardment went on around him, Dan turned his back on it. Taking out his night sight, and putting his NVGs on, he kept a lookout on the south side.

Up to five klicks out, the place was deserted. He scanned 180 degrees. The edge of the village on the right was still empty. He could not see any telltale flashes of light, nor any movement with the NVGs. That right side would be his trouble zone.

It was all part of a plan. They had at least one klick to get to the bunker where they had stashed the quad bikes. One klick of open ground. Best to do that while the mortars and guns were pumping away. Create a diversion.

Dan switched off his mic. It was time for radio silence. He ran down the stairs of the sangar. Roderick and Mariam were standing there, bags on their backs. Mariam had cut her gown off, exposing her legs from the knees down.

"Ready?" Dan asked. They both nodded silently. The hook ladder was flung over the wall. The night sky was lit up behind them with exploding mortar shells. Jones had now taken over. Dan ran back up the sangar, took out his M4 and scanned the ground, ready to fire for cover.

CHAPTER 15

Dan saw the dim outlines of the two figures drop down the last rung of the ladder, and flatten themselves on the ground. Everything was bathed in the green hue of his NVGs. The two figures got up and ran, bent at the waist. Roderick was grabbing Mariam's hand. Dan tracked to the right. The edge of the village. Still nothing.

The Taliban would come soon. Their return fire was now hitting hard, rattling the sangars. Heavy ordnance punctured the air thick with smoke, whining above their heads. Dan looked behind him. The sky was lit up like a bonfire night. Tracer rockets zigzagged up into the air, their lights dimming and falling just short of the compound with explosions that shook the thick perimeter wall.

Dan knew the Taliban would launch a counteroffensive, and it was happening now. They could not wait till the rockets were fired – if that happened, they were finished. They would take heavy casualties. No, they would try and stop it. As long as the Taliban knew they were holed up in the compound, they would try and get inside tonight. Kill them all, and take over the missile silo. Job done.

But not while Dan Roy was alive.

Dan turned the magnified night sight of his M4 to the village. He could see at least forty Taliban. Three streets away, by the bazaar. Fifty meters and closing.

Dan took one last look from the south wall. Mariam and Rod were close to the bunker. They would get on the quad now, and get to the LZ. He looked at his watch. Twenty minutes to ETA.

Dan came down, and ran across to sangar 3. Jones was still pumping the mortar shells.

Dan hoped his ears were ok. The compound walls were getting blasted with bullets. Dan had to do something about the forty fighters closing in. Their plan would be to target the main gate, where the walls dipped. Hook ladders, and they would be looking to get inside, under cover of heavy fire.

This was it. A desperate do-or-die.

Up in the sangar, Dan kept his head low against the volley of incoming fire. He grabbed the Gimpy, and checked it. He used his NVGs to locate the large group he had seen coming forward. For a while he could not see much. They would be sticking to the shadows, creeping in.

The sound of the blasting mortars masked all sound. The sky was lit up with the sight of distant and near explosions. Then he saw a movement. Close by. Twenty meters away. He could make out the snout of an RPG. Pointed straight at his sangar. Dan did not hesitate.

He let rip with the Gimpy, the heavy ordnance catching the RPG holder full in the chest, sending him flying off the ground. At close quarters, the power of the Gimpy was formidable. Dan literally shredded the remaining fighters who had dared to show their faces. He moved the Gimpy in an arc, the rounds smashing in through the mud walls of the huts, dislocating doors from their hinges.

He stopped after a while. He ran down, and tapped Jones on the shoulder. "Your turn," Dan said. "Go."

Jones went to get his rucksack, and Dan scrambled up the south wall sangar.

He heard a sound down below. Jones was now climbing up the ladder. Dan kept his lookout.

No movement from the right. He looked into the mid-distance. A small, black shape was moving away, fast. That must be Rod and Mariam on the quad bike, he thought with satisfaction. Below him, he saw Jones reach the other side, and then sprint across the open ground.

Only one left. Himself. Dan picked up his satellite phone.

"Alpha, this is Zero. Requesting FAS. Repeat requesting FAS." Fast air support. Maybe an F15, maybe a Reaper drone. Armed with enough Hellfire missiles to take out a small town.

Guptill's calm voice came on the line. "Zero, this is Alpha. 15 minutes to FAS. Do you copy?"

Shit. Shit.

Sweat poured down Dan's face. 15 minutes was too long. The Chinook would arrive on time to pick them up. But Dan had to stay behind to keep them at bay. If they were chased to the LZ, another firefight with the Chinook in the middle was not a prospect he looked forward to.

They could all die.

And with the Taliban closing in, 15 minutes was a long time. Dan could keep blasting away with the Gimpy, but he could not cover every angle.

"Alpha, I need it quicker. PID of multiple Tangos closing in."

"Negative, Zero. 15 minutes to FAS. Wait out."

Guptill hung up.

The compound was suddenly quiet. Bullets still poured in from outside, and loud explosions came from outside the perimeter wall. Dan came down the stairs quickly.

When the bombs fell on the compound, and the Scuds ignited, Dan knew he had to be at least one klick away. Otherwise he would not survive.

Dan caught a flicker of movement in the north-west perimeter wall. A shape. It became a head and shoulders, lifting itself above the parapet. Dan turned, and fired from his M4. There was a scream, and the figure fell backwards. Another explosion thundered against the perimeter wall, breaking off chunks of mud that rained down on the compound.

They were coming in. He saw more heads raising themselves above the parapet. He fired again from his M4, moving in an arc. More screams, and the sound of more bodies falling over.

He had no time to get to the Gimpy on sangar 3. He needed a vantage point, right now. He scurried up the stairs of the south wall sangar.

Dan ignored and kept firing. He sneaked a look at his watch.

13 minutes left.

He suddenly remembered the ILAW he had left. In the hut where he slept. Close to the base of the sangar he was on. Dan let off a long burst from his M4. He ran out of ammo, ejected the mag, unhooked a new one from his chest strap, and slapped it in. The he went down the stairs like lightning. He was inside the room in a flash. He got the rocket, and put it on his back using the straps.

He came out, and saw a figure at the edge of the compound. The first Taliban to make it inside. Dan fired before the man had time to react. The rounds shredded his chest, and he fell backwards. Without looking any further, Dan climbed. He needed to get up inside the sangar.

He got up there, and let loose a barrage of indiscriminate fire at the heads that kept popping up now all over the north wall of the compound.

Dan knew his position was insecure. He was exposed, for one thing. More dangerously, it would take the enemy only a second to figure out where the fire was coming from. Right on cue, rounds flew at him. Popping against the sandbags, bursting them open. Dan dived for cover. He heard a sudden loud whine and looked up in alarm.

An RPG, heading straight for him.

Dan needed to reach the wall behind him, with the ladder still dangling.

But there was no time. If this was a direct hit, he was dead. He ran to the rear of the sangar, ready to jump. He felt calm all of a sudden. This was it.

The way it was meant to happen. He had done his job.

The RPG streaked in with a hellish glare of orange-yellow and burst against the sangar.

CHAPTER 16

The grenade hit below the sandbags, on the long, wooden legs of the fortified position. The flames flew up into the sangar. Licks of hot fire burned his skin. Dust and smoke saturated the air around him. Dan felt the wooden floor shake, and then do a sudden lurch forward.

Dan fell backwards, the breath leaving his chest on the impact. He knew what was happening. The legs had given way. If the sangar crashed into the compound, and he was in it, the Taliban would be on him right away.

He would fight with his kukri. Till enough bullets had drilled holes in him. He was ready, but it also meant he would not be able to hold them for long.

He heard shouts and screams from the compound.

"Allah hu Akbar!"

Blindly, he groped for his M4. It was still fixed to his shoulder strap. He plugged two grenades into the UGL, and fired them into the compound. He sprayed bullets down as well, but then felt the sangar tipping further down, into the compound.

Dan ran to the back of the platform. He jumped on top of the sandbags outside, then used the wooden lip as a leverage to jump onto the perimeter wall. He was weighed down by the ILAW on his back, so he jumped as hard as he could.

He aimed for the hook ladder, praying it would take his weight. He landed on the wall, fingers scratching wildly for purchase. He slipped down. His hands clawed for the ladder desperately. His palms burned as he scraped the mud wall, falling down further. He stretched out a hand for the ladder, blind panic seizing him.

The fingers of his right hand closed around the rungs of the ladder. Then his left hand.

Behind him, the sangar was blazing with fire. With a loud groaning sound, it crashed down. Dan climbed. As fast as he could. He was over the wall, and climbing down to the other side when he heard the sounds. They had figured it out. They were climbing the ladder from the other side.

Dan jumped the last five feet. He rolled over and came up, pointing his weapon at the wall. A head appeared and Dan fired. A scream, a thud, and the head disappeared.

8 minutes left.

Dan turned and ran. His left leg held up suddenly, and he winced in pain. He looked down. The ankle was wet with warm liquid. Blood. He could still put pressure on it, but it was going to slow him.

He had to be one klick away when the Hellfire missiles hit. He was not going to make it. He heard the whine of bullets. They kicked up dust around his feet. Dan turned and returned fire.

One head dropped with a scream, but more appeared. Ladders were being set up on the wall. Dan knew what he had to do. He unhooked the ILAW, and put the weapon on the floor. Working quickly, he took the weapon out of its case and pointed it towards the wall. His earplugs had fallen off, and he did not have any spent shells to use. There was no time.

He knelt on one knee, ignoring the bullets that splattered dust around him. He aimed at the largest collection of shapes appearing over the wall, and squeezed the trigger.

There was an ear-splitting explosion as the missile left its launcher, streaking in a yellow haze towards the compound wall. A massive bang followed as the weapon tore through the wall of the compound, splitting the south wall in two. Sparks of white light flew in the air, as did the Taliban who had been caught in the blast. Screams filled the air, drowned out by the missile's furious noise.

Dan did not wait to see the result. He had stumbled forward from the force of the weapon, and his ears were deaf. All he could hear was a ringing sound. He turned and ran as fast as he could. He zigzagged, while maintaining a straight course, trying to present himself as as small a target as possible.

He switched on his radio as he ran. It chirped in his ear immediately. It was Roderick's voice.

"Zero, this is Bravo One, are you receiving?"

Dan gasped as he replied. "Receiving, over."

On the radio, Dan could hear a loud buzz, and Roderick having to shout over it. That would be the Chinook coming in. He felt a surge of hope. They would get out alive. He was not so sure about himself.

But he was a survivor. Dying was not an option.

"Where is Jones?" Dan panted.

"Just arrived…." Roderick said something else, but the sound was drowned out by the rotor waves of the big bird landing.

Dan ran as hard as his injured left leg would allow him. He only had his rucksack on the back now, so he could run faster, in theory. In practice, he realized he was limping.

He looked at his watch.

5 minutes left.

He was now close to the bunker where he had left his quad. He heaved a sigh of relief. Twenty meters away.

Movement. From the side wall of the bunker three figures appeared. Dan could barely make them out: his NVGs had fallen off. He could see them crouching, getting ready to fire.

Dan fired the M4 from his right hip with one hand. With the other he unhooked a frag grenade. He lobbed the grenade as hard as he could, and dived for the ground, still firing from the M4. He heard screams as his bullets found their mark. As soon as he hit the ground, the grenade went off with an orange fireball, shrapnel flying everywhere. He was just out of range, but he still kept his head down. In five seconds, he was firing again, staying flat on the ground. He ran out of ammo. He hooked another mag, and slapped it in. It was his last one.

3 minutes left.

Dan got up and ran as hard as he could. The noise came from behind him. They were chasing him. Bullets kicked up dust around his feet. They had found him. Dan cursed, and turned around. He saw them clearly in the IR vision of his M4 night sight. Five figures approaching, firing straight at him. At moments like this, when he was almost out of ammo, and outnumbered, calm was more important than a hot head.

It had saved his life every time. Dan aimed, picking out the one closest. He dropped him with a double tap to the face, then focused on the others. They went down before their throats, ripped apart by the bullets, could even make a sound.

But Dan did hear a sound. Behind him. He turned quickly. One of the survivors of the grenade blast had lurched closer. Five meters away. Dan could make out the headgear, and the loose dishdasha on his body. The man had a handgun, and he was starting to lift it. Dan fired, and the rounds carved out a hole in the man's chest. He fell backwards.

Feverishly, Dan glanced at his wrist.

1 minute left.

He looked up at the night sky. The drone was getting into position, high above. Had to be a drone, for he had not heard a fighter jet. He got up and ran. He could hear more shouts behind him. The reinforcements had found their fallen comrades, and were now chasing after him. Dan jumped over the dead bodies near the bunker, and headed behind it.

30 seconds.

Dan used the bunker wall as cover, and fired at the ones who were approaching. They were out in the open. It wasn't even a contest. He fired three bursts, then decided to save his ammo. He still had two grenades left. He took out the pin, and lobbed one, flat and hard. It exploded on impact, taking out three more.

15 seconds.

Dan ran like a madman. The bunker was approximately 800 meters away from the compound, so he needed to get another 200 meters. He put his head down, and pumped his muscular legs faster than he ever had in his life.

He saw a wadi on his left and turned into it, his chest heaving with the effort of the sprint. Sweat blinded his eyes.

The slopes of the wadi obscured a direct view of the compound – a dark hump in the background, fading around the bend. Dan's feet scattered stones as he ran along the dry riverbank.

Five seconds.

Four

Three

Two

One…

The sky was illuminated like it was daylight. Fissures spread along the horizon, crackling like white lightning. A thunderclap sounded, but very close, like it was next to his ears. The ground swelled and heaved around him like it was an ocean.

Dan screamed as he flew in the air. He landed in a heap, covering his head with his hands. The ground was soft, being a wadi, but the small stones stung him sharply. Debris rained down on him. The ground shook and thundered, the aftershock trembling through the bowels of earth deep below them. Dust covered the air.

Then there was silence. An eerie, total, absolute silence. Like a blackness without any light.

The silence of death.

Dan shook his head. Dust flew off his hair, choking him. He coughed and spat. He looked up. In the distance, a giant cloud was lifting up into the sky, lit up from below. Sparks of blue lightning flashed at its base. It was an ethereal sight.

Dan tried to stand up. He winced as his left ankle touched the ground. He checked his ammo. Not good news. Only eight rounds left, and one grenade. He fiddled with the radio. Thankfully, he got a signal. His GPS was still working. He got his bearings quickly, and started moving.

He glanced behind as he ran. Expecting bullets any minute. His radio chirped.

"Zero, this is Night Sky, do you copy?" It was the Chinook pilot. Dan breathed out.

"Loud and clear. Are the others ok?" Dan asked.

"Yes. Grouped at the LZ." A pause as the pilot checked the time. "We've got five minutes to evacuation."

"On my way," Dan said. He could not afford to slow down. The deathly quiet around him persisted, but he did not let that fool him. There could be Tangos all around. They had spread out already, hence they had been waiting near the bunker.

Dan ran fast. He ignored the pain in his left leg. His senses were alive to the night around him, expecting gunfire any second.

His main worry was the Chinook being targeted again. This whole area was now awake, and Taliban would be crawling around. Chances are, they had seen the Chinook already.

CHAPTER 17

Dan crested the top of a small hill, his fingers gripping the rocky surface. Below him, in the valley, he could see the outline of the Chinook. Its engine was off, and the rotors were silent.

They were waiting for him. Dan did not like it that the engines were off. If there was a contact, then it would take some time for the bird to fire up. He scrambled down the hill as fast as he could.

Roderick was the first one he saw. He, Derek, and two of the flight crew had formed a perimeter around the Chinook. Dan shouted out his name and call sign, and they put their weapons down.

Dan said urgently, "Get the bird moving, now. Tangos are on their way."

One of the flight crew picked up his weapon and ran back. Dan followed with the others. His throat was parched dry, and he could not swallow. His left leg was hurting like mad. But he, and the others, were still alive.

The Chinook's massive tailgate was lowered, and he clambered on-board.

"You took your time," a female voice said. Dan peered into the darkness, and saw Mariam. There was relief mixed with admiration on her face. Dan stepped up to her. She stood up.

"Take off your boots, and let me look at your leg," she said. Before Dan could answer, a shot rang out. More rounds followed, aimed for them. Dan grabbed Mariam and went down. He looked up, and his blood froze.

Roderick was on the floor, lying motionless.

Dan shouted, "Lift the tailgate, now!"

He lifted his weapon, and fired out even as the tailgate rose up. But it was slow. More rounds kept pinging inside.

"I need ammo," Dan shouted. Jones heard him, and lobbed him a new M4 rifle. Dan grabbed it and fired. He pulled Roderick in. It was an abdomen wound. Blood poured out of it. Dan looked at the back and found the exit wound. It was to the side. Below the level of the spleen. Chances were that it had missed the major abdominal organs and arteries. He put pressure on the wound.

"Hang in there, Rod!" he shouted at his pale face. Rod moved his lips but no sound came.

Bullets were raining on the Chinook now. Mariam appeared beside him.

She began to put a dressing on Roderick from the first aid box.

The rotors were moving. The engines of the mighty bird were loud, throbbing the inside of the carriage.

"Take the windows," Dan shouted at Jones. With one of the flight crew, they returned fire from each of the windows. The ground shook beneath their feet, and a blizzard of dust obscured their vision. But the firing continued.

With a huge lurch, the Chinook lifted off the ground. Within seconds it was airborne. Dan did not stop firing. He saw the convoy of cars that had appeared a hundred meters away. The bird lifted higher up, and soon the cars and enemy figures were smaller, like pins on the ground.

Dan threw his weapon down, and slumped backwards against the seat. He rolled over to Roderick. Mariam was still pressing on his wound. Dan checked: the blood seepage was less.

Jones handed Dan a flask of water. Gratefully, Dan downed it.

In half an hour, they had reached base. Roderick was carried out on a stretcher. Mariam met his eyes before she alighted. Dan looked at her and nodded. She smiled at him. Then she was led away by a uniformed private.

Dan staggered inside the base, and saw Guptill standing there. They walked into a room, where Dan sprawled in a chair.

"You did well," Guptill said.

Dan did not reply. Guptill said, "There's a new mission waiting for you."

Dan shook his head. It was always like this with Intercept. One mission faded into another. Like night into day. But right now, he needed to rest. Guptill knew that, too.

The older man said, "Have a sleep. Medics are waiting to look at you. Let me know tomorrow."

Dan said, "You knew about the compound, didn't you?"

Guptill paused. He opened his mouth to say something but then seemed to change his mind. He said, "Yes, we did. But we did not know for certain. The CIA guys could not confirm on radio."

"You could have given me a heads-up."

Guptill smiled. "I figured you would find out soon enough. I didn't want you to approach the mission any differently. That's why I kept it from you."

Guptill turned, and walked out the door.

Dan stood up. Every bone in his body ached. Tomorrow was another day. He would live to fight it, and whatever else came his way.

THE END

HIDDEN AGENDA

Dan Roy Series
Dan Roy Thriller 1

For Mersedeh, my secret, and special, agent

CHAPTER 1

Soho's narrow, crowded streets form the bustling heart of London city. Under its glaring neon lights, and inside its intimate, cozy pubs, gather the bohemians who give London its character.

The artists, the losers, the drug dealers. The nine-to-five single mothers who work in the lap dancing parlors in the evenings. The immigrants of Chinatown working for less than minimum wage in the glitter of Chinatown. The bankers stopping by for a drink, and perhaps a small bag of cocaine.

Dan Roy walked down the street into this melting pot. He kept his head low and tried to be inconspicuous, but being Dan Roy, that wasn't easy. He was a shade over six feet, two hundred and twenty pounds, with wide shoulders and biceps that strained the fabric of any shirt he wore. His brown hair was longer now, and it fell over his large, dark eyes. Eyes that were restless, but also expressive. They glinted like diamonds in the neon lights of London's underbelly.

In truth, Dan was scanning the crowd for signs of threat. He did not expect any danger, but looking for threats was part of Dan's DNA. He had spent years as a Black Ops specialist for the most secretive Black Ops organization of them all - Intercept. That experience had hard-wired anticipation of danger into his brain. He would and could kill without hesitation if the need arose. For self-protection, if nothing else.

But he did not want to.

The Army and Intercept had trained Dan to become a ruthless killer. It wasn't difficult, given that he was already a member of Squadron B, Delta Force, by the time Intercept came knocking on his door.

With Intercept, Dan had found his calling in life. He had been a warfighter already, but Black Ops took his skills to a different level. His kills became the stuff of legend.

But there was a price. His soul had no respite from constant war. The ravages of combat can be like claw marks on the mind. He had plenty of those.

He needed a break, like what he was enjoying now. He could not talk about what happened, but a clean break had made him sane again.

Dan saw the sign for the Duke of Edinburgh pub, and stepped inside. Soft, glowing lights and the warmth of human bodies standing close together enveloped him. He pushed his way to the noisy bar. The bar girl recognized him.

"Hey, Dan," the red-haired woman said. Their eyes met and her cheeks went red as Dan stared at her with his dark, intense eyes. Lucy Sparks was petite, no more than five feet six. Her figure was slender, but she was filled out in the right places. A figure that Dan liked. He stopped by the pub to chat to her, and often had his lunch there as well. Lucy was a student at Birkbeck College, doing a part-time PhD. She did her college in the mornings, and started work in the afternoon, staying till late at night.

"Hey, Lucy," Dan said. "How are things?" He had to raise his voice above the din.

"Busy," Lucy rolled her eyes. "How are you?"

"All the better for seeing you."

Lucy smiled, her cheeks touching crimson again. She did not disguise the fact that she had a thing for him. They flirted often, and Dan was on the verge of asking her out on a date.

"What can I get you?" Lucy asked.

"A pint of Camden Hells lager please." His mouth watered. When it came to craft beer, few places in the world topped London. Including Charlotte, NC, and that was saying something. He thanked Lucy, closed his eyes and took a long sip from the tall pint glass.

He looked around him carefully. The usual smattering of creative types, financial professionals, students and workers. He heard a cellphone buzz. It was nearby, but not his. Dan did not carry a cellphone. He did not want to be traced. He did not want to be called. He did not want to wake up and curl his fingers around the butt of his Sig Sauer P226 the second his eyes flew open.

He wanted to enjoy his drink in the company of strangers. This was the start of a trip for him. From London, he would fly to Morocco, and spend a week in Tangiers. From there he would fly to Mumbai, and taste the waters of the Arabian Sea with the hippies in Goa. Thailand beckoned after that. He had not planned any further. It was good not to have a plan, to go where his eyes would take him. He was looking forward to it.

Dan finished his drink, paid, winked at a blushing Lucy, and left. He would have two more drinks, catch a theater in the West End, then end up in a restaurant in Chinatown before going back to his small hotel on Charing Cross Road. A small en suite room cost a bomb, but the money he had made working for Intercept was more than adequate for his purposes.

Dan was close to Soho Square Gardens when he felt someone following him.

A shadow crossed the street ten yards behind. Dan stopped to buy a newspaper inside a kiosk. He looked but saw nothing apart from tourists. That alerted him further. A professional would not have fallen for that simple trick.

The gardens loomed in front of him. Dan went in, and the footsteps followed. Dan knew the park well. It was well maintained, with the help of London's high tax-paying public. He walked inside the gates quickly, then suddenly broke into a run.

He disappeared round the thick stump of a pine tree. He could hear the pounding feet now. Two men, running fast. Panicking that they had lost him.

Who? Why? Two questions he didn't have answers to. It didn't matter. Old reflexes took over.

Dan waited till the second man was about to pass him. In a blur of movement, he grabbed the man's midriff and pulled him under the tree. Dan slammed the man's head against an overhanging branch. He followed it up with a short arm jab to the right jaw. The blow sent the already dizzy man stumbling backwards. He sagged against the tree, unconscious.

Dan had dived for the ground in preparation for a bullet streaking towards him. The man's partner would have drawn his weapon. British cops did not carry guns, but Dan was willing to bet these guys were not British. He crawled behind the tree trunk and waited, his senses working overtime. It was quiet, the sounds of traffic now faded in the distance.

He didn't expect what he heard next. A voice he knew very well.

The voice said, "Dan, it's me. Come out and show yourself."

CHAPTER 2

Dan did not answer. After a beat, the voice spoke again.

"Don't be afraid, Dan. If I wanted you dead, there would be no need for this. I just want to talk."

The logic was irrefutable. The speaker was not one to make idle threats. Dan remembered his first mission as a Delta operative. This man had been his CO. Later on, his handler for Intercept. Major John Guptill. The man who had helped to sharpen his skills when he entered Delta and make him into a killing machine.

The only man Dan trusted implicitly. After all that had happened, his trust of intelligence agencies was broken. He would never trust any intelligence agency, big or small, ever again. They played games that had wrecked his life.

John Guptill had pulled him back when he had been staring at the dark abyss. The only one who had cared.

Guptill said, "We haven't got all night, Dan. Tell me, what's it gonna be?"

Dan stayed behind the tree and said, "Tell these guys to throw their weapons where I can see them."

Guptill gave out an order, and there was a sound of metal clattering on the floor. Dan saw a Colt M1911 and a Sig P226 handgun appear near him. They were close enough for him to reach. He saw a shadow appear. An average-sized man, slightly stooped and wearing a black overcoat. The figure spread its hands. It was John Guptill.

Dan stepped out. In the same movement, he picked up the Sig off the floor, and kicked the Colt to one side. He held the gun by his side.

Dan said, "You could have just tapped me on the shoulder."

"Where, inside a pub?"

"How long have you been following me for?"

Dan had spent the last month in London. He had traveled around Surrey and Berkshire, but not gone too far. He had got sloppy. He should have picked these guys up ages ago.

"The last two weeks," Guptill said.

"Why?"

"Shall we sit down?"

Guptill knew better than anyone else that Dan had left Intercept. He had done his final, exit interview. Promised his silence. A break of that promise was rewarded with death. He had also collected his last paycheck. He had not received all of it as yet: the money came to him in stages. Intercept wanted to be sure Dan did not divulge any critical information to the media or a foreign government before they paid him for the last time.

The question buzzed around his head. If Guptill knew this, then why was he here with two guys packing weapons?

His old CO seemed to read his mind. "First off, there was no other way to contact you. Your last known location was London, UK. These guys would not have harmed you. Their weapons are for my protection."

Dan looked at his mentor. Under the street lights, Guptill's silvery buzz cut appeared dull. But his blue eyes glinted.

Dan said, "You have an apartment in London, right? You come and go. Why do you need protection here?"

In answer Guptill reached a hand inside his jacket pocket. Anyone else did that movement, Dan would have stiffened. But this was the only man he trusted. Guptill sat down on the park bench close to the tree and pulled out a brown paper packet. He shone a flashlight on it. He took out a sheaf of photos and handed them over to Dan.

Dan looked up briefly. One of the men was helping his injured colleague up from the ground. They leaned against the tree trunk, keeping an eye on him. Dan looked away. He took the photos from Guptill's hand, who shone a light on them.

The photo showed a collection of black cylinders with yellow marks on them. Fins at the top and bottom. Hellfire missiles. Stacked next to a pile of Pathway missiles. Air-to-surface missiles used in Reaper drones, and also fired from a range of other aircraft. The next photo showed Heckler & Koch 417, and M4 SOPMOD carbines, all modified for Special Operations. But the locations were odd. They were on a mud floor, inside a mud hut.

Guptill said, "A Marine recon platoon chanced upon this in northeast Afghanistan. Inside a Taliban compound. Not controlled by us."

Dan said, "How did it get there?"

Guptill said, "The compound belongs to a senior Al-Qaeda commander, sheltered by the Taliban. That man is now on the run. We know where he is hiding." Guptill looked at Dan.

Dan knew where this was headed. He handed the photos back to Guptill.

He said, "No."

Guptill said, "These are our current weapons. Taliban have the capability to fire them from the Russian helicopters they have. It negates a huge tactical advantage for us."

Dan said, "Who is supplying them?"

"That's what I'm trying to find out. But first we need to get this guy, and confiscate the weapons."

Dan said again, "No. Get someone else."

"You'll get paid."

"I've already been paid."

"Not all of it. Plus, this time, you get a bonus."

"You could give anyone a bonus. Why me?"

Deep inside, Dan knew the answer. The man opposite him had been there on the last day of his Delta selection, when Dan almost died of dehydration. The notorious 40-mile hike with a 45-pound backpack through the remotest Appalachian Mountains. A feat that still disabled a soldier or two. Less than ten percent made the grade.

Dan was the first one in his group to make it back. He broke the all-time record for speed of completion of the final stage.

A record that still held firm.

Guptill had seen his potential and taken him under his wing. After his father's death, Guptill was the man who had become a father figure to him.

Guptill said, "The same reason I now have two bodyguards with me."

"You cannot trust anyone."

"Correct."

Dan sighed and rubbed his hands on his face. He said, "What do you know so far?"

"Not much. Somehow these weapons are getting up to Afghanistan. And if they can get up there, shit, they could potentially end up anywhere."

Dan understood. Any number of jihadis would love to get their hands on these weapons.

Guptill said, "Dan, this is a really big deal. JSOC contacted me. Remember Jim McBride?"

Dan nodded. He had heard of Lt. Colonel Jim "Fighter" McBride. One of the head honchos of Joint Special Operations Command at Fort Bragg, NC.

Guptill reached inside and took out another photo. Dan took it. It was a black and white photo of a man lying face-down in a pool of blood.

Guptill said, "That's the CIA agent who got me the photos. The cops found his body in London yesterday. They alerted MI5, who alerted the CIA."

Dan said, "Sir, you know I have left all this behind. If I do this, I get sucked back in."

Guptill leaned forward. "What if it was me in that photo you were holding, Dan?"

Dan stopped. What would he do? What *could* he do?

"I cannot trust anyone else on this. One last time. I swear I'll never call on you again. Not for anything like this."

Dan said, "There's something else. Intercept told you to come looking for me. You're not telling me the whole story."

Guptill sat back in the seat. The wooden slats creaked. He breathed out into the mild spring air. Dan waited.

Guptill said, "This is top secret. Officially, you don't have clearance anymore."

"Officially, you shouldn't be here asking me to go back to work. I quit, remember?"

"Whatever. Just remember what I said."

"I got it."

Guptill lowered his voice. "NSA, and GCHQ over here, have picked up a lot of chatter from online jihadi networks. A big attack is planned. In a European capital. Paris, Frankfurt or London. We don't know when."

"What does that have to do with this compound in 'Stan?"

"People who stashed those weapons there, you don't think they could use them here?"

Dan was quiet for a while. Then he said, "So getting the Al-Qaeda guy would help you to find the missing links."

"Right now, he's the only link we got. We need to get those weapons as well before the Taliban get to use them."

"And then what?"

Guptill asked, "What do you mean?"

Dan said, "What happens to me after the mission is over? Will Intercept cut me loose, or keep an eye on me?"

Dan had not planned to stay in London for long. He thought about the airline tickets he had bought. He had used cash, but someone must be keeping tabs on his bank account. The thought was unnerving. He might never be free of these guys. Dan was trained to be a killer. He seldom felt any emotion. But he did now.

Anger. Anger that they were still following him around, like he was some criminal.

He had done nothing wrong.

Dan stood up. He looked at Guptill who raised himself up slowly.

Dan said, "I guess you know where I'm staying. Well, I'm headed back. But I'm not *going* back, if you know what I mean."

Guptill stared at him for a while, then nodded. "I don't want to force you. It is your decision. I just told you the facts."

Dan said, "Thank you." He looked at the two guys, one of whom who was still rubbing his chin. He raised a hand.

"Sorry about that, guys. Next time, just come up and ask me. It's much easier."

CHAPTER 3

Dan went off to the nearby West End to catch an evening show. The show was enjoyable, but he watched it with half a mind only. After dinner in Chinatown, he headed back to his small hotel in Charing Cross Road. It was opposite Leicester Square, down an alley that dated back to the Victorian times. The front seemed like a shop that had shut down, and the sign was hidden behind a hanging basket of flowers. It was barely visible unless one looked hard. It was a narrow-terraced building, a common finding in London, and the interior was quaint beyond belief.

Dan stepped inside, and a doorbell chimed. The striped blue and gray wallpaper made the place even smaller than it was. Brits loved dark wallpaper. At the reception, the balding head of Rupert St John-Smythe, the proprietor in whose family the building had been for the last three generations, looked up as Dan came in.

"Ah, Mr Roy," Rupert said.

"Hey," Dan replied.

"Nice evening?"

"Caught up with some old friends."

"Splendid. However, and if you don't mind me saying so, you look rather tired."

Dan leaned against the table. "What you trying to say?"

A look of embarrassment passed Rupert's face. "Oh, nothing at all. Perhaps impertinent of me to suggest such a thing. I was merely…"

Dan said, "Rupert."

"Yes?"

"Chill. I was just busting your balls."

Rupert looked confused again, then his face cleared. "Ah, that expression. Means you speak in jest."

"I do."

Rupert said, "May I offer you a nightcap?"

It was just what Dan needed. He did not keep alcohol in his room. He did not want to rely on it. At night when he could not sleep, he went for a walk. The tourist areas of Central London were well lit and safe at night. And

85

common thugs or street gangs did not worry Dan.

Lately, he had spent many nights walking around the lonely streets. It had made him appreciate the city better, without the usual throng of tourists. At night, and on his own, the city was beautiful. He often walked down to Waterloo Bridge, and leaned against the stones, watching the rushing black river underneath. The tall spires of Westminster shone golden yellow like a dream in the street lights. The solitude gave him some respite from the visions in his head.

He said, "I would like that."

Rupert reached behind the desk and pulled out a bottle of Drambuie brandy. He poured two glasses and passed one to Dan.

Rupert said, "You know, this used to be The Queen Mother's favorite drink."

Dan knocked it back. The liquid burned his throat and warmed his insides. He shook his head. If it was good for The Queen Mother, it was good for him.

Rupert smiled, and poured another.

After three shots of Drambuie, Dan was ready for bed. He insisted on paying for the drinks, but Rupert said it was his personal supply. Dan went upstairs, put his sixteen-inch kukri knife under his pillow, and fell into a dark, dreamless sleep.

His eyes flew open when he heard the birds outside. His primal instinct, as always, was to reach for a weapon. A hardwired instinct. Then he relaxed, and sank back on the bed. It was strangely comforting to lie in that old bed in an old English Bed and Breakfast, and listen to the birds tweet outside. The first portent of spring. The first thawing of the ice in his soul. As he lay there, drifting in and out of sleep, he remembered that fateful day in Sanaa, the capital of Yemen.

Sanaa was a medieval fortress city of brown terracotta houses and white minarets. His mission: to blow up a bus carrying a local chapter of Al-Shabaab terrorists. He had staked out the bus garage for two days. He had surveyed the route. In the dead of night, he laid Claymore anti-personnel mines across the stretch of highway the bus would travel on. Next morning, he waited by the highway, hidden in the brush, detonator in hand.

As the bus got closer, he saw something that took the breath out of his chest. Little arms poking out the windows. The cries of children. He saw it clearly with his binoculars. For some reason, the route and transport had changed. This bus was taking kids to school. Thirty or forty kids, playing and screaming. His fingers were on the detonator, gripping it tightly. He had seconds to act. He heard the voice in his earphone.

"Take the bus out, now."

Intercept's support team. Dan's knuckles were white on the detonator. The bus came closer. He could still see it clearly – the eyes of a boy, about 8 years old, leaning out the bus, staring directly at him.

"Take the hit. DO IT!" the voice growled in his ear again.

Dan's eyes opened wide. His nostrils flared. The bus was ten yards away. He could hear the jingles of some music from the radio. Dan had never failed on a mission. A target was as good as dead when their folder was passed to his hands.

The cries of the children got louder. Dan's fingers were like claws. His hand shook. Within seconds, the bus was on him.

Now or never. That boy's eyes never left him. Dan would remember those eyes till the day he died. He saw them now, as he lay still on this English spring morning. Wide, innocent eyes. A face that would never harm him. A child who would never harm anyone. Dan Roy was a killer, but he did not kill children.

His fingers went slack. He lowered the detonator from his hand. The voice on his mic was going crazy. Dan ripped the earpiece off his ears, and lowered his head to the ground.

Early the next day, he was flown back to base. He wanted out. He promised his silence. They didn't like it, but they let him go. Dan knew there would never be a way back in. He had burned his bridges.

Till now. There was something odd about the whole thing. First off, Intercept were following him around. They knew where he was. Intercept always did things for a reason. In his heart of hearts, Dan had not wanted to leave after a failed mission. But he could not have fulfilled his last mission. If that is what Intercept wanted him to do…

But Intercept would know what was going on inside Dan's mind. He had been subjected to days of psychological profiling. Every thought of his was known to them. It had not bothered him before. Now, it made him uneasy as hell.

Guptill was sent for a reason. Dan would not listen to anyone else. They knew that. They also knew a mission like this – to potentially avoid a terrorist attack in a big city – would appeal to Dan. It could be his last chance to leave Intercept with a flawless record.

Well, maybe it was time to prove them wrong.

Dan showered and dried himself. His thick biceps, and the broad muscles of his back rippled as he went through a yoga routine afterwards. Then he dressed and went downstairs for breakfast.

Rupert had got the chef to make him a full English breakfast. He got stuck into sausages (called bangers in London), bacon, beans, tomatoes, toasted bread and black pudding. After breakfast, he slurped on his cup of Earl Grey Assam tea. Earl Grey English tea was cool, but not strong enough for him. Ever since he had started living in London, a whole new world of teas had opened up to him. The stronger ones worked almost like coffee.

As he walked out the door, he felt in his pockets to make sure he had everything. His fingers brushed the piece of paper on which Guptill had written down the cellphone number. Dan walked out towards the subway, or tube station of Leicester Square. He looked around him as he walked.

He picked up his first tail on the tube train as it rumbled through the underground. A middle-aged man with a newspaper. Dan came out on the other side of the river at Embankment, and walked down the river path towards the Tate Modern art gallery. Inside the gallery, it was easier to keep an eye on his tail. There were now two of them.

He had said no to Guptill. Why were they still following him?

CHAPTER 4

It was late afternoon by the time Dan had lunch and returned to Soho. He had managed to lose the two tails, but he was sure there would be others around. Inside the rabbit warren of Soho's narrow streets he could duck and dive, giving his followers the slip. Trained in countersurveillance, Dan used every trick in the book. He changed trains three times, caught a cab and jumped off at a traffic light, and doubled around himself till he got back to Soho.

Now he needed a drink. He watched the entrance of the Duke of Edinburgh pub for ten minutes. It was still early, but there were a fair number of people inside already. Through the windows, he could see Lucy cleaning the tables. She straightened, and tucked a loose strand of her ginger hair behind her ear. Dan could see that she was wearing a yellow tee shirt and jeans. When she leaned over the tables, he could see a flash of her cleavage. He smiled.

Dan took one last look around, then headed for the doors of the pub. Lucy looked up as he opened the door. She was twenty feet away from him. Dan stood at the doors of the pub, and smiled at her. She caught his eyes, put her hands on her hips, and tilted her head. She opened her mouth as if to say something.

The blast of heat exploded in a giant yellow fireball behind her. It ripped apart the long bar, flung tables, chairs and bodyparts out of the windows. Dan was lifted up in the shock wave and flew back from the door, which tore off from its hinges. His back smashed against the wall of a building opposite, more than ten feet away. He crumpled to the floor.

He was still alive. Breathing. He felt something hot and sticky coursing down his face. Glass and wooden debris rained down around him. He covered his head and let the falling fragments subside.

Silence. That total, awful silence immediately after an explosion. He looked up, and groaned as he pulled himself to his feet. There was a black, smoking hole where the doors had been. The two long windows had been smashed out. Hanging from the nearest window, a headless body lay upside down like a rag doll.

Dan's heart wrenched inside. He coughed and belched out smoke. He got to the doorway and leaned in. Black soot covered the floor. It hid the slick of blood, but not the charred, cut human remains. Dan ignored the ghastly sight around him. He limped over to where Lucy had been standing. There was no sign of her. He looked down in the smoke and haze, and heard the few groans that came from a survivor. At his feet, he found a pair of Doc Marten boots with purple laces, still smoking from the explosion. They were Lucy's shoes. Dan picked one up and pressed it against his chest.

A fearful pressure was building inside him. Rage, hurt, sorrow were mixing into a deadly cocktail, ready to burst out like a grenade. His fingers flicked down to his belt line. No, he did not have a weapon. He wanted one. He could smell blood, and felt something wet on his face. Not blood. Something lighter, and coming from his eyes.

He held the shoe tightly in his hand, and walked over to the nearest groaning survivor. His torso was half-blown off, and his left leg was missing. He would not survive long. Dan had done this before, but today it made him sick to the core. He rolled over a few bodies. It was horrible work.

He found her finally, slumped over the legs of a table. The left side of her body – the arm and legs, were missing. He knelt down and passed a hand over her red hair, now burned black. Dan was no stranger to death. He had pulled out corpses from demolished buildings before, and taken photos of kill targets as proof. He had not known Lucy for that long. But seeing her down there moved something inside him. He did not know what it was. Something like pain, an emotion that was alien to him.

He made a guttural, choking noise from his throat and stood up. His lungs were heaving. He opened his mouth, smelling the death and destruction around him. What he had lived for all his adult life. What made him who he was.

Did he bring this upon Lucy? And to the others inside this place – all human beings with a home and a family – now lying in a macabre assortment of flesh and bone. The thought came quickly and left. He could have been killed in any number of ways. Killing him like this would only bring attention upon his assassins.

This was a terrorist attack in the heart of London. The attack that Guptill had warned him about.

Dan heard a groaning noise above him. He looked up as dust fell on his eyes. The sound grew and something crashed down behind him. Dan lifted Lucy's half-body and ran for the door. The building, like most of Soho's structures, was an old one, and the ceiling had wooden rafters. They had cracked in the explosion and the heat was now bending them. A large black beam smashed down in front of him. With a huge groan, the windows started to cave inwards. Dust filled the air.

Dan dodged the falling plaster and bricks, and stumbled out. He laid Lucy's battered body on the road. A crowd had gathered. Sirens wailed, getting louder. Behind him, there was a huge crash, and the building collapsed completely. Dan picked Lucy up again, and stumbled out farther for protection. There was a whistle, and running boots indicated the arrival of policemen.

The next few hours were a blur to Dan. An ambulance arrived, and conducted the grisly task of taking the torn victims away. A paramedic arrived and spoke to Dan. She put a hand on his arm. He was holding Lucy's remaining arm tightly, and the paramedic gently removed it. A stretcher lifted her body into the ambulance.

Dan watched the ambulance thread its way out of the crowd. He knew her family would be notified and they would come down to see her body. Burial would be over the next few days. Dan hung his head. He put his hands inside his pockets.

When he took his right hand out, he was holding the piece of paper with Guptill's number on it.

CHAPTER 5

Guptill answered straight away. Dan was inside a typical, red, London telephone booth. He leaned against the side, wiping the sweat and blood from his face.

"It's me," Guptill said.

Dan swallowed, then said, "The mission. I am in."

Guptill did not answer for a while. Then he said, "Where are you?"

Dan did not reply. "The mission," he repeated like a robot. "I need the file."

Guptill was quiet again. Then he said, "Meet me at the north end of Hyde Park Corner. There's an oak tree next to the statue of Oliver Cromwell. I'll be wearing a black overcoat."

Dan said, "ETA one hour." He hung up.

He watched for a while from the phone booth. Then he slid out, and walked down a series of alleys. People and policemen rushed around him. He could hear human voices screaming, and the wail of more sirens. He stopped at a dead end alley, and walked to the end of it. There was a row of lock-up garages. Dan went to the last one, and inserted a key in the lock. He took one last look around him, then went inside. He shut the door, locked it and turned on the light switch. The space was roughly twenty by ten feet. In the middle rested the rusting hulk of a Austin Minor car from the 1920s.

The Cockney gangster who had sold Dan the garage had said the car was worth a lot of money if it was refurbished. Dan had replied that if it was, then the gangster would be doing it himself. The man had taken his money and left.

Dan knelt by the car, and slid under on his back. He had taken a screwdriver from a toolbox at the side. He worked for the next ten minutes, removing a portion of the chassis. When the last part came off, it showed a hollow space inside. The space was about four feet long. Inside, there was a black metal case. Dan removed the case. Then he crawled out of the car.

He went to the door and looked outside. The cul-de-sac was empty. He went back inside and leaned over the metal case. Inside, there was an M4 carbine rifle, one fitted out to the SOPMOD or Special Operations Peculiar

Modifications. Dan checked the night sight, the Underslung Grenade Launcher, and the various objects he could fit on the Picatinny rail. He also had a Sig Sauer P226, his favorite handgun. He expelled the magazine, slid back the breech, then sprung it back. Everything worked.

He checked the five boxes of ammo he had, for each weapon. To one side, he had another curved kukri knife, slightly shorter at eleven inches. He put the knife and the Sig in his belt line, and kept the M4 inside the metal case. He picked up the case, locked the door, and headed out into Soho.

*****

Guptill was waiting for him under the oak tree. He was sat on a bench. Dan couldn't see the other two men, but he knew they would be around.

Guptill looked up as Dan approached. "Jesus," he said. "What happened?"

Dan did not say anything. He sat down. Guptill stared at him for a while then said, "Shit. You were there."

Dan stared stonily ahead. His eyes saw nothing, he felt nothing. The only thing that mattered was the Sig and the kukri in his belt line. They gave him all the comfort he needed. Like an extension of his body that had been missing for a while.

Guptill said, "I'm sorry."

"Did you know?" Dan asked. He was aware that Guptill had turned to look at him, but he ignored it.

Guptill's voice hardened. "If that is what you believe, then walk the fuck away now. Don't come back."

Dan nodded. Guptill had not known about the specific location. That was all the confirmation he needed.

Guptill said, "You knew someone there." It was a statement, not a question. Dan did not respond.

"I can see it in your face," Guptill said. "You should not be on a mission for personal reasons. You know that."

"It's not personal."

"You sure about that?"

"Yes."

Guptill said, "Dan, I had to cover for you last time. Told them to leave you alone. This time around, I can't do that."

"Last time was different," Dan said.

"And this time won't be? Who was she?"

Dan stood up. "Do you want me on the job, or not?"

"Sit down. I need to make sure you are not distracted on this job. It's a big one. We need a kill and intel, or live target capture. You have to be firing on all cylinders."

"You know I will," Dan said. He caught Guptill's eye. He read the look. Guptill knew him well. Now he was seeing something new in Dan's eyes, and it was confusing him. But Guptill did not look angry or disappointed. There was curiosity in his eyes, and what seemed like an acceptance. Dan looked away.

Guptill said, "Give me your word, Dan. I need you to focus. For all our sakes."

Something in his voice made Dan stop. He looked at his old CO's face. There was an earnest plea in Guptill's tone. Dan knew he would not use it without good reason.

"I am focused. What time is the flight?" Dan asked.

"2000 hours. From RAF Brize Norton." Dan had flown on missions from that Royal Air Force base before.

"Who is my contact?"

"An Intercept guy called Rory Burns. Call him Burns. He's a good guy. You can trust him."

Dan had heard of Burns in the past, but never met him. He provided intel, and handled some of the operatives.

Guptill said, "Burns will meet you in Afghanistan. You fly out alone. Your kit will be there. At the RAF base there is a weapon armory. Pick what you want."

Dan said, "I need to pay my hotel bill. Pick me up in half-hour."

"Roger that," Guptill said. They both got up and walked off in different directions.

CHAPTER 6

Jalalabad Air Base
FOB (Forward Operating Base) Fenty
Afghanistan

It was weird being back in Afghanistan. It was dark inside his dorm room, a respite from the blinding yellow heat and relentless dust outside. That was one thing Dan never got used in the 'Stan. The constant dust, powdery and floating around in huge clouds. It got into his eyes, clotted up the valves of weapons, made his skin itch.

In the dead heat of the afternoon, Dan picked up his suppressed Heckler & Koch 416 assault rifle and looked down the ten-inch barrel.

The weapon had an EOTech optical red dot sight with a 3x magnifier mounted on top. He slid back the bolt and chambered a round, made sure the safety was on, and used the laser beam to light a pinpoint at the far end of his tent.

He checked the side pockets of his camouflage pants. In one he had his leather gloves for abseiling down ropes from whichever copter they would be flying in. Chances are it would be a Black Hawk Mi-17 or an Apache. In another pocket he had extra batteries. In the lower Cargo pants he kept his digital camera to take photos of kill targets and for intel. Wrapped round his left ankle he kept a small, snub-nosed, suppressed Sig for emergencies. The butt was thicker due to a rubber grip, and came easily into the hand. It had saved his life in the past.

He stood up and put his vest on. The ceramic armor plates weighed it down and the rest of his gear made it up to a full sixty pounds. On either side of his chest he had a radio. He tested the headphones to make sure he could hear the buzz of static, and the tiny digital microphone embedded in his right ear. Between the two radios he kept four extra magazines for the rifle, and a fragmentation grenade. Below that, on either side of the vest, he kept flashbangs, plastic lights, wire cutters and plastic handcuffs. He reached behind his back to make sure he could get the C-4 explosive fixed to the vest. It came off with a pull. The detonators were in a small pocket on his sleeve.

Then his hands slipped down to the curved, sixteen-inch kukri knife strapped to the belt line on his back. Presented to him by a Gurkha soldier, who had also shown him how to use it.

He hefted the kukri in his hand without taking it out of its black scabbard. Its long edge had been used with spectacular effect on a Taliban chieftain's neck. The head had separated from the body.

"Dan, are you there?" The voice came from outside the open door of his bunker. A tall, wiry man in a crumpled suit came in.

Rory Burns had a sallow, angular face with sunken cheeks. His gray eyes were bright and lit up when he talked. Dan had not met the guy before he had arrived at the base. Burns had taken care of his kit and acted as the liaison between them and the regiment billeted at FOB Fenty.

"Yes," Dan said.

Burns' head was bent, touching the top of the door frame. He stepped inside the room and blinked as his eyes adjusted to the dimness inside.

Burns said, "Time to debrief ten minutes. In HQ."

"Cool."

Burns sat on his haunches on the floor. There was an unexpected look of concern on his face. He said, "You okay?"

Dan could not keep the snap out of his voice. "Why shouldn't I be?"

Burns shrugged. "I spoke to Guptill. He said…"

Dan interrupted. "Said what?"

"Nothing. Just to keep an eye on you. Make sure you were cool."

"I don't need a nanny." Dan stood up, his broad bulk filling up the room. Burns stood up as well. He gave Dan another concerned look. Dan ignored him.

"See you out there," said Burns, and left.

Dan came out of his bunker, locked it, and walked across the dusty courtyard. The flat expanse of the silver hangars loomed in the backyard. He could hear the whine from the rotors of a large Chinook 47 as maintenance guys tested the machine. People in uniform moved in and out of squat buildings around him. There was a cafeteria and, adjacent to it, the military hospital. FOB Fenty was an annex to Jalalabad Airport, and much smaller than the larger camps in Afghanistan such as Camp Bastion. It was easy to spot people here, and as Dan came out he caught sight of Burns again. Burns waved at him and went inside the HQ building.

Dan opened the glass door of HQ and heard the suck of rubber gaskets as the doors shut. He was in an air-conditioned space with carpets and a hallway opening up to an office reception. The reception desk was empty. He turned down the hallway and knocked twice on the first door. Burns opened the door and Dan went in. An older man with salt-and-pepper hair stood next to a screen in the corner of the room. Apart from the three of them, the room was empty.

Dan and the older man stared back at each other. Then Dan remembered. He had seen the man on a TV screen before. Lieutenant Colonel Jim "Fighter" McBride. One of the deputy commanders at Joint Special Operations Command or JSOC, over at Fort Bragg, North Carolina. The guy who had spoken to Guptill about the operation. McBride was dressed in civilian clothes and was not here on official duty. No one in the Pentagon would know he was here, apart from the few who knew of Intercept's existence.

"Come in, Dan," McBride's voice was gentle, but it was obeyed instantly.

This room was soundproof, and secure. Inside this room they were Intercept. The US, or any other government, would deny their existence.

They were a highly secretive branch of elite soldiers, picked from the four squadrons of the Delta Force. The best of the best. Even their Delta colleagues did not know that they existed.

Their specialism was the shadowy world where DoD sanction was not needed, nor asked for. The Pentagon was tired of paying hundreds of millions to private military contractors, or PMCs. It was time they played the same game. The lawyers made sure their activities could never be traced back to the Army.

Dan saw the grid reference map as he sat down. The same map would be used by the support guys at base, hunched over screens showing live images from drone feeds and satellite images.

"The Person of Interest is holed up in the main building of this compound." McBride pointed to the cluster of buildings in the middle of the satellite image on the screen. "POI is a senior foreign fighter, Arab Al-Qaeda, but sheltered by the Taliban. Our mission is to destroy the compound, and take the POI alive if we can. If that's not possible, kill him if you have to. Intel thinks 20-30 fighters are in there. Expect a firefight. You will have air support on standby."

McBride shifted and continued. "You will be dropped two miles away at 2230 hours. Evacuation will be when you call for close air support." He stared at the two men in front of him. "Dan is front and center. Rest of you are backup."

They nodded. It was always like this. Dan would go out, do the recon, and complete the mission on his own. The others stayed back to assist if he landed in trouble.

Apart from the mission in Yemen, Dan Roy had never failed. He had spent several years of his childhood in a village near the base camp of Mount Everest, almost 30,000 feet above sea level. Running up the steepest mountain paths in the world from the age of seven had given him a level of physical fitness most humans did not have.

McBride asked, "Any questions?"

"No," said Dan.

CHAPTER 7

It was dark inside the Black Hawk. The rotor blades spun into a frenzy and the noise drowned out everything. The bird rose vertically, then its nose dipped as it picked up speed and roared through the desert night sky. The Helicopter Landing Site was half an hour's flight away. Dan was near the door and would be quick to rappel down. He checked the safety catch of his rifle. It had happened to some poor bastard once, inside a bird packed with kit and men. Rifle got knocked against wall and a chambered round went off by mistake. It all came down to standard operating procedures.

It was a good hour to the HLS in the Azrow Mountains, south-east from Kabul. Dan used the time to close his eyes and doze.

His mind drifted back to the cloud-wreathed mountains of his childhood. His parents lived as UN workers in a village in remote Nepal, before they had relocated back to the States.

His father waking him up at five o'clock, putting a doko bag around his head, and setting him off on his five-mile run up the goat path. He had the same routine as the hardy mountain men, the Gurkhas who lived in the village. The Gurkhas were renowned as legendary fighters, and made up three regiments of the British Army.

Mother calling him back in the evening, framed against the falling sun at the head of the rice fields. His mom forced him to study in the evenings. It was the only reason he did well in school. She was now dead, and so was his father.

Back in the US, he had joined the Army. After his basic training, he relished joining the 10th Mountain Division at Fort Drum, NY. Then he spent six years at a 75th Rangers Battalion, a proud "Bat Boy", rising from a rifleman to counterterrorism section leader. When the bearded and laid-back Delta Force NCO came calling, US Ranger Dan Roy was ready. He had trained for almost a year, preparing for the ultimate in selection tests.

He earned the Delta patch. It was in his locker, back at home in Virginia. He did not have any US Army-identifiable kit on him. Right now, officially, he did not exist.

Thoughts turned to a black mist in his head. His chin dropped forward onto his chest.

The pilot leaned back from his cockpit, close to Dan. His barking voice got through Dan's thin veil of slumber. The pilot lifted up one finger.

"One minute to HLS!" he shouted.

Dan switched his NVG on and everything became bathed in a green hue. These NVGs were new with a 180-degree field of vision. It was a vast improvement on the older ones, which did not allow any lateral sight. He adjusted the toggles on the side until the hills around him came into sharper focus. His radio chirped for the comms check. They were losing altitude rapidly. Before he knew it, the ground was rushing up to meet them.

Dan shook off the lanyard fixing him to the safety rail and jumped out. The area was deserted, but that didn't mean some resourceful Taliban watchman hadn't seen them coming and raised a signal.

A direct hit from an RPG would be all it took for the bird to go down.

He tried to run, but the rotor wash from the bird flattened him to the ground. He held his weapon ready and lay on his belly. Dust glinted on the rotor blades as the bird hovered inches above the ground, creating fire sparks. This was the most dangerous time. Those sparks were visible from a distance. But within seconds, it seemed, the helicopter raised itself up in a blaze of dust into the night air. Rapidly it became a distant speck in the sky, fading from sight.

Dan lay quietly as silence flooded back around him. The desert ground was hard and the smell of dust was everywhere. The radio came alive in his ears.

"This is Bravo One." That meant Burns, his handler for the mission.

Dan said, "Roger that. Proceeding to target."

He walked almost an hour before the small hills surrounding the compound came into view.

Dan did a last-minute check on his sixty-pound backpack. Breaching charge, check. Comms on the right channel, check. Tactical beacon attached to his left wrist in case he fell, check. Extra ammo, grenades, flashbangs where he could reach them – check, check and check. It was the mantra of all Special Forces warriors.

Never, ever skip on the basics. It made the difference between life and death.

Dan patrolled tactically. He ran a hundred yards, found shelter and scanned 360 degrees with his rifle night sight. Then he moved again. He found a small hillock within seventy yards of the target. Silent as a ghost, he scrambled up it.

Dan dropped to the ground and focused his NVG on the courtyard of the compound. A large building, presumably the residence, stood in the middle, flanked by two smaller buildings. The entire compound was roughly one hundred and fifty square feet in size. As he looked, Dan saw two figures, wearing loose kaftans and headgear typical of the Taliban, stroll out from one of the buildings. He took aim. The head of the first Taliban appeared in his cross hairs.

Soon, another figure came out of the main building. The lights were off, and the figures wouldn't have been visible without his NVGs. Lights flickered briefly, and Dan realized the guards had come out for a cigarette. Dan waited for a few more seconds, then waited some more. He wanted them close to each other again, like when they lit their smokes. In another twenty seconds that happened.

BOP.

The suppressed H&K jerked in Dan's hand once as the 5.56mm ordnance smashed into the head of one Taliban fighter. Dan had already aimed fractionally to his right before the figure hit the ground.

BOP.

Silence came back again. Dan waited. It was all about waiting. Wait for the enemy to show themselves. Wait for them to make the first mistake.

"Proceed to breach," Dan thought to himself.

Dan reached behind his back and detached the C-4 explosive. He slithered down the slopes into the flat ground leading up to the compound gates. A ten-foot-high, six-foot-thick mud wall, typical of Afghani compounds, surrounded the site. Dan went halfway up the open road and dropped, weapon trained on the door. He quickly set the explosives, making sure to dual-charge them, in case one detonator failed. Then he retreated thirty yards and surveyed.

A dog bayed in the distance, but not close. If there were dogs in the compound he was yet to see them. The moon vanished behind clouds making the night pitch black.

Dan slithered forward again, and went around to the rear. There was a small gate there. A black shape slumped near it. His NVG picked it up as a sentry guard. The man was asleep, but even as Dan looked, he straightened and sat up in his chair. He looked around.

Dan cursed. He went down, staying still as a statue. He couldn't aim and fire. First off, it would cause a movement, and nothing attracted more attention than movement.

Second, even the suppressed H&K would make a noise. If the man fell back against the gate he might make a crashing sound. Too risky.

Very slowly, Dan reached behind his back, and took out the sixteen-inch kukri knife.

Dan waited till the man was more settled in his chair. This guy also wore the typical Taliban headgear, and a dishdasha around his body. Something had caught his attention: hence he was looking around. But soon he lost interest. He lowered his head inside his dishdasha for some warmth.

It would be the last mistake of his life. Dan raised himself without a sound. He scurried towards his quarry, faster than a leopard. When he was within two feet of the man, he was startled and looked up. By then it was too late.

The man waking up helped Dan. He looked up and exposed his neck. That fraction of a second was all Dan needed. The kukri flashed in his hand, and buried itself to the hilt into the Taliban's neck. A gurgling, choking sound came, and warm blood pulsed over Dan's gloved hand. The eleven-inch blade cut the neck arteries, smashed the soft bones of the lower skull, and severed the cervical spinal cord at the back.

Apart from a soft pop and the choking, no other sound had been made. Dan lowered the body to the ground, and checked his G-Shock timer. Forty seconds to go. Hurriedly, he set the second charge, and faded back to his perimeter, circling around to the front of the compound.

The explosion lit up the night sky. A giant yellow and gold fireball erupted, flinging the door apart and crumbling a section of the wall. Shouts and screams came from inside. Dan crouched behind the rubble as he heard the whine of the heavier 7.62mm bullets the Taliban fired from their AK-47s. Some bullets splattered into the rubble in front. Dan lifted his head up briefly and saw muzzle flash up ahead.

He ducked his helmet down just in time to hear a bullet pass overhead. He waited for a lull in the firing, then got up and fired. Some of the guards in front fell and some scattered for cover. Dan took aim and let off some rounds in the direction of a new muzzle flash. He heard a distant scream as his rounds hit target.

The Taliban now poured out of the building and into the compound. Right on cue, the rear explosion shattered the back gate. Part of the compound wall crumbled. The charge had been heavier, and Dan felt the ground shake underneath him. The enemy was now disorientated by the twin front and rear explosions.

Agitated, some turned back. The others ran around, looking for a target.

They missed the figure lying silently on the ground, only a few feet away. Dan counted ten Taliban in total. He rose up, and locked onto his targets. He double-tapped the three closest to him. Then he advanced onto the compound. He used the Underslung Grenade Launcher (UGL) attached to the HK417. Three grenades were fired in an arc ahead of him. He took cover, turning around as they exploded.

There was nothing behind him. There was a sudden silence in the compound, punctuated by shrill scream from the wounded lying on the ground. They had never seen anything like this. The speed and ferocity of the attack had taken them by surprise.

Dan took his steps carefully, checking out every shadow in every corner. His senses were on fire. He crouched down and looked at the door of the outhouse. It was locked from the outside. He set his last small breach charge and moved away, out of range. When the charge breached, he went back in, shining his infrared torch. The room was empty. He chucked a couple of plastic chemical lights inside, which meant the room was clear.

It was ominously quiet. Dan didn't like it. If a senior Al-Qaeda was holed up here, where the hell were the other fighters? He had killed seven, maybe eight so far and wounded two or three, maybe more.

He went around the building and into the foyer. It was a two-story, four-bedroom house.

Dan peered against the wall of the first room, then kicked the door down. It fell off its hinges. His rifle light darted around the room. Mud walls. Folded mat in one corner. Two AK-47s. Rest empty. He darted around all the rooms on the ground floor. All clear.

He came out in the hallway and as he was about to go up the staircase, Dan saw a movement at the far end of the hallway. A figure slipped out a doorway in the back. Dan fired a round, but it missed, hitting the door frame. He ran to the back of the house and to the wall next to the doorway. He kicked it open, staying under cover. No gunfire came from outside.

He went out, weapon at the ready. He was in a courtyard, smaller than the front. The tall perimeter wall loomed at the back. Dan saw movement on his extreme right. He fired immediately and saw his target crumple to the ground. He ran forward. As he got closer, his heart jumped in his mouth. The prostrate figure on the ground was wearing a uniform. He recognized the blue shirt of the Afghan National Police. This was all wrong. This was a Taliban compound. What was ANP doing here?

Dan turned the body over. He flicked his light on the face. It looked familiar for some unknown reason. Dan snapped off two photos and looked at the body again. One arm was pointed straight, as if it was reaching for something. He looked, and found a large brass handle embedded in the ground.

The cries of the wounded had died away and the compound was strangely quiet.

Dan checked the trapdoor for any IEDs (Improvised Explosive Device), then grabbed hold and pulled. There was a splintering noise and he stopped.

"It's a cellar," he whispered to himself.

He pulled again, and this time, the loose earth on top fell off, revealing a chasm beneath his feet. He shone his IR torch on wooden steps descending into darkness. Dan leaned down, weapon still at the ready, and checked with the magnifying night scope mounted on his rifle. What he saw took his breath away.

Anti-aircraft guns. The DShKM, known as the Dushka, was a Soviet heavy machine gun on a tripod. There was a whole row of them, with mounds of coiled ammunition chains, on the floor of the basement. Dan had seen them before in Iraq. Insurgents still used them frequently.

He went down the steps. A long, wide room opened up below. Rifles were mounted on the walls and several short-range missiles lay on the floor. They looked Soviet-made with surface-to-air capability. In the corners, he found high, stacked piles of grenades with launchers. He got to the far end of the room and his hair stood up on end. Heckler & Koch rifles. G3, G6, 416,417, all sub-types. MP5 and 7 sub-machine guns.

These *weren't* Soviet-made.

He looked closer at the serial number on one HK. It was indistinct. He could smell the oxyacetylene blowtorch used to remove the serial number. Insurgents did this in Mosul, Iraq. His breath came fast and shallow. He'd found the evidence Guptill was looking for.

He flicked his light to the left. Long, black boxes with missiles inside them. He read the numbers on the Hellfire missiles. Next to it he saw stacks of boxes. The legends on them made him lean closer.

CL-20. State-of-the-art military explosives, more powerful than HMX. It was rumored that they could penetrate a ten-foot steel wall.

The Taliban were still using TNT and PETN, the least stable of all explosive compounds. If they got their hands on these…

Dan turned on his radio. "Bravo One, this is Tango One."

Burns replied immediately. "Receiving, over. What have you found?"

Dan told him. Burns said, "Good work. Take as much photographic intel as you can." Dan switched off and carried on taking photos.

In five minutes, his radio crackled into life again.

"Bravo One calling Tango One, respond. Over."

"Bravo One, this is Tango One. I have…" He didn't finish. Burns' normal calm voice seemed forced.

"Mission aborted. I repeat, mission aborted. Evacuate site and proceed to HLS. Do you copy? Over."

Dan stood in the silent blackness of the basement, thoughts running in his head.

"Roger that, Bravo One," he whispered into his radio.

He put his camera away, and prepared to get out of the basement. He poked his head out. The night air was silent. He heaved himself out, rifle ready to fire. Nothing. He patrolled out, then hurried along to the HLS.

CHAPTER 8

The flight back was quiet. Back at base, Dan clambered off the bird slowly. Burns was waiting. He came over and said, "There was a platoon-strength Taliban force headed your way. We had to evacuate you."

"What happened to the weapons?" Dan asked.

Burns said, "We've got a drone up there now. Any minute, the place will be blown sky-high. You being there would have compromised the mission. You did what you had to."

Dan said, "The POI was not there."

Burns said, "We don't know that for definite as yet. You might have killed him."

Dan shook his head. "This guy is important, right? He wouldn't have ten or twelve Taliban guarding him, there should be around fifty. I reckon he got wind and ran off."

Burns said, "McBride wants to see you. You got the photos?"

"Yes." They walked over to the HQ building. McBride was waiting for them in the same room.

"We are still not sure if the POI was there," McBride said quietly. "But at least you tried. I thank you for that." He looked at Dan and continued. "What did you find in the house?"

Dan reached inside the cargo pockets of his trousers and pulled out folded scrolls of paper. "I found maps, sir, of the large bases we have here and in Baghdad." It was a detailed map of Bagram airport and Camp Bastion.

"I understand you went around the back. Is that right?" McBride's eyes scanned Dan's face.

Dan explained to him about the basement and showed him the photos.

McBride looked at Dan's camera in silence, flicking through the images. He said, "I'm keeping this camera, Dan. I need to send these photos to HQ."

Dan opened his mouth and shut it.

"Yes, sir."

*****

Dan slept fitfully that night. Strange dreams filled his mind. He could see Lucy. Her red hair was falling over her face. Dan was holding her close to him. He bent forward to kiss her and she closed her eyes. The red curls of hair became rivulets of blood, wrapping tightly across her face. Lucy opened her eyes in alarm. She began to choke. She opened her mouth and shouted; Dan could hear a faint scream. She was saying something, and Dan strained his ears. Her voice was weak, faded.

"Let me in. Dan, let me in."

Dan was gasping. He yelled out, *"Yes, I will. I will."*

Lucy's voice came from far away. *"Open the door, Dan. Open the door."*

He awoke with a start. Someone was knocking on his door hard enough to make it rattle. He groaned and checked his watch. Seven o'clock. The sun was already bright. He swung his legs off the bunker and opened the door, stifling a yawn.

He blinked in surprise. Two Military Policemen were standing outside. They were stout, large men with meaty forearms hanging loose at the sides.

"You are Dan Roy?"

Dan rubbed his eyes and shook his head. "Yes. Why?"

"Come with us, now."

Dan held his ground. "What for?"

One of the MPs took a step forward. He was sweating. "Come with us and you'll find out. Now."

Dan put his combat shirt on and followed. They walked down the hallway towards the mess room and a row of lockers. Dan could hear Burns' voice. It was high-pitched, stressed.

Burns was saying, "It makes no sense. This is bullshit, right? Right?"

Dan frowned as he saw McBride and Burns standing next to his locker. McBride gave him a hard stare before looking away. One of the MPs opened his locker and reached inside. He pulled out a collection of folded papers. He opened one of them up. Dan stared in surprise, his heart thudding inside his chest.

It was a map of their base. He had no idea how it had ended up inside his locker, to which only he had keys. Before he could say anything, the MP pulled out another map. This was of Camp Bastion with portions circled in red.

Dan moved closer. "Hold up," he said. The MP had his hand inside the locker again. He stopped and looked at Dan. Dan met his eyes.

"I need to see inside my locker."

The MP moved aside. The locker was almost empty of kit, but Dan was on duty, so that was expected. But there were scrolls of maps, a laptop, and something else below it. Dan didn't touch anything. He turned to the officer and McBride.

"Sir, this stuff is not mine."

McBride said, "That map matches the ones we found in the compound last night. They're hand-drawn and the scale is the same. How did they end up in your locker?"

"I have no idea, sir. Why would you want to look in my locker anyway?"

"We didn't want to, Dan. But after last night's mission, I decided to check everyone's." A strange look passed in McBride's eyes. "We didn't expect to find this."

"It doesn't belong to me, sir," Dan repeated. A whirlwind of thoughts was passing through his head, but he kept his face impassive, giving nothing away.

Burns' face was working. He waved his hands in McBride's face. "Someone is trying to frame him! Damn it, can't you see that? Someone is trying to discredit Intercept." Burns jabbed a forefinger in Dan's direction. "By framing this guy."

McBride said, "Like who?"

Burns said, "Take your pick. The CIA, the government, other PMCs, they are all trying to get in on the act. All they see is the dollars we earn. No one thinks of the risks we take."

"You seriously think CIA will try to sabotage you guys?"

Burns leaned towards McBride. "Believe me, you have no idea how many feathers we have ruffled in the CIA. They call our operations illegal, even when they provide the damn intel!"

McBride gestured to the MP, and he resumed his search of the locker. He lifted the laptop and pulled something out. Dan tightened his jaw. His breath became shorter. It was a flat block of C-4 explosive with detonators on the side. He had used similar charges numerous times to breach into a target zone. But he had never kept anything like this in his locker.

"Where did you get this from, Dan?" McBride's voice seemed to come from far away. So did his own voice, when he finally found the strength to speak. Things were hazy in front of his eyes.

"I don't know, sir," he said.

CHAPTER 9

Dan sat on his bunker bed, his eyes staring straight ahead. A dull ache was gripping his head, like a hangover. His mind went back over the last two days. Arriving at FOB Fenty from Camp Bastion. Finding his barracks, bunker and locker. Debrief of the mission. Meeting the team. He couldn't place any time or event that had been odd, irregular. Apart from the mission itself.

What the hell was going on?

There was a knock on the door, then it pushed open before he could say anything. It was Burns. Their eyes met briefly before Dan looked away. Burns walked over to the corner of the room, lifting the curtain of the small box window to look at the blinding heat outside. Then he sat down on the beanbag in the corner. Neither of them spoke for a while.

"Dan?"

Dan rubbed his eyes and looked at his friend without speaking. Burns had a puzzled expression on his face.

"Who and why?" It was a statement, not a question.

"Damned if I fucking know," Dan whispered. He wasn't a paranoid person. He didn't think someone was out to get him. He killed his enemies. He knew who they were. But inside the barracks...

Burns sat down next to him on the bunk. "You reckon this has something to do with what you saw?"

Dan jerked his head towards him. The thought had appeared in his mind, too, but the potential ramifications were mind-boggling. He didn't want to go there. Dan frowned and focused on a mark on the wall, dead straight.

"Burns, I...I just have no idea right now." For the first time in his life, Dan felt helpless, a feeling he didn't like. Quickly, it turned to anger. He clenched his thick fingers, and slammed one fist into the other palm. The sound echoed in the room.

Burns said, "We will get to the bottom of this, Dan. I'll vouch for you, don't worry. You had nothing to gain from this."

Dan was silent. He did not know which way he could turn. Why had he come back? His thoughts turned to Guptill. If it hadn't been for him...Dan couldn't think anymore. He was getting a headache.

"What happens now?" he asked Burns.

Burns sighed. "Flight back to HQ. For both of us."

Dan's mind was working. "HQ in Virginia?" The Intercept HQ was near Fort Belvoir in Virginia.

Burns said, "I think so, yes."

Dan shook his head. "I need to go to London first, to see Guptill. Can you organize that for me?"

Burns chewed a nail. Then he said, "Leave it with me. I'll be back in a while. Pack your stuff up."

Burns got up and left. Dan stood up. He did not have much to pack. Whatever he had fit inside a small backpack.

Burns came back in fifteen minutes. He said, "I managed to get a deal. They want both of us back in Virginia. But I said Guptill will see you in London. I still have to head out to USA. The two MPs will escort you back to London."

It was better than nothing. Burns had done well to buy him some time. "Thanks," Dan said.

Burns stepped forward. He lowered his voice. "Do you think this has anything to do with what happened in Yemen?"

Dan had been thinking the same thing. Was Intercept betraying him? Maybe they needed to get rid of him. For good. Dan knew the high standards to which Intercept held every agent. Failure was never rewarded. Disobeying a direct order was the same as high treason. That was exactly what he had done in Yemen.

If they could show Dan was guilty, he had no hope of ever serving anywhere again. He might end up in jail. Or even worse, Dan thought grimly.

He said, "You work for Intercept, Burns. Why don't you try and find out?"

Burns said, "I believe you did the right thing in Yemen." He held up a finger. "It was me who asked Guptill to approach you. I knew that you had quit. But you showed in Yemen you had guts. You called Intercept's bluff. I needed a man like that for this mission. Someone who could use his own judgement. You saw what happened in London. This shit is serious, Dan. We need to get to the bottom of it."

Dan said, "There is someone inside Intercept. Someone told the POI we would be raiding the compound. That's why he escaped."

"Correct."

"Who is he, Burns?" Dan stared at Burns intently. The man shifted uneasily.

Burns said, "It's not me, Dan."

Dan said, "How do I know it's not you?"

Burns' face changed. He said, "If it was me, would I go out of the way to get you back in? I would try like hell to cover it up. I wouldn't even be here."

Dan nodded. It made sense. He asked, "What about Guptill?"

"You know your CO better than me, Dan. Do you think he'd do it? He approached you. You saw the photo of the dead CIA agent in London?"

Dan nodded. Burns said, "If Guptill was guilty, why would he show you all the photographic evidence?"

Dan was silent. Intercept was a shadowy, dark place. No one knew the top management or what they got up to. He asked Burns about them, but the fixer shook his head.

He said, "No one knows the top brass, Dan. No one ever will. All I can say is, I wouldn't want to be their enemy." He looked up at Dan. Their eyes met. Each knew what the other was thinking.

"I need to get out of here," Dan said.

Burns said, "You will get some breathing space in London. What you do with it is up to you."

"Yes," Dan said slowly.

*****

Dan had packed his gear the next morning and was waiting when they called for him. The same two MPs knocked on his door. He read their names this time, sewn into their shirts above their breast pockets. Smith and Sullivan. Sounded like two freaking talk show hosts. His weapons had already been confiscated. The rifles were gone, so were his Sig Sauer P226 handgun, and his 35mm Beretta. Only the kukri was left, and hell, that was all he needed to chop their heads off. He could feel its reassuring presence on his belt, the blade resting against the small of his back.

He hefted the bag on his shoulder and followed them without a word. The courtyard was deserted in the early morning, and the desert sun was just beginning to rear its malicious head. It was 0600 hours. They walked for fifteen minutes until they got to the hangar. In normal situations, they would have taken a bus.

A Chinook 47 was being loaded with supplies. Some were standard military ration boxes, and some weapon stacks for repairs. He clambered aboard. Maintenance guys shouted orders and checked lights, helped load boxes. Dan watched them. He knew his destination already. The two MPs would be traveling with him. It was back to Bagram Air Base, northeast of Kabul, then another plane back to London.

Then he needed to get some answers.

CHAPTER 10

The Ilyushin 76MD cargo plane started to flash its tail lights as it prepared for landing at Heydar Aliyev International Airport, twenty miles northeast of Baku, the capital city of Azerbaijan.

Robert Cranmer came off his seat in the huge, central aisle of the plane, empty now, but wide enough to fit two armored vehicles side by side. He walked towards the rear of the plane. A flight of stairs led down to the observation chamber below the plane's tail.

He stepped into a small room filled with screens of maps on the walls, radars and radio equipment stacked on the side desks. The floor was essentially see-through, a giant window that allowed 360-degree views of the country around. In the Soviet era, the Ilyushin served a dual purpose as the main transport for its airborne divisions, as well as a spy plane. Now, the planes were chartered out to various agencies for freight purposes.

Robert looked at the green mountains of Azerbaijan, and the vast, brown, flat plains stretching beyond them in the distance. To the east lay the gleaming blue waters of Caspian Sea, the largest lake in the world, but called a sea by the ancient Romans because of its salty waters.

The airport appeared, white in the afternoon sunlight reflecting off its domed buildings. Robert enjoyed coming down to the navigation chamber, watching the land below as if he was on a parachute. It gave him a certain sense of privilege.

The pilot's voice came on the loudspeaker. "Seats, *pazhalsta,* comrades. Preparing to land."

Robert clambered out and wobbled back to his seat, strapping his seat belt on. For such a large transport plane, the Ilyushin landed smoothly, its wheels barely bumping the runway. Robert stood up and grabbed his briefcase. Robert Cranmer was not his real name. Not many people knew his real name, and that was the way he liked it.

Robert strode into the check-in area and flashed his diplomatic badge at security. He was waved through. A few guards lounged around, leaning against the walls, AK-74 rifles hung casually round their shoulders. They barely lifted an eye as Robert walked past them. Robert walked to a row of counters in the corner of the Arrivals section and to his company office.

"Living Aid" specialized in transporting food and health items to countries with governments too weak to do it for themselves. Countries like Afghanistan and Angola handed out the logistics to private contractors. To men like Robert Cranmer.

The door was open and the man sitting at the only table, staring at his laptop, looked up and stood, grunting. He was considerably shorter than Robert's lanky six feet one.

"Robert," he extended his hand.

Robert shook the man's hand, feeling the weight.

"Hello, Yevgeny." Yevgeny Lutyenov was going past forty, his hair starting to bald and a pot belly growing on the formerly hard slabs of muscle. Strangely, that didn't mean he was out of shape, as Robert had seen him load huge cartons into pallets for the steel shipping containers. Beneath his eyebrows a pair of light brown eyes glinted, matching the color of his mustache.

Robert gestured at the laptop. "Any news?"

"Yes," said Yevgeny, and rubbed his hands. "New order from Vietnam."

"Good," said Robert, running eyes up and down the spreadsheet quickly, then he turned to Yevgeny and raised his eyebrows.

"Chilli powder?"

Yevgeny shrugged. "Guess they like it hot."

The two men met during the Anglo-Russian Chamber of Commerce Gala night, hosted in the sumptuous India Durbar of the Foreign and Commonwealth Office in Westminster, London. Yevgeny had a background in the KGB, but after 1991 became an importer of Western goods. Business had been slow at first, but as the inflation settled down in the late-1990s, Russia's import-export business went through a prolonged boom. When he heard Robert's business proposition, it hadn't taken them long to become colleagues.

Robert tapped his briefcase. "I have end-user certificates for Kabul, Democratic Republic of Congo and Vietnam."

"*Kharasho*, comrade," Yevgeny smiled.

"And I've put all of our planes on the flight schedule of Bagram and Jalalabad. So, from now on, you won't have any more problems."

Russian planes were not much loved in Afghanistan. The Afghani airports were littered with the rusting hulks of destroyed MiG fighters and a few of the old Ilyushins. One of the Living Aid planes had been boarded by the

Afghan Airport Authority after landing in Bagram last month, and the crew arrested. It had taken all of Robert's diplomatic skill to persuade the government to let them go.

"Are you sure about that?" Yevgeny said.

"*Konyeshna,* comrade." Robert switched to Russian when he wanted to make a point with Yevgeny. "Have I not just come back with an empty plane from Jalalabad? You have nothing to worry about anymore."

"I hope you are right," grumbled Yevgeny. "How did it go at the airbase?"

Robert paused for a moment before replying. "Yes, it was all fine."

Yevgeny seemed thoughtful. "Are you sure?"

"Yes, comrade. Don't worry. I am off to London now. See you later."

CHAPTER 11

The Chinook landed at the Royal Air Force base in Brize Norton. Dan yawned as the jolt of the landing bump awakened him. He looked out the window. It was summer, and apart from cloud cover, the weather did not look too bad. He got up, and packed his rucksack.

Dan stared out the black-tinted windows of the armored Range Rover as it speeded through the English countryside. Rolling green fields and gentle hillocks appeared, with white sheep dotted on them. Despite the bucolic surroundings, he couldn't help but wonder what was going to happen.

They suspected him of selling out to the other side. He would be grilled by intelligence officials whose names would never be disclosed.

Would they torture him? His own people?

They entered London. As they went down the old city's narrow streets, Dan recognized some of the sights. Then he saw the large, square building from a distance. He caught his breath. Grosvenor Square, Mayfair. One of the most expensive addresses in the entire world, and the location of the US Embassy in London. It was also the HQ of all clandestine CIA operations inside the UK.

But they drove past it. The car went straight down east, then banked south, heading for the River Thames. They drove past Hyde Park Corner, and the regal old buildings that faced the spacious green expanse. Soon they crossed the river at an unknown bridge, and the scenery changed. Industrial estates appeared, and they took a left after a grimy block of council houses, England's version of the Projects. Dan did not recognize these parts. He knew they were in South London, but not which part exactly.

The car stopped in front of what looked like an abandoned warehouse to the casual observer. But not to Dan. He could see the wide satellite receivers and tall antennas on the roof that marked a major communications hub. He also did not miss the men strolling around the front of the warehouse. Their shoulder bulges were well hidden but they did exist. Their eyes were hard and calculating. Paid mercenaries.

The warehouse backed onto the river. It was a gigantic structure, taking up almost one whole block. A row of warehouses merged into one building. A jetty on the river flashed by as they drove past. Dan could see two black, rigid inflatable boats or RIBs docked at the jetty, the military's choice of water transport. When the car came to a stop, two of the men loitering at the front ambled over.

IDs were checked, and security poked their heads in to look at the occupants—Dan, the driver and the two MPs. The bar lifted, the iron grill gate swung open, and the car swept inside the warehouse awning. Smith and Sullivan, the two MPs, both without uniform, and no doubt working on a private contract, stood on either side of Dan as he got out of the Range Rover.

The two suits gave Dan the once-over. One of them opened his jacket slightly to let Dan see the weapon inside. Dan stared back at the man, then walked past him.

Men were doing a search in front of a conveyor belt and X-ray machine. Dan dumped his rucksack in there and walked to the guards. He spread his arms and was patted down.

Dan looked around him as he walked inside. He was in a cavernous space, but one that crawled with people. Desks had been laid out, and large screens stood on the far walls, frequently changing pictures. Hallways branched off from the main atrium, men and women emerging from them with folders in their hands.

From the outside, he would never have known all these people were crammed inside. But he knew that was always the case in England. The British were masters of subtlety. A tiny building would go on for miles inside. A deserted warehouse by the river would turn out to be the Intercept HQ in London.

Dan was willing to bet money most of the agents inside were transported by riverboats from their homes. That left the roads empty. MI5 was probably on the take and they told local police to stay away.

Dan recognized the figure of Major Guptill walking towards him. He felt a sense of relief at the sight of his old CO. The only man he could trust.

Or could he? Guptill had not traveled to 'Stan with him this time. Burns had acted as his handler. Dan wondered why that was.

Neither man smiled at the other. Guptill glanced at Dan and gestured with his eyes to follow him. Dan walked down one side of the large atrium, looking at the men and women hunched over their screens, talking on phones. In one corner, a teleconference was going on. A man with a military buzz cut, but not in uniform, was telling the assembled group something from a giant screen. The face was well known to anyone who had worked in US Special Forces for any length of time.

Dan felt a surge of adrenaline. This *had* to be the Intercept's European HQ. He had so far been briefed 24 hours before his operations. In random locations. A folder would be left for him on a seat in a diner. It seemed risky, but the diner's staff would be trained. He had meetings with Guptill, his handler, at locations made known to him an hour before by a text. The locations were always different, irrespective of the country he was in. This was the first time he was attending HQ.

They headed off the main drag into a hallway. The two MPs were right behind him. Their boots clicked on the bare cement floor. They went down a flight of stairs and into a basement. Guptill pressed on the digital keypad next to a steel door and it swung open.

Guptill said to the MPs, "Stay here."

Dan walked inside. There was a table with two chairs inside. No windows. In another corner, there was a polygraph machine hooked up to the wall. There was something else in that corner, on another table, covered by a black cloth. A machine, Dan figured. He recognized an interrogation chamber when he saw one.

Dan sat down opposite Guptill.

Guptill said, "The plastic explosives found in your locker had Russian serial numbers."

Dan shrugged. "So do most weapons in Afghanistan."

"Remember your last trip to Russia?"

"Yes, to Belarus. On a reconnaissance mission to check their satellite station."

"Yes. It was an ISR mission with Delta." Intelligence, Surveillance and Recon.

Dan said, "You got me down here to talk about old times?"

Guptill stared at Dan for a while, then wrote something down on a piece of paper.

Then he said, "The investigation is still ongoing. We require you to be in London until it is finished." He fished inside his pocket and took out a cellphone. He slid it across the table to Dan, who did not touch it.

"Use this phone to contact me. And I will contact you. I don't have to remind you what happens if we can't contact you, or if you go AWOL."

He would be hunted down, and killed without hesitation.

It was a truth that was ingrained into the frontal lobe of every Intercept operative. They were the best of the best, but they were also held to a rigid code of silence.

"I know," Dan said.

"For what it's worth, I don't think you did it. Your career record is exceptional. You are one of our highest-value operators. You had nothing to gain."

Dan said, "Glad you see it that way." He pocketed the cellphone from the desk.

Guptill rose without a word. Dan followed. He knew when his former CO was giving him a silent order. Smith and Sullivan were still standing outside, silent and watchful. The four men went up the stairs. They walked back outside, and were waved through when Guptill flashed his badge.

They got back into the armored Range Rover. Guptill said something to one of the MPs and they pulled out into the empty street.

CHAPTER 12

They drove for a while and then joined traffic. Dan read the signs. They were in a part of town called Wandsworth. He did not know the place. They took a left and Dan saw the flash of muddy gray waters of the Thames again. The car came to a stop outside a section of the river that was empty of pedestrians. Guptill got out and Dan followed. The MPs stayed in the car.

There was a railing, beyond which a path ran down alongside the river. Heading up, Dan could see shiny new apartment complexes on both sides of the banks, and a hauling crane at a riverside dockyard. The sun had peeked out, and water rustled at the edges of the bank below them.

They stared at the swirls and eddies for a while.

Dan was the first to break the silence. "I didn't do it, sir."

Guptill didn't say anything. Dan waited.

"I know," Guptill said eventually.

Guptill gave Dan a hard stare, then nodded. Dan breathed out. He had served under Guptill in the Afghan war back in 2002. Then in Iraq and back in Afghanistan. As a Delta operator, then for Intercept. But the man who was his mentor didn't seem like the man standing opposite him now.

Dan said, "What's going on?"

"It's a shit game, this, you know?"

"Always has been. What's new?"

Guptill shook his head.

Dan pressed him. "I saw Special Forces rifles in there. H&Ks, adapted for our use. With NVGs. CL-20 explosives. You saw the photos."

Guptill's head jerked up. Dan held his eyes.

"Where is the camera I took the photos with?"

Guptill sighed. "Gone."

"Gone where?"

Guptill didn't say anything.

Dan said, "You're trying to protect me."

Guptill smiled for the first time. Then it vanished. "I don't know who to trust, Dan. You included."

"I told you. I didn't do it. Besides, if I was dirty, I would never make an error like that, would I?"

"You can't get into this, Dan. They are everywhere, up and down the country..." Guptill stopped, and looked away.

"I'm in this already," Dan said. "What do you want me to do? Roll over and give in?"

"Who's behind this?" he persisted.

Guptill didn't answer. Dan said, "You brought me here to tell me this gibberish?"

"Believe me, son, I have told you a lot more than I should have already."

Dan balled his fist in frustration. He gripped the iron bars of the railing. "What am I supposed to do with this clusterfuck?"

Guptill sighed and frowned. Dan could now see the conflict in his mentor. He wanted to help. But he did not know how far he could go.

Guptill regarded Dan for a few seconds. Then he leaned closer and whispered. "My apartment in Chelsea. Tomorrow evening. 1900 hours. Keep stag." He gave Dan the address.

Keeping stag was something they had picked up from the SAS guys. It meant surveillance. Dan nodded.

He heard a car pulling up. He looked behind him. An SUV had drawn up alongside, and the door was open. Guptill nodded at Dan, then walked to the car. He got in, the door shut, and they drove off.

Dan walked back to the Range Rover. He opened the back door and got in. Smith started the car and they pulled out.

"Where we going to?" Dan asked.

They didn't say anything. Dan figured they would take him back to base, and he would await orders there. He didn't have any money on him. He always traveled without ID. Either he needed to get some money, or Intercept had to find him some accommodation.

They drove for twenty minutes. Dan watched the traffic and read the signs. They were heading out of town and onto a road called the A3. The sign said they were heading for Portsmouth. Dan knew that was the south of England. Portsmouth had big docks and a Royal Navy base.

"Where we going to?" he repeated.

Sullivan replied, "A safe house for you."

Dan settled back in the seat. They got onto a faster dual carriageway. Soon it was countryside again. They hooked a left and went down a narrow, quintessentially English country lane. A car passed by on the opposite lane, inches from the Range Rover's wing mirror. After ten minutes, they pulled into the gravel drive of a country house. The front was shielded by a ten-foot-high fence, with tall pines in the middle. The building was set back and isolated from the road.

They parked, and Smith opened Dan's door. Dan got out. The two guys were flanking him. Dan looked at the house. A gray-brick building, two stories tall, old and imposing. It was very quiet here. He could not hear any cars. Some birds tweeted in the trees, and leaves rustled in a faint breeze.

Dan did not like it. Some unknown tension at the depths of his being was gnawing away inside him.

An instinct for danger. An instinct that had kept him alive all these years.

He met the eyes of the MPs. Eyes like stone. No feeling in them. One of them nodded towards the house. Smith walked ahead, while Sullivan walked behind Dan. Dan walked slowly, then stopped.

"I left something in the car," he said.

Smith, who was in front of Dan, took out his weapon. A suppressed Colt M1911. He flicked the safety off. The gun was pointed at Dan. The round, if fired, was going nowhere but his chest.

Dan turned, and saw Sullivan had drawn his weapon as well. The same Colt.

Sullivan was standing next to the back passenger door. Dan went to reach for the door, and the man was standing very close to it. Dan had already noticed his weapon's safety catch was on.

Dan turned as if he was reaching for the door handle, just as Sullivan stepped back. His right arm reached for the handle, but his left arm lashed out in the same movement, slapping Sullivan's gun arm away from him.

The movement was sudden, vicious and totally unexpected.

Sullivan swore and tried to bring his gun back, but Dan had already pivoted on his heels, and slammed his wide frame directly into Sullivan's chest. The man stumbled back. Dan grabbed his gun wrist, and drove his right fist straight up into the man's chin. The fist slammed against the bone, making a dull thud, and the man's head snapped back. The gun fired, the bullet picking up gravel dust at Dan's feet.

Dan was aware of movement behind his back. He pushed Sullivan backwards to the rear of the car even as a bullet smashed into the glass next to him. Dan dived forward, pulling Sullivan with him. That dive saved Dan, as he felt another round whistle over his head and blast into the side of the armored car. The round pinged off, and Dan rolled over to the other side of the Range Rover, the fallen man's Colt in his hand.

He had no time to stand up, turn around and aim. But he had the car's side as cover momentarily. Dan crawled on the gravel, hearing Smith run up behind him. He flattened himself on the ground, and looked underneath the car. He spotted the feet running up. He squeezed off two rounds, and heard the satisfying scream as they found their mark.

Even as the man fell on the gravel, Dan was up and moving.

He leaped onto the hood. He rolled over it, and came off firing at the figure lying on the gravel. Smith was ex-military, and he was no stranger to combat situations. But Dan's sudden move had taken him by surprise. He was aiming his gun underneath the car, searching for Dan.

Rule number one – Always do what your enemy does not expect.

Dan fired rapidly as he fell, the round streaking into the body on the floor. Smith realized at the last minute, but by then it was too late. Three rounds smashed into his skull and neck, and they erupted in a spurt of blood. His head fell back and he sagged sideways.

Dan fell on the gravel, feeling the stones pinch him sharply on the sides. He was up quickly, resting on one knee, gun arm straight at the elbow, scanning 360 degrees. No one else.

He went over to Sullivan, still lying on the gravel. He was starting to recover. Dan leaned over him, pointing his gun.

"Who sent you?" Dan asked.

In response, Sullivan spat at Dan. Dan turned his head just in time, missing the sputum. He kicked the man hard in the ribs. Sullivan rolled over, getting up on one knee. He reached inside his jacket and pulled out a small, snub-nosed 9mm gun. He never got the chance to use it.

Dan double-tapped him in the face and neck. Sullivan fell backwards, dead before he hit the ground.

Dan spun around, ready for more contact. Blood was roaring in his ears, and his chest was heaving, but inside, he was icy calm. This is what he thrived on.

If twenty men came charging down the road now, if they rappelled down from a Sikorsky bird above his head, he would fight them. He would fire till he ran out of ammo. Then he would pull out his kukri. If the kukri broke he would use his bare hands.

He would kill them all. He always had done.

But the surrounding quiet English countryside gave no indication of further threats. Dan did not let his awareness slip. He pulled the two bodies into the bushes at the side entrance to the garden. The gun had been suppressed, and there weren't any houses nearby, so hopefully he had avoided detection. Then he heard the buzzing sound. For a moment, he thought it was the cellphone that Burns had given him. But after a while he realized it was coming from one of the fallen men. He frisked the two bodies, and found a cellphone inside Smith's jacket.

He held the phone in his hand. Caller ID withheld. As he had expected.

If he answered, he was answering the question.

No, he's not dead.

Dan put the phone back inside the man's jacket. He frisked them both again, expecting to find nothing. Expectation fulfilled, he approached the front door. He nudged the door with his foot without touching it. Locked.

Dan did not want to waste time exploring the place. If these guys had been Intercept enforcers, then he knew they did not travel alone. That unanswered phone call would raise questions. He needed to put distance between himself and them.

He got into the car, and drove out. He headed straight down, looking for a sign. He found one that said "A3, London", and took it. He noted the right-hand drive, and drove carefully.

Once on the road, he allowed himself to think laterally.

Guptill did not travel back with him. Why was that? Burns had left for Virginia. It was Guptill who had wanted to see him in London.

Was Guptill showing fake concern for him?

Why had Guptill asked him to visit his apartment in Chelsea? So that he could finish the job?

Guptill, more than anyone else, would know that Dan could handle these two assassins.

Dan shook his head and gripped the steering wheel hard, till his knuckles were white.

What about Burns? Dan had kept the cellphone Burns had given him before leaving for the USA. But before Dan started the car, he had turned the phone off, and ripped the battery off the back. He kept them separate. His senses told him to throw the phone away. But it was his only link back to Intercept now.

No one had survived an Intercept hunt down. But they had not hunted Dan.

"Fuck you," Dan snarled under his breath. He changed lanes and speeded up on the A3. He was heading for Chelsea.

CHAPTER 13

Robert Cranmer watched the sunlight glinting off the Arghandab River far below his Sikorsky S-92 helicopter.

The Arghandab, one of the main rivers in southern Afghanistan, sprouted further up north in the mountains of Ghazni. It flowed four hundred kilometers down into the fertile valley of Helmand, before watering Panjwayi town, which was Robert's destination.

Robert sighed and looked back at the mountains rising in the distance. Afghanistan certainly had a dramatic landscape. He was in a wide, empty valley. The bare bones land shrugged itself into colossal stacks of granite mountains that rose forebodingly into a blue sky.

They were getting closer to Panjwayi. The first mud-thatched roofs appeared next to the river, with larger compounds of the richer inhabitants strewn around. Panjwayi was an important town in Helmand, not least because it used to be a Taliban stronghold. The Taliban had been beaten away, but only temporarily. Robert had no doubt that when the Allies left, they would move back in.

The rotor blades of the Sikorsky raised a storm of debris and the bird wobbled as it settled in the middle of the biggest compound. Children scattered for the cover of mud huts. It was stifling hot inside the cabin, all the windows shut to fend off the dust. Some of it still seeped in, making Cranmer cough. He put a handkerchief over his mouth. Afghanistan was much nicer from high above.

It was his second time back to the district HQ of the Panjwayi District. The Afghan National Police HQ and the local hospital were situated there— the only hospital in the surrounding hundred square miles—and a community care center, both staffed by US Marines. Scattered around the edges of the compound were residential quarters and storage warehouses. Two figures came out of the police HQ, a yellow, two-story clay building with antennas and satellite dishes. Two ANP snipers kept watch from bullet holes in the roof.

Robert got out of the helicopter. A portly figure in a brown uniform was making his way towards him, flanked by two ANP with AK-74 rifles. He extended his hand as they got closer.

"Mr Cranmer, what a lovely surprise," the fat Afghan man said in perfect English.

"Nice to see you again, Fatullah." The two men smiled and shook hands cordially. Commander Fatullah Zalaf waved expansively towards the police HQ.

"Some nice, cold, rose sherbet and sweets await you, my friend. Please come in."

"Ah, that's all I came for," Robert chuckled. Flanked by the guards again, the two men went inside.

Fatullah Zalaf's office was at the back of the building, on the cooler second floor, shaded by the branches of a pomegranate tree. There was no air conditioning. The windows were open, but it was still too early for the early evening winds. The room was hot and stuffy.

A boy came in carrying a stainless steel tray with two covered glasses and a plate of baklava and halawi sweets. Robert sat down and wiped his forehead with a handkerchief. Fatullah closed the door firmly after the boy. They were alone.

Fatullah organized some papers on the desk, pushed one glass and the plate of sweets towards Robert, then sat back in his chair. Robert took a long sip, watching Fatullah. He looked the same as last time. His cheeks had gone to fat, to match his ponderous belly. His luxurious black beard was longer if anything, and gleamed with oil.

"So, Robert, how is business?"

"Brisk, as it happens. We have orders in Africa and the Far East now. As well as here, of course."

"Good, good. So how can I help?"

"Well, it's about the vaccines. You know what happened with the last shipment."

Fatullah nodded. A Living Aid truck carrying vaccines had been seized by the Taliban three months ago.

Fatullah said. "After what happened in Abbottabad in 2011, any medical supplies are treated with suspicion, especially if they're vaccines."

"Yes," Robert frowned. "But this is us. They should know better."

Fatullah nodded. "Agreed."

When he didn't say any more, Robert said, "So what happened to the vaccines?"

"Robert, we *are* trying our best to find them. Searches are still…"

"I know all of that, Fatullah. But we had an understanding. I have to make excuses to the company directors about this. They're concerned. If it is the Taliban who took them, and not any other *mujaheddin* group, then surely you can talk to them?"

Fatullah was silent. Robert watched him carefully. Fatullah was a former Taliban commander, a mid-ranking one. At his peak, he had close to a hundred men under him. With the US-led war effort now coming to an end, the money for Taliban commanders was dwindling and pouring into the Afghan government instead. For those who joined the Taliban for money, such as Fatullah, it was time to switch sides.

"It is not easy, Robert."

"Then how can I guarantee the flow of supplies to you?"

It was a stalemate. Fatullah grasped and smoothed his beard, then sighed something in Arabic. He shook his head and looked askance at Robert.

"Yes, I know." Fatullah seemed lost in thought for a moment. "Okay, I will speak to them. But..." He raised his eyebrow and lifted a finger. "This remains between me and you, eh, *dost?*"

Robert grinned. "Of course, my friend—I mean, *dost.*"

CHAPTER 14

The May sun was fighting with the clouds as Dan stepped out of Sloane Square underground station. Underground or subway stations were called the tube in England. He had ditched the car almost as soon as he entered London and taken the tube. He guessed the car would have a tracking device.

It was six in the evening, surprisingly mild. The daylight would help him keep an eye on the apartment. Major Guptill's rental apartment was in Chelsea, a sought-after address in London. His Intercept salary paid for it.

Georgian colonial mansion houses adorned the street on both sides, with leafy trees at regular intervals. Dan kept one eye on the stunning architecture, and another on the people around him. He stopped every fifty yards, either to admire the scenery or to cross the street. He didn't see anything unusual. He took a left off Chelsea Bridge Road into Royal Hospital Road, heading for the river. Paradise Walk was a little street close to the river, just off Royal Hospital Road.

Did Guptill want him dead? His former CO?

Dan could not stop the question from surfacing in his mind. Snippets of his conversation with Guptill came back.

I don't know who to trust.

Up and down the country. Which country?

Dan came to the turning of Paradise Walk and stopped, looking at the spectacular red-brick, terraced buildings. Commuters were walking back from work. A woman was pushing a pram. Two women jogging. He leaned against the railings of a terrace. After ten minutes, he still saw nothing.

He doubled his way back up the other end of Paradise Walk. He was on the Chelsea Embankment now, opposite the river. Traffic was heavy. The sidewalk was wide on the Embankment, with benches to sit and admire the river scenery. He picked one from where the major's apartment was visible. The graceful, red and white terraced building was sandwiched between two others that looked exactly the same. He waited for longer this time, but again saw nothing unusual. Paradise Walk was a narrow street, and he couldn't monitor the building by getting too close. This was his best spot.

Why did Guptill not come back with him? Why did he get into another car? That car arrived like it had been prearranged.

Like they knew what was going down.

Dan kept watch until the sun was tilting in the west, casting long shadows of Chelsea Bridge over the Thames' muddy waters. Dan checked all around him, then got up. He felt the suppressed Colt against his back belt.

He sauntered along Paradise Walk to the double doors of number fourteen. They were tall and brown, the varnish on them shining, a speakerphone beside them. Dan pressed a button and waited. No response. He pressed again. After his third attempt, he gave up. He checked his watch. 1910 hours. He loitered around another ten minutes, then pressed again. Still no response.

Uneasiness began to eat away inside him. He checked his cellphone. No calls. Guptill would never call him on the phone anyway. Tracer magnets, he used to call them. Dan crossed the street and tried to look up at the third floor. The windows facing the street were open.

He waited. After a while, a woman in her mid-fifties approached the house. Dan stayed in the shadow of a doorway opposite and watched while the woman took out a set of keys. He crossed the street quickly.

The woman turned around in the hallway as she heard Dan come in behind her. Movement sensor lights came on in the ceiling, bathing the place in a white glow.

"Here for John Guptill, number thirty-two," Dan said cheerfully. "Have you seen him around?"

The woman ignored his question, mumbled a hello and turned away.

Dan looked around him carefully. No one present but him. He took the stairs up slowly, the Colt now in his hand, elbow ramrod straight.

Dan stepped off the third-floor landing and into the hallway. Fading sunlight streamed in through long windows at either end. The hallway was empty.

At Guptill's apartment, before he knocked, Dan checked around the door frame and the knob. No signs of breaking and entering. He put the Colt back in his belt. He put an ear to the wood. No sounds from inside. He stood on his tiptoes and passed a hand over the top of the door frame. No keys hidden there.

He knocked, then stepped back against the wall. No answer. He rapped the door again, heavily this time.

All of a sudden, his senses were twitching. His eyes jerked from side to side, up and down. His ears were picking up the faintest of sounds. He balled his fists. Something was wrong. He *knew* it. He considered his options.

If Guptill wanted him dead, he would be dead by now. A sniper would have picked him out. Or he would have been ambushed as soon as he stepped inside. Dan needed to find out what was happening. That was the only option. But he had to be ready for whatever lay behind that door.

He leaned on it hard. There was a splintering sound, but it was muffled. Dan grabbed at the handle, preventing the door from crashing in.

Before he went in, he took out his handkerchief and wiped the door handle. He listened. No sound from inside. Slowly he opened the door, but didn't go in. Still pin-drop silence.

No one would shoot him out here. They would wait for him to get inside.

He could see the hallway with two doors leading off it. One for the bathroom, another for the living room. Straight ahead, he could see the large, open-plan kitchen and reception area. The bedroom led off it. Silently, he closed the door behind him. It wouldn't shut, but that was okay. He bent down and crept along the hallway. His senses were tingling. The Colt was in his hand as he moved forward, pointing straight, ready to fire.

Someone's head. Grey-white hair. On the floor, lying face-down.

Dan felt like a mule had kicked him in the stomach. His chest was suddenly hollow, he couldn't breathe. Although the figure on the carpet was facing the other way, he knew it was Guptill.

Dan forgot everything else. Adrenaline took over. He flattened himself on the hallway carpet and searched for angles of fire.

He checked out the doorways ahead of him. Both doors were shut. No light underneath them. Curtains were drawn. The bathroom was further ahead, and the living room.

If the door opened suddenly, he could fire at the intruder's legs. He commando-crawled forward, elbows bunched by his side. A meter away from the reception, and three meters away from the figure on the floor, he stopped. A sofa was beside the motionless figure.

Next to the sofa, a door leading to the bedroom. It was ajar, and a light was on inside. That made him relax slightly. Only a fool would stand behind a door with a light on in the room. But it was still a possibility.

He rolled to his right. He could see the TV now, turned off. There was a glass bookcase stacked with books and magazines, and a minibar on the lowest shelf. A bottle of Chivas Regal on a tray with two crystal glasses. Guptill's favorite drink. His heart twisted at the memory.

He half-crouched and tried the handle of the living room door. He threw the door open, then sank back. The door banged against the opposite wall. No sound from inside. He peeked in, expecting gunfire. Nothing. Staying down, he moved into the room. It was empty, save for two lots of chairs and two glass bookcases again. He turned the lights on. The room was empty. Clear.

He repeated the same process with the bathroom. Clear.

He rushed to the bedroom. The major's clothes were on the bed, as if he was getting ready to go somewhere.

The whole process had taken a minute and a half. He turned quickly and bent down by the figure on the floor. Major Guptill's face was colorless, blood drained from it, his eyes wide and staring, his mouth open, saliva dribbling out. Dan needed gloves. Damn it. He took out his handkerchief and rolled it round his hand. He felt the carotid. A faint pulse, fast and thread-like. He didn't have long. Dan ran into the bathroom and returned with two small towels, rolling each around his hands, covering his fingers. Then he pulled the major onto his back. There was no blood. No signs of injury or assault. He checked the scalp, looked inside the lips.

"Felix...Felix."

Dan jerked his head back to the major's face. "Sir? Major? It's me, Dan. Dan Roy. What happened?"

Major Guptill's lips moved. Dan put his ear over his lips. "Yes, sir, I'm listening."

He stayed in that position for a few seconds before he realized there was no more sound coming from the major. Guptill's eyes were wide and fixed. His pupils were dilated. There was no flaring of the nostrils and his chest wasn't rising. Dan knew a dead man when he saw one. He didn't need to feel the carotid.

"Goodnight, Major," Dan whispered.

There wasn't anything else to say. He closed the major's eyes. He patted the body down. In the inside pocket of the vest, he found a wad of English banknotes. He put it in his pocket. Behind the notes he found a photo. He took it out. A young woman. Pretty, blond, in her twenties. She was smiling and looking at the camera. Her blue eyes matched Guptill's. She was young enough to be his daughter.

Dan knew that Guptill had an ex-wife who was a Brit. It made sense he could have a daughter.

The window behind looked out on the street, and it was open. A brief breeze blew in. Dan heard the slamming of car doors. He got up and stood to one side of the window behind the curtains, careful not to show his face. Two men in suits stood outside a Ford Mondeo.

They were looking up at the apartment. One of them signaled and they began to walk across the street, toward him. The knot of worry inside Dan's gut was growing, spreading into his limbs, making them ice-cold.

He had to escape. It was too late to go through the major's stuff. He stuffed the two towels in his pocket, and with his handkerchief wiped the handles of the bathroom, the living room and the main doors. He took one last look at the major, and then left. He was out on the landing of the third floor in less than fifteen seconds. One of the elevators was coming up. He looked down the stairwell. Empty, but he couldn't take the chance.

He jogged up one flight of stairs and looked down. He could see the elevator shaft from here. The two suits came out of the elevator. Dan knew he had seconds. He sprinted down the stairwell to the ground floor.

He came out on the street and headed down into the traffic of Chelsea Embankment.

CHAPTER 15

The buzz of the traffic and the pedestrians on Chelsea Embankment were a welcome distraction for Dan. His brain was numb, but his body was alive. He frequently did about-turns to look for danger. No one followed him. He was coiled like a wire spring and forced himself to breathe. Air rushed in from the Thames, smelling of mud and humidity.

He had to figure out what was happening. For that, he needed some space, and for everything to slow down. Briefly, he thought about stopping at one of the pubs to get a drink, but then changed his mind. He must get out of this place. The fewer people saw his face, the better. On the tube train he found a seat, put his head down and closed his eyes. The commuter rush was still going on. He was just another face among many. The crowd gave him some much-needed anonymity.

He changed at Waterloo, then got the train for Clapham Common in South London. He had been there once before, drinking at one of the pubs by the Common with some of his SAS friends. It was reasonably close to Chelsea. After some searching, he found a bed and breakfast. Known locally as a B&B, these places were England's version of a motel.

It was a nice B&B, in a large Victorian mansion by the Common. Dan paid in cash at reception, and went out to buy some cans of beer.

Dan's en suite bedroom was on the first floor, and the front windows opened out onto the green fields outside. He threw the shutters wide, got himself a cold Carlsberg can, and sat down in his armchair with his feet on the windowsill.

The evening sky was shrouding a cloak over the trees at the end of the green park. Darkness was claiming the air, and lights from the bars and pubs on the street were beginning to twinkle. He finished the Carlsberg in three long gulps, then went to the fridge and got himself another.

Major John Guptill. His old CO. One of the sharpest men he knew, and a man with connections. Who had killed him? Dan pressed his hands to his forehead. None of this made any sense.

Guptill had been like a father figure to him. The only man he could have trusted. His death made it unlikely that he had wanted Dan dead.

He thought back to how quickly the two suits had arrived. Who had called them? Had they come to dispose of the evidence, or were they cops?

Too many questions, not enough answers.

Dan forced himself to retrace his steps. Back to when he was trying to get into Guptill's apartment. There was no sign of forced entry in the doors or windows. He had no way of knowing if Guptill had a guest before he came in. Maybe he didn't. Guptill was wearing slippers. Had he stayed in the apartment all day? Had he been outside at all?

Dan remembered the pulse in the major's neck, and his breathing. He was still alive, so whatever happened had taken place shortly before Dan arrived. His lips twisted in frustration. While he was keeping stag, Guptill was dying, slowly…but how? As far as Dan knew, the major had no health conditions, he was fit as a fiddle, running two marathons a year. Dan closed his eyes. Guptill's pallid, white face jumped before his eyes. Very pale, drained of blood. But no sign of injury.

Heart attack? Possible. In a fifty-three-year-old man, non-smoker, minimal alcohol, and with his fitness levels? Maybe.

Then what? No bullet wounds. In the arms, Dan had looked for needle or knife stab marks. Zip. Nada. No blood anywhere.

*****

Dan woke up before sunrise. It was a habit. He was up in an instant, hand reaching for the weapon under his pillow. Then he remembered where he was. He relaxed but still kept his hand on the butt of the gun.

He still had the cellphone powered down, with the battery separate. He picked out the wad of notes and counted the money. One hundred and fifty pounds. That would not get him far in London. He washed his face, and did some yoga, as was his routine.

Then he looked out his open window. He had chosen the first-floor room deliberately. It gave him a good view of the surrounding streets. He could not see any cars that he had seen the night before.

It was 0830 by the time he got off at Sloane Square station. He paid the same attention to his surroundings as he headed down Chelsea Embankment. He walked down to the river end of Paradise Walk, casually passing the turning.

He stayed close to the riverside and looked on from the other side of the road. As he expected, the place was now a crime scene.

Yellow and black cross-marked police tape barricaded the entrance to the street. Two white police vans stood in front. As he watched, two men in white forensic suits came out the main door of the terraced house. A uniformed policeman followed. The forensics men went to the back of one van, took a briefcase out and went back into the house.

Dan sat down on a bench with the river behind him. After a while, he saw a woman. She came out and stood outside on the sidewalk. The uniformed policeman spoke to her.

The woman was in trouble. She covered her face with her hands, then allowed the policeman to help her to the squad car. She didn't get in, but took a tissue from the policeman and dabbed her eyes. Then she said something to the policeman, who nodded. The woman began to walk back up towards Royal Hospital Road.

She was blond and the younger side of thirty, Dan thought. From a distance, he couldn't tell her features very well. She wore a brown roll-neck jumper, and a dark blue skirt with black stockings. Her shoes were dark blue flats.

She looked just like the woman in Guptill's photograph. Dan got up and hurried in her direction.

CHAPTER 16

Dan didn't want to run: that gathered more attention than anything else. As he joined Chelsea Bridge Road, he saw the woman just ahead of him. Dan slowed his pace and kept people between them. The woman was about fifty yards ahead. As the tube station got closer, the number of pedestrians grew. More heads appeared between him and the woman. Dan increased his pace. He figured the woman wanted to get into the station, and if she did, he didn't want to lose her in the crowd. But a hundred yards from the Sloane Square underground, she turned into Sloane Avenue.

Sloane Avenue had tall, Art Deco buildings on either side of the street. They were all apartment blocks now, and Sloane Square being the fashionable heart of London, each apartment was worth millions.

Traffic there was less, and Dan hung back, following the woman at a leisurely pace on the same side of the street. She seemed in no hurry. Dan started feeling warm after a while and unfastened the top two buttons of his shirt. Sloane Avenue became full of elegant red-brick Victorian town houses. The terraced houses had elaborate cornices and balconies with curved railings and shutters in their windows. A maroon Lamborghini Diablo came down the road. Dan kept the woman in his sights.

Sloane Avenue turned into Brompton Road, a double-decker bus route, full of tourists and pedestrians. Boutique shops thronged the sides of the road. Dan increased his pace. They were approaching South Kensington. He was closer to the woman now, about forty yards away, when he saw her go into a clothes shop. He debated crossing the street, but decided against it. She could easily be keeping watch through the glass.

Dan bought a newspaper from a stand and pretended to read it. After a while, he peered inside the shop. He could not see the woman anywhere. He folded the newspaper and walked inside. He walked down the wide aisles. He looked at the back of the shop and saw another street exit.

He watched her shape flash against the door as she ran out into the street.

Dan swore to himself and walked fast. When he was out on the street, he caught sight of her, running down the steps of a tube station. Dan ran after her. She was at the ticket turnstiles, and went through as Dan watched.

Without looking back she went quickly down the elevator staircase. As the elevators descended, she turned slightly. Their eyes met and she looked away.

"Son of a bitch," Dan said, and ran towards the ticket counter. He did not have time to buy one: there was a queue in front of every counter. He got to the turnstiles and vaulted over them. He ignored the cries of a ticket collector.

He could not see the woman anywhere on the elevators. He ran down, pushing people out of the way. The elevators were crowded, but Dan managed.

A crowd of people came off the train. Dan pushed past them, searching in the windows for a glimpse. He found her in the fourth compartment, looking out sideways to see if she had been followed. Their eyes met again, and at that instant, the train doors began to shut.

Dan sprung forward. The doors had shut but he forced his hand through the rubber gaskets and prised the doors open. Dan got into the carriage, ignoring the disapproving gaze of the passengers, his eyes searching around.

He could not see her. He pushed past people again, determined not to lose her. He found her in the next compartment along. He could see her through the glass doors that separated one subway carriage from another. She was looking around, but could not see Dan.

That was what Dan wanted. He stayed out of her line of vision. She had found a seat. Dan remained standing, watching her. The train stopped at several stations, but she remained seated. Dan glanced at the map above his head. They were into East London.

The woman got off at a stop called Whitechapel. Dan followed a few people behind her. This time, she did not see him.

At street level, Dan noticed she glanced at her phone, then walked down a side road briskly. Dan followed. The traffic grew thin, then non-existent.

She was headed down an alley with old, derelict office blocks on either side. The alley was empty apart from the two of them. Dan stayed well back. He stopped behind a garbage can and peeked up just in time to see her vanishing into a building. Dan was against the front of the building in seconds. The entrance was wide, with revolving doors. There was scaffolding up the front of the building and it was undergoing renovation. Dan looked opposite and saw a similar office block with scaffolding.

He slipped in through the doors. The large lobby was empty. There weren't any carpets, and some old, disused chairs littered a corner. The reception desk was dirty and unused. Dan stepped carefully, on his tiptoes. Sound traveled loudly on cement.

The woman was not watching her step. Dan could hear the sound of her heels. He followed it to the stairwell next to the elevators. The elevators were out of order, and she was going up the stairs. Dan listened for a while, then followed her silently.

He heard her stop on the fifth floor, then go in. He stopped at the entrance and looked. There was a wide hallway, which opened out into an empty, open-plan room that was not yet built into an office. Opposite, Dan could see the windows of another office block.

Something lifted the hairs on the back of his neck. Automatically, his fingers curled around the butt of the Colt. He listened as hard as he could. The woman walked out into the middle of the open space, and stopped. She was halfway between Dan and the windows.

Dan came out of the landing and ran softly up to the walls. He raised his weapon up and listened. The woman was walking around. He looked in. She had her back to him and she glanced at her watch. She was waiting for someone.

There was no one there.

The realization hit him a split second before his worst fears were confirmed. A red dot danced around the walls. It came from one of the windows opposite. Quickly, Dan was out in the open. The woman turned around and her mouth opened in shock as her eyes traveled from him to his drawn weapon.

Dan bellowed at the top of his voice. "Get down!"

The red dot came off the walls and settled at the back of the woman's head. She was frozen, her eyes not leaving Dan. He threw caution to the wind and ran for her. She tried to move but Dan was swifter than the wind.

He grabbed her just as he heard the sound of a sharp crack. Then he was on top of her, covering her with his body. A few inches of wall protected them as the whining ricochet of bullets streamed in from the window.

"Get off me!" the woman screamed and fought, but Dan held her down. A bullet shattered a glass above their heads and the shards rained down on them. She stopped fighting.

Dan counted the bullets. Ten had been fired already. Most sniper rifles would have a 30-cartridge magazine.

And most sniper teams worked as a duo. When one ran out of ammo, the other took over, or handed a loaded gun to the shooter.

Dan would have to take those few seconds of respite. Dan counted another twenty rounds. They rolled around on the ground, getting closer to the wall and the hallway that separated them from the stairwell.

"When I say run, go for it. Go down the staircase. Right?" he whispered to the woman. Her fearful but beautiful blue eyes bulged out at him. She nodded in silence. Her blond hair was strewn around her head on the floor.

The bullets stopped suddenly. Dan screamed, "Now!"

The woman got up and ran as fast as she could.

But Dan did not run after her.

He raised himself, and took aim at the window from where he had seen the muzzle flash. A wisp of smoke still curled out of it. He fired three quick shots at it. The building was three hundred feet away at least. The rounds from the Colt would not have stopping power at that distance, but he could at least make them duck. Buy some precious seconds for himself.

He stood up from kneeling, shooting another two rounds at the window. Then he ran for the stairwell. The woman was waiting for him, halfway down the stairs.

They rushed down together. Dan stopped at the bottom of the staircase, and put his finger to his lips. He nudged her to a corner, and motioned to her to get down.

He could hear the faintest of sounds. Most normal men would not hear such sounds. But Dan was not a normal man. His senses were tuned to the movement of air around a body. To the whisper that a rubber-soled foot made on the ground.

Especially if that rubber-soled foot stepped on a piece of broken glass and withdrew quickly.

Dan checked his magazine. Three rounds left. He had another mag in his pocket, but he had no time to reload. Also, the click as the magazine went in would give him away.

Three bullets would have to do.

The footsteps approached the reception desk. Dan went to the ground. He was at an angle to the approaching men. They were to his left, and behind the stairwell door, about ten feet away. It was no good trying to come out of the door. They would shred him with bullets. Better to let them in.

Dan looked at the woman, and pointed upwards. She understood immediately. She got up silently, and took off her shoes. Then she padded up the stairs barefoot.

Dan pasted himself against the wall. He waited. The door opened slowly against him. He flinched backwards for the kick that would slam the door against him. It never came. A gun barrel poked through the door opening. Then a black, rubber-soled foot appeared.

Dan got up silently. As the figure came in through the doorway, Dan grabbed the gun. He pulled with all his strength. The man holding it was no weakling, which had the effect that Dan had desired.

The guy stumbled into the space. Without taking his hand off the gun muzzle, Dan fired point-blank with his other hand. The head mushroomed into a geyser of blood. As soon as he fired, Dan pulled the rifle off the man's hand, and dived for the protection of the wall.

Which was just as well. The wooden doors of the stairwell exploded under an avalanche of bullets. The firing was so ferocious that Dan could not lift up his head. Wooden fragments flew over his head, and covered him with sawdust. Dan knew what was coming next. He knew what he would do after such heavy fire. Lob in a grenade or a flashbang.

He would not give them that chance. He waited for the magazine to unload. The bullets stopped and there was a sudden, unnerving calm.

Dan did not wait. He kicked down the door, and the rattled structure flew off its hinges. He heard a grunt from the other side but he was firing blind already, teeth bared. He fired, then rolled into a ball on the floor, got up on one knee and fired again, moving the barrel side to side.

He stopped when he realized there was no return fire. The air was heavy with smoke and the sound of the rifle had deadened his ears. All he could hear was a ringing sound. As the dense smoke cleared, he looked at the floor.

The door had hit the man outside, and then he had been shredded by the bullets. It had been a two-man team. Enough to kill the woman, maybe.

But not enough for Dan Roy.

The man on the floor lay in a pool of blood. The silence was now total, a blanket of quietness that descends suddenly after vicious fighting. Dan heard a sound and cocked his gun up immediately.

It was the woman. Her forehead was plastered in sweat, and her eyes were wild with fear. Dan lowered the gun.

He said, "It's alright. You can come out."

She stepped out slowly. She stood to one corner, looking at the carnage around her. When her eyes saw the dead body on the floor she averted her gaze. Dan went through the unpleasant task of frisking the two men. He came up with nothing again. He lifted up the shirts from the belt line and then looked at their forearms.

His breath caught when he saw the tattoo on one of the men's deltoid muscles, near the shoulder. A red spearhead with the image of a black knife inside it. The Delta tattoo.

Sick at heart, Dan turned away.

He was used to killing. It did not bother him. He had never knowingly killed a woman or a child. He did not want that on his conscience. And neither had he ever knowingly killed one of his Delta brothers. Well, he had not known. That was what his rational mind told him. But his gut was telling him something else.

It's a shit game, son, John Guptill had said. Now he was lying cold in a grave. He should have added – Get out while you can. Otherwise, it might be you lying there one day.

"Hey, you okay?" It was the woman's voice.

Dan had been kneeling with his head against the wall. He felt nauseous and wanted to get the hell out of this place, more than anything else. He turned and straightened.

"Yes, I'm fine. What's your name?"

"Chloe Guptill."

"I thought so."

Chloe frowned. "What do you mean?"

Dan looked at the main exit, forty feet away, straight down the hallway. He said, "Let's get out of here alive, then I'll tell you."

CHAPTER 17

Chloe stayed behind Dan as they crept out of the building site. Once out, they ran for the main street. Dan felt safer with people around him. They ducked inside a coffee shop. They both used the restroom to make themselves more presentable.

When he came out, Chloe was already ordering. Dan got a large caramel macchiato, and with Chloe's cappuccino, they sat down away from the windows.

Her chest was still heaving up and down, and there was a light film of sweat on her forehead. Her blond hair came down to her shoulders. It wasn't dyed, he could tell by the non-darkened hair roots. Her eyes were wide, with long eyelashes. She had topaz eyes with dark, almost black irises. A small nose spread out into a generous mouth. She wasn't wearing much make-up and didn't have any lipstick on. She was very beautiful. Dan stared at her.

"Who are you?" Her voice was low, but direct. Dan had to admire her. Many people would have panicked and got themselves killed in the near-death situation that they had just been in. But Chloe had known how to handle herself. And right now, she was showing remarkable composure.

Dan didn't answer immediately, thinking of his best response.

"Who are you?" Chloe repeated. She was trying not to look scared.

Dan said, "I saw you coming out of the apartment block where Major Guptill lived. You spoke to the police officers, so I figured you had something to do with the major."

Chloe's face became a mixture of worry and curiosity. "Why were you watching me?"

"I wasn't watching you. I was looking out for the major. He used to be my commanding officer in the Delta Force, Squadron A."

She opened her mouth slightly, as if to say something, then shut it. She frowned heavily, and he could see the sadness in her eyes. Her voice trembled.

"He's dead." She lifted up her chin and sniffed, determined not to show emotion in front of a stranger. Dan could tell she was having a hard time.

"My name is Dan Roy. John Guptill was my mentor, ever since I joined the Force. Almost like a father figure. I'm very sorry."

Dan held her gaze. Eventually, she nodded.

Chloe had composed herself. "You are American, like Dad."

Dan nodded. She asked, "Did you recognize me from the photo?"

"Yes."

"Who told you to be there, Chloe?"

"I got a phone call. A woman's voice. She said Dad wanted me to meet someone. From the address, I didn't realize it was going to be that shithole. But I had to go, to find out what I could about Dad."

"What else did this woman say?"

"She said she was calling from Dad's law firm. I checked, they have a branch in London. They are a global firm. Dad wanted me to have some papers, but he wanted this person to give them to me at the location we were just in."

"Did that not strike you as suspicious?"

"Yes. But Dad did meet me in secret locations when he was in London."

Dan thought about that. "Did he ever tell you why?"

"No. But I got the impression he wanted to keep me away from everything. I know he worked for a firm whose name he couldn't tell me."

Dan nodded. Chloe said, "Do you work for the same firm?"

Dan hesitated. Chloe read his mind. "It's ok," she said, "you don't have to tell me. Need to know, right?"

"Right," Dan said, relieved. She was smart, he thought to himself.

"What happened in there…? You knew what to do."

Dan shrugged. "It's my job."

After a pause, he asked, "You live in London?"

Chloe said, "My parents divorced when I was young. I've lived with my mum and stepfather since then. In Reading, outside London, not far from Heathrow. Now I rent an apartment here, like Dad used to."

Dan asked, "Who called you about your father's death?"

"Scotland Yard. Guess they had my name down as next of kin."

"What did they tell you was the cause of death?" he asked.

"They didn't specify. He was found dead, and there was evidence of a break-in. No injuries on his body, however. They think there might have been an intruder, but they don't know how Dad died. Maybe a heart attack, they said, but no one knows." She grimaced. "They said the body would go to the coroner, and if he couldn't find a cause of death, then there would be an autopsy."

"Did they say it's now a criminal investigation?"

Chloe tucked a loose strand behind her ear as she took a sip of her cappuccino. "Yes, it is."

"Did the cops say how they heard of it?"

Chloe frowned. "Yes. They said a neighbor called when they found the body."

That was a lie. Dan tightened his jaw, but didn't say anything.

How could Guptill answer the door if he was lying dead on the floor? What sort of a neighbor would have keys to the apartment? And why had Dan not seen this neighbor?

Someone else had informed the cops. He thought of how rapidly the two detectives had arrived.

Someone who knew he would be there. Dan looked out the window. He hadn't been followed. But there were many other ways of keeping stag. A drone, for example. High above London's skies, invisible. His head became dizzy at the thought.

To get clearance for a drone feed someone needed access to the highest echelons of the intelligence service. Maybe it wasn't that. Maybe he was thinking about it too much. Maybe this was all fucked up beyond all recognition, and he was being played like a sucker.

Chloe coughed. "What do you make of it?"

"Sorry. I am confused at the moment, I have to say."

"Me, too. Do you really think someone broke into the apartment and…" She stopped. "Hang on, you said that the door was shut when you arrived?"

Dan nodded. Chloe said, "So the cops are lying?"

"No. The person calling them probably said he or she was a neighbor. Then they saw the door broken in when they came, found the body, and reached their own conclusion."

"Are you going to tell the cops?"

"No."

"But why not? It can help them with their investigation."

Dan shook his head. "There was no neighbor. The cops arrived while I was there. If a neighbor knew, they must have phoned the cops already. I can't see how the neighbor would have got into the apartment, unless…"

"Unless what?"

Unless the neighbor was the killer, Dan thought to himself. He shook his head. "Don't worry about it. What are you going to do now?"

A helpless look passed over Chloe's face. "I don't know. I didn't see Dad that often. I was ten when my parents divorced. But Dad came whenever he was on leave. I used to go on holidays with him." She became quiet.

"Are you staying in your apartment?" Dan asked gently.

"Yes," Chloe said.

"If you don't mind me asking, what do you do for a living?"

"I'm a journalist. I work for the *London Herald*."

"Interesting."

Chloe asked, "Why did Dad want to see you?"

"I don't know. I think it was something important, but not sure."

"What's going on here, Dan? You're holding back, I can tell. I need to know."

Dan sighed and nodded. Yes, she did need to know. But he had a problem. He couldn't tell her about his case, it was confidential.

He said, "I am in the dark as much as you are, Chloe."

She didn't seem convinced but didn't prod any further. "So, what do we do now?"

Dan said, "We need to find a cause of death. As you're next of kin, you have the right to demand an autopsy. Have you seen the body already?"

She lowered her face and nodded.

"I'm sorry," he said.

"Don't be. It's happened now. We need to find out what's going on."

"It's time to visit the morgue," Dan said.

CHAPTER 18

They were out on the street when Dan stopped.

"Do you know which coroner's office they've taken the body to?" he asked.

"Yes. The one next to Chelsea Crown Court. It's close to the Royal Brompton Hospital."

Dan said, "The coroner's report won't be ready for a day or two. I know you've identified the body already. I need to examine it more thoroughly. Are you sure you can handle that?"

If Chloe didn't understand what he meant, she didn't show it. She swallowed and nodded.

"Okay," Dan said. "Just close your eyes, if you find it disturbing. Without you, I can't access the body."

Chloe lifted her chin. "Don't worry about me, Dan. I'll be fine." Her upright posture, and the mild arrogance in the lifted chin suddenly reminded Dan of John Guptill. She certainly was his daughter.

At the morgue, a bored receptionist with a red Tina Turner hairdo stifled a yawn as they approached. Without speaking, she raised her eyebrows.

Chloe did the talking. "I need to see my father's body. His name is John Guptill."

"You are the next of kin?"

"That's right."

"Sign here, please," Tina Turner said. "And who's this?"

"My half-brother," Chloe said without missing a beat. Tina Turner glanced from Chloe to Dan and back to Chloe. The two women stared at each other for a few seconds. Then the receptionist pressed a button underneath the table.

"You'll see a guard at the gate of the basement. He'll take you down there."

"Thanks," Chloe said.

They walked through narrow, white hallways to the uniformed guard at the end. He nodded and opened a door, showing them a staircase.

In the basement below men in green overalls wheeled gurneys around, and pulled bodies out of drawers. It felt cold down there. On the walls, large air-conditioning machines whirred constantly. One of the green overalls approached them as a phone on the wall rang. The man answered it and spoke briefly, eyeing them. He hung up and came over.

"Chloe Guptill?"

"That's me," Chloe said.

"You wish to identify the body?"

"Yes," she said. Dan looked at her approvingly. She had identified the body already, but this guy didn't have to know that.

"Follow me."

They went down another hallway, dodging gurneys with stiffs on them. This nice part of London certainly had its fair share of dead bodies, Dan mused. They got into a cold, white room. The man checked a sheet of paper on a clipboard, running his finger down it. He thumped the clipboard gently, then turned and counted the square drawers on the wall. He found the one he wanted and pulled it out, revealing the white, cloth-covered body on the tray. "Do you just want to see, or spend some time?"

Dan looked at Chloe, who took a deep breath. "Spend some time," she said.

The man shrugged. From underneath the tray, he pulled two collapsible legs and set them on the floor.

"All yours," he said, with an understated cheeriness.

"Moron," Chloe muttered as the man shut the door behind him.

Dan exchanged a sympathetic glance with Chloe, opened his rucksack, and took out the latex gloves. He put them on.

"You don't have to look," he said.

"What are you going to do?" Chloe's voice betrayed her anxiety.

"I checked his body in the apartment. But his legs and arms were covered. I also need to check the spine, ears, and scalp."

"Okay," Chloe gulped.

"The quicker I do it, the sooner we get out of here."

Dan took the sheet off. The body was naked. Chloe had turned her back, facing the door. Dan moved his hand through the scalp. Guptill had a military buzz cut and he could see the scalp between the hair follicles. Perfect place, he knew, to hide an injection mark. A tiny, 28-gauge needle would leave almost no mark. Fieldcraft lessons, taught to him by CIA agents, when they worked together on missions.

He didn't find anything in the scalp. He moved down to the ears, checking the back of the lobes carefully, then looked inside. This was when an auroscope became useful, but he wasn't a doctor. He looked closely, but couldn't see any needle marks in the right ear. In the left ear, there wasn't any either, but he saw something else.

A small, black mark. He went over to the sink and wet a piece of tissue. Very gently, he touched the black spot. It flaked off. A blood clot. Beneath the clot, very close to the entrance of the inner ear, he found the smallest of puncture wounds.

So small, he would have missed it had it not been for the blood. He wondered if he had missed similar needle marks elsewhere. It didn't matter. He had found what he was looking for.

He checked Guptill's legs and between the toes of his feet quickly. There wasn't anything. Then he replaced the sheet, lifted the collapsible legs and trundled the tray back inside its square hole. He tore off his latex gloves, chucked them in the trash and washed his hands.

"Let's talk outside," he whispered to Chloe.

*****

Dan steered Chloe down the busy King's Road towards Fulham Broadway underground station.

He could feel Chloe's impatience.

"What did you find?" she asked eventually.

"I'll tell you later."

She wasn't happy with that. "Where are we going?"

"Back to my place, or to your apartment—it's up to you."

"My apartment, then."

Dan would have preferred his own place. Or a park bench, somewhere in the open.

"In which case," Chloe said, "we need to head down south."

"We'll take the tube," Dan said.

"It's not that long a walk."

Dan shook his head. "No, we take the tube."

The pavement was crowded. Easy for someone to hide and watch them, or for a sniper to pick them off a rooftop. He doubted that would happen in broad daylight on an open street, but after what just happened, he could not take any chances.

"Hold up," he told Chloe. "If someone just tried to kill you, chances are they have your apartment covered."

They had reached the crowded tube station. Chloe stopped, looking weary. "So, what do we do?"

Dan said, "They're after me as well. But all they know so far is that I escaped. They don't know where I am. So, it's best to go to the B&B I'm staying at."

Chloe looked defeated. Dan put a hand on her shoulder. "Hey, I know this is weird. But trust me, we will get to the bottom of this. Ok?"

Chloe nodded, and came off the wall. They took the elevator down to the trains.

At Clapham Common they walked to Dan's B&B. It took them ten minutes.

Chloe looked around the double bedroom, and out the window at the common. A soccer team was practicing outside on the green.

"So, what do we do now?" she asked.

Dan had figured this out already. "We need to find out more about what your father knew. I bet you the clues could be in his apartment already. I need to get back in there to check."

He sat down on a chair facing her and ran his hands through his hair.

"Chloe, have you heard of someone called Felix?"

Chloe frowned. "Felix?"

"Yes. Your dad said that word twice before he died. His last words. He was trying to make a point."

Chloe muttered the words under her breath. Then she looked up. "No. They don't ring a bell."

"I didn't see anyone enter or leave from the main door. Yet he was lying there, almost dead. There were no signs of a break-in."

"So the person who got in and killed my father was someone my father knew?"

"Looks like it, yes. Why would he open the door otherwise?"

"Alright. So how did he escape, if you were keeping watch, and you saw no one entering or leaving the apartment?"

"There's no way out the back, is there?" Dan had scoped this out already. There was a back garden, which led straight into the garden of another terraced apartment block.

"No."

"Two possibilities. He'd done the deed and left before I turned up for surveillance. Or, he left via the roof."

Chloe blinked at him in surprise. "What do you mean?"

Dan told Chloe how he had escaped when the cops turned up.

He asked, "You still have keys?"

"Yes."

"Then tonight I pay the apartment another visit."

CHAPTER 19

Chloe said, "I need to eat something."

"You read my mind," he said. He was famished. Apart from the coffee in the morning, he had had nothing to eat.

Chloe said, "If you need to see the apartment again, let's head down to Chelsea. I know a place where we can eat."

Dan looked at his watch. 1800 hours. He needed to get to the apartment under cover of darkness. The timing would be right. They walked out to the tube station and took the subway to Chelsea.

As they walked down, Chloe pointed down Chelsea Embankment towards the bend in the river. "This place is near Chelsea Harbour. Do you like seafood?"

"I eat any food. How far?"

"Fifteen, maybe twenty minutes' walk."

They crossed over to the riverside and walked down. Dan glanced around at the buildings, looking for open windows with curtains spread, and for sun glinting off metal.

"Tell me about your father," Dan said as they walked.

Chloe shrugged. "Like I said, I only saw him once or twice a year, but he stayed in touch. In many ways, we were close."

"I'm sorry."

"Don't be. He was a quiet person. Kept to himself. Never talked about his work."

Dan smiled. "All Army families have the same story. Soldiers lead crazy lives."

"I know."

The river stayed on their left, and bulbous, new, glass and steel residential and office blocks rose on the opposite bank.

On their side, the vintage buildings of Chelsea couldn't be torn down, but Battersea opposite was fair game, as most of its river front used to be dilapidated warehouses.

Soon they went past Prince Albert Bridge and the buildings on their side changed subtly. Chelsea Embankment had been left behind, and the graceful red-brick Victorian mansions made way for factories and warehouses that had recently been converted into residential apartment blocks. In between stood rows of smaller residential terraces, from Victorian times, but their less imposing façades meant they were for the clerks and servants of the lords and ladies who lived in Chelsea.

Chloe pointed at the smaller houses. "Three hundred years ago, this is where the normal people lived. The rich lot lived back there."

Dan smiled. "Not much has changed, then."

"Nope."

They reached Chelsea Harbour and a restaurant called Fisherman's Friend. The décor inside was dark and velvety, with oil paintings of marine life. Dim lights dotted the floor discreetly, lighting up the ceiling with soft haloes.

"Looks nice," Dan whispered as the waitress approached.

"It is."

It was Dan's turn to ask questions as they waited for their starters.

"Tell me about your job."

Chloe's eyes glinted in the low light. "I enjoy it, I have to say. Right now, the *Herald* is looking into the weapons industry."

Something distant tightened in Dan's mind. A sudden flash of the weapons catchment in that basement in Afghanistan. Then it was gone. He focused on Chloe.

"That sounds interesting. Tell me more."

"It *is* interesting. The weapon manufacturers in the UK are a very privileged group of private companies. The government has a support organization designed to help them sell their stuff to the rest of the world. It's called the Defence Support Organisation or the DSO."

"Surely the government helps other industries in the same way?"

Chloe shook her head. "I'm not talking about tax breaks or financial help here. The UK government actually does the marketing, publicizing and getting them contracts from foreign countries. What other industry does the government do that for?"

"So, what does the government actually do?"

"Diplomats speak to the Defense Ministers of Middle East countries. The Saudis are our biggest weapon buyers. There is even a so-called Export Support Team, a group of ex-military men who advise foreign governments which weapons to buy from us."

Dan had heard about this. "But that's all above board. What's your angle?"

"The angle is Britain's huge arms sales to Middle East countries that are using these arms to fight their own wars. Just pick one. The fight against ISIS, in Syria against the government, in Yemen against the Houthi rebels."

Dan pursed his lips. "I don't want to sound insensitive. But if there is a war, then someone has to supply the weapons, right?"

"That's not the point, Dan. Anyone can supply weapons. The point is, when the regimes we supply weapons to use them in blatant human rights violations, then we're doing something illegal. There is actually a law that prohibits us from doing that. So why do we keep doing it?"

Dan lifted his eyebrows. "When these countries buy the weapons from us, they don't tell us they'll bomb civilians, do they? So how is it our fault?"

Chloe sighed. "Dan, even a ten-year-old child will tell you which countries in the world we shouldn't be selling weapons to. And yet, they happen to be our biggest customers. In fact, they make us the second-largest exporter of weapons in the world."

"Okay. I get it. But let's come back to your angle."

"Right. We have concrete evidence that British-made cluster bombs, now declared illegal by NATO, have landed in farms in Yemen."

Dan kept quiet. Delivering weapons and training to rebel groups was something Special Forces had always done. Dan himself had played a part in training Afghan Special Forces when he was with Delta. No one ever asked where the weapons came from. It was a given that they would be there when needed.

Chloe continued. "As the cluster bombs are banned, several newspapers in the UK are putting pressure on the DSO to negotiate their return from the countries they sold them to originally."

Their starters had arrived and they tucked in. "I doubt that's going to work," Dan said, taking a mouthful of squid.

Chloe wiped her lips and waved her hands. "Maybe. Maybe not. But Dad was going to introduce me to someone in the US Embassy who knows about this."

Dan stopped chewing his food. He swallowed quickly and refocused.

"Wait," he said. "Your father said someone in the Embassy would talk to you about this?"

"Yes."

"Why?"

"What do you mean why? Because he's my dad."

"No. I mean why would this person speak to you?"

Chloe shrugged. "I guessed that he would speak anonymously. It happens a lot."

Dan frowned. "Yeah, but if this guy *works* in the US Embassy, I bet my bottom dollar he's actually CIA. What's his name?"

"Simon Renwick."

Dan thought about the name. It did not mean anything to him. But he felt uneasy. His mind was tangled up in knots.

Chloe sipped her white wine.

"Penny for your thoughts," she said.

Dan said, "Did you ring the Embassy asking for this guy, Renwick?"

Chloe pursed her lips. "Why do you ask?"

"Because I need to know. Did you, Chloe?"

"Yes."

"When?"

"Two days ago."

"When did this woman ring you from your dad's law firm?"

"Yesterday. You think there's a connection?"

Dan sat back in his chair. His brows were furrowed. "Maybe."

CHAPTER 20

By the time they came out of the restaurant, it was past nine o'clock.

"Did you ever know your father's lawyer?"

"No. Why?"

"Call them tomorrow. Ask them about this woman who called you. See if this call was genuine."

Chloe said, "I checked already. I never got the woman's name. The partner who's looking after Dad's assets in the UK is going to get in touch with me."

"But they don't know about what happened this afternoon."

"No. I spoke to them yesterday."

Dan said, "You need to call a cab now. Head back to the B&B. I'll see you tomorrow morning."

"I thought you were going back to Dad's apartment."

"I am. And I need the keys." Dan stretched his hand out.

"Maybe I should come with you," Chloe said. An image flashed before Dan's eyes. Lucy, standing with her hands on her hips inside the pub. Just before *it* happened. With an effort, he suppressed the sense of dread that rose up inside him.

Dan shook his head. "No. There's every chance someone is keeping an eye on the place. If there's any trouble I don't want you to get caught up in it."

"Will you be okay?" she asked softly. Dan looked at her and smiled.

"Don't worry about me. I know how to take care of myself."

*****

Dan watched the tail light of Chloe's cab glow a dull red in the distance, then fade from view. He retreated to the cement balustrades by the river, and reached inside his pocket. He took out the cellphone Guptill had given him. He stuck the battery on and powered the phone up.

He had one missed call.

He thumbed down the list of contacts. There was always only one number stored in these phones. Dan dialed it, and heard it ring four times before he heard Burns' voice.

Dan said, "It's me."

Burns said, "Been trying to get hold of you."

"Guptill's dead."

Burns asked, "I know. How did you find out?"

"He told me to meet him at his apartment. He was dead when I turned up."

Burns said, "Shit. This has to be the same guy who killed the CIA agent."

Dan asked, "What happened in Virginia?"

"Not good, Dan. They want to see you, and find out what the hell is going on. With Guptill now dead, things are more dicey. What are you gonna do?"

Dan thought for a while. He could run, but Intercept would come after him. He had no wish to go back. He wanted to be free. But free on his own terms. Not with a death sentence hanging over him.

He said, "I need to resolve this first. I need to clear my name."

Burns said softly, "Ok, I get that. But you have to be careful."

After a pause, Burns asked, "Who killed the guards who went with you to the safe house?"

"I did. They tried to kill me."

Burns whispered, "Jesus." He paused and said, "We need to meet."

"Yes," Dan said. "Where are you?"

"At the office."

There was a large hotel opposite where Dan was standing. Its lights fell on the Thames, reflecting in the waters. The Millennium & Copthorne Hotel. A Rolls-Royce Phantom V16 came to a stop outside as Dan watched. A man in an expensive tuxedo helped out a woman in a tiny red dress. The woman pouted and smiled. Then she swung her shapely bottom up the marble staircase. She was half her escort's age.

"Meet me inside the Millennium & Copthorne Hotel lobby. Chelsea." Dan hung up.

When Burns turned up in half an hour, Dan was inside the hotel, waiting at the bar. They found two armchairs behind an enormous vase containing a palm tree. Shaded from the other guests, but surrounded by people. Just what Dan wanted.

"Talk," Burns said.

Dan told him what happened. Burns leaned back in his chair. "Fuck."

He looked at Dan. "We've been infiltrated. Let me state the obvious here. Someone is trying to silence you. They got to Guptill already."

"Because of what I saw in that compound. And maybe because of what happened in Yemen."

Burns said, "Yes. Unless there is something else from the past."

Dan racked his brains. Making enemies was a by-product of what he did. He had killed one of the biggest heroin dealers in Iran six months ago. Blown up their factory, too. Iran had become one of the largest conduits of heroin from Afghanistan into Europe. This dealer had been close to the Ayatollah's Republican Guards, who had put a price on Dan's head.

Dan asked, "What did Guptill know?"

Burns shook his head slowly. "I don't know. Now we'll never find out."

"I think you can, if you try."

Burns' tone was sharp. "What do you mean?"

"I reckon you are our connection to the US Government. Maybe you worked for the CIA in the past."

Burns' tone was soft. "How do you figure that?"

"You were there when the shit hit the fan with me. You sort these things out, right?"

"Even if that were true, what's your point?"

Dan said, "So I think you are tight with the powers that be. You can ask favors. Find out what Guptill was up to."

They stared at each other for a few seconds. Then Burns smiled. "Guptill and McBride spoke highly of you. I can see why."

"So will you ask around about Guptill?"

Burns said, "Alright. I'll ask around, I promise. But remember, someone is inside Intercept. The camera you took photos with has disappeared. I could have taken that straight to the CIA."

"I know that."

"Dan, you need to be careful of who you trust. So do I. I don't know which way this thing's gonna go next."

Dan was thinking about Burns. "What are you gonna do?"

Burns said, "This shit is deep. I mean, without clearance no can even access these weapons, right? And I'm talking about a base that we control."

Dan nodded. "Yes. I checked the Hellfire missiles in 'Stan. Sure as hell said 'US Army' on the side."

Burns said, "So we are dealing with someone high up. I need to go back to Virginia soon, to give them a report. Intercept suspect you, Dan. But I know they are looking all around, too. If there is someone inside, they will find him."

Dan said, "I need money. I can access my checking account, but I would rather use the expenses." Every Intercept agent had an expenses account.

"And I also need a weapon. A Sig Sauer P226, with a box of extra ammo. 7.62mm NATO rounds. A Heckler & Koch 417 rifle with all the mod cons we are used to. NVGs and a compass. Can you get that?"

Burns nodded. "We need to be careful with our phones. You shouldn't call me again from the one I gave you."

"Makes sense."

"Use a new one with a new SIM card for every call you make to me from now on."

Dan rose. Burns rose with him. He said, "See you back here tomorrow, same time. I will have the money and a bag with the weapons with me. Do not meet anyone else from Intercept apart from me."

Dan said, "Roger that."

Burns said, "I got something for you." He pulled out a briefcase and opened the lid a fraction. Dan peered inside and smiled. He pulled out his eleven-inch-long, curved kukri knife. He stuffed the knife in his back pocket.

"Thanks."

Burns asked, "Where you headed now?"

"To find the infiltrator."

*****

Dan waited for ten minutes after Burns left.

At 2200 hours, he came down the stairs. He was out the main door in less than five seconds, and on the street immediately after that.

He didn't see any cars waiting at the curb opposite, and he relaxed. He walked quickly, keeping his face low. No one followed him. Orange street lights glowed brightly in the warm night air. He slowed down as he approached Paradise Walk. The yellow and orange police tape was still strung from one end of the street to the other. He kept watch again. After ten minutes, he hadn't seen anything unusual. A couple of residents sauntered out of one of the apartments and then went back in. A couple came out for a walk along the Embankment. Dan stayed in the shadow of a tree, almost invisible in the darkness.

Half an hour later he made his move. He strolled casually up to Paradise Walk, and did what the residents had done. He bent below the police tape and walked on, keeping to the same side of the street as Guptill's apartment. Some of the lights were on in the windows of the four-story building. There was a light on at the main entrance as well, but he didn't see any security cameras.

He let himself in with the key. The hallway was deserted. He padded up the staircase to the second floor. The landing was in darkness. The elevator shaft was open and the lights indicated an elevator was waiting. He went to the double doors and peered through the glass box. The hallway to the apartments was empty. Lights were placed on the wall at regular intervals. Dan waited for a minute. He didn't want to wait too long in case someone came up the stairs or the elevator. He put his latex gloves on.

Three lines of the police tape were stuck across the door frame of Guptill's apartment. The door was ajar. Beyond the door—total blackness. Dan knelt down and removed the tape rather than break it. Staying down, he pushed the door gently. It swung open into silence. He let his eyes adjust.

Then he was inside the apartment. He took the ends of the sticky tape and reattached them to the door frame. He would have to repeat that procedure when he left. He reached into his bag and took out the flashlight, putting it in his pocket for future use.

He could make out shapes. He saw the doors on his right and left. Bathroom and living room. He opened each one and peered inside. Then he went inside each one and, staying down, turned the flashlight around. Clear again.

In total silence, he moved into the reception area. A faint ray of street light let itself in through the window shutters. He saw the furniture, but nothing else. He crept towards the bedroom. At the door, he listened. If there was anyone inside, they were being very quiet. It was almost impossible that they had heard him.

Almost. There was always a danger. He couldn't afford to be complacent. Slowly, he reached out a gloved hand and turned the door handle. It was well oiled. He opened the door soundlessly, and shrank back from the opening, back against the wall. Then he looked inside. Darkness again, but in the broken shafts of street light falling in the reception area, he could make out the bed. The clothes were gone. Staying crouched, holding the flashlight in his hand, Dan walked into the bedroom. He left the door open behind him, so he could escape if something happened.

There was a wardrobe. Dan stood up and shifted his kukri scabbard from his back belt to the front of his waist. He could remove it easily from the scabbard now if he needed to. He opened the wardrobe door and looked inside. An array of suits were neatly arranged inside. Below that, a similar collection of dress shoes. Dan moved the suits and found some shirts. He looked under and, apart from the shoes, he found some slippers. Two travel bags for the suits, both of which were empty. He found two shoeboxes as well, with nothing inside them. He stood up and looked at the suits again. Savile Row. Bespoke and expensive.

He lifted up each suit jacket, shook them slightly, then put them back in. There were six suit jackets in total, and the fourth one seemed heavier. Dan passed his hands over it. Not much there. He turned the torchlight off and put the jacket on. Immediately he felt it. On his left, something inside the lining. He peeled the jacket off and slashed at the sides of the expensive fabric. The lining fell open. Inside, he found a silver wig that would suit an older man. He also found an envelope with three passports inside. A red EU, a navy blue American, and a maroon Egyptian. He used his phone to take photos of everything, then stuffed the passports and wig inside his bag.

Then he heard the noise. He froze.

CHAPTER 21

It had been very faint, maybe a creak of a footstep, Dan thought. But it was definitely something. On the balls of his feet, swift but silent, he moved to the door.

There was no further sound from outside. Whoever was out there had gone quiet. He felt for the kukri. He balled his fists, dropped his shoulders. How many? One or two? Maybe another waiting outside on the landing. If this was a full team, then another in the car.

The darkness suddenly exploded. The bedroom door was savagely kicked open. It smashed against him, and he had his arms lifted up like a boxer's. As the door bounced off him, he saw the gun appear and the hand holding it. Dan grabbed it and pulled up and away from him, and a round went off whining into the ceiling. A suppressed gun, he hardly heard the sound.

Dan kicked the door shut, making the man stumble into the room. Keeping his hand firmly on the gun wrist, Dan punched the man as hard as he could in the stomach. He heard the groan, but by that time his other hand had found the man's hair. Dan grabbed hold of a generous grip and pulled the head down to his rising knee with lethal force. Another round went off into the ceiling. There was a squelching sound, like a large grape being squashed under a shoe, and a muffled scream. The man would need a new nasal septum.

The man used his body weight to crash into Dan, throwing him off balance. They both fell backwards, landing on the bed. The man was on top, blood dripping onto Dan's face. Dan still had a vice-like grip on the man's right wrist holding the gun. With his free hand, the man clawed Dan's face, reaching for his eyes. Dan punched the man in the jaw. He connected solidly and felt the bone crunch. He delivered the same blow again. This time with a soft pop, he heard the TMJ snap. The man screamed this time, loudly. It sounded strange and guttural, like he had lost his voice. Dan rolled on top of him and punched him once more to render him unconscious. He felt the body go slack and the gun came out in Dan's hand. Dan lowered the body gently off the bed. The man might be out cold, but not for long. And if he had backup…

Dan rolled off the bed and, gun in hand, listened by the doorway. Total silence again. His eyes bore into shadows, searching movement: his ears listened to every sound in the night. He could hear water dripping somewhere, a cat's meow. But nothing else. He gripped the unfamiliar butt of the gun. He fell to the floor and crawled his way out into the living room. He was now in a direct straight line with the open door, and he didn't like it. He rolled over and stood up near the window, staying away from the frame, and peered down the side into the street.

He saw the car. On the same side, further down. Lights and engine off, but he hadn't seen the car before he came in. It was a foreign make, probably a Lada or Škoda. He took a deep breath. For a few seconds, he kept his eyes on the car. Then he saw the movement inside. The driver, who took out a cellphone, stared at the screen, then put the phone down. Dan got an idea. He crept over to the glass shelf at the other end of the room. He found a bottle of whiskey. Staying below the window, he opened it a fraction, just enough to put the bottle on the ledge. Then he walked to the doorway and loosened the police tapes. He came back to the window and tipped the full bottle of whiskey out. It fell, landing with a crash on the empty street below.

Dan ran. He came out of the apartment, sprinted down the landing, and took the steps four at a time. In ten seconds, he was at the ground floor. He ran to the wall next to the main door and flattened himself against it, sinking down to the floor. He still had the gun in his hand. He didn't know what type it was, but it had a level of suppression he hadn't come across before. Which was unusual, because he had used most of the common, suppressed handguns.

Ten seconds for the guy in the car to figure out something was wrong. Another ten seconds to get out of the car, lock it and hurry down. Dan counted down. He had ten seconds in hand. Right on cue, there was a sound at the door. A key turned. The door opened gently. A shaft of dull yellow street light fell into the hallway. Dan tightened his grip on the weapon. He couldn't extend his elbow to raise it, but he turned it so it was facing the open door.

A tall, wide man stepped in. Black jacket falling to his knees. He kicked the door shut gently with his heel. Dan got a flash of his face in the street light. Swarthy, dark hair, and with a weapon in his right hand. Only six feet separated Dan from him. Dan could hear his heart squeeze against his ribs. A trickle of sweat found its way past his eyebrows into his left eye. He couldn't move to wipe it off.

The man stared into the darkness ahead, then strode forward. He put a hand on the stair railings, ready to climb upstairs. Then he waited. Dan couldn't see him anymore. He knew the man had one foot on the stair. Listening and waiting. Dan extended his right elbow and moved slightly forward. He would get the first round in.

He heard a stair creak. Then another. Dan kept his elbow extended, and moved it up along the underside of the staircase. The steps kept going further up. Dan listened till he couldn't hear any more.

Then he got to his feet quickly. He opened the door with his key, shutting it gently behind him. He ran over to the car and took a photo of the license plates. Then he turned towards the rustling waters of the Thames and sprinted down the road.

CHAPTER 22

Dan ran down the side streets, avoiding the main avenues of Chelsea Bridge and Royal Hospital Road. As he got near Sloane Square tube station, he was able to flag down a minicab. The driver rolled down his window. He was of Middle Eastern origin, in his late-forties, his teeth stained yellow. Dan looked him over quickly. Then he jumped in the back and gave him directions to Clapham, straight down Chelsea Bridge.

He got out of the cab five hundred yards from the hotel, paid the driver, and walked the rest of the way. It was 0100 hours. He slowed down as he approached the hotel, watching for a minute. The reception light was on. The rest of the building was sunk in darkness, including his room.

Dan stepped into the reception. The owner was dozing at the desk, but he looked up with a start as Dan approached. He recognized Dan and smiled. Dan went up to his room and knocked. Chloe opened the door on the chain, and relaxed when she saw Dan.

Dan felt Chloe's eyes on him as he peeled off his sweaty black vest and went into the bathroom for a quick shower. He put on a dressing gown, then sat down with the bag on his lap. Chloe put the table lamp on and sat down next to him.

Dan told her what had happened. Chloe's hand went to her throat. She looked beautiful in that small gesture of vulnerability. Dan stared at her, then looked away, embarrassed.

She said, "But you are ok, aren't you?"

Something in her voice made Dan look up. "Yes, I am." Chloe did not meet his eyes. She looked down and said, "This is what you do, right? I mean, for a living."

"You mean kill people."

"I didn't say that."

She said, "You are good at what you do."

"I'll take that as a compliment. Thanks."

Chloe looked away. Dan felt a little bad, he was being defensive. This was a big deal for her, and she had probably never met anyone like him.

Dan said, "I grew up in the highest mountain ranges in the world. In

Nepal. The Himalayas. Not far from the base camp of Mount Everest. The Gurkhas live there, and they have a fitness beyond the average human being. The reason is the low concentration of oxygen at those levels. I trained myself to do what they did. I ran five miles up and down the mountain path every day from when I was seven years old, till I came back to Bethesda."

"Jesus. That sounds hard."

"I know. But you should see the Gurkha kids. They carried forty-pound weights on their backs and did the same distance as me in the same time. I could, too, but only after hard training. It gave me a level of fitness most humans don't have, and one of the reasons I got picked to join, uh, where your dad worked."

Dan fell silent. He had already said too much. He did not wish to speak about his operations. He never could. The things he had seen and done...he would take them to his grave.

Dan exhaled, stretched, then picked up the passports from the bedside table.

"You got this from my dad's place?" Chloe asked.

"Yes," Dan said.

He took out the gun first. He held the butt with a kitchen towel, not touching the weapon. It was a squat, ugly thing. Almost snub-nosed in appearance. For a small handgun, it was heavy. Using the towel, he pressed the magazine switch. Six-round clip—small for a modern handgun. But his eyes widened when he saw the size of the rounds. 7.62mm standard NATO issue ordnance. This small gun packed a punch. He remembered the soft whistling sound the gun made, far softer than any gun he had used.

He put the gun to one side and took out the wig and the passports.

John Guptill's face stared out of the American passport's photo page. He looked through the Egyptian passport. Guptill again, with a beard, glasses, and the wig. He peered closely at the photo. Guptill's eyes looked different. Contact lenses. His normal light gray eyes looked black. His face was also more tanned: he looked darker. Overall, one would assume the man in the photo was Middle Eastern.

Dan looked at the red EU passport last. He had lost the glasses, and had brown contacts to disguise his blue eyes, along with a light beard. He wasn't wearing the wig.

Chloe reached out and took the three passports from where Dan had put them. Her face was a mask of shock as she looked through them.

She said, "What did Dad do with these?"

"We do all sorts of clandestine work, Chloe. Most of our actions are deniable if we are caught. But that still means trouble. For us and our country. Hence, we often have fake identities when we are abroad. But, I have to say, you father was very well prepared."

"For what?"

"I don't know. What with the disguise and these passports, I have a feeling he was working for some intelligence agency."

"Like the CIA?"

"Maybe."

Dan looked at Chloe. "Listen," he said softly. "Get some sleep. We can talk about this in the morning." He looked at the bed.

"You sleep on the bed," he said, feeling awkward. "I'll take the couch."

Chloe took the bed, and turned the lights out. She was asleep soon. Dan closed his eyes, but he saw one of two faces constantly. Lucy, then Guptill. He tossed and turned, the two faces keeping him awake.

*****

When Dan woke up, Chloe was up already. She was wearing a light pink, knee-length skirt, a lilac, sleeveless vest with a light blue cardigan that almost matched her eyes. Her hair was tied back in a ponytail. Her eyes had make-up on, but they were lined with lack of sleep.

"Hey, Dan," she said brightly.

Dan made an attempt at a smile. He got up from the couch. "Sleep well?"

A shadow passed across her face.

Chloe waved her hands. "It's nothing. I need to get busy with the funeral, and do my job assignment as well. It will be good for me. But last night," she looked at him, "I just kept thinking about Dad, and…"

She was being brave, holding it in. He remembered how he felt when his father had died.

"It's alright. It gets better, I promise. My dad died, too."

She sniffed and wiped her nose with a tissue, and took a deep breath. "You know, he spoke about you."

"What? Really?"

"Yes. He said you were very tough. And loyal. A good friend to have in a fight."

"Did he mention anyone else?"

"Yes. He spoke once about an older man, Colonel McBride?"

Fighter McBride. Dan remembered him from the night of the debrief in

Afghanistan, before the botched operation.

"What did he say about him?"

"Said he was a good man. He enjoyed working with him."

Dan thought for a moment. "I know this is hard for you, Chloe. But I want you to think about something for a moment. Did your father ever mention something, or someone, called Felix?"

Chloe frowned. "You asked me this before, right?"

"Yes."

"No, don't think so."

"Alright."

"Chloe, there's something else I have to tell you."

"About what?"

Dan told her about what happened on his mission in Afghanistan. When he finished, she looked shocked. "Dad suspended you?"

"I don't think it was his decision."

"But he didn't believe you?"

"At the time, maybe he didn't. But, later when we talked by the river, he knew. He wanted to tell me something. That moment never came."

Dan leaned forward. "Something happened last night when I was at your dad's apartment." Dan told her about the men inside. Her face was a mask of shock again.

Dan said, "Chloe, all of this stays between you and me. You understand that? We need to tread very carefully now. I might even have to disappear for a while, in order to find things out."

CHAPTER 23

Dan walked out of the hotel on his own. He walked to the tube station, and got off at Westminster. He went inside a red telephone booth and dialed the landline number that Burns had given him. He answered on the first ring.

Burns said, "We have a problem."

His tone was urgent. Dan asked, "What?"

"Scotland Yard have put out a circular on TV and print media for a man who matches your description. You were seen the first night you went there. An old woman saw you. I rang MI5 and made some discreet enquiries."

Dan remembered the old woman. He had snuck in behind her.

"Shit," he said.

"Yup. Not good. You need to lie low."

Dan told Burns briefly what had happened the night before.

Burns was silent for a while and said, "You got the number plate of the car?"

Dan read it out to him. Burns said, "That sounds like a diplomatic number plate."

"And I got some weapons off them, too. Do we still have our armory guy?"

"Yes."

The armory guy was an old man who supplied them with unmarked weapons. His name was Spikey, and he was an SAS veteran. He had his own makeshift ballistics lab in his backyard. English laws made it difficult for soldiers in the UK to purchase weapons. Spikey got around that problem. He supplied some of the PMCs in London, and soon he had come under Intercept's radar.

Dan asked, "You got his address?"

Burns gave it to him.

Dan broke the connection, but he waited for a while inside the booth, keeping the phone receiver to his ear. He looked around. It took him almost three minutes, but finally he saw it. The one car that wasn't moving. A black car, and it looked like a Lada or a Škoda. Eastern European, probably Russian. Very similar to what he'd seen on Paradise Walk last night. A man got out of the driving seat. Even from a distance, Dan could see the white bandage on his nose. Someone else was in the car in the passenger seat.

The same two men who had been at the apartment last night. Dan had come here by tube and hadn't been followed, he knew that. How did they know he was here?

Dan came out of the booth and walked towards Waterloo Bridge. Sure enough, the black car moved out into the traffic to follow. He could see the two men clearly now.

Dan turned around and ran.

*****

Chloe caught the look on his face as she opened the door. Dan brushed past her into the hotel room.

"What's the matter, Dan?"

Dan went over to the windows and pulled the curtains. The room became dark. He flicked the light switches.

"They were waiting for me," he said.

"Who?"

Dan told her about the two men, and then about the police.

Chloe said, "So they're calling you a suspect in Dad's death?"

Dan shrugged. "Apparently, it was natural causes. We need to see the coroner."

"Why?"

Dan decided Chloe needed to know. Things were getting worse very quickly. When he wasn't around, she needed to be able to protect herself.

"Chloe, I think your father was killed."

Chloe's face went rigid. "How do you know?"

"I don't, but when I examined his body in the morgue, I found a small needle puncture wound in his left ear. I remembered one of the CIA guys talking about it once. Toxic compounds can be injected through needles in places like the scalp, ears, between toes, in the rectum. Where it can be hard for the coroner to find."

Chloe had her arms wrapped around herself. "And you found something like that on my father?"

"I'm sorry. Yes, I did. In his left ear, there was a puncture wound at the entrance of the inner ear. Very hard to see, even with a microscope. The guy who told me about this mentioned how the KGB used this as a killing tactic."

"The *KGB?*"

Dan held his hands up. "Don't run with that. We don't know anything for certain as yet. But those two guys following me, the gun they had, the car they drive, all of it does point to something foreign."

Chloe sat down on the bed and clasped her hands in her lap. "You know the car registration, don't you?"

"I remember it."

"Our newspaper has a database of car registration numbers. I can ring them and find out, or call the Driver and Vehicle Licensing Agency."

"Burns is looking for it already. The DVLA will tell us about the car, but not where it comes from or who it's registered to."

"Good point," Chloe said.

She opened her cellphone and made the call. She scribbled something as she spoke. Then she thanked the person and hung up.

"It's a diplomatic corps number," she said. "The car is registered to Kensington Palace Gardens, London."

"The Russian Embassy," he said softly. Burns had been right. "Ok, let's do this in order. Did you go through your father's bank statements?"

Chloe's eyes brightened. "For the last three months, I did, yes. You'll never guess what I found."

"Hit me."

"Apart from his monthly pay from the organization you both worked for, he was also getting paid a lump sum every quarter from a company called Wellington. I looked into it. The money was transferred by a BACS payment, like most salaries in the UK. I called HSBC and they gave me the identifier for the BACS. It turns out Wellington International Services is an overseas company, based in Jersey."

"Jersey is a tax haven for the super-rich."

"Yes, but not just for the super-rich and hedge funds. The island belongs to the British Crown, but doesn't have to answer to British laws. A huge number of companies are based in Jersey, because they can enjoy offshore status, buy and sell tax-free, and not have to disclose their business to anyone."

"These guys run more scams than any criminal I know. But sounds like you hit a barrier there."

"Yup," Chloe grimaced. "Wellington International Services is run by a board of trustees. Exactly who the bloody trustees are, no one seems to know. But finally, I did find something. The board of trustees are represented by a law firm."

"And?"

"Well, the law firm happens to be based in London. I'm going to visit them tomorrow."

Dan considered this. "You have to be careful. People like these—they don't like people like you who ask questions."

"Hey, I'm a journalist. It's my job to ask questions." Chloe smiled and Dan couldn't help smiling back.

"Anything else?" he asked. "Emails, cellphone?"

"I can't get into his email. It's a dot Army domain, so I rang the Ministry of Defence. They're looking into it."

Dan raised his eyebrows. "You *have* been busy."

"Totally. Cellphone, similar story. Held by Scotland Yard right now."

"They should hand it back, if they're saying this is *not* a murder investigation."

"There's something else. Dad had a car."

"He did?"

"It's still in the garage. Not sure if the police have looked at it. But from his papers I found the address where it was last sent for repairs. I'm guessing it's still there."

Dan's mind was turning over. "We need to get to the car before the police do. And at the same time, we need to visit the coroner. I want to ask him about the cause of death."

He sat down in front of Chloe, crossing his arms. He was wearing a half-sleeve, button-down shirt and he noticed Chloe stare at his forearms. Her cheeks flared a little rosier, then the color died. She smelled nice, Dan thought. He didn't know what the hell it was, but it was flowery and fresh.

He said, "Right. The way I see it, we need to find out about those passport identities that your father had. Maybe you could make some phone calls, ask some questions. But please be very careful about who you go to see. Don't go to the garage, for instance. I want to come with you."

"And what will you do?"

Dan pointed at the plastic bag containing the pistol. He grinned, then his face became serious. "I need to get myself a gun."

Chloe said, "I need to see this man at the US Embassy. Simon Renwick."

"Whoa. You think that's a good idea?"

"It's the US Embassy, Dan. Who's going to kill me there?"

Dan considered this. The logic was irrefutable. Nobody wanted an international incident on their hands.

"Ok," he said. "Just be careful."

*****

Chloe Guptill got off the tube station at Hyde Park Corner and walked to Mayfair. She was heading for Grosvenor Square, to the US Embassy.

She was looking forward to meeting Simon Renwick.

Chloe was one step below becoming a subeditor for her newspaper. A big feature story on this would make her career. Deep inside, Chloe felt her father, despite his military background, had supported her. John Guptill had been a soldier, through and through. He fought his wars on the battlefield. Politics had never been his cup of tea. He had an intense dislike of the DoD in America, and the MOD in England, whose budget cuts, Guptill said, hurt a soldier's life more than a bullet did.

She felt a tug in her heart as she thought of her dad. A constant emptiness. He was gone. She would never see him again or hear his voice. The sunlight turned to rust, and the breeze flowing in from the Thames turned cold and frosty. Chloe hastily put her sunglasses on. She blinked away tears.

At Grosvenor Square, there was a steel barricade, and a ring of US Marines with MP5 sub-machine guns. They stopped every pedestrian attempting to enter the steel barricade. The checkpoints were busy. Chloe waited in the queue for half an hour, getting impatient. When she finally got inside, and showed her newspaper ID and the letter her dad had written for Simon Renwick, she was asked to take a seat.

Soon she was led from her seat and taken to a bank of elevators. She went up to the third floor and stood in front of a door that blocked a hallway. She had to press the buzzer three times before it was answered. A middle-aged, bespectacled woman opened the door. She told Chloe to sit in the reception while she went to look for Mr Renwick. Chloe hadn't expected anything glamorous, but the plain green chairs, the dying plants on the window ledge, and the slightly musty air of the old building all pointed to an atmosphere that could be improved.

An array of posters adorned the wall. Exhibitions and event advertisements. There was an aircraft exhibition coming up at Farnborough, and an armored car expo in Kent. For both events, the DSO would act as brokers to introduce defense companies to the relevant officials in foreign Defense Ministries.

"Miss Guptill?"

The voice came from behind her. Chloe turned around. The man she saw was younger than she had imagined. She'd only spoken to him on the phone, and the man had a heavy voice.

"Simon Renwick. How do you do?"

Mr Renwick had a sallow complexion, sunken cheeks and square glasses. The glasses gave him a slightly nerdy look, but his smart suit and easy manners made up for that. His dark hair was short and brushed back. When he smiled, his eyes remained blank. His face was tanned, with lines in the forehead from the sun. He had an American accent, as she had expected. She imagined he was a well-travelled man. She shook hands with him, and then followed him up to his office.

A large desk in the middle of the room took up most of the available space. A set of windows looked over one of the many Grosvenor courtyards.

"Have a seat please, Miss Guptill."

"Thank you."

He tapped a few buttons on the keyboard in front of him and looked at the screen briefly before turning to her. He was smiling, but his eyes remained untouched by mirth.

"How can I help?"

"Well, my father advised me to see you. His name was John Guptill."

The smile vanished slowly from Renwick's face. "You are John Guptill's daughter?"

"Yes," Chloe said slowly.

Renwick's face cleared. "Ah, right, I see. What is it that you want to know?"

Chloe said, "You knew my father, right?"

"Yes, I did."

"He asked me to see you about the weapons industry in the UK. About the DSO in particular."

Renwick said, "I am sorry, Miss Guptill. I am an American. It would not be wise to comment on UK policy."

"Your name does not have to be mentioned. Ever read a newspaper article quoting a source in Washington or London? You could be that source."

"I know that. But these things have a habit of coming around. Like I said, I am sorry. And I am sorry about your father, too. I will miss him."

Chloe stared intently at the man. "Exactly how did you know my father?"

"That information is classified. But we became friends. We played golf together." Renwick pressed his lips and looked out the window. Then he glanced at Chloe.

Chloe got the impression that she was done here. It was a blind alley. She would not get anything more out of Renwick, and nor did she care about his attitude. She got up.

"Goodbye, Mr Renwick."

"Thank you for coming, Miss Guptill."

CHAPTER 24

Dan took the bus to the far south-east corner of London. It was more run-down here, a grimy collection of tall, brown-brick council estate buildings, all built in the 1960s, designed to herd as many deprived families into one place as they could. Upturned shopping trolleys and trash cans littered the streets. In a basketball court, teenagers smoked cannabis and played their MP3 players loudly. Rap music blasted at Dan, along with a few taunting calls asking him if he was scared. He walked on.

After fifteen minutes he came to a shabby building called Ferguson House. The timber- and glass-paneled doorway had been kicked a few times. Glass lay scattered on the floor. Graffiti adorned the walls, inside and outside. Dan approached the doorway and looked at the calling buttons for the apartments. The building had seventy-four apartments. He pressed the buzzer and waited. After the second buzz, a voice came crackling on the intercom.

"Who is this?"

"Spikey, it's Dan."

"Dan who?"

"Dan Roy. The one with the kukri."

Dan took the cramped elevator to the fifth floor and knocked on number forty-three. After a fumble with the lock, the door opened.

The man who stared at Dan was well into his sixties. He was shorter than Dan, but even now, his impressive girth was a reminder of how physically strong he had once been. His eyes were hooded but attentive. His scalp was bald, and his skin wizened and leathery from many years of service in deserts and jungles. Spikey Dobson, so called because he was short and an expert in using the bayonet to kill at close quarters, smirked at Dan and walked back slowly, leaving the door open.

The apartment was cramped. Photographs of old escapades hung on the walls. Dan pushed his way past two tables overflowing with papers and books, and two sofas with foam leaking out of them. Spikey slouched in an armchair, the TV on some game show.

"To what do I owe the pleasure of this visit, Mr Shady American?" Spikey said, moving his head from the TV screen to stare at Dan.

Spikey was an old boy. A former SAS man, he served in the 22nd Regiment in Northern Ireland, the Falklands, and the Balkans. He also had a lot of decommissioned weapons in his personal possession that he'd accumulated over the years.

Spikey had become an institution, known only to a handful of men. If any of that select few needed a weapon, they came to Spikey. No questions asked, no answers given.

Dan suspected Spikey had contacts with the criminal underworld as well, but he never asked. He had wanted a Dragunov sniper rifle as a memento once, having used a discarded one in Afghanistan a few times. Spikey had been the man to get him one.

Dan took out the plastic bag containing the handgun and threw it on Spikey's lap.

"Hey!" Spikey looked up with a frown. "What you playing at?"

"Don't worry. The safety's on."

Spikey sat up in his chair, grumbling. "To hell with safety." He took the gun out and caressed the butt, looking at the weapon closely. Then he whistled.

"Wow," Spikey said. "Where the hell did you get this?"

Dan tapped the side of his nose. "That would be telling, Spikey. Can you tell me what it is?"

"This is a PSS silent pistol. Jacketed, steel core outside, internal automatic bolt mechanism inside. It's designed for use by a certain country's Special Forces. It's one of the most silent guns in the market. Do you want to know why?"

"Why?"

"It uses a heavy 7.62mm cartridge. But the cartridge is coated with a chemical called SP-4, which absorbs all the gas that explodes when the cartridge is fired. Hence, unlike a traditional suppressed gun, none of the exploding gasses are released. So, the sound you get is more like a soft whistle than a loud BOP or BAM from a suppressed gun."

"So the gun only works with this special ammunition."

"Yup. It's called the 7.62x41mm, SP-4 ordnance." Spikey's voice was suddenly quiet. "Do you know who it's used by?"

Dan had an inkling of the answer already, but he didn't like it. He really didn't like it.

"Go on, then," he said.

"Spetsnaz," Spikey said.

Russian Special Forces. The Spetsnaz were equivalent to the Delta, Navy SEALS and the SAS.

Dan sat down on the tattered sofa. "Yes, that figures."

If Spikey wondered what Dan was talking about, he kept it to himself.

Dan said, "So after these four bullets have gone, I can't get any more."

"I didn't say that. If you know anyone in the Russian Mafia, I'm sure they can sort you out. I don't think the Spetsnaz will give you any, though, even if you ask them nicely."

Dan rolled his eyes, then looked at Spikey carefully. "I need a weapon."

"What do you want?"

"A Sig Sauer really. P226 if possible. Or a Glock. If neither of those two available, then I'll settle for a Beretta or an H&K handgun. But not too old."

"Don't ask for much, do you?"

"Have you got anything?"

"Yes. A Sig Sauer P226, as it happens. But a few years old. Automatic, sixteen-cartridge magazine, good condition. Cost ya."

"How much?"

"Two hundred."

"Come on, Spikey. It's a handgun, not a rifle."

"I know, but you're asking for a specific gun you lads use. They're harder to find. You want a Glock or a Colt, I can get one for less than hundred."

They settled for one hundred and seventy-five, with extra ammunition. As Dan was leaving, Spikey shuffled closer to him. The old man lifted his face to Dan. "Be careful, kiddo. The Spetsnaz don't like their weapons being nicked."

"Yeah, well," Dan pulled the rucksack on his shoulders. "Neither do I. See you around, Spikey."

*****

As Dan approached the hotel on Clapham Common he saw a black Lada car parked nearby. It looked brand new with gleaming, metallic paint. The car was facing away from him. The number plate was different this time and he tried hard to read it. Another diplomatic number. He could make out two men seated in the front. The car was parked on the same side of the road as his apartment, a few doors behind.

Dan walked past the car, keeping his eyes straight ahead. He got into his room quickly, looked around, it was empty.

Chloe was still at the US Embassy. That was good.

From his bag he took out the PSS silent gun and put it in his front jeans pocket. He stripped off, put the Sig Sauer in a shoulder holster and wore a brown shirt on top. He took two extra magazines and stuck them in his sock. His kukri remained on his back-belt line. He stashed the remainder of the 5.56mm ammunition underneath a floorboard in the room.

He got his rental bike from the hallway, locked the door and made his way north-west, towards the river and Battersea Park.

CHAPTER 25

As he put foot on the pedal, Dan heard the growl of the engine behind him. Traffic was moderately heavy, evening peak hour was approaching. Around most of London, the next two hours would see its narrow roads gridlocked.

Battersea Bridge rose up ahead, but Dan was heading right. The road ended in a T-junction underneath another railway bridge. To the right, next to the railway bridge, there was a disused factory. Dan turned right.

He heard the Lada's engine: it was catching up on him to see which way he would turn. Dan speeded up, and as he came up to the gate of the derelict factory, he skidded off his bike.

Leaving the bike on the pavement, he ran into the factory. The building was large, and its corrugated-iron roof extended back more than a hundred yards.

There was a pair of large, iron double doors in the front covered in moss and plants. Broken pipes and smashed beer bottles littered the floor around. A smaller workers' entrance lay to one side. It was rusty as hell and one solid kick was all it took for the door to fall off its hinges. It would clearly give his position away, but that was exactly what Dan wanted. He heard the Lada screech to a stop behind him, car doors slamming and running footsteps. He didn't have much time.

He did a SitRep. The floor in front of him was about fifty yards wide and more than a hundred yards long. Three hulking, rusting machinery blocks lay in the middle. Fire escape stairs led up into a balcony snaking around the entire periphery of the upper floor. Shafts of dull sunlight came in from the broken skylights above and through gaps in the roof.

Dan ran inside. He came to the first machine. It had chains and pulleys, and an old tractor sat in the middle. Everything smelled of old grease and stale urine. Dan ran around the back, took out the PSS silent pistol and lay down flat on the floor, gun arm extended. To anyone coming in through the door, he would be practically invisible on the garbage-strewn floor, hidden behind the machine. But someone entering through that doorway would be framed in the sunlight, presenting an ideal target.

He waited. His ears were attuned to the sides of the warehouse and behind him. If these guys had any sense they would split up and one of them would come either from behind or down the side.

They didn't. Dan saw the small guy enter first, crouching down, holding his weapon straight. Dan fired, gripping the PSS gun tightly with both hands, as he couldn't guess the recoil. It was just as well. The butt jumped in Dan's grip. The sound was like a soft squelch of air from his bike tire. The man crouching in the doorway screamed and went down. Dan fired two more rounds, both of which hit the door.

The taller man leaned his weapon into the entrance and fired a burst inside the warehouse. The ordnance splintered across the warehouse, chopping up dust and whining as they ricocheted against the scattered metal. The sound was suppressed, but Dan still recognized the firepower. An MP5 or MP7, set to automatic. In an enclosed space, a firefight would be deadly. With his Sig Sauer, he wouldn't win.

Dan had already dropped back into cover behind the tractor. He took out his trusted Sig. A foot crunched on paper, followed by another burst of gunfire. Dan slid further down the floor, the rounds whining above his head. He used the noise to turn around.

Now he could see the taller man. He was inside the warehouse, but he had backed into a corner. His gun was pointed up and he was looking around the balcony, jerking his arm around. That made sense. If Dan had the time to go up the fire escapes, laying down fire from a height could be fatal for the man.

The man had his gun pointed to the walkway above. Dan picked up the PSS pistol. Lying on his back, he threw the gun as hard as he could, upwards and to the left. It clattered against one of the iron fire escapes, making a sound that echoed around in the silence. The man turned to his right immediately and let loose a burst from his MP7. At the same time, Dan rolled on the ground to his right.

He was out in the open now. He came to a rest on his chest, both hands gripping the Sig. He had the man straight in his sights.

Because of his height, he was an easy target. The man saw the flash of movement from the corner of his eye. He started to bring the MP7 around, but he wasn't quick enough. Two 5.56mm rounds slammed into his chest, pushing him back against the wall. He grunted and still tried to raise his weapon. Dan squeezed the trigger again. This time the bullet found the head. Blood and bone splattered in a red eruption on the wall behind him. The man slid down to the floor. Dan rolled back to the cover of the machine. He listened for three seconds. No sound.

He crouched and came out into the open. The man he shot first was still on the floor, but he was moving. Dan could see him trying to raise his arm to reach his gun, a few inches away from him. He saw Dan coming and made a desperate lunge. Dan fired instinctively. The bullet went in the man's neck. He shuddered once, then was still. Dan swore and ran forward. He wanted one of them alive—to make them talk. He felt the carotid pulse. Gone. The other attacker had half his head blown away. He wasn't talking to anyone.

Dan frisked the body and found no ID. Dan searched the man thoroughly. In a shoulder holster he found a larger weapon. He whistled as he took it out. He had seen this little monster before, in an operation against government forces in Syria.

It was a KEDR, perhaps the most compact and lightweight sub-machine gun in the world. He hefted the thing in his hand. It was like a feather compared to an MP7. He took the magazine box out. It had 9x18mm ordnance in a thirty-box mag. Capable of firing 800 rounds per minute. An absolute killer in close quarters battle. The KEDR was exclusively used by the Russian secret service and Spetsnaz.

He put the KEDR under his arm and went over to the other corpse. An MP7 lay on the ground next to him. In this man's pocket Dan found something interesting. A small, dark glass bottle with a liquid inside it. Dan held it up to the light, but he couldn't see a great deal. The bottle had a tight screw top. He put it in his pocket.

Dan went back and picked up the PSS. He wiped the butt clean. He did the same with the KEDR. He put the PSS in his back pocket and the KEDR, which had a strap, over his shoulder.

The street outside was empty. He got on his bike and pedaled away, fast.

CHAPTER 26

Dan stashed the bike in the hallway, and paid the hotel manager for its rental. He was relieved he hadn't damaged the bike.

Chloe was waiting for him when he got up to the room.

"Guess what I found?" Chloe said as soon as Dan walked in.

"Tell me."

Chloe held out the fake American passport that belonged to one of her father's identities. "This man's name is Lee Hill."

"So?"

"So I looked him up in the telephone directory. There are three American Lee Hills in London who have the same DOBs. Only one of them wasn't available to talk to me. I spoke to the others. In fact, I spoke to their wives first. They were both at home, enjoying some time off with the family."

"And the third?"

"The third lives at Hyde Park Corner. I visited the apartment. No one has lived there for the last six months, according to the landlady."

"Interesting."

"It gets better." Chloe waved the passport under Dan's nose. "Where do you think this Lee Hill works?"

Dan thought for a while, then frowned. "Same place your dad gets all the money from?"

"Yes, Wellington International Services. They even have a damn motto—relationships are our business." Chloe rolled her eyes.

"How did you find out where he worked?"

Chloe narrowed her eyes. "You need to keep a secret."

Dan smiled. "Sure."

"I saw a letter poking out of his letter box. Actually, there was a bundle of them. They'd been gathering dust for the last few months, I guess. I picked up the whole bunch. Most of it was mail order crap, but I did find a letter from his employer. It shows his tax return for the year."

"Quite the detective, aren't you? Or should I say journalist?"

"Tricks of the trade, nothing more."

Dan sat down on the bed, thinking. "Wellington International Services," he said to himself.

Chloe came and sat down in front of him. "I haven't finished," she said. "I rang the lawyer firm of Wellington as well. No reply from them. I left several messages."

"Don't bother. We need to visit them. It might need more direct action."

"Where have *you* been?"

"I went up to see an old friend."

"Were you followed?"

Dan hesitated. "Yes," he said shortly.

"What happened?"

Dan stood up and went to the window. "I guess you can say they've retired from their jobs."

Chloe didn't say anything for a while. "What's going on, Dan?"

Dan paused. "Something weird. A mixed bunch. All I know is that we need to get to the bottom of it, and fast."

"Something strange is going on, that's for sure."

Dan picked up the newspaper on the desk. It was one of London's daily tabloids. He read the screaming headline with the lurid photo of a bearded Taliban soldier holding a rocket launcher on his shoulder:

"Senior Taliban commander responsible for bombing stadium in Peshawar killed by drone strike."

Dan read a few lines of the report, then threw the newspaper back on the table. Chloe was sitting on the bed with her legs folded under her. Dan stared for longer than he intended, he couldn't help it. He met her eyes, then looked away to pace the room. Eventually he stopped and looked at her again. He didn't miss the faint blush on her cheeks, which made her look prettier, he thought.

"Okay, so let's see what we have." He made a fist and he flicked one finger up after another. "We have Wellington, the car, the coroner, and the passports."

"Right. Let's do this. In that order?"

"Yes, there's something about Wellington that I don't like. But I need to speak to the coroner first. Then let's hit their lawyer."

"Sure."

Dan took the small bottle he had got from the dead Spetsnaz agent, and wrapped it carefully in some tissue. He put the bottle in his inside pocket. They walked to the tube station, and traveled to Chelsea and Westminster

Hospital, which was a short walk from Fulham Broadway tube station.

They went inside the large, sunny atrium of the hospital and followed signs to Pathology. At the reception, Chloe asked for Dr Sherman, the coroner who had given the cause of death. They were provided with a copy of the death certificate. Chloe took a while to go through it while they waited to see the doctor. Dan frowned as he read. "Septic shock following alcohol toxicity. Leading to cardiac arrest."

Chloe was surprised and saddened. "So he'd been drinking?"

Dan shook his head. "I didn't smell alcohol on him. And I got up pretty close." He needed to ask the doctor some questions. He reached into his pocket and took out the small bottle.

Dr Sherman arrived. They both stood up as the white-coated figure approached them. The doctor was into his fifties, with a mop of white hair. He had kind, blue eyes that crinkled into crow's-feet at the corners. He smiled gravely at them.

"Sorry for your loss, Miss Guptill," Sherman said. "What did you wish to speak to me about?"

Dan said, "My name is Dan Roy. I'm a member of the same Army unit the major belonged to." They shook hands.

"Yes, Mr Roy. Did you wish to say anything?"

"Would it be possible to speak in your office, Dr Sherman?"

"Yes, of course," the doctor said.

In his office they sat facing the doctor across his desk. A life-size skeleton stood next to Dan's chair.

Dan couldn't tell the truth. Not without implicating himself in the murder. He held out the bottle. "I need to find out what this is, Dr Sherman. The major gave it to me the last time I visited him. He wanted me to have it tested to see what it was. He was helping in an investigation with contraband drugs."

The doctor took the bottle, turned it around.

"I see. Sure. I need to run a couple of tests on it. I can tell the lab guys to do it right now. Are you okay to wait for a few minutes?"

"Is there a coffee place around here?" Chloe asked. "I could use some."

The doctor said, "Ground floor on your right. There's a Starbucks."

Dan and Chloe went to get their coffees. The main atrium in the hospital was busy. They stood in a queue to get their coffee, then went back to the office. Chloe nervously sipped her coffee. Dan squeezed her shoulders. "Hey, it's going to be alright, don't worry."

Chloe's face was pale and drawn. "Let's face it. It can't get much worse than now."

Dan sighed and held her hand. In a few minutes, Sherman returned. He looked at Dan, a curious expression on his face. Dan stood up.

"What did you find, doc?"

Sherman closed the door and sat down slowly in his chair. He steepled his fingers in front of his face. "Where did the major find this bottle, Mr Roy?"

"He received it during the course of an investigation. I believe he was trying to get it checked, but you know what happened. Could you please tell me what it might be?"

Sherman paused for effect before continuing.

"The liquid in the bottle is a chemical called diphenhydramine. It can be used as a sedative antihistamine in the right dose. What people take for hay fever, right?" Dan and Chloe nodded.

"But in such pure form as what you have here, and injected in the right amount, it can cause respiratory and cardiac arrest. Its effect is potentiated by the presence of alcohol. But the critical thing about diphenhydramine is this—the molecule disintegrates in the body very quickly. About an hour after injection into the bloodstream, there's no further trace of the chemical. It simply breaks down."

"So, no trace of it is found in the body?" Dan asked.

"None whatsoever."

Dan and Chloe rose and shook hands with the doctor. Dan said, "Thank you very much, Dr Sherman. You've been a great help."

They left the office and went out to the back of the building where there was a garden and a seating area. Dan breathed out and spoke first.

"Right, let's suppose that the major was drinking that afternoon. With someone who came to see him. Maybe more than one person. I'm going out on limb here. He became sleepy, maybe they put something in his drink."

"A few drops of that stuff would do the job," Chloe whispered.

"Then, when he was drowsy, they put the drug in a syringe and injected him in the ear. The effect was enhanced by the alcohol. He stopped breathing. The drug broke down and no trace of it was found in the post-mortem."

Chloe and Dan sat in silence, thinking. After a while, Chloe spoke.

"Who was it?"

"Probably the man I got it from. There were two of them. The same two I met in the apartment the night before."

Chloe looked at the floor when she asked the next question. "What happened to them, Dan?"

"They're dead, Chloe," Dan said quietly.

Chloe leaned back in her seat. After a while, she stood up and walked away. Dan drained his cup, threw it in the trash, and followed.

He caught up as she was coming out of the main hospital exit. He settled into a walk next to her and when the street was quieter, he touched her arm.

"Chloe, wait."

She stopped and looked at him, rubbing her arm.

"Look," Dan said. "I know this is weird. But someone framed me in Afghanistan, and then someone killed your dad. I took photos of what I found in Afghanistan and that camera has disappeared. I'm not saying they're connected. But there are a lot of loose ends we need to tie up. I don't know where this is going to lead to. But I know it's going to get a lot worse before it gets better."

"I know that. But shouldn't we tell the police?"

"I'm under investigation already. They won't believe me. Trust me, we need to do this ourselves. Once I get enough evidence, then we involve the cops."

Chloe looked vulnerable. Dan put his arm around her shoulders gently, and she didn't resist.

"We'll get to the bottom of this, I promise you."

They walked in silence for a while. "Where to now?" Chloe asked.

"We need to check out Wellington."

"I have the address of their law firm."

CHAPTER 27

The law firm was called Overmeyer and Sons, and it was close to a tube station called Temple, in the financial district of London. Temple was on the eastern edge of the city and it took them a while to get there. The tube station was packed and it was slow coming out onto street level. They walked for ten minutes, going past the shining tower blocks with clumps of young men and women in suits standing outside smoking. Finally, they came to an alleyway, at the corner of a street with a pub. The alleyway looked empty.

Dan asked, "This is the place?"

Chloe checked her phone. "That's what it says on the website."

They went into the alley. London was full of small alleys such as these, often a conduit from one large street to another, sometimes merely a dead end that might have been a courtyard in the distant past.

The back-end of the pub took up most of the alley, and behind it, there was a small, two-story building with a glass door and a small, silver plaque beside it. Chloe bent down to read the names.

"Here it is. Overmeyer and Sons. That's Wellington's lawyers."

She pressed the buzzer and the door slid open soundlessly. Inside, plush green carpet swallowed their footsteps. Air conditioning hummed unobtrusively and sculptures on pedestals adorned the small lobby. Beyond that, Dan could see the reception. A thin blond, dressed in a tight dress suit, looked up as they approached.

Chloe told her, "We would like to see Mr Overmeyer, please."

"Certainly. And the name is…?"

"Chloe Guptill."

"Please take a seat."

The reception area was recessed into the wall. They sat down in a corner from where they could watch the reception desk, but they couldn't be seen. After five minutes, Chloe suddenly clutched Dan's arm.

"Look!" she whispered.

A man was passing through reception to the outside. Dan only saw him from the back.

Chloe stood up. "What is it?" Dan asked. She started for the door.

"It's that man I met at the Embassy."

"Who?" Dan was still confused.

"Simon Renwick. The man who knew Dad."

The secretary saw them leaving and reached for the telephone.

Dan followed Chloe as she rushed into the alley. They saw a flash of the dark suit as Renwick turned the corner, heading right into the road. Dan lowered his voice.

"We might have to split up. Two of us following him looks suspicious." Chloe nodded.

"You go first, then," she said. "He knows what I look like and you can guard me, if he turns around."

The crowd was helping Dan keep out of sight, but he also kept losing sight of Renwick, who was heading for the trains. For the moment everyone was at a standstill, waiting for the pedestrian lights to change. Renwick smoothed his hair back, then turned round to look, checking. The traffic lights changed. The mass of commuters surged forward.

Dan saw Renwick turn up ahead. He took a sharp left, leaving the crowd of commuters. Chloe was now ahead of Dan, and he saw her turn and follow. Renwick was walking faster now, glancing at his watch. Chloe speeded up.

Renwick took another turn off the main thoroughfare. This road was quieter, facing the back of large department stores and some restaurants. Dan caught sight of Chloe before she disappeared round another right corner at the end of the road.

Dan broke into a run. It was a maze of streets. Original old City, as the financial district was known. Ahead, he was just in time to see Chloe turn another corner. The sounds of traffic had faded now. Dan surged forward and took the turn Chloe had just taken.

Then he stopped short.

It was a dead end. A tall brick wall blocked the alley. He had no hope of scaling it. Against the wall there was a row of three men holding KEDR submachine guns. They were heavy, swarthy, similar to the Spetsnaz men he had seen. The guns had suppressors attached. Chloe was standing in front of them. As Dan came skidding to a halt, she turned around, her mouth open in shock.

Renwick was nowhere to be seen.

Dan heard a screech of tires behind him. A black SUV had come to a stop, and men piled out of it. These men were bearded, heavily armed and agile. They held MP7s, and handguns tucked in their waistbands. Three of them. Not Russian. But with the Russians, they formed a combined team.

Six in total. He was held in a crossfire, with Chloe in the middle.

"Put your gun down," came the shout from behind Dan. Dan stood still, watching around him. Chloe stood near him. Six men circled them, guns pointed. Dan did not recognize any faces. He felt a barrel poke him in the back. In the next instant, the heavy butt of a gun smashed against the side of his skull. The sound of the impact was like a pistol going off, reverberating against the walls of the alley.

Most men would have fallen unconscious. Not Dan Roy.

A yellow ball of pain zoomed across his head, and he felt his eyes get hazy. He stumbled forward, but did not fall. He rectified himself quickly, and swung around, fist raised. Another blow, from something similarly heavy, crashed against the other side of his neck.

Agony exploded inside his brain. Dan grunted, and lurched forward, feeling a wave of nausea. He shook his head, bent at the waist. Through blurry eyes, he saw two of the men grab Chloe from behind. They tied her hands. A shape appeared before him. Tall and dressed entirely in black. Dan stood up but he was too late.

A heavy fist swung and brushed against his right jaw, aimed to poleaxe him. Dan had leaned back at the last minute, and he did not feel the full impact of the blow.

His instinct was to fight back. But his head was telling him he needed to be calm. If Chloe had not been here, he would have gone for it. They were too close to him. Bunched together. With his Sig he could have unleashed mayhem.

The man in front of Dan raised his fist again.

"Enough!" A voice rang out.

Dan turned. One of the men from the car was out, and he seemed to be in charge. His face was bearded, and he wore black glasses, hiding his face. A black cap hid his hair.

"We need him alive. Put him in the car, with the girl." The accent was American.

Dan felt his hands being tied behind his back. He was patted down, and his guns and knife were removed. He shook his head twice again. The ringing sound was less, and his eyes were clearing. The left side of his face felt numb. He saw Chloe being bundled into the car. Anger flared inside him. But he controlled it. His time would come.

As usual, they had made a mistake by not killing him.

The three Russians got into another car and waited, engine purring. This car was a ZiL limousine, Dan noted. Beloved of the Kremlin upper classes. In the SUV, he saw a driver up front, with a man in the passenger seat. Chloe was in the back, next to a man by the window. One man got into the rear seat of the SUV by lifting the trunk door. Dan was shoved next to Chloe, and the other man, who seemed to be the leader, got inside next to Dan. Dan watched them carefully. He noted the knife in its scabbard, and the keys of the plastic cuff next to it, in the man's belt.

"Go," the man ordered.

There were two men up front, including the driver. Two in the back with them, and one in the rear. Total five, in this car. Four in the Zil. Dan glanced at Chloe. Her eyes were wide with fear. Dan pointed down with his eyes. She gave an imperceptible nod. In the rear-view mirror, Dan could see the Zil following them.

The driver was playing with the sat nav. The leader lifted up a hand.

"Take the left," he said. They drove fast, threading their way through traffic. Dan saw the flash of water. They were in a deserted stretch of disused factories by the river. Somewhere in East London. The cars came to a halt.

Dan was covered by an MP7 from the front, rear and sides as he alighted. Chloe came after him. The factory had a steel roller door. One of the men lifted it up. Inside was a large area with old, rusting machines. Clumps of grass grew in the deserted space. They entered. Two more men with MP7 sub-machine guns were waiting for them.

Dan said, "I need to pee."

The leader gestured to one of his men. A gun barrel prodded Dan in the back. Another man moved to his front. The leader faced Dan. He still had his black glasses on.

He said, "You try anything funny, we kill the girl." Chloe was thrust forward into his vision, a gun to her head. Dan nodded, his cold eyes giving nothing away.

The gun shoved Dan further down the yard. Dan walked slowly, looking up at the ceiling, taking in the surroundings. There was no walkway up there, it was bare, corrugated-iron roof with great holes poking out to the sky. They went outside through a rickety door. Shrubs and weeds grew tall around them.

One of the men faced Dan. His back was slouched. His finger was not on the trigger. Dan felt the gun shift behind him, and keys slot into his handcuffs. He felt them turn. His handcuffs fell away. The man in front of Dan was in the process of lighting a cigarette.

Amateurs.

As soon as his arms were free, Dan spun on his heels. He crashed into the man behind him, moving the gun barrel away from his back. He grabbed a handful of the man's shirt, leaned his head back, then slammed his wide, thick forehead into the man's face. Teeth and bone fragments exploded out of the man's mouth. Dan repeated the process, and the man sagged to one side, unconscious.

Dan picked up the knife from the man's belt as he fell. The other guy had dropped his cigarette and lighter and tried to rush Dan.

Dan let him come. He stood half-turned, and still. When the man was about to grab him, Dan ducked down, and used his attacker's momentum to lift him above his shoulders. Then he slammed him down on the ground, the soft grass absorbing the sound. The knife stabbed deep inside the man's neck, severing his trachea. Blood spurted in an arch. Dan held his face down, avoiding any sounds.

The whole thing had taken no more than five seconds.

Like a cat, he crouched and turned. Observed. Waited. No sounds, no witness. But they would come out soon.

He picked up both rifles, and strapped one on his back, and checked the other one. Heckler & Koch 416, both with 30-round mags. A waste of a weapon on these jokers, but a weapon he liked using.

There was a fire escape going up the side. He thought about it, but then decided against it. He needed to be on the same level as Chloe.

He opened the door a fraction and peered in. They had not moved. The man with his gun to Chloe's head was farthest from him. But he had a clear shot. The leader was to his side, looking around, alert. The rest of the men were lounging around. The Russians were on the floor, leaning against a wall, smoking. Five in total.

Dan spreadeagled himself on the floor, and extended the rifle across the crack of the doorway. He had the man holding the gun to Chloe's head in the gunsight. His finger caressed the trigger.

But the man moved. Dan jerked his eyes off the rifle. The leader shouted an order, and was heading straight for the door. His eyes had still not fallen on the gun barrel sticking up from the floor. Any second now, he would.

Worse, his body was now blocking Chloe. As the leader's eyes moved down the door, he shouted again. He had seen the rifle. The leader drew his weapon, pointing it at Dan.

Dan had no time. He fired. The 5.56mm ordnance hit the man in the chest, and Dan followed it up with a headshot as he fell.

The shouts had already alerted the men, and they had their weapons out. Dan ignored them. He had a few seconds in which to take decisive action.

In these split-second situations, it came down to priorities.

He shifted his attention to Chloe. The man holding her had turned his back to him. Dan fired, and saw the head erupt in a cloud of red mist. He shot him again in the back, and the body toppled forward. He saw Chloe spread out on the floor, lying very still.

Dan's heart jumped in his mouth.

A bullet jarred the iron door above him. Dan turned the gun a fraction. Three men were aiming at him, but they never stood a chance. Dan was partially concealed, and they were out in the open. Dan double-tapped them twice in the chest, and they went down like they had been hit by sledgehammers.

The remaining gunman had hidden himself behind an old oil barrel. He fired, and the round smashed inches past Dan's right arm into the ground, kicking up dust. Dan swore, and aimed at the source. Two of his bullets hit the top and base of the barrel. Then he stopped, and waited. Waiting in a firefight was often the best option.

It worked. The man thought Dan was out of ammo, or loading his weapon. He lifted his head up to aim and fire, but Dan was waiting. The round made a mockery of the man's face. He fell backwards, dead instantly.

Dan scrambled up and ran towards Chloe. A horrible, sick emptiness was clutching his guts. There was no blood around her body, save what was seeping out from the skull of the man lying dead next to her.

Gently, Dan supported her neck and turned her over. Her eyes were shut. The chest was rising and falling. He checked her head, neck and scalp. No injuries. He ran his hands and eyes down the rest of her.

Then he lifted her off the floor, and held her against him. Her eyelids fluttered open. Dan heaved a huge sigh of relief. She had fainted.

She blinked. "Dan?"

"Can you stand up?" Dan asked. She could. Once her eyes were open, she was steady on her feet, and alert. Dan ran around the dead bodies, frisking them quickly. No ID, as usual. He found a six-inch knife on one of them and took that. He took off the dead leader's glasses. Caucasian, but no one he knew. He checked him for tattoos. Nothing. But he did find a Sig P226 handgun on him. Dan discarded the rifle and checked the Sig's magazine. It was full. He put the gun in his back belt.

Chloe followed him outside. Dan had concealed the rifle inside his jacket.

They came out of the disused industrial area. They skirted around old, broken warehouses, and came out onto the main road. Traffic was flowing and the pavement was busy with pedestrians.

Hand in hand, they walked quickly to the nearest tube station. Traffic grew in volume. They walked till they came to a station called Shoreditch.

"Where now?" Chloe asked.

Dan's face was tight. "You are going back to the hotel. I need to see Simon Renwick at the Embassy."

CHAPTER 28

They sat down at a café on the pavement opposite the US Embassy, from where they had a good view of the building. Chloe stirred her cappuccino and took a long sip.

"I needed that."

Dan looked at her critically. He was worried about her. She had never lived the life he had. She was a civilian. It was a lot for her to go through. Either she was hiding her true feelings, or she had some of her father's natural toughness.

He decided it was the latter. Chloe put her cup down.

"No, I'm not going back to the hotel," she said.

"Excuse me?" They had had this conversation already, and they weren't getting anywhere.

"I told you about this guy. Now I want to see it through."

"What if we get ambushed again?"

"I didn't pay attention last time. I lost him too easily. It won't happen again."

Dan's voice was gentle but firm. "No, Chloe. I cannot have that on my conscience. Do you understand?"

Chloe said, "I can look after myself."

Dan looked down at his cup. The vision of carrying out Lucy's torn body rose up like a nightmare, shrouding his mind in a black shadow. A frown passed across his face.

Chloe said, "What is it, Dan?"

Dan stirred his cup in silence. He did not answer. He raised the cup and finished his drink.

He said, "It's nothing."

He stared at the hulking building opposite. They had been sitting there for half an hour. One car had left the entrance in that time.

Dan told her, "There is something you can help me with. If you keep watch for five minutes, I need to do some shopping."

"Shopping? Really?"

Dan stood up. "Five minutes. Call me, if you see him leave."

He returned wearing a new black tee shirt, baseball cap and sunglasses. He had gone into a nearby sportswear shop, and got changed inside a McDonald's toilet.

"You look different," she said.

"Good. That's the impression I need to give this guy. If he's a CIA field agent, he will notice patterns."

Dan glanced at his watch. 1400 hours. "Let's move," he said. They paid the bill and left.

"Shall I head back to the hotel, then?" Chloe asked. Dan nodded. Chloe took Dan's discarded jacket and vest and Dan waved her goodbye at the train station. Then he walked around.

Further across from the Embassy there was a building site, which looked empty. A two-meter-high wooden enclosure surrounded it. Dan could see the top of a large, earth-digging JCB machine poking above the enclosure. As he approached the building site he kept a close eye on movement in and out of it. There was a door to the enclosure, but it was probably locked.

Dan pulled out his knife. To anyone looking from the street, it would look as if he was reaching for his key. The lock on the door was flimsy. He leaned on the door with his hands. It gave way slightly. Dan pushed harder and there was a crack. A splinter appeared at the top of the makeshift doorway, and it swung open. Dan stepped in quickly.

Dan put a brick against the bottom of the door. That would have to do for now. The area was a rough rectangular shape, thirty by fifty yards approximately. The ground was being dug up, no doubt to put down foundations for yet another building. The giant claw of the JCB machine yawned in front of him like the jaws of a Tyrannosaurus. Dan went to the eastern edge of the enclosure and climbed a small mound. From here, over the fence, he had a good view of the sidewalk ahead and the Embassy building

Dan settled down to wait. It was 1500 hours. A fresh breeze across the Thames dragged in black clouds that scuttled across the sun. A few drops of rain fell on Dan's face. Well, if he had to get wet, then so be it. He took out his kukri and began to sharpen the blade against a stone. Time passed slowly. His knees grew stiff. Once his kukri was razor-sharp at the tip, he climbed down from the mound and carved an eyehole at the base of the fence. He could lie down spreadeagled now and keep watch on the street ahead of him. With any luck, no one would notice it.

Half hour later two figures emerged from the Embassy gates. One of them was Simon Renwick. His colleague said something to Renwick, then turned and walked away. Dan watched as Renwick pressed the button on the traffic light.

Dan didn't wait any longer. Renwick was heading back to Vauxhall station. Dan got up, dusted himself clean, adjusted the baseball cap and his sunglasses, then left.

Traffic was heavy. The lights wouldn't turn red, despite him pushing the button repeatedly. Ahead of him, Renwick reached the other end of the four-lane road and was walking towards the station concourse. Dan sprinted across to the island in the middle, dodging cars. One driver put his window down and shook his fist at him, shouting. At the station steps Dan couldn't see Renwick anymore.

He took his sunglasses off, and walked slowly into the station lobby. Without moving his head, he swiveled his eyes back and forth. There was a crowd of commuters. Dan took his time and inched forward.

Renwick was in the queue at the automated counter. Dan sighed in relief. He made sure it was Renwick, then he put the sunglasses in his pocket. Renwick took the Victoria line headed north. Dan stayed in the same carriage. He got off at Notting Hill Gate following his target.

Dan bought himself a newspaper, letting Renwick get ahead of him as he walked up Holland Park Avenue. It was getting quieter, and Dan was hanging back forty yards now to make sure he wasn't spotted. Renwick passed a small park and turned into a cul-de-sac. Dan hesitated. A blind ending. Was Renwick creating a trap for him again?

Dan walked past, watching. Renwick was fumbling with house keys. But he wasn't alone. Opposite him, the doors of a car were opening. Renwick was oblivious. Dan's breath caught as he recognized the type of car.

A black Lada. He didn't recognize the number plates. The two men who came out wore black suits, and Dan could see the telltale bulge of shoulder holsters. Russians. Probably Spetsnaz: Dan knew just by looking at them. Arms hanging loose at their sides, walking lightly on the balls of their feet, they approached Renwick, who had his back to them.

They didn't lock the car, and the engine was running.

CHAPTER 29

Dan took the kukri out and shoved it into his front waistband. The Sig would make too much noise. The men had got to Renwick now and he turned around, a mixture of alarm and surprise on his face. Dan knew exactly what was going to happen if he didn't act fast.

"Simon!" Dan cried out, waving his arms. His face broke into a wide grin. "Hey, man, how are you?"

All three faces turned to look at Dan. He kept the smile on his face and let a friendly gaze pass over them. He had been ten yards away and closed the gap quickly. Five. Three. He saw one of the men frown and reach inside his suit jacket.

Two yards. Dan spread his arms wide. "Simon, how long has it been?"

Renwick was to his left, and the two men were to his right. Dan catapulted into the man closest to him, wrapping his arms around the man's waist. He stayed low and propelled his shoulders forward, the momentum pushing the man onto his companion who was trying to get his weapon out. Dan felt Renwick scatter backwards, falling against the steps.

The two Russians collided into each other, tripping up and falling. Dan and the two men went down in a tangle of bodies. Dan felt a blow land on his side, crashing into his ribs. It was a good hit, into his kidneys, and it made him wince. He pushed his knee into the man below him, pinning him down, and punched him hard on the jaw, snapping his head back, hitting concrete. The man grunted and tried to get up, but Dan followed through with his fist, making a bone-crunching connection just below the man's forehead. His eyes rolled back.

Like a sumo wrestler, the other guy crashed into Dan. Dan saw him coming and crouched down. The man's head smashed into Dan's chest, exploding air out of it. They rolled back, tumbling onto the ground. Dan was trapped between the man's legs. He was above Dan, and brought his fist down for the knockout blow. Dan moved his head at the last instant and the knuckles glanced off the side of his ear.

It jarred his skull. Dan heaved with his waist, trying to dislodge the man. He was fat and bulky.

He managed to get an arm below the man's thigh. But the man had got his weapon out. Dan recognized the menacing, snub-nosed barrel of the PSS silent pistol. With every ounce of strength in his body, Dan heaved up with his arm, bucking his waist at the same time. The man fired, but the bullet went whistling above Dan's head.

His body fell backwards and Dan leaped on top of him. He grabbed the gun hand, forcing it back, and brought his forehead down on the man's face with savage force. The man fired again, and screamed as his nose was smashed. He hit Dan on the side, but it bounced off Dan's midriff. It was Dan's turn to deliver the knockout punch. He pushed his knee forward and trapped the man's arm. He hit the man with an uppercut, jolting his chin back with a cracking sound.

The man's eyes clouded over and closed. The gun became loose in his fist and Dan took it.

He looked behind him, and his blood turned to ice.

Renwick was lying in a pool of blood. He was looking at Dan, the glasses still on his face. Dan checked the other thug quickly. He was out cold. Dan removed his weapon, the same PSS silent gun. Then he crouched next to Renwick. He had been hit in the abdomen and Dan could see two entry wounds.

Dan ripped open the blood-soaked shirt. He checked the back. No exit wounds. Damn. Damn it all. The large arteries in the abdomen were probably shredded by the 7.62mm bullets. Dan felt the neck pulse. Almost non-existent. Dan took out his phone and dialed 999.

Dan pressed on the wounds, trying to stem the flow of blood. He crooked his elbow underneath Renwick's neck and lifted his head up.

"Simon, my name is Dan Roy. I work for Intercept."

Renwick's face was mottled gray. Dan could feel the body turning cold. The man didn't have long left. Slowly, he nodded. "I know who you are. The man who worked with John."

"How did you know John Guptill?"

"We were…" Renwick closed his eyes then opened them again. "We worked together." His chest heaved and he was getting exhausted. Dan spoke urgently.

"Who is Felix?"

Renwick's eyes flew open. His mouth opened. Fright covered his face, then a look of anguish. "Felix…"

Dan leaned closer. "Who is he, Simon? Tell me."

"Dangerous. Very…very dangerous."

Simon's eyes closed again. Dan shook him, but Simon didn't wake up. He was still breathing. Dan felt his neck again. The pulse was present, but fast and threading, implying significant loss of blood. If Renwick could get to a trauma surgeon quickly he might still live. Dan heard sirens in the distance. He took one last look at Renwick and checked his pockets. He found his wallet and pocketed it.

The cul-de-sac was still deserted. If someone had passed by they hadn't stopped. Dan took one last look around him. He picked up his baseball cap and put it on.

"Good luck, Simon," he whispered.

*****

Dan retraced his steps back towards Notting Hill. When he was in a secluded, leafy street, he stood underneath a tree with low branches and took his phone out. He flicked to his self-image and looked himself up and down. There was blood on his hands, his jeans and the black tee shirt. He couldn't go back like this. He walked another five minutes and found a phone booth. He didn't want to use his own phone to call Chloe. Opposite the phone booth was a café. He gave Chloe the address and hung up.

He went into the café, ordered a beer and used their toilet to get changed. He peeled off the tee shirt and washed it under the tap. He took off his jeans, where the bloodstains were turning black and were obvious. He washed the blood patches the best he could, then put the jeans and tee shirt back on. When he came out, he took the beer and sat down near the window, watching the street. He heard police sirens. Two patrol cars rushed down the road, heading for the crime scene.

Dan lifted the beer and in a long gulp half-emptied the pint glass. He needed that. One of the waiters looked out the door as another police car screamed past. Dan breathed softly. The waiter smiled at Dan, then turned and went back to the counter. Dan took out Simon Renwick's wallet. He counted one hundred pounds in twenty-pound notes. He took out the cards. Credit and bank cards, along with an ID card for the US Embassy. Dan stopped at the next card and studied it carefully.

It was a Royal Air Force card, printed for a base in Welford, near Berkshire. Dan hadn't known that the RAF had a base in Welford.

The name on the card was Major John Guptill, SFOD-D. An old card bearing the major's old job title.

He wondered why a Delta Force major had an ID card for an RAF base.

There was no photo on the card, but there was a magnetic strip on the back, which he knew would contain most of the holder's personal details. Dan put the card in his pocket, and the rest of the money and cards back in the wallet.

He saw Chloe peering in from the door. He waved her over. Chloe spoke to the waiter and ordered a cappuccino. Dan took his vest, jacket and a pair of slacks from her and disappeared into the bathroom. When he came out, Chloe was sitting at the table, sipping her drink.

The café had three more customers, but more were coming in for evening meals. He slid in next to Chloe and downed the rest of his beer.

"What happened?" Chloe asked.

"Simon Renwick might be dead. I couldn't save him." Her mouth was open in shock. She looked down at her coffee in silence. Another couple came in. Dan took a twenty-pound note from the wallet and put it on the table. He brushed Chloe's arm.

"We need to get out of here," Dan said.

They headed towards Holland Park tube station. Their train was tunneling towards Chelsea within minutes. They got off at Victoria station and by the time they were back in the B&B it was nearly eight o'clock. Dan had a shower and came out to find Chloe sitting at the mirror, combing her hair. She put the comb down and looked at Dan as he came out, fully dressed. He was toweling his hair.

"What happened out there, Dan?"

Dan told her the best he could. Chloe gripped her forehead. "But why? Why would someone want to abduct or kill him?"

"He knew something. I'm guessing it's about Felix. Whoever that is."

"But did Renwick not try to lead us into an ambush?"

Dan had been thinking about that. He sat down. "Did you actually see Renwick's face when we left the lawyer's office?"

"No, just his side profile and back. It looked like him."

"So, someone could have been impersonating him."

Chloe frowned. "But why?"

Dan said, "To get more information out of the lawyers."

Dan sat down on the bed. He didn't like the way people were being taken out. First Guptill, now Renwick. Chloe or he would be next. He hardened his jaw. It would not be Chloe. He would take a bullet to his brain to save her.

He asked, "Your dad's car. Do you know exactly where it is?"

"Yes, I have the address."

"Good. Tomorrow we get the car. Then I have to drive to a place. I have a feeling I'll find something there."

"Where?"

"RAF Welford," Dan said quietly.

He said, "Better get some sleep. I need to go and see a friend." Dan needed to see Burns.

She stared at him for a while without speaking. Dan didn't look away.

Chloe whispered, "Would you mind not going out tonight?" She brushed her hair back and Dan could see the redness working its way up her neck. "It's just with what's been happening, I...I just wonder if someone is looking for us, too...maybe we're finding out more than we can handle and..."

Dan held her. She was shivering, and her breathing was rapid. She placed her head against his chest and Dan tucked it under his chin. She smelled nice, that same flowery, soft scent that suffused his tense muscles with a looseness, uncoiling his tight sinews.

She looked up at him, her eyes shining in the light, lips inches from his mouth. He couldn't take his eyes away from her face. Faintly, he was aware of his own breathing, suddenly labored and harsh.

"Stay tonight, Dan," Chloe whispered.

Dan's lips were pulled to hers. The first touch was electric, it sent shivers down his body and spine. She gripped him tighter, her hand pressing on his wide chest, fingers digging in gently. Her mouth opened further, and slowly their tongues met and entwined. Dan lost himself in the sensation. He stood up without realizing, lifting her up, too, their lips still locked in a kiss. He put her gently down on the bed, then Chloe pulled him down on top of her.

CHAPTER 30

Dan woke early the next morning. He looked over at Chloe, who was still asleep, her head nestled in her folded arm. He leaned over and moved a strand of hair away from her face. She was beautiful.

He looked out the window. The spring sunlight was brightening up the room. Despite all that had happened in the last few days, he felt a strange peace. Like he was floating in a warm swimming pool on his own. The cold cage that enclosed his heart was melting. The hard edges were blurred, softened.

But an anxiety burned inside him. He could not let Chloe be harmed. Come what may, he had to protect her.

He lay there thinking for a while, preparing himself for the day ahead. He needed to meet Burns. There he was a lot he had to discuss with him.

He got up, splashed water on his face, and performed his yoga routine. He did it most mornings, particularly when he didn't have time to go on his usual five-mile run.

"Wow. Never knew you were into yoga." Chloe was still in bed, watching him.

"Yup, don't blink."

Chloe went for a shower, and when she returned, Dan was looking through his phone.

"Where is the car garage?" Dan asked.

"A place called Balham, in South London."

"Yes, I know it. Not far from Clapham and Battersea. Who gave you the address?"

"Mr Mortimer, the lawyer."

"Okay. Is it as simple as showing your ID and picking it up?"

"Nope, not even that. It's a lock-up garage. We just need to pick it up." Chloe finished latching her earrings and picked up a set of keys from the dressing table.

"Excellent."

As Chloe got dressed, Dan came up behind her. Chloe saw him in the mirror. "What is it?" she asked.

"Do you have a hat? Or anything, to hide your blond hair?"

Dan was the first one to leave, and he spent some time as usual checking out the lobby. The road opposite was empty except for a few tourists. Dan walked ahead on his own, then sat down on a bench, keeping an eye on Chloe. No one followed her.

It took them almost half an hour to get to the garage. The road was lined with Victorian terraced houses, but suddenly gave way in the middle to an apartment block.

"This is it." Chloe said, checking the address. The car park was behind the block. Rows of lock-up garages lined the space.

"Number 55," Chloe said. They found the right one and unlocked the single door, then slid the garage door up. The space was for a single car. A maroon-colored Toyota Celica stood inside. The car was a two-door coupe. It looked new, but had a sheen of dust, like it had traveled but not been touched in a while. Dan saw flecks of mud on the bumpers. The tires looked good. There weren't any dents in the bodywork. Chloe handed the keys to Dan.

"Thanks," he said. "But wait." In the cramped space, it was difficult for him to get down. Something bugged him. In Iraq and 'Stan, it was a favorite ploy of the enemy to put improvised explosive devices in cars. Grunting, he poked his head underneath the car, then lay down and slid under. He couldn't see any obvious wires, scratch marks or tampering.

"Let's go outside." He shut the garage door and moved twenty meters away. "Stand behind me."

Dan pressed the unlock button. The Toyota beeped once, and the car unlocked. Dan opened the garage door again. Lights had come on inside the vehicle. He looked at the car one last time, then opened the driver's side carefully. The leather seat was worn with use. He slid in, while Chloe got in the passenger side.

He turned the ignition on. Half a tank full. Dan flicked his eyes to the sat nav and went through the controls. He found the stored addresses.

The first one said, Bickersteth Road. EC14 0RN. East Central 14. That meant somewhere in East London. He could look that up later. He went through the list. Two other addresses made up the bulk of the list, interspersed with Bickersteth Road.

Neither of the two addresses that turned up frequently had road names, only zip codes. One was RG20 7EY. The other, IP11 3ST. Dan scrolled down the list, but he couldn't see any other addresses.

"Looks like this car traveled between these three addresses a lot," he said.

Chloe was leaning over to him, looking at the screen. "Yes."

"Did your dad have another car?"

"Not that I know of."

Dan looked at her raised eyebrows and smiled. She had taken off the wide-brim straw hat and her hair fell on her shoulder.

He said, "It will be fun driving this car. But it will be me alone." Chloe's face clouded over.

"It's for the best," Dan said gently. "Look, I can hire a car, if you want. But I still need to see where your dad went."

Chloe shrugged. "I'm not worried about the car."

He reached across and put his hand on her thigh. She covered it with her own, her lips pressed together.

"I don't want anything to happen to you."

"Nothing will. Don't worry."

As they drove back Dan did a Google search for the zip codes. He didn't find the exact location, but he did find a location on RG20 that got his attention.

RAF Welford. Something prickled the back of his neck.

The ID card he had got from Simon Renwick. It belonged to the major, and it was for RAF Welford.

He did a search for the base. It was run by the US Air Force. USAF 420th Munitions Squadron, to be specific. It was the largest depot of heavy ammunition for the USAF in Western Europe.

A black cloud of worry was beginning to form at the edge of Dan's mind. He did a search for the second address. It was in Ipswich, near the coast of Norfolk, in the east of England.

He had to make some urgent phone calls when he got back to the hotel.

*****

After they parked and paid a royal ransom in parking fees for one whole hour, Dan jogged to the nearest tube station. He got off after ten minutes and made a phone call to Burns.

He got back on the tube and came off at Piccadilly Circus. He walked on foot, passing the Royal Academy of Arts. He went to the nearest hotel on Regent Street. He waited outside, watching.

Burns drove up in a black BMW. He parked and went inside the lobby. Dan watched around him for a while, then followed him inside.

Burns was sitting next to a piano. He was facing the doors and saw Dan coming in. This hotel was smaller but still had plenty of people around. Burns had a briefcase on his lap.

Dan sat down facing him and the door. He asked, "You know of an RAF base called Welford, in Berkshire?"

Burns nodded. "Big place. Missile storage. Hellfire, Pathfinders, for Apaches, MiGs, F-35s. Also light ammunition, rifles, handguns. It's the 501st Tactical Missile Wing of the USAF and NATO Air Force."

Dan digested the information. A tactical missile wing was a big deal.

"Is it true that RAF Welford is the largest heavy ammunition depot for the USAF in Western Europe?"

"Yes, mainly for the missiles and heavy ordnance. Why do you want to know?"

Dan hesitated. Burns said, "I'm not liking this, Dan. Not liking this at all."

"Neither am I. We found Guptill's car. He traveled to this place on a regular basis."

Dan told Burns about Chloe and what happened last night. He did not mention Simon Renwick by name. When he finished, Burns said, "Anything else?"

"No."

Burns said, "Jesus Christ, Dan, you could have told me. Guptill's daughter. You know we've been looking for her. Thought she was dead, damn it."

"The first time I met her, she had a red dot dancing on her head. I didn't know who I could trust. What could I have done?"

Burns clicked open his briefcase. He took out some photos and gave them to Dan. They were photos of Simon Renwick.

Dan said, "Shit."

Burns looked up. "You know this guy?"

Dan told him. Burns was angry. "Come on, Dan. What else you holding back? We got the Russians on our tail, someone's hunting you down, Guptill's dead, what the fuck?"

Dan told him about the Delta tattoo on the man who had tried to kill Chloe. Burns said, "Are you sure?"

"Positive."

Burns was thoughtful. He asked, "Do you have a photo?"

"No. Did not have a phone on me that day. You think that two-man team for Chloe came from Intercept?"

Burns frowned and stroked his chin. "Where else would it be from?"

Dan said, "Tell me about Renwick."

"We did a global search on face recognition software for Guptill. We found a match at the US Embassy here. The Embassy let us look at their photos. That's what you have in your hands."

"Why did they try to kill Renwick?"

Burns said, "He led you into an ambush, right?"

"Maybe."

"Once he did his job, they took him out. To silence him. Unfortunately for them, you were there."

"What's happened to Renwick now?"

Burns flipped out his cell. He read Dan's look. "It's not traceable, don't worry." He talked on the phone for a few minutes.

Then he said, "Renwick is alive. In an intensive care unit, but still breathing."

Burns reached inside his briefcase and took out a wad of notes.

"I figured you would want cash instead of plastic." Dan nodded.

"Thanks."

"Now what?"

"I need to check out the RAF base in Welford. Can you get me in?"

Burns nodded. "No problem. Give me till tomorrow morning."

Dan said, "Tell me where you're gonna be. I can pick up the creds on my way in." He tossed the ID card that Guptill had. "This might not work."

Burns inspected the card. "This is an MOD card. British Ministry of Defence. It means Guptill had clearance from MI6."

"That's what I thought."

"And Simon Renwick had it in his possession. A CIA agent."

"So Simon used this card, or he had clearance from the MOD as well. Have you checked with MI6?"

Burns said, "Yes. But MI6 are keeping a lid on it. Thanks for this. Now I can go back to them and say hey, how the hell does an ex-Delta major get RAF creds?" Burns smiled. "That should crack them."

Dan rose up. "You better tell them we are on the same side on this one. Otherwise the cracks are gonna spread."

*****

Dan got back to the hotel and told Chloe of his plans for the next day.

Chloe said, "While you're away, I'm going to find out what happened to Simon Renwick."

"Whoa."

"What?"

"You think the men who tried to kill or abduct him won't be keeping watch?"

Chloe shrugged. "He's going to be in a hospital, right? If he's still alive. Even if he died, he would have been taken to a hospital. The closest hospital is Chelsea and Westminster. Chances are someone there will know."

"Are you sure about this?"

Chloe nodded. Her features hardened. "Don't forget that I met this guy. I think he wanted to tell me more than he could. He knew Dad well. I need to see him."

"In that case, I can get someone to help. I know which hospital he's at."

Chloe raised her eyebrows. "Someone from your organization told you?"

"Yes."

Dan rubbed her shoulder. "Don't go as yourself. Do something to change the way you look."

"Yes, I know." She spread her arms. "Besides, he might not be in a state to talk anyway. If he's still alive."

"Exactly. So no point in taking risks yourself." He fixed her with a stare. "If anything happens to you, Chelsea will burn down. You know that, right?"

Chloe hugged him. "Yes, I know."

CHAPTER 31

Dan pressed on the gas and the engine growled. Not been let out in a while, Dan thought with satisfaction. He met Burns at Shepherd's Bush, a place in West London.

Burns parked his car and walked over to the Nissan. He sat down and said, "I don't like this, Dan. I don't think you should go to this RAF base."

"Why not?"

"For starters, even with the MOD creds, you are an outsider. You will be noticed. Think of what's happened so far. These guys know what you saw in that compound in Afghanistan. Only you saw it. You were the only witness. These guys are hunting you down. You don't think they're gonna be waiting for you at the RAF base?"

"There's no other way."

"That's not all. Scotland Yard have an alert out for you. They will have your details at every Army depot in the UK."

Dan was silent. Burns leaned over and handed him a small, black cylindrical object.

"What's this?"

"A GPS beacon. In case you're in trouble, and you need exfiltration. Just press the switch, we'll pick the signal up at HQ."

Burns handed over the creds to Dan as well. He said, "Be careful, and get the hell out if there's trouble."

*****

Traffic was heavy heading down west towards the M25. He traveled north, then took the exit for the M4, heading out towards Berkshire and the West Country.

Something about the zip code bothered him. It wasn't on Google Maps, but the surrounding area was. On the sat nav map it was blacked out. He could see where it was. Close to Welford village, whose surrounding land had been converted into the RAF base during the Second World War.

It was in Berkshire county, which began roughly forty miles outside the western edge of London. Small and gently rolling hills appeared on either side of the M4 as the car cruised. Cattle dotted the green land around him.

In half an hour, Dan was getting close to his destination. He took the traffic circle, and as his exit approached, he frowned. It was marked, NO ACCESS, WORK UNITS ONLY. Normally with an RAF base, there would be a clear sign to mention the base. What the hell was this works unit sign for?

Dan drove in. After driving for more than fifteen minutes, he saw the familiar gray iron grill fence that surrounded an RAF base. Sentry boxes at regular intervals. It looked similar to RAF Credenhill, where the SAS HQ was based.

He was coming down the slope of a hill and he could see large, rectangular structures in the middle of the base, which looked like giant Lego box shapes arranged neatly in a line next to each other. There were four or five rows of these, extending almost all the way across the base. They looked strange.

He got to the gates. Two guards with M4 carbines stopped him. Dan gave them the ID that he got from Burns. The guard looked at it, and showed it to his friend. He nodded.

The bar lifted and he waved the car in. Dan drove slowly. Cylindrical dome-shaped mess houses with corrugated-iron roofs appeared on his left. To his right, another electric barrier, this time unmanned. He took the left at the T-junction. Right in front was the football pitch. Next to it, a canteen with a large sign that said, "American Diner".

Dan drove past the canteen. Two men in gray RAF overalls strolled past the canteen, eyeing Dan and the car. Dan drove around the football pitch. A bunch of men, some in uniform and some in soccer football kit, walked down the road towards the office and the spectator stands. Dan drove past them until he found the soccer pitch car park.

Three cars were parked already, all empty. Dan got out and locked the car. A two-story brick building lay ahead, next to a clubhouse and bar area. The stands were next to it. The men from the road walked in, and Dan fell in behind them, smiling in greeting to the few looks cast in his direction. There was a reception area inside, and double doors leading to the bar opposite. The men turned towards the bar, but Dan followed the sign that said "Changing Rooms". He almost barged into two men in soccer gear coming out.

"Sorry," Dan said, and walked past them into the changing rooms. One person was getting changed. A row of lockers along the periphery of the room. Benches all around and in the middle. Dan instantly saw what he was looking for.

Gray overalls hanging on a wall hook. Dan started taking his clothes off. The man on the other side of the room finished dressing and left. Dan stripped quickly and tried the overalls on. It was a tight fit. He packed his clothes under his arm and went back to the car, putting his clothes in the trunk.

He went past the canteen and kept going until a clearing appeared. He could see the giant Lego box structures in front of him, and they looked extraordinary. What he had thought were rectangular boxes were in fact a neatly lined row of hillocks. Each one about ten yards wide and separated by about the same distance. A road ran alongside.

Each hillock opened out to a hollow in the middle, like a giant claw had eaten half the hill away. A truck rumbled past Dan, stopping at the first hillock and reversing into the hollow. Two men opened the rear and jumped out of the tailgate.

The truck was unmarked. Rows of artillery shells were stacked out in the middle of the hollow. He recognized them—155mm shells for heavy guns, like the self-propelled AS-90. One hell of a monster. He had seen rows of them pummel the life out of the Iraqi Army outside Baghdad, back in '03. Steel rain, bring the pain, baby. His lips twitched at the memory.

The two men were pulling down cages of more shells from the truck. At the back of the hollow, carved into the green hillock, were two giant doors. The doors were open, and Dan could see the cages stacked in order inside.

Another hillock also had a truck in front being unloaded. These weapons had three familiar yellow stripes at equal intervals on the black body. The three black fins at the back. He had seen these strapped under wings of attack Apache and Cobra helicopters.

Hellfire missiles. The best air-to-surface missiles he knew. One of the men unloading looked over at him and waved. Dan waved back. Opposite, the same long stretch of the hillocks. Dan saw another truck in the distance and walked towards it. He moved to the back of the truck.

"You guys need a hand?" he asked the two sweating men taking the cages out. Each missile took two or three men to lift. And these were packed inside their gray metal cases, which made them heavier.

"No, we're okay, pal," one of the men said.

Dan gave them a thumbs-up and went to the front of the truck. Instead of going back on the road he sat down near the front wheel of the truck to tie his shoelaces. From here, he had a side-angle view.

The storage was being emptied, loaded on the truck. The reverse of what was happening in the other sites around him. That could be normal, ammunition being transferred from one site to another. Dan thought about weapons moving out of a large munitions base. A base that Guptill traveled to frequently, maybe with Renwick. He decided to see where this truck was going to.

The two men wore RAF overalls and were loading the truck with artillery shells, SAMs and flat black boxes, which, judging from their size, contained light weapons. Probably rifles. The two men didn't look familiar. The manner in which they worked suggested they had done this job before, and knew the place well.

Dan knew he couldn't stay here for long. He watched as the two men finished loading the truck and shut the tailgates. They got into the cabin, slammed the doors shut and reversed out onto the road. The truck beeped its horn once and the men opposite waved back. Dan remained behind the truck, following slowly on the opposite side of the road.

CHAPTER 32

Dan watched the truck lumber out in front of the soccer pitch of RAF Welford, and turn towards the American Diner. It was moving slowly. Dan hurried back to his car. As he drove out on the road circling the pitch, he saw the truck in the distance stopping at the diner. Dan parked nearby, walked in and ordered a burger. He came back out while the order was being made.

The truck driver's door was open. One of the men was checking the lashings around the side. He went around and checked the tailgate as well. Dan went back inside, picked up his order and ran back to the car. The truck was still standing by the road. Dan watched it as he munched on his burger.

There was rumble of multiple engines. A convoy appeared on the main road leading out to the gates. He counted six trucks, all unmarked and identical. One by one, they left the base. The driver of the truck Dan was following waited for another five minutes. Dan was slurping on his Coke when the truck got into gear and drove towards the main gate. Dan put his drink down and eased the Toyota out onto the main road.

Once he was out on the main perimeter road, Dan could see the truck ahead of him. The rear red lights of the convoy were getting dimmer in the distance. The barrier lifted and the truck swung out on the road directly ahead. Dan gunned his engine. He approached the barrier slowly. The same guard leaned in the window. He frowned at Dan, pointing at his overalls.

"Borrowing some clothes, are we?"

"We had a knock around on the pitch and my civvies got dirty."

The young man didn't seem convinced, but lifted the barrier and waved Dan through.

He couldn't see the truck anymore. But the truck could only go one way at the end of the road—the M4 motorway.

He continued, rarely raising the speed above thirty mph. The country lane, with empty fields on either side, came to an end. Dan could hear the rush of the motorway traffic as he wound the window down. He couldn't see the truck anymore. He speeded up slightly. The motorway was ahead of him, cars zipping across at breakneck speed.

He was impatient to join up, and find where the truck had gone. He was about to pull out when out of the corner of his eye, he saw the truck speeding along the other side of the motorway, heading in the opposite direction.

Dan swore and pulled out into the traffic. He put pedal to metal and the engine responded, growling as it picked up speed. Dan got into the fast lane and accelerated. In a minute, he could see an exit approaching. He veered to the left, and at the traffic circle joined the motorway headed west into London. The truck couldn't have gone far, he figured, unless it had gone into an exit.

For five minutes, he didn't speed. It attracted attention, and police cars patrolled this road often. He kept a steady pace in the middle lane, overtaking the slower cars. Finally, he saw the truck, four cars ahead, in the slower left lane. Dan breathed in relief.

The truck trundled on and the mass of machines and humans grew denser as the M4 approached London. But the truck headed north on the London Orbital M25, the motorway surrounding the capital like a spider's web. Dan almost missed the truck as it veered off to the left. He stayed four or five vehicles behind. The truck traveled onto the west of the country towards the coast. They joined a single-lane road, stopping frequently in the traffic.

Two and a half hours later they were close to Ipswich. He sat up straighter. One of the addresses on the sat nav of Guptill's car had been near Ipswich. He opened the screen and scrolled down.

Ipswich came and went as the truck drove past it. After fifteen minutes, they neared Felixstowe Port, the UK's largest container port. But the name had never meant much to him until now.

Felixstowe. *Felix.*

Dan clutched the steering wheel tightly. He was two trucks behind his mark, and watched as all three trucks indicated for the Port exit. Thoughts were swarming around his head. He got a flashback of Major Guptill's contorted face as he died.

The last word he spoke.

Felix.

A chill ran down Dan's spine.

Guptill had traveled down here from Welford and London several times. That was clear from the sat nav. Why? Had he followed a similar truck? Or had he been tailing someone?

The truck Dan was following now was filled with weapons and missiles. Felixstowe was a civilian port, and it dealt with civilian goods. The realization hit him suddenly like a screaming train crashing into his head.

There was hardly any security in Felixstowe.

True, he couldn't just waltz in, but no way would there be armed guards or customs checks. Container ports were famous for being porous. Most contraband drugs found their way into the country through ports such as Felixstowe. The port workers were in the pay of organized gangs that delivered these drugs to their larger networks.

Dan bared his teeth.

That lax security was the reason why this truck was headed into the port. No one would search inside. No one would question where the goods were going.

From Felixstowe, the contents of that truck could go anywhere in the world.

Into that compound in Afghanistan.

Felix.

Is that what Guptill had tried to tell him? About the port? Yes, and something more. Dan let out a ragged breath. It was a code name. Foreign agents were often given names like these. Felix was the cover for a spy. Possibly a double agent, and Guptill had discovered his identity.

He remembered what Burns had told him. *We have an infiltrator.*

Dan bunched his jaws tight and gripped the wheel. He was getting closer to some answers.

He watched as the trucks ahead slowed and turned left into a lane that said "Delivery-Arrivals Only". A number of other trucks had formed a queue in the wide, multi-lane space. Counters stood at each lane, like tollbooths on a bridge.

Drivers leaned out from the cabins and handed over paperwork or shouted out numbers to the people inside the booths. Some drivers disembarked, and so did the booth operators. The Volvo truck swung down the side and stopped at a far lane behind a bigger vehicle. Dan memorized the registration.

Dan knew he couldn't get in. As the only car, he would be spotted instantly. Traffic was slow, and he moved forward at barely twenty mph, straight past the exit for the trucks. He needed to get out of this road and turn back on himself to get into the port. After ten minutes' driving, he saw the sign he needed. "Non-delivery and other vehicles."

Dan took the exit. Traffic was lighter here and he soon approached the tollbooth. The bar remained lowered as a woman in a Port Authority uniform approached him.

"What's your VRN?" she asked, looking at Dan and the car.

"Sorry, what's that?"

"First time here?"

Dan smiled. "It shows, doesn't it?"

"You American?"

"Yup."

"Hope you're having a good time here."

"I am, thanks." *One hell of a good time.*

"You need a vehicle registration number in order to get in here. Register at the website."

"I see. Is there any other way, like a tourist section? I don't have to get inside, but just wanted to see the large freighters."

The woman nodded. "If you keep going down the way you came, there's a sign for the Port Authority Education Trust. It's for school trips and families, but it's on the water, with a café, benches and so on. You can see the ships docking and sailing up and down as well."

Dan thanked the woman and turned the car around. Another fifteen minutes later he saw the sign. There was no traffic here and he speeded up. Then Dan saw the glimmer of water. The broad sweep of the rivers Stour and Orwell, according to his sat nav, joining the great wash of the North Sea.

Dan parked in the visitors' car park and went over to the café and Port Museum building. Waves lapped at the pebbly beach. Large freighters were docked at the port. Giant rigs rose high in the air over the berthed ships, picking up shipping containers from their decks in steel claws.

A monstrous floating castle was putting slowly in from the North Sea, its deck and forecastle stacked high with multicolored shipping containers. The ship blotted out the sun as it got closer. On amphibian tours of duty Dan had seen large destroyer vessels, and he'd been on the USS *Nimrod*, the US Navy aircraft carrier in the Persian Gulf. The ship he was watching seemed as big as the aircraft carrier.

The courtyard of the café was sprinkled with people watching the ships. The pebbly beach of Felixstowe Port stretched out towards the fence, separating the beach from the first deep berths.

CHAPTER 33

It was 1845 hours. Another hour and a half of light, if that. He needed to see what was happening with the truck inside the port.

Dan made his mind up. He went back to the car park and bought an overnight ticket. He opened the trunk and took his clothes out. He put the Sig on his back belt, next to the kukri. He lifted the floor of the trunk and peered inside the wheel well. He took the floor out, and unscrewed the reserve wheel.

He took the KEDR sub-machine gun, and slotted out the breech, magazine and barrel. He stored the individual parts in the corners of the wheel well, then refixed the wheel and put the floor back on. He put an extra magazine of the Sig in his pocket, and the Nite-Glo torch in the other. He shut the car and went to the bathroom in the café. He used one of the cubicles to get changed into his jeans and button-down shirt. He dropped off the RAF overalls in the trunk of the car, and then looked around him. The car park was empty.

He walked to the side of the parking lot. The fence was low there and he vaulted across it to the low ground that led to the pebble beach. He cut straight across, heading to the port, walking quickly across the shrub and grassland. A line of low trees near the port fence gave him cover. He studied the wire fence. It was about ten feet tall, with regularly spaced posts, and he couldn't see any signs of electricity. There wasn't any barbed wire at the top, which made his life a lot easier.

He grabbed the wire mesh and shook it. It was firm and would take his weight. He wrapped his legs around a post and pulled himself up with both hands, using it like a fast rope. He crouched over the top and jumped down. The brick wall of a building lay in front of him. He could hear an engine wheezing and what sounded like train railway tracks. Then he saw the freight trains. A small path went past several buildings to the first berth.

The brick wall had a sign. Wickenden House. He came out onto a wide-pitched road. Men in high-visibility, red overalls and hats walked along. He looked at them carefully. They wore steel-toe boots with ID badges dangling from the neck. Opposite him there stood a cluster of buildings, one of them belonging to the Port Authority Police.

Dan headed back out towards the fence. He could keep going down the back of the buildings instead of the road. Eventually he found a clearing with a train station. A freight train was being loaded by fixed electric rigs on the side. A stack of twenty-foot-long, ten-foot-high shipping containers lay opposite, arranged in rows as far as the eye could see. Signs on the containers read: China Shipping, MSC, Lundberg, Evergreen—and many were labeled Maersk.

"You alright there, mate?" a voice called out from behind him.

Dan turned around. A worker with his sleeveless, high-visibility jacket, helmet and glasses stood there smoking a cigarette. He looked Dan up and down.

"Fine, thanks," Dan said. "I came with my brother who is a hauler. He gave me the number of a container in the train docks, and asked me to check if it's arrived. Then I got lost."

The man walked closer. He kept puffing on his cigarette.

"What truck is he driving?"

"A black Volvo."

"So, you don't work here?"

Dan shook his head. "No."

"You American?"

Dan smiled. "Yeah. Not seen my bro in years, so thought I'd come down and see where he worked. Going for a beer with the guys later."

"I see," the man said.

Dan asked, "Do you know how I get back to back to the truck loading zone?"

The man threw his cigarette away. "Yeah. Follow me."

They walked past the train platform. A container landed with a soft thud and screech on the train. The huge claws separated and lifted up.

They crossed a clearing with more buildings. HMRC Office, and then Tomlinson House, P&O Shipping lines. Beyond that, Dan found himself in an open space the size of multiple football fields, all stacked with shipping containers in their white marked berths. Far to his left lay the rigs and waters of the port. The man stopped and pointed.

"Head for behind the containers. That's where the main hauler route comes in. The stations are numbered. Which one were you?"

"Eight."

"One of the last ones then. Keep walking."

Dan pointed to the man's high-visibility jacket. "Do you know where I can find one like that?"

"At the reception desk beside the Customs center." He jerked his thumb backwards.

"Thanks," Dan said. He breathed out a sigh of relief, and watched the man disappear behind a row of containers. Then he went to the reception desk. A surly, old woman jabbed a finger at a stack of old and dusty red jackets piled up on the floor. He found an old white helmet, too. Dan picked one up, thanked the woman and left.

A few trucks were standing in line, and a forklift loading transporter moved between them. The transporter stopped at one truck and lowered its long arm from which hung a wide, double-pronged hook. The hook clanged around the sides of the container on the truck and lifted it up. The transporter drove up to the stack of containers, the container swaying in the air between the two hooks on either side.

It took Dan twenty minutes to find the Volvo truck. It was in the middle hauler park. More trucks stood side-by-side, with enough space in between for another forklift transporter to maneuver.

Dan stepped in behind a truck opposite and watched the Volvo. The cabin was empty. The lashings had been taken off, and the cover removed from a shipping container that bore the legend *"Living Aid"* on its sides. The name didn't ring any bells. There was a sound of gears clashing and the forklift transporter moved past him to the first truck in the line, at the far end. It lifted the container off the truck and moved away.

He could find out where the container was destined for, if he followed the transporter. And maybe, what cargo the Volvo would be taking back. Most of the trucks had empty cabins. The two on either side of the Volvo were definitely vacant. He crossed the distance quickly.

When he was between two vehicles, he looked below the truck. Two sets of legs at the far end, where he could hear the transporter coming back with its load. Dan reached up and tried the handle of the Volvo. Locked. He walked around the back and tried the passenger side. Locked as well.

He heard a sound from the other end. Another forklift transporter was making its way up the line. The driver climbed off. Then he heard voices. Very close. Coming up to the Volvo, and getting louder. Dan was trapped. He dropped to the ground and rolled underneath the truck.

He went forward and pressed himself against the underside of the front chassis. The two drivers came up to the Volvo. One threw down a cigarette on the ground and stamped on it. The cabin door opened on the passenger side. Before the man could get on, Dan heard another voice. A man came up from the rear of the truck.

"Hello, chaps. What have we got here today, then?" The forklift operator. Dan could see up to the man's belt line. He pressed himself further against the chassis.

"The usual cargo. Vaccines."

The forklift guy scribbled something on the clipboard he was holding. "Oh yes. For Karachi again?"

"Yes, Karachi."

"And what about the pick-up?"

The same voice spoke again. Dan assumed it was the driver. "Same again." There was a slight delay, then the voice said, "Container number PV 346756 from Karachi."

Forklift scribbled again. "Yes, got that, too. Okay, chaps, looks like you're third in line now. Just wait." The man was about to turn away when the driver spoke to him again.

"We need to check it. Like last time."

Forklift came forward again. "Now chaps, you know I can't let you do that."

Dan could see the driver reach into his pants pocket and pull out a wad of notes. He peeled off several and handed them to the forklift operator. His voice was lower now, almost a whisper. "We can make it worth your while. Just like last time."

Forklift hesitated. Then he put the money into his pocket. His voice was now a whisper as well.

"Alright. But we go before I take the vaccines off. Come with me when I'm unloading the second truck. Yeah, the MAN truck. Check what you have to, then I come back to take this bitch off. Don't follow me, come back your own way."

Forklift sauntered off. Dan watched the driver and his helper walk down to the rear wheels of the Volvo. They stopped there, watching the second truck being offloaded at the front of the queue. They lit cigarettes and waited. Dan kept himself plastered against the chassis. Silently, he took the Sig out and screwed the suppressor on. He held the butt in both hands, finger loose on the trigger.

He tracked the men as they moved around the truck. If they peeped in, or checked the tires, Dan would shoot first. He would get a headshot on one. No more than one shot would be necessary. Then he could drag the body inside.

CHAPTER 34

The whine of the forklift transporter got louder. One truck along, the container was being lifted. That was the signal. Dan watched as the men threw their cigarettes away and walked after the transporter. The long shaft raised itself from the body of the transporter like the turret of a machine gun. It's widely spaced claws at either end held the container securely, but that didn't stop it from swaying slightly. Dan gave the men a head start, then he rolled out the side of the Volvo and followed.

They moved into a miniature city of shipping containers, piled up to five high. Dan craned his neck up and around. They went around a block of Maersk containers. Dan stopped at the edge. He heard the gears of the transporter shifting, then a loud clang as the container was deposited. The engine died down. He heard the forklift guy speaking in a low voice, but couldn't make out any words. Footsteps receded and he tiptoed around. He caught them just as they were coming out the far end. He ran, and poked his neck past the last container.

The damn place was like a rabbit warren. After another turn, he heard them stop. Dan flattened himself against a container and peered across. The three men were standing in front of a dark blue container. He watched as they unlocked it. The driver lifted some bolts in the front of each door, pulled the long camshafts, and opened both doors. Then the driver and his helper went inside.

Dan shifted back. He was just in time. The forklift guy was looking around fearfully. He called out to them. They emerged in five minutes. They said something to the forklift guy, then locked the doors. Dan got ready to sprint back. To his relief, the men didn't retrace their steps. They went left and Dan followed. They were headed back to the trucks. He ducked back inside the container city.

Dan found the blue container quickly. The bolts were down, but the central lock was still open. He opened one door like he had seen the forklift guy do, stepped inside, and shut it without locking it. He needed to be quick. Mr Forklift operator would be back soon.

It was pitch black inside. He shone his torch around.

218

Bicycles. Piled on one another, up to the ceiling. Mostly mountain bikes with fat wheels and tubes.

What the hell?

Mountain bikes from Karachi? It didn't make sense. He got closer to the bikes. He put the flashlight between his teeth and grabbed the nearest. It weighed like a mountain bike should. Admittedly, these were sturdy bikes, with wheels larger than normal...

Hold it.

Dan shone the torch down the bike carefully. He tapped the steel tubes. A dull sound. His heart beat faster. He got down to the fat tires. He squeezed one. Tight as a bamboo pole. Ok, it might be pressured. But still... he took his kukri out and stabbed the tire. There was a hiss of air, but only slightly. Dan cut down with the kukri, slashing the rubber. He felt something inside. He shone the torch. Pay dirt.

A plastic tube was wrapped around the inside of the tire. Dan used the tip of the kukri to cut it. Under the torchlight, a gray-brown dusty material poured out. Dan sniffed at it—a pungent, sharp smell. He had smelled this before. When the memory jogged, his spine whiplashed straight.

Eight years ago. Helmand Province, Afghanistan, inside a poppy farmer's hut. The poppy harvest had just finished and farmers were gathering the poppy resin to be sold in the market. Some farmers, like the one whose hut they were raiding, went further. They actually reduced the resin and boiled it with chemicals, then dried it in the sun to form a dry powder.

Heroin.

Dan stared at the powder in his hand, then at the plastic tube hanging from the inside of the tire. Powder was still pouring out, forming a conical tower on the floor. He got up and tapped the steel tubes. The handlebars came off with some effort. More plastic tubes with the same gray-brown stuff inside...

Bicycles were packed inside the container. The HMRC (Her Majesty's Revenue and Customs) man would look at the bikes, tick a box and move on. No one would suspect the millions of dollars' worth of heroin secreted inside the frames and tires.

Dan poked around in the back of the container, but it was all the same. He listened at the door for five seconds, then stuck his head out. He heard the sound of an engine. The forklift transporter was returning. He came out and locked the doors quickly, went around the corner and hid. The forklift made a massive moaning sound as it trundled into the space.

It was carrying the *Living Aid* container. With a loud sound and a cloud of dust, it put the container on the ground. The crane lifted up from the middle of the transporter, and the two claws on either side grabbed the container above the one that Dan had just been in. Finally, the forklift lifted the container from Karachi, and the transporter turned around and left for the hauler park. Dan watched it go around the corner and vanish from view.

He ran over to the *Living Aid* container, got in and took his flashlight out. Shelves lined the space inside. He had a small area in the middle to move around in.

He noted the Hellfire and Pathfinder missiles. H&K rifles lined one whole wall. He swore under his breath when he saw the NVGs. They were the older generation, but they were still of key tactical advantage.

Why the hell were these bound for Karachi? Pakistan's largest port? Now he knew the answer.

He had just discovered a weapon-smuggling ring. From the RAF base, via Felixstowe Port, to Karachi, and then into Taliban hands.

The weapons were paid for by contraband drugs, and cash. He suspected the contraband was worth more than the cash was.

Dan felt sick inside. He thought of the men he had seen die in Afghanistan. He had carried back the wounded from the battlefield. Many of them, for the last time. Is this what those men had died for?

He thought of the young men on the streets, wasting their lives as junkies.

Someone was profiting from this. These weapons would be worth a lot of money to the Taliban.

A rage grew inside him, and so did a conviction. He would get them for this. Dead or alive, he would get them. He was the scapegoat, being framed for smuggling weapons. But they had picked on the wrong person.

He flashed the torch around, searching. Finally, on the lowest rung of a back shelf he found it. The entire shelf was lined with suitcases of C-4 explosives. He picked a hundred-pound bag and opened it. The putty-like explosive was lined in one corner with a fuse wire, a timer and detonator. As explosives went, it was pretty basic, but it would more than do the job.

Dan picked the suitcase up. It was heavy, but he could manage. He was about to step out when he heard the sound outside. It was the forklift operator again, but he was much closer this time.

Dan cursed. He had taken too long to check the equipment. He opened the door a fraction. The forklift transporter was coming around the bend. The wide jaws of its crane were empty, possibly the reason why it had come back quicker. It was now going to stack the containers back in their place, ready to be picked up when their ship was ready.

Dan shut the door almost fully, leaving a small sliver through which he could see. The transporter went slowly past the *Living Aid* container. Dan heard it stop. Footsteps approached. Slowly, Dan put the suitcase down. It would take the forklift driver a few seconds to realize the door was ajar.

Dan had those few seconds in which to act.

He waited until the man came right up to the door and stopped. In that instant Dan pushed the door back with all his might. There was dull thwack as the heavy steel door smashed into the forklift driver's face. Dan pivoted on his feet, and hopped out of the container at the same time. The driver was on the ground, his face a bloody mess. Dan knelt down. The man was out cold.

Then he heard another voice behind him.

"Well, well, what do we have here?"

CHAPTER 35

Dan got up, and slowly turned around.

Four men circled him.

"You didn't think you would get away that easy, did ya?" the tallest of the men smirked. Cockney accent. From London's East End, where most of its criminal underworld congregated.

Dan stood there silently, watching the men form a ring around him.

The tall man was about two inches shorter than him. He was wide at the shoulders, and his long arms hung loose at the sides. He carried himself on the balls of his feet, suggesting a boxer's stance. Dan wondered who had sent them.

The two men on either side of him were shorter and squatter, thick around the neck and shoulders. Their shifting eyes and pock-marked faces identified them as veterans of street fighting. Part of the dockside gang, maybe, who had been hired as protection. They did not have the cold, calculating eyes of men like Dan.

If they had, Dan would have been dead by now.

One of them had stepped behind Dan. He was not worried, he had his measure already. Similar to the two in front, on either side of their leader. He knew they were armed, and that they would not hesitate to use it if necessary.

He was not worried about that. He was more worried about the passage of time.

He needed to get on that damned truck. It would lead him to the source of all his troubles.

He calculated how much time he needed to get through these men, and stayed silent like a statue, watching them closely.

"Throw your weapon and empty your pockets!" the leader snarled, taking a step closer.

Without moving his body, Dan shook his head slowly from side to side.

No. Come closer to me, asshole.

He watched the leader's hands. The gangster's right hand snaked inside his right coat pocket. He lunged forward suddenly, a gun appearing like magic in his right fist. Looked like a Glock 19. Dan was prepared. He stepped back quickly. With his left hand he struck the gangster's right hand down, hard as he could. The gun went scattering on the floor, out of sight underneath a container box.

Immediately he felt the man behind him hook his elbow around his neck. Dan did not mind that. He had a broad neck, with thick muscles. He bunched his neck muscles, bringing his head down. The man was strong, and he tried to bring Dan down with a wrestler's grip round his neck.

Dan allowed the man to pull him back, but only till he was leaning against the man. Then he used his support to heave his legs off the ground.

His boots smashed into the leader's face, blood erupting from his broken nose. The other foot hit another man in the chest, sending him sprawling against some rattling garbage bins.

Dan hooked his fingers round the elbow that was gripping his neck. He went down on his knees, kneeling forward like he was doing a somersault. The forward jerk made the man fly off him, landing on his friend on the floor, who was still winded from Dan's foot landing on his chest.

It had all happened in the blink of an eye.

The leader was slowly getting off his knees, searching for his gun on the ground, clutching his bleeding nose with his left hand.

The remaining gangster uttered a vile oath and flew in with his fists. Big mistake. The man was wide and thick, and all his power was in his shoulders and neck. His knockout punch sailed harmlessly past Dan's face as he calmly sidestepped. The man stumbled and Dan kicked his feet, bringing him down. Dan quickly stepped behind him and grabbed his hair, bending his neck back. He hit the man as hard as he could just below the right ear, aiming for the jaw angle.

The man screamed and jerked, but Dan held him tight by the hair, and hit him again, in exactly the same spot, feeling the blow reverberate up his forearm this time. Dan let go of the man. Screaming, he went down to the floor.

From the corner of his eye, Dan saw the leader. Blood flowed like a pair of curtains down either side of his face, covering his mouth and chin in a red mask. His eyes were wide, and a knife had appeared in his right hand. He circled Dan, hatred filling his face. The two others had got off the floor as well, and joined their leader. Then they rushed Dan in a triangle formation.

This time, the leader slashed at Dan from below, aiming for his midriff. Dan high-kicked with his left leg, a move that surprised the leader. It surprised most knife fighters, who rely on their arms to parry and block.

The leader cried out as the kick flung his right hand out of the way, dislodging the knife. The cry died in his throat as Dan's fist landed square on his jaw, crunching bone. The man was knocked out cold, but Dan grabbed his shirt even as his two mates rushed him from either side.

Holding the unconscious leader like a shield, Dan turned left and cannoned into his attacker.

Three of them went down in a heap, with the last gangster behind them. Dan rolled off and was on his feet in the same movement.

The gangster on his feet kicked hard and caught Dan in the midriff, winding him. It was a heavy blow, but Dan did not let go of his leg. He lifted till the man came off his feet and landed on his back. Dan straddled his chest instantly and double-punched him. The man's eyes rolled back as Dan lifted him up by the collar and head-butted him with savage force, spraying bone and cartilage from his nose.

Dan was on his feet just as the last gangster got to his.

One-on-one. Dan wanted to glance at his watch. He was dangerously short of time now.

The drivers could be getting back to the truck any minute now, and Dan couldn't let them drive off without him.

The thick, heavy-set face of the gangster curled up in hate as he lifted his fists and approached Dan.

The man feinted with his left and punched hard with his right. It caught Dan on the shoulder as he ducked. But the blow was good. It turned Dan around, and he stumbled backwards.

Dan swayed out of the way as another punch came for his face. The man had put too much into the blow, and it was his turn to stumble in the follow-through.

Dan hit him hard in the midriff just below the sternum. The man doubled up as the breath left his chest. Dan grabbed his head and brought his right knee up, smashing the face down. The neck loosened. The limp body sagged uselessly to the floor.

Dan glanced at the parking lot. The trucks were still there. He ignored the four bodies lying on the floor. They would be out cold for a while.

He went back inside the container and began dragging out the steel cages that held the explosives, missiles and rifles. He took the missiles out of their shelves and put them on the floor. Anyone who came up here would see the container had been tampered with and should raise the alarm.

And they sure as hell would not miss the four bodies.

He picked up the suitcase of C-4 explosive and jumped on the forklift transporter. The machine had an ignition and a steering wheel. He turned the ignition key and the engine purred smoothly to life. With the suitcase at his feet, Dan drove around the *Living Aid* container and headed out to the hauler park.

He flicked the light switches of the transporter on. It was 2100 hours now, and the sun had set, leaving the sky in deepening shades of black. The hauler park was dark. Lights farther away lit up the road.

The Volvo was still there. Three of the other trucks had left. The Volvo's cabin was still empty. Dan got closer. The truck was loaded with the deep blue container full of mountain bikes.

Lashings had secured it tightly to the truck bed. Lights in the cabin were off and Dan figured the men were having dinner.

He worked quickly. He put the C4 suitcase on the ground and used the steel claws of the transporter to grab it and lift the suitcase to the roof of the Volvo's container. He drove away and parked the transporter back near the stack of containers.

Dan returned to the Volvo, grabbed the lashings at the back of the container and pulled himself up. Using the bolts and camshafts as leverage, he climbed upwards, and heaved himself onto the roof of the container. He could see the suitcase. He crawled towards it, pushed the suitcase out to the middle, and pulled two lashings till they covered the suitcase like a strap holder. Then he lay down spreadeagled.

He didn't have to wait long. The drivers came back, smoking and cracking jokes. They got into the cabin and flicked on the light switches. The ignition fired, gears clashed and with a deep rumble the leviathan pulled out of the park.

CHAPTER 36

The Volvo moved slowly out of Felixstowe Port. Once it hit the dual lanes of the A12, the road heading back to London, it picked up speed. Traffic was lighter now, but the twelve-wheel machine wasn't built for speed. It rumbled along at 40mph, Dan estimated.

He was holding onto the lashings on either side of him. The steel surface was recessed and cut into his stomach and legs. Dan did a quick calculation. When they joined the M25, the truck would pick up speed. When it came off the M25 at the other end, there would be traffic on London's roads. There always was. He looked behind him. One car, lights blazing, overtook the slower Volvo. Then it left the road in darkness, lit up only by the truck's headlights. He wouldn't get a better chance than this.

Dan let go of the lashing with one hand, and pulled out the Sig. The suppressor was still screwed on. Then he slid forward on his belly, using the recesses on the steel. He got close to the side of the container.

Black asphalt flashed below him. Wind whipped at the lashings. The blurry white line on the road ran along the side of the huge tires.

He steadied himself, transferring his weight back. He looked behind briefly. The road was still empty. Dan leaned his gun arm over the side, extended his elbow and aimed for the side-view mirrors. The rattling of the container wasn't helping. Neither was the wind. He held the gun butt tighter. Then he fired. The round went into the road, picking up a puff of dust. Dan swore and refocused his arm. This time the shot cracked into the mirror, destroying it.

He had been prepared for the swerve, but when it came it still surprised him. He almost went over the side as the truck moved sharply to the left, but he managed to hold onto the lashings and pull himself in.

He knew how important side-view mirrors were for a truck driver. They did the job of rear-view mirrors. The driver was now blind on the right side. As Dan expected, the truck moved onto the hard shoulder, decelerating. He glanced at the suitcase, it was secure. As the truck came to a stop, Dan was already at the back. His feet were on the camshaft bolts, and he slid down lower, holding onto the lashings. As the truck belched out a final puff of exhaust and shuddered to a stop, Dan dropped down to the road. The headlights went off and it was very dark all of a sudden.

He crouched behind the rear wheel. The driver's cabin door opened, but the man didn't come down. Instead, Dan could just about make out the muzzle of a rifle. The rifle poked out further, and Dan could see the man turned around inside the cabin, twisting his body so he could use his weapon. Dan heard the passenger side open and the other man jump down. He would have a weapon as well, and would come around Dan's back.

He couldn't allow that to happen. He had to maintain the element of surprise.

There was no wind now and he was rock-still. He could see half of the driver leaning out with the rifle. That was enough. He fired, and the sound of the strike was like the squashing of a watermelon under a hammer. The driver screamed and fell out the cabin, breaking his fall against the door. The rifle clattered uselessly to the ground. Dan ran forward, firing again. The bullet made contact, somewhere in the upper body. It was hard to tell in the dark. The body collapsed on the ground and was still.

Dan heard a sound behind him and threw himself on the ground. The first bullet whined over his head. Dan rolled to the front of the truck as another bullet kicked up dirt on the asphalt. He could hear the man running. Dan ran around the side of the vehicle and threw himself under it. The man's legs appeared on the other side. Dan squeezed off two rounds and heard the dull smack of impact. The man screamed as the rounds tore into his calf muscles. He went down and Dan fired twice more, aiming for the head. Both bullets found their mark. The body slammed on the road, jerked once, then was still.

The motorway was still empty. Dan grabbed both bodies by the collar and pulled them over to the grass verge. He shone the flashlight on them. The driver was hit in the chest and neck. He was close to being finished. The second guy had met a 5.56mm NATO round with his head, and the result wasn't pretty. Dan looked behind him. The grass verge rose up four feet, then a steel fence appeared. He checked the men's pockets, and found their RAF identity cards and cellphones. Then he picked up the bodies and dumped them over the fence.

He went around the back of the truck and climbed back up to the roof. He got the suitcase and brought it down. It wasn't easy. He dangled with one hand on the camshaft bolt of the container door, while the other held the heavy case. He jumped to the ground and fell over, bruising his shoulder. He put the suitcase in the cabin and got into the driver's seat.

CHAPTER 37

The nurse tapped the keyboard. She spoke without taking her eyes off the screen.

"BIBA yesterday, you said? Gunshot wound?"

Chloe was standing in Chelsea and Westminster Hospital's Accident and Emergency Department, a long queue of disgruntled people behind her. It was 8 am, but the queues had already started. She had tied her hair up in a bun, and was wearing a baseball cap.

"Was he brought in by ambulance?" the nurse asked Chloe impatiently. BIBA. Chloe twigged.

"Yes," she said hastily. "Name is Simon Renwick."

"And you are?"

"Close friend."

"Wait here." The nurse got up and left. Chloe looked around. On either side were receptionists and nurses manning the desks. Behind her, a large space was lined with seats, filled with the muffled coughs and occasional groans of the sick and needy. The nurse came back and this time she had a doctor with her.

"Come to this side, please," the nurse said. The doctor opened a door, and Chloe walked through.

The doctor was Asian, in his early thirties, with closely cut black hair. He regarded Chloe with interest.

"How can I help you?"

Chloe repeated herself, and this time she described Renwick as well. The doctor frowned.

"Someone matching that description was brought in yesterday. One hell of a trauma. Heavy bleeding, but we managed to stabilize him with four liters of blood. They took him to theater. He was very lucky. The two bullets missed the major arteries. Part of his liver had to be removed, its blood supply had died."

"Where is he now?"

"In ITU. Intensive therapy unit, I mean. He is still in a critical state. I must ask you again, what is your relation to this man?"

Something in the doctor's voice bothered Chloe. She kept her face passive and met his gaze. "I met him in the course of my job, we had an important professional connection. He knew my father well. I'm concerned about him."

The doctor sighed. "Look, I don't mean to cause offense. But there was a big police presence when this guy turned up. His condition was critical, but we were also told not to allow any visitors, or *anyone* for that matter, near him. Don't ask me why."

Chloe nodded. "I see. So, you don't think I'll be allowed to see him?"

"I very much doubt it."

Chloe took the elevator to the first floor and followed directions to the ITU. It was at the end of a long concourse, lined by wide windows that looked down onto a leafy Japanese garden below with a fountain and stream. Two RMP-uniformed men with machine guns stood on either side of the doors. They stared at Chloe as she approached. One of them put a hand out.

"Can we help you?"

"I'm here to see a patient. Simon Renwick."

"Wait here."

One of the guards went inside and came out with a nurse.

"Mr Renwick is not allowed any visitors," the nurse said, looking a little flustered. Chloe didn't miss the glance the two guards exchanged, and how they tightened the grip on their weapons.

"Is there a reason why not?"

"His condition is still critical. Touch and go. Next of kin have been informed. We can inform you, too, if you leave us your details."

Chloe shook her head. "No, thank you. I'll contact the next of kin myself and come back at a suitable time."

"As you wish," the nurse said.

Chloe went back down the concourse, thinking to herself. The Royal Military Police were guarding Simon Renwick. Someone high up was protecting him. Well, they must have realized now that he was at risk. After he almost died. If it hadn't been for Dan...

Chloe felt Renwick knew what this was all about. Her father dying, Dan getting framed. What Dan had seen in that compound. The weapons. She thought hard about her meeting with Renwick. The DSO was promoting new military hardware like fighter jets and satellites. There was an air show in Farnborough, which was the UK's largest trade—which meant weapons and associated technology—and public air show.

Billions of dollars' worth of sales were made each year. She had seen the advertisement on the wall while she was waiting for Renwick.

And today was the first day of the air show.

She had intended to cover it for *London Herald*. Several MoD officials would be there, most of them in senior positions. Last year, even the Secretary of Defence had been there. But the trade fair was held on separate days, when members of the public weren't allowed. Chloe came out of the hospital and called her office. Her name was already down on the press list. All she had to do was get her ID badge from the hotel room and head down to Farnborough.

*****

The sun was shining as Chloe approached the Press Exhibitor's counter of the Farnborough International Airshow. Her ID was checked, and she was given a new ID necklace, which she had to wear at all times. At the final check-in counter her handbag was searched and Chloe was patted down by a female guard inside a room.

Outside, she gaped at the massive spectacle in front of her. Chloe was facing the Outdoor Exhibition Area, a huge, three-square-kilometer enclave which included a runway. Several commercial jet airplanes were parked on the grass verge, their massive bodies glinting in the sun. People milled around them like ants. She saw Boeing and Airbus jets of various sizes. After the commercial passenger planes, the line of military airships started. The first stall was so big she mistook it for a new section of the show.

It was the area dedicated to BAE Systems, the largest weapon manufacturer in Europe, and the third-largest in the world. Headquartered in London, BAE Systems were the builders of everything from all-terrain vehicles to the latest warplanes. Chloe walked slowly around the new Solaris drone, its twenty-meter body so slim and streamlined it seemed almost impossible such a thing could fly at thirty thousand feet.

That was until she saw the range of missiles attached to the underbelly of its wings. A man in a suit, standing in front of the machine, was explaining the drone's abilities enthusiastically to a group of foreigners, including an Arab dressed in a white *dishdasha* and the traditional *keffiyeh*.

She came to the Cyclone jets, the next generation of traditional fighter jets. The relatively small size of the cockpit, and the enormous wingspan attracted her attention most. Machine guns were mounted on the wings, built in so that only the muzzles protruded. Beneath the wings, she saw a stunning array of missiles. The man explaining was pointing to the missiles, and indicated inside the plane's belly where more bombs lay hidden. The jet seemed like an airborne weapons depot, designed to fly anywhere in the world, ready to drop its seeds of destruction.

After a while, Chloe was feeling dizzy. She stopped at a drinks counter and sipped on a Diet Coke. She decided to head inside to the Indoor Exhibition Area. An enormous, dome-shaped tent had been created to house it. The cool hum of the air-conditioners was a welcome relief after the heat and bustle outside.

She headed for the toilets. She followed the signs, and went inside. It was empty. Chloe stood in front of the mirror, and took out her make-up bag. She took out her lipstick and froze.

In the mirror, behind her, she could see a large man. He had a grin on his face. Chloe opened her mouth to scream, but she was too late.

In one swift movement, the man stepped forward and wrapped his hand around her mouth, pulling her into his chest. Chloe fought back. She managed to lift her upper lip above the hand clamping down on her mouth. It smelled of cigarettes.

She bit down hard on the hand, feeling the bone crunch.

"Bitch!" the man screamed. He let go of his hand and spun Chloe around. A fist smacked against her face, and Chloe fell backwards, her eyes going black.

CHAPTER 38

Dan was parked in a street opposite the Intercept HQ.

He had found a café nearby for breakfast. He had barely slept, and the tiredness was giving him a headache.

He flipped open the cellphone that Burns had given him, connecting the battery to the phone.

Burns did not answer. Dan got off and went to a nearby store to buy himself a drink.

As he was walking to the truck, his cellphone beeped. He took it out and stared at it. Chloe's number. He pressed answer.

"Chloe?"

There was a pause, then Dan heard a man's voice. A voice he knew.

It was Burns. "Hey, Dan, it's me."

Dan frowned, then felt his heart suddenly hammer against his chest. He had difficulty speaking. "Burns."

"Yes, buddy, it's me." Burns' voice was light, relaxed.

"What are you doing with Chloe's phone?" A dreaded chill was spreading through Dan's body. He tried to fight it off. But it kept coming back. His rational mind kept trying to find a reason why Burns would have Chloe's phone. It couldn't find one.

Burns said, "You got the truck, Dan?"

Dan opened his mouth and forced himself to breathe. Words were frozen in his mouth.

"How do you know about the truck?"

"I know everything, Dan."

Dan leaned against the truck, feeling the ground opening up beneath his feet. The cellphone. The GPS beacon. The truck had a satellite feed. They could track him, and Burns had given him every single item.

"Where's Chloe?"

"Oh my, wouldn't you like to see her?"

"You're bluffing. She's not there. You just found her phone."

There was a scuffle, and some muffled voices. Dan could hear his heart pumping.

"Dan? Dan, is that you?"

He closed his eyes. It was Chloe. She sounded scared. He spoke quickly.

"Yes, it's me. Don't worry. I'm on my way. They won't do anything to you."

"Go straight to the police, Dan..." Another scuffle as the phone was ripped off her hand.

The same voice came down the phone. "Believe me now?"

"Felix."

There was a pause at the other end. Burns' voice hardened. "We need to meet up, Dan. Tonight. After dark, at 10 pm. I'm giving you an address. Don't even think of going anywhere else. The truck has a tracker, and I can see it on my screen as we speak."

"Let her go first."

"Negative. You bring the truck into the address. Leave the truck here and take the girl."

"And let you kill us both?"

"I guess that is a chance you will have to take, Dan. Unless you want the girl to die a slow and horrible death. After my boys have had some fun, of course." He laughed, a derisive, high-pitched snort, and Dan could hear other voices laughing in the background.

"You are a dead man, Burns," Dan said softly.

"Spare me the hero talk. I will call you at 9 pm to give you the address. If you're not here, we start playing with the girl. I can see on my screen where the truck is. If you start moving around, or if you tamper with the truck's GPS tracker, the girl dies. Do you understand?"

"Got it."

"I know what you are trying to do. If you go inside Intercept, or go to the cops, or the US Embassy, if you speak to anyone at all, you know what's going to happen."

Dan didn't say anything. He could hear Burns breathing on the other side.

"Wait for my call." Burns hung up.

Dan gripped the phone tightly in his hand. He had no options. He hopped out of the truck cabin. He locked it, and took the tube back to Clapham Common. Inside his hotel room, he assembled his weapons and checked them. He sat down to wait.

As darkness claimed the skies over London, Dan left to get back in the truck. He had packed all his weapons on him, with extra ammo. He was sitting inside the truck at 2100 hours when his cellphone rang. Caller ID withheld. Dan put the phone to his ear on the second ring.

"It's me," he said.

"Dan, how nice to hear your voice again." Burns said.

"I want to speak to her."

There was a delay, then Chloe's voice came on the line. "Dan."

"I'm coming. Hang on."

"Dan, I..." Chloe could not complete her sentence. Dan heard a faint scream. He closed his eyes and hardened his jaw.

Burns came back on the line. "Hope you are satisfied now, Dan. Here is the address: number 345, Bickersteth Road, E14 3ST." The line went dead.

Dan flicked through his phone. He knew the address. It was one of the three addresses on the sat nav of Guptill's car. He sat for a moment, collecting his thoughts.

He looked at Google Maps and checked the satellite image of the address. It was a warehouse. He would have to go inside with the truck, there was no space to unload it in the courtyard. Dan glanced at the seats in the truck cabin.

He bent down and had a look at the side of the seat. There was a catch, and if he released it, the seat lifted up. He found another gun in the hollow inside, an M4 carbine rifle. He took it out and emptied the contents of the suitcase. He sliced the top of the wire casing with his kukri and fitted the detonator. He put the C-4 explosive next to it and shut the seat.

He picked up the empty suitcase, went to the back of the truck and opened the container doors.

*****

It was close to 2230 hours when Dan approached East Central London. It was the area around Canary Wharf, the heart of the city's financial district. The bright lights in the skyscrapers sparkled, turning night into day. Dan nosed the truck past the State Street and J.P.Morgan buildings, heading south towards the Isle of Dogs, where the Thames formed a tight noose of land, hanging over a thin line of its muddy waters.

He got closer to the river. A sharp turn led him into the flat, drab expanse of an industrial estate. Warehouses lined both sides of the road. Number 345 lay smack bang in the middle, next to a waste recycling center. It seemed as if the plot opposite also belonged to the waste center—it was lined with waste disposal trucks. Dan peered at the structure in front of him. A triangular, aluminum-frame roof enclosed the warehouse.

There was a small courtyard in the front. Three black Lada's were parked there with diplomatic number plates. As Dan watched, two men in black suits came out the front door, illuminated by the headlights. One of them gestured to Dan to cut the lights, and he obeyed.

In the dim street light he could make out the men pushing the front gates. There was a loud whirring noise, and the entire front of the warehouse opened up to reveal a hangar-like structure inside. The men pointed to Dan, and he slowly eased the Volvo into the yawning darkness.

"Turn the lights on!" one of the men shouted. Blinding lights came on instantly. The place seemed smaller with the truck in there. Pallets of goods were placed around the warehouse. In the far corner, and near the gates, he saw two offices. Two more cars were parked inside, both black Range Rovers. Four men, all in suits, leaned against them.

Burns stood a few steps in front of the Range Rovers. Dan couldn't see Chloe. He wound the window down. He took his time to light a cigarette that belonged to the dead driver. He took a drag, then turned back to them, blowing out smoke.

"Where is she?" he asked.

Burns smiled. He lifted his hand. One of the four men behind him opened the back door of a Range Rover and pulled Chloe out. Dan's heart jumped when he saw her. She looked calm and unhurt. Her hair was crumpled over her face, and black stains lined her eyes and cheeks. She stared at Dan. He glanced at her briefly, nodded, then looked around. In the far-right corner, he could see the back door. It had a bolt on it. The front door had been shut after he came in. There was no other way out.

Burns said, "I know what you're thinking. But let me save you the trouble. There's no way out. Now, why don't you throw your guns out the window and come down very slowly, with your hands in the air?"

Dan threw the two guns belonging to the dead men. They dropped with a clatter on the ground.

"And *your* weapon," Burns said.

He threw the Sig down, too.

"Can I keep my cigarette?"

"No, throw that down as well." Dan did as he was told.

He opened the cabin door. Four men were circling him. Each one had an MP7 sub-machine gun pointed at him. Dan jumped down onto the floor and raised his arms. One of the men came forward, went around to his back and searched till he found the kukri. He chucked it at his boss's feet. He picked it up.

"Interesting," Burns said, looking at the knife. "A kukri, I believe." He threw the knife casually behind his back. Dan noticed there was now one man with Chloe. Another had come to stand next to his boss. Four were surrounding him. Seven men, including Burns. All with MP7s, apart from Burns, who certainly had a weapon. And Dan didn't even have his kukri. He didn't like the odds.

"My name is Robert Cranmer." Burns said.

Dan said, "You sure that's your real name?"

"Hey, you got to have a couple, right?" Burns smiled. Dan didn't like it. Burns looked relaxed, easy, like he had done the hard work.

Dan said, "Or is your name Felix?"

"Ah. A nickname I never knew I had. Rather fetching, don't you think?"

Dan said, "You were in Afghanistan waiting for me when the mission started. You pulled strings to make sure the terrorist wouldn't be there."

"That's right."

"Guptill gave the mission the green light. You wanted to stop it, but you couldn't. I found out all about it, and took the photos. You destroyed the camera, didn't you?"

"Correct again, Dan."

"You kept me alive all this time to see what I could find out about Guptill's investigation. Who was he working for? CIA? With Renwick?"

"Well, Dan, you're gonna be dead soon, so you might as well know. Yes, Guptill had become an undercover CIA agent. Renwick was a CIA agent as well. Both were making life difficult for me. Of course, they didn't know who I really was."

A rage was building inside Dan. But he kept his voice even. Losing it now would not help him. He said, "You put the bomb in that pub, didn't you? Where Lucy worked."

Burns smiled thinly. "I enjoyed that," he said. "Got everyone shook up, but also showed my clients what I could do for them."

"You're a traitor. Selling weapons to the enemy."

Burns smiled. "But also getting closer to the enemy, Dan. Who do you think provides the intel on their whereabouts? All these drone strikes. I sell them weapons, they tell me where the big dogs are hiding. Just a little give and take."

"Selling our weapons for heroin, that's what you call give and take?"

"It's how you win a war, Dan. Divide the enemy. Make them fight against each other."

Dan snorted. "You only live for yourself. You use the Russian Mafia to sell your drugs on the streets." Dan indicated the Russians around him. "And the cash you get, you keep for yourself."

A voice spoke up from behind Cranmer. "These men are Spetsnaz. Not the Mafia."

Cranmer said, "Meet my business partner, Yevgeny Lutyenov."

"Everyone knows about the Kremlin's links with the Russian Mafia. Spetsnaz doing your dirty work does not exactly surprise me," Dan said.

Dan came a step closer. The four machine gun bearers shuffled forward with him.

Dan was now standing within an arm's length of Burns, who hadn't moved. There was silence for a second, punctuated by their heavy breathing.

"You're a clever man, Dan," Burns said softly. "You should be working for me. Shame you have to die tonight."

Dan looked past him at Chloe. She was staring at him with wide eyes.

Dan said. "You are insane."

Burns laughed. Two men dug their rifles into Dan's chest and pushed him back.

Burns said, "Goodbye, Dan. Believe me, I have more important things to attend to. It was nice knowing you."

"How much you making, Burns? A few million a year?"

Burns said, "You really think this weapon selling is my main thing? This is just a sideline."

Burns looked at Dan, and Dan felt someone squeeze his heart in a vice-like grip. What Burns had told him a minute ago flashed across his mind like a meteor.

Got everyone shook up, but also showed my clients what I could do for them.

Burns stepped forward. His eyes blazed. "I will make billions, Dan. 2.5 billion dollars to be exact. When this shit goes down, the whole world will come down with it."

Dan's heart was hammering in his chest. He remembered the CL-20 explosives he had seen in the compound. Burns had access to the latest in military-grade explosives.

He said, "What are you talking about?" He needed to keep Burns talking, stall for time.

"When it happens Dan, you will know. Trust me. Fingers will point everywhere, and nuclear weapons will be flying around. It will be the end of the world."

"You're gonna use the CL-20 in some public place," Dan said. "Somewhere prominent. In London."

Burns smiled again. A hard, calculating smile. "My, my, haven't we got our thinking hats on today."

An ice-cold fear gripped Dan. He felt his legs buckle as the realization hit him like a sledgehammer.

He looked at Burns with wide eyes. "No," Dan whispered.

Burns cocked his head to one side. "Excuse me?"

Dan said, "The US Embassy. You can get in there, right? I bet you have the right creds."

Dan was talking faster now, the words tumbling out of him. "We will blame the Middle East, and your Russian friend here will leave a trail that leads to the Kremlin."

"Aha," Burns said.

"We retaliate against Russia.... and..."

Burns clapped his hands together. "Bang," he said. "So, you finally figured it out. Well, it's too little and too late," Burns sneered. "Goodbye, Dan."

Dan asked again, "How can you do this?"

Burns said, "Because I look after myself, Dan. This has been planned for a long time. Tonight is the big show."

Burns indicated to Yevgeny. A forklift truck whined and lifted a pallet onto the back of a waiting truck. It repeated the process four times. Dan watched with a sick feeling in his heart.

He knew what was in those pallets. Burns gave Dan a last look of contempt, then turned and left the warehouse.

Five men were left inside. One of them held Chloe by the open car door.

A tall, wide guy approached Dan. Two men held Dan's arms. The man hit Dan hard in the face. A broken tooth and some blood spurted out of Dan's lips. A raw, blistering pain lashed across his face.

Dan straightened himself. He looked at Chloe and nodded to her.

The man in front of him smiled. "Say goodbye to your girlfriend." He pulled out a handgun. A Colt M1911. He pointed it straight at Dan's head.

"It's time for you to die," he said.

"No," said Dan, raising his voice so Chloe could hear him.

"It's time for *you* to die."

CHAPTER 39

Before anyone could move, Dan pulled his arms around together as hard as he could. He heaved using every ounce of strength in his colossal shoulders. The two men holding him turned and smacked together in the middle.

As they collided, the fuse that Dan had lit while lighting the cigarette sparked the detonator. It exploded instantly, firing the one hundred pounds of C-4 explosive hidden inside the front seat of the truck.

The shattering explosion blasted Dan off his feet.

He flew in the air, dimly aware of an orange fireball erupting in waves around him. Debris cascaded in the air, and a heavy object hit him in the head, knocking him down. He smashed against the side of the car where Chloe had been standing and crumpled to the floor.

A charred, burning smell was in his nose and mouth. He felt dizzy. He tried to open his eyes, but his head swam. He forced his eyes open. Apart from the black fumes and a fireball where the truck's front cabin had been, he couldn't see anything else. The pallets of goods had been blown apart. They were used weapons. Components of old Kalashnikovs and heavier Russian guns lay strewn on the floor.

One of the Spetsnaz guys lay face-up on the floor. He wasn't moving. Dan rolled over and removed the KEDR from his hands.

Dan saw movement to his extreme right. An arm raised itself, and pointed the muzzle of a gun at him. Dan fired a long burst from the KEDR, the gun's recoil surprisingly light. The figure went down. Dan crept along the floor, past the dead bodies, until he saw another man lift his head. He fired another burst into that body. The man shook as the rounds pumped into him, then he was still.

Dan felt an arm reach over his neck and pull him back. One of the men on the floor had sneaked up on him. Dan leaned forward, and the man tightened his grip. Dan saw double. The room swam before his eyes. His breath came in gasps, and the man was now leaning forward. Dan wanted that. He was holding the KEDR with both hands, but the sub-machine gun was light. He pointed it backwards past his own midriff. At point-blank range, he fired. The bullets tore into the man, sending him spiraling backwards. Dan fell forward, retching and coughing. He looked around, trying to catch his breath, ready to fire again. The bodies remained still.

He needed to find Chloe, but all he saw was inert bodies.

His heart stopped when he looked beneath the car and saw wisps of blond hair. It was Chloe. Dan removed another body in the way and reached for her. He grabbed her soot-blackened finger, then pulled her arm, but she didn't stir. Dan dragged her out of the car. She was breathing and her mouth was open. He moved the hair from around her face. Dan slapped her cheek lightly. After what seemed an eternity, her eyes fluttered open.

"Chloe. Can you hear me?"

"D…Dan?"

He held her with one hand and lifted the KEDR to point at the destruction in front of him. None of the bodies on the floor moved. Flames were licking the truck and starting to move back towards the fuselage. With an effort, he stood, picking Chloe up.

"We need to get out of here. Now."

He lifted Chloe with a fireman's lift onto his shoulder. When he tried to walk, he realized he was dragging his left leg. Blood trailed on the floor, seeping from a lower leg wound. The leg felt numb. He grit his teeth and picked up his pace. He went past the dead bodies, the burning truck, and into the open. He reached the gates, pushed them open and walked out. He wanted to run, but couldn't. Somehow, he kept putting one foot in front of another.

He'd gone a hundred meters when the Volvo's fuselage ignited. The explosion lifted up the roof of the warehouse, sending a mushroom of gray cloud rising into the night air. The sonic wave made the ground shake under his feet and he sank to his knees. Chloe came off his shoulders, and she pulled him into the perimeter wall of a vacant warehouse opposite. Shards of aluminum and other debris clattered on the road in the distance. They crouched as the rumbles faded.

Chloe was on her knees, facing him. She wiped a hand across his face. It came away red with blood.

"Dan," she said weakly. "Your head's bleeding."

He looked at her and managed a smile. "I've been through worse," he said.

Dan grabbed the wall and pulled himself upright. He looked around him wildly. Then he stumbled out to the middle of the road. Fire crackled in a yellow blaze where the warehouse stood.

Dan fished inside his pocket and smiled. He pulled out a black, cylindrical object.

It was the GPS beacon that Burns had given him. Dan pointed it upwards and pressed the buzzer.

"What is that?" Chloe asked.

"Something Burns will regret giving me." Dan ran towards the wreck. He could feel Chloe coming after him. He stopped.

He said, "No, you stay here when the helicopter comes. I need to get myself a weapon."

Dan gave her the beacon. "Here, hold this. If you point it up, it sends up an infrared beam which the pilot will be able to see."

Chloe did as she was told. Dan stumbled inside the wreck. The heat hit him like a wall. His left leg was hurting like mad, making him limp. He fought the flames, looking around for a weapon.

He also kept an eye out for a stray bullet. Just in case they were not all dead. He rummaged around in the hellish carnage, till he found an MP5 sub-machine gun that still worked. He slid the mag out and slapped it back in. He fired a shot. For good measure, he picked up a handgun as well. It looked like a Colt, and it still fired.

As he was heading back to the road, he heard the sound of the rotor blades above. They grew louder, and he was suddenly bathed in a brilliant glow of yellow light. Dan pointed to a vacant spot, moving his hands till the bird shifted. It was an MH-17. The bird landed on the road, and the pilot kept the engine running. The sound was deafening, making the warehouses shake.

A technician dropped down from the cabin and hurried towards them. Dan cupped his hands over the man's ear.

"The US Embassy is under attack!" He shouted the words twice till the man understood.

They got on the bird, and Dan waited till they hooked him up to the comms system.

Dan said, "Terrorist attack on US Embassy London, Grosvenor Square, Mayfair. Head there, now. Pilot, do you copy?"

The pilot nodded and gave Dan a thumbs-up. The rotor blades whined louder and the bird lifted up in the sky.

The technician in the cabin with Dan was getting flares and rockets ready to be fired if they were engaged. Dan went over to the 0.50-caliber mounted machine gun at the doorway. He checked the weapon was ready.

London's lights glittered brightly under them like a blanket of jewelry. At any other time, the sight would have been beautiful. Now it was ignored.

Dan stared ahead. He nodded to Chloe, who was curled up at the back. She nodded back.

The pilot's voice came in Dan's ear. "Embassy approaching. Instructions to land?"

"Damn right," Dan said. "Hurry up. They are in there already. We are losing time."

Dan listened as the pilot got in touch with air control. They hovered over the Embassy's helipad.

"Alpha Two Zero requesting permission to land, over."

The pilot repeated his message twice before he was answered by the Embassy's air control.

"Identify yourself, Alpha Two Zero."

Dan was on the radio, and he broke in. "My name is Dan Roy. Ex-Delta Force. The Embassy is under attack. I repeat, under attack. A terrorist is inside. His name is Michael Burns, but he could have an alias of Robert Cranmer. He has credentials. Let us land. Repeat, let us land."

The controller was not getting the urgency. He said, "Negative, Alpha Two Zero. What is your authority?"

Dan could have screamed in frustration. But shouting would only make it worse.

"This is an emergency…." Dan continued. The bird did rounds in the air above the Embassy, wasting precious time. Dan groaned inside as the pilot argued for landing with the controller. Below him, he could see a flurry of movement as security guards ran out with their weapons.

That gave him an idea. He told the pilot, "Get me Colonel McBride. Fort Bragg, NC."

Dan chewed his lips as the pilot searched the number. It would be afternoon in Fort Bragg. With any luck, McBride would be in.

An eternity seemed to pass, and sweat poured down Dan's face. He was starting to hate this wait. Then his earphone crackled into life.

"This is Jim McBride. Who the hell is this?"

"Sir, this is Dan Roy. Intercept. We met in Afghanistan, sir."

"Yes, I remember. What's going on, Dan?"

Dan told him as fast as he could. He heard McBride's voice change.

"My God. And you know he is in there?"

"He has to be. The basement would be the best place to plant the CL-20. He'll have it on a timer, and explode it later tonight. He will be far away by then."

"Ok, give me five," McBride said. He hung up.

Another age seemed to pass, while the pilot engaged his radio again. Dan sat there, fists clenched, shaking his head.

Eventually, the controller got back to the pilot. Slowly, the bird began to descend. Dan felt the blood surge in his veins as the *H* sign of the helipad rushed up to meet them. He checked his weapons. Then he waved to Chloe, who nodded at him.

In a flash, Dan realized what was happening.

He was on the most important mission of his life. Failure was not an option.

When the bird was inches from the ground, Dan jumped on the roof of the Embassy.

CHAPTER 41

Dan ran as fast as he could to the rooftop entrance. The door was locked. He pulled out the Colt and fired twice, making the lock snap. He kicked the door open and rushed down the stairwell.

All of a sudden it was quiet. Lights buzzed into life around him. Motion sensors. He was in a sterile, white stairwell, with stairs going straight down. Dan took three at a time.

He was on the tenth floor. On the third floor the doors burst open and Dan raised the MP5, ready to fire. But it was one of the security guards, and another appeared behind him. They pointed their rifles at Dan and screamed. Dan put his rifle down and raised his hands up.

"I came from the bird!" Dan shouted. "The Embassy is under attack." The guards shuffled closer and lowered their weapons when they realized Dan was telling the truth.

"Did you see a black Range Rover come in, say, 30 minutes ago?" Dan demanded. One of the guards spoke on the radio and nodded.

He said, "We are checking the car as we speak."

Dan said, "The guy who came in the car could blow this place sky-high any minute. How many men have you got?"

"We got a team of twenty guarding the property."

Dan said, "Get a team onto the rooftop to guard the bird. They could try to fly it out. You two, come with me to the basement."

They descended rapidly. Apart from the occasional chatter on the radio, the silence around them was getting deeper. As they got to the doors of the basement, Dan motioned to the guards to turn their radios off.

Dan put himself at the front. He motioned with his fingers. He would go first, and the guards would take either side. Dan looked in through the glass panel on the door.

The space outside was a corridor, and it went around in a circle. Dan was first out, heading for the room directly opposite.

This, the guards had told him, was the plant engine room. It housed the boiler machines that plumbed the heating system to the entire property. Next to it they had the room that stored the main electric circuit boards.

Dan nudged the door open with his rifle. It was dark inside, but there was a light source deep inside the room that cast a hazy glow. Dan could see shadows of pipes crossing the ceiling. Large machines hissed steam. Water dripped somewhere, the sound loud in the silence.

He listened, then crept in. Stealthily, he advanced, rifle raised, butt on his shoulder.

The cages of machinery made a maze inside. Behind him, in the distance, he heard muffled shouts, then the unmistakable sound of gun fire. Dan ignored it.

A sixth sense kept moving him forward.

A sudden metallic sound. Like a spanner hitting a metal surface. Dan froze. It was silent again. The sound had come from his right, behind the hump of several dark machines. Light did not reach there.

Dan dropped to the ground. He crawled as fast as he could, to the right, then to the left, dodging the big metal cages. Then he saw it. A black shadow, scurrying behind a corner. Dan got to his feet. Before he could move any further, the darkness was shattered by the ear-splitting sound of automatic gun fire. Bullets whined above his head and kicked up dust around him.

Dan dived backwards and crawled against a cage. The heavy gun fire continued, the rounds falling to his left. He waited for a while, making sure he had the angle of fire correct. Then he got up, and ran to his right, then straight ahead. He would have to box them, and sneak up from behind.

The gun fire was less, and then stopped. Dan came upon a water tank. It was big, and he had to circle around it. He stopped and looked upwards. Electric wires. He looked to the ground around him. He saw cans of oil used to grease the machines. He picked one up and sniffed. Kerosene. Dan felt in his pockets. His Zippo lighter was still with him. He picked up the smaller of the kerosene cans.

Then he continued to box around. Another burst of gunfire. They were worried that Dan was creeping up on them. Their friends were being engaged by the security guards outside.

By firing that weapon, they had given their position away again. Dan surged to the left. He knew exactly where they were, and what he would have to do.

"Dan!"

The loud shout stopped him in his tracks. It was Burns' voice.

"Dan, I know it's you. Answer me."

Dan stayed silent, and moved towards the sound. The light was slightly better now. A bulb glowed in the far corner.

Burns shouted again. "I want to tell you this. This place is going up tonight. You will die, and so will your girlfriend on the roof. Is that what you want, Dan?"

Dan found a machine with ladders by its side. He tested a rung. It took his weight. He climbed up carefully till he could see them. Four of them were crouched next to one of the wooden pallets. He guessed the pallet was full of CL-20, enough explosive to send this building into orbit.

To bring the world to an end.

"I have the trigger in my hand, Dan. Show yourself, unless you want to die."

More sound of muffled gunfire. Dan guessed they had put more of the pallets elsewhere in the basement. The guards had found them.

Dan aimed at the body farthest away from him. At an angle against the wall. If they moved, that would be his first miss.

This MP5 rifle did not have a suppressor. It made a loud bang as the round left the barrel, the sound exploding in the darkness. Dan saw the body slump, and he fired rapidly. The advantage of surprise was gone. He got two of them, but the other two returned fire. Dan ducked his head, but he still had a view and fired back. The third body went down.

One left. He was doing most of the firing. Before Dan could take even partial aim, a bullet streaked close to him, and he flinched. The round slammed into his left shoulder. He felt the sharp, hot burn of metal in his flesh. He cried out, and the gun fell from his hands. He lost his balance on the ladder, and fell backwards heavily.

He landed on his back. Air exploded out of his lungs, and he couldn't breathe all of a sudden. The pain in his left shoulder was excruciating. Black shapes swam before his eyes. Waves of nausea hit him. He put his right hand to the shoulder wound and it came away sticky.

He tried to get up. His left leg gave way, and he fell again. With a superhuman effort, gritting his teeth, he raised himself. Bullets whined above his head. He had lost his rifle in the dark. But he still had the Colt in his back belt.

A round pinged off the metal cage next to him. He crouched down, hand over his head. He needed cover. As he stumbled away, he heard a skittering sound. Something sliding towards him.

He looked down towards his feet, and his worst fears were confirmed.

A flashbang grenade. The cylindrical object was about ten feet away from him.

Adrenaline pulsed into every fiber of his body. His eyes opened wide. From a deep corner inside his soul, the strength of survival ripped apart the darkness and pain.

He *was* a survivor. A warrior.

A shout emanated from his lungs as his legs found purchase on the ground. He was moving, running, flying across. Arms outstretched, he was airborne.

The flashbang lit up the space in an orange and red glow. The sound was cataclysmic, and the explosion caught Dan in its grip, hurling him further away. His shoulder smashed against the corner of a metal grid and he collapsed against the corner.

He couldn't see anything. His ears were ringing. The pain in his head and shoulders was back. He shook his head and tried to crawl. It was useless. His body felt heavy like lead. He lay there, panting.

His fingers touched something wet on the ground. He sniffed his hand. Water had spilled from the water tank.

"Dan." It was Burns. "Don't try to hide, I'm right behind you."

Through a mist of pain and dizziness, Dan craned his neck upwards. He shook his head repeatedly. He could just make out, in the hazy smoke, the thick, electric cables above. He lifted up his gun, and fired. Electric sparks flew in the air. He fired again, and again, till the cables gave away.

The cables swung like sparkling fireworks as they fell to the ground. Dan crawled away.

"Oh, Dan," Burns' voice was playful. "I can see you." Dan wondered how he could see.

Dan felt a kick in his ribs, a blow that sent shards of pain through his body. He grunted and tried to move, but this time the kick came to the side of his head.

Dan fell back, his eyes suddenly black again. There was a roaring sound in his ears, replacing the ringing. He blinked his eyes open. A few feet away, there was a dark shape. A man. He was pointing a gun straight at Dan.

"I have the detonator in my hand, Dan. You might as well know, I'm going to set this thing up for tonight. Sure, I need to give myself some time to get out of here. Then it's time for fireworks."

Dan lifted himself on one elbow. He could not see well; the smoke was still stinging his eyes. But through the haze, he could make out that Burns was wearing a gas mask. Which meant he had perfect vision, and he didn't have to breathe the noxious fumes of the flashbang.

Burns wrenched the gas mask off his face. He said, "I have to give it to you

Dan, you are tenacious. As soon as my men told me a helicopter was hovering overhead, I knew it had to be you. Giving you that beacon was a mistake. Hey, I can correct it now."

Burns smiled. He raised his gun. Sweat was pouring off Dan's head.

He panted, "How could you do this, Burns? How could you become a traitor?"

"Oh please, Dan. You don't think our country plays games? You have no idea."

Dan tried to sit up. "When war breaks out over this, and we die, what about your family, Burns? You don't care about them either?"

Something changed in Burns' face. He came a few steps closer. Dan watched him carefully.

"My family were wiped out in a terrorist attack, Dan. No one did anything. Why the hell should I care?"

Dan needed to keep him talking. "How did they die?"

Burns' face wasn't visible, but the bitterness in his voice radiated across to Dan. "They were in a convoy of SUVs, heading out of Baghdad. Their car got hit by a drone. Wrong intel and wrong target."

"I'm sorry about what happened. I know nothing will bring them back. But think about what you are doing now. You're going to kill us all."

"Sorry?" Burns gave a cold, maniacal laugh that chilled Dan to the bone. "All they said was sorry. No one really cared. No one did anything."

Dan shouted at him, "How can you say no one did anything? Nothing hits the media, no one gets to know. That doesn't mean it's not happening. You of all people should know better."

"I do know better. That's why I've got more money than I will ever need. You will die in this hell hole, while I live like a king. So, fuck you, and everyone else."

"You know what your problem is, Burns?"

Dan shifted back, and Burns stepped forward again, following him with the gun. Dan's right arm was in darkness, but he was gripping something. Something Burns couldn't see.

Burns was right where Dan wanted him. Five feet away from him.

Burns took aim with the gun. He held the detonator in his other hand. He said, "Enough talk, asshole. Time to die. So will your bitch, up on the roof."

"You never knew the importance of your position," Dan said.

Burns frowned. "What did you say?"

"I said, you never knew the importance of your position."
Burns threw his head back and laughed. "What position?"
Dan smiled at him. "Your position now, motherfucker."

CHAPTER 42

Burns was standing over a puddle of water next to the water tank. The water stopped two feet away from Dan. In the shadows, Dan's right hand was gripping one of the electric cables that he had shot down from the ceiling.

In a flash of movement, Dan threw the live electric cable into the puddle of water. The move was unexpected.

Burns did not have time to react.

240 volts of live blue electricity streaked through the water and ignited into Burns' body.

There was a sudden flash of white and blue lightning, then Burns shook like a rag doll. He screamed but the sound died in his throat. His body glowed, bolts of blue flashing through his legs, arms, eventually lighting up his face.

But he had already fired his gun. It was a reflex shot when he saw Dan move. Dan had recoiled as soon as he threw the wire, but the bullet still hit him. It was a wild shot, and it grazed his lower leg. He felt the hot burn of metal again, and he rolled away as fast as he could.

He looked up at the ghastly scene before him. The last blue sparks were still flying off the top of Burns' head. His hair was charred and sticking up straight. The smell of burned flesh floated into Dan's nose. Burns stood standing for a few seconds more, a look of utter incomprehension on his destroyed and burned face.

Then he dropped to his knees and fell forward, face down in the puddle of water. His body jerked as flashes of electricity still pulsed through him.

There was a sound at the doorway. Dan looked up. He pointed his gun, and lifted himself on one knee, then the other. He managed to stand up. The last wound was a minor graze injury. He gripped the gun in his right hand, wincing at the pain in his left shoulder.

A loud voice shouted, "Who's in there?"

A terrorist would not announce his arrival. Dan shouted back, "It's Dan Roy. I came in the bird."

Running feet, and one of the security guards came into view, rifle raised at his shoulder. He stopped when he saw the scene in front of him.

"Jesus Christ," he said.

Dan said, "Turn off the electric mains. You know where they are?"

The man nodded and ran off. Dan heard the electricity wind down with a hum. The shooting blue sparks from the wire faded, then died completely.

Dan stood in the darkness with the gun in his hand, listening hard to the sound of silence.

Strobes of flashlight danced in the air. It was the security guards again.

Dan directed them away from the scene, and towards where he had seen the wooden pallet. They found the explosives and secured them.

Dan walked around the rest of the basement with the guards, looking at all the other pallets. They were stacked full of CL-20 explosives. He shuddered inside when he thought of the mayhem this would have created.

It would have resulted in World War III.

The pain was surging through his body and his headache had returned. His shoulder and leg were bleeding. He rode the elevator up to the roof. The bird had powered down, its rotors still in the night air.

Chloe jumped down and ran towards him. She put an arm under his shoulder and helped him up into the cabin. The technician put a bandage on his wounds while Chloe fed him some painkillers.

Dan hooked himself onto the comms channel. McBride's voice crackled in his ears.

"SitRep, Dan."

"Threat neutralized. Evacuation in process. Over and out."

Dan took the headphones off his ears. The pilot fired up the engine. The rotors whined into a deafening sound and dust flew up around them. The bird's nose dipped as it gathered speed, then it rose vertically up in the air, flying over the night lights of London once again.

*****

Sun streamed in through the huge windows of Heathrow Airport. The massive, black nose of a Boeing 777-300 Jumbo jet gleamed in the sun outside the window, several feet away from where Chloe and Dan were sitting.

Chloe's hands were in Dan's. They all but disappeared inside his large palm. She stroked the rough surface of his knuckles. Dan lifted up her hand and kissed it gently. Dan's left arm was in a sling, supporting his shoulder.

Chloe said, "What about your job?"

Dan shook his head. "I retired already. This was always going to be a one-off, and now it's over."

"What will you do?"

"Just get on the road. See where it takes me."

Chloe looked down at their entwined hands. Dan put his right arm around her shoulders.

"Hey," he said. They had talked about this. Dan needed to get out of London, and sort out his affairs back home in Bethesda, West Virginia.

Intercept had agreed to let him go. He had his last meeting with McBride and another man he did not recognize, but whose aura of real power put McBride in the pale. They had listened to him, looked at the evidence, and absolved him of any wrongdoing.

Now, he was free. Free from the life he had led for so many years. Free from the relentless cycles of combat and training. He longed to be on the road.

Chloe could not come. She had her own life in London. But they would always be friends. Chloe had been the best thing that had happened to him in a long time. She had made him feel human again. He would never be able to express what that meant to him. She knew regardless, and that was all he cared about.

The last call for the flight to Dulles Airport came on the PA. Dan stood, and picked up his backpack. The only piece of luggage he possessed.

They embraced. He saw tears in her eyes, and he wiped them with his fingers. Then he kissed her on the forehead, feeling a lump in his throat.

He walked to the end of the line, limping on his left leg. Then looked back. Chloe was standing there.

He waved, and she waved back.

Dan ducked into the passage that took him into the plane. He sat down and closed his eyes, feeling a pain behind them. Eventually the plane took off.

He stared at England, the green isle spread out below him. Then he looked ahead. The plane was streaking through the clouds.

Somewhere out there, far away from all the madness, lay his freedom. He did not know if he was going to find it, but at least he was free to try.

THE END

DARK WATER

Dan Roy Series
Dan Roy Thriller 2

PROLOGUE

South west Atlanta
Georgia, USA

Vyalchek Ivanov, nickname Val, wondered if he should start torturing his captive now. The man was a whimpering mess already. He looked sick, eyes sunken, his forehead covered in sweat. A pallid crimson colored his cheeks, but otherwise the man's face was white as a sheet. He wore a suit two sizes too big on him. It had been a nice suit once, but now the elbows were threadbare, the cuffs frayed. His prominent Adam's apple bobbed over the loose collar.

Val controlled himself with an effort. The man didn't know who he was. It was better that way. He was a businessman, looking to complete a deal. Val tried to smile and spread his hands.

"Mr Longworth, I thought we had a deal."

The man swallowed and opened his mouth, then closed it, like a fish out of water. He looked at the three men at the table next to them. Val's men. His *Bratok*. They all wore suits and had their eyes fixed on the door. Apart from the five of them, the restaurant was empty. It belonged to one of the *Bratok's* cousins. A safe place to conduct business. A waiter appeared, discreetly clearing up dishes at a table before going into the kitchen, avoiding everyone's eyes.

"Are... are these men with you?" Philip Longworth finally spoke, his voice weak. He sniffed and wiped his nose with the back of his hand.

"They are my colleagues, yes." Val regarded the man with distaste. What was he putting up his nose?

"What did you say your business was again?"

Val leaned forward slightly. Vyalchek had an imposing presence. Six four and two hundred and twenty pounds, blond hair with high cheekbones and light grey eyes. Eyes that were dull, dead. Utterly devoid of feeling.

"Mr Longworth. We have been through this already. I represent a client. Our common friend has put us in contact. My client wishes to use your expertise to further his business. As proof of your abilities, he would like to know the location of the job you are currently doing." Val sat back in his chair, not wishing to intimidate the man further. There would enough scope for that later. He held his finger up. "Make no mistake, my client is a big player in your field of work. A very big player. He would compensate you handsomely."

"How much?"

"Name your price."

Longworth looked around like he expected a grizzly bear to come out from a corner and jump on him. He caught the eyes of one of the men, who looked back at him dispassionately.

"Uh… I…"

"How about a hundred grand for starters?" Val said.

Longworth stared at him like there was a halo around his head. "A hundred grand?"

"To start with. When we check the information, if it's all there, another hundred."

Longworth was silent for a second, considering something. "How about five hundred grand, all in one go, when I get you the information?"

Val took a deep breath. *Pashli na khui*, he thought to himself. Longworth wasn't stupid. He cursed again in silence. The man looked like a junkie. Hell, he *was* a junkie—but he had brains, somehow figuring how badly Val needed this.

If this deal went down, the whole of the *Bratva* would know Val's name. Never mind the US of A. Never mind the Russkies of Brighton Beach. His name would spread to *Moskva*. To the *Krasni Ploshad*. Inside the Kremlin. For the first time he would have political connections. Real power. He took a sip of water and kept his face impassive.

"A hundred grand. That is all you are getting. You give us the information and you get the rest."

"If I give you the information and you vanish, who will I chase after?" Longworth indicated the other three men. "Your colleagues here? I don't even know the name or identity of your client. You tell me, what security do I have that you won't just vanish with the information?"

Val narrowed his eyes. "Is that why you did not bring the drive with you today?"

Longworth nodded. "Understand my position. I'm a sole operator. If I sell you the goods, and you're not happy, you can come after me. So I don't want to sell you a dud. But if I give you the goods and wait for the money, I have no guarantee that you'll pay." He coughed and the spasm became a prolonged bout. He pulled out a handkerchief and wheezed into it. He wiped his face, mucus trailing from his lips. Val looked away in disgust. He made a pretense of checking his platinum Rolex Daytona. It was 9:30 p.m.

He asked Longworth, "Are you alright?"

"Thank you for your concern. Yes, I am."

Val lifted his chin. Was the asshole being sarcastic? He sighed. It didn't matter. "Listen to me. I can give one hundred in cash right now. In hundred dollar bills. Totally legit money. We can pick you up tomorrow, like we did today. You must have the hard drive tomorrow. When we have it, we check it on a laptop here." Val was stabbing his finger on the table. "If it's all good, then you have the remaining money."

"I want four hundred."

"What?"

Longworth made a sound like he was choking. He cleared his throat and swallowed noisily. Val grimaced.

"Four hundred tomorrow on delivery. Otherwise, I don't want your money."

"If I say no?"

"Then the deal is off." Longworth put his hat on and got up slowly. Val didn't move a muscle. He glanced sideways at one of his *Bratok*, who stood up to get in Longworth's face. The man had a barrel chest, and his jacket moved to reveal the gun inside a shoulder holster. Longworth stopped, alarmed.

"Who *are* you guys?"

"You can ask your friend. I just want to know if we have a deal or not?"

"For four hundred on delivery, yes we do."

Val shut his eyes a moment. A few choice Russian phrases came to his mind. "Okay. Four hundred, if we can check it here on delivery tomorrow. There will be a map, yes?"

Longworth nodded. "Yes, there will be. I want the hundred now."

Val reached inside his jacket. Longworth's eyes bulged in fear for a second, then calmed when he saw the key. Val who motioned to one of his men and gave him the key. The man reached a hand underneath the table and pulled out a briefcase. He unlocked it, snapped it open and put the briefcase in front of Longworth.

Val eyed Longworth closely. "It's all in there. You can count it if you want."

Longworth raised his eyes to Val. "I'm sure it's all there." Val did not change his expression.

Longworth coughed. "Do you mind if I use the bathroom?"

Val gestured to another of his *Bratok*, as broad as the last one. "He will show you."

"Thanks."

They walked to the rear of the restaurant. The place was small, about thirty tables laid out in a square formation. A sign outside said, "St Petersburg, Authentic Russian Cuisine". The interior was simple, red and blue curtains hanging above windows with neon lights. A selection of Russian dolls adorned the main counter. Longworth and the man moved through a beaded curtain at the back. Val sat, tapping the desk with his fingers.

There was a crashing sound, then a shout from the rear. A car engine roared, tires screeching. More shouts. Val was up and out the front door before any of his men, his 0.357 Smith and Wesson in his hand. He ran around the corner just in time to see a blue car, belching smoke, take a right at the end of the road. The *Bratok* supposed to guard Longworth came running, pointing at a window.

"He opened the bathroom window and jumped. Jesus Christ. The car was waiting for him. He planned the whole thing!"

Val turned on him, his face a mask of hatred. His fist lashed out, making solid connection with the man's chin. The *Bratok* stumbled backwards. Val punched him in the head again and the man went down. Snarling with fury, Val began kicking until the face was a mess of blood and bone.

Then he aimed his gun at the unmoving body and squeezed the trigger twice. The man's body jerked as the rounds slammed into it. Val swung the gun towards the other men, who stepped back.

"Find him!" Val screamed. "Or all of you are dead!"

CHAPTER 1

North Bethesda, Virginia
Present day

Dan Roy stood with his head bowed.

The little cemetery faced the church. It was August, and high above, white clouds sailed in a silent blue sky. The church was pretty, with a spire rising above the green trees hanging around it. Around him, Dan could hear the chirping of birds. Up here, there was no sound of traffic. He was alone in the cemetery.

Every year, he made this journey. For him, it was a pilgrimage. He kneeled, and put the two bouquets of flowers by the two gravestones that stood side by side. Rita and Duncan Roy. His parents. They had given him the best life they could. It seemed like a long time ago.

The sadness he got used to, but the sense of loss was ever present. A chasm that would never be filled. He arranged the flowers around, and touched the gravestones.

Dan whispered, "Words will never express how much I miss you."

He touched his hands on the gravestones and kept them there for a while. It felt cold. He swallowed hard, and felt the sting behind his eyes. He got up, turned around and left.

It was the only emotion he allowed himself. Years in the Delta Force, and then in black ops for Intercept, had made him an automaton. A fighting machine. The best that Intercept, one of the most powerful black ops outfits, had in their possession.

But a machine nevertheless. Deployed globally, working solo, and at short notice. There was never time for himself, or his own thoughts. He came here once every year, in rain, snow and sunshine. Somehow, it allowed him to heal, and to feel a peace.

Some things in life lasted for ever.

*****

Dan got into his car and roared down the highway. His hands gripped the steering wheel lightly. As he drove, his dark eyes glanced at the rear-view, checking out the cars driving behind him.

As the Virginia countryside flashed by, he wondered what direction his life would take in the future. He was in the process of selling his parents` house in Bethesda. Once that was done, the last physical bond he had would disappear. He was free to go where he wanted.

It was not merely new vistas that he wanted to see. He wanted to open new doors in his mind too. Look at the world with new eyes. Constant violence had wrapped a wintry cloak around his soul.

He *was* a man of violence, he could not deny that. But he was also a human being. One with sorrow, regrets, happiness like everyone else. For too long, he had been forced to operate like a machine. A part of him liked that. It was who he was. But another part of him wanted…wanted some warmth. Some life.

That process had started in London, two months ago. But it had not lasted long. He had been framed for a crime he did not commit, and the true perpetrator had killed his old commanding officer. Like a crazed bull, Dan had fought back.

That had been the final break. Intercept had agreed to let him go. He needed to have one last meeting with the man who had become his new handler. A man called McBride, but he suspected that might not be his real name. It did not matter. McBride possessed real power in the corridors of the Pentagon, and in Capitol Hill. Like most of the handlers of Intercept did.

Dan drove down south from Arlington. Straight down the I-95, and to a town adjacent to Fort Belvoir. He drove past the Davison Airfield, a military airport he had taken flights from in the past. He felt a familiar tightness in his stomach. That pre-mission coiling of the limbs. The smell of impending combat.

He would miss it. It was what he did. He was a warrior, and always would be. Dan parked the car on the street where was due to meet McBride. After five minutes of waiting, he saw two black Ford SUV`s park at the end of the street. Dan watched them park, and turn their lights off.

He got out and stretched his six feet, two-hundred-and-twenty-pound frame. The width of his shoulders and chest accounted for most of that. He locked his car, then approached the second of the two SUV`s. The door slid open. Inside, he saw an older man, in his late fifties. His salt and pepper hair was brushed back neatly. He was dressed in a black suit, which seemed to be the unofficial uniform for Intercept employees. Only, McBride was much more than an employee. It was rumoured he was high up in the Pentagon.

Dan would never know his real identity, and he did not care.

More than anything, Dan wanted to be free.

"Close the door, Dan," McBride said.

Dan sat down next to him. The older man said, "Sorry to hear you are leaving. Any particular reason?"

Dan said, "Nothing particular."

"I am sorry about Guptill, too. I know he was your CO."

Dan did not say anything. John Guptill had been Dan's handler in Intercept, and his mentor when he had joined Squadron B, SFOD-D, as the Delta Forces were known. Last year, Guptill had been killed. Dan had found the killer.

Dan did not mind risking his life. Hell, he lived for it. But he wasn't so crazy about the games intelligence agencies and politicians played. Those games wrecked lives.

McBride leaned forward. His slate grey eyes were steely. "You know this is your exit interview, right?"

Dan nodded. Every Intercept agent had one. They were held to a code of silence so strict, any break of it resulted in certain death. Not just death. A disappearance. The bodies were never found.

For the next half hour, Dan answered questions about his motives and future plans. At the end, McBride leaned back. He opened the window. He clipped the end of a cigar and lit it up. There was a sign in the car that said no smoking, but not many people told McBride what he could or could not do.

Dan liked that about him.

Between puffs of fragrant tobacco, McBride said, "Head out to the south. Georgia or Florida. Catch some rays."

Dan said, "I'll think about it."

"Hey, as part of your bonus, we'll get you a one-way flight."

They had talked about money already. A healthy seven figure sum. The price paid for conducting the most dangerous, and deniable missions in hotspots around the world.

And the price of silence.

Dan made for the door. "Like I said, I'll think about it."

CHAPTER 2

Val Ivanov looked out the tinted windows of his Cadillac as the car smoothly pulled up outside the warehouse in Marietta. The capital of Cobb county, northwest of Atlanta, and prime Mexican gang land. A gang called Z9, or Zapato 9 as they were better known, had called for this meeting. Val hadn't agreed initially until he heard their request. It was of mutual benefit. Besides, alliances between the *Bratva* and the large Mexican gangs weren't uncommon. In California, Nevada, Texas, all the way down to Florida, wise guys had to work with Mexican gangs. They ruled the turf. They were well-organized and by sheer numbers they threatened everybody. Working with them opened up multiple revenue pathways. Something the Cosa Nostra hadn't learnt yet. Alliances between the Sicilians and Mexicans were rare. Well, Val thought, their mistake was his opportunity.

Val glanced at the *Bratok* next to him. Artin was his personal bodyguard. He was lightning quick with a Glock, and equally skilled with an AK-74. He had saved Val's life more than once.

"How many men at the back?" Val asked.

"Three. And three opposite the front and sides. We have the place surrounded. Anything happens to us, no one leaves alive."

Another Cadillac stopped in front and four of his men were out, stretching. None wore suits today, including Val. He was pleased with the precautions they had taken, but he knew the Mexicans wouldn't try anything. They didn't want to start a war. It interrupted business and helped no one.

The front door of the warehouse opened and a Hispanic kid stepped out. His forearms were covered in tattoos. Indigo, maroon and blue, with Latin inscriptions. A gun was stuck in plain view in his belt. He waved at them. Val waited until Artin got out the other side, came to his door and opened it. It was good to make an entrance. He was a *Pakhan*, after all. A general, a godfather. Eight cells under his control in Atlanta and Jacksonville. Damn right he was going to make an entrance.

Val stepped out eventually, dwarfing the other men around him. They knew the drill. Two stood to either side of him, one in front, the rest at the back. In that formation, they approached the lone gang member. Val had to duck inside the door as one of his men held it open.

It was a darker inside, but light streamed in through the windows on the roof. Val guessed the gang used this warehouse as a meeting point. It was clean and well-maintained. A stairway went around the sides, circling the perimeter. He spotted two men with rifles. In the middle of the floor, a table had been laid out with simple wooden chairs. Four men sat around it. All of them looked older than the kid who greeted them. From their late twenties to early forties, he guessed. The man in the middle wore a red bandana and he seemed the oldest. At the back there was an open door with another gang member standing guard.

Val approached the four men, who stood up. The man with the red bandana was the first to shake his hand.

"Manolo," Val said. Manolo Estefan. A mid-ranking captain who was making moves for the top. Val pointed at the armed men above.

"You expecting trouble?"

"Only if it`s coming our way," Manolo said, his hard, glittering black eyes not leaving Val`s face. The men on either sides of him started to look around. Val`s men had formed a loose semi-circle around him.

Val shrugged. "Putting snipers around us is not a great way to start a meeting."

"Do you expect me to believe you have not surrounded the place with your own men?"

They stared at each other in silence. Above them, there was a soft clicking sound. Safety catches on rifles being released. It all happened very quickly. In a blur of movement, men had their guns out. There was a shout from the back, and the snipers leaned over the rails with their rifles trained.

Val shook his head, his face blank. "You start this, Manolo, we go all the way. It never stops. I promise you."

Manolo smiled. "This is our territory. If all of us spit on you, you will drown."

"Won`t matter to you, if you`re dead. You know who I am. I don't make empty threats."

"My boys are angry. The gringo robbed them."

"Then let`s talk business."

Manolo stared at him for another second, then signaled to his men. The guns were lowered slowly.

"Stand down," Val told Artin. He sat down, while his men stood behind him. The four Mexicans sat down facing him.

"Tell me what the gringo has done to you."

"Half a kilo of coca has gone. The gringo was selling for us. He never paid us. He was going to turn up with the money. He never did."

Val breathed out. Philip Longworth had guts. Taking on the Z9. And now the *Bratva*. Well, he was going to pay for it.

"What has he done to you?" Manolo asked. Val told him.

Manolo said, "What do we do now?"

Val shifted in his chair. Damn thing was uncomfortable. "We start with his house. Ransack the place. Top to bottom. Your half kilo might well be there hidden."

And maybe what we need as well, he thought to himself.

Manolo nodded. "Let's do it."

CHAPTER 3

The woman in front of Dan stumbled over her suitcase. Dan leaned forward and picked it up for her. She had been in the seat next to him in the flight from Washington Dulles to Atlanta. Her dark hair was tied back in a ponytail. Her skin was tanned from the sun, and she had brown eyes. In her fifties, he guessed. She had bags under her eyes, and looked tired.

Hartsfield-Jackson airport was busy. The air conditioning was keeping the place cool, but Dan knew it was hot outside. High eighties, he reckoned from the sun that beamed in through the windows. They had just taken their luggage off the conveyor belt when the woman had slipped. Dan had his usual single rucksack. All his belongings in one place.

The woman said, "Thank you."

"No problem," Dan said. The woman flashed him a tired smile, then went on her way towards the exit. Dan followed at a more leisurely pace. Although the airport pulsed with activity, Dan was relaxed. It was his first holiday in years. Intercept worked very much like Delta Forces – when not deployed he had to undertake constant training and mock battles. This time, he would go where he wanted to, and just drift as far down south as he could. All the way to the Florida Keys. He was looking forward to it.

He came outside, and felt the heat hit him immediately. The sun was blinding. He wiped sweat off his forehead. Should have got a handkerchief. Hell, it felt like he needed a sweatband. Must be in the mid-nineties at least, he thought. His cream T-shirt—he had deliberately chosen a light color— was sticking to his back like a second skin. He passed a billboard where the date, time and weather were displayed. Ninety-four degrees. Seventy-two percent humidity.

He walked to the queue for cabs. While he was waiting, he looked opposite, where car drivers were picking up their loved ones. Hugs and hellos. Something Dan had never experienced. Apart from his parents he had no family. He had always travelled alone.

As he watched, he noticed the same woman standing at the far corner. Near the edge of the sidewalk with her suitcase, like she was waiting for someone. She looked in Dan's direction, and their eyes met. Then she looked away.

He saw the snout of a tan Chevrolet sedan appear around the corner. The car stopped in front of the woman. She did not move. Dan saw a tall blonde man step out. He was dressed in a suit. His movements were slow and deliberate. Two other men stepped out from the back. Also in suits. Shorter, but wider, with bulges of shoulder holsters at their armpits. Their eyes darted around, looking at cars, people.

Dan knew bodyguards when he saw them. The tall blond man towered over the woman, who seemed to shrink away from him. He spoke to her, and Dan could see her shaking her head. The tall man said something again, which drew the same response. One of the bodyguards was standing behind the woman. The driver was in the car, engine running, and the kerbside back door was open.

It happened in a flash. That corner of the sidewalk was empty. No one noticed.

The bodyguard clamped a meaty hand over the woman's face. He almost lifted her up, and propelled her inside the back seat. Before she disappeared inside the car, she raised her head. She looked up and met Dan's eyes once more. For the briefest of seconds. But enough to communicate a vital message.

Help me.

The trunk was opened and the woman's suitcase was chucked inside. With a slam of doors and a screech of tires, the sedan took off towards the exit.

Dan had a split second to decide his next course of action. He had the choice of not doing anything. But if he did, then, potentially, the vortex of death and violence would open for him again.

Dan was almost at the head of the queue. There was a guy ahead of him. A single man. Dan acted quickly. As the cab drew up, Dan pushed the man to one side.

"Hey", the man shouted, as he stumbled to the side.

Dan said, "I'm sorry, but there's an emergency."

The man had fallen over, and he was scrambling to his feet as Dan got inside the cab and slammed the door shut.

"Drive, now," he said to the driver. The cab pulled out, and the man Dan had pushed to one side stood up, shouting and shaking his fist.

The driver looked at Dan in the rear view. "Lookin' for someone, mister?"

"Yes. A tan sedan. Chevrolet. Took the downtown exit."

"I'm on it," said the driver. Dan kept a look out the window. Several cars had slowed down ahead, looking for the right turn to take. Dan's driver zipped around them expertly. Soon he pointed up ahead.

"Tan sedan, three cars up on left lane."

Dan followed his gaze and saw the car. The same one with the woman in it. He could see the shape of the two bodyguards on either side with someone in between.

"Stay on this lane and follow them," Dan said.

"No sweat," said the driver. "You an undercover cop?"

"If I was I couldn't tell you, could I?"

The man smiled in the rear-view mirror. "Cool."

Traffic seemed to be flowing okay. They passed industrial estates, then lush grasslands on either side. They probably belonged to the colleges. Farther north, in the distance he could see the shining towers of downtown winking in the sunlight. They passed Georgia State University. Traffic began to get heavier as they approached downtown.

The sedan took a turn soon. Dan`s driver waited and then followed. This part of downtown did not seem so salubrious. Derelict buildings stood on either side. Shopping trolleys and trash cans littered the small green parks. They drove through till they came to an intersection. They stopped at a warehouse, and the gates opened. The sedan drove in. Dan`s cab had stopped at the mouth of the street. Dan waited for ten seconds after the gates shut. He paid the driver with a fifty-dollar bill and got out.

"Keep the change," Dan said, when the driver wound the window down.

"You be careful, pal," the driver said. He drove off. Dan hitched both straps of the rucksack on his back. He stood for a while against a disused shop awning. The walls of the warehouse were two metres tall. Inside he could see the steel roof of the main building. The warehouse was used, but it had no signs in front. There was a path going around the back.

Dan headed for the path. He took a trash can and turned it around, emptying it. Then he used it to stand up on the back wall of the warehouse. No barbed wire. There was a row of short spikes, but he could climb over that easily. He looked over. Six feet fall, roughly. A cluster of refuse sacks below. He would fall on them, that would mask the sound. Was there an alarm? If there was, it might be off in daytime. He would have to take that chance. Against the main warehouse building, he could see the parked sedan. It was empty.

Dan lifted himself up, and pushed himself on the wall. He vaulted over the spikes, sailing through air. His arm was to land on his feet, but roll over quickly so his feet did not take whole impact. He landed on the black refuse sacks. He slid down and was on his feet quickly. Two smaller outbuildings flanked the main warehouse. He noticed the cameras on either side of the warehouse, facing front and back. He was being watched. Not much he could do about that.

Dan flitted across the courtyard like a shadow. He was against the door of the warehouse. It was a glass double door, and it did not seem locked. He crouched against the side wall. No one came in or out. Staying crouched, Dan pushed the glass door and went inside. There was a lobby, with a desk, but it was dark. A door at the end which led to main atrium of the warehouse. Dan crawled forward on his hands and knees.

He came against the door and lifted his head up to peek in the glass panel. Suddenly, something was jammed against his back. The muzzle of a gun.

"Stay quiet," a voice said. "Get your hands in the air."

CHAPTER 4

Dan stood very still. He had been listening out for movement, but this guy had been very quiet. He was good.

The voice said with more menace, "Get your fucking hands up. Or I shoot."

Slowly Dan lifted his hands up. He felt himself being patted down. Dan listened hard. He turned his head sideways. He could not see anyone. The lights were off but there was sunlight coming from outside. Enough to afford visibility. The man was on his own. While he was searching Dan, he had moved his gun from Dan's back. He was bending down on his knees, searching Dan's legs for a concealed weapon.

His own weapon was in the air. Dan had a second, maybe two. It was all the time Dan needed. He kicked out backwards, the heel of his boot catching the man's gun arm. The movement was totally unexpected. The man grunted as his arm was thrown back. In the same movement, Dan turned sideways and fell on top of the man.

He saw Dan coming, and raised the gun. But Dan was quicker, and he had gravity on his side. Their bodies collided, and Dan reached for the gun arm. His fingers curled around the man's wrist, and smashed it against the floor. Dan felt a sharp punch land against his right ribs. The blow was vicious, but Dan ignored it. He lifted up the gun wrist and smashed it down on the carpeted floor again. The gun flew out of the man's hand.

Before the man could punch again, Dan had drawn his right arm back. He crashed it down with a straight punch aimed at the jaw. The man's head snapped sideways. He reached his arm up and tried to hook his fingers into Dan's eyes. Dan felt the nails scrape his cheek. He lifted himself up and straddled the man on his chest. Two quick blows, using both fists, rocked the man's head from side to side like a rag doll. Dan felt bone crunch against the jaws, and the body became still.

Dan came off him, and picked up the gun. A Colt M191. He checked the rounds. Six left. He slid back the safety and approached the door again. Three men inside. The bodyguards. He couldn't see the tall blond guy. The woman was in the middle. She was tied to a chair. One of the men was talking to her.

The other two stood to the side. Dan craned his neck up. A steel cage walkway went around the perimeter. It was empty. There was no one else inside.

Dan looked behind. This guy would wake up soon. Then it would be four against one, minimum. He had to act now. He pushed open the door a fraction. He went to the floor and slowly crawled out.

The woman saw him first. The man talking to her followed her gaze. With a shout, he reached for his shoulder holster. He did not get the chance to draw it. Dan fired, double tapping the man on the face. His head exploded into a geyser of blood and bone, and some of the tissue fell on the woman. She screamed.

Four rounds left. No margin for error.

The other two men had turned. One of them was half pointing his gun at Dan, when the slug tore into him. It hit him on the neck, and he went down. The gun fired, the round going high in the air. Dan could not kill him now, while the other guy had enough time to take his weapon out and aim.

The sound of the unsuppressed weapons were like small explosions. Another loud bang, and a piece of wood inches from Dan's face flew off the door. Dan rolled over, knowing the man would have to re aim for him. He came up shooting. His aim was off as a result. He caught the man in the shoulder with the first round, spinning him backwards. He screamed, and tried to fire again, but this time Dan shot him between the eyes. He toppled back and fell with a crash. Dan had turned his weapon already to the remaining guy. He was still twitching. His arm still held the weapon.

All of six seconds had elapsed since Dan fired the first shot.

Dan walked over calmly. He ignored the woman, who was staring at him with open eyes. He kicked the gun away from the man's hand. The bullet had gone through the side of the neck and come out the other side. It had severed the man's cervical spinal cord in the neck. He was trying to move, but all he could do was twitch. Dan bent down over him.

"Who do you work for?" he asked.

The man's eyes were glazed. They looked at Dan without seeing. Dan had seen the look before. Brainstem death. The man could not speak if he tried. Death would come soon as the lungs stopped inflating.

Dan walked over to the door. The man was still out cold. Dan slapped him on the cheek. Hard, twice. Still out cold. He fished around in his pockets. He found a six inch K bar knife in the front belt. He took it, and walked back to the woman. He cut through her ropes quickly. The woman finally found her voice.

"Who are you?" she gasped. Dan was leaning over the guy, frisking him. He stood up, having found nothing.

"We need to get out of here, quickly." Dan ran over to the remaining body and searched. Apart from another Colt he found nothing. He grabbed the older woman's hand. She came willingly. They crossed over the guy who was out cold on the reception floor.

The sedan was open. "Get in," Dan said. The keys were in the ignition. He fired the engine. He took the two Colts out, and put one between his legs on the car seat. He checked the other one – five rounds left. He gave it to the woman.

He asked, "You fired a gun before?"

"No."

"Just hold the butt, don't touch the trigger. Get your head below the window. Give me the gun when I ask for it."

Dumbly, the woman nodded. Dan turned the sedan and approached the gate. As he had expected, the steel gates slid open into a recess in the walls. Dan drove out fast.

CHAPTER 4

"Where do you live?" Dan asked the woman. They were in downtown traffic now, and she was sitting up straighter. Dan kept a look out in all directions as he drove. He did not get an answer from her.

He said, "Hey. Are you ok?"

The woman was staring ahead, and she turned at his voice. Dan saw the fear in her eyes. She swallowed and said, "Yes, uh, I`m fine."

"What`s your name?"

"Jody. Jody Longworth."

"Jody where do you live?"

She pressed her hands against her forehead. "Up from downtown. Towards Virginia Highlands. Just head north."

Dan checked the signs. He was headed in the right direction. He gave Jody a few minutes. Traffic was light in the midmorning hour.

Then he said, "My name is Dan Roy."

The woman sniffed into a piece of tissue, and nodded. "Hi, Dan."

"Why were those men after you?"

Jody did not reply for several seconds. Then she said, "It`s a long story. I…" She looked at Dan. "I don't even know who you are."

Just someone who has habit of getting into trouble, Dan thought to himself.

Out loud, he said, "Just here on vacation."

"Vacation, huh?"

"Yeah."

"Where did you learn to shoot like that?"

Dan said, "I used to be in the army."

Jody was silent. Dan was wondering if they should head to the nearest police station. He never had much luck with police. They would not believe him, and probably arrest him. He never carried any creds. With Intercept, he was not *allowed* any creds. Still, the police would give the woman some safety.

He said, "Maybe we should go to the cops."

The look of fear returned on the woman`s eyes. "No," she shook her head.

"You scared of those guys?"

Jody was silent again. Dan sneaked a glance at her. Her face was lowered and her hands were knotted on her lap. He tried a different approach.

He asked, "Have you ever seen these guys before?"

Jody pointed with her hand. "It's this turning up here," she said.

Dan indicated and said, "You didn't answer my question."

"Like I said, long story."

"Must be, for them to grab you the way they did."

Jody did not answer. Dan drove up a narrow, secluded road, following the signs for Virginia Highlands.

"This is me," Jody said, and Dan pulled to a stop outside a house set way back from the road. Jody opened the passenger door and got out. She shut it gently and looked at Dan.

She said, "Listen Dan, I really appreciate what you did back there. I don't know how to thank you. Would you like to come in for a cup of coffee?"

The front lawn was overgrown. The letterbox was bare. Jody must have emptied it recently. The house was modern, what realtors liked calling the Bauhaus style. It had a wooden front that matched the surrounding tall trees. A balcony with a glass railing ran around the top floor. The curtains were open, the garage door shut. Pine trees creaked high above. It smelled of musk, earth and acorns. It was very quiet. Similar houses on either side. Some bigger, some smaller.

The street was deserted. Dan watched the pine trees move in the breeze. Funny, seeing pine trees in Atlanta. Planted in this suburban neighborhood for effect. The thick branches brushed against the distant blue sky, pulling white clouds in their wake.

Dan said, "I don't want to impose on you. You have family in there?"

A shadow passed over Jody's face. "Not now, no. My husband is away right now."

Dan said, "Well, guess I'll leave you to it, then."

Jody turned to him. "No, honestly, it's no problem. You must want some coffee, right?"

Dan nodded. "I could use a cup of coffee."

Jody gave him a tired smile. "Of course. Come on in."

She opened the car door and stepped out. Dan did the same and locked the car. Jody was standing by the car, looking around her. Not normal behavior for someone who'd just got home, Dan thought. He walked around the front of the car.

Dan said, "You ok, Jody?"

She had that look on her face again. The frightened, hunted look.

"Yes, fine. Come on." She started to walk up the brick path in the front garden. She looked left and right. Dan walked behind her, watching the movements. Jody went up to the front door and paused. A brown oakwood front door. Thick and heavy. Jody hesitated for a few seconds, then dug into her pocket, searching for a key.

While she was doing that, Dan stepped to the side and peered in through the living room window. He stopped short.

"Jody," he called out. She flinched at her name being called.

Dan said, "Don't open the door."

CHAPTER 5

Jody tiptoed over, and joined Dan by the window. The room was clearly visible through a gap in the curtains. Without saying anything, Dan pointed.

The room was large, thirty by twenty feet. L-shaped comfortable sofas were arranged around a flat screen TV. The TV was face-down on the carpet. The sofas had their cushions removed and it looked like someone had taken a knife and sliced round the edges. Foam spilled out on the threadbare carpet. Framed photos from the wall had been taken down and smashed on the floor.

Dan could feel Jody shivering next to him. Her hand was at her throat. "Oh my God," she said. Her voice trembled. Dan gave her the car keys.

He spoke in a gentle voice. "Go and sit down in the car Jody. I wanna take a look around."

Jody did not seem to hear him. She was looking at the scene inside, transfixed.

"Oh my God," she repeated. Dan had not lived in a home for most of his adult life. He wondered what it was like coming home to see it trashed like this. He grabbed her elbow. He guided her back to the car. She walked down without saying a word.

Dan left her in the car, took the house keys from her, and walked back up to the front door.

He checked the window and door frames. No sign of forced entry.

To the left of the front garden, there was a path that went around to the rear. Dan walked around the house. The kitchen had cabinet doors on the walls above the sink and on the sides, all open, plates smashed on the floor. Dan picked up his pace.

Bi-folding doors opened up the kitchen and dining area into the patio. He stood on the patio and looked out at the garden. It was smaller than he had imagined. Maybe the front lawn took up too much of the land. The pine trees continued in the back, screening the end of the garden. It was similar for all the houses.

He went back around to the front door, unlocked it and gently pushed it open, listening intently. No sound, apart from the pine trees swaying in the breeze. If there was someone still in there, they were being mighty quiet.

He stepped in. The alarm didn't go off. He had expected that. It only reinforced his heightened state of awareness. His hand went to his beltline automatically, but he did not have a weapon with him. Not even his kukri knife.

Silence around him still. He crept down the hallway. He didn't go into the living room. Straight ahead, the staircase, and the entrance to the kitchen. He bent his knees, lowering himself to offer a smaller target if someone emerged from the kitchen. On his tiptoes, he went forward. The floorboards had seen better days. A couple creaked and Dan grimaced.

He stayed low and entered the kitchen. It was a large space. The table hadn't been touched, but the cushions of the chairs had been knifed. The walls had some modern art, framed and tasteful. He had no idea about modern art, but these looked nice. All the drawers had been opened. He found a kitchen knife and stuck it in his back belt.

Next, Dan crept up the stairs. It felt like clearing a house in Iraq or Afghanistan. Only this time he didn't have his trusted Heckler and Koch 416 rifle. He tested each stair before he put his full weight on them. At the top of the stairs was the master bedroom with the balcony in the front. The back bedroom probably had one as well. To his right a small corridor. He craned his neck. It led to a bathroom and another bedroom. The silence was pin-drop, the sound of the pine trees left outside.

To be safe, he dropped and crawled into the master bedroom. The bedding was on the floor and the bed frame had been taken apart. The wardrobe doors were open, clothes spilled on the floor. He checked the other bedrooms quickly. All had been systemically turned out and searched. Paintings and framed photos had been taken off walls. Floorboards had been lifted up. Air conditioners in every room had been loosened from their wall sockets.

This was a professional job. Not some ordinary burglar.

He went to the room next to the bathroom. It was a study, the walls lined with shelves. Books had been tipped off the shelf and lay in a disorderly pile on the floor. He picked one up. It was a bound version of a technical journal, *Optical Fibers*. He waded through the strewn books and magazines on the floor. He picked up one glossy magazine and flipped through it. It was called *Communications*. A page inside had been folded on an article called, *Network processing in high pressure marine environment*. Whatever the hell that meant.

He looked at the authors' names in the credits. Philip Longworth was the top one. Must be Jody's husband. It seemed as if Philip was a cable engineer.

He must have been an important one to write articles.

At the desk he saw the wires for the broadband modem. There was a window above the table that faced the road outside. He peered underneath. Telephone wires sticking out, and a panel of electric sockets. He checked the drawers of the table. All empty. There was a filing cabinet with its doors open. No laptop.

Dan got up and walked around the first floor. He went out on the back-bedroom balcony and looked at the garden. Then he went downstairs, and walked out to the car.

Jody was sitting inside, biting her nails. She looked up as Dan approached. Dan walked over to the driver's seat and shut the door.

He said, "We need to call the cops."

Jody's voice was strained. "What's happened in there? I need to see."

Dan said, "Someone has taken the place apart, Jody. You wanna tell me what they were looking for?"

Her face was ashen. "I...I don't know," she said.

Dan sighed. "Ok, Jody, we can do this two ways. Either you tell me, and then we think about what to do next, or I drive to the nearest cop precinct and leave you there to tell them."

Jody had her hands folded on her lap, and her neck was bowed.

Dan spoke softly. "It's those same guys, right? Are they after your husband? He owes them money?"

Jody's head shot up. She looked at Dan with wide eyes. "What do you know about my husband?"

"Nothing," Dan said. "I think his study upstairs has been trashed. I saw a magazine with his name on it. Philp Longworth, right?"

"Yes."

"I'm just guessing here, Jody. When this kind of stuff happens, it's either for money or something valuable."

Jody was silent. She looked at house, then at the road, then back at the house again. Like she was trying to gather up the courage to go inside, but not sure she wanted to.

Dan said, "Who were those guys at the airport, Jody?"

"I have never seen them before."

"You sure?"

She nodded, her eye downcast again. "Never seen them, but..."

"But?"

"Seen some other guys...two of them. They used to park here, outside, opposite the house." Jody pointed with a finger.

"What sort of a car did they drive?"

"A blue Chrysler."

Jody wiped her eyes and sniffed.

"Philip`s been very busy with work lately. Gets up early, comes home late. He said he had something important to do in Barnham, near the coast, and headed out there. That`s the last I heard of him."

"Where`s Barnham?" Dan asked.

"It's a small town not far from St Mary`s." Dan knew of the little historic town, near the ocean in Georgia.

"Was something bothering him?" Dan asked.

"He never said anything."

Dan said, "These two men waiting in the Chrysler, what did they look like?"

"Hispanic, I think. Can`t be sure. But I saw them all the time, sitting in their car on the kerb opposite. Watching me."

"Did you tell the cops?"

Jody shook her head. "No."

"Why not?"

Jody pursed her lips. Dan said, "Jody, the sooner we get to the bottom of this the better. We've come this far, don't hold out on me now."

Jody's face was ashen. "You don't understand." Her voice trembled. She sniffed and Dan turned to look at her. Jody`s face was chalk white. Her nose became red and tears welled in her eyes.

Dan fished around in his pockets and came out with a handkerchief. He gave it to her. She accepted it without a word.

Jody said, "You can't help me. And I can't go to the cops."

Dan lowered his voice. "Why not?"

"Because they'll kill my little girl."

CHAPTER 6

Dan rested his head back on the seat. It made sense. The old woman had no family, and these scumbags had threatened her daughter's life to keep her quiet. Dan waited, giving Jody space.

After a while, she spoke again. "I was going out grocery shopping one day. The men in the blue Chrysler drove after me. I stopped by at a drugstore on the way. It was quiet in the parking lot and they came up to me. They had tattoos all over them. One of them wanted to see my husband. I told them, he was gone with work. At first, I denied knowing where he was. But then I had to tell them the truth."

Dan said, "When they mentioned your daughter?"

"Yes. I don't know how they found out about her. But they did. So I had to tell them what I knew about Philip's whereabouts. It's funny though."

"What is?"

"They seemed to know about him being at Barnham. They kept asking where else. I didn't have a clue."

Dan thought for a while. "Who did Philip work for?"

"A cable company. They make cables for data transmission. Synchrony Communications."

"Did you call them?"

"Yes. They said Philip was involved in county-wide, Wi-Fi infrastructure planning. But they couldn't tell me how long it was going on for. They weren't very helpful."

"Well, they should know. Where are they based?"

"In Atlanta."

"Did you speak to Philip after he left for Barnham?"

"No. He said he was going to be back in a week, and its now been 2 weeks. He doesn't call or answer his cell. I've emailed him, but he doesn't reply."

"And his work say they don't know here he is?"

"No. Apparently, he's left Barnham. He finished his work there, then just...vanished."

Dan did not say anything for a while. His spell was broken by Jody.

The older woman said, "It's not what you think."

"What am I thinking?"

"You're thinking there's another woman. Or there's gambling, drugs. But Philip wasn't like that. We were a happy family. Well, Tanya went off to college, but she visits all the time. Emory isn't far."

"Tell me about your daughter. What's her name?"

"Tanya. She's 21, at college in Emory. Doing a biology major."

"Does she know about her dad disappearing?"

"No. I don't want her to know either."

Dan said slowly, "Emory's a big college. Must be expensive, right?"

Jody wiped her eyes. "A cool 60 grand a year. Of which 36 grand is tuition fees. But she got a scholarship. She's a smart girl." Jody turned to look at Dan. "The only girl I have."

Dan tapped a finger on the steering wheel. He didn't want to say it, but he knew he had to. "Did Philip have money troubles? You know, for the tuition fees."

Jody held her forehead. "Oh Jesus."

"Tell me," Dan said.

"The scholarship only covers ten percent of the tuition fees. None of the living costs. She's our only child, right? Want to give her the best and all that. She had her heart set on that Biology major. One of the best in the country."

"Right," Dan said. He had no idea about biology majors.

Jody whispered, "I don't know if the fall semester fees have been paid yet."

"You can't check Philip's account?"

"No. He keeps the outgoings for the mortgage and tuition fees on a separate account. I don't have the password. He didn't have any savings plan for the college fees, I know that. He pays it every term."

Dan said, "So, if the fall fees are not paid…"

"They give her one term's grace, then she's out."

"When are the fees due?"

"This week."

Dan did some quick calculations in his head. He had a seven-figure sum left over from his Intercept final salary and bonus. And a house in Bethesda.

Dan asked, "You can ring the college and find out if the fees have been paid, can't you?"

Jody said, "Yes, I can. Why?"

"I can pay this semester's fees."

Jody's mouth fell open. She looked at Dan with wide eyes. "What?"

Dan said, "It's okay Jody. I can see you're in trouble here."

Jody shook her head. "No. I cannot let you do that, Dan."

"It's alright," Dan said.

Jody opened the car door and stepped out. "Thank you for offering, Dan. But I cannot accept that from someone I just met."

Jody walked over to the house. Dan locked the car and followed. Jody opened the front door slowly, like she expected something terrifying to happen. She stood silently for a while, then stepped inside. Dan walked in quickly.

Jody was standing inside the living room. Her chest rose and fell, and her nostrils flared. She turned to Dan. He noticed the paleness of her face, skin stretched tight between the bones. Her dark blue eyes glazed over, and she blinked. Her straggly brown hair was pulled back in a ponytail.

Dan asked again, "Do you have any idea what they might be looking for, Jody?"

She moved her head from side to side. Dan could sense the torment in her. She was a strong woman. Holding it in. Feeling the panic but not letting it overcome her. Slowly, she walked past Dan, into the hallway. Dan followed her into the kitchen. From there, upstairs. She couldn't bear standing in the bedroom. She ran down the stairs. Dan caught up with her at the base. Jody went into the kitchen, opened the bi fold doors with a set of keys, and stepped out into the garden.

The garden was more than forty feet in length. Pine trees rose up in the background, followed by a forest. Jody stepped off the patio and sat down. She lowered her head into her hands.

Dan said, "Let's get out of here."

Jody looked up. "Go where?"

Dan was looking into his phone. "There's a place downtown that we could visit."

Jody looked bewildered. "Like where?"

Dan smiled. "Lock up and let's get back in the car."

In fifteen minutes, Dan was pulling up at the grandiose entrance of the Ritz Carlton in downtown Atlanta. He chucked the keys to the valet. The valet stared dubiously at the car, but grinned when Dan pressed a twenty-dollar bill into his hand.

Jody was open mouthed again. She stuttered. "Dan, what...what the hell is this?"

Dan walked her to the concierge. He got a single room, and gave Jody the keys.

"This is where you`ll be staying tonight."

Jody was shaking her head again. "No. No way. You hardly know me." She gave the keys back to Dan. "You can't do this."

Dan knew the type. She had morals. She had a sense of honor.

"Jody," he said quietly, "It's too dangerous for you to go back to that house tonight."

They had walked over to a table by the bar area. "What do you mean?" Jody asked.

"I mean, if I was them, and I knew that you were back in town, I would hit the house again tonight."

CHAPTER 7

It was early evening by the time Dan got back to Jody's house in Virginia Highland. He parked at the beginning of the avenue, more than a hundred meters from the house. Sunlight was fading but he could still see. He couldn't see a blue Chrysler anywhere on the road. After ten minutes, he drove up and parked in the driveway.

He let himself in with the key he had got from Jody. He shut the door and stopped. Something was biting away at the back of his mind and he realized what it was. There was no sign of a break in. Whoever had come in had entered with a set of keys.

Who did they get the keys from?

Dan took out his cell phone and a piece of paper. Jody had written down the number of Philip's employer.

Dan listened to the phone ring three times before a sing-song female voice picked up.

"Synchrony Communications. How can we help today?"

"I'm looking for a missing person who is an employee at your office."

Sing-song became downbeat, lost her rhythm. "Who is speaking?"

"I need to speak to the boss of Philip Longworth. You sent him out on a job a week ago and now he's missing. Have the cops been?"

"Sir, I know nothing…"

"I'm sorry, I need to speak to your boss. Can you get him for me, please?"

"Hold on for a moment, sir."

Dan waited twenty seconds before a male voice came on the line. Deep set and heavy. "This is Marcus Schopp. Who is this?"

Dan explained everything.

Schopp listened without interruption, then said, "We win contracts to lay cables, Mr. Roy. That's why people get satellite TV in their homes. A new township is being built in Barnham and we are working there. Philip should be back anytime soon. He's a big boy, he can look after himself."

"How long was his assignment for?"

A slight hesitation. "Two days, I think."

"Then doesn't it strike you as odd that he hasn't been home for more than

2 weeks? He's not called, not replied to his emails, or SMS."

"What do you want me to do, Mr Roy? Hold his hand? Shall I spank him when he comes back, tell him not to do it again?"

A brief silence in which Dan could hear heavy breathing.

Schopp said, "I don't know what's bugging Philip, Mr Roy. He's not done this before. I understand his wife and family are worried. For the record, cops say most missing men eventually come back on their own. Maybe you should just wait till he does so."

Dan said, "Have you called the cops?"

Schopp countered, "No, I have not. Haven't you, seeing that you are so concerned and all for Philip? Who are you, anyway?"

"A friend of the family."

"Alright, Mr Roy, I think I have told you as much as I know. You still go questions, by all means, go to the cops." He hung up.

Dan picked his way around the destroyed house again. He had only cast a cursory glance at the third bedroom before. He went inside now. The walls were colored a light pink, and it looked like the girl's room. Tanya Longworth. She must have all her stuff at college, because there wasn't much in the wardrobes which had been opened and trashed. Dan lifted up the ripped carpet and checked underneath the floorboards, like he had with the other rooms.

Nothing. If there was, then it was probably taken by the men who had already been.

Downstairs a stack of bills caught his eye. From the Carter Medical Centre. The invoice wasn't itemized, but they were stamped in red as being unpaid— twenty grand worth of unpaid medical bills. He made a note of the address of Carter Medical Centre. He found a photo from a broken frame. Tanya, Jody and Philip in happier days. They were dressed in anoraks and hiking gear. There was a blue sea sparkling behind them and they were on a white sandy hill. Somewhere on the coast, probably in Georgia. There was another photo of Philip in the same place, blue sea, same white sandy dune. It was close enough to see his face well. Dan put both photos in his pocket.

He was about to turn away from the main hallway when from the side of his eyes he caught a flicker of movement outside. A patrol car. Police. Atlanta PD. The car didn't flash its lights or sound the siren. Two half sleeved blue uniformed policemen got out and slammed the doors shut, heading straight for the house.

CHAPTER 8

There wasn't much time to think. It had to be one of the neighbors who called them. Dan would have to present himself as a family friend. They might not believe him, and maybe arrest him on the spot. There was one way of avoiding that. He strode to the front door and flung it open. The two uniforms coming up the drive stopped short, their hands reaching for the guns on their belts.

"Hello," Dan said, his face impassive. He filled up the doorway with his wide bulk. It would put them off. He stood to one side, holding the door open for them. He nodded at them.

"Come in, please."

It was a man and a woman. Both young patrollers. They looked at each other, keeping their hands on their weapons.

"I'm a friend of the woman who lives in this house. Jody Longworth. Her husband's missing. I came down to check on the house."

The man asked, "What's your name?"

"Dan Roy." He waited for a second. "Look, if it bugs you that much, I can step outside while you have a look inside the house. It's been trashed."

The man whispered something to his partner. She nodded and stared at Dan.

"After you," the officer said. Dan could see the man's badge. The uniform and car looked genuine. He didn't like the idea of a man with a gun coming up behind him, but he needed to put this guy at ease.

"Okay," he said. He walked down the hallway, into the living room, the patrolman behind him.

"Jesus Christ," the officer said. Dan said nothing. He let the man observe for a few minutes, then took him round to the open plan kitchen area. Dan tested the bifolding doors, then leaned against them. He let the man take his time, seeing the mess.

"Upstairs is similar," Dan said.

"You stay here. I'm going up to check."

Dan shrugged and fiddled with the lock of the bifolding patio doors. It was open. He stepped out into the garden. The humidity seeped inside the broken space. Dan used his sleeve to wipe the sweat off his forehead. He heard a sound and looked back to see both cops in the dining room with their guns drawn. Double hands on their weapons, elbows extended, pointed straight at him. The man did the talking.

"You need to come with us to the station. You can come of your own volition or we'll have to arrest you."

"I got some questions myself. Can I lock up here first?"

"No," the cop said. "Keep your hands where we can see them. My partner will lock up."

Dan waited as the woman walked past him to the patio door. The cop kept his gun trained on Dan.

Dan said, "I need to set the alarm too. You can't do that, and I'm not giving you the password."

The cop frowned. "We can set the alarm. It's not a problem. Give us the password."

Dan stood very still, his face impassive. "No."

The cop's face changed. He tightened the grip on his gun. "Then leave the alarm. We can lock the front door."

Dan said, "Listen to me. Whoever came in to wreck this place had keys for the door. The alarm could not have been set, or it would have gone off. Or they had the code for the alarm as well, I don't know. Either way, setting the alarm is not going to hurt. I need to do it."

The cop began to sweat. Dan waited, cool as a cucumber. The woman came around and whispered in her partner's ear. He took a deep breath, then nodded.

"OK," the cop said. The collar of his blue uniform was damp. "Just watch it. I don't want to shoot you. But I might have to."

Dan wanted to put the young guy at his ease. But he knew his words would not matter. Cops were the same the world over. But to their credit, they had given him the option of coming to the station of his own free will. That was better than an arrest.

Not the ideal way to begin a holiday. But he had faced far worse situations.

The guy covered him from the back, while the woman went outside the front door and watched him from the porch. Dan noticed she had not drawn her weapon, but kept her hand on it lightly. Less strung up than her partner.

Once Dan had set the alarm, he waited for the woman to lock the door. Then he stretched his hands out. "Keys, please," he said.

The male cop was between them in a flash. "No," he said. "First we need to take a statement off you at the station. If charges are placed against you, then you might not get the keys back."

The man was getting tiresome. But Dan kept his thoughts to himself. Dan turned on his heels and walked up to the police car.

It was a blue Ford Taurus. There was an extra stick out bumper at the front and back. It was black with Atlanta PD written on it in red letters. On the side of the car it said the same thing, with two extra words in white paint. Police Interceptor. LED flashlights on top. Dan leaned against the side, next to the rear doors.

The young cop came up, raised his eyebrows at him, and opened the door. Dan got in and the door slammed shut. It was hot, stuffy inside, with the smell of old leather. They got in at the front, and drove off slowly.

Dan lowered his window. It smelled of pine trees and fresh earth. They drove out of the neighborhood, and headed south, towards downtown. They used the backroads, and stopped in front of a red brick building that said "Atlanta Police Department Zone 1".

He was led to the front counter, where he had to give his name, address and ID. The officer checked his ID, looked interested and checked Dan out. Dan kept his eyes on the man without saying a word. He put his ID back in his pocket and walked to the reception area. He sat for ten minutes, then was called by the female cop who had come to the house. He followed her down a corridor into an interrogation room on the left. She knocked and entered. When Dan entered the room, she went out and shut the door.

CHAPTER 9

The room had whitewashed walls, a metal table with the legs screwed into the floor and two fold up metal chairs on either side. Two suits sat at the table. One of them stood. He had light sandy hair, a lined face that had seen better days, and wore an open collar suit that hung loose on him. He flashed his badge.

"I'm Detective Brown, and this is Detective Harris." Harris nodded. "Sit down, Mr Roy."

Dan sat, facing the two detectives. Harris looked sharper. He was younger, mid-thirties, with busy dark eyes that looked Dan up and down.

Harris said, "You are Daniel Roy, is that right?"

"Yes."

Harris looked at a paper in his hand. "From Bethesda, Virginia. Says here US Army. You used to be in the Delta Forces, but that was seven years ago." Harris put the papers down. "Where have you been all this time, Mr Roy?"

"Been abroad. With work."

Harris said, "What sort of work?"

Killing people. Blowing up compounds. Stopping the US Embassy from getting bombed sky high.

That kind of work.

Dan said, "Jody Longworth is a friend of mine. Her house was ransacked and her husband's disappeared. She wants to know why."

Harris frowned at him. He looked at his partner, who shrugged. "As far as I know, there's not been any report of a missing person called Philip Longworth." Harris wrote something down, and pressed the buzzer. The female cop came back, and Harris handed her the paper while muttering some words.

The other detective, Andy Brown turned to Dan. "How did you meet Jody Longworth this time?"

Dan considered. He said, "At the airport. She was coming back from New Jersey." Dan had already asked Jody this. She had been to Nutley, NJ to see her sister. She had caught the flight back from Newark when she bumped into Dan at Atlanta airport.

Dan said, "The front door was locked. The windows hadn't been forced. The bi-folding doors at the back were open. Maybe whoever came in had to leave quickly. They definitely had keys. They left via the garden. When Jody and I came back, we might even have surprised them. There`s a pine forest at the back. They escaped through there."

He waited for the detectives to digest this. "Maybe that's what the neighbor saw. Someone running out the back. Or he or she got worried that two strange men were entering via the front door."

The two officers were holding something back. Dan knew it.

"Who did the neighbor see?" Dan persisted. The two cops stared back at him.

"I`m not a suspect, am I?" Dan asked. Harris looked at Brown again, who shrugged.

"Alright Mr Roy," Harris said. "The neighbor saw a tall, Caucasian male enter the building this morning. With a group of four men. About three hours before your arrival. Yes, they did see the same guys run out the back as well, just when you arrived."

"What was the tall guy wearing?"

Harris looked at his notes again. "A black shirt and dark brown pants. Blond hair. Big guy."

A tall, white man wearing dark clothes. The description matched the man Dan had seen at the airport. The man who kidnapped Jody.

"Thank you," Dan said. "Did the neighbors hear an alarm going off?"

Brown said, "Not that we heard of."

Dan asked, "Were the other men with the tall guy Hispanic? Or Mexican?"

Harris said, "Yes. One of the neighbors mentioned that."

Brown said, "Where is Jody Longworth now?"

"Somewhere safe."

Harris leaned forward. "Let me remind you something here, Mr. Roy. We can arrest on suspicion of a felony. You do understand that right?"

Dan did not reply. Harris continued. "That being the case, and given that we are answering your questions, which we don't have to, some cooperation would be in order."

Dan said, "This was an inside job. Someone had Philip`s keys. Probably knew the alarm key code as well. Philip would not just hand them over. He might have been tortured. This is not about me. We need to find Philip."

"What did you do before you joined Delta?" Brown asked.

"US Ranger."

Brown smiled. "A Bat Boy, huh?"

"A proud one as well. Why do you wanna know?"

"Ex-US Army. Airborne as well. 82nd Airborne Division."

Dan nodded. The 82nd Airborne Division had been deployed all over the world. They played a major role in all combat theatres, and were also based at Fort Bragg, NC, where Dan had been billeted during his Delta years.

"Hooyah," Brown said. Dan smirked.

"I knew you were a tough guy when I saw you," Brown said. "You don't fit the bill of a regular army grunt." He shifted in his seat and sat up. "So tell me, Mr Roy. Since you left Delta, what the hell have you been up to? And what brings you to Atlanta?"

Dan said, "Like I said, I had work overseas. Running a business. I came to Atlanta on holiday. Just happened to bump into Jody at the airport."

"Just like that?"

"Yup."

"Anything else?"

"Weather reminds me of Iraq."

Brown smiled. "I'm not a fool, Mr Roy. I can tell you are still a fighting man. You have that look in your eyes. I don't know what you are playing at, or what authority you have. Are you working for the FBI?"

It was Dan's turn to smile. Not wanting to work for a giant bureaucracy was exactly the reason he had left the Army in the first place. "No. I'm definitely not working for the FBI."

The two detectives seemed to relax at his answer. There was a knock at the door, and the female cop returned with a folder. She whispered something in Harris' ears then went out.

Dan waited while the two men read the file. He asked, "Any news?"

Harris said, "If you mean any viewings or sighting matching his description, then no. We know that his credit card was used to purchase a return ticket to Barnham from Atlanta Rail Station. Card's not been used after that. Barnham PD has no records of him."

"Hotel registrations? Car hires? In Barnham, I mean. He's there for work. Has to be eating, drinking somewhere."

"Must be using cash, Mr Roy." Dan thought about the bank statement he had seen in Philip's study. It didn't look like the man had a load of cash at his disposal.

"Any cash withdrawals from his bank account?"

"Nope. We checked. Checked with his employer as well. No issues there."

"Are you putting out an APB?"

Harris sighed and looked at his colleague. Brown stayed reclined in his seat, like all of this was an effort. But his eyes examined Dan closely.

"An APB is for people who are missing for prolonged periods, Mr Roy. Not two weeks. He's probably soaking up some rays somewhere. Found a friend. I don't know. We see this a lot. Middle-aged man, needs a break from life. He should be back soon."

"How long is soon?"

Brown shrugged. "A month, maybe two."

"You know the house was trashed. Someone used a fine toothcomb, searching for something. That doesn't bother you?"

Harris said, "That's new evidence. Yes, we have to evaluate the case in that light now, but there's no plan of putting out an APB."

Harris scraped his chair back. All three stood up. Brown extended his hand.

"First name is Andy. Here's my card. Call me if you think of anything."

"Nice to meet you, Andy."

Dan shook his hand, feeling the hard grip. He smiled. He shook hands with Harris and walked out.

CHAPTER 10

North Atlantic Ocean
268 miles west of Jacksonville, Georgia, USA
West of US continental shelf
2nd August 2015

Captain Mikhail Shevchenko gripped the railings on the foredeck of the *Nimika* and stared out at the ocean. The research vessel was on its maiden voyage. The sun was out and seagulls scoured the clear skies overhead. He patted the railings affectionately. He had waited seven long years for this ship to be built at the Yantar shipyard in Kaliningrad on the Baltic Sea. As yet, there was no other ship like it.

Ships such as the *Nimika* had to be sturdy, often battling with severe conditions including gales and cyclones. This ship was virtually unsinkable and had satellite locators which, when activated, fed its location with pin-point precision to patrolling Russian ships on the African coast. Its GPS signal was on a frequency that couldn't be jammed. But that wasn't why the *Nimika* was special. It had the next generation of sonar screens to pick up very low frequencies, and the latest biological sensors to find even a few molecules of radioactive waste a nuclear submarine might leave behind. By virtue of its two bow thrusters it could achieve speeds of eighteen knots, unheard-of for a heavy research vessel. The ship dragged a load of sonar screens on a platform behind it, and on the stern there was a white dome-shaped sonar receiver that looked like a giant golf ball.

Shevchenko patted his beard and moved aft, spreading his legs to adjust against the swell. He spent a few seconds there, then walked back towards the bridge. Behind and above the bridge was a helipad, but the Kremlin's machinations meant he wasn't allowed a helicopter on this voyage. Still, he had something far more powerful at his disposal.

In the bridge, the young OR-5 Sergeant, as junior Petty Officers in the Russian Navy were known, put down his binoculars and saluted when he saw Shevchenko enter.

"Good morning, Alexeyivich," Shevchenko murmured, taking up position next to him. Alexander Alexeyivich, known as Sasha, was a graduate of the Kuznetsov Naval Academy. The same Academy in St Petersburg from which every Russian naval officer graduated, including Shevchenko himself.

"Beautiful weather today, Captain," Sasha said.

"Yes indeed," Shevchenko mumbled. He turned around and headed down the spiral staircase to the ship's main body. Sasha, aware of his master's moods, followed without comment. They descended into the heart of the ship where in a large dry dock, taking up almost half the size of the interior, lay their two most prized possessions.

*****

Shevchenko walked forward and patted the hull of the 20 feet long, and 1400-pound heavy large submersible carried in a cradle, attached to the slings of a crane, ready for lifting.

"Today would be a good day for it, Captain," Sasha said.

Shevchenko smiled to himself. The impetuousness of youth.

"Today would not be a good day for it, young Sasha, because we do not have all the information as yet. Do not lose sight of the mission objective." He looked up at the young man and raised his eyebrows. "But, it could be the day for a test run."

A smile appeared on Sasha's face. "Yes, sir."

Sasha put out a call on the intercom and crew members rushed into the dry dock. As Shevchenko watched, Sasha barked out orders and the men went through the drills. A groaning noise started and the crane tightened the rubber straps. The men did a quick, last minute check on the sides of submersible, called the *Guboki*—Russian for "deep". Of particular importance to Shevchenko was the removable data storage module. He made sure it was secure, then stepped back. He nodded to Sasha and the men moved away.

The floor began to vibrate. A circular area in the middle began to recede, moving back all the way to reveal the ocean below. The cranes whined louder and the *Guboki* was lifted out of its cradle. It wobbled in the air slightly, then began to descend towards the water.

Shevchenko and Sasha returned to the bridge. The room adjacent had been set up as the control room for the submersible and two scientists were already there, fiddling with the keyboards, facing a large dashboard of screens. An acoustic monitor beeped occasionally.

One of them turned to Shevchenko. "What depth, Captain?"

Shevchenko thought to himself. The geophysical assessments of yesterday showed the depth of the sea bed to be almost 3000 meters. This was beyond the continental shelf and he was expecting four kilometers, so three wasn't bad. Time to push the *Guboki* to live up to its name—to go deep. It had withstood sea pressure of 4500 meters in its simulations.

"Descend to 1000 meters, comrade Pushkin."

Pushkin flicked buttons. "1000 meters, Captain. What speed?"

"Depends on the currents. They do not appear strong, but start with two-and-half knots." That was good for a machine of this size. The *Guboki* could achieve up to six knots. "Gradually descend to the floor at 3000 metres approximately. Then surface at twenty kilometer intervals , just as a test to make sure it`s all okay. Do a circle with a radius of seventy kilometers, then come back to base."

"Yes, Captain."

Sasha said excitedly, "Its test voyage in the Mediterranean lasted for five hundred miles and two hundred hours, Captain."

"Yes, Sasha," Shevchenko said patiently. "It travelled under a US Navy aircraft carrier and they did not even find it. I know that."

Sasha gulped. "What I meant, Comrade Captain, is that it should be easily able to complete this mission."

"No, Sasha," Shevchenko said. "This mission is more difficult. We do not know of American capabilities in these waters. That is why we need that information. It should be here soon. But hopefully before that, we can find what we are looking for."

"And then we can start?"

"Yes, we can start."

"With any luck, Captain, the effect will be a calamity for America."

Shevchenko suppressed a smile. These young guns were full of the new party bluster. In some ways, it reminded him of his younger days.

"With any luck, yes."

"*Soveitski Syoz, Darogi Kapitan.*" To the Soviet Union, my dear Captain. A common Russian toast, tinted with nostalgia for greater days now firmly in the past.

"*Sovietski Syoz, Maladoi Chelovek.*"

A young man indeed, Shevchenko thought. Lucky to be on such a revolutionary voyage.

CHAPTER 11

Dan got a ride back in the same patrol car. At the house he walked around to the back and stood in the patio, then stepped into the garden. Mown a few weeks ago. Grass brushed against his ankles. He walked to the end where a waist-high fence separated the property from the pine forest beyond. He turned and looked back at the house. The rear elevation had the balcony on the back bedroom as well. The sloped roof could have a loft conversion. He thought about that. He needed to check if there was a loft space. The man had been searching for something. He left everything else it seemed, apart from Philip's laptop.

Dan checked the garden. The dry turf, some of it bleached in the sun, didn't show anything. No footprints. No cartridge cases. No drops of blackened blood.

He went back inside and cleaned up the kitchen the best he could, then called a cab and headed out to the nearest supermarket.

He came back with some groceries and cut some fennel, onions and mushrooms. He turned on the oven and put them in. He raided the larder, it was well stocked. He took out the soya sauce and honey. There was a packet of pork chops in the fridge. He rubbed a honey and soya mixture on the meat and put them in the hot oven. Below the pork chops he put in the vegetables. He put the beer in the fridge to cool.

He went upstairs and looked at the ceiling above the landing, and in each on the bedrooms. He went out on the balcony at the back. There was no access to the loft space above. He went to the balcony in the front bedroom, picking his way through the foam ripped up from the bed and the wardrobe doors on the floor. The telephone had been ripped off their sockets. He put his hands on the balcony and looked out. A couple was walking down the street.

Then he saw the blue Chrysler in the distance.

He wouldn't have seen it unless he'd looked carefully. He could see the front of the car, the driver and a passenger. There could be others in the back. Dan went back inside. It would be a dark in an hour, around 9:00 p.m.

Back in the kitchen he took out the pork chops, sprinkled rock salt and pepper from the dispenser. The fennel onions and mushroom were a bit well done, but edible. He ate on the table and washed it down with a beer. Thirty minutes had passed. He checked the back. The garden was empty.

He went upstairs and got one of Philip`s old jackets, an anorak with multiple pockets. He put a long kitchen knife in the inside pocket and stuck a smaller one in his front belt. In the garden shed he found a hammer. It had a heavy metal head and a thick rubber grip. He put that into one of the anorak pockets. Outside it was still warm, the sky darkening with shades of pink and violet.

Another fifteen minutes, he figured. Maybe half an hour.

From the front bedroom, he could still see the blue Chrysler. With the curtains open, he put the lights on in the bedroom and the study. Then he went back downstairs and into the garden.

Dan crept down the side of the house and along the fence. He lay down flat on the ground, resting on the side entrance. The darkness grew around him. A car passed by, then silence returned to the street.

He heard the engine before he saw anything.

Lights off, the Chrysler came slowly up to the front of the house. Four men got out, closing the doors gently. Light streamed on them from the bedroom above and Dan could make out their faces. All of them looked Hispanic. The driver seemed to be the leader. He had tattoos on his arms and neck, and a piercing on his eyebrow. He took a gun out and released the safety. Dan crept farther back, then threw himself down in a plant bed, crawling under the bushes. One man approached the garden from the side. He walked out to the patio, took out a handgun and looked around. Someone knocked on the bi-folding doors and he spun around, gun raised. He relaxed when he saw one of his own and waved.

Dan kept his head down as the man in the garden stepped off the patio onto the grass. He came towards the plants. Dan kept very still. He could barely see. The footsteps stopped two meters away. Dan could hear the man shuffle closer. He tensed his muscles. Had he seen something? Maybe Dan`s boots, sticking out the back? Dan heard another shuffling sound, and then more footsteps. But fading now.

Silently, Dan uncoiled himself. He raised himself to his knees, staying low. The hammer came out. He hefted the heavy object in his hand. The knife would kill the man, but he might fight first. The hammer was better. Dan crept out, following. The man had no idea. He was looking ahead, towards the garden shade. When he was close, Dan charged, hitting the side of the man's face and hearing the cheekbone crack. As the man fell, Dan grabbed his neck and jumped on top of him. He raised the hammer high up and smashed it down on the side of the temple, where important blood vessels travelled up the side of the ear. It was the best place to hit someone on the skull. Another crunching sound. The body jerked once, then was still. Dan felt for the gun on the grass. A Glock 22. He released the breech and the magazine dropped out. He couldn't see in the dark, but he was pretty sure it was a fifteen round magazine. It wasn't suppressed.

He left the body and stole out to the side entrance. He put the Glock in a pocket and held the hammer in his hand. He spread-eagled himself on the floor. The Chrysler was in front of him, and leaning against the side he could see the silhouette of a man. That meant two were inside the house. The light in the bedroom above had been turned off. The man at the car was facing the house, and his left side was turned slightly away from Dan. He probably had his gun out. It was safer to assume that. Dan couldn't use his weapon. It would make too much noise. Besides, he wanted at least one of them alive and to use some field interrogation techniques on the survivor. Make him talk, before he died.

With this guy, Dan had one problem. He was jammed between the car and the side entrance. It was an awkward space to navigate, if he had to get up to the man undetected. Dan crouched forward on one knee like a sniper. He had a clear view of the man's head from the side. He threw the hammer as hard as he could. At the same time, he moved. The hammer smashed into the man's head just as Dan slammed into the man's waist, trapping him against himself and the car. Dan frantically fell for the man's hand, searching for a gun. There was no need. The hammer had found its target and the man crumpled to the ground. He was dazed, and Dan hit him again, in the same spot on the temple.

He looked up towards the house and saw a flashlight briefly in the study. He stepped over the prostrate body and went to the door. It was ajar. He sank to his knees and looked in. Completely dark. He stayed in that position and heard a whispered voice from near the staircase. Then the creaking of stairs. They were coming down.

CHAPTER 12

Dan sank down low. The door opened. One man stepped out, then another. Dan didn't give them a chance to see the dead man. He brought the hammer up with savage ferocity, aiming for the side of the man`s face in front of him. There was a thud, a grunt, and the blow almost lifted the smaller man off his feet. Dan was charging, heading low for the man in front, probably the leader. He cannoned into the man just as he was turning to find out what happened behind him.

He stumbled and fell forward, and Dan spread his legs to sit astride his back. The man`s gun arm was caught underneath him. Dan took out the Glock and pushed it against the man`s ear.

"*Que pasa, hombre?* Move and you die. Who sent you?"

The man`s cheek was squashed against the floor. He spoke between his teeth. "Fuck you."

"Wrong answer."

Dan leaned on the man`s head with his arm. He caught a whiff of stale sweat and cannabis. He hooked his hand around and used his fingers like claws to dig inside the man`s eyes. The man shouted something in Spanish and thrashed around. Dan realized he couldn't do this in the open. He needed to drag the man inside. He grabbed his collar and lowered his voice.

"I am going to let you stand up. If you don't do as I tell you, then I will blow your brains out. Do you understand?"

"Yes."

"Give me your gun. Take your arm out slowly." He pushed the pistol harder against the man`s skull. The man moved his arm out from below him. He did it slowly. Dan twisted his neck to watch him. He had raised his foot, ready to kick the gun hand, if needed. When the gun was fully out the man suddenly cocked his wrist, aiming at Dan. He wasn't fast enough. Dan's boot slammed down on the hand and the round went up into the sky. The shot ran out, echoing against the houses. Dan hit the man with the butt of the Glock. Two hefty blows on the mastoid bone at the back of the ears and the man was still.

The guy who was first out the door hadn't moved. All four down.

298

Dan dragged all the bodies inside the house, put the lights on and searched them. They all had tattoos. He ripped open the shirt of one. Lots more tattoos on the chest and trunk, many with Spanish inscriptions. Down the middle, Z9 written in large letters. A street gang, with a penitentiary chapter, more than likely.

Dan called Detective Brown. He picked up at the second ring.

"Detective Brown speaking."

Dan explained what had happened. Fifteen minutes later, an unmarked police car pulled up outside the house. Brown was wearing his suit and he had a flashlight. Dan opened the door for him. Brown had his Glock raised. He lowered it when he saw Dan.

"This their car?" Brown indicated the Chrysler. Dan nodded.

Brown followed Dan into the kitchen. He looked at the bodies, then at Dan. "Jesus Christ, you did this?"

"Self-defense," Dan said. "It was me or them."

Brown kneeled down and looked at the tattoos. He put a finger on their necks to feel for a pulse. "Jesus Christ," he said again.

"What is Z9?" Dan asked.

"Zapato 9. Named after their leader, Zapato Mares, now locked up in El Salvador." Brown looked up. "These guys are all over the place. Up and down the country." He stood up.

"Drugs, extortion, what else?"

"They're big on human trafficking as well. Sell Mexican girls as slaves. Cocaine, too. Those are their two main businesses—cocaine and prostitution." Brown shook his head. "If Longworth was mixed up with them, then it's bad news."

"You reckon Philip was selling for them on the side? I can't see him being mixed up with prostitution."

Brown let out a long breath. "How do you know? A middle-class white guy in the 'burbs is exactly the kind of guy these gangs want to act as a front for them. It's happened before. Mainly with narcotics, but you would be surprised of the filthy shit we uncover sometimes."

"They want something from him."

"Money, probably."

"What doesn't figure is the tall blond guy."

"No, it doesn't. But don't forget these gangs operate here because there's demand. They deal in weapons, they act as enforcers for biker gangs and organized crime families. So the blond guy is mixed up with them. I bet you."

"No one matching his description ever been on your radar?"

"Not that I recall. But the Mexican gangs, especially these guys, have become more active in Atlanta recently. They use the city as a major transit route for cocaine they bring in from Peru and El Salvador, via Texas. The business had died down, but now it's up and running again."

Dan said, "Can you clear this up for me?"

Brown was silent for a while, then nodded. "This changes everything. Now we have new angles. Might have to get the FBI involved as well."

"Or the DEA." Dan ran his hand through his hair. This was getting worse.

"Yes," Brown said shortly. "I'm calling an ambulance. We can say they were trying to rob an empty house. You got back late and found them inside. You acted in self-defense. But this becomes a crime scene now. The lab guys will come around to do their thing." He looked at Dan. "What are you gonna do?"

"I need to check out the employer."

Brown felt inside his pant pockets. There was a film of sweat on his brow. He pulled out a packet of Marlboro cigarettes and headed outside the folding doors of the kitchen. He lit a cigarette, took a deep drag and blew out smoke.

After a pause, Dan joined him outside.

Brown offered him the pack. "Smoke?"

Dan said, "No thanks. You alright?"

Brown swallowed and said, "Yeah, fine." He cracked a smile. "See dead bodies all the time, right? Sometimes it's like half of this city is dying."

Dan kept his voice gentle. "You get those dreams? Flashbacks?"

Brown took another lung full of smoke. "Used to. Got past it, now."

"That why you left the Army?"

Brown kept his eyes averted from Dan and nodded. "Kind of. You know what it's like, right?"

"Yeah. Never had it myself, but I know others." After a beat, Dan said, "But you're gonna be OK, man. You're holding down a job, doing well for yourself."

Brown took a deep drag. "Some ain't so lucky, right?"

"Right." Dan turned to leave. Brown called him.

"Dan."

Dan stopped. "Yeah?"

"Thanks, dude."

Dan nodded. Only soldiers knew what it was like. Combat left scars on the mind. Scars no one could see. And professional soldiers were expected to settle down to civilian life like nothing had happened.

Brown said, "You be careful out there. I don't like what's happening here."

"That which does not kill me," Dan said, "makes me stronger."

CHAPTER 13

After Brown left, the crime scene guys arrived. They set up tape around the house, put on their white suits and got to work. Dan found himself a corner in one of the bedrooms upstairs and tried to catch some sleep. Before he turned in, he rang Jody and brought her up to speed. He promised he would come and see her the next day, and told her not to leave the hotel. He didn't forget to take her daughter's cell number.

Dan was up and out early the next morning.

He walked past the World of Coca Cola and down the steps of the Centennial Olympic Park. The fountain was sprouting high and he caught some spray as he walked close. He preferred to walk. The heat was sapping, even at 10:00 a.m. He had a baseball cap on, and sunglasses. No one followed him. He headed south, looking for a road called Edgewood Avenue. He found it after another ten minutes, guided by his phone.

The avenue had a tramline on the left strip and cars on the right. He needed number 1430. The building turned out to be a single floor, blue-tinted glass and metallic structure opposite a faded red brick Victorian building. A curious juxtaposition of the old and new. Commercial buildings lined the road, but next to the Victorian building there was a modern two-story structure with Greek letters in a pediment on top. Probably an off-campus sorority house. There was a parking lot next to it, with Fords and BMW's closest to the street.

Number 1430 looked average, nothing special. There was no street entry door and it took him a while to find it around the back. There was a car park, and next to it, an entrance to the building. Dan stopped. The guard at the doorway looked heavy. He was standing still, feet planted apart. He wore a black baseball cap, black fatigues and a bullet-proof Kevlar vest. A Heckler and Koch MP5 submachine gun was held loosely in his hands, but his finger was on the trigger. He saw Dan coming and the MP5 came up, barrel pointing straight at Dan. The butt was against his midriff, but he was comfortable. Dan knew a sniper when he saw one. This was no ordinary security guard.

"Yes?" the guard asked.

"I am here to see Marcus Schopp. The boss."

"Stop there," the guard called. Dan did. The MP5 barrel lifted until the man had it on a shoulder stance, pointed straight at Dan`s head.

"What do you want from him?"

"I'm a friend of Philip Longworth. He's missing, and the cops are coming here after me. They have some questions for Mr Schopp."

The gun didn't go down. Dan heard a sound behind him and he turned around. Another gun barrel. Same weapon. H&K MP5. This guard was wearing a similar black uniform, baseball cap, and he was less than five feet away from Dan. Close enough for Dan to see the weapon was switched to automatic mode. A squeeze on the trigger would literally blow Dan away.

"Against the wall. *Now.*"

Dan turned around and raised his hands. Hands pushed him against the wall. He spread his legs. These guys would ask him to, if he didn't. He could guess who they were. Ex Rangers or Delta, maybe even Seals, now working as private military contractors. The hands frisked him and up down expertly.

"Turn around," the guard said.

Dan turned to see both guns aimed straight at his chest. The men stared at Dan without blinking. One of them went to the intercom and buzzed. He looked back at Dan. "What`s the name?"

"Dan Roy."

The guard spoke in a low voice at the intercom. Then he turned to his colleague and nodded. The second man indicated with his gun, and moved towards the double doors.

Dan walked past them and through the double doors that had swung open silently. He was in a brightly lit white hallway. There was no reception desk and he didn't know which way to turn. There were wooden framed photos of suspension bridges and cables.

A woman in nice white shoes walked past him and he caught her eye. Pretty. Smoky green eyes, five eight, navy blue skirt suit trimmed around the bust and waist, accentuating her figure. Dark hair, falling in waves at the shoulder. She smiled and Dan smiled back. He kept his eyes on her as she walked to the end of the hallway and turned a corner without looking back at him.

"Mr Roy." Another woman, older this time, with a bowed back, was waiting for him. A man in a similar black uniform to the guards outside was standing behind her. He kept his steely eyes on Dan, and Dan stared back at him as he walked up. He was holding a Heckler and Koch 416 assault rifle.

Dan's weapon of choice. The H&K handgun was strapped to the right thigh, the extra ammunition in the center of the chest piece. Another hand gun at the left waistline. These guys were well-equipped, and more than normal security. Dan following the woman down the hallway. They went through another set of double doors and into a waiting room.

"Have a seat here, please. I will let Mr Schopp know that you have arrived."

He knew already, Dan thought. He nodded and sat down. He picked up a copy of the *Atlanta Gazette*. The Democratic Party's computers had been hacked. Confidential emails between senators leaked out, including many between supposed rivals on the other side. Republican senators were quick to fault the Democrat's cyber systems and were denying all knowledge of the emails. Politics.

The circus continued, with the best jokers in the nation. Or worst jokers, depending how you saw it. Financed by the tax dollars of millions of hard working Americans.

"Mr Schopp will see you now," the secretary announced.

Dan stood up and followed her. The office was spacious, more photos of cabling and engineering projects on the walls. His feet sank in the carpet. A series of tall windows at the back lit the room up.

Next to the windows, at a huge mahogany desk, sat a man who could be summed up in one word—round. Marcus Schopp was in his sixties, with a round face, bald round scalp and rounded shoulders. He stepped out from behind the desk and Dan saw the prominent gut, held up by two small legs. He looked like a large penguin in a black suit. They stared at each other for a while.

"You are Philip's friend?" Schopp asked in that gravelly voice that Dan heard on the phone.

"Yes."

Schopp made a noise in his throat that was between a growl and a choke. He curled his lips up in disdain, like Dan had somehow brought a bad smell into the room.

"I told you on the phone. I have nothing else to add."

"How about turning Philip's house inside out, searching it with a fine toothcomb, then sending four Latino gang members around?"

The corners of Schopp's eyes crinkled. For an instant, there was a lack of control. Rage. Then it was gone.

"What the hell are you talking about?"

Dan told him. Schopp's black eyes stayed focused on Dan, giving nothing away. Dan could see other movements. His thumb on the desk kept rubbing against his forefinger. His ankle twitched up and down. All the signs of a nervous man.

"Tell me about Philip," Dan said.

Schopp rolled his eyes. "This is a rat's ass, you know that? What do you want, a character reference?"

"What I told you just now makes no difference? I want to know what he was like the days before he went off to Barnham. How he acted. Did he come to see you?"

"Hell, no. I don't have time to see all my employees. Look, if he's mixed up in something bad with these gangs, that's his problem. Not mine, and not my company's."

"He had money worries. Mortgage and college fees. How much was he being paid?"

"That's confidential information."

"You couldn't have been paying him much. He was way in the red in his checking account."

"Like I said. Get his bank statements and find out."

Dan tried a different tack. "Tell me about Barnham."

Schopp sighed. "Again, like I said..."

"Laying cables for Wi-Fi across the county, I know that," Dan interrupted. "He got a one-way ticket to there. Didn't seem like he was coming back in a hurry."

"And?"

"Why would he do that?"

"I don't know." The look on his face was stubborn. Dan wouldn't get anywhere like this. Marcus Schopp knew something, but either he was scared to tell him, or didn't want to.

"You are next, Schopp. They're coming after you," Dan said softly.

Schopp's face turned purple. "Get out!" he shouted.

Dan turned on his heels and left.

CHAPTER 14

Dan came out of the office, walked through the empty waiting area and into the open hallway. The hallway was empty. Dan looked around him. The corridor bent round the corners on either side, the building was in the shape of a doughnut. In front of him there was a door. Behind, steps going down to what seemed like the basement.

Dan went through and down the stairs, coming to a corridor that was a replica of the one above. Here a white door had a small glass window near the top. He looked inside. Rows of computer screens with a few people hunched over them. The door didn't have a handle, only a retina screening machine and, next to it, a larger device in the shape of a human hand. A *Vein map*.

Dan had seen these before in the CIA office in Langley, and also at the Intercept office. Fingerprints could be forged, but no two individuals had the same pattern of veins in their hands.

He moved on. A door on the opposite side was a janitor's cabinet. The corridor was empty. Dan opened the cabinet door. There was a small space inside it. He shut the door, and turned the light on. Inside, a uniform hung on the wall. He put it on quickly. Luckily the janitor was a big man. He took out a broom and bucket, filled the bucket with water, and dragged them out into the corridor.

He walked around in a circle. The room with the white door took up a lot of the ground floor. On his left he found a door that opened into a hallway. At the end - two offices. The place was empty. Dan put the broom and bucket against the wall. He took out a piece of cloth and started to rub the windows.

He could see the security camera above the door as he came in. He got a chair and stood on it. A wide angle lens. Keeping his face hidden below the camera, he took out the black glass cover. It was a screw top. He tied the piece of cloth around the camera lens. Then he screwed the cover back on. He got off the chair and put it back in place.

The office doors did not have any signs on them. Dan tried one. It was open. The room was dark. He turned the light on revealing a table with a laptop in the middle and a larger screen to one side. He went to the table.

Two folders on the top. Both were stamped Classified, USN, US Navy.

Dan opened the folders. Numbers, diagrams and flowcharts that he would have to read through.

He flipped out his cell phone and started taking pictures. When he finished, he opened up the laptop. He needed a password. He looked around the room. Two filing cabinets behind the table. He was going to move towards it when he stopped short.

Two male voices. Heading for the office. Dan went to the wall and turned the light off. He stole back to the filing cabinets. Behind them there was an alcove against the wall. Dan pressed against it and sank down to his knees.

The door handle turned, then stopped. He could hear the voices clearly now and one of them belonged to Marcus Schopp. He stopped at the entrance of the door, speaking to someone outside.

"He says he's a friend, but how do you know? I mean, how the hell do you know? He could be anyone," Schopp's voice was frustrated. The person at the other end said something.

"Yeah, you gotta be careful. I'll see you upstairs." Schopp said, and came inside the room.

He flicked the light switch on. Dan drew his knees closer and breathed as softly as possible.

There was a creaking sound and a grunt as Schopp sat down in the leather chair. He rustled the papers in the folder. Then Dan heard the sound of the chair being shoved back. Padded footsteps approached the filling cabinet.

Dan flexed his jaws. His knuckles were white. The cabinet was six doors tall and he could see Marcus's shoes around the corner.

He was standing on his tiptoes. Marcus said something to himself, took some papers out of the cabinet, then slammed the cabinet shut. He went back to the table. Dan breathed. Marcus picked up the files and went to the door. He flicked off the lights and left.

Dan crawled out from behind the filing cabinet. He let his eyes get used to the dark, then tried the top drawer. It was locked. He looked at the table. Marcus had taken the folders. He went to the door and put his ear against it. Silence. He opened the door a crack. The reception area was empty. He got his broom and bucket off the wall and went back to the janitor's cupboard. He passed the white door and glanced in again. The same people were sat there, eyes focused intently on the screen. One of the screens facing Dan had a map of USA with flashing lights on the east and west coast.

Dan turned away. He changed quickly in the janitor's cupboard and made his way back to the upstairs corridor.

He walked straight into the same woman he had seen earlier in the hallway. Sea green, smoky eyes, nice blue dress and very attractive.

"Just been to see Marcus?" she asked.

Dan kept his face impassive. "Who wants to know?"

"Lisa Chandler." She extended her hand. She smelled of lavender and sandalwood. Her hair was dark chestnut, and it contrasted with her light eyes watching him, moving from his chest to his shoulders.

"Dan Roy." They shook hands.

"You work here?" Dan asked.

"Yup. I needed to see Marcus myself, but was told he has a visitor. Guess that must have been you."

"Yes. He`s free now."

Lisa shrugged. "It makes no difference really. He`s always in a bad mood. Luckily, he leaves us alone most of the time."

"You been here long?"

"Coming up to five years. Yeah, it feels long."

"You might have known my friend. Guy called Philip Longworth."

Lisa frowned. "You know Philip?"

"Yes, he`s been missing for a week now, so I'm helping my aunt look for him."

Lisa`s eyes flicked behind Dan. He guessed a guard was moving up behind him.

Dan said "These guards always around?"

"Uh-huh. More in the last six months. There`s two more on the other side."

"Why does a cable company need security like this?"

"We do a lot of work for the DoD. Military applications."

"Fair enough. But these aren't any ordinary guards."

Lisa nodded. She dropped her voice. "I`m on my lunch break. Do you want to go for a quick coffee?"

"Sure, let`s do that."

CHAPTER 15

Lisa knew a place behind the Centennial Olympic Park. The sun was high and the heat was like a haze around them. Dan had bought a pair of handkerchiefs on his way down. He felt like he needed a towel.

Lisa watched him wipe his forehead. "Not used to the heat, huh?"

"You could say that. It`s more the humidity, actually," he added.

"Are you from around here?"

"From Virginia, originally. But spent a lot of time abroad. When I was a kid, I lived with my parents in Nepal."

"You lived in Nepal?"

"Yes. You know where Nepal is?"

She looked at him like he had asked a stupid question. "Mountain kingdom in the Himalayas, north of India. Capital Kathmandu. Favorite haunt of the hippies in the sixties. Best trekking in the world and white-water rafting. That Nepal?"

Dan pressed his lips together. "Alright, I`m sorry. Guess you know about Nepal. We lived in a Gurkha village. My dad trained me in physical labor like the Gurkha kids."

"The Gurkhas are a warrior tribe aren't they? The fought for the British, I think."

"They still do. Five regiments in the Brigade of Gurkhas. We left when I was sixteen and came back to Virginia." Dan did not want to say anything more.

Lisa asked "And then?"

"Joined the Army. Saw the world."

He could feel Lisa's eyes on his face. She wanted more elaboration from him, he could tell. But Dan felt uncomfortable speaking to anyone about his life in the Army and thereafter.

They found a café and sat down. It was lunchtime and workers with their lunch boxes and take away food were slowly filling the park. It was school holidays and some kids ran around, playing tag. Dan ordered a caramel macchiato and Lisa got herself a skinny latte.

He asked, "How well did you know Philip?"

"I saw him around. We worked on different projects most of the time. He spent a lot of time away. But when I saw him lately he seemed distracted."

"How do you mean, distracted?"

Lisa shrugged. "Like he had something on his mind. I also heard him arguing with Marcus once."

"Marcus, the boss?"

"Yes."

"Did you know what it was about?"

Lisa shook her head. "No, I was waiting outside and I could hear raised voices inside Marcus's room. Then Philip came out, his face flushed. He slammed the door shut and stormed out."

"What was Marcus like afterwards?"

"Cool as a cucumber. It didn't seem to bother him."

"Did you know that Philip left for Barnham?"

Lisa nodded. "Yes, he said he was going. That was right after he had the argument with Marcus."

"I see." Dan said after a pause, "Did you know that he got a one-way ticket to Barnham? It's on his credit card bill."

"No, I didn't know that. I wonder why?"

"Me too."

"It's like he wasn't planning on coming back."

Dan nodded. "Would you say Marcus and Philip were not the best of colleagues?"

"Yes, based on what I saw. You know," Lisa leaned closer, "it's not the first time that Marcus has ruffled someone's feathers."

"What do you mean?"

"He's a bully. He likes to push people around till he gets what he wants. You know he's ex-army, don't you?"

This was news to Dan. He thought of the gravelly voice and the haughty manner. It wouldn't surprise him. Probably an officer, not an NCO like himself. "I didn't know that," he said.

"He was on track to become a one-star general, apparently. But they took him off it. Some corruption scandal about preferential treatment of a defense contractor. Marcus used to be a director on the board of that company."

Dan sat back. "Interesting."

"He left the army and set up this company. Some say he still uses his old contacts to get business."

"So, what do you do for them?"

"I look after the amplifiers in the optical fibers that form the cables. They increase the data signal as light is passed through the fibers."

"You lost me."

Lisa smiled. "Sorry to get technical, but you asked. Basically, my job is to help design the connectors in the cables. Make sure the signal is loud and strong when they get to the other end."

"That's better. So what did Philip do?"

"He was in overall charge of the network. What distance the lines would cover, how much data they could hold, over what sort of geography, stuff like that."

Dan ran his finger across his lower lip, rubbing it slowly. "He was like the designer of the network?"

"Uh-huh, you could say that."

Dan thought of the books in Philip's study. The laptop that had clearly been removed—and not by the cops. The folders on Marcus's desk. Something was rotten here and it was Synchrony Communications that smelt the worst.

"You like your job?," he asked Lisa.

"It pays the bills."

"Must be more than that. It sounds technical. Did you go to school for it?"

She nodded. "Yes, I majored in solid state technology at Atlanta Clarke, then followed it up with a masters at GSU."

Dan was impressed.

"You got brains," Dan said. And looks to match, he thought silently. "Local girl, then? Grew up around here? You don't have an accent though."

She shook her head. "I grew up in Chicago. Went to high school there. My dad was an engineer as well. He worked for an electric company, making pylons. My mom was a home-maker. Guess I always wanted to follow in my dad's footsteps."

"Makes sense," Dan said. "Listen, you know of a place to stay around here?"

"In Atlanta? Yeah, heaps. What sort of place did you have in mind?"

He couldn't go back to sleep at the house in Virginia Highlands. Just pick up his stuff, then find a safer place.

"Somewhere cheap. A midtown hotel would do. I need to stay a couple of nights, then I'll head out to Barnham."

Lisa thought for a while. "Let me ask around. A couple of my friends have apartments where they have spare rooms. They might want a lodger."

"That would be cool," Dan said. "Listen, I need to ask you something. Your office has a basement floor. Guess you knew that."

"Yes."

"They have a room there with piles of computer screens. Hand vein locks and retinal scanners. That seems pretty secure to me."

Lisa raised her eyebrows. "You went for a stroll?"

Dan shrugged.

"That room is guarded like Fort Knox," Lisa said. "They have their own secure internet server that allows access only to needed sites. All other sites are blocked."

"Like an internal network," Dan said.

"Yes, and none of the workers in there are allowed in with their phones. They have to hand them in before they start."

"How do you know this?"

"Philip used to work in there. He told me."

"What are they doing in there?"

"That's the bit he wouldn't talk about."

Lisa checked her watch and stood up. "I better head back. What will you do?"

Dan took his time before replying.

"I need to do some digging on this Marcus guy and go see Philip's daughter as well. She's a student at Emory. I might need your help with finding out about Marcus."

Lisa said, "No problem. There's something weird about this and I figure Marcus knows more. Let me know how I can help."

"Sure thing."

Dan paid the bill, said good bye to Lisa and called a cab on his phone.

CHAPTER 16

Fort Gordon
Georgia
780th Military Intelligence Brigade

Susan Gardner, MASINT (Measurement and Signature Intelligence) specialist, hunched over the two large computer screens in front of her and frowned.

She clicked on the keyboard and brought up several images, extracted data from them and superimposed them on each other. Susan`s work, like that of many others in the 780th MIB, was to monitor internet signals flowing in and out of continental USA. She found cyber threats, and dealt with them. Another group in her brigade was responsible for launching cyber attacks on the hackers around the world that threatened US military installations.

Susan opened up MS Excel and used it to form a spreadsheet chart of the data she had found. Most times, she did not need fancy computer programs. She stared at the chart in front of her and her frown deepened.

Susan printed off the charts and got up from her desk. She walked across the darkened office, with analysts poring over computer screens all around her.

She knocked on the door of her Commanding Officer, Major Becker. A male voice told her to enter. Major Becker was alone. Susan brushed back some strands of her brown hair and straightened herself as she entered. She was dressed in office garb, navy blue skirt suit and black tights. Her brown hair was tied back in a ponytail. She put the spreadsheets in front of her boss. Becker looked at them.

"What is this?" he asked.

Susan said, "Sir, these are charts of signal lapses in our network servers."

"All networks have signal lapses, Sargent Gardner. You know that."

"Yes sir. But these all occur at certain times of the day. Early in the morning and mid day. Apart from the timings, there are other similarities. They last for the same lengths of time. I looked into several – their amplitudes are identical."

313

Becker raised his eyebrows. "What are you saying?"

"That there is a pattern here, sir. There is no smoke without fire, and I believe these signal lapses are not a fault of the servers. They are coming from an external source."

"You think so?" Becker was frowning.

"So I looked around."

"Did you? Anything interesting?"

"Several things, sir. As you know, the Democrat convention's emails have been hacked. Some senators' emails, from both sides, have been leaked out. No one actually knows if the senators in question even had these emails. But the leaks show the same IP address as the senators' website."

"That could be a result of a hacking attack. The emails might not exist at all. Hackers copied them and sent it from that IP address."

"Exactly. So I looked at the signals in the convention servers, and also the senators offices. They had similar signal lapses, at the same time of the day as us. Same amplitude. Has to be the same machine that is causing them."

Becker leaned forward and put his elbows on the desk. "Sit down Sargent."

"Thank you, sir." Susan smoothed her skirt and sat down opposite her boss.

"What else have you found?"

"You know there was an internet outage in parts of New York and New Jersey?"

Becker said, "Near Bellport and the coast of NJ?"

"Yes. I looked into those outages as well. Similar story. Before the outages happened, they had similar signal lapses. But these lapses became progressively longer, till there was no transmission at all. The outage lasted for ten hours before it was fixed."

"So why doesn't it happen to us? The outage, I mean."

"Because of our dedicated dual servers. They are different from civilian ones. If one of our server's go down, another takes over. Plus, our cables are different too. Civilian cables are easier to disrupt."

"But our infrastructure can go down, and then we have an outage of our own."

Susan was silent. Becker said, "Who else have you told about this?"

"You are the first to know, sir."

Becker tapped his lips for a while, staring at the ceiling. Then he passed a hand over his head.

"You sure about the validity of the MASINT?" Becker asked.

"Yes sir. 110%"

Becker reached for the red phone on his desk. "Get me Lt. Colonel Stanley, Deputy Director of the DIA," he said.

*****

Joint Base Anacostia Bollings
Washington DC
HQ, Defense Intelligence Agency (DIA)

Lt. Colonel Chuck Stanley looked at the three men and one woman inside his office. He knew all of them, including Major Becker of the 780th MIB. The woman, Sargent Gardner, he had not seen before. And she was the one doing all the talking.

Stanley said "So what are you trying to say, Becker? That what happened in New Jersey and down in Georgia are related?"

Much to Stanley`s irritation, Becker deferred to the woman again. Stanley preferred to speak to the ranking officer.

Susan said, "Sir, this was done by a machine. The software that did it has to be the same. Our coders can verify that."

Stanley said, "So where the hell is this machine, Sargent?"

"That's what we need to find out, sir."

Stanley sighed. "So you are here to tell me you have no idea of the source of the problem?"

Becker took over. "Neither HUMINT or MASINT have come up with anything so far. If it is a machine, then it is unlike anything we have encountered so far. And that research has been done in collaboration with your guys here, sir."

Stanley said, "By machine you mean a computer. How can it be so hard to find a computer? Find the same IP address. It might be hidden or encrypted, well, just break the code."

Susan said, "It's actually not that simple sir. A microchip could code for this software and the chip could be hidden anywhere capable of transmitting the program. It could be in a satellite for all we know."

Chuck Stanley looked at the woman briefly. Pretty, and a nice dress. But her words hit home. She made sense, and she did not seem fazed by his presence. Most of his men found him intimidating, but not Susan Gardner. Stanley was developing a grudging respect for her.

He said, "So we are sure that these…incidents, are linked?"

Both Becker and Susan nodded. Susan said, "Yes, sir."

Stanley looked to his left, at his Sargent in Command. "Joel, call a conference of our analysts." Joel saluted and got up to leave.

Stanley called him back. "And Joel, get the Secretary of Defense as well. Tell him it's me."

CHAPTER 17

Dan got off at Emory's main campus in Druid Hill. The sprawling university occupied hundreds of acres. He had Tanya's cell number, and he had called her twice but the line was engaged once and the phone was off the second time.

The buildings were a combination of classical and modern, and were very well maintained. There was a complex of restaurants and a large public arts theatre. Young people strolled around, as carefree as one could be in a school that cost sixty thousand dollars a year to attend, and admitted just above a quarter of those who applied.

He asked in the main office for Tanya's halls of residence. He had the address from Jody already. As he walked down, he thought about what he was going to say. Hey, I'm a stranger who met your mom at the airport. By the way, your dad's gone missing, your mom is literally having a fit, and I came down here to look for him. He sighed. Maybe this was a bad idea.

He got to the college dormitory and stood outside, watching a gaggle of girls stream out the door, followed by two football jocks. Jocks looked the same the world over. Beefy, broad and permanently vacant eyes. They smiled at Dan, who didn't smile back.

He went in through the door and looked for Room 215. Second floor. He took the stairs to the landing and waited again for some students to come out of the double doors. They stood there talking, books in hand, hands gesticulating, holding up the hallway. What was it with students? They had too much time on their hands. Or was he just an old grump bag?

Dan suddenly realized how odd he must look. He was clearly not a freshman, way beyond a sophomore, more than a senior... maybe he looked someone's dad. The thought was mortifying. He ducked his head and walked into the hallway. Loud music came from one of the rooms. Rap. Jah Rule bleating about how big he was. He got to the door of 215 and knocked. There was no answer. He put one ear against the wood. Apart from the dull thud of the rap music, he couldn't hear anything. The room was empty. He should have rung. He knocked again.

"Can I help you?" a female voice asked from behind him.

Dan turned around. An interesting sight.

Three young women faced him. They wore mini-skirts and tops that finished below the breasts, showing their toned midriff and abdomen. All three had long legs, and he couldn't help but move his eyes vertically once. Perfect. Long legs and great figures. All three were smoking hot. The middle one was blonde with "Dooley's" written in red on her white top and cheerleader written all over her face. The other two were shorter, with darker hair, and just as hot. All three must be cheerleaders, Dan guessed. Tanya was a bookworm, Jody had informed him. Dan took that to mean a nerd. Well, to get in here on a scholarship one had to be a nerd. He wondered what the cheerleaders wanted from Tanya.

He cleared his throat and tried to look nonchalant. He was the older—much older, guy here.

"I am looking for Tanya Longworth. Is she here?"

The two girls at the side exchanged glances, but the one in the middle was frowning at him. The tall, really hot one. She stepped forward, her eyes narrowed.

"I am Tanya," she said. "Who are you?"

Dan stared back at the three women in front of him. When he looked closer at the blonde girl, he saw dark blue eyes that reminded him of Jody. He swallowed.

"My name is Dan. Dan Roy. I am a friend of your father's."

Tanya's eyes were suspicious. "I didn't know you were dad's friend. And why are you here?"

Her face cleared suddenly. "Is dad ok?"

Dan looked at the room. "Can we talk inside please, Tanya?"

Tanya thought for a while, then exchanged a glance with her friends. "Give me a second," she told Dan. The three women went a few paces out and talked in whispers. Dan didn't blame them. He was a total stranger. But there was no other way. From what he had seen so far, the guys out to hurt Jody meant business. Tanya was in danger, and she needed to know that.

After a while, the women came back. Dan noticed all three of them look him up and down. He was thirty-five and these girls were what, twenty years old?

He felt the heat rise to his face. He looked down and put a finger inside his collar. He scratched his head.

This was absurd. Dan cleared his throat and folded his thick arms across his chest.

Tanya said, "Alright. Come inside and tell me quickly what you have to say. My friends will stand outside. If I'm not out in five minutes they'll call security."

Dan followed Tanya inside. It was a typical college dorm room. Two beds lay on either end of the large room, with desks by their side. Bookshelves lined the wall space above the beds and the desks. A poster of Leonardo di Caprio looked down at him, smiling. Tanya flounced on the bed, and her skirt rode up dangerously high. She patted it down and folded her long legs. Dan breathed out and looked away.

In a guarded voice, Tanya said, "So what did you want to say?"

Dan told her about meeting Jody, and what happened after. He left nothing out. Tanya listened, open mouthed, shock and disbelief battling for place on her face.

She spoke immediately when Dan stopped. "What`s happened to Daddy? Is he alright?" The concern in her voice was palpable.

Dan tried his best to look supportive. "I'm sure he is. Don't worry. But he went somewhere with work, and he hasn't come back as yet." He put his hands up. "But he will be back soon, I bet you."

"How do you know that? And who the hell are these people following my mom around?" Tanya was standing up straight, and looking at him sharply.

"I don't know, Tanya. But I'm trying to find out."

Tanya was breathing heavily. "And who the hell are you?"

Dan could feel the situation slipping out of control. He pulled out his cell phone. He dialed Jody's number and gave Tanya the phone. "Here, this is your mom. Speak to her. It's ringing."

Jody looked at the screen, then pressed the phone to her ear. Dan hoped and prayed Jody would answer.

"Hello, mom?" Tanya said. Dan felt relief course through him. Tanya listened intently as her mother spoke. Several times, Tanya lifted her eyes to look at Dan. Each time, Dan lowered his eyes.

Finally, Tanya hung up. She gave the phone back to Dan. Her face was more controlled. She brushed her hair back with her hands. "Thank you."

Dan said, "It's nothing, honestly. I'm in this now, too. The cops suspect me. The men who came to get your mother are now after me."

"So what do we do?"

"Tanya, listen to me. I want you to think very carefully. Do you remember seeing anything unusual in the weeks before? Was your dad acting weird? Anything you can remember would be useful."

After a while, she nodded to herself. "There was, in fact. One evening, I saw him walk to the end of our street. I was in his study, printing something. He got into a car and drove off with a couple of guys I've never seen before."

"Can you remember the car? Color, registration, make anything."

"Yeah, I do. The car was blue and it looked like a Chrysler. It was weird, because he's never done it before."

Dan felt a hammering inside his head, like someone was hitting the sides of his skull nonstop. There was a tightness in his neck and an ache behind his eyes.

"You sure it was a blue Chrysler?"

"Yes, positive."

"Anything else?"

"A man came to see him one evening. It was Friday. I had come home to pick up a dress—I had a sorority dinner that night. I opened the door to this man. He said he wanted to speak to Daddy."

"What did he look like?"

"Shorter than average, but chunky. You know, fat. He had a round face and he wore a black suit, I think. He even told me his name, when I asked him. Damn if I can remember it now."

The throbbing inside Dan's head was getting worse. "Marcus. Marcus Schopp? Is that what he said his name was?"

"Yes, that's right. How did you know?"

"He's your dad's boss. Was your mother in when these things happened? She never told me anything."

"Yes, she was. But maybe she didn't notice."

Tanya sat down again and held her head. "I can't believe this is happening."

Something in her tone bothered Dan. "Tanya?" he asked gently.

She spoke in a low voice. "I have never seen you before. But what the hell. You might as well know. Mom and Daddy don't get along anymore. They try to keep up appearances in front of me, but I know. I know."

Dan said, "It's alright."

"No, it's not. They've been drifting apart for years, really. They just act in front of me. Dad sleeps in the couch when he comes back late. I used to find him in the mornings. But it meant a lot to both of them that I came to this school. Daddy started working harder. I think that drove them apart." She picked at an invisible thread in the bed linen.

Dan came off his chair and knelt on the floor in order to face her. "You are right, Tanya. We are strangers. I know nothing about you. But let me tell you something. You coming here had nothing to do with your parents having trouble. Do you hear me? Absolutely nothing. Your parents are proud of who you are. Of who you have become."

"Yeah? Then why has Daddy disappeared?"

She was gazing at him and he saw the sadness build up until it broke over the wall and crashed out of her eyes. She put her hands on her face and sobbed. Dan felt awkward. He wanted to comfort her, but it didn't feel right. He sat there, staring at the floor.

Tanya got up and went to the bathroom. He heard her blow her nose and she came out with a tissue, drying her eyes.

"God, I'm sorry, Dan." She looked embarrassed.

Dan let out a big sigh. "Don't be. It's my fault. I should have warned you. Your mom didn't want you to know. But I had to know if you could shed any light on the matter. As it is, you've helped plenty."

"What do you mean?"

"What you told me so far. I need to look into it." He paused for a second. "Just one thing. When Marcus came around, did you hear any of their conversation?"

"No, they went into the living room and shut the door." She was standing near the window, looking out at the sunshine streaming through the trees. "Dad called me, you know."

"Really?" Dan stood up. "Since he disappeared?"

"Last week." She frowned, trying to think. "No, week before. Ten days ago."

"What did he say?"

"It was weird. He said he loved me, and everything would be alright. He told me not to speak to anyone, and not to tell anyone he called."

"Did he say where he was?" Tanya shook her head.

"Okay, Tanya, I want you to think about this. Could you hear any background sounds? Anything particular?"

Tanya was quiet for a while. "Yes, it was windy, I could hear it between his words. And a high-pitched sound, like a horse."

"A horse?"

Tanya shrugged. "Sounded like that. Who knows what it was."

"What number did her call from?"

"His own cell."

Dan thought for a while. Every cell phone call was recorded. Philip would have known that, and the fact that he could be traced from that call. Yet, he had taken that risk, maybe because he wanted to hear his daughter's voice.

Why? Was it for the last time?

"And he didn't leave any messages?"

"No."

Tanya turned around to face Dan. "Can you find my father?"

All of a sudden, she seemed like a lost girl, eyes streaked with tears, asking for help.

Dan felt a tightness in his limbs, and the slow spread of an anger that burned across his chest. He flexed his jaws before he spoke.

"I'll find him. I promise."

CHAPTER 18

"Captain!"

Mikhail Shevchenko turned at the voice behind him. He had his laptop open and was reading one of the emails sent from Kremlin. He shut the page and closed the laptop.

"Yes, Sasha."

Sasha looked excited. "The *Guboki* has returned. It's in the dock now."

"Very well, I am coming."

Shevchenko walked sedately down the gangplank as Sasha scurried ahead of him. As Shevchenko descended the stairs and entered the vast room, he heard the high whine of the crane and felt the tremor of the floor as it slid back in its semi-circle. He stood near the doorway and observed quietly. The glistening hull of the *Guboki* was resting on its holds. The crane straps were still fastened. There was a loud thud as the remainder of the floor locked into place. The number of men on the floor increased, mostly congregating around the machine.

Shevchenko strode over. Near the head of the machine, he peered closely at the removable data storage module. He gestured to Sasha, who came over and barked some orders. A man at the console chamber at the back punched some orders into a keyboard, and the clasps that hooked on the RDSM sprung free with a click. Shevchenko picked it up, and took the module out of its waterproof box. He headed towards the bridge.

"Come with me, Sasha," he ordered. The boy needed to learn.

They went up to the scientists' room next to the bridge. The two P's, they called them. Pavel and Pushkin. They took the RDSM from Shevchenko and plugged it into their system. The data was varied. It included atmospheric pressure, chemical samples and digital photographs. Most of it was technical, but the photographs and videos were what Shevchenko was most interested in. After some time, Pushkin bought up one of the images on the large screen. The pictures were dark, but as Pushkin went through the series, they became clearer. The *Guboki* had gotten closer to the ocean bed, its flashlight reflecting off the sand. Images of a long black line emerged on the seabed, stretching out into the murky distance.

"It's there," Sasha said.

"Yes," Shevchenko murmured. "But we expected that." He watched some more, chin in his hand. "Switch to video mode and keep it on a slow frame." After a while, Shevchenko looked at his protégé.

"This stretch looks alright as well. The *Guboki* needs a rest. Can the *Krasnaya* go down later tonight?"

Sasha nodded. "Of course, Captain. I will see to it at once."

"Do not send it down without me being there, Sasha. I want to check the RDSM first."

"No problem, Captain." Sasha said. "By the way, the sonar technician wants to see you."

Together, they went to the big white golf ball on the aft deck. The sonar guys had an office next to it. The senior technician was a man called Yuri. Shevchenko patted him on the back. Yuri took his headphones off. He pointed to a screen where a graph was continuously plotting out the sound waves coming from under the ocean.

"Small sounds coming from two hundred miles away, Sir. Not whales or other big fish. Too small to be a submarine. Don't know what they are."

Shevchenko peered closely. "Keep monitoring this. Can you keep a copy of the charts and see if there is a pattern?"

"No problem, Captain."

Shevchenko's phone rang. He took his cell out and looked at the screen. He excused himself and went down the ladder into the bowels of the *Nimika*. Within five minutes he was in his room with the door shut securely. As was the usual practice, the phone rang again. He answered it this time. Both of them waited for a second as the click of the encryption came on.

"Hello, it's me," the voice said. It was Val Ivanov.

"Yes, comrade. Have you got the information?"

There was a pause. "No, but it should not be long. We have one lead that we are pursuing actively. How are you doing?"

Shevchenko sighed. The longer he stayed out here in the middle of the Atlantic the greater the chances of him being spotted. He probably had been already. His voice became impatient.

"We are going ahead as planned. But as you know, this is the secondary role of the mission. We still await the important co-ordinates."

"And they will come, I promise you. Continue to show us what you can do. There is no indication the Americans suspect anything. Not as yet. Even when they do, it will take them a few days to get to you. Do not worry. You will be warned in advance."

"Please remember what I carry. My ship contains two of the most advanced machines in the entire Russian Navy."

"I know that. That is why you were chosen for this mission, Captain. For your experience with them. Now that you are here, let us make the mission successful."

"We need to hurry up."

"Do not worry."

"Listen to me. Our propellers and engine make a huge amount of noise. Any passing submarine will pick us up on their passive sonar easily. We can always pretend we are doing research and nothing else. After all, we are more than two hundred miles away from US shores. However, we do not want the attention. I do not have to tell you the catastrophe that will begin, if these machines fall into American hands."

There was a pause at the other end. Shevchenko knew Val was digesting it slowly, and wondering if there was a threat in what Shevchenko had said. There was, he had meant it, but he wasn't afraid. Shevchenko had powerful friends in Kremlin. He wouldn't be pushed by some criminal, however powerful *he* was.

"You don't have to remind me, Captain," Val said in a soft voice.

"Good." Shevchenko hung up.

He returned to the bridge. Sasha was waiting for him.

"The *Krasnaya* is ready for departure, Captain."

"Very good. Let us go." They went down to the dry dock and checked what was needed. When Shevchenko was up with the scientists, he had his laptop with him. He opened his emails and peered at the one he wanted.

"What depth and speed, Captain?"

"Same depth and speed as the previous dive. But this time we need to do this as well."

He pointed at his laptop. Sasha and the scientists leaned closer.

"Very good, Captain," said Pushkin with a smile.

*****

Val stared at the cell phone in his hand. He was forced into being nice to Shevchenko, and he hated it. He should be threatening the old man, telling him to shut up and do his job. But Shevchenko did have a point. They needed the information as soon as possible. Sooner or later, the US Navy would realize what the *Nimika* was up to. They didn't have much time. The phone beeped.

"It's me," Val said shortly.

"Any news of him?" Direct and to the point as usual.

"No, still looking." The voice at the other end made an impatient clucking sound.

"He's hiding somewhere in Barnham."

Val was starting to get the same impression. They had looked in Atlanta and in the counties around. Neither the Mexicans nor his men had found any trace of Longworth. The man was obviously using the cash he had stolen from Val. He wasn't calling on his cell, and probably using a fake name. He could be anywhere. But yes, it made sense he was in Barnham.

"There are still a few places around here where we have eyes," Val said. "Then we can head down to Barnham."

"You need to keep this as a priority."

"It *is* a priority." Val didn't like being told what to do.

"He was delivered to you, and you let him get away. Now this other guy has joined the search."

Val grimaced. He resented the tone, but he also knew about the new guy. The one who had smoked four Mexicans inside the house. Without using a gun. The man did sound interesting. Val wanted to meet the guy—and kill him slowly.

"Don't worry about either of them," Val growled. "Neither will be alive for much longer."

CHAPTER 19

Dan decided to take a bus back to Morningside. There was a stop on Virginia Highlands and he could walk from there. He sat by the window and stared out as the ornate buildings of the campus flashed by.

Number one. Philip had been in that blue Chrysler. With the Latino gang-bangers. What was he doing? Regardless of the answer, it was bad news. He thought of the men who had come to the house. They were now in the morgue. He needed to stop by and see Detective Brown. Find out where the ganglands were in Atlanta. Andy might have new evidence from the house, too.

Number two. Marcus Schopp. Who the hell was he? Sounded like he had a dark past. And he came around to Philip`s house. Must have been something urgent. They had a shouting match in the office as well.

Number three. The tall, blond guy.

Too many questions, not enough answers. He got off the bus and jogged the last twenty minutes to the house. He hadn't run for the last week, and he was used to running five miles a day. He got to Virginia Highland covered in sweat. A short run, no more than three kilometers, but he felt better. There was white tape around the outside of the house.

Philip and Jody`s American Dream. They had woken up one morning and the dream wasn't there anymore. He picked his way past the white tape and unlocked the front door. Not much had been cleaned up. The bodies in the kitchen had gone, leaving a stale smell of sweat behind. His black bag was still in the cupboard under the staircase. He walked through the kitchen area. There was a door leading out to the garage. He opened it and turned the light on.

The garage was large enough for two cars, but there was only one. A black Lincoln town car. Looked in good shape, too. Dan ran his hand down the side, onto the bonnet. No dust. The fenders gleamed. He tried the front door and it opened. It smelled of the leather seats inside. He made himself comfortable in the spacious driver's seat and looked around. There was no key in the ignition. He found it inside the dashboard drawer, tucked into the corner under some CD`s. The engine sprang to life. He pressed on the gas and the engine responded. The fuel tank was almost full.

He left the engine running and went to get changed. Upstairs was still the same. Clothes and torn carpet everywhere. He took out a change of clothes from his bag: a grey shirt and blue Chinos. Then he ran down and shut the engine off. He took the keys and went back upstairs. Time for a quick shower. As he rubbed himself dry, he went to the front bedroom. He saw it almost instantly.

A car that hadn't been there before. A maroon Buick salon. Two men in the front. Parked opposite the house, but both men were checking the house out.

Had they followed him? He hadn't seen anyone on the bus. He got dressed quickly and went downstairs. The hammer and knives were missing. He picked up a smaller kitchen knife and his bag. He went to the living room. He stayed away from the windows, but could see the maroon Buick clearly. It had seen better days.

Two Mexican guys in the front seat. The driver had tattoos up the side of his neck. As he watched, the car pulled out and headed down the avenue. Dan ran into the garage. He chucked the bag in the rear seat and pressed the remote for the garage door. The Lincoln leaped out into the driveway and churned up dust as it swerved onto the street.

Ahead of him, he could see the Buick at the end of the road. It indicated and turned left, heading for downtown. Dan kept four cars behind. Traffic was light. After twenty minutes driving, the Buick nosed up north. Dan recognized some of the land around, mainly because he could see the glint of sun on the Chattahoochee River in the far left. The Buick kept pushing up, and Dan saw signs for Cobb County soon. They were leaving Atlanta.

The air conditioner was on full blast. The sky was cloudier today, and judging from the black smear around the edges of the horizon, a storm was coming. He turned on the radio to a news channel.

There was a lot of noise about a senator`s connection with the Russians. His email had been hacked and some of his emails were sent to The Atlanta Herald, a local newspaper. The senator had extensive contacts with Russian businessmen, arranged trips for them to come over from Moscow, and all of these businessmen had powerful contacts in the Kremlin`s Red Square. His opponents were calling for him to resign. The senator was denying all knowledge of these emails, and a nationwide hunt had begun for the hacker. Dan half-listened. His eyes were on the Buick four cars ahead. It stayed on the I75, steadfastly heading northwest.

He remembered hearing something last week on the news about the Democrat convention being hacked. A national telecommunications company was in trouble, too. Bellport, a seaside town in New York state, had suffered a blackout of its internet communication. After Bellport, several counties in New York reported similar outages. Dan shook his head. Bad news got all the headlines.

As was his habit, he flicked channels for international news. If there was a terrorist attack or hostage situation he liked to know. Not that it was his concern anymore, but old habits die hard. It seemed almost weird that he wasn't operational anymore. But then again, he wanted to be free.

He rolled down the window and a blast of warm, humid air came in through the window. They passed by an airfield on the left. He didn't know the name.

Almost an hour later, he saw signs for the city of Marietta. Capital of Cobb county. The Buick rolled off a turnpike and descended into the city. A truck trundled past Dan and he kept behind it. They were at the outer limits of Marietta, and the Buick bumped along an industrial road with warehouses on both sides. Dan stayed behind the truck, the Buick one car ahead of it. Soon the Buick indicated right and turned into a warehouse. Dan drove past it, then did a hard left and pulled into the car park of a large building. It was a meat packing factory.

He locked the Lincoln and walked out, heading for the warehouse. The sky had darkened above and he could hear the rumble of thunder. He checked his watch. 1500 hours. He stopped at an overgrown bush before the gates of the warehouse. He could see the Buick in there, along with two other cars. All three were empty. Gang members, having a meeting. Probably some of the shot-callers. The front door was shut and he could see the steel bar outside, which could lock the door.

There was a path snaking around to the back. There was no one at the front of the warehouse courtyard to see him. He vaulted over the gates and landed on his toes. He moved quickly. He flattened himself against the corrugated iron sides of the warehouse. The place wasn't big. A fire escape led up to a door at the top. Windows too, but they were too high up to see. He tested the fire escape stairs, then stole his way up. At the landing, he paused. He put his ear to the door. Voices inside, some being raised. Muffled; they must be on the ground. Gently, he tried the door handle. It was open. A slight crack allowed him to see inside.

Six gang members were sat around a table on the ground floor. One of them wore a red bandana. All of them had their arms and necks covered in tattoos. As he watched, one of them got up, said something, and walked to the rear of the warehouse, where he opened a door. Dan shut the fire door and sprinted down the fire escape. He ran to the back and, shielding himself against the side, he looked around the corner. The man was taking a leak. The door behind him was shut. Dan took out the knife in his belt.

He crouched down low, his face almost touching the overgrown grass. Soundlessly, he traversed the distance between them. The man was just finishing. He zipped up and Dan was right behind him, his arm clamping around the man's face, jerking him back against him. The knife edge was thrust against the carotid artery in the soft part of the neck. The man grunted and went for his gun. Dan kicked with his knee, moving the hand away. He increased pressure on the knife.

"Move again, asshole, and this knife is going all the way in," he whispered. The man went still. "Do you understand?" The man mumbled something and nodded.

"Throw your gun on the floor. Do it! Slowly!" Dan pushed the knife in. A trickle of blood wound its way down the man's neck. Dan watched as the man fumbled in his belt, took out his gun and dropped it on the floor. Dan jerked the man around till he was facing the door.

"We're going in. Take it easy. Not only will I stick the knife in, but then use your body as a shield to get out, if they start shooting. Got that?" The man nodded. Sweat poured down his face, dampening Dan's hand clamped over his mouth.

"Open the door," Dan ordered.

Together, they walked in, Dan keeping a rigid clamp on the man's face. The five men around the table didn't notice at first until one of them pointed and stood up.

Dan was less than thirty feet away from the front door. He shuffled closer. He looked at the men, all of whom were now on their feet, guns drawn.

"Sit down," Dan shouted. They ignored him.

"You want him to die? He's going to die, I promise you." Dan removed his hand from the man' mouth and pulled his head back by his hair. "Tell them asshole," he whispered. The man broke into a frightened yelp of Spanish. There was shouting at the table, with hands and guns waving. Two of the guns remained calm and pointed straight at him. He kept shuffling back until he was six feet from the front door.

The man with the red bandana shouted at the rest in Spanish. Dan guessed he was the leader. The others shouted back and he pointed his gun at them and screamed. Two of them looked down. Red bandana looked towards Dan.

"If you kill him, you will die as well." His voice was calm, unhurried.

"Okay, let me kill him then." Dan put pressure on the knife and another drop of blood tricked down. The man screamed and kicked with his legs, but Dan held him firm.

"What do you want?" Red bandana said.

"Philip Longworth. Where is he?"

The man smiled. "The gringo? You are here for him?" He shook his head. "You are a fool. The gringo is dead already."

Dan ignored that. "Was he selling for you? Cocaine?"

A snarl came up on red bandana's face. "Yes, he was." He spat on the floor. "*Puta madre*. Then he vanished without paying us."

"You don't know where he is? So why do you think he's dead?"

The man smiled, a hard, cruel smile. One of the men spoke and he snapped back at him.

Dan said, "Atlanta PD, the FBI and the DEA are on this case now. If you tell me what the hell is going on, I might be able to cut you on a deal."

Another man shouted at the leader, who shouted back. For a while, they screamed at each other, waving their guns. Something was wrong here, Dan thought. This was more than gang business. The men calmed down and the leader looked at Dan again. Dan had used the time to move closer to the front door. He dragged the whimpering gang member with him. Less than four feet away now.

"How much money does Philip owe you?"

"More than fifty grand. You got that money, *cabron*?"

Jesus Christ. Philip, you asshole. What the fuck did you do?

"Who is the tall, blond guy?" Dan asked.

The leader's eyes narrowed and he didn't say anything. One of the men shouted at him again and they went off into another verbal match. Dan cleared the remaining space to the door and kicked it open. He shoved the man inside, who stumbled and sprawled on the ground. Dan shut the front door and used the bar to lock it. He sprinted towards the meat packer's factory. He could hear shouts and screams inside the warehouse. He got into the Lincoln, fired the engine and reversed it into the road. He slammed his foot on the gas. The wheels spun and the big car plunged forward. He was hurtling past the warehouse when the gang members came running out the side. They fired at him. Dan ducked low and kept the steering steady. A bullet tore into the body work, and another two whined overhead. Then he was past the warehouse and heading for the highway.

CHAPTER 20

McBride adjusted his hat and stared at the muddy waters of the Potomac river. It was turning warm in Washington. He liked coming to this park, where he often met his contacts. It was nice to stroll around as well. He heard the laughter of children behind him. He heard footsteps too, headed his way. He knew his men were keeping watch around him. On his earphones, he had not heard a warning. Instead, he heard something else.

"Greystalk approaching, now," a voice chirped in his left ear. McBride nodded, and waited in silence.

When politicians came to ask for help from Intercept, they never gave out their true names. Neither did they send their secretary. They came in person. Part of the reason was Intercept's deep connections in Capitol Hill. The other reason was to be safe. A brief, anonymous talk with another man in a park was safer than an official who could be bribed later by the media.

Greystalk sat down on the bench, next to McBride. They said hello.

Greystalk said, "Secretary of Defense called a meeting. A cyber-attack is underway."

McBride listened in silence. He said, "This have anything to do with that agent we spoke of last time?"

"Yes. A lot." They talked some more.

Greystalk said, "All our internet communications rely on those undersea cables. You know that. But the ones being targeted are actually the dark ones."

McBride said, "The cables for military use."

"Yes."

"We need to know how they got the location. Supposed to be a secret."

McBride said, "There is a mole. Also, you know about the ship? 200 miles out from our Atlantic coast. Russian research vehicle. It's a cover, obviously. It was near Bellport last week."

"Yes. A big line of cables land at Bellport. Right from London. One of our most important communication links to Western Europe."

They were silent for a few seconds.

McBride said, "What do you want?"

"Bring it to an end. Whatever it takes. But keep it silent. The President does not want to activate any federal units. No special forces. Delta and Navy SEAL's are out. This is a strictly deniable mission. Got that?"

"No political fall-out."

"Yes."

"Do you have anyone down there?"

McBride allowed himself a grim smile. "As a matter of fact, I think we do."

*****

Dan kept to the speed limit and drove steadily down the I-75. The first few drops of rain arrived, and thunder grumbled overhead. He kept an eye on the rearview, but there was nothing. He wasn't being followed. His cell beeped and he looked at the screen. He didn't recognize the number.

"Hello?"

"Dan, this is Lisa. Where are you?"

"Just heading back from Marietta. What's up?"

"I had a look into Marcus's old files from the DoD. They were classified, so I had to get a friend who works in DoD's Washington DC records office to release them to me."

"You didn't have to do that."

"Yes, I did. If there is something weird going on, I need to know. Marcus might go down, then the company might fold. I'm going to lose my job. This is about me as well."

"Alright. Why don't we meet up to talk about it?"

"Cool. Same café?"

In one hour, he was back in downtown Atlanta. Rain was falling in a constant drizzle now. Lightning flashed as he parked the car and walked out towards the Centennial Park. Lisa was waiting inside. She had an umbrella folded behind her seat.

"Jeez, you're wet."

Dan shrugged. "Just a little drizzle, that's all. You ordered?" He was suddenly hungry.

They got coffee and Dan ordered a turkey and cheese melt. He sipped the coffee and closed his eyes. He had needed that.

"Are you okay?" Lisa asked.

"Yes, fine. What did you find out about Marcus?"

"It's interesting. He was based in the Pentagon after he was discharged from active duty. There were no concerns while he was deployed. When he came back, he worked for some defense contractors, then applied for the Pentagon. His first job as an adjutant lieutenant colonel was to procure a license for long-range mortar shells. Well, one of the contractors he had worked for made the shells, and despite a competitive tendering process, they got it." Lisa clasped her hands together and looked thoughtful. "That's not all. This pattern repeated itself over the next two years. He was rumbled finally, and kicked out."

"Do you have the reports with you?"

"I couldn't print them out. But I have them at home on my laptop. You're welcome to have a look."

"Thanks."

"Are you still looking for a place to stay?"

Dan nodded.

"Well," she said. "If it`s only for a night or two, you can rest on my couch."

Dan wiped his mouth and shook his head. "No, I don't want to inconvenience you."

"You won't be, I promise. By the way, have you seen this?" Lisa took out a folded newspaper from her bag. It was the Atlanta Herald. The front page was news of the senator who was being accused of being a Russian spy. She turned to one of middle pages and handed the paper to Dan.

It was a report on the four gang members he had killed at Philip's house. There was a photo of the exterior of the house.

"That's Philip`s house, isn't it?" Lisa asked.

Dan told her what had happened. Her hand went to her neck. It stayed there, massaging nervously.

"My God. Do you think other gang members will come back?"

Dan sighed and told her about what he had just learned about Philip. She listened with wide eyes. When Dan had finished, she held her forehead. "Philip was selling drugs? Cocaine?"

Dan nodded. "And it looks like he owed them money as well."

"Why would he be selling cocaine?"

Dan shrugged. "To make money. He was in debt, and I don't think he was earning enough. It's a dumb plan, but maybe he got sucked into it and carried away."

"So now what?"

"We still have to find him. I need to see Marcus again. First off, can I come to your place and see the reports?"

It was six o'clock and Lisa had finished work. They drank their coffee and headed out to her apartment. Lisa lived north of Midtown, near the Botanical Gardens. Dan drove up through the line of red tail lights smudged in the rain-splattered windscreen. The air-con was on and the wipers worked full time. It took them almost an hour to get to Lisa's place.

It was a new apartment complex two blocks away from the gardens. It was made of white and black marble, with a garden courtyard at the front. Blue, red and yellow lights lit up the plants and trees. What the realtors liked calling a luxury development. Dan drove in and parked at the underground lot. He followed Lisa up into the apartment. The place was smart and minimal, with two bedrooms, a balcony and a bathroom.

"Have a seat," Lisa indicated the couch in the reception in front of the TV.

"Thanks," Dan said. He sat down, looking at the art work on the wall. Lisa returned with her laptop. She showed Dan the emails from her colleague at the DoD. Dan clicked on the attachments. The reports looked genuine enough. They were details of disciplinary actions against Marcus Shoppe. He had been warned not to carry out preferential canvassing for contracts, but had continued to do so. Eventually, military police had got involved, and he had been court martialed. Scant evidence was found against him, and he was let off with a light sentence.

"Very hard to prove any actual wrongdoing," Lisa said, as she watched Dan read the last report.

He nodded. "Yes. Apart from the fact that he worked for those companies. What time does Marcus leave the office?"

"About now, sometimes later."

"Do you know what car he drives?"

"A blue Toyota salon."

Dan stood up. "It's time I paid him another visit."

Lisa gave him a key for the apartment. Dan told her not to wait up for him. She showed him the smaller bedroom he would be sleeping in. It was next to hers. He thanked her and left.

CHAPTER 21

He parked in the red brick Victorian house opposite Schopp's office. He turned off the ignition and the lights and waited. The rain was letting up, and the roads were slick. Lights were still on inside, and he saw one of the guards strolling around in the courtyard. He checked his phone and gave Jody a quick call.

He needed to get Jody and Tanya out of Atlanta, but he didn't want to explain that on the phone. He spoke to Jody briefly, not divulging what he had learnt about Philip just now. He hung up and continued to wait. He turned the radio on. More on the news about the slow upload speeds that were affecting most of Georgia. Important emails were not getting sent. Computers were crashing across the state, worse in Atlanta than anywhere else. Dan turned up the news, listening.

At 8:00 p.m. all the lights in the office went off. Shortly after, a black pick-up truck left. Dan figured that contained the guards. The next car to leave was a Toyota salon. In the streetlights he could see the dark blue color. He waited a beat, then followed.

Traffic was less now and soon they were up in leafy DeKalb Avenue. There was no car between them. Dan stayed fifty meters behind, but it was pretty obvious that the two cars were headed in the same direction. Signs for a development called Lakeside Views appeared and the Toyota turned in. Dan drove past, then pulled onto the dirt sidewalk. After ten minutes he drove back towards the development. It was a gated community. The guards at the security room flagged him down. Dan lowered his window as the guard stepped out.

"Message for Marcus Schopp. Philip Longworth has been found, and wants to speak to him urgently. Tell him it's Dan, Philip's friend."

The guard looked at Dan and the car, then went up the steps. He spoke on the phone, then came back.

"Okay, he'll see you. Its number fourteen, the third house on the left." Dan gave the guard a thumbs-up, and drove in through the open gates.

It was a detached modern villa, Spanish style. The rest of the buildings were similar. Dan ran up the steps and pressed the bell. The door opened, but it was on a chain. The round figure of Marcus Shoppe stood framed in the light.

"You alone?" Schopp drawled in his low voice.

"Yes."

Schopp peered out through the door. Then he took the chain off and opened it. Dan shut the door behind him.

"In here," Schopp said. Dan followed him into an opulent drawing room. Chandeliers hung from the ceiling. Schopp pressed a button on a remote and steel blinds came down over the windows. He turned to Dan. He was still wearing his blue work suit. His features were softer, but his eyes were wary.

"You found Philip?"

"No, I lied. I couldn't get in here otherwise."

Schopp's face swelled and turned purple. His eyes became black slits and a vein popped in his forehead. "You son of a bitch!" he screamed. He threw the remote on a sofa. "I can't believe I listened to your shit. You son of a bitch."

Dan regarded him calmly. "You need to tell me what you know about Philip, Marcus."

Schopp was staring at the floor, shaking his head. "You don't know shit. You're going to get us all killed. God damn it." He began to pace up and down the room.

"You know Philip was selling cocaine, didn't you?"

Schopp came to an abrupt halt. He stared at Dan. "You don't know anything. Nothing."

Dan stepped forward. He thought of Tanya, blaming herself for her parent's marriage and now for her father's disappearance. He thought of Jodie, sitting in that hotel room, scared and worried.

"Listen to me. I told you already, four gang-bangers came into Philip's house last night. They wanted Philip. I dealt with them. Today, I followed their friends to Marietta. I found out how much Philip owes them. He's got a daughter and wife who are also in danger."

Schopp was pacing around again. "What do you want me to do?"

"Who is the tall, blond guy?"

Schopp stopped again. There was that fear in his eyes that Dan had seen before. He swallowed, began to say something, then walked away again.

"You had an argument with Philip in the office before he left for Barnham. Before that, you went to see him at his house. What for?"

Schopp sat down heavily on the sofa and covered his face in his hands. He mumbled something.

"Talk to me, Marcus."

Schopp turned to him and smiled. That surprised Dan. It was an ironic smile. "You call yourself a friend, and you don't know anything about Philip."

"Then tell me. His daughter and wife deserve to know."

Schopp sighed heavily. "Yes, Philip had started selling cocaine. It`s not hard. There are plenty of dealers on every street corner. Mainly the Latino gangs. Plenty of demand as well. You wouldn't believe how popular that white powder is in this city. Philip had to do something. His life was spiraling out of control."

Dan waited. Schopp passed a hand over his bald head and stared down at the carpet.

"He had cancer. Of the glands, and in his blood. Lymphoma or leukemia—some shit like that. He didn't tell his family, because he didn't want them to worry. He needed money for the medical bills. Chemotherapy and shit. He couldn't get insurance. No one would give him a loan against the house. So he had to do this."

Dan felt a throbbing headache inside his skull. He closed his eyes, feeling the pressure behind them. He remembered the stacks of unpaid medical bills on the floor of Philip`s study.

"Why did he tell you?"

Marcus said, "I was his only friend. He helped me set the company up after Dynamic Corp, my previous company, failed."

"What else?" Dan said.

Schopp shook his head. "Listen to me. Go back and wait for him to return. You're going to get us all killed."

"Is Philip still alive?"

"I don't know," Schopp whispered. He looked up at Dan. "I`m begging you. Leave this alone."

"What`s going on, Marcus?"

"You're way in over your head in this. I`m telling you, you'll get us all killed. Now get the hell out of here."

CHAPTER 22

Lisa was in bed by the time Dan got back. He let himself in with her key. He got changed and lay down on the small bed. He had difficulty fitting into it. He gave up after a while, got up and transferred the bedding to the floor. He lay down and sighed. Much more comfortable. He thought of Philip. He wondered if Jody knew anything about his illness. Philip probably hid it all. Couldn't speak to anyone… apart from Marcus Schopp, it seemed. He saw his life slowly wither away and fade, like he was watching it from a train speeding away. Then it took a life of its own, dark and maleficent.

There was a lot Schopp was hiding. He was scared. Something bigger, much bigger than the cocaine. Maybe something related to Marcus` past. Dan thought until he couldn't think anymore, then fell asleep.

He woke up once at 5:00 a.m., then fell back asleep. Bright light spilling in through the open window woke him up again. He got up and stretched. Eight o'clock. He had slept for a good eight hours. He went out into the kitchen. There was a note on the counter.

"Off to work. Croissants out, and OJ in the fridge. Help yourself to coffee. Lisa."

Dan started by doing some yoga. He did some Pranayama to cleanse his lungs out, drawing the air in to the pits of his stomach before letting it go slowly. He flexed the small joints—wrists, elbows, ankles and then did the fourteen steps of the *karthik asana*. He was sweating by the time he finished. He showered and ate breakfast, then left.

He fired up the Lincoln and drove down to Atlanta PD. He called Andy Brown on the way in. He was at the office. Dan was shown in. Brown sat in an open cubicle, next to Harris and in a line with other detectives. A patrolman pulled someone in handcuffs and orange jail suit ahead of Dan as he walked in. Brown stood up and shook hands with Dan.

"Found anything yet?" he asked. Dan took a seat next to him.

"I was going to ask you the same question," Dan said.

"Fingerprints and DNA showed the gang members. There are other DNA samples, but nothing shows up on our databases."

"Nationally?"

"Nothing." He leaned closer to Dan and jerked a thumb. "By the way, the chief wanted to interview you. I submitted a statement on your behalf. It was an act of self-defense, and there are no relatives lining up to press charges. I took care of it."

"Thanks," Dan said. He told Brown about Philip and the cocaine, and about Marcus. Brown raised his eyebrows as he listened. Then he shook his head. "Poor bastard. You reckon this is all true?"

"The part about Philip's illness is true. I saw those unpaid medical bills myself. I could ask Carter Medical, but I know they won't give away confidential information."

"So what's left?"

"I need to head down to Barnham. See what Philip was up to there."

"You know where to go?"

Dan nodded. "Lisa will get me the address of the place. It's a small town anyway." He glanced at his watch. He said goodbye to Brown and got going.

He drove south, heading for Hartfield-Jackson Airport. Fifteen minutes of traffic later he was in Grove Park. He drove through a wide avenue with tall Project buildings on the left and dilapidated brown brick houses on the right. Clumps of young men hung around in street corners. Dan drove into a drug store parking lot and pulled up. He counted the money he had. One hundred and fifty. Should be enough for what he needed. He rang Tanya and spoke to her. She was in-between classes, and they spoke quickly.

He went into the drug store. The owner was Asian, middle-aged, spiky hair with glasses. He looked at Dan and rubbed his eyes inside his glasses. Dan slid him a five-dollar bill.

"Where's the nearest gun store?"

The man looked at the bill and smoothed it. He put it in his pocket.

"Union Street and Haven junction. Down left, five minutes' walk."

"Thanks. Can I leave my car here for ten minutes?"

The gun shop was down an alley. He looked around him, then went in. The iron grill door chimed when he opened it. A squat, fat man with large eyes stared at him.

"I need a Sig Sauer P226, suppressed. Fifteen clip magazine, and two boxes of extra rounds."

The man scratched his belly. "Let me have a look," he grumbled.

He came back in a few seconds. He put a box on the counter, opened it and picked out the grey gun. Dan took it. The familiar weight and feel in his hand was comforting. He slipped the magazine out. Empty as expected. He checked the serial number. Intact. He nodded at the man.

"What round does this take?"

"I got two Sig P226`s. One chambers the 0.40 Smith Wesson round, and another for 0.357 Sig. Hang on." He walked off and came back in a minute. "I got the 9mm as well. Which one do you want?"

"You got all three?"

The man raised his eyebrows and smiled. He had two front teeth missing. "We got it all, man" he said. "Which one do you want?"

Dan thought for a while. He wanted a heavier round than the 9mm. He wanted to carry an assault rifle, but it would be much harder to disguise. "I'll go for the 0.357."

The man grinned at Dan again. "Heavy duty, huh?"

Dan stared at him impassively until he stopped smiling. He ducked underneath the counter and came out with two boxes. Dan checked them. 357 V crown nickel plated cartridges. Hollow tip. 20 in each box. He took four of them.

"How much?"

"One hundred twenty-five."

"I need a knife as well."

"What type?"

"A kukri."

"A what?"

A forlorn hope. "Never mind. Have you got a Force Recon commander, about 12 inches with handle?"

"Think so."

"That will do for now."

The knife was in a black nylon and Dan pulled it out. The grip felt good. Not as good as his kukri, but it would more than do the job. He swung his right wrist around in circles, flashing the knife in different directions.

The shop keeper was watching him. "You a knife man, huh?"

"You could say that."

He walked back to the parking lot. A couple of kids were trying to look inside the driver's side window. Dan approached them slowly.

"Can I help you?" The kids turned around and looked at Dan, a grin on their faces. Dan stared back at them, and the grin faded. They shrugged and walked off. Dan got into his car and drove out, heading up towards Druid Hill. It was past eleven o'clock and the traffic was thickening. He got to the turn before Emory University and parked the car in a side road where he could still see the street ahead coming down the hill from the college. He put the loaded Sig in his glove box. He wound both front windows down. The folded knife was in his front belt line.

He waited. After ten minutes he saw Tanya, coming slowly down the hill. She was dressed in blue jeans and a pink half sleeve top. Dan put the windows up and took the Sig in his hand. A few moments later, he saw them. Two men, walking faster. As they went past the side road, Dan locked the car, put the Sig in his back pocket and sprinted after them. He turned left, down the hill. Ahead of him, he could see the two men. They wore dark jeans with holes in them, and leather jackets. In front of them, he could see Tanya. There was a nature reserve at the bottom of the hill, and Tanya headed into the woods. The two men followed. Dan increased his pace. As he got into the woods, he spotted the two men in front.

They were spread apart, looking around. He couldn't see Tanya.

CHAPTER 23

Dan stepped behind a tree as one of the men turned around. He heard their footsteps moving ahead in the silence, and peered out. They were going deeper into the forest. He followed, keeping close to the trees, crouching down low so the men didn't see him. The Sig was out in his right hand. The path dipped in the middle and he saw a flash of blonde hair ahead. Tanya. The men had seen her too, and increased their pace. In the seclusion of the woods, the sound of footsteps was loud. Tanya looked back. She saw the men and broke into a run. So did the men, and behind them, Dan. Tanya was fit, and she ran fast. The men were slower. There was a stream in the way and Tanya jumped over it, but she slipped and fell on the other side.

The men splashed into the water. Tanya got up and ran again. The path curved upwards, dense green foliage on either side. It was slippery as well, and it slowed her down. She held on to a tree trunk and pulled herself up.

The men had crossed the stream when one of them caught his friend's arm and pointed back. Dan was running behind them openly now. They took their guns out. One man stayed behind while the other ran after Tanya. The one who stayed pointed his gun at Dan. Dan dropped to his knee, Sig held in both his hands.

He aimed at the midriff and squeezed off two shots just as he heard the man's non-suppressed weapon crash out a round. He had rolled over by then, and the round whizzed over his head. Dan was on the ground now, wet with mud, but ready for the kill shot. He didn't need it. His previous rounds had found their mark. The man was on the ground. His arms were twitching. Dan fired another two and the body shook, then stilled.

Dan heard a woman's scream. He got up and ran, jumping over the stream. He fell on the other side, rolled over and ran up the path. Above him, the man had almost caught up with Tanya. She was finding it hard on the slippery path. Her running trainers gave her no grip, and she was on all fours, going up slowly. The man looked behind, saw Dan, and fired. Dan fell to the ground and rolled into the bushes. The shot thundered and zipped into the bushes harmlessly, but he slipped and fell further back.

He clawed with his hands, fighting for purchase on the ground. The man was standing, realizing Dan's predicament. He was aiming his gun at him. Dan didn't have any time. He dug his boots into the ground, slowing himself. He fired twice in quick succession. One shot up, one down. The man's head snapped back like he had been punched by a heavyweight boxer, the gun arm dropped and his legs buckled. A red mist sprayed up where his head had been.

Dan grabbed a heavy root. The slope wasn't too steep, but his weight meant he slid easily down unless he stopped himself. His feet found support in a rock and he lifted himself back up on the path. He swung the gun around. No one else following. He allowed himself a few seconds, breathing hard, staring at the stream below. Nothing. He looked up and saw Tanya's mud-stained face peeking out the bushes. He reached her, and squeezed her shoulder.

"You okay?" Dan asked her.

She nodded in silence, her face drawn and white. "You did well. Really well," Dan said.

He crouched in front of the first dead man. He had stopped a bullet with his face. Result—not much face left. Dan patted him down and found a Glock 22. He used his shirt to pick the weapon up and put it in his pocket. The man had a wallet with some bills and change. No ID. He lifted the shirt and had a look at the chest. No tattoos. Same on the hands and neck. They went down to the other man, sprawled on his back near the stream. Dan looked closely at the face. Caucasian. Swarthy, heavy built. Could be Russian or Eastern European. There was a tattoo on his left wrist. Something written in Cyrillic letters. Probably Russian.

Dan frisked him quickly. The wallet had some money again, but no driving license, credit card or social security card. He had a Glock 22 as well. Dan picked it up and checked the serial number. He put the gun in his back pocket too, again using his shirt to pick the weapon up by the butt. He picked up all the shell cases from the rounds.

They walked down towards the road. Dan glanced at Tanya. She was very quiet. Withdrawn. She could be in shock, but overall, she was taking it very well.

Tanya pushed back the hair falling on her face. She nodded. "Okay, I guess." She looked around her.

"Where to now?"

"Reckon we can go back to your dorm room to clean up?"

"I guess so."

Where the nature reserve ended and the roads began, Dan stopped and checked the street. No cars parked with a driver sitting, waiting, watching. He grabbed Tanya's hand and they walked back up the hill towards the university. They got some funny looks as they went into her dorm. Inside her room, Dan let Tanya get changed.

When she came out, she was running her hand through her long hair, head bent to one side. She asked him, "How did you know?"

"I had my doubts when they turned up at your parent's house after I left you. I figured they must have followed me. More worrying, they were keeping an eye on you. I needed to flush them out." He looked at her. "You did well," he repeated.

She sat down next to him. "What's going on, Dan?"

"I am starting to find out, I think. But it will still take time. For now, it's important that you're somewhere safe."

"If I stay on campus, I should be safe."

"Maybe, but you can't stay on campus like a hermit. Your friends might want to party in town, and you could go with them. Until this blows over, I think you should stay somewhere else."

"Like where?"

"Where your mom is right now, at the hotel."

Tanya packed the things she needed, then they headed out towards downtown. Dan drove carefully, keeping an eye out for any tails. If there was, they were damn good, because he saw nothing.

In the hotel, Jody was cautious about opening the door. Her eyes lit up when she saw her daughter. They hugged, and the tears fell spontaneously. Dan stepped inside and shut the door.

He cleared his throat. The two women looked at him. Dan said, "You need to get out of Atlanta for a while."

Jody said, "Why?"

"Because it's not safe. There are gangs everywhere in this city, and I have a feeling we are looking at a combination of different gangs that are after you. Well, after Philip." His mind raced over, wondering if he should bring up Philip's drug dealing. Then he decided against it. Jody did not seem to know a lot about her husband's life. Even if she did know about the drugs, there wasn't a great deal she could tell Dan. But one thing was bothering him still.

"Jody, when they got into your house, they had keys. Had your or Philip's keys been stolen or lost before Philip disappeared?"

Jody thought, then shook her head. "No. I don't think so."

Tanya was silent for a while, staring down at her hands. Her eyes were clear when she looked up at Dan.

"What was Daddy mixed up in?"

"I don't know yet," he said.

"Is he dead?" Her voice was flat.

"I don't know."

She looked away and tightened her jaws. "Damn it."

Tanya said, "You can't do this on your own. You need my help."

Dan smiled. "I'll try and do as much as I can. I'll call when I need your help. Right now, I want you to be safe."

"But where?"

Dan looked at both of them and said, "I have a house in Bethesda. It's not been lived in a great deal in the last few years as I have mostly worked abroad. But you are welcome to stay there till this blows over."

Jody seemed to do a double take. "You're gonna let us stay in your house?"

"There's no one else staying there, Jody. Might as well get used. Unless you have family that you can stay with."

Jody looked at Dan and shook her head. "No, we don't."

Jody came forward. She reached out and held Dan's hand. Her touch was warm, and Dan felt a hint of embarrassment.

Jody said, "You're a kind man, Dan. You don't show your true feelings, but your actions speak louder than any words."

Dan didn't say anything. He took out his cellphone and called his realtor in Bethesda. She was still in the office. Dan explained that he wanted his house to be opened for the Longworths' and agreed on a time and place for them to meet.

Tanya helped Jody pack, and the three of them went downstairs to the car park.

CHAPTER 24

Val Ivanov stood by the stream in the woods and looked down at the dead body. There was another one further up the path. Val kicked the body.

"Idiot," he hissed. He could guess what had happened. Small footprints of a girl's sneakers were everywhere. They had followed the girl without checking if someone was following *them*. He walked up the slope to where the other body lay crumpled. Artin was going through his pockets.

"Wallet and gun gone," Artin said, looking up at Val. Val squatted. The man's face was non-existent. He looked around the body and further out in the grass. No shell cases. The killer was meticulous. He turned to Artin.

"How did we find them?"

"Two *Bratok* came to look for them. They were late for the evening hand-over. Took them a while to find the bodies."

"What about the girl?"

"We sent a man inside, dressed like a college kid. She's not in her dorm."

"Now she's missing too?"

Artin stood up slowly and backed away. "We will keep looking..."

"Shut up!" Val turned and stormed down the path. The three men at the bottom scattered. Val clamped down on his jaws. Goddamn it. The girl had a protector, and he knew who it was. That man who came to look for Philip. Dan Roy. He had wasted the Mexicans, and now his own *Bratok*. It was time he paid the price. Val turned to Artin.

"That big bastard who's been hanging around Longworth's house. It's time we had a meeting."

*****

Dan drove Tanya and Jody down to Hartfield-Jackson and dropped them off at the boarding gates. Dan felt embarrassed when Tanya hugged him. He let go quickly, turned around and left. They had the keys to his house, and from Dulles Airport would take the train to Bethesda. Dan felt relieved that they were out of harm's way. He could now concentrate on the job at hand.

Dan was walking back to the short stay car park when his cell buzzed. Caller ID hidden. He answered.

"It's me, Brown."

"What's the matter?"

"Where are you?"

"Heading back uptown."

"I need to tell you something." Dan didn't like the tone of Brown's voice. He waited.

"Marcus Schopp is dead. A patrolman found his body inside a car registered to him. Two shots to the head, close range."

Dan felt a cold numbness spreading into his limbs. He leaned against a concrete post in the parking lot.

"Where and when?"

"On a quiet street, mid-town. Found this morning around 8:00 a.m. Dead for an hour, at least. His cell phone and wallet were gone. Keys were in the ignition."

Dan thought quickly. "Any damage to the car?"

"No."

"Any sign of struggle?"

"No."

"Forensics?"

"Nada. Going through it now, but nothing exciting. I'll keep you in the loop, if something turns up."

"Thanks for letting me know."

"You went to see him last night, didn't you?"

There was no point in denying it. The security had seen him, and he might have been spotted by the neighbors as well.

"Yes, I did."

Brown sighed. "Look, I gotta call you in. Just give me a statement. Keep the captain happy. No one's pressing charges."

"Do you want me to come now?"

"Yes. And Dan?"

"Yeah?"

"Be careful, buddy." Brown hung up.

Dan got to the Lincoln and sat, clutching the steering wheel as he thought to himself. He needed to get in touch with Lisa. Make sure she was okay.

"Hello?" It was a relief to hear her voice. She sounded loud.

"Marcus Shoppe is dead."

"I heard. I was just about to call you." Her voice was strident, anxious.

"Are you okay?" Dan said.

"No, I'm not. What the hell is going on, Dan? You went to see the guy last night and this morning he's wound up dead." She stopped. "Sorry, I know how that sounded. I didn't mean it like that. I'm worried, Dan. Just really worried. About you, more than anything else. I don't know what to do." The high pitch had come back in her voice. She was losing it, he could tell. He gripped the phone harder.

"Hey, calm down. I'm fine. Just take it easy. Where are you?"

"At the office."

"Why don't I meet you for a coffee? At the usual place?"

Lisa agreed. Dan hung up.

As he sat stewing in the traffic and ruminating over the day's events, he noticed the car. A red Ford, about four cars behind on the second lane. The driver was a woman, and she had a passenger in the back. He had seen the car as he had come out of the parking lot at the airport. As they nudged up slowly on the black asphalt river of motors and humanity, Dan changed lanes. The car stayed in the same lane. Past downtown, the traffic was less, and he speeded up. The Ford accelerated and stayed four cars behind. Dan took the turnpike to get on the road for Lisa's apartment. The car followed. As he went into Lisa's road, the car drove past, speeding around the bend.

Dan went into Lisa's apartment and got changed. Then he drove back downtown. The rain had relented and the humidity was less. Dark clouds still scudded low across the sky. That didn't stop the heat, however. It was still hot. Maybe not in the nineties, but still high eighties, he reckoned. Lisa was sitting at an outside table, waiting for him. She waved at him.

Dan slid into a seat and gazed at her. "Are you alright?"

She looked down and picked her nails. "Sorry about earlier."

"No problem. I know this is weird."

"I feel bad. I checked the guy out, thought he was up to something. Now he winds up dead."

"Lisa, he *was* up to something. So was Philip. Marcus was running scared. I reckon Philip is, too. If he's still alive."

"You think he is?"

"Yes, I think so. If he was dead they would have found him by now." He shrugged. "Or maybe they just haven't found his body as yet. Look, all I know is that I need to keep looking."

The waitress came and they ordered coffees. As Lisa sipped hers she said, "Let's head back to my apartment after this."

Dan shook his head. "I have to go to the police station." Dan told her about his conversation with Brown.

"Jeez, Dan. This keeps getting worse."

"You aren't going back to work?" Dan asked.

"I don't have to. I've taken the rest of the week off."

"I reckon that's good for you. Get a break, while things cool down."

"It's not just that. I don't even know if the company will remain open now that Marcus is dead."

Dan leaned forward. "Hey, I'm sure it will. Don't worry."

They finished their coffees and left. As they drove, Dan glanced at her.

"Do you mind if I stay one more night at yours?"

Her face was impassive. "Sure, no problem."

"But tomorrow morning I'll be gone."

"Gone where?"

"I need to head down to Barnham, where Philip was last seen."

Lisa stared out the window at the traffic. "I'm coming with you."

"No, Lisa. I'll be looking around, asking questions. If Philip is hurt, then the men responsible will come after me. I can't have you around there as well."

"I can look after myself."

"I know you can," he said gently. "This is not about that. If something happened to you, I wouldn't forgive myself."

"I *said* I can handle myself, Dan. Look, I have three days leave. I can sit at home and worry about what you're doing, or I can come and sit by the seaside, catch some rays. You know what I'm saying?"

Dan sighed. "You aren't going to listen to me, are you?"

She grinned for the first time. "Hell no."

*****

Dan drove down to the police station and presented himself to the desk. In an interview room Andy Brown stood up and shook hands. There was a woman Dan hadn't seen before. She wore blue pants and a blue jacket. She showed Dan her badge.

"Captain Andrea Hodge," the woman said in a flat voice. Hodge had a sharp beak of a nose and flat, black eyes that went with her voice. Her hair was raven black too, her skin tanned. Dan stared at her briefly, then at Brown. Dan was getting a bad feeling.

"Sit down," Hodge said. "Can you say your name for the recorder?"

"Am I under arrest?"

"No, you are not," Hodge said. "But we need to ask you questions."

Dan looked at them in turn. Brown shrugged, trying to put Dan at ease. "Where were you the morning Marcus Schopp was murdered?"

"Sleeping."

Hodge gave Dan a cold look. "Don't get funny on me, Mr. Roy. There's been a murder and you are a suspect."

"I was sleeping at a friend's house in Atlanta."

"Can this friend vouch for you?"

"She can, yes."

Hodge wrote something down and nodded. "Why did you go to see the deceased the night before?"

"I'm here to look for my aunt's husband, who is missing. He worked for Marcus, hence I went to see him."

"It's a gated compound. How did you get in?"

Easy does it. "I said I had information that was important to him."

"What information?"

Dan shrugged. "About Philip. He let me in."

Hodge had that dead-eyed fish stare that Dan didn't like. "Then what happened?"

"He said he couldn't help me. So I left."

"Bullshit," Hodge said. She leaned forward. "You told him you had information on Philip so he let you in. What information?"

"He was in financial difficulty. Bills and college fees."

"What else?"

"That's it."

Hodge sat back in her chair and glanced at Brown. He didn't say anything.

"Why are you holding back?" Hodge said softly.

Dan folded his hands across his chest. Hodge's eyes flickered over his body. "I'm not," Dan said.

"Let me tell you something, Mr. Roy. I got a call from the FBI today. They want to know what happened to Marcus Schopp. Do you know why the FBI is interested?"

Dan shook his head. "No."

"The FBI got a call from the Pentagon. They would send Military Police, but Marcus was a civilian. Do you follow?"

Dan nodded. "MP would not investigate the death of a civilian, even if he was ex-Army."

"So why the hell is the Pentagon so interested in a cable engineer?"

"I don't know," Dan said.

Hodge flexed her jaws. Brown remained silent. "You arrive in Atlanta, and Philip Longworth's house gets trashed."

"Correction," Dan said. "I surprised them."

"Whatever. Then they come back, and you," she paused for effect. "You single-handedly blow them away. I got four dead gang members, a dead former army guy, and another guy missing. Not to mention his wife and daughter. His wife has not filed a report. Don't you find that a little odd?"

Dan didn't answer that. Brown scratched his lower lip and did his bored look.

"What I'm trying to say, Mr Roy," Hodge said, "is that we have the FBI involved in this now. We have pressure. To find things out. And you are holding back."

Pressure. "If I knew something, I would tell you."

Hodge scraped her chair back. She flicked the digital tape recorder off. She gave Dan one last dead stare.

"Get him out of here," she told Brown.

Brown walked Dan to the door and down the steps. "Sorry about that," he said.

"Don't be. This shit's gone far enough."

"This is something big, Dan. Really big. I don't know what exactly, but the FBI is pretty pissed. Apparently this guy Marcus was someone important. I don't know why. The Feds are being the Feds, keeping their cards close to their chests. There *is* something the Captain doesn't know yet."

"Like what?"

"The fingerprints finally came up with something. We had to go global. Interpol gave us this guy. Vyalchek Ivanov. Second generation Russian immigrant. From Brighton Beach in New York. Big kahuna in the Russian organized crime ring. They call themselves the *Bratok,* or Brotherhood. Got chapters in every major American city. Drugs, prostitution, extortion, you name it. This guy's a real douche bag. There's a rumor he killed one of his own men a few weeks ago, 'cos he let someone escape. He's been in a couple of times himself, for armed robbery, then extortion."

"Who knows?"

"Harris and myself. I have to tell the captain soon. Thought you would like to know."

Dan nodded. "Thanks." He told Brown about the two men he had just killed. Brown put his hands on his hips and looked up at the sky. "Jesus Christ."

"One of them had a tattoo on his wrist. Pretty sure the writing on the tattoo was Russian."

CHAPTER 25

Dan headed back to Lisa`s. He spotted the red Ford again. The driver was holding back now, staying six cars behind. Dan drove slowly, making sure he kept the car in his sights. When he pulled into Lisa`s apartment complex the red Ford was gone.

Dan let himself in with the key. Lisa was sitting in the sofa, her feet up on the coffee table, her eyes on her laptop. She glanced up as Dan entered. Her hair was tied up in a ponytail, and she was wearing pink shorts that showed off her shapely legs. Dan felt his eyes travel up and down her.

"Hey," Lisa said. "How'd it go with the cops?"

Dan told her, including the part about Tanya. Lisa`s eye widened.

"They attacked your cousin?"

"The Russian mob is on the case as well. It`s getting serious."

"Dan, I reckon you should let the cops handle this now."

Dan shook his head. "Until I turned up, they'd done sweet FA."

"What does that mean? Sweet FA?"

"Sweet fuck all."

Lisa threw her head back and laughed. "Where did you learn that from?"

"Something the guys used to say in England."

"What, the soldiers?"

"Civilians too."

"Sweet FA. That`s got to be my favorite Brit term of all time."

Lisa turned her attention back to the laptop. The broadband connection was slow. Google maps wouldn't upload. Lisa checked her modem and router. The laptop seemed to be working fine, but the green light in the router was flashing yellow.

"That normally means poor connection," Lisa said. "It's been like this the whole week. At work too, most of our computers are either down or working slowly."

"Let`s get old school," Dan said. "You got any atlases?"

Lisa did. They took out a map and pored over the pages. Lisa found it. She stabbed her finger on a small point of the long coast where Georgia met the ocean.

"Here it is. Barnham."

"Just below St Mary's."

Lisa said, "St Mary is a nice little historic town. Popular tourist place."

Dan wanted to get going. But it was 1800 hours already and from the map it looked like a long, five-hour drive. The door bell sounded.

"You expecting someone?" he asked.

Lisa was biting her lower lip. "No."

Dan thought about the red Ford.

Twice, it had seen him near Lisa's apartment. Followed him around.

He went to his bag and took out the Sig. Lisa's eyes widened when she saw the weapon. Dan raised his finger to his lips and gestured. Lisa got up, took her laptop and went inside her bedroom. She opened the door a fraction and peeped out. Dan turned the lights out. In darkness, he stepped over to the door. He looked out through the door peep hole. It was a woman. Blonde hair. As she lifted her face, Dan felt the earth vanish from below his feet. His breath was suddenly coiled and tight in his chest.

It was Tanya.

Dan switched the lights back on. He opened the door and stared at Tanya for a second. Then he yanked her inside the apartment. Tanya stumbled inside. Her rucksack on her shoulder, and her hair was tied back in a pony-tail. She glared at Dan defiantly. Dan shut the door and put the Sig in his waistline.

"What do you think you're doing?" he hissed.

Tanya met his gaze. "He's my father. I'm not leaving him. I'll do whatever it takes."

Dan ran his hand over his face. "Tanya, I thought we agreed on this."

Tanya's eyes flashed. "Yes, we did. But then I thought about what was really going on. My dad would never leave me, if I was in trouble. He needs my help now. And I'll be there."

"Was it you in the red Ford?"

"I called one of my friends at the airport. She was nearby and we were lucky to catch you."

Dan's shoulder's dropped. "Oh, Tanya. What about your mom?"

"She's gone. She agreed to let me go when I told her I was going to come and see you."

"Hi there." Dan and Tanya whirled around as they heard Lisa's voice. The two women were staring at each other. Checking each other out. There was a long silence.

Dan said, "Lisa, this is Tanya...Philip Longworth's daughter."

Tanya asked, "Is this your girlfriend?" She looked at Dan crossly. "She knows about my dad too?"

Lisa said, "I am *not* his girlfriend. And I only recently found out about your father. I used to work with him.

Tanya said, "So, you knew my dad?"

"Yes," Lisa said. A look passed between the two women. Lisa added. "We knew each other as professional colleagues. Nothing else."

Tanya pointed to Dan and asked Lisa, "So, he's not your boyfriend, but he's still living with you?"

Dan intervened. "Tanya, Lisa was kind enough to offer me a place to sleep over till I found my own place."

The two women looked each other up and down again. Dan wiped his brow, wishing he had his handkerchief on him. Embarrassment fanned his face with heat.

"Lisa, I went to meet Tanya earlier today. Right now, she is meant to be on a flight." Dan narrowed his eyes at Tanya.

"Well," Lisa said. "She is *not* on a flight."

Dan said, "Can you please give us a minute?" He grabbed hold of Tanya's arm and steered her towards the door.

"Where are you going?" Lisa asked.

"I just need to speak to her. Back in a moment." He took Tanya out in the hallway, made sure he had the keys to his Lincoln, and shut the door.

He said, "Those two guys I killed today were the Russian Mafia. They are after you, because they think you might know where your dad is."

"I know that. Don't talk to me like I'm a child." Her chin came up.

"Did anyone follow you?"

"What? No."

"Are you sure?"

She paused, bravado all over her face. "Yes."

"Tanya, I know you think you're doing the right thing. I appreciate that. But believe me, this shit has hit the fan. The FBI and the Pentagon are involved. There's a lot more to this now than just your father disappearing. Today, his boss was killed."

"His boss?"

"Yes. The fat guy who came to your house. Him. Can you see? They're killing off the people close to him. Who do you think is next?"

She tried to shrug and act cool. But the flash in her eye was gone. "I don't care. Don't you get it? I love him. I can't just leave him out there. I…" her voice trembled slightly. "I also think he's sick. He lost a lot of weight in the last three months. Just like that. When I asked him, he said he joined a gym. He hates gyms."

Dan clenched his jaws and his fists. *Damn it. Damn you, Philip.*

Aloud, he said, "Let's go back to your dorm."

"My dorm?"

"Yes. To talk."

"I want to help you, Dan."

Dan held up his hands. "You have. And you will," he added hurriedly. "Just give me a chance to find out more. Then I'll call you. Promise me you won't follow me around anymore. It's bloody dangerous."

Her eyes were crafty. "Only if you promise you *will* call, and let me join you."

"I promise."

Tanya stayed in the elevator while Dan walked around the parking lot. A Honda Civic came in and parked. A woman got out, smiled at Dan and headed for the elevator. Dan signaled, and Tanya came out to join him. They got into the Lincoln.

"Give me your cell." Tanya frowned, but gave it to him. Dan turned the phone off and ripped out the battery. He gave both back to Tanya.

"Hey," she said. Dan took out his cell phone and did the same. They drove off into the gathering gloom of the close, humid evening. Orange, red and white lights were shining in the towers of downtown.

*****

Dan got back late, but Lisa was still awake. She was on the couch again, her arm draped over the side. Jimmy Fallon was cracking jokes on TV. She turned her head and gazed at Dan expectantly.

"What happened?"

"I found her another flight," Dan said, sounding relieved. He was. He wanted to crack open a beer, but this was not his home. "This time, I made sure I saw her board the damn thing."

"She did?"

"Yes, I even waited until the bloody thing took off."

"So what now?"

"Now we head for Barnham."

Dan was up early the next morning, packing the few belongings he had.

He went through his yoga routine. Then he checked the Sig P226. He loaded the magazine full. It was all working fine. The Sig didn't have a safety catch. Instead it had a decocker. A round was always chambered and all he had to do was pull out the gun and fire. He liked that about the Sig. He put the gun in his front trouser pocket. Lisa knocked on his door. Her bag was a small suitcase.

"Got everything?" Dan asked.

She smiled sweetly. "Yup, including the bikini." She seemed more relaxed than yesterday, Dan thought. He drove the Lincoln to a gas station and filled it up. He checked the tire pressures. It was 0930 hours, and the morning traffic rush was subsiding. They headed out west and south, aiming for the I-75 to take them towards the sea.

After three hours of driving, Dan needed a break. They were approaching the seaside town of Savannah. He checked into a service station motel and they had lunch. The second leg of the journey was nicer. Dan wound his window down. The wind was fresher, less humid. He could see the blue glint of the Atlantic. It was past 1500 hours when they came off the I-75, and saw the first signs for Barnham town. The population was 120,000.

"Not as small as I thought," Dan said.

CHAPTER 26

Dan dropped his speed and they drove slowly into town. White shops and boutiques lined the main parade. Some of the houses were painted blue, red and yellow.

"Looks pretty," Lisa said.

"Where are we going?"

Dan took out a piece of paper.

"2334 Lynch Avenue, that`s what Marcus`s secretary told me. Hope she got it right."

"We need a town map," Dan said. He tried his phone again, but his, like Lisa`s refused to upload Google maps. Dan pulled up at a motel and got a map from the reception counter. The seaside was next to the main town parade. He parked the Lincoln at the nearest lot and they both got out and stretched. The sun was shining on the sea. Seagulls soared overhead. The air was heavy with saline mist. Dan stared at the sparkling water. It was beautiful being this close to the sea again.

Dan spread the map out on the bonnet. There was an A to Z at the back. He found the street name, and then got it on the map. He took out a pen and circled it. It was further in from the main parade. He turned to Lisa.

"You need a place to stay." She pointed at the motel. "It looks alright."

Dan shrugged. They got back inside the car and drove. The motel was big, new and shiny. It was called Motel 10, and was over two floors. Rooms radiated across a balcony on each floor. There was a large parking lot in front. They parked, took their bags and went inside. The large reception area was mostly empty. A small Indian man was sitting behind the desk, his eyes on a computer screen. Above him a sign said "Sea view rooms with free views." As Lisa and Dan approached the man clicked his tongue and shook his head. He took his eyes off the screen and looked at them. His lips split into a smile.

"Hello, welcome to Motel 10."

They signed in for a double room. The reception man turned his attention to the screen again. "Darned broadband not working again."

Dan said, "Problem here as well?"

"Most of Georgia, it seems. Where have you guys come from?"

"Atlanta."

The man shook his head. "So slow it`s easier to just pick up the phone and ask someone." He looked at Dan curiously. "Any problems there with the internet?"

"Slow as you have it down here."

"God knows what`s going on." The man picked up some keys. "Let me show you to your rooms."

Dan picked up the bags. They took the stairs up to the first floor. The sea sparkled between the trees in the distance. When they were inside and the man had left, Dan stood by the door with his bag in his hands. Lisa went over to the sliding glass door and checked out the balcony overlooking the sea. She came back and stared at him.

"What are you doing?"

"I`m going to check out a few things. See you soon."

"Hang on. I`m coming with you."

Dan shook his head. "No. Too dangerous. I`m sure they're here. Keep your phone on, I'll call."

He went out the door, down the stairs, and checked the location of Lynch Avenue with the motel keeper once. In the parking lot, he opened the trunk of the Lincoln and put his bag in. He stuck the Sig inside his front belt, next to the knife. He got into the car and looked around him. The parking lot had three cars excluding his. One Dodge van, a pick up, and a Honda coupe. He hadn't seen any of the cars before. If someone was following him, they were doing one hell of a good job. That, or they were waiting for him.

He stopped at a service station, refueled, and bought a bacon cheese burger, two cans of soda, a packet of biscuits and a takeaway coffee. He ate the burger and drank the coffee in the car.

He followed the map up to Lynch Avenue, but didn't go into the street. He circled around. The avenue was on a crisscross grid of streets at the top of a hill that overlooked the ocean. It was windy and fresh. He parked the car two streets down, under a tree. He walked past Lynch Avenue twice, noting the parked cars and any pedestrians. The street was empty. Mostly rental holiday homes, he guessed.

As he walked back on one of his circles, the blue ocean faced him. He could see a white ship with its stern open, a large crane on its deck raised like a question mark. The crane had a pulley that was revolving, laying something on the water. A fishing trawler, he guessed. But from this distance he could not see clearly.

He walked into Lynch Avenue after a while and headed for number 2334. The property was similar to most on the street. Two-story, post-colonial, with warm colors. Steps went up to a wood porch with an empty recliner. The two houses on either side had cars in the drive. As he watched a man came out, smiled at Dan, and got into the car. Dan watched as the man reversed out, then he walked up the drive. He waited until the car had gone before he rang the bell. The bell chimed. Twice. There was no answer. He knocked. No response.

He came down the porch stairs and down the side. The garden went to the edge of the hill then slid down after a fence. Dan tried the back entrance. He peered in through the window, it was the kitchen door. The door was locked. He hadn't seen an alarm at the front wall or the back. He took out the knife and his credit card. He kneeled down and jiggled the lock with the knife, while trying for the bolt with the credit card. After five minutes of trying he gave up.

He got up and looked around. The houses on either side couldn't see him. He leaned against the door, then pushed. He pushed harder, and with a crack, the lock split from the door frame. He tensed himself for an alarm he hadn't seen, but there was no sound. He breathed easy and let the door swing inside. He waited for a beat, then stepped inside. It was dead quiet.

The kitchen was medium-sized. Two dishes rested in the sink. The cupboards were all open. Plates, pots and pans had been dragged out and lay in a heap on the floor. The dining table in the middle was overturned. One of the chairs had its leg broken. He took out his Sig. He stepped around the mess until he came out in the hallway. Carpets had been ripped up, showing bare floorboards. He checked the living room. Two sofas upturned, foam slashed in broad knife strokes. Similar to Philip's house. He kept the gun raised and crept upstairs. Same carnage. Carpets lifted, floorboards loose. There were three bedrooms upstairs, of which only one was used. All the doors were open; every room had been trashed. Dan put his gun away.

He looked around the house and found nothing. On the upstairs landing, he checked the window facing the street. The neighbor he had seen leaving was parking his car in the drive again. He looked up and down the street and saw something new. A black Cadillac. Parked three houses down to the left, on the opposite side. He could see two men in the front. Maybe more in the back. The men sat there, watching.

Dan came away from the window. He went downstairs and opened the main door. The porch creaked under his boots. He looked at the neighbor by his car. He was closing the trunk. Dan glanced at the Cadillac. Four guys at the very least. Staring directly at him. He walked over to the neighbor, a middle-aged man with light grey and white hair. The man stopped as Dan approached.

"Hello there," Dan said. He jerked a thumb towards the house. "Here to see Philip Longworth. He used to live there."

The neighbor thought for a while. Then his eyes cleared. "Ah, yes. To be honest, a few people come and go from that house every year. It's a rental home. But I remember the last guy there. If that's who you mean. What did he look like?"

Dan took out the photo of Philip with his family on the hiking trail. The one he had taken from Philip's study.

"Yes," the neighbor said. "That's him. How do you know him?"

"A friend of the family." The rest he didn't need to know.

"I see. You know, I gotta mention it, he seemed kinda odd. Kept to himself. Tall chap, and always walked bent over. Quite pale. Was he sick?"

Dan nodded, keeping his face straight. "Yes, he was. Do you remember anything particular about him? Like his car, or what time he came home from work. Anything really."

"Well, he never had a car. He always took the bus from the end of the road, where it joins the Corinthian Road. That's the main road that heads down to St Mary's."

"Okay, did he take the bus every morning?"

"I reckon so, yes. Came home pretty late I guess, I never saw him."

"Did he have visitors?"

The man shook his head. "No, he was a loner."

"You live here alone?"

"No, with my wife. Kids are in college. You're welcome to ask her, but she wouldn't have seen anything else."

"Thank you," Dan said. "By any chance, you wouldn't know which bus he took, would you?"

"As a matter of fact, I do. I drove past him a few times as he was boarding it. He took Number 37. That goes to town and does a loop back here."

"Thanks, you've been a big help."

Dan glanced over the man's shoulder. The Cadillac was still there. He returned to the Lincoln and drove off. He took the main road back to the motel by the Broadway. A check on the rear view mirror confirmed it—the Cadillac was following him. He drove inside the parking lot of the motel, and as he parked, the Cadillac flashed past. The passenger side window was lowered and a blond-haired man was staring out. They caught each other's eyes.

CHAPTER 27

Dan went inside the motel. It was the same guy at reception. There was a TV above the counter as well and CNN was on. Three people were standing around and listening to the news. Dan watched. The senator whose emails had been hacked had resigned. Oppostion lawyers were pressing charges against him. The senator had links with Russian criminals who were close to powerful figures in Kremlin. Capitol Hill was in uproar. The hacker was still mysteriously absent. The two parties were blaming each other and Congress had come to a standstill as first the Democrat, then the Republican senators had walked out.

Dan shook his head. The whole thing was a big mess. The three men who Dan thought were guests looked at him and moved back. The Indian guy behind the counter smirked at Dan.

"See what these idiots are up to?"

"Like Dumb and Dumber," Dan said. "I need to find the Town Hall. Do you know where it is?"

Dan got the directions and went back to the car. He thought of checking on Lisa, but figured she would be either be resting or getting a tan on the balcony. He opened the trunk, and took extra ammunition for the Sig. He had a feeling he was going to need it soon.

After ten minutes of driving he was out on a country lane. Farmland appeared on the left and the ocean to the right. He saw the white ship again, the crane on its deck, and some other machinery. He drove on and came into a small complex. It had the town hall and sheriff's office. He pulled into the parking lot of the town hall. A bored-looking woman at the reception looked up as he entered. She was in her fifties, red hair tied up in a bun at the back, eyes behind thick-rimmed glasses that looked at Dan blankly.

"Can I help you?" she asked.

"Yes, there's an internet cable project going on here. A company called Synchrony Communications is in charge. They're based in Atlanta. I need to speak to someone dealing with them."

"What for?"

Dan put his elbows on the counter and leaned over. "The man Synchrony sent over has disappeared. The cops are looking for him. He's my friend and I'm here to look for him. Now if you don't mind, I need to speak to someone who knows more about this."

The woman reached for the phone. "Have a seat there, please. Let me see who I can get for you."

"You do that," Dan said.

He sat down on a worn leather sofa by the window, looking at the ocean sparkling in the distance like gems had been scattered on the water. A bunch of cars were parked in the parking lot. The land beyond dipped over a hill. He could see the white ship ploughing the water far away. Dan became aware of a presence beside him. He looked up to see a pot-bellied, middle-aged man standing with a curious look on his face. Dan stood up. The man took a step back, then composed himself.

"I'm Richard Maxwell. In charge of town infrastructure planning. I understand you need to speak to someone about Synchrony Communications."

"Yes." Dan introduced himself and they shook hands.

"Please, come into my office."

They sat down in the air-conditioned office, facing each other.

"How can I help you?" Maxwell asked. Dan told him about Philip.

"Did you meet him?" Dan asked.

"Once in the beginning, yes. After that, he got busy with the project and we never saw each other again. What do the police think is happening?"

"They're still looking for clues," Dan said. Maxwell had seen better days. The flesh on his cheeks hung loosely over his jowls, his hair was almost nonexistent, and he had a tired hang-dog expression.

Dan said, "Did you know that the CEO of Synchrony Communications has died?"

Maxwell blinked and controlled himself. "He died?"

Dan was suddenly wary. Maxwell knew something and he was hiding it, just like Marcus Schopp had done. "Shot dead in his car. Two bullets to the head. The evening before, he told me if I didn't stop looking for Philip, I would get everyone killed."

Maxwell looked around the room like a trapped animal. He licked his lips.

"That's strange. I mean, I don't know why…" He looked at Dan. "Why are you telling me this?"

"Because I'm trying to find Philip. Tell me about this project, Mr Maxwell. Is it about broadband cables or something else?"

Maxwell didn't answer. Dan said, "Philip's house in Atlanta and the place he rented over here have both been trashed. Like someone was looking for something. You know anything about that?"

Maxwell stood up and pulled the blinds down. He folded his hands on the desk.

"Look, I don't know who you are. I don't know what happened to Philip. This project is like others up and down the country, nothing special."

"Why does a defense military contractor handle a civilian infrastructure project like this?" Dan asked.

Maxwell closed his eyes and opened them, like he was exhausted. When he spoke, his voice croaked.

"Mr. Roy, there is nothing else I can tell you. If you visit our website, there is enough information about the project."

Dan stood up. "Remember what happened to Marcus, Mr Maxwell. Might be better if you came clean with me now."

"Goodbye, Mr. Roy."

Outside, Dan pulled his cell phone out and called Andy Brown.

"Any news on Marcus?" Dan asked.

"Something came up from his previous records. He used to work for DARPA," Andy said.

"That research place?"

"Defense Advanced Research Projects Agency. It's like the NASA for the military. They build on ideas from scientists and defense contractors by providing funding. They came up with stuff like the stealth planes and the miniature GPS you can put in a phone."

Dan remembered an old article in a military gadgets magazine. "Yeah, I got it. So, what did Marcus do for them?"

"It gets a bit vague there. It says he was the office supervisor for a branch of the Tactical Technology Office in Atlanta. Then he left and opened up Synchrony."

"Alright. Listen, I need your help with something."

"Shoot."

"I don't know if you intended that pun, but that's precisely what I might need. If it gets rough down here I might need a hand. Is it cool for you to come down here? I have a feeling Philip is somewhere around."

"Maybe. Let me check with the chief. If it's for this case, she might be okay with it."

Dan hung up and went into the police station. If Barnham had a problem with crime, it didn't show in its offices. Dan had never visited a more pristine, well-organized police station. It felt like an office block. The air conditioner hummed out cool air, the walls were covered in nice paintings, the seats were leather and comfortable. A uniformed man was at the counter. He carried on writing something until Dan was right up at the desk.

"This the right place to ask about a missing person?" Dan said. The police officer was in his late twenties to early thirties. He had black hair and a pale complexion that had turned ruddy in the coastal sun. His dark eyes stared back at Dan.

"Has a report been filed?" he asked.

"Philip Longworth. Atlanta PD should have been in touch."

The policeman picked up his coffee and tapped a few buttons on his computer.

"Yes," he said eventually. "Philip Longworth of 2334 Lynch Avenue. That correct?"

"Yup. Any news?"

The man grimaced and stretched his arms, like he had all the time in the world. "Nope. We get them once in a while."

Once in a while, Dan thought. "Do their houses get trashed and their bosses get killed once in a while, as well?"

That got his attention. "Say what?"

"You got a police chief here?"

The chief's office was at the back, surrounded by cactus and other long leaf green plants in pots. Dan stood while the sulky young man knocked on the door. A sign on the glass panel said, Greg Radomski, Police Chief, Barnham Town. The police officer shut the door, leaving Dan outside. In a few minutes, he came back out.

"He'll see you now." He jerked a thumb towards the office.

A broad-shouldered, beefy man sat at the desk. He looked at Dan without smiling and didn't offer to shake his hand.

"Who are you?" Chief Radomski asked.

Dan told him. He repeated what he had told the young officer, and left out everything in between. He mentioned Brown in Atlanta. Radomski grunted.

"You see a connection between his boss`s murder and his disappearance?"

Dan said, "I went to ask him myself. He was evasive. He died the next day."

Radomski said, "We mounted a county-wide patrol car search for him.

Showed his photo to residents. Radio and TV ads. Found nothing so far. And now the internet is playing up. Things are slow."

"Nothing so far?"

"Zip."

Dan changed tack. "What do you know about the broadband cable job?"

Radomski curled up his nose. "Far as I knew we had broadband already. Folks in the town hall were vague about it. I figured it was something political, so I stayed out of it."

Vagueness was exactly what he got from Maxwell, but evasion, too. The man had fobbed him off. Looks like he had fobbed the police off as well. It wouldn't be hard. In a small town, an infrastructure project meant jobs.

"You know where Philip worked around here?"

"Sure. By the water. Take the Corinthian Road towards St Mary`s."

"Yeah, I heard." A thought struck Dan. "St Mary`s is close to the King`s Bay submarine base, isn't it?"

"Yes. Nuclear submarine base. Cumberland Island is close by. You been there? Nice place. Got wild horses and shit."

Dan's eyes flared. A sudden memory hit the sides of his skull like an explosion, blowing every other thought apart. He caught his breath.

"What did you say?"

Radomski stopped when he caught the look in Dan`s eyes. "About the submarine base?"

Dan`s voice was urgent. "No, about the horses."

"Oh, that`s Cumberland Island. The place has wild horses that no one gets close to. They bite and stuff."

"Goodbye, Chief. I`ll be in touch."

CHAPTER 28

Dan drove fast. Streets flashed past on his right, with the ocean opposite. The white ship had come into the harbor, berthed offshore.

The horse's neighs.

The sound that Tanya had heard when Philip had called her.

The place had been windy, probably a beach. Philip was in Cumberland Island. He knew the hiking trails well. The family went there regularly. Philip would know where to hide.

Dan looked in his rear-view mirror. He had company. The Cadillac and another car were following about fifty meters behind. Dan pressed on the gas, pushing the needle up to a hundred. The Lincoln surged in response. The Cadillac was keeping pace, and if anything, getting closer. Dan pushed the speed past one hundred and ten. The Lincoln and the car directly behind speeded up, too.

The Cadillac was more powerful. The Lincoln was a town car, but Dan guessed from the Cadillac's shape it was a sports model. As he watched, the Cadillac moved out to the empty lane on the left and accelerated. Dan realized their plan. The Cadillac was trying to outflank him. Behind him, the other car leapt into view in the rear view mirror. It was a blue Chrysler. The car came closer and Dan could see the red bandana of the driver. The Z9 gang. The Mexican gang-banger he had seen in the warehouse in Marietta. Dan reached into the glove box and put his phone in his shirt pocket.

They would try to force him off the road.

The Cadillac moved closer. Dan could hear the growl of its engine. The driver he didn't recognize, but the passenger was tall and blond. Dan took his foot off the accelerator and pulled the Sig out. He lowered the window on the passenger side. The wind roared inside the Lincoln, bringing dust and sand, and Dan blinked as some of it went into his eyes.

He drove with his left hand. On his right hand, he held the Sig, balanced against his other forearm. Dan fired twice, quickly. The Cadillac's driver's window shattered. The car went forward, swerving on the road. Then it overtook Dan and began to slow down. Dan wound down his window and fired another two shots, aiming for the rear tires. Behind him he heard a crashing sound and he ducked down in his seat. The Mexicans were firing at him.

Bullets popped in the back and his rear wind screen smashed into a thousand shards of glass. The Chrysler moved forward.

Dan was trapped. The Cadillac ahead of him was slowing him down, and the Chrysler behind him was moving in for the kill. He crouched as low as he could and gritted his teeth. He jolted as his front bumper smashed against the Cadillac's rear. He made up his mind up in an instant. He swung the wheel a hard left.

The Lincoln's tires skidded and the front bumpers ground against the Cadillac, metal tearing against metal. The car came off the road onto the dirt. Dust flew in through the open windows, blinding him momentarily. Dan wrenched the wheel back straight, then to the left again. He wanted to raise up more dust. The trees weren't far away now, a row of tall, old oaks up ahead. He screeched to a stop in a cloud of dust. He could hear the whine of tires against asphalt as the other cars braked and came off the road.

Dan kicked open the passenger side door and slid out head-first. He rolled on the ground and was up in an instant. Using the car as a shield, he shot three times at the Chrysler, and three more towards the Russians. Visibility was poor in the dust swirl and he could barely make out the shapes. He heard two screams from the Russian car.

Then he turned and ran, diving into the trees.

The foliage was dense. Shrubs covered the ground and the trees were wet with moss. He knew the ocean was close, but he couldn't see it. Daylight became shaded as he went deeper. He could hear shouts behind him. He stopped for a moment behind the trunk of a thick oak. No dog barks. That was good. A dog would have moved much quicker through the forest than a human. He heard another shout, an order to spread out. He ran again, moving swiftly between the trees. He wanted to stop and shoot, but he needed distance from them first, and shooting would give his position away too quickly.

As he ran, he considered the numbers. Four in each car. Eight against one at a minimum. Could be more. He had hit one, maybe. He could take down some more, but they could outflank him.

He stopped. The trees in front were getting lighter and ahead of him he could see sand dunes. Beyond that, the sea. He could hide in the sand dunes. But after that, all he had was the open beach. He didn't like the idea of a firefight on an open beach. He could bog them down on the sand dunes. He had four extra clips of ammo on him. But so would they.

The forest stretched out in either direction. He couldn't hear them anymore. He ran again, flitting between the trees. They had spread out and the farther he went, the more chances he had of coming up on one of them alone. He liked the forest terrain. It gave him options. Twice, he heard a sound and dropped to the ground, crawling on his elbows. Nobody. He kept up this routine of hiding, listening, running until sweat covered his body.

He paused for rest behind a tree and looked. The ground was dry and he was careful not to step on branches. A sound grabbed his attention. Five o'clock. A man, moving slowly between the trees. His gun arm was hanging by his side and he had lit a cigarette. Dan crouched low and looked behind him to the other side. In the distance, he could see another figure. Eight o'clock. But he was further away.

Dan put the Sig into his pocket and took the knife out. He flicked it open. There was a fallen tree and he lay down flat behind it. His shirt was getting wet from the moss. When he looked up, the man diagonally to his right had moved up. Twenty meters, at the most. Still smoking his cigarette. Careless. Dan let him pass by. Then he slithered over the tree and followed.

He came closer. When Dan was two meters behind him, the man stumbled against a tree trunk. He cursed and began to straighten himself. Dan crept up behind him and put his hand over the mouth, pulling the man into his chest. In the same movement the serrated edge of the curved knife slid inside the anterior angle of the neck, above the neck muscles. It destroyed the trachea, shred the carotid artery and jugular vein and crushed the soft bones of the sinuses. Blood spurted through the nose and mouth. Dan twisted the knife once, grinding deeper into the lower skull. The body twitched and jerked, but he held it steady. Then he lowered it gently to the ground. He wiped his arm on the man`s pants. He was carrying a Smith Wesson 0.357. Dan pocketed the gun.

The forest was silent, save the chirping of birds high above. Dan ran behind a tree and looked around. He couldn't see the man to his left anymore. He guessed he had moved up ahead. Dan ran from tree to tree again, keeping low. He retraced his path, running back towards the car. By now, the gangsters would be near the sand dune, facing the ocean. Soon, they would realize that Dan wasn't there. Then they would head back. Dan kept up his routine of hiding and running. In five minutes he was near the road. He could see the three cars between the trees. He dropped to the ground and observed.

Movement. Next to the Cadillac. He saw the barrel of a gun.

CHAPTER 29

An M4 assault rifle, hung from the shoulder of a man who came around the Cadillac. He put his feet apart and stared at the forest. Bad news. If that gun went off, someone would hear the sound. But the man had one serious disadvantage. He was out in the open ground. He had no shelter. To a sniper, he was dead meat. Moments like these, Dan missed his Heckler and Koch 417 rifle. But he had the Sig, and he had a 357 round chambered in it. Nice, heavy ordnance. Dan stayed low and got into range.

The man was to his right, two o'clock. He had the rifle ready, and he was staring straight ahead. Dan stayed flat on the ground and took out the handgun. He held it in both hands, elbows straight, finger on the trigger. He had to aim between the trees. He had to hurry up too, if the man moved he would miss his mark. He slowed his breathing. He was less than forty meters away. Dan increased pressure on the trigger. The man moved. He turned his head, then his body, and looked straight towards Dan. Dan was spread-eagled on the ground, and the man's view passed over him. Dan swore and adjusted. Now or never. He fired.

The round slammed into the mouth and exited out the back of the skull, blowing the back of the head away. A gust of red mist and bone fragments, and the body slumped to the ground. Dan was on his feet and moving before the body hit the ground. He picked up the M4, searched quickly for extra ammo, which he found in the front of the dead man's jacket. He took out his knife and ran to the Chrysler. He plunged the knife in the two rear tires, and did the same to the Lincoln.

He jerked his head up as he heard a sound. Behind him. Feet crunching leaves. They were coming back. Dan ran to the front of the Cadillac. The keys were in the ignition. He slid the M4 on the passenger side seat and jumped in. The engine growled. There were shouts and screams, and he ducked as he heard the whine of a round. Then came the chatter of automatic fire. Dan pressed on the gas and turned the wheel.

The car leaped up the road and behind him, there was an explosion. It was one of the rear tires. They were shooting for it. Dan drove desperately, but there was another explosion and a black cloud engulfed the vehicle. The second rear tire and the exhaust gone. Dan could feel the drag as the car slowed, despite him pushing the gas pedal to metal.

He didn't have many options. He checked the lane opposite. A pick up whizzed by, then the lane was empty. Dan picked up the M4, checked his Sig and the Smith and Wesson, made sure the knife was still tucked into his belt. With the car still running, he opened the driver's side door and turned the steering wheel.

With screeches of protest, the burst tires flapped on the asphalt. The car turned around in a semi-circle. He jammed on the brakes and tumbled out of the seat onto the road. Bullets were slamming into the car, but he had the car as a shield between him and the gangsters. He counted six of them. All had their handguns raised and were firing at will. There was another explosion as one of the front tires burst. The men were spread out in a line. Dan aimed with the M4 and picked out the man in the middle. He was wearing the red bandana. He double-tapped him on the head and chest and the man crumpled to the ground.

The firing got heavy. As bullets whizzed overhead he crept out the side of the car, staying low. As he had expected, one of the men on the right was trying to move in. A quick burst felled him. Four still approaching.

Dan rolled over to the other side of the car. A bullet found the window above him and showered him with glass. He shook his head free of the fragments. He located the man on the extreme left this time. The gangster had his gun raised firing at the car. But he wasn't pointing low, where Dan was hiding, and he wasn't watching his shots. Two head shots dropped him dead. Three left.

Dan quickly did a sitrep. It was one of the worst things in combat, not to have circumferential awareness. If they had more than eight, one or two could easily have gone around and shot him in the back. In front of him, several bullets slammed into the bonnet of the car and picked up puffs of dust on the asphalt on the side.

Movement from the other side. Shit. Shit.

Dan saw a shadow flit through the trees to his right. Behind him. With his back to the car, Dan lifted the gun and aimed. Four o'clock. He didn't switch the rifle to automatic. He let off three shots and he saw the shadow fall. Then it got back up again and ran forwards. Dan whirled to the opposite side. Goddamn. Another shadow, running fast. Eight o'clock. They had managed to outflank him. There was no escape. He lifted the M4, aiming for the man on the left.

Then he stopped. The man carried a rifle, but it wasn't aimed at him. As Dan watched, the man fired directly over Dan's head, towards the gangsters. Dan heard a sound and looked up. He knew that sound very well. The rotor blades of a helicopter.

The bird flew in from the ocean, staying well above firing range. It hovered above, then swept across, blades flashing in the sun. Dan whirled his head left and right. He couldn't hear firing from the gangsters anymore. Two black shadows emerged from the trees. On each side. Four in total. They approached in arrow formation, ten meters behind each other, guns trained on Dan. They all had beards, about two to three month's growth.

"Put your weapon down," the lead man on the right shouted. Dan looked at him carefully. Black combat pants and top. Knee pads for sniping. The rifle looked like a suppressed Hecker and Koch. Microphone in one ear. Handgun in thigh holster. Kevlar vest and fragmentation grenades on the belt. These were not gangsters, nor were they rank and file soldiers. He didn't have a hope in hell.

"Put the gun down," the man shouted again. They were ten meters away now. Dan saw the two men at the back peel off to the sides and advance towards the gangsters. He couldn't hear a peep from behind him.

It was suddenly deathly quiet. A breeze rushed in through the trees. Dan put the M4 down. He lifted up his hands. He turned on his knees and stayed like that, arms spread up. The two front men approached him. One of them searched Dan for weapons and removed the two hand guns and the knife. The other kept his rifle on Dan's face. He motioned with his rifle, and Dan stood up slowly. He patted Dan down, then stood back and shoved him forward. Dan stumbled, but kept his balance.

The two who had recced out to the sides came back. Dan hadn't heard any further shots. The surviving gangsters had escaped, or they were dead. The four men circled Dan, each with their rifles trained on him, fingers on triggers. Dan didn't lower his hands.

"My name is Dan Roy," he said. "I could be wrong, but I think I'm on the same side as you."

"Shut the fuck up," the lead man said. He lowered Dan's hands and tied them in a plastic handcuff. He produced a cloth bag and draped it over Dan's head. The world turned black before Dan's eyes. It was hard to breathe. He felt a rifle prod him in the back.

"Move," a voice barked.

CHAPTER 30

"There, there it is!" Shevchenko tried to keep the excitement from his voice, but failed. Both the *Krasnaya* and the *Gobuki* were down at the sea bed today. Sasha craned his neck to look at the large screen above the scientists' head. The picture quality was excellent. The screen showed the fiber optic cable that carried information from the east coast of USA to mainland Europe. This particular cable was brand new, having taken more than a year and almost a billion dollars to complete. Its landing station was in Jacksonville, Florida and on the other side, almost four thousand miles away, in the northern coast of France.

They had found the cable three days ago. Right now, their main source of excitement was the object that had detached itself from a console on the side of the *Gobuki* and fixed itself like a hook on the cable. It was a clip-on coupler, a type widely available commercially, routinely used to check signal in the fiber and ensure internet traffic, including voice and video communication flows optimally.

These were also used for eavesdropping, often in the name of network maintenance.

Shevchenko leaned back in his seat, a satisfied smile on his face. The most gratifying thing was that the transducers had been bought on Ebay, the coupler from a New Jersey company, and the software was downloaded for free.

It had taken them a week to sort through all the data. Then the Democrat Head Office emails were hacked. From there, getting into a Republican senator's emails hadn't been difficult. One thing the coupler couldn't do was transmit information. Wi-Fi was impossible under water, although work was progressing towards achieving that. From an office in Sporchivniya, Moscow, bogus emails from Russian businessmen were filling the mail inbox of this Republican senator. Shevchenko almost felt sorry for the man.

But worse was to come. When the final information arrived, then the *Krasnaya* and the *Gobuki*—the Russian Navy's premier unmanned undersea vehicles or UUV's—would go into combat mode. No, they couldn't start a war. But they could disrupt the American plans. Simple sabotage in multiple places would go a long way. Shevchenko wasn't really interested in these cables.

The real game awaited them. He breathed out with impatience as he thought of the delay. Despite how the Kremlin had vouched for their agent, Shevchenko wasn't convinced. These agents, assets, spies, whatever one wanted to call them, always ended up either getting caught or blabbing their secrets. Take that Edward Snowden, for instance. If he was Russian, would he even be alive today?

Impulsively, he checked his cell phone. No calls. No SMS. Still waiting. He was about to yawn when the alarm sounded, almost knocking him off his chair. The two scientists jumped and removed their headphones. Shevchenko went out the door onto the bridge. Men were running on the deck outside. He noticed a figure rushing out of the sonar receiver on the aft deck. Shevchenko shimmied down the staircase and fought his way out on the open deck. A man saluted.

"What is it?" Shevchenko demanded. "And shut that damned alarm off. It's not like we have been hit by a torpedo."

"Sir, it's the telescopes. And it's been confirmed by our satellite feed trying to jam their GPS frequency. There's an American plane over us."

Shevchenko craned his neck up, but couldn't see anything. It was what Shevchenko had feared. It was what the idiots in Kremlin, and the idiot criminal this agent was forcing him to rely on, would never understand.

Durakh, he thought bitterly. *Durakh*.

He hurried to the telescope chamber and looked through them. He spotted the thing finally. He magnified the image. It was a long plane with a huge wingspan. Grey in color, with white numbers on it. He had seen this plane's images on recon photos in the past.

"A Poseidon P8A plane. Belongs to the US Navy," he muttered to himself. He felt a presence behind him. It was Sasha. He asked, "Any updates?"

"Yes, Captain. Sonobouys were dropped from the aircraft at 1310 hours. It is 1312 now."

"Sonobuoys," Shevchenko repeated. Passive sonar receivers to catch their sound waves. Sonobuoys were very versatile and could fire sound waves as well, using their echo to build an image of what they were hitting.

He told Sasha, "It is possible they have been watching us for a while. We probably have a drone on top as we speak. That does not worry me. The drone cannot see through the titanium roof of the dry dock. But I don't know how powerful these sonobouys are. If they can get a glimpse of our UUV then we are done for."

There was a shout from the bridge. It became persistent. A sailor rushed in, sweat pouring down his face.

"Sir, the scientists want to see you."

Shevchenko and Sasha dashed upstairs. Pavel pointed at the screen as they burst into the control room.

"This just came back from our pencil beam sonar collision avoidance system on the *Gobuki*," Pavel said. Shevchenko peered closely at the screen. The pencil beam sent out sound waves to see if there was any object in its way. The vehicle caught the echo coming off any obstruction, and then navigated around it. But the data it sent back was grainy and vague. It was something large, whatever it was.

"Could it be the continental shelf, Captain?" Pavel suggested.

Shevchenko scrunched his face. Something disturbing was lurking at the back of his mind. "Turn the collision systems off. From now on, we do not send any active sonar out."

He left the scientists and went to the sonar technician's office. They were sat hunched over the assortment of screen in front of them, eyes moving, a blue glow on their faces. He tapped Yuri on the shoulder.

"Did you keep a record of those small sounds you picked up on the spectrograph analysis?"

"Yes, Captain." He flicked back through the screens to bring up the images. He laid them out in rows on a large display.

"Can you get the time these sounds appear?" he asked Yuri. The man pressed a few keys and the data came up.

Shevchenko pointed to the screen. "Can you see the pattern? These sounds occur at morning and..." he stopped. Yuri looked at him, his mouth open. The senior technician knew perfectly what his Captain was saying. Blood drained from Shevchenko`s face. Beads of sweat formed on his forehead.

"These are transient sounds. From a submarine." He didn't have to explain any further to Yuri. Both nuclear and diesel submarines were known for being very quiet. Their propellers and engines made hardly any sound. They could never be picked up by passive sonar. But the sounds the crew made—banging toilet seats down, walking around, washing—all of these sounds produced detectable sound waves. So called transient sounds were often what gave a submarine`s position away.

"They are here. I think it`s an Ohio class nuclear one, stationed at the Kings Bay Naval Yard." Shevchenko swallowed hard. "Sasha, get those UUV`s out of the water right now. They might engage us." He set his face in a grim look. "Prepare our torpedoes. If they make adverse contact, then we respond with force. I am not surrendering this ship."

CHAPTER 31

Dan stumbled along the ground, his boots kicking small pebbles. The barrel of the rifle jammed into his back frequently. He couldn't see anything and breathing was difficult with the bag over his face. It was ironic that he had used similar methods when he had captured insurgents in Iraq and Afghanistan. He wondered what sort of interrogation he would be subjected to, and if they would employ so-called advanced techniques. Dan had been trained both to interrogate and resist questioning. He hoped like hell he would not have to use any of those skills now.

He listened hard. These guys had saved him. Why? Did they think he knew something? If they did, then he would definitely be facing advanced techniques. Which would also mean they were the enemy.

Well, he sure as hell wouldn't be telling them a word. He would rather die. Slowly, if necessary.

He could hear the birds again. It was darker. They must be in the forest. The ground became crunchy with fallen leaves and branches. A wind picked up, blowing the cloth against his face. Sea salt. A moment later, he heard the sound of surf. His boots sank into something soft and warm. Sand. They were on the beach. The sand became firmer after a while and they kept walking. The team pushed him until he was walking on something harder. Felt like duck planks laid along a beach. They turned away from the ocean and he felt the wind on his back now. His head was pressed down and he guessed it was to go through a doorway. He hesitated for a second, but there was no point in resisting.

A door slammed and it was pitch black. A light came on, bright even against his covered eyes. He was pushed, and judging by the sounds, he was in a narrow hallway. They kept moving until he was finally shoved into a room. The bag was lifted from his eyes. The room was dark, but it was still daylight outside. A small grill window let in sunlight. Dan blinked until his eyes got used to the light. He looked around the room. A heavy steel door was open at the front. One of the men with stood there with his rifle down, but trigger finger on guard. He looked at Dan, his face devoid of expression. There was another man in the room with him. He had short ginger hair, and freckles covered his face and forearms. It was the same man who had cuffed him. He stood behind Dan and unlocked the handcuffs. He stepped back. Dan turned around slowly.

The man had a gun pointed at Dan`s belly.

"Any trouble and we shoot you first, ask questions later. Do you understand?"

Dan cleared his throat. "Yes."

The man went out, keeping his gun trained on Dan. He slammed the door shut and keys turned in the lock. Dan staggered back against the cold wall. It was made of metal, probably steel. There was a musty smell inside, which the tiny grill window at the top did nothing to relieve. He sat down and massaged his wrists. His throat was parched dry. He wiped the sweat off his brow and lay down on the cold floor. He tried to sleep, feeling thirstier than he had ever done in his life.

It was 1700 hours. After fifteen minutes, he heard a key turn in the lock. A man he had never seen before came in. He was younger, clean shaven, and wore a navy working uniform. He carried a tray of food. Behind him, one of the bearded men came in and pointed his rifle at Dan. Dan grabbed the bottle of water on the tray and chugged it down in one gulp. He looked at the food and grimaced.

"Oh man, not an MRE," Dan said. They tasted horrid, but as in a combat situation, he had little choice now. He grabbed the packet.

The MRE was black bean and rice burritos. The packet had dried peaches, a fruit bar, pan cakes and the burrito. It wasn't that bad. He hadn't eaten since that morning and an MRE had never tasted this good. Not when he was on holiday, anyway. He leaned back against the wall. They had taken his cell. Even without the battery, he had no doubt they would try and go through it.

When two of the bearded guys came back, they simply opened the door and signaled at Dan. Their rifles were drawn. Dan followed one of them, while the other stayed behind him. In that formation, they walked down the narrow corridor. Wind blew against the sides of the wall. A panel of flat rectangular windows opened high above his head, more than three meters high. That wind must be coming from the ocean, he thought.

They passed a series of doors until they came to one and knocked. A voice told them to enter. Dan walked in and blinked in surprise. An older man with silvery hair was sat at the table. McBride.

McBride indicated to the two men. They left the room and shut the door. McBride stood up. His skin was leathery from the sun, and his slate grey eyes quick and sharp.

Dan said, "Fancy seeing you here."

"Do you know why I'm here?" McBride countered.

Dan was thinking. After a few seconds pause, he said, "You bought me the ticket for that plane to Atlanta. Guess I fell for it."

"What do you mean?"

"You knew that Jody Longworth would be on that flight."

McBride said, "Yes, I did."

Dan asked, "What else?"

"Nothing else, Dan. It was a shot in the dark. I had a feeling something might happen, but I did not know for sure."

"You knew they were after here."

"Yes, I did."

Dan sighed. "Can we stop playing games here? Pretty sure you have been listening to my cell phone, so you must know where Jody and Tanya are. Just tell me the rest already."

"What do you think is going on?" McBride asked.

"Philip Longworth knew something important. It's not about broadband cables. That's a cover. The two folders I picked up from Marcus Schopp's desk were classified information from the Navy. They were about clandestine undersea platforms. Designed for unmanned undersea vehicles. Philip must have known something critical about them."

"What else?"

"Synchrony Communications has to be a front company for the DoD. They work closely with DARPA, and Marcus used to work for DARPA."

McBride said, "That's right. Marcus Schopp was the head of the Tactical Technology Office. He got to know Philip while DARPA was funding the work of another company called Dynamic Corp."

"Yes, that was the company that went bankrupt."

"Correct. They became close friends. Philip had money worries and Marcus got him to work for him."

"What did Philip do exactly?"

McBride paused and went back to his chair. He put some folders inside a drawer and locked it. "Follow me, son."

CHAPTER 32

Dan hurried down the corridor behind McBride. They walked out into a clearing. The ocean lay behind them. They crossed the clearing into a huge warehouse. The guards at the front saluted and let them in.

The place was so vast that Dan couldn't see the end. Its width was easily more than a hundred meters, he guessed. Dozens of workshops lined the floor space. Precision engineering machines hummed over large yellow objects that looked like overturned boats. Dan watched a machine wheel up, driven by a man controlling robotic arms. He used the arms to fix something on the overturned boat closest to them, then went down the line, fixing all of them. McBride pointed to them.

"Undersea pods," he said, as if that explained everything.

"What does that mean?" Dan asked.

"These pods are meant to lie on the sea bed, and I mean deep sea bed, more than four kilometers down. They hold drones inside them. They can lie there for years, if need be. If they get disturbed, or get a signal, then the pods hatch."

"Hatch?"

"Yes, Dan. They hatch and rise to the surface. Like bubbles. At the surface of the ocean, the pod snaps open and the drone pops out. It lifts into the air and does its survey, sending data in real time. On identifying a target, the drones will carry missiles that can be activated."

Dan digested this in silence.

"So they're like ISR tools?" ISR stood for intelligence, survey and reconnaissance.

"Yes, precisely," McBride said. "We can't monitor all the oceans. Our nuclear subs are out on deterrent missions all the time. But that's a defensive arrangement and not an adequate one. We need to be more proactive. The new class of nuclear submarines the Russians and Chinese have are so silent, even our extensive sonar receivers aren't picking them up in time."

Dan had been on the nuclear submarine SSGN *Georgia* once as they had been evacuated from *Bandar Khalifa*, a port in Iraq. He remembered how the entire sea seemed to rise up around the RIB to which they clung for life. It had been night time, and he couldn't see a great deal, but the experience of boarding and then being on the nuclear submarine had been etched on his mind. He had great respect for submariners. Those men and women spent months under the oceans, ex-communicated from the rest of the world. They were an exclusive set.

"We don't want to be notified of a Chinese nuclear sub lurking one hundred miles out of Norfolk," Dan said aloud.

"Damn right, son. That's where these pods come in. They have pressure transducers that can be activated by the water displacement of a nuclear sub. They can be powered by ocean currents."

McBride looked at Dan. "Tell me what the problem is here."

Dan thought for a while, then shrugged. "Communication?"

McBride smiled for once. "Good. Salt water doesn't allow radio waves. Hence we don't have Wi-Fi and GPS under water. It is very hard to communicate from land to deployed submarines. So these pods become critical. Once activated, we can get all sorts of information from the airborne drones about what's lurking under the sea."

"What else do you think the pods can do?" McBride asked.

"I don't know."

"Well, they can carry unmanned undersea vehicles. Whole swarms of them. When activated, these undersea drones can carry out a variety of missions."

Dan whistled. "So we don't need submarines anymore?"

"No, we do. But in far fewer numbers."

"I'm guessing these pods and drones will be one hell of a lot cheaper than traditional nuclear subs."

"Think billions of dollars."

"Eyes on the ocean floor," Dan said. "Is this what those folders on Marcus' desk were all about?"

"To a certain extent, yes. But there's more."

Dan asked, "So now we have all these UUV's or drones under water, searching for enemy subs and other threats. How far can they travel?"

"Depends on their fuel, but two to three hundred miles is not impossible."

Dan said, "I think these drones are battery charged, aren't they?"

Mc Bride clicked his fingers. His face became animated. "And batteries run out quickly. Even the most powerful iridium batteries on a UUV won't last for more than a week."

Dan was beginning to see. "I get it. You want to keep these pods as docking stations. They can have electric chargers that can recharge the drone batteries."

"Bingo! So imagine a network of unmanned undersea pods where roving UUV`s could stop to recharge their batteries. At the same time, they could securely upload the intelligence they've been collecting, which could be transmitted to a nearby command post on a ship."

"I get it. So that`s why you mentioned the communications. A submarine can't communicate with land easily, not without the risk of being detected. But if the pods are detected, the worse that can happen is that they get destroyed.

"Exactly."

"And the pods will hold drones as well?"

"Yes. They'll have multiple functions. They are forward-deployed battle stations really. UUV`s can dock, recharge, upload and be on their way again. If a threat is perceived, the pods can release a float to the surface, which releases the drone."

Dan shook his head. He had not understood much of this from reading the folders, but hearing it from McBride made it sound real.

"I still don't get what you needed Philip for. He is a cable engineer, right?"

McBride lifted a finger. "More than that. He was a specialist in deep sea fiber optic cabling. Ninety-five percent of our internet data comes from these deep sea cables. Without them, we are powerless. Think of a world without Google, email. That`s what would happen if someone severed the cables."

"So these drones could guard the cables?"

"It`s time we went outside," McBride said.

CHAPTER 33

They walked past the clearing towards another giant warehouse. Beyond that, Dan could see the ocean, dark now in the late afternoon light, white top waves fighting over each other restlessly.

They emerged on a pitched road. Four trucks were parked on the side. Where the road ended, there was a long harbor. Dan recognized the ship moored at the harbor. It was the white ship with the open stern he had seen while driving around Barnham. It looked bigger close up. The giant crane loomed over the open back, like a colossal sewing spool. A massive circle of cable was attached to it.

Guards let them enter and McBride walked briskly up the gangplank. Dan craned his neck up at the crane. It was a monster and the huge spool of cable it held in its maw swayed ominously in the breeze.

On the deck, Dan stared at a huge machine in front of him. It was made of yellow painted steel and looked like a tank. It had a plow on one end.

"That is our sea bed plow, Dan." McBride slapped the side of the machine. "This big boy weights thirty-two tons, it's ten meters long and five meters high."

Dan said, "It digs holes for the pods to be placed in."

"Yes." McBride pointed out to sea. "This undersea network is the future of anti-submarine warfare, Dan. Most nukes the Chinese and Russians have are hidden in their submarines. With this network, we can find out where these enemy submarines are. You can imagine how much they would like to get their hands on the whereabouts of this network."

"And Philip was in charge of designing which part of the network?"

"Not all of it, obviously. Mainly the locations of where the pods would be. See, the pods are charged by the ocean currents. Movement is converted into electrical energy. That in turn charges the drones. So, we need to place the pods in places where ocean currents are strong. But that is the critical part. If the location of this distributed network falls into enemy hands…"

"They can destroy them with torpedoes. All this effort is in vain."

McBride turned to him. "Do you understand now why Philip is so important?"

"So he has all this data?"

"Philip and Marcus were the only two with access to the data. All the files were destroyed, and Philip was the only one with the hard drive. He helped in designing the pods as well. He has extensive experience of working in these conditions. Many people are involved in this, but Philip came up with a location map for the first wave of these undersea pods. Then he vanished with the data."

Dan looked at McBride steadily. "Philip wasn't just a cable engineer."

"Correct."

Dan's mind was working hard. "If the Russian mafia and the Mexican gangs were not threatening Philip and his family, I would say Philip was the bad guy. He was a mole, the spy who was also the scientist."

"Good thinking."

"I want to know how the Russians got to know that Philip had this data. But once they knew, they came after him. They threatened his family. Philip disappeared with the data. Then they killed Marcus."

"Right on."

"Who was Philip really working for?"

McBride said, "FBI."

"Really?"

"Yes, really. Many military technology secrets were ending up in the hands of Russians. We suspected a mole within the Pentagon, or inside some defense contractors. This isn't that rare actually. Defense contractors are technical companies and they often employ talent from abroad. Some foreign scientists have turned out to be spies in the past."

"Hang on. I don't get it. How can Philip be a cable network engineer and an FBI agent?"

"He wasn't an FBI agent. He was helping them. And he was working undercover."

"So he spread word that he had this secret information, and the Russian gangsters came for him?"

"Something like that."

Dan frowned. "What about the cocaine?"

McBride shrugged. "The Mexicans acted as the enforcers for the Russians. When Philip realized, he played a dangerous double game. He tried to become a dealer for the Mexicans. To see if he could find out who sent them. The plan backfired."

Dan thought for a while then said, "You know he was sick, don't you?"

"Yes. That was sad."

"The pressure of having to work undercover isn't easy either. There was too much on his shoulders."

"Yeah." McBride stared at the horizon, where light was fading in banks of grey and red clouds. "I don't know how this is going to end, Dan. But we need to find Philip and the data. Fast. Before the enemy get to him."

"I know where he is."

McBride spun around. "Are you serious?"

"I think I know, sir. We have to go and see." Dan told him about Cumberland Island. McBride listened with a grim face.

"What do you need to do?" he asked when Dan had finished.

Dan laid out his plan, something he had been working on since he left the town hall and police station. McBride listened without interrupting. "Okay. Let me send a crew with you."

Dan shook his head. "No, he's spooked already. If we turn up with the cavalry, he might run again. He needs to trust someone."

Dan levelled a gaze at McBride. "What I want now is you to be honest with me. You dragged me into this. Is there anything else I need to know?"

McBride shook his head. "You know everything I know. People much higher up than me are on this Dan. Make no mistake, this is the highest national security issue at the moment."

A phone rang somewhere. Dan looked towards McBride, who frowned and patted his uniform jacket. He produced a cell phone, checked the number, and answered. Dan watched his face change. He listened, then turned away from Dan. He spoke briefly, then hung up.

"Things just got a whole lot worse," McBride said. His weather-beaten face was pinched, and his voice was edgy. "A Russian research ship has been seen in the Atlantic, a few meters from where we have important data cables. An Ohio class nuclear sub is on its way. That ship being there can't be a coincidence, Dan. This could be a shit storm in the making. You better find Philip, and find him fast."

CHAPTER 34

Dan got his cell phone back from the guys who arrested him. They were Delta operatives.

The ginger-haired leader said, "I'm sorry we had to do that. But we didn't know who the hell you were."

Dan shook hands with him. "No problem. You did your job. Name's Dan, by the way."

"Fisher. I know your name."

Dan made two phone calls, then called Lisa. She picked up at the first ring.

"Dan, where the hell have you been? Your phone's been silent, like, forever."

Dan explained to her about the car chase.

"Jeez, are you ok?"

"Yes, I'm coming over to get some stuff. Talk to you then." He hung up. He went to the next room, where McBride was debriefing the four Delta guys. They all turned as Dan came in.

Dan walked over to the table where they had opened up a map. Cumberland Island, seventeen miles long and three miles wide, was a ferry ride away from the town of St Mary's and not far from the King's Bay Naval Base. McBride circled the island with a pen. It had a long shape, thin at the bottom and broad at the top. It bent around the contours of the coastline and offered protection to the naval base.

"Where do you think he might be?" McBride asked.

"I don't know," Dan said. "But the island is a national park and gets visitors. I reckon he will head for the northern end, which is more remote. Can we have an RIB in these waters that I can call on?"

"That's easy," Mc Bride said. "You can have two."

"What else?"

"I want an infra-red painter, but I can use one attached to a rifle. I will need extra ammo, too. A GPS tracker would be good."

McBride said, "You need a GPS signal for sure. There's going to be a drone above."

"Really?"

"This is important, Dan. We need to get it right the first time. To do that, I want eyes on you."

Dan nodded. It made sense. But he needed to clarify something. "The drone won't have a payload, will it?"

McBride fixed his steely eyes on Dan. "Not if you don't want it to."

Dan shook his head. "Too dangerous. Could be a blue on blue."

"Alright. I've got something for you." McBride leaned across the desk and opened a drawer. He took out a long, curved knife in its scabbard. The handle was thick, with a black rubber grip. It was long, fifteen and half inches, and was more of a machete than a knife.

Dan exclaimed, "A kukri!" McBride handed it to him. Dan took the knife and removed the scabbard. The blade was made of black steel.

"That's a KA Bar kukri made in USA. Thought you might like one."

Dan gripped the weapon and looked at it reverently.

"Thank you, sir. I owe you one." He smiled gratefully at McBride. He strapped the kukri on his back belt. The familiar presence was reassuring.

"You need a car, right?" McBride asked.

Fisher spoke. "There's one waiting for you outside, by the trucks."

Dan said, "I need a gun."

"Follow me," Fisher said. They went down the corridor to the men's quarters. The armory was a walk-in cabinet, locked by a steel wheel safe. Dan looked at the weapons rack and whistled.

"You got anti-tank weapons in here?"

Fisher said, "Prepared for every situation, man."

Dan chose a suppressed Hecker and Koch 417, with the medium range, sixteen inch barrel. He took a detachable thirty round magazine, each round a full-powered 7.62x51mm NATO ordnance. He took five extra ammo boxes. He chose a Sig Tac CP-4x optical sight for the rifle, and a pair of NVG's for himself.

"Nice choice," said Fisher.

"Gas checked?" Dan asked, indicating the rifle.

"Yup. Ready for battle."

The car outside was a civilian Cherokee jeep. Dan had the rifle and ammo in a shoulder bag. He had taken some extra ammo for the Sig as well. He had the Glock from the gangster he had killed. Along with his kukri, he felt he finally had a decent arsenal.

He shook hands with Fisher and the other Delta guys, then faced McBride.

"Good luck, Dan" the older man said.

Dan said, "For the last time. Right?"

"Right."

Dan got in the Cherokee and drove back to the motel. He left the guns in the trunk and went upstairs. Lisa opened the door before he knocked.

"I heard you coming," she said. Sunlight fell on her face, making her green eyes dance. She wore a white sleeveless vest and shorts. She touched his arm. "You okay?"

"Need to get changed," Dan said as he walked in. "I must stink like a road kill."

Lisa smiled. "After what just happened, I think we can forgive you for that."

Dan took his shirt off and threw it in the bathroom. He noticed Lisa staring at his chest.

"You need to get packed. We might be camping for the night."

"Where are we going?"

"Cumberland Island." Dan told her what happened as he wrapped a towel around himself. "Pack your full sleeves and boots. Take a hat. You might need to get some bug spray as well. It`s a wild island."

He had a quick shower while Lisa got ready. He changed into the dark clothes he had in his rucksack, then they both headed downstairs.

CHAPTER 35

They were too late to catch the ferry, but Dan chartered a private boat to taken them across from the mainland visitor`s center at St Mary`s.

He checked his new GPS watch that the Delta guys had given him. 1800 hours. The sky was still bright, but the sun was a pale shadow over the horizon, shimmering its last light on the sea. Lisa and Dan clambered onto the twenty-foot motorboat. Lisa sat close to Dan and shivered. The captain fired the engines and the boat shook, then chugged forward into the water. They could see the island, a dim, blue shape at the mouth of St Mary`s river. As they advanced, a black shape crossed ahead of them. It was very long and a turret rose high above the water, dwarfing the boat.

"That`s a submarine," Dan pointed.

"Gosh, it's big."

"Hmm. Pretty special inside, too." Dan told her of the time he had been on the SSGN *Georgia*.

They got off at the Sea Camp dock on the island and waved the boatman goodbye. Dan looked around him.

"We can stay at the Sea Camp tonight, if you want. We'll be hiking tomorrow anyway, so best to get a night`s sleep."

"Sure thing," Lisa said.

As they walked off the dock, Dan saw another private boat arrive. They had moved about five hundred yards, but he looked back before they left the dock. A number of men were lifting bags out of the boat. He counted the men. Six in total. He had no problem in recognizing the tall blond man who was helped up by one of the men. Dan ducked into the path at the end of the dock, joining Lisa and dropping out of sight. He grabbed her hand.

"We gotta go," he said.

"What`s going on?," Lisa asked, matching her steps to his.

"They're here. The men who tried to kill me." Lisa didn't say anything. She squeezed Dan`s hand and hurried alongside him. They checked into a double bedroom at the Sea Camp. Once they were inside, Dan took out his Sig and went near the window. The lights were off. He could see the main entrance of the camp. He waited, but didn't see any of the men coming in. A light sprang up behind him. It was Lisa coming out of the bathroom. Dan closed the curtains.

"Lisa," he said, "this is going to get nasty. I want you to get out of here now."

"I've come all this way. I want to see this to the end."

Dan shook his head. "No, you don't understand these people. They will kill both of us given half a chance. Tomorrow morning, I want you to take the ferry back to the mainland."

"And what will you do?"

"Start hiking. I need to find Philip. And they'll come after me."

"Give me a gun. I grew up on a farm. I know how to fire one."

"These wild animals shoot back. It's not the same."

Lisa stepped into his face. She was inches away and he could feel the heat of her body. She put a hand on his chest. Dan swallowed. She looked up at him, her emerald eyes full of a mild question.

"We do this together," she whispered. "Do you understand? Two pairs of eyes are better than one. And trust me, I know how to handle myself."

Dan closed his eyes. "Okay, but you stick by me and do exactly as I tell you. Right?"

Lisa nodded slowly. "Like I said, I know how to use a gun. I've done range fighting contests before. If you have a spare one, I could use it."

Dan nodded. "Okay, you could use the Glock. I'll show you tomorrow." He smiled at her. "Now go to sleep."

"How about you?"

Dan pointed to the packed sandwiches they had taken out of Lisa's bag. "I need to eat something, then I'm keeping guard."

"Okay partner. Wake me up at 3:00 a.m., and I'll take over."

Dan sat down on the floor as Lisa got ready for bed. He kept his eyes averted, but didn't miss the stolen looks that Lisa darted in his direction. He munched on the turkey, mustard and gherkin sandwiches they had picked up from the shopping mart on the way.

Night fell.

He could hear waves crashing on the beach outside. Insects buzzed by the lights nearby. He listened hard, waiting for footsteps. The Sig was between his legs. The kukri was strapped to his left thigh. The Glock was on his back belt. He was ready.

He wondered what it was like outside. On the beach, with the waves rushing in, the stars out over the sea like a moth-eaten blanket. Where was

Philip? Somewhere near. He would find out tomorrow. He rubbed his eyes and yawned. That sandwich had made him full. His cell was off and separated from his battery. He went and sat near the window and parted the curtains gently. Yellow light showed the log planks on the pathway outside. Two cabins on either side of him, and the entrance at the front. It was deserted.

He almost dozed off a couple of times, but every time he felt like it, he got up and paced around. He wished he had some coffee. After what seemed like a long time, he felt a movement behind him and he turned around with a start. The Sig was instantly in his hand.

"Whoa!" he heard a female voice cry. Lisa. There was muffled sound. His watch had a light and Dan turned it on. It was bright as a flashlight. Lisa had fallen back on the bed.

"I'm sorry," Dan said, giving her a hand. She caught it and stood up.

"Are you alright?" Dan asked. "Sorry, you startled me."

Lisa went to turn on the bedside light. Dan stopped her.

"I don't want anyone to see inside," he said. Lisa nodded.

"It's my turn for watch," she said.

"Are you sure?" Dan asked.

Lisa said, "Yes, catch some sleep."

Dan needed that. He had a long day tomorrow. He put the weapons under his pillow and tried to sleep.

*****

Morning came bright and boisterous. Dan woke up to find the room bright from sunlight filtering in through gaps in the curtains. Lisa was asleep on the twin bed next to his. 0600 hours. He swung his legs off the bed. The door was shut as it had been all night. He checked it carefully. By the time he had brushed and come out of the bathroom Lisa was up and stretching.

"No sight of the tango's?" he asked.

Lisa was momentarily confused, then her face cleared. "You mean the bad guys. Nope. Guess they need to sleep too."

"Yes, but they won't be far. We need to be switched on today."

Dan packed food, bottles of water, his flashlight, a length of nylon rope and his tatty leather gloves into the rucksack. The palm leather gloves were old and had seen use all over the world. The last time had been in Afghanistan, abseiling down from an MH-6 helicopter into a Taliban commander's compound. The mission had been one of his last, and a success. After the end of his combat days, Dan had kept his leather gloves. It was his little piece of luck. He had his old army issue kukri too, but getting on a civilian plane with that was impossible these days.

Lisa came out, wearing her hiking gear. They walked to the Sea Camp offices first, where there was a camping shop. Dan bought a two-man tent, in case they spent the night out in the open. There was every possibility. He got a map and pored over it with Lisa.

"We are here," Dan pointed at the southern tip of the island. "We got a long hike up. These are the hiking trails."

"Look, there's a road that goes up north. Stops halfway up the island. Maybe we can hire bikes," Lisa suggested.

"Good idea," Dan said. They went to the bike hire, Dan keeping his eyes peeled. He reckoned the men would have split up, and dressed like the other holiday makers. It was easy to spot a clump of six men in a camp of families and couples.

He paid for the bikes, then they set off. The sun was climbing and the morning rays were refreshing. They could see the ocean's blue glint up ahead. They passed a crumbling ruin. It had once been a vast building, but only columns of bricks and bare walls remained. Dan looked behind him as he cycled. He cycled slower, deliberately, to let Lisa go ahead, and also to keep watch behind him. In the distance he could see a number of cyclists. It was impossible to be sure if they were being followed.

They took a break at 9:00 a.m., and then cycled again. An hour later they had come to the end of the road. A hiking trail went inside the island, and the same road curved into a branch that led to the white sand dunes by the sea.

Lisa was off her bike and down on the hiking trail. "Jeez, I am pooped."

Dan nodded. "We rest here." He handed her a water bottle. He got off his bike and looked behind him. A couple of bikers went past. Looked like a family. Others were coming up behind. All seemed to be following the road.

He looked at his watch. "Our path is straight up from here, if we want to go to the northern tip of the island."

Lisa took a gulp of water and wiped her mouth. "Let's go."

They walked up a few paces on the trail, then Dan took their bikes and put them behind an oak tree. He chopped some bush with his kukri and scattered the leaves and twigs over the bikes, concealing them.

CHAPTER 36

The ocean on either side had turned grey against grey clouds that had claimed the sky. Dan didn't mind. If they had to hike, a blistering noonday sun was the last thing he needed. Especially with Lisa with him. It wasn't like he could leave her to rest. The Russians weren't far behind.

The trail led deeper into the trees covered with Spanish moss, and soon they had lost sight of the ocean. Branches and twigs leaned over the path. The oak trees were twisted, and palmetto fronds crowded around their roots. The gnarled branches and the light filtering in through the leaves made the place look strange, mythical.

Dan took out his kukri and hacked at the branches, making it easier for Lisa to walk.

"Looks like you done this before," Lisa panted.

"Many times. I did operations in Borneo, south Asia. Basically I was let loose in a tropical forest in the middle of monsoon, to track down the leader of an estranged group. That bloody place was full of leeches, snakes and swamps. Once you live through that, the rest becomes easy."

"Glad you feel that way."

Dan stopped and glanced back. "Are you okay?"

Before Lisa answered, there was a scurrying noise in the bushes below. A long, oval-shaped creature emerged near their feet, its long snout pointing at their feet. Lisa screamed and jumped on Dan. Dan caught her easily and lifted her up.

"Don't worry," he said. "That's just an armadillo."

"Jesus Christ, that scared me," Lisa looked embarrassed. She got off from Dan, brushing her legs. "Sorry."

"Don't be." He pointed a few feet away. It was a pile of horse manure.

"That's horse dung, but I think they have other animals, too. I can tell by the paw marks." Dan showed her. "That's either deer or hogs."

Lisa crinkled her nose. "Smells," she said.

A flight of birds got Dan's attention. It came from a clump of oak trees that they had left behind. About a hundred meters away. He clamped his jaws tight. He took out his Glock and showed Lisa how to use it.

"You walk ahead now," he said. "We might have company. Keep looking all around you, not just ahead. But be careful of your arc of fire." He made a semi-circle with his hands and Lisa nodded.

They walked quicker with Dan glancing back frequently. The forest around them was dense. Some animal trails branched off from the path, but none wide enough for humans. Dan had the kukri back in its scabbard. The Heckler and Koch was in his arms now, trigger finger where it should be. He moved in circles as he followed Lisa, pointing the rifle in 360 degree arcs.

Sounds came from around them. A quick rustle of steps to his left stopped Dan in his tracks. The gangsters would move into the bush, he knew that. They would try and attack them from the sides. Behind him, Lisa had heard it as well. Her Glock arm was extended.

"Keep moving," he hissed. "Stay low."

The rustle came again and Dan raised his weapon, head up from the optical sight, ready to fire at will. A horse broke out from the shrub. Dan sighed and lowered his weapon. He scanned around him. Nothing. He stepped back, facing the other way to Lisa.

"Move," he said.

They kept walking, eyes and ears tuned to every sound in the forest. The trees above them started to get thinner. The ground had been flat, but it started to climb a trail. They pushed on. Several times, they heard sounds, and they squatted down, guns ready. But apart from animals, they saw nothing. Dan was uneasy. He knew they were being followed. They had probably found the bikes. Just how far down they were, he didn't know. After last time, they were keeping their distance and biding their time.

The path trailed down again and Dan heard the faint sound of galloping hooves and neighs. He looked down. Lisa had stopped.

The ocean was closer to their left and the hill sloped down to meet the white dunes on the beach. Scattered at the bottom of the hill were large felled oak trees, their branches sticking up like accusing fingers. The beach was very wide, perhaps the widest expanse of free beach Dan had seen. The clouds were less and the light had changed, making the ocean appear more blue. White crested waves charged to the beach and Dan`s eyes followed the pack of wild horses that ran across, splashing water and neighing loudly. It was remote and forsaken, nature at its primordial, inchoate, best. At any other time, he would have sat down to enjoy the spectacular view.

Then he saw the huts.

In the shade of the hill`s slope, to the extreme right. They caught his eye as he followed the horses. Three dilapidated log cabins, Spanish moss heavy on the walls, sitting on wooden platforms. Although old and not maintained, they were sturdy and had withstood the vagaries of nature. Dan signaled to Lisa. They left the trail and waded into the bush. Dan went first. He took the Sig in his right hand and held the kukri in the left. He slashed hard at the bush around him, taking care at his feet.

"Look out for snakes," he said to Lisa. "Don't jump over if you see one. Give it a wide berth and walk around."

"Rattlesnakes?"

"Yup."

Lisa's face said it all. Dan looked behind him. If the Russians were following, they were doing a damn good job of hiding. They arrived at the base of the hill unhurt. Dan was the first to jump on the powdery white beach. He helped Lisa down.

They crouched and observed. The three huts were about fifty meters away. He indicated, and Lisa moved first. Dan looked up and back as soon as Lisa was mobile. He crept forward with his back to her. The rifle was back in his hands, pointing up at the forest above and behind him. The huge expanse of the beach was totally empty. The ocean lay in the distance with the rolling sound of the breakers. He looked behind—Lisa was close to the first cabin. He ran, his feet digging into the powdery white sand.

Together, they stared at it. It looked much worse close up. Moss grew all over it. Moisture had rotted most of the timber and a section of the roof had fallen in. The two windows that faced the ocean were shut. Wooden shutters. The door too was closed. Dan indicated, and Lisa sank to her knees, gun arm extended. Dan crept forward. The smell of animal waste was strong. The platform creaked under his feet. He got up to the door. It was locked. He took a step back and kicked it hard. There was a splintering sound, and the door crashed inwards. Dan had leaped to one side already, back pressed to the logs. He looked at Lisa, who nodded.

Dan peered in. It was hard to see in the gloom inside. He took his flashlight out. It was empty inside. Old wood, overgrown with moss, and a stench that came from being shut for decades came from within. Dan stepped in and flashed the light around. No one had been in this room apart from the wind and some critters.

Lisa was out already and rushing to the next cabin. Dan followed. Lisa seemed to be a quick learner. She sank to her knees outside the cabin, gun raised. Dan ran past her and kicked the door down. The door crashed open.

The smell of waste was less this time. On Lisa`s signal, he went in. This cabin was better preserved. It was sandwiched between the two and its side walls were in good shape. There was a hole in the roof, through which light penetrated, and a damp spot had formed in the middle from rain.

In one corner, Dan found what he expected. A camping bed on the floor. Two bottles of water to one side of it, and a laptop.

He flashed his light over it. He knelt down. Under the pillow, he found a cell phone that was turned off. He picked up the laptop. It had a remote battery charger connected to it. He heard a sound behind him and saw Lisa come in.

"Put your hands in the air, Dan," Lisa said.

CHAPTER 37

Dan stopped. He put the cell and the laptop under the pillow. He stayed kneeling on the floor.

"I said, put your hands in the air, damn it." Lisa`s voice was harsh.

Dan slowly put his hands up.

"Turn around. Easy." Lisa said.

Dan did as he was told. He stood up, and the room suddenly seemed small with both of them in it. Lisa was standing with her feet apart, in line with her shoulders. The Glock was pointed straight at Dan`s head. At this close range, he knew she wouldn't miss.

"Take off your backpack and the rifle. Very slowly."

Dan did as he was told, not taking his eyes off Lisa.

"Now the Sig. Kick them all to me. Any funny moves and I fire."

Dan took his Sig out and put it on the floor, next to the rifle and rucksack. He nudged them towards her with his foot.

"Now kneel back down, and put your hands behind your head."

Dan knelt. "You're the double agent, aren't your Lisa?" he asked. Lisa didn't reply.

Dan said, "It was you who introduced Philip to the Russian gangster. When Philip realized who the gangster was, he made a run for it. Yes, he was sick. He needed money. For medical bills and college fees. You preyed on him and got him to meet the Russians."

Lisa remained motionless, her gun not wavering.

"Only, you got it wrong, Lisa. You underestimated Philip. He agreed to meet with your man, because he wanted to flush them out. That was why he had an escape plotted out."

"Shut up," Lisa said, frowning.

"You spies are all the same. You think you're so goddamn clever. But you`re actually stupid. The Mexicans followed me back from Tanya`s college after I told you I was going there. That was a giveaway. Marcus was shot dead that morning I was in your apartment. You left early, way early. I saw you slip out of the apartment. He was shot dead in his car that morning. That was why you knew about it before anyone else. Andy Brown told me on the phone and no one else knew. No one at Synchrony. No one in the media. How the hell did you know? That was pretty dumb of you."

Lisa's face had lost some of its composure. She came forward, her jaws working. "You don't know what the hell you're talking about, Dan. Save your breath, 'cos you're going to die soon."

Dan smirked. "Those DoD reports you showed me about Marcus? The ones from the Pentagon? They were fakes. Good ones, but fakes. I took photos of them on my cell phone. I sent them to my friends. You were trying to convince me Marcus was the bad guy, when Marcus was actually the only friend Philip had. I bet you he was the one who helped Philip escape. He might also have been the only one who knew where Philip was. That was why you had to kill him."

"You son of a bitch. Should have killed you too, when I had the chance."

"Yes, you should have. Because, you know what? You're not going to get that data. Ever. You'd better tell that research ship out there to turn back unless it wants to get blown sky-high."

Lisa bared her teeth. "Wrong, dickhead. All the data is in that laptop right there. I just need to take it." She paused. "By the way, if you're so darned smart, then why did you let me come all the way with you here?"

"To get the Russians out of Barnham. I didn't want them lurking around the base. I knew they would follow us. And, I wanted *you* right where I could keep an eye on you."

Dan smiled again, and Lisa didn't like it. Her eyes snaked to the bed, then back to Dan.

"You want the laptop, you have to get through me first," said Dan, and stood up. Lisa fired. The hollow clicks of the pin on the chamber sounded twice.

Lisa looked like she had been punched in the gut. She fired again and the hollow click sounded again.

Dan put his hand inside his pockets and took out the rounds.

"I took them out last night. That's why I waited until today to give you the gun." He threw the rounds on the floor. They clattered around Lisa's feet.

Lisa snarled and jumped on Dan. She punched him. He ducked and the blow glanced off his shoulder. He straightened and caught her on the chin with an upper cut. Lisa went flying across the room and crashed against the wall. She slid to the floor, dazed. Dan knelt by the rucksack. He removed the nylon rope and tied her hands together, then used the same length of rope to tie her hands to her legs. He ripped off a piece of the bedding with his kukri and stuffed her mouth with it. She could still breathe through her nose.

It was an acutely sharpened auditory sense that made him duck the split second he heard the sound.

A battle-hardened sixth sense wired inside him for life. It saved him, as it had done in the past.

The heavy round smashed in through the window on the side, and thudded into the woodwork where a second before, his head had been.

Bop. Bop. Bop.

He recognized the sound of suppressed rounds—they burst in from the window. Dan looked towards the door. He could hide from the window, but the door was the danger zone. If they came in through there, he was good as dead. That would be their plan: pin him down with fire, and send a killer to the door.

He looked for the guns. They were by his feet. The bullets kept coming in from the window, whining and banging inside. He ignored it. He backed up against wall, the Heckler and Koch pointed at the door. The doorframe moved, and then was kicked open. Dan fired from the hip. His first rounds caught the man in the doorway square on the chest, spinning him backwards. The man behind him had no chance either. Dan had shuffled forward on the floor. As the front man fell, Dan was firing already. Two 7.62mm NATO rounds made mincemeat of the second man's face. The third guy was standing with his back to the wall outside. He thought he had his chance now. But he was wrong.

This was close-quarter battle and Dan had never fought it with one weapon. The rifle was too heavy to move quickly. The third guy knew this. He exposed himself, pointing his gun at Dan. But he had not expected Dan to be so close to him.

Too late, he saw the snout of the Sig Sauer pointing at him, a mere five feet away. Shot one blew his face away, and shot two severed the spine below the neck, so the automatic impulse that made him squeeze the trigger, even after he was brain dead, was no longer a factor.

There was no one else outside. The shots coming in from the window had stopped. Dan heard a volley of shots from further out, up in the hill. Sounded like a different weapon. He knew who that was. Andy Brown. That was one of the phone calls he had made after speaking to McBride. The other had been to Tanya. Dan looked around the beach, then rolled out of the hut. He turned and scrambled to the base of the hill. Holding the rifle aloft with one hand, he hoisted himself up on the slope. He rushed up, rifle at the shoulder now, scanning around. He heard more shots up front. A round whined above his head. He dropped flat, then threw himself against the trunk of an oak tree. He needed to find the source of fire.

More rounds came. He leaned out the side and let out a volley himself. Then he ran for the next tree. He wasn't fast enough, but he got lucky.

A thick branch snapped in two in a burst of fire at hip height, just as he got to the cover of the tree trunk. Shrapnel and dust exploded into his face. That round was headed straight for his liver. He thanked the tree and laid down heavy fire in that direction. His ammo ran out. He clipped another thirty round magazine and began firing. He didn't stop, and the clump of trees he was firing to became pockmarked with dark spots as chunks of the trees blew away. He emptied the magazine, reloaded and laid down rapid fire again.

There was a method to his madness. He had counted six last night at the harbor. Three were dead. If the other three were holed up here, then he could finish the job now.

He had Andy Brown bringing up the rear. If he could distract the gangsters, they wouldn't hear Brown coming up behind them, and Brown could waste them all. With any luck. He spotted a flash of white against the trees in front and fired. There was a scream and he was fired upon immediately.

Dan heard more screams, and the sound of new fire came in. That was Brown. The familiar sound of the M4 assault rifle came again and Dan heard more screams. The gangsters were trapped and had to escape. Dan was ready. One of the gangsters made a run for it. Dan tracked him for two seconds, then got him with a head shot. He saw a blur of movement to his left, but he was too late to aim and fire. Then he heard another burst of M4. The man went down in a heap. Four and five. Which left one.

CHAPTER 38

Silence. All of a sudden, there was no sound. The smell of gunfire hung heavy in the air. Dan did a sitrep. All clear.

He listened for a while. Apart from the surf breaking below, the forest was quiet. Dan chewed his lower lip. If the last one was there, it could be trouble. There would be no way of smoking him out unless he moved. Dan knew the art of laying in silence for hours. Targets moved sooner or later. More often than not, it was their last move.

The silence was shattered by the M4 again. Dan gripped his rifle. He didn't have any ammo left. He took the Sig out. Then he heard a shout.

"Dan, are you there?" It was Brown. "Dan?" Definitely his voice. But still, he was careful. He relaxed when a girl's voice sounded.

"Dan, it's Tanya." Shouting meant giving his position away. But now he knew it was them. He leaned out and shouted back.

"There's one left. Have you seen him?"

"No," Brown said. "But we got the two dead ones here."

Dan crawled out of his position. He crawled over the brush to the bodies. Three heads popped up in front of him. Tanya looked scared, but her face cleared when she saw him. He felt sorry for her being here, but there was no way Philip would have gone with Brown.

Next to Brown, he saw an old man. Philip Longworth. The man looked like a ghost. The skin on his face was stretched so tight it seemed to shine. His cheeks were hollows, and so were the holes that were his eyes. A few wisps of hair stuck out from the sides of his scalp. With difficulty, Dan identified him to the man he had seen in the photo. Dan nodded at him. Philip nodded slowly back, staring at him.

The time for pleasantries would be later. They still had an unfinished job. Dan got closer to them.

"Where is he?" he asked them. All three of them shrugged.

"There was a tall, blond guy near the edge of the hill," Tanya pointed towards the ocean. They were far into the forest. Dan suddenly thought of the bullets that were fired at the cabin. They couldn't have been fired by someone here. They had to be at the edge. The leader. The tall guy. He had been taking the shots.

In a flash, he realized. "He's down at the cabin. Might have figured out I'm holding Lisa in there. He wants to get the laptop as well."

"Don't worry about the laptop," Philip said in a low voice, and coughed into his hands. "I have the data in a drive." He reached inside his shirt and showed them a necklace with a pendant at the end. The pendant was a removable disk drive.

"Suits you, sir," Dan said. "You guys stay here to keep watch. I'm going down. Andy, you get up to the edge of that hill now. Use your height to fire on him. Got that?" Andy nodded.

Dan got up and ran to the edge of the hill, then scrambled down to the beach. He ran towards the cabins. His rifle was without ammo. He took out his Sig and slowed down. As he approached the middle cabin, through the window he could see movement inside. A face looked up and saw him.

Dan fired, but not before he had been fired upon. He threw himself on the sand. Another shot whined overhead. Dan got up and ran towards the cabin. He was out in the open, while the blonde guy was inside. He needed to get cover.

Dan fired twice at the window to keep the man quiet. He ran towards the door, but the door opened before he could get there. A tall blond man stepped out. He was big, almost six five, and broad. The wooden platform sagged under his weight. He aimed at Dan, but Dan was quicker. The Sig jerked twice in his hand and the man screamed. Dan had aimed for his gun hand. A splash of red appeared and the gun flew away. Dan fired again, but the Sig was out of ammo. He was out of ammo, period. The blonde guy realized. With an oath, he used his good hand and scrambled for his gun. He had to turn his back to Dan to do so. Dan had seconds to act. He ran up and cannoned into him.

The cabin shook on its foundation as the two men collided. Dan was up first. He kicked the man's Glock pistol into the sand.

Valcheck Ivanov stood up behind Dan. With his good left hand, he took out a long knife from his belt strap. Dan turned around just as Val thrust forward with the blade. The serrated edge flashed in the sun. Dan stepped aside, but the knife ripped along the side of his forearm. Dan winced in pain. A red gash appeared on his shirt and blood dripped into his hand.

Dan pivoted, slammed into Val and the two men rolled off the platform onto the sand. Dan fought to grab Val's knife hand. He got a hand around it, then lifted his other elbow and brought it down with savage force on Val's chin. Val grunted and tried to punch Dan back. Dan lifted himself off Val and ran. Val got up and followed. He thought Dan was searching for the Glock. But he was mistaken.

Dan took out his kukri with a flourish. Blood dripped down his arm, soaking his grip on the knife. Val snarled as he stood up. They circled each other. The ocean roared behind them. Val's right hand was a bloody mess, but his left arm was strong. Dan suspected the man was ambidextrous, hence the knife had been in his left belt. Val was bending down low. He feinted at Dan, who swayed away easily. He feinted again, lower this time. In a blur of movement, his injured hand grabbed sand and flung it into Dan's face.

Dan coughed and stumbled back. He fell and rolled over, a red mist in his eyes.

He could see Val above him, bearing down for the killer blow. Dan kicked his legs as hard as he could. He caught Val at the knees and they folded. Dan was up as Val lost his balance. The sand was still in his eyes, but he could see. Val rushed him, aiming low again, as most knife fighters did. Dan slapped the knife away with his free hand, and slashed at Val's neck. The longer, hooked blade of the kukri smashed into the neck with a tearing force, severing the arteries immediately. Blood spurted up in a high arch as the kukri cut open the windpipe and came out the other side.

Valchek Ivanov fell to his knees. His hands clutched his neck, but they couldn't stop the blood gushing out onto the soft, white sand.

He stared uncomprehendingly at Dan for a second, then slowly his eyes glazed. His body tilted forward and he slumped face-down.

Dan stepped back, panting. Sweat was pouring down his face. He wiped his forehead with the kukri hand. Sweat mixed with blood appeared on his sleeve.

"Goodbye, Dan," a female voice said behind him. He was facing the ocean, and he turned around slowly. Lisa had come out from the cabin. Someone had cut through her ropes. It must have been Val. She had Val's Glock in her hands. It was pointed straight at Dan's head, held in both her hands.

"Are you going to shoot me?" Dan asked.

"You bastard. You spoilt everything."

Dan saw her fingers tighten, and he moved to the left and down. Lisa was right-handed. If the bullet hit his arm or his shoulder, he might still survive. The gun exploded. Dan buried his face in the sand, expecting the sudden stab of pain that came with a bullet wound.

From this range, it would be last his last bullet wound.

It didn't come. There was another explosion, this time from closer by. These shots were coming from behind Lisa. Dan looked up. Lisa was on the sand. A red circle was spreading on her back. The second shot had hit higher up, near the shoulder. Dan saw movement. Andy Brown jumped down from the hill and clambered towards him in the sand.

Dan took the Glock away from Lisa. He turned her over. Her eyes were still open. They flickered as she looked at Dan. Dan shook his head. He checked her wounds. One bullet was inside her chest. Heavy internal bleeding. The other had hit the left shoulder and exited. He pressed on the chest wound, stemming the blood flow.

She might be saved, if there was a helicopter to take her away. Dan took out the GPS locator from his pant pocket and pressed a button. He continued to put pressure on Lisa's chest wound. A sound of motors came from the ocean. An RIB, its black nose rising up above the waves, was bobbing over to the beach at high speed. It landed and Dan watched the four Delta guys pull the boat to shore. He turned to Andy Brown.

"Thank you," he said. Andy only had a revolver in his hand.

"He fired," Andy pointed behind him. Dan looked to see Philip stumbling towards them, the M4 assault rifle pointed towards the sand. He seemed to be weighed down by the gun. But hatred sparkled in his eyes.

When he came up to them, he panted, "Is that the bitch who tried to kidnap my girl? I`ll kill her!" he shouted, raising the gun. Dan stepped between them.

"Philip," he said, raising his voice, but keeping himself calm. "She`s half-dead already. She`s going to get her due, don't worry. If she lives, she can answer a lot of questions. It's better to have her alive."

Tanya was watching with a scared expression on her face. Philip looked wildly from Lisa to Dan.

"It`s over Philip. I know what she did. But it`s over," Dan repeated. "Look at me."

Philip stared at Dan, who grabbed the muzzle of the gun. He pulled it gently. Philip resisted, but then gave it up.

Tanya came up and put her arm around her father. Then she pointed to Dan`s arm.

"You`re hurt."

Dan was still holding the kukri. He wiped the blade and put it back in its scabbard. He smiled at Tanya. "This? It`s nothing. You`re safe, that's what matters." Her face was drawn and lined with worry. She left her father and came over to hug Dan. He closed his eyes. Relief washed over him. If anything had happened to her, he would never have forgiven himself.

"I couldn't have done it without you," Dan said.

Tanya said, "I`m just glad it`s over."

He nodded. "Me, too." He glanced over at Philip. He was a shell of the man he once had been. His back was stooped, his cheeks were caved in. He could barely stand up.

"You okay?" he asked. Philip mumbled something incoherent, and flopped down onto the sand.

The medic in the Delta team gave Lisa emergency aid and called a bird to airlift her. Dan and the others took shelter inside the cabin as the Blackhawk bird touched down. It was back up within seconds, heading for the nearest ER. They wanted Lisa alive.

They picked up Philip`s stuff and walked back to the RIB with the remaining two Delta guys. They fired the boat up and it ploughed into the ocean, cutting through the waves powerfully. The boat circled around the mouth of St Mary`s river and headed for King`s Bay Naval Base. Two men in white uniforms were waiting for them. They escorted them inside. Dan shook hands with the Delta guys. As they walked into the base, he fell in step with Philip.

"I am Dan Roy, he said.

Philip nodded. "Yes, I know who you are. Tanya told me." Philip stopped, and raised his yellow eyes to Dan. "Thank you for looking after my family."

"No problem", Dan said.

"Why did you start buying cocaine off the Mexicans?" Dan asked.

"They were following me around. I wanted to find out why. That's why I approached them. It didn't work out."

Dan said, "That's what I figured."

CHAPTER 39

"Captain, what are we going to do?" Sasha looked at Shevchenko.

They were standing on the bridge, staring out the large glass screens. Men lifted machine parts in the front deck below them. They were being moved out of sight. Shevchenko had a pair of binoculars and he was staring at the thumb-sized speck that had appeared on the north east horizon. The shape was moving. He lowered the binoculars.

"That is a US Navy destroyer. Not just any other ship," he said quietly. "Did you call the Kremlin?"

"Yes, Captain. They want us to respond, if we are engaged."

"Respond?" Shevchenko sighed. The earlier fight had gone out of him. "Respond against a nuclear submarine and a destroyer with torpedoes?"

"But Captain, you said you did not want this ship to fall into enemy hands."

"Yes, I did. But only if they engaged us. I don't think they will. We are more than two hundred miles away, out of the exclusive economic zone the Americans have from their shores. They suspect us of something, but they will not want an international incident by boarding us, or firing."

"So what do we do?"

"We are in international waters. We hold our ground."

The telephone jangled on the wall. Sasha picked it up. He listened, then turned to Shevchenko.

"Captain, they have located our bandwidth. The Americans are contacting us."

Shevchenko swore under his breath. It had to happen sooner or later. They were listening to all their conversations. With any luck, they hadn't broken the encryption code. But one could never be sure. Without speaking a word, he took the receiver from Sasha`s hand.

"This is Captain Mikhail Shevchenko of the Russian Deep Water Research Agency speaking," he said in perfect English.

There was a pause, and some static, then a voice came through the phone. "This is Admiral John Sims of the United States Navy. Do you copy?"

"Yes I do." An Admiral. That was serious. Probably calling from a land link and not actually on the destroyer. Shevchenko had a sick feeling in the pit of his stomach.

"I know who you are, Captain. I need to tell you something important. Your agent is dead. We know everything about your operation." He paused. "You have two options. One, to head back immediately where you came from. We will be tracking you. If you, or any Russian submarines, are not clear from these waters in the next hour, then you will face option two."

Shevchenko said, "Which is what?"

Another pause, then Admiral Sims continued. "We will confiscate your ship and crew. If you try to resist, we will use force. Your actions are harmful to American interests and we have proof of that. I know you are in international waters, but the Unites States Navy has the right to respond to dangerous intent with force, and by any means necessary. Do you understand?"

"What do you think will happen, Admiral, if you confiscate our ship? Do you think the Russian Navy will sit quietly and allow it?"

"We have assets in the ocean now which are capable of using lethal force against any naval units. This is not a negotiation. We have the absolute right to protect ourselves. Take this as a final warning."

Shevchenko was quiet. He felt old suddenly, and weary. Admiral Sims spoke crisply on the phone again.

"One hour, Captain." He hung up.

Shevchenko handed the receiver back to Sasha.

"What happened, Captain?"

Shevchenko didn't speak for several seconds. He stared out at the choppy blue waves, their white tops curling over like never-ending question marks.

"Sometimes, Sasha, discretion is the better part of valor." He turned and clasped his hands behind his back.

"It is time to go home."

CHAPTER 40

Philip Longworth and Dan sat with McBride in a parked car in downtown Atlanta. Two black SUV`s were positioned in front and behind them. A black suited agent was out of each car, keeping an eye on the otherwise vacant street.

"The Russian diplomat has been summoned to the White House," McBride said. "The guy you killed, Vyalchek Ivanov, has an uncle who is the secretary to the First Minister of the Russian Navy. The Kremlin is, of course, denying all knowledge of any links. But this is not the first time the Russian mafia has worked with Kremlin. The *Bratva* is an efficient and well-connected global network."

He looked at Dan and Philip and said, "I cannot tell you the name of individuals. But know this: the principal resident of the White House sends his personal regards."

"I appreciate that" Dan said. Men like him never got medals. They died in cold graves in foreign lands. Dan did not care about politicians. He never would. But he had been able to avoid a calamity for his country – that was the only gratification he needed.

"Were the town hall people of Barnham in on this?" Dan asked.

Philip answered before McBride could. "Yes. We had to take them on board. They fed the usual news to the media. But all they knew was that it was a confidential site. They didn't have details."

Dan asked Philip, "So did you suspect Lisa Chandler from the beginning?"

"She tried to get close to me all the time. She knew I was in charge of the network design and location. I began to leave hints about my financial problems. That`s when it became obvious she was crooked."

"Did she know you had the only copy?"

"She figured it out eventually. No one is allowed copies from the secure room."

"Who is she?"

"A deep undercover agent of the former KGB. Been in this country for fifteen years." Philip coughed into his hands, a hack that bent his back.

"Are you alright?" Dan asked. Philip nodded, getting his breath back.

McBride said. "Her real name is Lydia Vasilevina. By the way, she's alive."

Dan nodded. "Philip needs to get back to the medical center."

"All bills will be paid by us, Philip," McBride said. "When we told the FBI your medical bills weren't coming out of their budget, they loved you even more."

Dan said to McBride, "I need to have a word with you."

McBride said, "Let's step outside." Philip remained in the car.

Dan and McBride walked a few steps away from the car. Dan said, "It ends here."

McBride said, "Yes, I know."

"Like hell you do. Don't play games with me, McBride. I'm not one of your agents anymore. Stop acting like I am one. You should have told me the truth from the beginning. Instead, you let me fall into the shit."

McBride was silent. Dan said, "If Jody asked me for help, you knew I would not refuse." Dan breathed out. "The days of you guys taking advantage of me are over. Do you understand?"

McBride smiled ruefully. "And what about you, Dan? Will you be happy? What the hell are you gonna do with your life?"

Dan said harshly, "That's my god damned business. All I want is you, and the rest of Washington, and the Government to stay the hell out of my business."

McBride nodded. "Roger that."

Dan walked back to the car. The door opened and Philip stepped out. He stuck his hand out at Dan.

Philip said, "Thank you for everything, Dan."

Dan shook hands with Philip. "Take care of yourself, and your family, Philip," he said.

Philip's eyes were misty. "Words cannot express how I feel."

Dan held Philip's thin shoulder. "It's alright. I understand. Say goodbye to Jody and Tanya for me."

"I definitely will. Where are you headed, Dan?"

Dan said, "Where my two eyes take me. I want to vanish for a while. Where no one can find me."

Dan lifted the backpack on his shoulder, the only luggage he ever carried. He walked to the end of the street, and hailed down a cab. Before he got in, he looked back once. McBride was standing there, looking at him. Their eyes met one last time. Then Dan was in the car, telling the driver to head for the airport.

THE END

THE TONKIN PROTOCOL

Dan Roy Series
Dan Roy Thriller 3

This book is dedicated to the people of Myanmar.

AUTHOR'S PREFACE

The Gulf of Tonkin (*Tong Quing*) lies between the Hainan Island in South China Sea and the coast of Vietnam in South East Asia.

From May 1950, US Naval Forces were present in these waters to show support for the Republic of Vietnam. China and Russia were both involved in the consolidation of Communism in North Vietnam and Indochina.

On August 2, 1964, the US Destroyer *Maddox* was patrolling those waters, conducting signals intelligence. Troubles were already widespread in the region.

Allegedly, the *Maddox* was fired upon by three North Vietnamese gunboats. It responded, and the incident became known in the annals of history as the Gulf of Tonkin Incident. Evidence remained scanty, and controversy about the Incident reigns to this day.

But one thing is undeniable – the Gulf of Tonkin Incident was the official beginning of the Vietnam War.

This much we know is history.

Now, fast forward to fiction.

PROLOGUE

Malacca Straits
South of Singapore
Present day

David Harris was watching with his telescope from the high-rise apartment on the tip of the Singapore peninsula. This was the highest point of the island, and with the telescope, he could clearly see the *Lunar Smile* oil tanker. The tanker was in excess of 1400 feet long, and carried almost 2 million barrels of oil. That equated to 84 million gallons.

The colossal ship had left port at the southern Iranian oil city of Bandar Abbas, where it had loaded up. It had travelled down the Strait of Hormuz, a narrow Persian Gulf Channel through which trillions of barrels of oil passed every day, delivered to the rest of the world. From there, the *Lunar Smile* had moved into the Gulf of Oman, and then south into the vast expanse of the Arabian Sea, along India's south coast.

The *Lunar Smile* was headed for China, specifically for the Hainan Island, connected to the Guangxi province of southern China. Hainan Island was the major nuclear submarine base of the Chinese Army, and also the site of critical pipelines that carried oil into mainland China.

Oil that China needed to function on a daily basis.

David adjusted the magnifier on the telescope and sharpened the image. The irritating bush fires from the jungles of Sumatra were a nuisance at this time of the year, blowing huge hazy clouds across the narrow 550 mile Malacca Strait. Not to mention the shallowness of the waters here, less than 85 feet, which meant the larger ships like the *Lunar Smile* had to travel slowly.

The radio in David's ear crackled into life. "Lotus 1 we are in position."

David waited for a second, then heard the beep of the scrambler. Then he said, "Copy that Lotus 2. How much longer?"

"90 seconds to ETA."

"Roger that, out."

A dense archipelago of islands south of Singapore narrowed the world's most important oil tanker channel even further. The Malacca Straits was East

Asia's oil lifeline, and the only waterway that linked the Indian Ocean to the South China Sea.

A vital waterway for China. And a key patrol zone for the US Navy 7th Fleet, based in Yokosuka, Japan.

Last night, a team of scuba divers had left by boat from one of the Sumatra islands. They had waited under cover of darkness till the *Lunar Smile's* bow was visible, a few hundred yards away. They had travelled by rigid inflatable boats (RIB) across the Malacca Straits choppy waters, close to the ship. The 250 Kg of plastic explosives, dual fitted with a timer, was attached to the ship's hull by the scuba diver team. Then they had moved back to land, undetected.

David counted the seconds in the timer held in his left hand. When twenty seconds was left, he trained his telescope on the ship again. A small yellow ball appeared briefly at the starboard hull of the ship. The explosion was not enough to breach the massive hull of the ship, especially as the Chinese reinforced their oil tankers with missile proof titanium. But it would stop the ship, and instead of moving into the South China Sea, the stricken vessel would have to take port at Singapore.

David saw the smoke haze lift up briefly. The *Lunar Smile* had stopped, and it was leaning slightly to starboard. He turned his eyes away. He fished inside his pocket and pulled out his cell phone.

His call to the number was routed through five countries of Central Asia before it got to its destination, inside a small office in Fort Belvoir, Virginia. He heard someone pick up the phone. Again, David waited for the scrambler.

He said, "Tonkin Protocol is activated. Repeat activated."

A silence followed. Then a gruff voice said, "Copy that, Lotus 1. Proceed as planned."

CHAPTER 1

Northern Shan State
Myanmar
100 miles from China-Myanmar Border
1 month later

David Harris gritted his teeth as the jeep rattled over the stony tract that led higher into the mountainous jungles.

This region, in the eastern corner of Myanmar, was under the control of the Shan ethnic people. Numbering over a million and half of Myanmar's population of fifty-one million, the Shan's had fought several wars with the *Tatmadaw*, as the Burmese Army was known. As a result, the Shan's had their own army, aptly called the Shan State Army. Their vision of carving out their own state from Myanmar, or Burma of the old days, had never become a reality. But that did not mean they had stopped trying.

Only recently, gunfire had broken out in the state line between Shan state and Mandalay, over the ambush of a Shan State Army patrol. Mandalay was the epicenter of the vast plains dotted with mystical pagoda spires, dating from the 6th century. The *Tatmadaw* blamed the Shan State Army, and vice versa. Neither side believed they were to blame, and that was not far from the truth.

David Harris knew who was to blame. But for now, that knowledge would remain secure inside his brain. As the jeep lurched to the left, David tightened his grip on the dashboard handle. A towel hung conveniently from it – used to wipe sweat in the humid jungle. He glanced down, and immediately wished he hadn't.

A steep ravine loomed to his right, a fall of more than a hundred feet. At the base, and as far as the eyes could see, was a canopy of dense green foliage. Beyond that, in the distance, grey clouds floated in a hazy blue sky. They said rain was never distant in these high eastern plateaus. Heavy clouds got stuck in the monsoon, and it rained for weeks without end.

David gritted his teeth. He couldn't care less about the rain. It was April, and the damn place was too hot. Not to mention the hazardous driving conditions. There was nothing but open air to his right. If any of the wheels slipped on these stones...

After an hour of tortuous travel, they had arrived. The jeep dived to the left, and plunged into a jungle. Massive baobab and teak trees dominated the space around them. Sunlight struggled to get through the dense green vines, looping endlessly above. In the green expanse, David saw colorful orchid flowers, throwing splashes of red and orange into the greenery.

The jeep slowed as the jungle grew dense. The smell of damp earth was strong and refreshing, an earthly, nascent smell that had remained the same for countless centuries.

David felt something above his head. He looked up to see tubular brown structures hanging from a tall tree. He patted the driver next to him on the forearm.

"*Maung* Thin," David shouted above the sound of the engine. "What is that?" He pointed upwards. *Maung*, or young as the prefix meant, glanced up quickly, a worried look on his face. Then he smiled.

"Tamarind fruit, *Baw* David. Tangy taste. Very nice." Baw was the common prefix used for a foreigner.

David said, "I see."

Thin shouted back, "You made me think it was snake." He grinned.

David did not grin. He hated snakes. "What do you mean?" He asked.

"I mean, like a python. You see them sometimes here."

David closed his eyes and looked away. All of a sudden, all he could think about was a long red-green serpent hanging from a tree above him, forked tongue sliding out...

"We here," *Maung* Thin said.

David shook his head, dispelling the image from his mind. He followed the direction of Thin's outstretched hand. There was a clearing ahead. The teak and shimul trees had been hacked down, and the land levelled. A row of brown thatched huts stood on rigged bamboo posts. Sunlight, unfettered by the thick canopy of rainforest, illuminated the area.

As they bounced closer, David saw the flash of brown uniform, and a cluster of watchful guards, all with AK-47's on shoulder straps. The guards flagged the jeep down. David blinked as the jeep trundled out of the semi-darkness into bright sunlight.

After some questions, they were allowed through. The jeep came to a stop outside a row of the huts. Men in the typical brown uniform of the Shan State Army (SSA) walked around, armed to the teeth. Anti-aircraft guns and

Chinese FN6 Surface to Air Missiles (SAM) were scattered around the periphery. The thick forests started beyond the perimeter, undulating over the hills to the far horizon. Close by, to the east, lay the Yunnan province of China.

"You should see the place at night, *Baw* David," A voice spoke behind him. David turned around. A Burmese man in his forties, dressed in uniform jacket and combat trouser, and a deep tanned, weather lined face stood facing him. His hands were clasped behind his back, and his spine was ramrod straight.

David bowed his head. "*U* Khin Nyunt, it is a pleasure to meet you again." The prefix U stood as a term of respect for an elder. Which Khin Nyunt certainly was, in military terms at least. A former commander of the *Tatmadaw* jungle infantry, he had left to join his people's army. The state border had advanced into Mandalay under his command, and had stayed that way.

Nyunt pointed at the trees. "On a clear night, the fireflies light up the forest. Above them, we have the stars. It is very beautiful. Maybe you shall see it, one day."

The two men shook hands. "Maybe I will," David said.

They walked into the thatched hut that served as Nyunt's office. Underground cable wires brought electricity inside. An air conditioner hummed, providing a cool respite. A laptop was open, with a fax machine and printer next to it on the table.

Nynut closed the door, then opened a drawer. He spread out a map of the region on the table. Myanmar was broad in the middle, and compressed at the sides. To the left lay the deep waters of the Bay of Bengal, and to the right, Eastern China. That's where they were right now, close to the Chinese border. A series of crosses had been marked on the map, showing a line travelling from the Bay of Bengal into China. Nyunt laid a thick forefinger on the map and traced the line.

"There it is," he said. David was seeing it for the first time. He shook his head, then looked up at Nyunt.

David asked, "Is it operational already?"

"Damn right it is."

Nynut continued. "It runs between Pangshang and Mong Pawk. You know what they are?"

David said, "Correct me if I'm wrong, *U* Nyunt. Both are towns at the eastern edge of the lower Shan state, right at the border with China. Both are controlled by the United Wa Army, which is heavily supported by the Chinese National Army. China provides all their weapons and money."

"Correct, *Baw* David. Pangshang in particular is a little party town, with a 24-hour casino, ten pin bowling alleys, busy night life. Lots of girls from the villages go there." Nynut stopped and grinned. "Because *Baws* like you go there for fun."

David said, "Also because of the opium."

Nynut shook his head. "It's true that the United Wa Army are still the biggest heroin traffickers of Southeast Asia. But with Chinese help a lot of the opium farms are being shut down. China does not want opium in Yunnan. The new drug in town is *yaa baa*."

"I heard of this. Methamphetamine."

"Yes. Crystal Meth. More than a hundred labs along that border manufacture it, and push it south down to Thailand."

David said, "Let's get down to business. Do you think we can do this?"

Nyunt folded the map and put it in the drawer. Then he locked it. He took out a bottle of clear liquid and two small glasses. Without asking, he put a glass in front of David. He splashed a measure out of the bottle into the glass.

"What's this?" David asked. He knew he could not refuse. In Myanmar, it is rude to refuse a drink when offered by the host.

"*Shwe le ma.* Toddy juice, made from fermented palm sugar." Nynut held up the glass. "Cheers!" He knocked the glass back.

David took a sip. The strong alcohol burnt the back of his throat and he coughed and spluttered. His face went red. He looked up into the amused face of Nynut.

"Are you OK?"

David said, "Just need to get used to it, that's all." Nynut suppressed a smile.

They talked business for a while.

Nynut said, "If this goes ahead, you know there will be a massive crackdown. Not just on the Shans. The Kachin, Rohingya, all of us. You know the Wa Army supplies all the insurgent groups in Burma with weapons. Without weapons we cannot defend ourselves."

David leaned forward. "How would you like some drones?"

Nyunt raised his eyebrows. "You're bluffing."

"No I am not. Tomorrow I can prove it. You have airfields. You have internet connections. Supplying you with drones is much easier for us than providing aircraft or other heavy weapons that Chinese drones flying overhead can easily see. On top, we will provide modern rifles like Heckler and Koch, and the latest special ops capable M4's. Not to mention NVG's."

"Seriously? How will you get the drones into Myanmar without the Tatmadaw knowing?"

"By land, through India." Myanmar shared a long north-western border with India.

David said, "Trust me, we have plenty of assets in India at the moment. The Rohingya's are ready to help us. A convoy of UN trucks will make the delivery."

Nyunt tapped his lower lips thoughtfully. "Tell me more."

*****

Night fell with a cloak of darkness so dense that David could not see his hands. As they moved in formation, he looked up at the sky, and realized Nyunt was right. Fireflies glowed against the dark expanse of the trees, and stars studded a black sky like pin point diamonds.

They moved deeper into the dense trees. They left the trails behind, and plunged into the heart of the jungle. Two trackers in the lead separated the foliage and listened for the big cats. The brown leopards and the black mountain lions were the main predators, but generally they left human beings alone.

Serpents were another problem. The pythons stayed coiled on thick branches or on the ground. They never bothered anyone unless they were hungry. The smaller cobras were far more dangerous. An accidental step on their tail could mean death unless the flesh wound was cut off with a knife immediately. Even then, it seldom worked. The silent hooded cobra was a fearful creature.

After an hour of marching they stopped, and drank water. Then the march started again. When the lead man halted them, David could already a light breeze on his face. They went to ground, and crept forward. They were at the top of a hill, the ground beneath them giving way to the familiar panoply of forest. The moon was out, and the whole scene was washed in a silvery white glow, giving the rainforest an ethereal, enchanted atmosphere.

In the valley below, yellow lights glowed and construction workers moved around. David grabbed his NVG binoculars and looked. He saw Chinese armored vehicles dotted around the valley. Soldiers leaned against them, smoking.

Nynut was next to him. David turned his head, and the darkness around him exploded into a fireball of orange yellow heat. The explosion lifted David clear off the ground and hurled him against the sturdy trunk of a teak tree. His head cracked against it, and he crumpled to the ground, dazed.

Gunfire erupted all around him. The jungle reverberated with screams of wounded soldiers. More explosions sounded, and the night was lit up with flashes of gunfire.

David reached for the pistol on his belt. He heard the crunching of leaves. He removed the gun, but he was too late. A heavy boot landed on his arm, and then kicked his gun arm. David fell back. The butt of a rifle smashed into the side of his face, knocking his head back. He felt sticky, warm liquid pour down his face.

Gunfire and shouts continued around him. Above him, David felt a presence. A flashlight shone on his face. Someone exclaimed, and there was an urgent whisper. More footsteps arrived.

David felt someone kneeling in front of him.

"Who are you?" a voice said in heavily accented English. Another light appeared. David fought the nausea and bile that rose to his mouth. He swallowed. When he looked up, the breath caught in his chest.

He was looking up at a pale skinned face. Oriental features. A deep scar ran from the side of the left eye to the left lip. But what held him were the eyes. For a moment David thought the man was blind. The pale irises were almost the same color as the whites. Then the eyes blinked. David realized the eyes had no expression in them. Utterly blank.

"Who are you?" the man said again. David was silent.

The man got up, and said something. A boot crashed into the center of David's chest. Pain mushroomed in his ribs, and he could not breath. Another vicious kick, then strong arms lifted him to his feet. A punch to the abdomen followed, bending him over. Rope was tied over his hands. Then he was dragged liked an animal. He fell to his feet, but got up and stumbled. Wounded soldiers moaned around him in the sudden silence of the jungle.

CHAPTER 2

Kimberly Smith looked up at the dark shapes that were hunched above her in the meeting room. She could not see any of their faces, but she knew her face was illuminated by the screen. She pointed with the infra-red dot on the map screen.

"This is the Guanxi Island, which is 100 miles south east of Hainan Island on the South China Sea. The Chinese have built this, it's man made. It has a deep water port, and what is interesting is the vessel that has berthed in its wet dock recently."

Kimberly clicked a button and a series of photos appeared. She heard the audience behind her shift in their seats. They all knew what the photo showed.

"That's right, gentlemen." Because they were all men, she thought to herself. As more than often in her career, she was the only woman in the room.

"This is a *Nimitz II* type Russian Navy nuclear submarine. Docked at a secret island of the Chinese Navy. We want to know why, obviously. Our passive radars have not picked anything up as yet, and we are sending out our UUV's to map the seabed with active sonar."

Kimberly indicated, and the lights came on in the room. She blinked in the sudden brightness. Around the long table, a cluster of faces looked back at her. Ten in total. Kim knew them all from previous operations. As a member of the National Clandestine Service (NCS) East Asia Division, it was her job to update the National Security Advisory team with any new developments.

An Admiral cleared his throat and asked Kim, "So, why do we think the Russian submarine is there, Miss Smith?"

Kim said, "This would not be the first time that the Russian Navy have held joint exercises with the Chinese. Just like we do with South Korea and Japan. But it would be the first time a ballistic missile capable Russian submarine has secretly arrived at a Chinese port."

Kim's boss, the neatly dressed Solomon Barney caught her eye. Solomon had his habitual three piece black suit on. The sharp suit reminded Kim of a Wall Street banker rather than a federal government employee. His mannerism however, was far from that of a banker. Solomon, director of the East Asia Division, and overall in charge below the Deputy Director (DD), was one of the humblest people she had met.

Solomon said, "So, you are saying the Russians wanted to hide that they had arrived. But why?"

"Sir, that might have something to do with the explosion on board the Chinese mega tanker, the *Lunar Smile*. No one knows who did it, and the Chinese aren't buying the story about engine trouble."

Solomon raised his eyebrows. "There's no way that we benefit from pulling stunts like that. Hell," he tapped the laptop in front of him, "my computer parts won't get made if we starve China of oil."

A light wave of joviality swept the room. Kim set her jaws. Her blonde hair was pulled back in a ponytail, and her light brown eyes narrowed slightly. Her strong cheekbones and chin accentuated the natural assertiveness of her posture.

"Regardless," she said "the Russian ship being there coincides with the opening of a 4,000-mile-long pipeline from Siberia, via Mongolia, coming in to Beijing. It's a big deal for China, and Russia too. Russia is bearing the bulk of the cost to get the pipeline built."

Solomon said, "And China has agreed to ten years forward oil prices. That means billions for Russia. I get that. But why the submarine?"

Kim said, "Sir, that brings us back to the incident on the *Lunar Smile*. I reckon China is trying to show us that they can borrow some Russian muscle if they need to."

"In other words," Solomon said, "this naval exercise shows how close the two countries are."

"Exactly."

Kim took some more questions from the audience. After a while, one by one, they left. Only Solomon and her were left. He walked over to her. Kim pretended not to notice. She gathered up her files, and put them inside her folder. She detached the flash drive from the laptop.

"Are you OK?" Solomon asked.

Kim looked at him. "Why would I not be?"

Solomon held her gaze and remained silent. "The Deputy DDO wants to speak to us."

CHAPTER 3

Kim raised her eyebrows. The Deputy Director of the Directorate of Operations was high up in the food chain of the National Clandestine Service. She gathered up her folder and was followed out the door by Solomon.

"Anything serious?" Kim asked.

"Not sure," Solomon said. "He's not giving much away."

They rode the elevator up to the fourth floor of the cavernous Langley building. The NCS was situated in the Old Headquarters (OHB) side of the George Bush Center of Intelligence, separate from the New Headquarter building (NHB).

The DD was waiting for them in his office. John Hymers was in his fifties, with short cut hair that had gone to white. He was of medium height, and sported a goatee beard on his face. He shook hands with both of them. They sat down at one end of the large gleaming desk, facing Hymers.

Hymers said, "We have a situation in Myanmar. Or Burma, as it used to be known."

Kim and Solomon waited. Hymers continued in a calm, unhurried voice. "As you know, we established an office at the US Embassy in Yangon 4 years ago, when Myanmar introduced democratic elections."

"One of the operations officers from the NCS office in Myanmar has gone missing. His name is David Harris. These are his details." Kim glanced at the file that Hymers gave to her. She noted that Solomon was not given a file.

"Last known whereabouts?" Kim asked.

"In the eastern Shan states near the border with China. Presumably, he had gone there to develop some HUMINT."

Gathering human assets, or HUMINT, was one of the key tasks of NCS agents

"Why was he there?" Kim looked up from the file.

Hymers said, "That's where it gets tricky. He did not leave any word of his whereabouts. Went on his own, too. Do we have many assets in the region?"

Kim thought for a few seconds. As a South East Asia specialist, and fluent in Mandarin and Urdu, she had lived in India and China for several years.

She had been a young journalist then, and her language skills had meant the CIA had been eager to recruit her when she returned home. But she had never been to Myanmar.

Kim said, "I need to look into it, sir. Myanmar butts into Yunnan province in the west of China. Pretty sure we have some assets there."

Hymers tapped his cheek, then leaned forward. His eyes bore into Kim's. "I want you to head down there. Can you handle that?"

Kim's nostrils flared, and she breathed deeply. Solomon stirred next to her. He said, "Is that necessary, John?"

Hymers looked at Solomon. "You have anyone else who can do it?" Solomon fell silent. Kim knew the NCS had several agents who could take her place. But none of them had her language skills, or experience.

Kim fought with herself. Her fingers were clutching the chair handles, and she lowered them into her lap. She kept her face impassive.

Don't show emotion. That's what he is looking for.

The suppressed visions rose up into her mind like a nightmare. Long, black shadows that remained hidden in the recesses of her mind. Kim swallowed.

"Yes, sir. Of course, I can."

Hymers looked at her closely for a few seconds, then nodded. "You will fly direct to Yangon, from Dulles. The Embassy there will have list of contacts who might have seen David. Your job will be to develop the assets, then provide intel to the Special Operations Group who will be sent down eventually."

"Copy that, sir," Kim said. Hymers nodded at both of them. Kim and Solomon left the room. Once they were outside, Kim turned on Solomon.

"You knew." Her tone was angry.

Solomon's voice was apologetic. "He approached me. Told me not to break the whole thing to you. I didn't know he was going to ask you to fly down there."

Solomon held her eyes. Kim breathed out. "If you are worried about me," she said, "Then don't waste your time. I can do this." She turned on her heels and walked away. Partly in anger, partly because she wanted to get away.

She got into her office and slammed the door shut, then locked it. She lowered the blinds.

Sarah's photo was on the table. It was an old one, from her early teens. Eleven or twelve years old. It was one of Kim's favorite photos, and she had it framed. Sarah had dark looks that contrasted with Kim's fairness. In the photo, her deep brown hair was long, her almost black eyes were smiling, and she had freckles on her face.

But they still looked like sisters.

Kim sat down heavily on her desk, and took the photo in her hand. The metallic frame was cold on her fingers.

Impotent guilt and grief surged inside her. It clutched her insides in an iron grip, squeezing the breath out of her chest remorselessly. Her head throbbed and her vision dimmed to black. Panting, she put the photo down on the desk. Sarah's eyes stared at her. Asking her why.

November 27, Mumbai, 2008. The Taj Palace Hotel. After almost a decade, the two sisters were meant to be on holiday together. Sarah had flown out after her graduation to join Kim, who was older by six years. Kim, having lived in Mumbai for a year by then, knew the city like the back of her hand. She was working for the NCS already, as a field officer. Mumbai's proximity to Karachi, Pakistan's biggest port, had a lot to do with her being in Mumbai. But when Sarah came down, she was overdue some down time.

The screams and sounds from that night came back to her like bolts of lightning. Kim sank back in her chair.

They had been in the bar area, dressed casually, when the first sound of gunfire filtered in. It had sounded like firecrackers. But Kim had known immediately. When the grenades exploded in the lobby, Kim had hooked an arm around Sarah and dropped to the floor, covering Sarah with her body. More explosions followed. The bar area was reasonably full with tourists on that warm, balmy night by the Arabian Sea.

When the gunman arrived at the door, Kim had hauled Sarah up, and they had run for the exit before anyone else.

Kim gripped her forehead.

What should she have done? Should she have laid still? Would the gunman have fired a burst and then left? Was it her fault that Sarah was...

The terrorist sprayed bullets around, and by a miracle, they missed Kim. But not her sister. Sarah, the better athlete, had sprinted for the exit. A hail of bullets had mowed her down. Then came the yellow flash of the grenade, the sound of smashing glass and furniture, and the world had gone dark in Kim's eyes.

She had been lucky to escape. She heard later how the gunman came in after the grenade explosion, and shot several more tourists as they pleaded for their lives.

Kim shook her head, took a deep breath and stood up. She was suffocating. She needed air. She opened the door and walked quickly across the hallway, keeping her head down. She took the stairs down, avoiding the elevators. Outside, she walked to one of the park benches and sat down. Sunlight warmed her face.

Guilt was rising up to her mind like a tidal wave again. There had been intelligence. An attack on Indian soil was forthcoming. Somewhere in a big city. No one knew where, and New Delhi, India's capital, had been on high alert.

But not a soft tourist spot like the Taj, arguably the most iconic hotel in India. And try as they might, the CIA had no jurisdiction anywhere else in the world. Getting the Indian authorities to coordinate a safety program would have been a gargantuan task, at the best of times. And one could not act on every shard of intelligence. The manpower to do that simply did not exist.

She knew all of this. But should *she* have acted? Should she have been more careful? Maybe inviting Sarah down had not been a good idea. Hindsight was a terrible thing.

She would do this for the rest of her life.

Kim looked up into the foliage of the oak tree above her, and the dapple of sunlight around it. Her breathing was calmer, but the heavy weight at the back of her throat would not budge. She sniffed, and felt the tears roll down her cheeks. She wiped them away slowly. She had counselling, and went through a bout of drinking whiskey every night for two weeks after she came back. The Agency had looked after her. She had almost a month off on bereavement leave.

She had never set foot in Asia again. She did not want to. But that was six years ago. Time had healed some wounds, but there was a corner of her soul, hidden even from herself, that would never heal.

And now, her country needed her. It was time again to pick herself up, harden her heart, and put her shoulder to the wheel. Kim walked back and climbed the steps up to the huge building. As she did so, Sarah's face flashed before her one last time.

I am sorry. Dear God, I am so sorry.

CHAPTER 4

Yangon
Yangon District, Myanmar
Present day

The heat in Yangon was stifling in April. Dan Roy used the handkerchief he had bought for a hundred kyat and wiped his forehead.

He looked around the restaurant. The doors and windows were wide open, now that it was late afternoon. Between 12 and 3pm, the entire city dozed in the heat. Windows were shut to keep the heat out, and opened when the sun relented.

The Blue Orchid restaurant was full. There was a smattering of tanned white faces, mixed with Burmese. The fans spun in the ceiling with rheumatic groans, but only the fresh breeze blowing in from outside relieved the heat. The aroma of frying spices and barbecued meat filled the air. Neon lights glowed in bars and restaurants outside. This was the SanHsein Township, in downtown Yangon, a main backpacker tourist drag. Rickshaws jostled with yellow taxi cabs on the crowded street, blowing their horns loudly.

A street market had formed outside, one of many in downtown Yangon. Sellers squatted with their vegetarian and meat produce on the sides of the road. From where he was sitting, Dan could see mounds of mangoes, papaya and stacked sugar cane for sale. Sugar cane juice, freshly pressed in a roadside stall, had become his favorite drink.

There was no Starbucks here. Dan liked that.

A flicker of movement to his right got his attention. The waitress had brought his food over. Her red, yellow and green bangles jingled as she put the plates on the table. She put down the bowl in front of Dan. It was a dish called Mohinga – rice noodles in a thick fish soup. A half boiled egg was next to the noodles and pieces of fish. It was topped with deep fried chick pea fritters, crumbled on top. The soup was slightly spiced and salty. A good bowl of Mohinga could last him many hours. In the evenings, a wide array of Burmese meat and fish curries awaited him.

These days, Dan' idea of culinary heaven.

Dan glanced at the waitress. "*Mingalaba*, Maya." The traditional Burmese greeting meant a combination of hello and blessings.

Maya' face split into a grin. She was ten years old. Her chestnut brown eyes danced with mirth, and her long black hair fell almost to her waist. Her skin was the color of pale coffee, and her smile was infectious. She had a small jasmine flower in her hair. She was a beautiful little girl.

Maya said, "*Mingalaba*, sir. How are you?"

Dan glanced at his watch. "Have you been to school today?"

Maya's smiled faltered. "School does not pay."

Dan spread the napkin on his lap. "Now, we have had this conversation already, haven't we?"

Maya poured some mineral water into a glass for Dan. "If I go to school, then I can get a good job?"

"Yes."

Maya said, "Sir, there are no jobs. My aunt says all the boys with degrees are looking for jobs."

Dan slurped some noodles inside his mouth. With a spoon, he broke into the yellow yolk of the egg.

He chewed his food, then said, "By the time you graduate, there will be. You can go anywhere for jobs, right?"

Maya's eyes were shining. "If I go to school, maybe I will become someone important like you?"

Dan smiled. "I am no one important."

"But you are American. Aunt says normal people in America are important. In our country, the politicians don't care about us."

Dan snorted. "Believe me, American politicians are the same."

"Really?"

"Yes, politicians are the same everywhere."

There was a shout from the kitchen area. Maya's face changed. "I have to go, sir. Restaurant is busy."

Dan said, "Don't forget your tip."

Maya smiled uncertainly and left. Dan watched her as she threaded her way around the tables, picking up orders. She wore a full sleeve red cotton shirt, with the thin baggy pants that came with it. Despite not going to school, she had picked up English, which meant she was smart. Dan ate at the Blue Orchid every evening, and over the last few weeks, had become good friends with Maya. He tipped her handsomely every night.

As he was finishing his meal, Maya came back. She collected his plates and came back with the bill. Dan left her a hundred-kyat tip. Maya put it in her pocket quickly. Maya lived with her aunt after her parents had died. Her aunt had no other family.

Maya looked at Dan curiously. "What do you do?"

"You asked me that question before."

"And you didn't answer."

"Because there's nothing to say. I don't do anything right now. I take it easy."

Maya made a face. "Ok, then, what did you do *before?*"

Visions flashed in the back of Dan's mind. The blood-soaked face of his dead targets. The chatter of machine gun fire. His breath warm on the barrel of a Heckler and Koch 416 rifle, eyes fixed on the cross hairs of the target scope.

As the highest value operator for Intercept, the most powerful Black Ops organization there was, he was entrusted with the most politically sensitive, time critical missions. He had never failed, till in Sanaa, the capital of Yemen, he was told to blow up a bus full of children.

He refused.

He quit, but Intercept found ways of entangling him in more operations. Finally, he had left. Thrown away his worldly possessions and gone incognito. He had taken a one way flight from Atlanta, USA, to London. He stayed one night in London, just enough time to board a flight to Mumbai, India. From there he had dropped further south to the golden beaches of Goa, and the warm waters of the Arabian Sea. After 3 months, he had decided to leave for Thailand and Myanmar. Calcutta, in the east of India, provided the ideal springboard for travel to the far east of Asia.

Yangon, the capital of Myanmar was fascinating. Teeming with pagoda temples, street markets and beautiful lakes, the place had also had streets full of sumptuous colonial buildings left by the British. But the nicest thing about the place was its friendly people, who made him feel welcome.

Dan said to Maya, "I used to be an instructor."

"What does that mean?"

"Means I told people what to do."

"Like a teacher?"

"You could say that. Promise me you will go to school tomorrow."

"You always ask me that," Maya said, pouting.

Dan was about to reply when he saw a white woman enter the restaurant from the main road entrance. Most female foreign tourists did not travel alone. The woman had blonde hair, falling loosely around her shoulders. She wore a white bush shirt that stuck to her back, and white crops that came down to her calves. She was not accompanied by a man.

She sat down to the right of Dan, three tables away. Their eyes met briefly. Mid-thirties, brownish eyes, skin tanned almost light brown from the sun. Toned arms and legs. Quite attractive. She looked away from Dan and picked up the menu. Most men would not have noticed the small bag that hung from her shoulder. But Dan was more observant. He noticed a black object poking out from the mouth of the bag. The woman zipped it up as she sat down.

Dan knew the butt of a gun when he saw one. The bulge in the small bag was also evident. The woman did not wear any make up. She wore slippers on her feet, the open toe sandals typical of south Asia. She had a cell phone in her hand, and was looking at the screen.

Maya was watching his face. "Do you know her?" she blurted.

Dan looked at her and suppressed a smile. "Why do you think I know her?"

"You keep looking at her…," Maya's voice faded off into shyness, and she looked down.

Dan pressed another hundred kyat note into her hand. Maya looked at him big eyes. "Thank you," she said.

Dan scraped his chair back and stood up. "I'll swing by tomorrow morning. You should be in school, not serving breakfast."

Maya looked unhappy. Without saying anything, she waved at Dan. Her bangles tinkled. Dan nodded, and walked outside.

CHAPTER 5

Dan stepped into the human melee of people, rickshaws and human beings, lit up by garish neon lights from the shop fronts. His dark, restless eyes swept in 180 degree arcs. The market area was busy. Shoppers jostled around him, rubbing shoulders, many looking up as the wide shouldered, tall foreigner walked past them. Dan's dark hair had grown long, and he had a four-day stubble on his cheeks.

A truck was parked to one side, and crates of fresh vegetable were being unloaded from it. Wooden stalls sold betel nuts wrapped with spices in green leaves, often with tobacco mixed in. Burmese men chewed on these all day, spitting out red juice from their mouths frequently. Dan had tried one, and the taste was not to his liking.

But he did like the Chinese green tea. A stall keeper, sat cross legged on his wooden seat, called out to him, holding a small glass. Dan nodded and passed the man some money. He took the glass and sat down on the rickety bench to sip his green tea. The river of humanity flowed around him endlessly.

He saw a shape that looked vaguely familiar. He turned his head and saw the blonde woman from the restaurant. Their eyes met again, and she looked away quickly. She clutched her purse bag tightly. Her steps were fast and she walked into the jumble of human bodies, fading from sight. On an impulse, Dan followed.

He was about forty meters behind the woman. She was easily visible with her blonde hair. She was walking towards the red brick Victorian Gothic building of Hogg Market, built in 1874. Named after a certain Sir Stuart Hogg. Dan had been inside. It was a fascinating rabbit warren of shops, giving way to a central square where farmers sold fresh produce. Chickens squawked inside cages, and carcasses of goats and lambs hung from hooks.

The crowd thinned as they left the street market. The woman stopped and looked around. Then she walked rapidly again, heading for the red brick Hogg Market entrance. The sky was darkening above. Dan quickened his pace. Inside the market there was every chance of losing the woman in the maze of alleys, and the habitual throng of humanity made worse by the narrowness of said alleys.

433

He picked her up as she entered and walked straight through. Then he noticed something else. A man slipped out of an alley, and started to follow her. Dan hung back. The man was short, with almost spiky black hair and Oriental features. Either Chinese, or Burmese. The man walked fast, keeping pace with the woman. She obviously had a destination in mind.

They left the jungle of shops and shoppers behind them. The sounds faded as they came into the square. It was darker now, apart from some yellow bulbs hanging from long wires. The square was almost deserted. The stalls were closed or being shut as farmers closed up for the day.

A second man joined the first one. He was slightly taller, but had similar oriental features. If the woman knew she was being followed, she gave no indication. She walked through the square, heading for the dark opening to the outside.

Dan's senses kicked into high alert. Every sight, sound and smell was acutely palpable to him suddenly. He balled his fists. He stopped for a second behind a chicken coop and watched as the two oriental men followed the woman through the door into the darkness outside.

Then he burst into a run. At the door way, he stopped. It was a big arched exit. Dan knew what lay on the other side. A few small alleys that led to the clothes shops. At this hour, they would be closed. The alleys would be dark.

A bulb glowed up ahead, and he picked up the two men, walking purposefully behind the woman. The alley ended up ahead, and the woman was close to the end. As Dan watched, a dark figure loomed there. It was joined by another one. The two figures blocked the end of the alley. The woman stopped. She looked behind and saw the two men. She was trapped. Her head swung from side to side.

Dan frowned. The woman did not seem frightened. She stood still, a hand inside her bag. The four men converged on her. She had not seen Dan. But the two men behind her had. One of them nudged his companion. They turned to look at Dan. Dan increased his pace. It didn't look good. The alley was narrow, brick walls covered by the same corrugated iron roof that swept over the whole market. There was no escape. The element of surprise was lost.

The men at the end of the alley had approached the woman. She was speaking to them, her hand still inside her bag. They turned and saw the two oriental men. Dan saw the men stiffen and point at them. One of the oriental men reached inside his pocket. Dan saw the glint of metal in the bulb light.

He exploded into action. In five long steps, his six feet two hundred and twenty pound frame crossed the gap. One of the oriental men had pulled his gun out, pointing it at the woman. The other one was crouching, facing Dan, reaching into his back pocket. He didn't get a chance to get his weapon out. Dan bent his knees and propelled himself into the air for the last two feet. He smashed into them, his arms hooking around their midriffs, bringing both men down in a football tackle.

But he was too late to stop the first bullet. The suppressed round was fired just as Dan crashed into them, heading for the woman. Dan grabbed the collar of the man who had fired, and banged his face into the cement ground. The nose exploded with a squelching sound. The man screamed and tried to claw upwards with his hand, but Dan repeated the process. The body went still. His partner swung a fist into Dan's face. It was a good hit. It caught Dan below his right jaw, making him grunt. But Dan had thick bones, and large hands to go with it. The blow sent a frisson of sharp pain radiating into his head, but his right arm came up in the same instant. He backslapped the man on the face, sending him reeling towards the wall. The man came off the wall just as Dan got to his feet.

One on one. Against Dan Roy. Most men did not stand a chance, and this one was no different.

He shouted an oath, and tried a karate move. He crouched and spun, kicking high in the air. Dan dropped to his feet and rolled under the kick. He shot up, and smashed his right elbow against the man's face. The face snapped back with a tearing sound. The body slumped to the floor, useless.

Dan crouched, and looked for the woman. She was standing with her gun drawn. A body lay prostrate at her feet. The other man had vanished. The woman lifted the gun and pointed it straight at Dan.

"Who are you?" She asked in English. American.

Dan lifted his arms up. "Name is Dan Roy. Here on holiday. Saw you were in a tight spot and came to help."

The woman did not lower her weapon. She said, "Drop any weapon you have. Come forward where I can see you."

"I don't have a weapon." Dan walked forward with his hands raised.

CHAPTER 6

"Stop!", the woman said. Dan was five feet away. He came to a standstill.

Her blonde hair was plastered across her sweaty forehead. Her chest was heaving up and down. But the gun did not waver in her hand. Dan recognized the weapon as being a Taser.

"Can I put my hands down?" Dan asked.

"No. Why were you following me?"

A good question. Dan could lie, but he decided to opt for the truth.

"I don't know. There was something about you. You carried a weapon, and most tourists in this part of the world don't do that. Most women don't travel alone either. Then I saw these two following you. You know the rest."

The woman did not lower her weapon. She seemed to be considering his answer.

Dan said, "If I lower my hands, you're not gonna shoot me, are you?"

The woman didn't answer. Watching her carefully, Dan slowly lowered his arms. After a beat, the woman lowered her weapon too.

Dan said, "These guys will come to, soon. We need to head out of here."

"You know this place?"

"A little, yes. It's Pyaw Street outside these alleys. We could walk down and head for the Myint Park."

"The Press Club is near the Myint Park."

"I think so, yes," Dan said. "But seeing as its getting dark, best to get a taxi there."

The woman put her gun inside her bag. She came forward.

"My name is Kim. Short for Kimberly. Smith is the last name."

"Hi Kim."

Dan shook her hand. Then he bent down, and turned over the two men at his feet. In the yellow haze of the bulb, they appeared Chinese. It could be confusing, as some Northern Burmese could look Chinese. He frisked their pockets and found nothing. He checked their weapons. Browning semi-automatics. He put both weapons in his pocket.

He turned to the other man, only to find Kim was frisking him already. The man had been tasered. He looked oriental as well, but different from the other two.

Kim said, "No ID."

Dan stood up. "Let's get out of here."

They walked out to the end of the alley and peered outside. It was a quiet back road. Cars and rickshaws were parked outside dark shop fronts. Dan watched an old man cross the road, body bent almost in double. The man did not straighten, and walked slowly. Dan kept an eye on the figure. After another crossing, they came to the bright lights and traffic of Pyaw Street.

No one waited for traffic lights in Yongan. They waited for a lull in the traffic, then crossed the wide avenue quickly. The unlit park loomed ahead of them. To the right, the bell shaped tower of the Shwedagon Pagoda rose 99 metres into the sky. Made entirely in gold, with 5,448 diamonds encrusting the tip, the Pagoda was a stunning sight, its golden halo shimmering in the air.

Dan asked, "How long have you been here?"

"Two days. How about you?"

"More than 4 weeks now. Looking for a flight to take me to Bangkok. There's plenty, but this place is chilled out. Kind of like it here."

"Are you on vacation?"

"Yes."

Dan looked away, searching for a cab. He hoped that would end the discussion. It didn't.

Kim asked, "Where did you learn to fight like that?"

Dan shrugged. "College football."

Kim said, "Didn't know footballers took down men with guns. Your college must have been special."

Dan didn't answer. In the yellowish penumbra of streetlight, he couldn't see Kim's face well, but he heard the heavy sarcasm in her voice.

Dan said, "Why do you wanna go to the Press Club?"

"I'm a journalist."

"I see."

"You don't believe me." It was a statement, not a question.

Dan said, "I want to drop you off there. Unless you would rather go somewhere else."

"You don't have to baby sit me. But the Press Club is fine."

Dan nodded. Kim was being smart. He was a stranger, and not showing him which hotel she was at was a wise move.

Finally, a yellow Nissan screeched to a stop in front of them. He sat down on the old leather seat as Kim told the driver where to go.

In ten minutes, they had arrived at the parking lot of the Press Club. There was security at the gates, and the building itself was an old Golf club, again left by the British. The Club had its own golf course and swimming pool. The rifle bearing guard struck a salute and opened the door as Kim presented her credentials. The lobby was small, but the main attraction was the outside balcony and bar. A few people mingled with drinks.

Dan said, "This is where I say goodbye."

Kim hesitated. "Would you let me buy you a drink? Just to say thank you."

"OK." He could use a beer. A waiter came around and they ordered. Western beers were available, but Dan had developed a taste for Kalyani Black Label, which despite sounding like a fake whiskey, passed for a surprisingly nice hoppy beer. When the drinks arrived, Kim sipped on her rum and coke and eyed Dan.

"So, where are you staying?" she asked.

"Kenley Lodge. A backpacker hotel near SanHsein Township, north of Downtown."

"I see."

Dan said, "Those men will come back for you. The two Chinese who followed you."

"You think so?"

"I don't know who you were meeting. But the Chinese think you know something."

Dan left his statement hanging in the air. Kim didn't owe him an explanation. And really, what business was it of his? He needed to board that flight, and get the hell out of this place.

Kim was looking around her. The cool, dark expanse of the golf course lay in front of them. A ring of lights stuck on wooden posts went around the perimeter before they vanished from sight. The guests were a mixture of foreign journalists, and some Burmese. One Burmese man in a blue suit was explaining something to a group of men at a table. The heat was less in the evening, but the humidity still remained. Dan wiped a trickle of sweat going down the back of his head.

Kim leaned forward. "The men I met had news about the conflicts going on in the east of the country."

Dan said, "That's near the Chinese Yunnan province. You will find most of the areas are called the Black Zones – no foreigners are allowed there."

"Correct."

Dan took a long swig of his beer. "So how did they reach out to you?"

Kim smiled. "Reporters have sources, right? They knew someone who knows me. Another journalist based in Myanmar, actually."

"Which newspaper do you work for?"

"It's a news agency. Press Trust of America. PTA. I'm their south Asia correspondent."

"Uh-huh. You speak any of the languages?"

"Fluent in Mandarin and Urdu. I used to live in New Delhi for about five years." Kim's voice faltered. She looked away into the darkness of the night sky. If Dan noticed anything, he did not show it.

After a pause, Dan said, "Interesting. So, if you were meeting a Burmese man, why were the Chinese there?"

Kim frowned. "That's the bit I need to figure out."

"Pardon me for saying so, but there's a lot you need to figure out. These men were not kidding around. They came to kill your informer. And you as well."

"I should tell the cops."

"Yes, you should. And your employer too." Dan drained his glass and stood up. "Thanks for the drink. I'll be heading back."

CHAPTER 6

Henry Deng crunched grass as he walked in the forest clearing. All around him tall deciduous trees formed a virtually impenetrable barrier to any casual observer. The clearing was huge, spread over two square miles. A number of huts dotted the clearing. Smoke came out from their chimneys. Several had long steel pipes emerging from the thatched rooves, blowing out the excess of hydrochloric acid.

"Henry!" Someone called his name. In the silence of the forest, sound travelled far, so they spoke softly. This voice was not loud. Henry turned instantly. His face broke into a grin.

"Li Yonping," Henry said. They shook hands.

Henry said, "How are you doing, cousin Li?"

Both Henry and Li lived in the Wu state, close to Myanmar's border with China. Although born in Burma, they were the Wa people, who were ethnic Han, the same ethnic group that formed the majority of China's population. They considered themselves Han first, and Burmese second. Both, like most people of their state, were fluent in Burmese and Mandarin.

Li Yonping said, "A nice day, isn't it?"

Henry looked up at the sky. It was April, and it was hot, and the monsoon was still far away. The sky was a spotless blue. In the distance, he heard the call of a barking deer, a long, rasping sound. The jungle pressed all around them, teeming with wildlife.

A man with an Ak-74 slung across his back walked past them. He lowered his head in respect as he went past Deng. Deng nodded briefly.

Deng said, "It will be a nice day if you got what you needed."

Li said, "Oh yes, I did."

"Well, let's see it then."

Together they walked to a hut near the perimeter of the compound. It was raised on stilts, like most of the huts. That protected against the wet soil in the long monsoon season, which caused landslides, and brought the long snakes and other animals into the compound.

They climbed up the stairs, where two armed guards stood on each side with QBZ-95 assault rifles in their hand. The bullpup style assault rifles were ubiquitous in the People's Liberation Army, as China's standing Army was known. The PLA provided arms to the United Wa State Army, or UWSA, to which both Henry and Li belonged.

They entered the room, where another armed guard stood near the window, keeping watch outside. His lips were red from chewing betel nut leaf, and he was slouching, with his hand on the window sill. He stood up hurriedly and bowed as Deng and Li entered.

Deng said, "Outside."

"Yes, *Zhu* Deng." The guard left the room, shutting the thick bamboo door behind him.

Li went forward and opened the trunk. Sun reflected off the shiny surface, lighting up the long, deep scar that ran from Li's left eye to the corner of his left lip.

Deng glanced briefly at the stacks of US hundred dollar bills. "Have you checked the serial numbers?"

"We checked every bundle at Kunming. They are all legit."

As much as they relied on China for weapons and finance, Deng knew the Triads were not above stealing from them. They had been sneaky in the past. When Deng had met with the Triads, he had threatened with stopping supply. That, apart from bullets, was the only threat the Triads would listen to.

Li said, "There is one problem however, cousin."

"What is that?"

"General Sein Tho."

Deng frowned. "He is on board."

"Maybe. But he has stopped one of our trucks near the Pyutaw river bridge."

The Pyutaw river was one of many that formed shallow channels between Myanmar and China. None of them were guarded, with wild jungles on either side. Ideal ground for the small-time smugglers, but not enough for Henry Deng. They needed big trucks, and for that they needed a bridge across the river.

Deng said, "Is the truck loaded?"

"Yes."

"What does he want?"

"What does everyone want?"

Deng thought for a while. Without the General's help, it would be difficult to control the bridge.

Li said, "They know about this new place," he indicated his hand at the compound outside. It was the latest of several methamphetamines producing hubs that Deng possessed. "And that's not all. He also had something to say about the railway line."

Deng's head shot up. His tone became sharper. "What do you mean?"

"The contract for the railway is in trouble."

Deng swore. "Does the *Baw* we caught have anything to do with this?"

"The *Baw* works for the CIA, I'm sure of it. But we have no proof. In any case, I don't know. All the General said is there is trouble in Parliament over it."

Deng frowned. "It's time we went to Naypyidaw." Naypyidaw was the new capital of Myanmar, where the Government offices were situated.

"What are we doing with the *Baw*?"

Deng shrugged. "It's not like anyone has come to claim him, have they? Which means he is working undercover. Yes, that does worry me."

Deng opened the door. Li locked it and they went down the stairs. A fresh breeze moved in over the trees, warm and dry. Deng looked to the east where the jungle hills sloped down to the meandering yellow river, whose waters flowed thick and sluggish.

Li said, "We cannot hold the *Baw* forever. You know what they are like. Sooner or later, they will send a team of their own, or the *Tatmadaw*.

Deng breathed the jungle smell deeply. He squared his shoulders. "Then we can go and see the *Tatmadaw* first," he said.

*****

Naypyidaw, the new capital of Myanmar, is north of Yangon, the traditional capital of the country. As Deng looked at the five lanes of empty highway that his Zil limousine was driving through, the familiar feeling of incredulity emerged. The highway opposite, also of five lanes, ten lanes in total, was empty apart from his vehicle. It was surreal, like driving through a post-apocalyptic city.

The airport where he had landed half an hour ago, did not have any queues anywhere. Glistening shops of duty free merchandise, Rolex watches, even a Ferrari dealership lined the Arrivals lounge as he walked through it. He was not alone. All of four men came off the plane with him.

Five of them walked through the gigantic airport, their footsteps echoing along the hallway. Only two passenger planes arrived daily. Both domestic planes, and in Deng's experience, they only held a handful of passengers. This time had been no different.

Yangon remained the main port of entry for foreigners coming to Myanmar. In Naypyidaw, the only planes Deng saw were military.

He saw the huge detached buildings as they approached the downtown center. Most of them were empty too, he knew. The only busy building in the whole of this bizarre town was the huge sprawl of the Parliament building. Both the military and civilian governments had their offices here. Deng came rarely, when he had a problem with one of his business contracts. It seemed the place was only for the few thousand government officials who worked in the office where he was headed.

Two of the street cleaners looked up as Deng's stretch limo zipped past them. They wore triangular bamboo hats and the loose kaftans typical of the village people around Naypyidaw. Deng grunted. At least he saw two human beings. This place gave him the creeps. Why bother employing street cleaners when there was zero traffic and pedestrians?

Still, they wanted to waste the money Deng gave them doing this shit - then it was up to them.

As long as they did not stop Deng doing what he wanted to do.

The Parliament building was off limits to everyone. The place was surrounded by a moat. Deng's car was checked over with sniffer dogs, then Deng had to step out and be searched himself.

Then they were allowed through. The Lower Parliament rose above them like a vast Tibetan palace, with white and green curled cornices, and statues of giant, golden Buddhist lions at every corner. The entire structure was built of white marble, and the gold was mined from Myanmar's northern Shan state, where the riverbeds glistened with the yellow metal.

They drove past the Lower Parliament into a squat, wide building that seemed to go on for miles. They went inside the first entrance, and after more checks, down a tunnel. These tunnels, Deng knew, were built with the help of the North Koreans. Built to help the military conduct their affairs in underground bunkers, in case a pro-democracy revolution happened, and American ships made port in Yangon, right next to the Indian Ocean.

The limousine went straight down, and into an underground road that seemed a lot like a smaller version of the highway above. Only two lanes this time, lit by bright LED lamps. It was weird, like having a city underneath a city.

At least this time he saw more cars - military jeeps zipping up and down the opposite lane. It was a privilege to be down here, he knew that. Only the hardcore supporters of the military were allowed, and recently, some of the democratically elected government ministers. A privilege that Deng could not care less about.

Deng finally arrived at his destination. A subterranean office block. Deng waited while his driver opened the trunk, and took out the two heavy suitcases. He pulled them on their wheels with both hands. Flanked by armed guards, they went down a further flight of stairs into a spacious, well-lit lobby. A receptionist rose up from behind her desk, bowed at Deng, who bowed back slightly. They stood waiting while the reception knocked on the door. She went inside, then came out and held the door open for them.

CHAPTER 7

Khyan Hsein, the Minister of Interior, rose up as Deng entered. Her hair was turning silvery, but her bearing was erect, almost regal. She eyed Deng with distaste, like Deng had somehow brought a bad smell to the room. Deng stopped and bowed deeply. His driver left the two suitcase by the door and exited.

"Henry Deng," Khyan Hsein said. "Or should I say Hisaw Tun Khaing?"

Deng kept the smile on his face. He hated his Burmese name. "Deng is easier, *Daw* Hsein." *Daw* was a respectful prefix for an elder lady.

Hsein driver sat down and asked him briskly, "What do you want?"

Deng sat down. "The railway line from Sittwe to Pongkham, and then to Kunming, in China."

"What about it?"

"It has come to my attention that there might be a problem with it."

Hsein leaned back and let a satisfied smile come to her face. "Ah, I see. Worried about your merchandise not flowing across the border into China, are you?"

"*Daw* Hsein, I am but a simple trader. But as you know, Beijing's Ministry of State is willing to provide both finance and manpower for the project."

Hsein said, "Do you suggest we give all our infrastructure projects to China, *Ko* Deng? Is Myanmar's destiny to become a state of China in all but name?"

"Of course not, *Daw* Hsein," Deng said in a soothing voice. "All I want is for commerce to flourish in this country. If we can import our minerals across the border, there is a huge market waiting for us."

The elderly lady smiled unexpectedly. "You mean a huge market for your illicit drugs, *Ko* Deng?"

"I don't know what you mean, *Daw*. We mine jade and amethyst in our hills. You know how much the Chinese love their jade."

Hsein's voice became sharper. "You don't fool me, Mr. Deng. I know about your jungle laboratories. Every year they are churning out millions of methamphetamine pills. Your gang of pharmacists steal ephedrine from our hospitals, depriving our people of medications. Then they use it to make these pills. In fact, your business is now so big that Myanmar has become the methamphetamine capital of Asia."

Deng lowered his head. "*Daw* Hsein. These are only rumors, perpetrated by enemies who are envious of my success. Ask your Ministers and Generals."

Hseins nostrils flared in anger. Her voice rose a notch. "They are all in it with you. You don't think I know? How the hell do your trucks go across the border into Thailand without being checked?"

"*Daw*, please…"

Hsein stood up. "Our meeting is at an end, Mr. Deng."

Deng stood up and bowed. Then he hurried to one of the suitcases by the door. He wheeled one over to the desk. He kneeled on the floor and opened it up. The 25Kg suitcase was stacked inside with hundred dollar bills.

"*Daw*, there are 2.5 million US dollars in here. And same again in the other suitcase." Deng stood up and bowed again. "All I ask is that you advise the Lower House to pass this bill. This train line will be extremely useful for both Burma and China."

Hsein walked around her desk. Her black eyes glittered with hate. "You bastard," she whispered. "You think I am one of your sycophants who will roll over at the sight of money? I know you corrupt all our officials with cash. But your bribe will not work with me!"

Deng went to say something but Hsein raised her finger. "Listen to me. Do you know the American DEA is interested in you? That they want to know where all the party pills in Tokyo are coming from?"

Deng stayed calm. "Are you threatening me, *Daw* Hsein?"

"Get out, now!" Hsein rang a bell on her table.

Deng locked the suitcase up. He bowed deeply again. "Goodbye, *Daw* Hsein," he said.

*****

Khyan Hsein finished her day's work and stretched. Myanmar's problems were many, but a lack of suitors was not one of them. The fertile soil of the country was blessed with gold, tin, tungsten, jade and other precious minerals. The seas in its eastern and southern coast had oil. This abundance of natural resources was the main reason the world's two superpowers were interested in her country.

Of the two, Hsein was more wary of her giant eastern neighbor. The People's Republic of China. Even the Generals were afraid. Her personal choice would be an alliance with the West. As democracy arrived in

Myanmar, the opening of the US Embassy in Yangon had been a useful stepping stone in that direction. But Hsein knew the path was littered with minefields. The Generals of the *Tatmadaw* would have to be appeased first, and she did not foresee that happening easily.

Hsein told her secretary to call the driver. The Range Rover arrived, and she got into it, carrying a folder of the day's work with her. Hsein lived in the Ministerial circle of Naypyidaw, where a number of her colleagues also resided.

The route to the exclusive estate in the hills climbed over lush green hills that contained tea farms. Hsein liked to draw the window down, and feel the fresh breeze on her face, with the scent of the tea leaves infusing the air. Rolling green hills melted into grey and blue clouds of the horizon far away. Hsein watched the scenery, and thought about her visitor that afternoon.

Anger flared in her. Because of idiots like him, pretending to be fighting for a cause, this country had so many problems. If only...she sighed. "If Only's" ran high on her wish list for her nation.

Hsein heard a droning sound getting louder. Her driver glanced in the rear view as well. It was a motorbike, coming up the mountain path. Had to be a powerful one to be travelling fast up the hill. The Range Rover slowed.

Hsein asked the driver, "What are you doing?"

"Letting this guy pass."

Hsein relaxed. It would be nice without that annoying droning sound. She looked outside again. The hills became more numerous the higher up they went. She felt the car slowing again. This time, before she could speak to the driver, the car was pulled over on the verge. Scarcely ten feet away the hillside rolled away to the bottom - a fall of several hundred feet, to the jagged rocks of a river bed. The river was so far below it was invisible.

Hsein snapped, "What are you doing?"

The droning was louder behind her, but she paid it no attention. If the driver needed to take a leak, he could have just asked her.

She watched open mouthed as the driver opened the door and run straight up the hill road, leaving the car door open. Hsein scrambled to open her door.

She did not get the chance. A motorbike pulled over, and two men dressed entirely in black leather and black helmets, jumped off it. One of them slammed the door shut, and the other pressed a keypad. The car doors locked shut with a snap.

Hsein broke out in a sweat. She hammered on the black tinted windows. "Let me out!" she screamed.

The man with the digital key pad leaned closer to the window. His helmet reflected a distorted, wide angle view of the car. The man lifted one hand and waved her goodbye. Hsein felt the car lurch behind her.

"No!" she screamed. The man who waved at her now ran back and joined his friend. Together they pushed the car forward. The hood of the Range Rover tipped over, and Hsein slammed forward between the seats, hitting her head against the driver's seat.

The car pushed forward further. Hsein's stomach lurched in her mouth as she saw the teeth of jagged rocks far, far below, and the tall trees rising up like giant arrows. Words were frozen in her mouth.

She screamed, but the sound was lost as the car finally lost to gravity, and hurtled down in space to its dusty grave.

One of the men leaned at the edge of the cliff. He took his helmet off. The scar running from his left eye to the left lip twisted as he smiled. There was a muffled explosion as the car ignited into a fireball, several hundred feet below.

CHAPTER 8

Kim got off the yellow Nissan taxi that seemed to be ubiquitous in Yangon, and paid the driver. A fresh breeze, smelling of rain, ruffled the long fronds on the palm trees on either side of the road. Kim felt the wind on her face. It was soothing in the humid heat. Downtown Yangon was not far from the warm, emerald waters of the Indian Ocean, and Myanmar was full of unspoilt, white sand beaches. Someday, she would explore. For now, she had work to do.

Black and metal office buildings stood on either side. Kim was headed for the first building on her left. The US Embassy of Myanmar. The US Military Police stopped her at the gates, although they recognized her. They checked her creds, then nodded and waved her through.

The US Embassy was in a grand old red brick colonial building left behind by the British. A twelve feet high fence circled the perimeter, topped with barbed wire. The pretty building had green vine growing on it. It had white gables and cornices, and the railings of the numerous balconies were also painted white, standing out against the red bricks.

Kim walked into the air-conditioned lobby, and went up to the second floor. She pressed her ID against the digital pad on the doorway for three seconds. Her biometric details were processed by a mainframe computer more than three thousand miles away at a USAF military base in Okinawa, Japan. Then the pad beeped and the door fell open.

Kim walked into an office with series of monitors showing maps, figures and faces. Three rows of analysts sat hunched over their screens, some of them punching their keyboards.

Mary and Estefan, the two analysts who had been assigned to her, walked over to her desk as she sat down.

Estefan said, "We found nothing in David Harris' apartment. Went through it with a fine toothcomb. In fact, it seemed as though he was hardly there." Mary and Estefan had both been in Myanmar for longer than Kim. Estefan in particular, had been in the CIA branch of the Embassy as an analyst for the last two years.

Estefan asked, "You sure this guy worked for the NCS?"

Kim frowned. "Yes, you have seen his file, right? His whole record is there."

Estefan waved his hand. "Yes, seen all that. I'm just saying, this guy hardly ever came to office. No one seems to remember him well."

Mary said, "Well, he was a field operative. His job was to develop assets. But yeah, he must have had a base here, right?"

The three of them looked at each other. It was a problem Kim had faced right from the start. No one seemed to have much of an idea about David Harris. He kept to himself. That could have been his brief. National Clandestine Service agents after all, were expected to work under cover.

Kim asked, "Any news from the Rohingya contacts?"

The two men she had met last night, before she was interrupted, had been informers from the Rohingya community in the province of Arakan. Estefan had tracked them down through one of his assets in the Arakan State Army. Myanmar's identity was a fractured one. Although the central Buddhist majority ruled the country, the states in the west, east and north all vied for independence.

Estefan said, "I thought you met them last night. What happened?"

Kim turned to him. She could not keep out the harshness in her voice. "It was a trap, Estefan. I was compromised right from the start." Kim told them the story.

Estefan held his head in his hands. "Jesus. I'm so sorry."

Kim looked at him hard. In the shadowy world in which they operated, trust was never a given commodity. Estefan had been here the longest, which also made him vulnerable to overtures from the Chinese. Myanmar's porous eastern border with China meant agents of the Ministry of State Security (MSS), the Chinese Secret Service, were always present in Myanmar.

Mary said, "I managed to hack into his emails however."

Kim asked, "You did?"

"Yes. I found a bunch of emails that were encrypted with a key that no one knows about."

"Tried the NSA? They must have a cryptographer who can do it."

"I tried. No dice. But they did decipher the subject line, which was a different code. If the servers don't recognize the subject line, then they can delete the emails."

"What was it?"

"The Tonkin Protocol."

All three of them looked at each other. Estefan said, "The what?"

Mary shrugged. "That's what it said. It was on more than one email so it can't be a fluke."

Mary continued. "I did a search for it. Found nothing on our databases."

Kim said, "I need to ask Solomon. Thanks Mary."

They rose, but Estefan lingered. Kim looked at him. "Yes?"

Estefan said, "I have other assets. This time, we go for extreme vetting. If you want, I can go myself."

Kim said nothing for a while, then nodded. "Do the vetting. See what turns up."

Kim glanced at her emails and replied to some of them. Mary had arranged for her to see one of the politicians of the ruling party tomorrow. The man did not know her real identity, and Kim would have to be careful of how she approached him. It was rumoured that the politician was close to the United Wa State Army, the Army of the Wa state on Myanmar's eastern border with China. Kim finished going through her emails, then called Solomon Barney in Langley. She waited for the beep that signified that the line was encrypted.

Solomon asked, "Any news?"

Kim told him. "Have you heard of the Tonkin Protocol?"

"The what?"

Kim repeated herself.

Solomon said, "Doesn't ring any bells. Where did you get this from?" Kim told him.

Kim knew Solomon. When he was thinking something over he had a habit of smacking his lips together and whistling through his teeth. He said, "What the hell was this kid mixed up in?"

"That's the other thing. No one here seems to know much about him."

"He's one of ours, don't forget that."

Kim sighed. Internal rivalries *did* exist in the CIA. The Directorate of Operations, or DO, under whom the NCS worked, thought themselves as the Secret Service of the CIA. Kim thought it was all bullshit.

She said, "If he's one of ours, how come no one knows about him?"

"I don't know," Solomon said. "But it's time to dig deeper. You know what it's like."

Kim did. Every search on the Agency database put up a flag. Trying to access old classified documents meant jumping through numerous hoops. And someone could always trace those flags, thereby knowing who had tried to access the files.

"Do your best," Kim said.

There was a pause. Solomon's voice was gentle. "You don't have to prove anything. If it gets hot, I'm taking you out."

Kim said, "You can't take me out. The Director's controlling this."

Solomon said, "And he is my first port of call. Don't take any risks you don't have to. Let me see what I can get here."

Kim hung up. She chewed her nails for a while.

Her thoughts returned again to the handsome stranger who had saved her. There was something about him. He was ex-military obviously. One hell of a fighter. A man who was retired, way early. That intrigued her. And his hard, dark looks. The longish brown hair, the strong cheekbones, and those dark, intense eyes that seemed to look right into her. She had tried her best to be casual about sneaking looks at him, but each time, she had failed. He had caught her.

He had also told her where he was staying.

Kim woke up early next morning. She was staying at an enclosed block of apartments in the diplomatic enclave. Mary lived in the block, in the floor below her. From her apartment window, Kim could see the blue waters of the Inya Lake with the palace on its banks. To her extreme left, she could just make out the gold minaret of the huge Shwedagon Pagoda complex. More than two thousand five hundred years old, and made of solid gold, the Pagoda attracted thousands of monks in the Buddhist season. The inner sanctum was reputed to have strands of Buddha's hair. Kim couldn't wait to see it.

She thought about Dan Roy again. Why did he follow her? He had told her, but could she believe him?

Actions spoke louder than words. He had been there when things got rough. She probably could have handled it herself, but Dan being there had definitely made it easier. She felt safe around him last night. None of her dangers radars had sounded anything.

And, he could be useful. Kim had worked with many special forces men in her career, and Dan was better than all of them. But, she reminded herself, she still did not know who he was. She needed to find out more about why he was here. Her gut told her he was speaking the truth. Maybe she needed to check him out more, and find out if he was being honest with her.

CHAPTER 9

Dan opened his eyes as the sounds of morning reached his eyes. His hands automatically reached for under his pillow where he had put one of the Browning hand guns. The wooden shutters of the window was shut, but shafts of bright sunlight forced their way in. The traffic noises were starting, and as the day wore on, would rise to a cacophony.

Dan's room was simple. A bed, table and a wardrobe. On the table he had a laptop. The walls had old paint. The floor was made of flat wooden planks. A fan hung from the ceiling. Dan went to the bathroom and got dressed. By the time he came down to street level, the rickshaw squawks were competing with the bleating horns of the buses. The sun was stronger.

Dan walked over to the Blue Orchid restaurant. Kim was standing outside. She was wearing a straw hat that hid her blonde hair. She tipped her face up when she saw Dan.

"Thought I might find you here," she said with a smile.

Dan said, "You thought right." He thought she looked very pretty in her hat. "Shall we go inside?"

The restaurant was not too busy at this time of the morning. They found a seat close to the counter. Dan kept looking for Maya, and getting happier by the minute that he couldn't see her. He hoped she was in school. Then he sighed in exasperation.

Maya sailed out the kitchen carrying a tray that was clearly too big for her. Her large expressive eyes were a mask of concentration as she walked out to the table. The tray was loaded with plates and cups, and the table she was walking to had five men sitting on it.

Maya got Dan's eye, then averted her gaze. The tray wobbled in her hands. She took a few more steps. One of the plates, heaped high with eggs and bread, slid to the corner of the tray. Maya tried to correct it, but gravity won. The plate slid out, and landed on the floor with a crash. The tray tilted, and a tea cup followed the plate, landing with another crash. The owner came out, cursing.

"You stupid girl," he shouted at Maya. Maya was on the floor, cleaning up the mess. The man strode out and grabbed Maya by the ear. He pulled her to standing.

"No pay for you today," he shouted, and then lifted up an arm to slap her. The arm never came down. Dan was between them in a flash, grabbing the man's arm in mid-air. Dan pulled the man's arm, and he stumbled backwards. He tripped over Dan's feet and fell. Cursing loudly, the man stood up. His black eyes were fired up. Sweat poured down his head.

"You fucking *firang!*" he shouted. "I'll teach you a lesson you won't forget."

Dan said mildly, "It's you who needs a lesson. You shouldn't be employing under aged children. And you definitely shouldn't be hitting them."

Out of the corner of his eye Dan saw the five men at the table stand up. One glance was enough to assure him these men were not ordinary locals. They were thick, heavy set Burmese with wide shoulders. The look in their eyes was cold, and it was directed at Dan. The tallest of them, about the same height as Dan, approached them. The owner stuck his hand out and said something quickly. The leader stopped and looked at Dan, then walked back. The men left the table. They stood outside, as if waiting for Dan.

The owner turned to Dan. He had a nasty sneer on his face. "You are done here, whoever you are. Get out!"

Dan ignored him. He looked at his table. Kim was watching apprehensively, clutching her straw hat. Dan noticed she had her bag in her hand. He couldn't see Maya anywhere. He did a 360 degree. She was gone.

The owner said, "And that bitch isn't coming back here either. Plenty more where she came from."

Dan turned on the man, rage suddenly boiling in him. He opened his mouth to say something, but felt a soft touch on his arm. It was Kim.

"Let's get out of here, Dan," she whispered. Kim kept her hand on Dan's and pulled him out on the street. A couple of curious onlookers had gathered, drawn by the shouting. The five men had gone. Dan was looking for Maya still. They walked further down the road. Dan stood, arms on his hips. He saw two other working girls, and a boy carrying a basket of vegetables on his head. But he could not see Maya.

"Mister!"

Dan turned at the voice. It came from a stall to their left. A wizened old man, naked from the waist up, wearing a *lyongi*, or sarong, was waving at him. Dan and Kim approached.

The old man bared his yellow teeth. "You looking for the little girl who works in the restaurant?"

Dan said, "Yes."

The man pointed down the road to the left. "She went that way." He looked at Dan speculatively. "I know where she lives."

Dan took out a hundred kyat note and handed it to the man. "Where?"

The old man reached out a skinny arm with flesh hanging loosely off it. "Behind Hogg Market. There's a place called Sula's Bazar. She lived there with her aunt last year. Should be there still." The man gave Dan directions.

Dan turned to Kim. "You don't have to come with me. I feel sorry for that girl. I cost her the job."

Kim said, "I have to see a politician later on but I got an hour to kill. I'll come with you."

They walked around Hogg Market till the sounds of traffic became less. A mass of shanty huts loomed ahead of them. There was a dusty clearing with some boys kicking a football around. The brick walls of two houses on either side, with white chalk drawings on them served as goalposts. They stopped when they saw Dan and Kim.

One of the boys, aged around eight, came up to them, his eyes big with curiosity. Tourists stuck to the tourist trail, it was rare to see them around here. The boy's friends stopped playing, and gathered around them. Dan sat down on one knee.

"You speak English?" he asked the boy. He nodded.

"A girl called Maya lives here with her aunt. Do you know where?"

"Over there," the boy pointed.

Kim smiled at him. "Can you be more specific?" she asked. The boy looked at Kim, perplexed.

Dan said, "Straight ahead, left, or right?" Realization dawned in the boy's eyes.

"Straight down, then take the third, no fourth, left. There is a...a..."

One of his friends shouted, "Pond."

The boy spoke hurriedly. "Yes, a pond, then more small houses. She lives in one of those."

Dan stood up. He looked at Kim, who was smiling still. "Very specific," she said. They walked around the clearing. The boys watched them leave.

The alley was narrow, the houses crowding over. Several leaned so far forward they seemed in danger of falling. On the balcony of one house a woman was combing very long jet black hair. She stopped to watch them pass. Dan observed everything. His dark eyes moved rapidly, watching the huts and alleys for any signs of danger.

It would be easy to walk into a trap here. Kim had shown she could handle herself with the Taser gun. He had one of the Browning guns on him, magazine full. But women and children lived here. He could not fire his weapon.

They went deeper into the shanty town. Naked babies, sucking their thumbs, came out of doorways to gape at them. They went past the pond. They came to the tin roof hut the boy had pointed out. There was an open drain next to the hut, and the door was nothing more than a flimsy lean to. Palm trees rose in the back, and around the hut. Dan reached forward and knocked on the tin door. It made a rattling sound.

After a pause there was a sound from inside. Then the door cautiously opened. Maya's face appeared in the doorway. She gasped, and rapidly disappeared behind the door.

CHAPTER 10

David Harris tried to open his eyes. It was difficult, as they were stuck together. Blood and sweat mixed to form a grit that was smeared over his face. His hands were tied behind his back, and his feet were tied too. He was lying on the floor of a mud hut. His left cheek was on the hard, packed floor, and he could smell the earth. He wanted to sit up. And he needed a drink.

A shaft of sunlight fell from the thatched roof, and lit up his face. David tried again, and his left eyelid fluttered open. The floor stretched out ahead of him. The hut had a bamboo door with a wooden log that worked as a latch. He knew there was a padlock attached to the latch, as he heard the guards open it when they bought him drink.

David licked his dry, cracked lips. A drink would be good. So would an Anadin, to get rid of the headache. He had not eaten for two days, and hunger rumbled his stomach. He lifted his head, and the vertigo hit him like a sledgehammer. Nausea rose up inside him, sending bile to his mouth. He moaned, and his head fell back on the floor. He tried to move his feet. Stuck together. Hands – same. His cheeks were swollen and bruised, and pain flowed with hot sparks every time he tried to move a limb.

The beatings had started two nights ago. He was strapped to a chair, and used as a punching bag. Then he had been hung upside down from a tree in the jungle and left overnight. That had been the worst of it. He could hear the snakes slithering, and several times large animals had come to sniff his face. His head had been covered in black cloth, and he could not see anything. He could not shout, for fear of attracting more wildlife.

In the morning, they had dropped him, tied a noose around his hands, and dragged him back to the compound. He had actually not seen anything, as the black bag was still around his face. Then the beatings started again.

David heard a sound. Keys in the lock outside. Then voices. The door opened, and he screwed up his face as the bright sunlight hit him. Strong arms lifted him up as he cried out in pain. Roughly, he was pushed against the side of the hut. He leaned on the wall, trying not to squash his fingers.

"Tch, tch, look what they have done to you." The man in the cream colored, half sleeved safari suit sat down in front of him.

David opened his swollen eyelids further. It was this man who had interrogated him the first night. After the initial beating.

The man said, "I don't believe I introduced myself the last time, did I? How rude of me. My name is Henry Deng."

The man spoke with a thick accent. David tilted his head back on the wall. Behind Deng he could see another man. He recognized the strange face. The light colored eyes, and the long, deep scar that disfigured the left side of his face.

David licked his lips again, and tried to speak. All he could vocalize was a dry rasp. Deng frowned and snapped his thumbs. A soldier came forward, and put an earthen tumbler to David's lips. David drank greedily, and emptied the tumbler, water splashing over his chin into his blood soaked chest. He bent his head, gasping.

"Feel better?" Deng asked. David kept his head lowered, and remained silent. A hand grabbed his hair and pulled his head up.

David looked at Deng. After a pause he said, "Henry Deng. Nice to meet you."

Deng smiled. "There you go. See, we are not all that bad, are we? Just a little cooperation, and we can be friends. Soon, we can let you go back."

David said, "How about now?"

Deng shook his head. "I would love to, Mr…"

"Call me Ted."

"Ok, Mr. Ted. I can let you go, as soon you tell us what you were doing here."

"Like I told you, I work for an NGO. Our base is in Yangon. We are here to help the villagers stuck in the forest while you guys fight the Government."

"Please," Deng said in a low voice. "We have checked your NGO. Of course, they back up your story. But we also know there are many NGO's and charities who are merely fronts for the western intelligence agencies. From your accent, I can tell you are American, yes?"

David did not reply. Deng said, "What sort of an NGO hides in the forest at night with a fully armed platoon of the Shan State Army, Mr. Ted?"

David said, "What are you building down there, Mr. Deng? Looked like a railway line to me. Do you have authority from the Burmese government?"

Deng smiled. "Oh, believe me, we have authority." Behind him, the man with the scarred face smiled as well.

Ted said, "You guys are not friends with the Shan. You must be the Wu Army, right?"

"We are the citizens of the Wu State, yes."

"That also means you are closely allied to China."

"What is your point, Mr Ted?"

David went silent again. He felt a jarring blow to the side of head, almost knocking him down sideways. The man next to him grabbed his hair and straightened him again. Mucus dribbled down David's face.

Deng said, "You are helping the Shan. Spying on our work. We found C4 and RTX explosives with the Shan platoon. I think you are here to cause damage to what we are doing."

David said, "There are many people who know I am here."

Deng sat back, and motioned to the man with the scar. He came forward with a small cage, the type used to transport pets. The man opened the top, and lifted up an object. David looked, and his eyes widened.

It was the head of Khin Nyunt. The eyes were closed, and dried blood blackened the face. Nerves and ligaments hung like tendrils from the bottom of the severed head. David looked down and retched. He spat out bile, his chest heaving with the effort.

Deng said softly, "The people who knew you are here are all dead, Mr. Ted. Just tell us what we want, and we will leave you by the roadside in the morning. A bus will carry you back to the nearest town."

David breathed heavily, then said, "I have seen your face, Deng. I know you are going to kill me."

Deng smiled again, "You guys. So full of your Hollywood films." Deng leaned forward. "Down here, Mr. Ted, a man's reputation is everything. People fear me for a reason."

Deng paused then said, "One last time. Tell me who you are, and what you were doing with the Shan."

David remained silent. Deng stood up. He turned to the man behind him. "Another night in the jungle, Li. Don't cover his face this time. If he gets his eyes clawed out, maybe he'll talk tomorrow."

Li Yonping smiled.

*****

Fear was gripping David. Hanging upside down, his face was swollen like a water filled balloon. His vision was hazy, but his eyes had got used to the dark. He tried to close his eyes, but the jungle at night was full of sounds. He heard the snap of twigs, and the call of barking deer. Then something else. A soft, slithery sound. Almost like a hiss. David twisted, but he could not move. His legs were tied to a branch overhead, and his hands were tied behind his back. Sweat poured down his head, dripping to the jungle floor.

Then he saw the eyes. They glowed green in the dark. David went absolutely still. His vision was reversed, but he could still make out an animal. The eyes were above a bush, but then the animal padded out softly. David could smell it. A beastly, thick smell. He didn't know what it was, but a big jungle cat like a leopard would be his best guess.

Panic surged through him, but he forced himself to remain still. He felt the animal come closer. It was so silent, he could barely hear it. Just the smell. David tried to stop breathing, but it was no good. He gasped. Then he realized his best chance was to scare it away. He jerked his feet on the rope and screamed.

"Hey!" The action seemed to have the desired effect. The animal stepped back, its eye glowing like emeralds in the dark. Then David heard the growl. It was soft at first, then grew louder.

Uh-oh.

Fear and adrenaline coursed through him. He twisted wildly, shaking the branch above him. The animal growled louder and got closer, realizing he was trapped. David saw the beast crouch, getting ready to launch itself at him.

David let loose with his voice. "Help," he screamed. His voice broke. "Somebody help me!"

The animal growled louder, and then David heard another sound. A displacement of air, like a swishing sound. It was followed by another, then another. Then he heard dull thuds, and the animal yelped. It ran off into the dark, bounding over the bush.

David went quiet. His heart was pounding in his mouth. He heard a scurry of feet, then a human face appeared close to his.

"*Baw* David," the voice whispered. "It's me, *Maung* Thin. Your driver, remember?"

David could barely speak. He watched as Thin's black shape climbed swiftly up the tree, silent as a snake. David felt his feet become loose. Then Thin came back down and hacked the rest of the rope away. Gently, he lowered David to the floor. He cut the ropes at the back of David's hand.

Thin whispered in David's ear. "The *Wu* are everywhere, *Baw* David. We need to get out of here right now. Can you stand up? Here let me help you."

David stifled back a curse of pain as he stood up. He leaned against the tree, panting. Thin put his arm around David's back.

"One step at a time. Let us move," he said.

David had no idea where they were headed. After an hour of painstaking walk, they collapsed on the floor. Thin gave David a bottle of water. He sucked from it greedily.

Thin said, "I managed to escape. I came back after they had left. The bastards left the dead bodies there for the animals. But I found something on Nyunt's body."

"What?"

Thin's eyes glistened in the dark. "The map."

CHAPTER 11

Dan said, "Maya, I'm sorry. I just want to talk."

Maya did not say anything. But neither had she shut the door. Dan repeated himself.

Maya's face peered out of the door. Fear was etched in her beautiful chestnut brown eyes. "You should not have come here," she whispered.

"Why not?"

"Just go away. Right now!"

"Can I please come in?" Dan asked. "I swear we won't take up too much of your time."

Maya opened the door wider and beckoned them inside. Dan noticed her looking out the door, trying to see if anyone had seen them.

The floor was made of hardened mud, with rugs spread over them. A wooden oven in a corner outside was burning coal.

Dan said, "You on your own?"

Maya looked down at the floor. "Yes, aunt is at work."

She looked up to them and said, "Did anyone follow you here?"

"No," said Dan. "What are you afraid of?"

Maya said, "The owner of the restaurant is the brother of an Army General. They say he also…" Maya's voice trailed off.

"Also what?" Dan asked.

"They sell pills." Dan nodded slowly. He had heard backpacker tourists mention how easy it was to score "pills" on the street. They were mostly contraband amphetamine. Myanmar was a hub for the crystal meth trade in Asia.

Dan said gently, "Will he make trouble for you?"

Maya frowned. "You should not have come here. The neighbors will now know. Those men are like his bodyguards."

Maya said to Dan, "They go around collecting money from people who live here. They call it rent, but this is not rental land. This is owned by the Government."

Kim said, "An extortion racket."

Kim could not stop staring at Maya. Something about the way she looked, walked, and spoke was sparking a memory inside her. The memory of a little girl she had once known. But it was impossible. A long-abandoned door in her heart opened and shut, and a brief light flared in her heart like a sunset over the sea. It illuminated every scarred portion of her heart, then died. She shook her head.

It was strange, and evocative. She could not put her finger on it, but Maya somehow reminded her of Sarah. When Sarah was a child. She had long dark hair, she bent her head and stared at everyone just like this…this little girl did. Maya caught Kim looking at her. Kim looked away, embarrassed.

Dan asked Maya, "Do they do the same from the shops around here?"

Maya nodded, and looked at the floor. "We are poor. If we get kicked out from here, we have nowhere to go. And those men can kick us out."

Dan said, "Don't worry. That won't happen."

Maya said, "There's nothing you can do." She looked at Dan and Kim in turn, a helpless look in her face. Kim felt a wave of sadness wash over her, mingling with a sense of wonder as she gazed at Maya.

She said to Maya, "Like Dan said, you won't get kicked out. Don't worry."

Maya shook her head. "You don't understand. Please leave now, and don't come back."

*****

Kim and Dan walked back in the mid-afternoon heat haze. Their clothes were sticking to their backs. The humidity was sapping. Despite the heat, the sun was playing hide and seek with a bank of grey clouds.

Kim said, "I'm going to ask at the office. The name of the government minister in charge of this area can't be hard to find, I'm sure."

"Be careful," Dan said. "Ministers here have their own private armies."

They flagged down a cab. Before they got to the address, the cab stopped. Streets were clogged with traffic. The entire road was at a standstill.

"What's happening?" Dan asked the cab driver.

"Big procession," the man said in his broken English. "For election. Many men march with banners."

Dan said, "We better get off here and walk. These rallies can go on for a long time."

Kim agreed. "This rally started way back, and it's going to end at the town hall. That's where the press conference will be."

They threaded their way through the usual log jam of sweating bodies, three wheel covered scooters called auto-rickshaws, and the perennial dust raised by hundreds of feet.

They stopped to have a fresh coconut. The juice inside was sucked out with a straw. Apart from the pressed sugarcane juice, this was Dan's favorite drink. It was salty sweet, and just what his body needed. Kim gave him a thumbs up as their eyes met, straws in their mouth.

Crowds had spilled outside the town hall. Loudspeakers tied to bamboo poles and streetlights with rope blared out a commentary. It was in Burmese, and Dan didn't understand a word of it. He asked Kim if she did. She had to shout her response.

"A few words, that's all," she said.

Dan sighed. Sure as hell made American politics look boring. The atmosphere on the street was almost festive, like a carnival. He spotted the entrance to the town hall. He indicated to Kim. There was a crowd looking to enter. As they approached the gates, Dan stiffened. One of the five men he had seen at Blue Orchid restaurant was standing as security. He had a red ribbon tied around his left bicep. It was the leader. He was taller than most people around him, and his eyes were scanning the crowd. They fell on Dan. Dan returned his gaze, not looking away. The man turned and melted to the back of the building. Dan pulled on Kim's arm.

"I've been spotted," Dan said. "I'm not going in. Don't want to make trouble for you."

Dan looked towards the gates, only a few paces away. Another man had appeared. Shorter, oriental features. He looked Chinese. That was not the only reason he caught Dan's attention. He had a scar that travelled from his left eye all the way down his face. A deep scar. The kind a knife blade would cause.

His eyes fixated on Dan. Not much unnerved Dan. He had looked into the eyes of the coldest killers. He recognized a killer now. But what he found strange was the lack of intensity. Men who were killers had hard, cruel eyes. This man seemed to have...nothing. No animosity. No sensation. Like the world could end right now and he would smile and carry on.

Eyes that did not belong to a human being. Dan looked away. When he looked again, the man was still there, still staring at him. But he now had the touch of a smile on his lips. It wasn't mirth. It was more of a sneer.

CHAPTER 12

Dan said goodbye to Kim and threaded his way out of the crowd. Once he was thirty yards or so out of the main entrance of the town hall, he looked back. Kim had gone in. There was still a raucous gathering around him, but it was ordinary evening traffic.

The skies had darkened suddenly, and there a fresh breeze. The breeze got stronger, and became a wind that slapped the tin doors of the hawker stalls against one another. A dust storm raised up in the middle of the street. Lightning flashed overhead. There was a murmur in the street. The wind was incredibly refreshing, cooling his fevered brow, and Dan's sigh seemed to join a mutual exhalation that rose up from the street. Distant thunder rumbled.

A thunderstorm. Could even be a cyclone. Dan quickened his step, heading back towards his hotel.

He went down an alley, and the red brick Goth façade of the colonial market opened up in front of him. He came out into the square. It was quiet apart from a few shopwallahs packing up their stuff. Dan felt the fresh wind, smelling of rain, and soon after, the first fat drop on his forehead.

A whisper carried in the storm wind, a susurrus of something a few feet away from face. Getting louder instantly, like a tiger about to pounce on his back.

Dan trusted his instinct. He threw himself down, rolling on the ground, hands covering his head. Glass smashed behind him, hitting the alley wall. Then the wall burst into flames. Dan smelt the fumes and knew what it was. A Molotov cocktail. Simple, and effective. He reached for the weapon in his back, but someone grabbed his right arm.

Dan swung around, bending his elbow and pulling his attacker from behind him. The man stumbled out to Dan's front. Dan recognized him as one of the five men from the restaurant. Dan's left fist came up instantly, making solid connection with the man's jaw. A crack, the head snapped back and the man's knees folded. But he had picked Dan's gun up. The gun fell to the floor, and Dan was about to pick it up when a pair of shoes kicked the gun away. Dan looked up to find the leader of the pack. The man was thick around the shoulder, with heavy, long arms. He made his fists into claws and approached Dan, circling him. Dan noticed the other three appear on his periphery. Two in front, and one behind him.

The leader put his arms wide. A wrestler's stance. He would look to grab Dan around the midriff and pin him to the floor. The man was big. Heavy. Dan stood still and let him approach. Five feet away. Four feet. Then the man pounced. He went for the grab, but all he grabbed was empty air. Dan was light on his feet. He rolled on the ground and was back up as the heavy man stumbled. He had his chance. It was now Dan's turn.

Lighting quick, Dan swept the man's legs from under him with a vicious kick. As the thug fell face first, Dan was on his back. He straddled the man, and grabbed his head. He had long hair. There's a reason for the military buzzcut. In a close fight, opponents cannot get a hold on the head easily. Dan pulled the hair, and the man's screamed as his neck was stretched back. Dan's heavy fist came down like a mini bulldozer, smashing into the side of his face, rupturing the temporomandibular joint, pushing blood into the eye socket.

Dan stood up, a dull roar in his ears, a fire burning in his limbs. He didn't like to admit to himself. His conscious mind would not accept it either. But this feeling was what he lived for. The sudden explosion of strength that flooded his limbs, made him feel invincible. He crouched, soft on his toes like a cat, and swivelled around.

How many? Two, three, five? Ten? He would take them all, go down fighting till they tore his limbs off his body.

Only the three men faced him. They approached him, looking uncertain. One of them shouted an oath, and flew in. Something flashed in his hand, and Dan recognized the sliver of a switchblade knife. He slashed at Dan from above, and he swayed away. The knife swished inches past his face. The knife man was good. He did not allow the forward momentum to carry him. His body remained erect, and he snapped his arm up like a backhand tennis shot, the knife flicking up for Dan's face.

Dan leaned back, stumbling, almost falling. He felt the knife graze the side of his chin, and a sharp sting. He regained his balance, and his attacker came in again, fast, this time thrusting from low down. Dan noticed the other two were moving behind him. If he stumbled back again, they would grab him, push him down. Or maybe just shoot him in the back.

The knife was below his waist level, when Dan kicked high with his left leg. It was too quick for the knife man to make an adjustment. He shouted as his hand flew up, and the knife left his fingers. Dan folded his right arm, and hit him hard with the elbow. The head snapped back like it had been hit by a train, and the man collapsed.

Dan turned swiftly to the men at his back. He saw them instantly and his blood froze. One of them had a weapon trained on him. It was the gun Dan had dropped. The man had a wolfish smile on his face.

"*Bas!*"

The shout rang out from behind Dan. He turned. A car had pulled in at the edge of the square. The back door was open. Two tall men flanked a much shorter man, who was clearly the boss. The two guards stood silent and watchful as the shorter man approached. He barked out another order, and the two men behind Dan scattered.

The three men stopped thirty yards away. Dan could not make out their features well, but he did recognize the man with the left sided scar. He stood very still, not taking his eyes off Dan.

Dan felt the man was scrutinizing his face, memorizing it for later. Then he stepped back, turned and left with his entourage of hoodlums.

The rain picked up, and soon it was pouring. Dan took shelter inside a hawker stall, then ran towards Downtown. He got drenched, but saw the blue neon sign of a bar and dived in. The interior was dark and cool. A few locals lounged in tables with a few foreigners at the side. Dan looked carefully. No one he knew. He ordered a Tsingtao beer at the bar and sat down. He pondered over the day's events.

He had no wish to get caught up in something. He was on a damned holiday, and that was how he was going to keep it. He wished he was back in Goa, watching the sun set, eating prawns on stick, and downing it with rum. Maybe he just needed to get out of the city. Once he was on the road again, he would be alright. He thought of the woman. He didn't believe a word of her cover as a journalist. Since when did a journalist carry a Taser gun?

But there was something about her. Her large eyes were beautiful, and there was a certain vulnerability in them. When she looked at him, he caught his breath. Dan closed his eyes. Once he had left, Kim Smith would be a memory, nothing else. It was the best way.

Dan finished his beer, paid and left.

CHAPTER 13

Henry Deng observed the plane's landing lights flash in the dark clouds gathering on the horizon. It was far from monsoon, but the clouds were still dramatic, ominous grey beasts that rose up from below and threatened to cover the sky. The plane's wheels emerged, and it did a smooth landing on the tarmac of the runway.

It was the afternoon, and there was still some light in the sky. As the passengers started to disembark, Deng put the binocular to his eyes. He spotted the man as soon as he stepped out. He was wearing a navy blue suit, matched by a blue hat. Deng followed the man as he climbed down, then was greeted by Li Yonping, his cousin. They shook hands, and Li ushered the man into a waiting Mercedes Benz. Deng put his bino's away and hurried out of the arrivals lobby.

He met them just as they were coming in through the door. Den strode forward with a smile on his face.

"Sung Min Lee, how nice to see you again." Both men shook hands. Sung Min kept his hat on, and wide glasses covered his eyes. His normal silvery hair was cut short, hidden under the blue hat. Four guards covered the men back and front, and the group approached customs, where Sung Min's passport was barely noticed by the immigration official. They were waved through quickly.

Once they were in the car Sung Min Lee took his hat off. He removed his dark glasses. He was one of the leading scientists of the Democratic People's Republic of Korea. He was in his fifties, with inquisitive eyes and a sallow complexion. He had known Deng from previous business transactions. Not many people knew that Sung Min was here. The passport he had just shown to the customs official had a deceased Chinese businessman's details. Sung Min Lee was travelling undercover.

Lee said, "So, Henry, I hear business is going well."

Deng smiled. "It is, but with your help we can scale heights not deemed possible."

"Have you informed the Government of your plans?"

The smile faded from Deng's face. "As you know, this is a private agreement between us. I do not see what the Government has to do with it."

"The Chinese or the Burmese Government?"

"Either one," Deng said, and frowned. "Sung Min, I need to know if you are fully on board with this. I have explained this to you, and you already have in excess of a million US dollars in your anonymous Swiss account in Zurich."

Lee stared at the intense eyes of the younger man for a while, then dropped his gaze. "Yes, I know. As long as you realize that the final outcome will need a lot more resources than any private individual can provide."

Deng nodded. "I know, don't worry. When the time is right, both Governments will be made aware. There is no other option."

Lee appeared relieved. "Good. Glad you see it that way."

After an hour's drive they reached their destination. Li led the way, and the others followed with armed guards. The giant white structure loomed above them, encircling a wide area. They walked around in a semi-circle, then stopped at a metallic door.

Li opened the door and they stepped in. A grill walkway led to stairs that led down to the lower level floor. From there, they took the elevator which went down several levels. Hard hats were passed around, along with bright orange protective wear. The elevator doors opened to the loud sound of drilling machines and hammers. They walked down a central passage till they got to the main chamber.

Deng bent down and picked up a black rock. Blue and yellow grains ran inside it. Light caught the blue glint inside the rocks. He handed it to Sung Min Lee. The older man turned the object round in his hand, examining it. Lee looked up and his eyes wandered over the lines of men with protective eye wear and lamps shining from their helmets.

Most of them were pushing drills into the walls of the cave they had descended into. Like the men, Lee and the others wore ear plugs. The sound was still loud, and the ground shook beneath their feet. At the end of the massive, dome shaped cave complex, narrow gauge train tracks took the mined rocks to a central loading area. A system of conveyor belts lifted the rocks to the surface.

Deng was watching Lee's face. Lee turned to him. "Good, Henry. I can see that you are making progress."

Deng said, "Let's head upstairs."

When they stepped off the elevator, and the noise was quieter, Lee asked, "Did the Chinese man deliver?"

Deng smiled. "Yes. I must say that is where you proved your worth, Sung Min."

"Excellent. As you know, without those centrifuge tubes, the whole operation is useless. You can try the gas diffusion method, but the yield is only 2-5%."

They strolled around the giant space, noting the tractors that carried the crushed rocks on for further processing. They walked through the large space till they came to a series of doors leading to another chamber. This place was almost silent, and air conditioned. Blue floor lights cast a glow on the ceiling. On each of the rows stood hundreds of three feet tall tubular structures. Deng motioned to one of his men, and spoke to him in a whisper.

Lee asked, "If you have a load ready, I would like to see how they are working."

Deng said, "That was exactly what I was just discussing. Time for an exhibition."

The lights overhead dimmed even further till the whole chamber was pitch black. Then a humming began, soft at first, then gradually louder. The buzz spread down the rows till there was a uniform rotating movement in all of the cylinders. Red and yellow lights glowed down the side of the cylinder as they rotated at ultrasonic speed. The motion became faster, till the entire room seemed to be spinning in a yellow and red daze. The sound never got above a gentle, pervasive hum that was easy on the ears.

Lee nodded. "Good shock absorbers. I told you these machines were good."

After a while, the humming began to subside. Their yellow and red stripes, stretching in long rows across the room, began to blink, then went dark. The blue floor light came up again, basking the ceiling in a light that had a soft, aquatic quality.

"Good," Lee said. Deng beamed. "Thank you."

They left the room and filed outside. They took the elevator above, and Sung Min Lee went off to do some sightseeing.

Li Yonping and Deng watched his car pull away.

Deng said, "This is it, cousin. Once we have this material, we will be unstoppable. The Politburo in Beijing will have to speak to us. The Burmese will be falling at our feet. We play off one against the other."

Li said, "And then?"

"Then we cement our authority. The Deng family will become as powerful as the Triads across the border."

"We are para-military already, cousin, the Triads are scared of us."

Deng said, "They are, but not in China. Believe me, the political influence we will possess will open new doors for us. All across China the Triads will pay respect to us."

Li Yonping looked to the yellow dust at their feet, then at the trees above. He said, "Henry, do you remember when we helped *Biyu Muqin* carry her snake fangs and elephant tusks up the hills into Kunming?"

Biyu Muqin, or Mother Biyu was the name by which Li had always called Deng's mother – his aunt. Biyu had raised Li as her own child after his parents had died. As a single mother with two boys in Pangshang, life had not been easy. But they had survived, and flourished later, thanks to Biyu.

Deng lit a cigarette and took a deep drag. He smiled at the memory. "Yes, of course. Long time ago. Why do you ask?"

"Remember how small Biyu's business was. She made it grow slowly, and with time, it became big."

"What are you trying to say?"

Li sighed. They walked together, and Li raised an arm and draped it around his cousin's shoulder. "Biyu always said: the longest journey is made up of the smallest steps. Remember?"

Deng rolled his eyes. "Are you trying to give me a lecture, Li?"

"No, cousin. I know you, you always plan big. You want to get up that mountain, and then go across it. But when we play with politicians, we have to be careful. What we are doing now is different. Our *Ya Ba* business has made us powerful. It gave us friends in the Government and military. But this…this has the potential of destroying us."

"Or making us powerful beyond our wildest dreams. I don't want to sell *Ya Ba* all my life, Li. I want power. *Real* power. *Zhenshi Liliang.*"

Deng stopped and faced his cousin. "*Ni mingbai ma?*" Do you understand?

Li nodded, and shrugged. "*Shi de wo mingbai.*" Yes, I do understand.

They turned as they heard a shout from behind. One of their men came running up.

"U Tay Zo is here, *Zhu* Deng. He says he needs to see you right now."

Deng and Li exchanged a glance. Tay Zo was a mining tycoon, a powerful businessman who had seen the potential in Myanmar's resource laden hills, and gone to work in his dad's tin mine as a young man. He now owned several mines.

Deng had negotiated with him to buy a portion of a mine, and Zo had agreed. But increasingly, Zo wanted more money, and more insight into what Deng was doing. That was dangerous. If Zo spoke to someone in the Government, or the *Tatmadaw*, it could spell disaster.

Deng said, "Tell him I shall see him. Make him wait. He can come in, but only with us."

The man bowed. "Yes, *Zhu* Deng." He adjusted the rifle on his shoulder and ran off.

Deng and Li walked back in a leisurely fashion. Two Jeeps were waiting, with a black Range Rover. A portly, average height Burmese man stepped out of the Range Rover as Deng approached. Tay Zo was dressed in an expensive blue suit, with a handkerchief knotted at the left breast pocket. His silk shirt strained at the belly, and the top two buttons were undone to reveal a hairy chest and a heavy gold necklace.

Deng spread his arms, then clasped his palms together under his chin. He bowed slightly. "U Tay Zo. How nice of you to pay us a visit."

Zo heaved himself towards Deng. He wiped his balding scalp with the handkerchief, not returning the greeting.

"I call you, and you don't answer, Deng. At the factories, your men say you are away." Zo waved behind him. His jacket hitched up, showing his sweaty armpits. "This place, you keep secret from everyone. I only found out from one of the engineers who needed an old plan. I didn't even know you opening up here was in our agreement."

"Come, come now, U Zo. I have paid you every cent you were promised…"

Zo interrupted, and raised a finger. "But we didn't agree on how far you could come. Every month, you advance by another mile. And this…what the hell are you doing here?"

Li coughed politely. Deng looked and Li nodded imperceptibly. Deng said, "Why don't you come downstairs, and I can show you?"

Zo looked around him. Doubt was written all over his face. Deng said, "If you wish, bring your men with you. With their weapons. I have no wish to fight you, U Zo. I am a business man. Like you said, let us get to an agreement. How about that?"

Zo relaxed. "If I am not back home this evening, my wife knows to call the President's office. Do you understand?"

Deng smiled. "Perfectly."

Zo's men came out of the two jeeps. They followed down in a single file to the elevator. As they walked around the space below, Zo's mouth opened.

"This is huge, Deng. How long have you been planning this for?"

"A long time," Deng said. Li had moved up ahead. Zo's guards were behind them. Their weapons were out, and they were keeping a look around.

"Up here," Deng said. He steered Zo by the elbow.

Without warning, he pushed Zo with all his might, throwing the corpulent man on the floor. From either side, and above, four Type 80, 7.62mm sub machine guns of the PLA (People's Liberation Army) opened up, shattering the silence. Deng watched the men behind him jerk as the heavy ordnance shredded their bodies. Within a minute the carnage was over. The men lay on the floor in a bloodied heap.

Li appeared. He grabbed Zo by the collar and heaved him up. He pulled Zo to a large circular vat of boiling, 100% proof nitric acid. A chain pulley was lowered, with a heavy hook at the end, designed to lift industrial goods. Li attached the collar of Zo's suit to the hook. Zo fought back but Li punched him twice in the face, both blows knocking the man's head back.

A machine sprang to life, and gears clashed. The pulley whined, and the chain lifted, dragging Zo up in the air. The fat man screamed and kicked his legs. The pulley moved direction, and hovered right above the middle of the vat. Acid spat upwards, sending noxious vapors in the air. The heat rising from it was palpable.

Deng had to shout to make himself heard. "Goodbye, U Zo. It was nice doing business with you."

Zo's face was red, sweat pouring off it. "Deng, you won't get away with this. I have friends in the Army. My wife knows…"

"Your wife will meet with an unfortunate accident soon, you fat bastard. My men are already on their way. Soon, there will be no trace of you, or your family."

Zo twisted and turned. "No, Deng, I can make you rich. Take my mines. I will give you…"

Deng said, "I don't negotiate, Zo. I take what I want. If you understood that, you wouldn't be in this position now."

"No, Deng, please, no…" Zo's voice rose to a high-pitched scream as the pulley lowered, slowly dropping the man towards the acid. His screams became continuous, rising to an agonizing crescendo, as his feet lowered into the acid, followed by the rest of his body.

CHAPTER 14

Kim breathed a sigh of relief as she came out of the packed town hall. The hall had been air conditioned, but people were packed in it like sardines in a tin can. Luckily, there had been an enclosure for the press up at the front. She listened with her earphones on the digital voice recorder and translator. But her attention was elsewhere.

At the back of the stage, she could see three Chinese men. They kept an eye on her, and she acted like she was ignoring them. But as she jotted on her notebook, she used the pen camera to take photos of them.

Now, she looked outside carefully. People were filtering out of the hall and walking into the warm night. The Chinese men were not around. Neither could she see any of her contacts. So much for developing assets. The two Burmese men she was meant to see had not got back in touch with her.

Her mind went back to that night. She was capable of protecting herself, but Dan being there had definitely helped. The way he had fought, his movements, everything pointed to him being ex-military. There was a hardness in his dark eyes that she had seen in others. Dan Roy was no stranger to death, or in the dealing of it. This man had killed, many times.

And yet, he had a strangely soft side. He was protective of that girl, almost as if it was his duty. He acted like he would do anything for her.

And, Kim admitted to herself with a tingle of warmth, his masculinity was having an effect on her. The way his brown hair flopped over his forehead, and the glitter in his intense eyes as he looked at her. Her heart skipped a beat as she thought about it now.

Over the last six years, since Sarah's death, she had not allowed herself much male company. She had been on dates, and had a couple of transient relationships, nothing meaningful. She was 33 now, and her life, she knew, would be in service of her country. She wondered if Dan believed her cover as a journalist. Her gut told her he did not. But for now, he was not asking her about it.

Kim looked at the dark corners of the alleyways, at the gaps between the shops. She kept a hand on the Taser in her purse. She was on the main street of downtown Yangon, the Sule Pagoda Road. Her hotel was another ten minutes' walk away. She was sweating by the time she got to it. For some reason, she felt eyes on her as soon as she landed in Yangon. She did not know why. But she trusted her instincts.

The guard opened the door for her and saluted. Kim went through the double doors into the diplomatic enclave, nestled in the hills of North Yangon that sloped down to the Inle Lake. Most of the CIA, and foreign embassy staff lived here. She had three messages. She took them up to her room. All of them were from the CIA team based at the US Embassy. They had sourced new assets within the Rohingya refugees.

Kim made two phone calls. Another man had agreed to speak to her. This guy, like the others, spoke English. He was going to meet Kim at a hotel called Kenilworth International. The address was downtown. Kim spoke to Mary and Estefan for ten minutes, then got ready for bed.

*****

Kim woke up early the next morning. Two faxed files had arrived for her, and she took time to read through them. Both related to her current assignment.

As she read, her thoughts returned to Dan. He had left, and she had not checked on him. He did not have a cell phone. If she wanted to see him again, she would have to go to his hotel. She hoped he was OK. Deep inside, she fought conflicting feelings.

She had no reason to involve Dan in her work. Her mission – to develop these assets and find out what happened to David Harris – was front and center in her mind. But yet, having Dan around had helped.

The question covered her mind like a black shadow. Was she about to put Dan into harm's way? He had shown he could handle himself, but that was not the point. There was always a possibility something could happen to Dan, just like it had done to Sarah…

Kim looked down and bit her lower lip. No, she scolded herself. Whatever Dan's background was, to her he was a civilian. She had no right to drag him into this. A forlorn wind blew across her mind, scattering against the walls of her heart. Perhaps she could not get close to anyone, after what had happened to Sarah. Maybe she would always be this way, worried and anxious.

At least, she owed Dan a goodbye. Kim made her mind up. She needed to concentrate on her job, and not let Dan distract her anymore. She would go to his hotel, say goodbye then put him out of her mind.

She got ready, wearing a light, white cotton shirt and pants that covered her arms and legs. She called for a cab, and waited outside the gates.

The cab dropped Kim outside the ramshackle wooden building that was Dan's hotel. A longhaired hippy came out, saw her and stopped. Kim was looking up, shading her eyes against the sun. The building had a balcony at every level, and went up to four storeys.

"You cool there, honey?" The tall hippy drawled. He wore a blue and red bandana on his head, and had a beard. He reminded Kim of the singer, Willie Nelson. A long white cigarette hung from his lips. The odour of cannabis wafted in the air to Kim.

Kim gave him a hard look without saying anything. She walked past Willie into the lobby. She took the stairs up to Dan's room. The wooden door was shut, and it rattled even when she knocked lightly on it.

There was a sound from inside. A bed creaked. Kim suddenly wondered if she had done the right thing here. Dan might not be alone. He could be…before she could finish her thoughts the door had been flung open. Kim's mouth hung open too, but she did not realize it.

Dan was standing in the doorway, dressed in his pants. He was bare from the waist up. Kim knew that was not unusual in Burma, where local men often walked around in sarongs and nothing else. But she had not expected to see Dan without a shirt. She tried to avert her gaze, but could not help her eyes from lingering over the breadth of his shoulders, the chiselled biceps of his arms, the flat six pack of his abdominal muscles.

"Hey, Good Morning," Dan said. There was a smile on his face. She looked away, embarrassed. Heat fanned her face.

Dan said, "Why don't you come inside?"

Kim managed a weak smile, and scratched the inside of her neck. She stepped inside the simple room. The windows had been opened, and looked out over the brown roofs of houses and hotels outside. The sun was pulsing, and green and grey blue hills rose up in the shimmering horizon. The room was simple, consisting of one bed, a table chair, and a wardrobe.

Dan said, "It's not the Ritz, is it?"

Kim said, "I didn't say that."

"I don't need much. Things weigh you down. This place is basic, but it's all I need right now."

Kim said, "If it makes you happy then why not, I guess. Did you get back home OK last night?"

"Met up with some new friends." Dan told her what had happened.

Kim's heart turned to ice as she listened. It was what she had feared. Could no one be close to her and not get hurt anymore?

Dan read the look on her face. He stepped closer. He had pulled a shirt on now, but he hadn't buttoned it up. She could smell his deep, musky scent. Kim swallowed.

Dan said in a low voice, "Hey, you alright?"

Kim walked to the chair and sat down. She put her file on the table. "I'm sorry. I should have known after Maya told me. All the politicians here have their own personal guards."

"You mean thugs."

"Yes. Whatever. I shouldn't have taken you to the rally last night."

Dan said, "You weren't to know. It's fine. But there are some things I can't figure out."

"Like what?"

"Like what the Chinese were doing there. And why they attacked you."

"There are a lot of Chinese who live in Myanmar."

"I know. But most of them lead normal, peaceful lives. They don't attack foreigners."

Kim knotted her fingers on her lap. She was aware that Dan was watching her. He sat down on the bed across from her. The bed creaked.

Kim looked up and said, "Dan, I...I can't involve you in what I'm doing any more. It's best if we don't meet any more." As soon as she said it, she felt bad. But she had to.

Dan said softly, "You're no journalist, are you?"

Kim did not answer. Dan said, "Do you work for the CIA?"

Kim tried to act nonchalant, but he saw through it. She looked out the window and sighed.

Dan said again, "Those Chinese men would have killed you. Killing a foreigner in Yangon is a big deal. They needed to kill you for a reason. I'm thinking you know something that's pretty important to them."

Kim looked down at her lap again. He had figured out a lot without her saying a word. And yet, she did not resent it. If anything, she felt safer that he knew. He had put himself in harm's way for her. If he belonged to the other side, he wouldn't have done that.

She looked at him. His hair was brushed back with his hands, and he had a four-day stubble. His dark eyes glinted at her. She could not take her eyes away.

"It's alright," Dan said in a soft voice. "I know you can't tell me."

Kim fought the myriad of emotions that fluttered inside her chest. She matched his low voice. "It takes one to know one, Dan. What secrets have you got?"

Their eyes connected. His eyes widened slightly, as if he was trying to delve inside her mind. In that instant, Kim knew she wanted him. Badly. But she couldn't do it. She had more important things to worry about now. She averted her eyes, and stood up. She grabbed her file in front of her, as if it gave her protection.

I am only afraid of myself, she thought. Not you.

Dan stood up with her. "Where are you going?"

Kim said, "To work. Enjoy your holiday."

"I guess this is goodbye, then." He had moved close to her again, and she breathed in his scent. It made her feel giddy.

She firmed her voice. "I guess it is." She went to the door, and stepped outside. Dan made no effort to follow her. Kim went down the stairs without looking back.

CHAPTER 15

Dan watched her go. An uneasiness was gnawing at the back of his mind. Kim had come for a reason. She did not want to drag him into this any further. Which meant she could be in trouble.

Dan threw on a shirt, and changed into his jeans. He checked the magazine of the Browning hand gun. Six rounds left. He put the gun in his back belt, then let his shirt fall over it. He locked the door and took the stairs three at a time, heading down.

Sule Pagoda Road, the main street outside, was full of rickshaws, cars, scooters, and pedestrians jostling for space. Rickshaws squawked raucously, cars blasted their horns, and traffic was gridlocked. Dan knew Kim would not have gone far.

The morning was hot, a sweaty, humid heat that made Dan's forehead exude water like a pressed sponge. He walked fast, dodging between the hawkers with wicker baskets of food on their heads, and the throng of general public.

After ten minutes, he caught sight of her. She was getting into a cab. He saw a flash of her blonde hair, and the white bush shirt she was wearing. The cab inched along on the traffic.

Dan managed to flag down a three-wheeled auto rickshaw. He got into the back and extended his arm out. The white Nissan cab was just about visible.

"Follow that car," Dan said. "Do you understand?"

The driver grinned and nodded. "Speak English."

He honked his horn, shouted obscenities and weaved between the cars as he crept up on the white Nissan. Dan held on to the sides as the auto rickshaw sped up. Traffic began to move, and the cab sped up as well. The driver squeezed the engine, revving it up to its maximum. Dan watched as the white cab took a turn into a wide avenue lined with trees.

To his right, in the distance, he could see the massive gold dome and tower of the Shwedagon Pagoda. The enormous Buddhist temple was almost half a mile away, but the sun still caught its golden colours, and made it sparkle like a thousand diamonds. The tip of the pagoda, Dan knew, held exactly that: 5,448 diamonds.

Kim's cab slowed in front of a large, walled garden with gates and a sweeping driveway leading up to tall, wide building. The sign outside said Kenilworth International Five Star Hotel. Kim's cab drove inside the hotel.

Dan got off the auto, and paid the man. The white building needed a lick of paint. The gardens were getting overgrown. He walked in through the glass doors of the lobby that squeaked as they were pulled apart by a uniformed doorman.

Dan looked around the lobby. It was mostly empty. The marble floor reflected the sunlight, and tribal artwork on the wall hung in glass cases. Two hippies with long, Rastafarian hair were paying their bill at the counter. One of them had a chillum, or ganja pipe, hanging from his backpack.

A Chinese man walked past. Dan watched him. He wore a sarong and brown shirt, and came out of a side door. He looked like a hotel employee. He saw Dan, smiled and bowed slightly. Dan nodded. Harmless.

He could not see Kim anywhere. He tried not to panic. The elevators were opposite to him. The concierge was busy, and paid Dan no attention. Dan walked over to the elevators. Both the elevators were climbing. He saw one stop at the 7th floor. Dan heard voices behind him. He looked behind, and froze.

The Chinese men he had seen when Kim was attacked. One of them had a bandage around his head, where Dan's fist had made a good connection. Dan turned his back to them, but he heard more voices. The two men were not alone. Out of the corner of his eye, he saw a group break up and head for the stairs.

There was no way he could escape discovery, Dan realized. He set his jaws tight. If it came to that, he would have to fight his way out. His instincts had been correct.

Kim had just walked right into a trap.

Dan got ready. Any second now, those two men would be upon him, and they would recognize him. There was a ping on the wall above him, and the elevator doors opened. To Dan's relief, a crowd of tourists popped out. Many of them were Western, and Dan huddled between them, and walked out into the lobby. Behind him, the two Chinese men got into the empty elevator.

Dan hung back as the elevator door closed. He saw it rise up to the 7th floor and stop. Dan turned, and sprinted for the staircase. Without breaking stride, he ran up to the 7th floor. He slammed against the wall when he got there, taking in great lung fulls of air. He took the Browning out, and released the safety catch. Then he looked at the hallway. The hotel room doors were all shut. Dan opened the door separating the stairwell from the hallway, and peered inside.

Two men were standing outside a door. Their beltlines bulged with weapons. As Dan watched, the door opened. His heart skipped a beat. Two men appeared, followed by Kim. Her face was drawn and haggard. Behind her, another three men filed out. It was obvious that the man right behind Kim was holding a weapon to her back. 7 in total, 8 including Kim.

Dan realized the score. There was only one exit. They had to either take the elevators, or take the stairs. The group were advancing directly towards him. Dan slowly retreated back to the stairwell. Two of the men peeled off and came towards him.

The remainder stayed with Kim for the elevator. Dan made his decision quickly. The two men were about ten feet away from him. He needed to take these two out first. Make his job a little easier.

He ran down the stairs. Above him, he heard the men talking and descending. Dan pressed himself against the door that led to the 5th floor hallway. He hoped and prayed no tourists would disturb him. Through the peephole he saw the two men coming down. They were moving quickly. Dan jumped out into the landing just as they arrived.

The men had their backs turned to Dan. The element of surprise was in Dan's favor. They spun around at the sound. One of them dropped their hand to their beltline. But they were too late. Dan grabbed the back of their shirt collars and slammed the two men together like they were rag dolls. Their skulls knocked together, and one of the men fell, dazed.

But the other was quicker. He had lowered his head as Dan hit them, and now he pivoted against Dan, spinning around to his right. Dan tried to grab his arm but the man was too fast. In a blur of movement he had his gun out, and pointing it at Dan at almost point blank range.

Dan moved inside the gun arm, slapping the arm upwards. The wrist holding the gun flicked up, and the bullet meant for Dan screamed into the wall above, picking out a small chunk of masonry.

The gun was small and compact, smaller than a Glock. The man tried to bring the weapon down to bear on Dan, but they were too close. Dan gripped the gun arm in his hand now, pointing it straight up. With his right fist, Dan punched the man at the angle of the jaw. He crunched bone, and the head snapped back. Dan hit him again, and the eyes rolled back in the head, and the man sagged down to the floor.

Dan glanced at his companion quickly. The man was out cold. But they would be up soon. He considered killing them. He felt no remorse. They would do the same to him in the blink of an eye.

And to Kim.

But the bullets had fired already. More unsuppressed rounds would bring unwanted attention. Dan took both their weapons and put them in his belt. Then he ran down the stairs as fast as he could. At the base of the staircase he paused. He looked out at the marble floors of the main lobby. Directly opposite him, a large golden statue of the Buddha sat peacefully against the wall.

There wouldn't be much peace if Dan went into the lobby and found the group waiting there for him. And he could not fire. Not without running the risk of hitting Kim. Dan peeked out the door, opening it a fraction.

He saw them immediately. They were standing in the alcove next to the elevators. Three behind Kim, two flanking her on either side. Smart, Dan thought. No one would dare fire at them. Kim's face was calm. But her eyes were sharp, scanning around.

She's looking for a break.

The men were looking around as well. The group leader, a taller man who was standing close behind Kim, gave out an order. The two men flanking Kim started walking towards the stairwell. Dan shrank back against the door. He let them approach. Then swiftly, he ran one flight up the stairs.

The men were coming to look for their friends.

One of the men had pulled out his gun. He opened the door slightly and called out. Silence, he called out again. Dan heard footsteps climbing up the stairs. He was lying flat on the landing. He saw the man's head appear, then his shoulders. The man turned, as if to say something to his friend behind him.

Dan didn't know how many of them had come up to check. He would have to take that chance. He didn't waste any time. In that fraction of a second while the man's head was turned, Dan sprang into action.

He put his palms on the floor and lifted himself up. Like a sprinter coming off the starting block, Dan launched himself at the man. The guy was about ten feet away. He looked up as a massive shadow loomed over him. There was a shout behind him. But the element of surprise worked in Dan's favor.

Dan's two hundred twenty frame slammed into the man in a flying tackle. Dan grabbed the guy around the midriff, and he fell backwards onto his friend. The friend had taken his gun out, but as all three of them fell backwards the gun tumbled out of his hand and clattered on the landing floor.

Even as he fell, Dan had his fist bunched up against the man's neck. His opponent's fingers were locked in Dan's hair, pulling Dan's head back. Dan was the first up, keeping his grip on the man's neck. He felt a jarring blow to his lower abdomen. Lights swam in Dan's eyes. He refocused. He had the man by the neck, but he was using his knees to kick Dan. In a flash, Dan recognized the move. Thai style kick boxing. They boxed, but also used their legs to kick.

Dan ignored the pain and slammed his broad forehead into the man's face. At close quarters, the guy could not use his legs well. And Dan had a forehead hard enough to crack bone. Blood and cartilage spurted out of the man's face, and he screamed. Dan bent his arm, and hooked an upper right elbow into the man's face. He staggered back and slumped against the wall, out cold.

The other guy was up, and he was behind Dan. He bent his legs, and jumped around in a high kick. But Dan had seen it coming. As soon as Dan had felled the man in front, he tumbled to the floor. The kick sailed over his head. Dan used his leg to sweep the man's legs out from under him. The man crashed down on his back. Dan was up on his feet, but he saw the man's fingers inches away from the gun on the floor.

The man grunted, and reached for the gun. Dan dived on top of him. His fingers reached out and grabbed the man's arm. But the guy had the gun's butt already. Dan lifted his arm high and delivered a massive blow to the man's face. The head knocked back against the concrete floor. His eyes glazed over but he still had the gun in his hand. He tried to bring the gun arm around, but Dan's hand closed around his wrist, and slammed it to the floor. He did it once again and the gun fell from the man's arm. In the same motion, Dan punched the guy again. This time the head rolled back. Blood trickled out of the man's ear.

Chest heaving, Dan stood up. He wiped sweat off his face. He listened, and looked. Silence again. He could see the main door at the base of the stairwell. Any moment now. The others would now know something was wrong. 4 down. 3 to go. If these guys had brains, they would take their captive and make a run for it.

Dan took the men's guns out, and ejected the magazines. They were all the same handguns. Browning, chambered in what seemed like 9mm rounds. 12 round magazines, and the guns had Chinese letters inscribed on the barrel. The guns were heavy in his hand, and they felt like his usual Sig Sauer P226. He put the magazines in his pant pocket, and left the guns. He stole down the stairs. His weapon was out, elbow ram rod straight. Now, he would shoot to kill.

He peered out the door again. They had gone. He came out in to the lobby putting the gun inside his belt. A bright yellow slab of sunlight lit up the entrance outside. He caught a glimpse of blonde hair. The three remaining men were hurrying Kim outside the door. He heard the screech of tires, and a black Mercedes pulled outside the entrance.

Dan broke into a run.

CHAPTER 16

Kim stiffened herself as the muzzle of the gun bore harder into her back. She was not afraid. She was hopeful. Something had happened to the four gangsters who had gone into the stairwell, and not returned. They had to be gangsters, given the tattoos they had on the arms and necks. She had last seen ink like this on Mexican gangs when she had been a field agent in Tijarillo.

The remaining three gangsters were worried now. That's why they were hurrying towards the main entrance. One of them had pulled out his cell and spoke urgently into it. Seconds later, the Mercedes pulled up. They pushed Kim towards the gate.

Kim moved, but she pretended to stumble and fall. She wasn't afraid of the guy holding the gun behind her. These hand guns were an old make, and they all had safety catches. The gun boring into her back did not have the safety catch released. That made her think they wanted her alive. Plus, if they did want her dead, they could have done that easily in the apartment. She had walked into a blood bath. Both the Burmese men who were waiting for her had been hacked to death with a machete.

As Kim fell, she rolled on the ground. The three men had not expected the move. One of them tried to grab her, but Kim scooted, then dived for the corner wall. During her four week long intensive Basic Army Training Fitness at the Farm in Quantico, Kim had been one of the fastest runners in her class. That was more than a decade ago, but she was still quick on her feet.

Even as she did so, she heard the sound she was waiting to hear. The crashing sound of an explosion behind her.

She looked up, and saw one of the men slump to the floor, the back of his head blown out into a cavity of blood and bone. Before the men could move the gun behind had exploded again, and the man closest to her took a bullet to the chest. He had his gun in his hand and tried to raise it, but a bullet in the head finished him off.

Kim made herself into as tight a ball as possible and looked at the source of the gunfire. It was Dan. He was crouched under a big statue of the Buddha, taking cover, but from her angle she could see him. The third gangster had jumped for cover, behind the glass doors. Kim got to her feet, ready to make a move towards Dan. She saw Dan move out on his tiptoes, legs bent at the knees. He came out into the center, his gun arm straight, scanning around. Their eyes met.

Kim heard a sound, and looked behind her. Her blood froze. About a dozen or so armed gangsters had poured out of another two cars that had screeched to a stop. She recognized the weapons. Uzi sub machine guns and Ak-47's. All set to full automatic mode.

Kim stopped, and slipped on the marble floor. Dan was out in the open, facing a line-up of snarling men about to open fire with their weapons. Time froze, and it all seemed to happen in slow motion.

"Dan!", Kim screamed. Her shout reverberated along the walls. Even as the guns sprouted yellow orange blasts of fire from their muzzles, she saw Dan move. She had never seen a man move so quick. He turned to the left and ran three steps towards the concierge desk ahead of her.

Bullets pockmarked the wall, blowing out chunks of masonry as Dan dived, and rolled over the desk to the other side. The ground shook with the sound of gunfire. Kim felt dizzy. Her ears were literally getting blown out. She wasn't armed. But she saw something close by. One of the handguns from the dead gangsters. Kim crawled towards it, bullets flying over her head.

She didn't see it coming. The stock of a rifle landed on the side of her skull, jarring her vision. Pain ripped her skull apart, and her eyes went black. Someone shouted, and she felt two pair of arms lift her up from both sides. She felt the sunlight in her eyes. Then she was bundled inside a car. Doors slammed and she felt the car pull out with a screech of tires.

*****

Dan raised his head as he heard the cars. A hail of bullets greeted him, whining against the walls, blowing pockmarks in the wooden concierge desk. Dan went back down. On the floor, curled up into a tight ball, was the concierge manager. The man was literally urinating with fear, and he whimpered when Dan grabbed his shoulder. The man was unharmed. He looked at Dan with wide eyes, his breathing erratic. His chest badge said Sen Thein, Daytime Manager.

"Listen", Dan whispered urgently. "These men want me, not you. If there is a back way, then tell me now. If I escape, then the firing might stop."

The Manager's eye became wider still. He blinked. "Behind the stairwell doors there is the servant's entrance. It leads to the restaurant. You can go out the delivery route."

Bullets drowned out the Manager's last words. Dan raised his arm and fired back a volley blindly. He was out of ammo. He checked – 3 magazines left on him. He released, clipped a fresh one, and fired again. He emptied half the magazine. It wouldn't stop them, but it would buy him precious seconds.

"Thanks," Dan said to the Manager, who was staring at him with fearful eyes. Swift as lightning, Dan crawled out behind the concierge desk. Staying low, he ran towards the stairwell. He knew they couldn't see him, unless they had moved around the back already. That's what he would have done.

If they had, he was dead meat. But Dan had to take that chance. He still had rounds left. He might die, but he would take his shooters with him. Dan scanned the marble lobby ahead of him. Gunfire rattled sporadically behind him. But it was slowing down. It was a matter of seconds before they realized Dan was not returning fire.

The service door was ajar. Dan ran through it. There was a yelp of fright. He had almost barged into a woman who was carrying a tray full of food.

"I wouldn't go out there if I were you," Dan said as he went past her. The woman said something in Burmese, and she stopped in her tracks.

Dan ran through another set of doors and he came into the steaming hotel kitchen. Huge brass and steel pots hung from the ceiling and massive fires blazed. The aroma of fried chicken hit his nostrils, but he did not care right now. Chefs in white hats and aprons shouted as Dan pushed them to one side. He had to get out of here. He needed to find Kim.

There was a loud crash as a stack of dishes and cutlery, stacked more than four feet high crashed to the floor. Dan ran over it and saw the doors to the exit in front. He ran into them full tilt, almost ripping the doors off their hinges.

He was out in the open. He took deep breaths of the humid air. He was in a courtyard, with a parking lot ahead of him, and a fence running along the perimeter. Beyond the perimeter, he could see the main road. Traffic was stuck, cars were honking. Dan heard a crash behind him and he spun around, weapon ready.

It was one of the gangsters. He was lifting his Uzi to his shoulder, pointing at Dan. Dan fired immediately, from instinct more than from aim. The bullet caught the man in the shoulder, and Dan shot him in the face before he went down. Dan had no time. His friends would be right behind him. And Dan did not know how many.

He ran to the cars, and jumped on top of a blue sedan. He climbed on the roof, bent his knees and jumped again, using all the strength in his rippling thigh muscles. His palms landed on the lip of the concrete fence, and he heaved himself up using the power in his wide shoulders.

He heard another shout behind him, and the whine of a bullet. He felt the buzz of a round close to his ear and ducked. He looked below. He was right on top of a freeway. There was no place to land. Traffic was moving slowly. A truck appeared below him. Its green roof was covered in tarpaulin, pulled tight with rope. The fall was more than ten feet. If he rolled off the truck, there was every chance one of the cars would run him over.

Dan heard the sound of another round, but he did not wait to see the result.

He jumped. Once he was airborne, he spread his arms to balance himself. He landed on the truck, and rolled forward, trying to grab the ropes. His feet slipped and he fell heavily on his side, sliding out to the side of the truck. Desperately, his fingers crawled for the ropes.

He grabbed one finally, just as he swayed out to the side, one hand clutching the rope. He slammed against the side of truck again, but he did not let go. He used both hands to hold on to the rope. Thankfully, it held its weight.

A man poked his head out the passenger side of the truck cabin.

Please be someone friendly.

The man said something loudly in Burmese that Dan did not understand. Then he ducked his head inside the cabin. Dan turned his head to look around him. The four lane freeway was girdled with traffic. He twisted front and back. Sweat blinded his eyes. The rope was burning his hand.

Then he saw it. A black Mercedes SUV. The car that arrived at the hotel to take Kim away. On the far-left lane, moving slowly. Dan checked the cars behind and around him. All moving at the same pace as the truck. He slid down the rope further. Then he jumped on the road. He could run, but he would lose the Mercedes. Traffic might speed up too, then he would be in trouble. Dan lifted himself up into the truck cabin door.

Two astonished Burmese men, skin tanned brown in the sun, both with cigarettes dangling from their lips, stared at him.

"Hey," Dan said. "Care to give me a lift?"

CHAPTER 17

The cabin door was open. Dan climbed aboard. The passenger protested, and Dan showed him his gun.

"I'm sorry to do this, but I need your ride."

The two men still looked at him like he had landed from another planet.

"Best if I do this alone," Dan said. He motioned with his gun. The driver understood, and frowned.

"No," he said in English.

Dan said, "Please don't make this hard for me."

The driver said in broken English, "My truck." He pointed to his bare chest.

"I know," Dan said. He kept his gun pointed at them and fished in his pockets. The two men stared back at him. Dan found some dollar bills, and pushed them towards the men. More than a hundred bucks, he guessed.

"Take it," Dan said. The passenger spoke to the driver. Eventually, the man took the money from Dan's hand.

Dan waved the gun again. "Now go. Move it!" The men stepped out of the carriage into the road.

Dan grabbed the gear stick and clashed it into place. With a roar, the truck lurched forward. Dan did not know what the truck had in the back. From its size, and the smell of timber, he guessed it was teak logs felled in the forests around Yangon.

The front bumper of the truck smashed against the car in front. Dan was going across the slow moving lanes. Cars honked and metal tore against metal with a ripping sound. Dan pressed the truck's horn. It was a loud shrill sound, like the whistle of a steam train. He yanked the massive wheel sharply to the left. A car slammed on its brakes behind him and went into his back. The tires of the car exploded with a deafening sound.

Dan continued to turn the wheel, then he pressed on the accelerator, heading diagonally across the mass of cars. He honked on the truck's horn repeatedly to warn the vehicles. Cars saw him coming and collided against each other in blind panic. Dan's left front bumper smashed into the fender of an SUV, ripping it off.

"Sorry," Dan shouted, as the driver came out on the road, shaking his fist. Dan kept his eyes on the black Mercedes. He was still two lanes away. Ahead of him, there was a turning off the freeway. This part of Yangon had been modernised recently. Far off to the right he could see sun glinting off the gold walls of the Shwedagon Pagoda, and flashing on the waters of Kandawgyi lake.

The roads were new, and Dan knew he had to get to the Mercedes before the car took the turning. Dan pressed on the gas again, and the truck surged forward like a behemoth. Again, he hit cars left and right, carving out a path of destruction ahead of him, leaving a trail of broken glass and ripped metal.

Dan wasn't worried about the cops. This was Myanmar. The cops would take their time coming, and when they did, they would be far less well armed than the gangsters up ahead.

The Mercedes began to move. Dan cursed. They had seen him. Dan honked his loud horn again, and cars began to move out of his way. The Mercedes backed up, then turned left on the emergency lane. It was heading for the turning. Dan clashed against several bumpers before he was finally free. He was just in time to see the Mercedes black rear disappear down the turning. Dan pressed on the gas, and the truck hurtled down the road.

Four cars ahead he could see the Mercedes. Traffic was thinner on this road. To his left, up ahead, stretched a huge expanse of corrugated tin and iron sheet buildings. A shanty town. Dan saw high rise metallic buildings on his right. They were going past downtown. The new modernised downtown of Yangon.

Sirens.

Dan looked in the rear-view and cursed. Two red police jeeps were behind him. Dan swung the big wheel, and pressed on the gas. Ahead of him, the Mercedes swung too, making a beeline for an exit ramp. Dan had three cars in front of him, one of them a slow moving van. The police jeep was getting closer. Dan swung out of his lane.

He crashed into the side of another car who could not get out of the way in time. It was a Honda, and it's tail pushed out into the lane, sending it into a spin. The Honda did two circles, tires leaving black marks on the asphalt, then slammed into a pickup truck on the other lane. A sedan behind the Honda pummelled into its back. The first police jeep was coming up too fast and could not avoid the collision. The three cars collided one after the other, the police jeep hitting the hardest.

Dan glanced in the rear-view at the exact moment of the police jeep colliding. He saw a policeman in his brown khaki uniform go flying in the air, arms outstretched. Dan turned into the ramp, leaving the carnage on the road behind. He wiped his palm across his forehead. The Mercedes was swerving in and out of traffic.

Industrial warehouses sprouted on the sides of the road. Ramshackle shanty buildings filled the gaps between them, with roadside bamboo huts serving snacks. They were going deeper into one of the many market streets of south Yangon. Soon, Dan knew, the throng of people would mean he would have to ditch the truck. The Mercedes would also have to stop. Which meant they were close to their destination.

The shops on the roadside became thicker, and human beings more numerous. Men in sarongs and bare chests, Hawaii T shirts, and women in their red yellow and orange *Htameins*, the colorful skirts that came down to cover their feet.

Dan barely registered any of it. His attention was focused on the Mercedes. He had come to a standstill. There was nowhere now for a truck this size to move. He watched in despair as the Mercedes beeped at people, and turned down a similarly crowded side road. Dan turned off the engine, put the keys in his pocket, and climbed down from the cabin. He ran to the left. The crowds were thicker still, but they had parted to let the Mercedes through. It had surged up ahead. Dan pushed his way through the crowd.

The Burmese are not a tall race, and Dan could see above their heads. More than two hundred feet away, Dan saw the Mercedes stop and the gangsters pile out. Their weapons were concealed. One of the them opened the back door, and four others lined up alongside, blocking Dan's view. But he caught a glimpse of Kim as she was pulled out of the rear. She stumbled, then straightened herself.

The men pulled her inside an alley. They disappeared from view again. Dan increased his pace, pushing past people as fast as he could. At the mouth of the alley, there was a wooden alcove built in, and a man sat inside with his legs folded, spreading tamarind juice on betel nut leaves. Triangular clay cups of green tea were laid outside on circular stands.

The alley was quieter inside. It was narrow, barely wide enough for three men to walk side by side. An open drain ran down the middle. Balconies and windows of buildings towered above Dan, He looked up and saw a little sliver of sky above. Dan took the gun out and released the safety catch. Anyone could fire on him from above.

Dan stopped and did a Sit Rep. The alley was empty, but the street behind him was crowded. That told him there was trouble ahead. He slowed his breathing, and gripped the butt of the Browning tighter. He stepped into the alley, scanning his arm around, looking for threats. He looked carefully at all the windows and balconies. He moved rapidly, and got to the end of the alley.

Beyond it, Dan faced a crossroad. All manner of corrugated iron and tin huts lay against one another in haphazard fashion. To his left, he saw a warehouse. The street was empty again. All the traffic noise and shops seemed to be behind him.

Dan watched the warehouse. Two men sauntered out from the open doorway. Both had AK-74's slung on their backs. The wore their shirts over it, but it was obvious. The men had tattoos on their arms, chest and neck. Dan faded behind the alley wall to hide himself.

He could shoot and take the two guards out. Easy. But his gun was not supressed and the sound would warn anyone inside. More importantly, they could whisk Kim away to another place. She was probably drugged, or beaten up. Dan tightened his jaws. He needed to move.

Dan leaned out a fraction and watched the guards again. They were smoking and talking. If they looked around they would see Dan on their far right. But they did not care.

Dan came out and walked casually across the road. The guards were about seventy yards to his left. He kept his head low and walked slowly. Fast movements attracted attention. Panic gave the game away. If they did recognize him, all he had to do was point and shoot. From this range, he would not miss.

Sweaty palm on the butt of the Browning in his pocket, Dan walked across the road. With a sigh of relief, he reached the other side.

The huts now covered him from view. He looked up across the huts at the warehouse. Not very big. About fifty yards in length. Dan spotted a window on the second floor. He could see lights and a fan in the ceiling. He went behind the huts and came out into the street. The guards were around the corner now, out of sight. They should be going around the perimeter, not smoking and chatting. Their mistake was his opportunity.

There was a fire escape. Dan went up it silently. He tried the door at the top, but it was locked. The window he had seen was next to the door.

Dan glanced down. If anyone looked up from the road, they would see him. He had to be quick. He stood up on the railing of the fire escape. He leaned out and his fingers reached the ledge of the window. He strained his neck. From what he could see, the room was an office. It was empty, but the fan was on, and papers were strewn on the table.

Dan grabbed the ledge with both hands, and jumped off. Now he was dangling from the window ledge, nothing but empty air below him for forty feet.

With the power of his shoulders, he pulled himself up like he was doing a body lift in the gym. The window ledge creaked. Dan got to the top, and hooked his right elbow over it. He got more leverage, and used his feet to lift himself up. He straddled the ledge, then swung his legs into the room.

He stood there panting. A table and a chair, with a bookshelf behind him. A map of Myanmar on the wall with portions marked in red.

Then the door opened, and a tall, wide man walked in.

CHAPTER 18

The man had Burmese features. He wore a sleeveless top, and his thick arms were covered in tattoos. He frowned, then opened his mouth to shout.

Dan had a second to think. Firing was out of the question. Men with sub machine guns would come running, and he would be trapped inside the room. Not a good idea.

He glanced down and saw a heavy crystal paper weight on the table. In a blur of movement, Dan picked up the object and hurled it across the room. His aim was good. The heavy weight struck the man between the eyes. He grunted and clutched his forehead. Dan crossed to the door in two quick steps and grabbed the man by the front of his vest. He pulled him in, kicking the door shut in the same movement. The man was dazed but he recovered quickly. He snarled as he fell against Dan's body. He grabbed Dan's shirt and the two of them tumbled over the table and onto the floor.

The man had thick biceps and his grip was strong. He bunched his knuckles into Dan's throat. Dan gagged and his nostrils flared. He hooked his fingers into the man's eyes. The man screamed and released his grip on Dan's throat. Instantly, Dan's right fist slammed like a sledgehammer to the side of the man's face. Dan followed it up with a series of right and left hooks, slamming the man's face from side to side like a punching bag. The man's arms fell useless to the side, and he slid down to the floor, eyes closed.

Dan stood up, dripping with sweat. He checked his weapons. He found a 6 inch knife on the man's belt line and put it in his own. He paused by the doorway. He could hear sounds outside, but the door was still closed. He opened it a fraction. The room opened out into a steel walkway that wrapped around the warehouse.

On the floor below, a group of men were unloading boxes from pallets. Two trucks stood side by side, their back doors open. The pallets was their load. Dan looked at the boxes on the pallets carefully. They were covered in a white cloth, with the initials WY99 inscribed on them. A lot more of the boxes were stacked in the far corner. Another team was stacking the boxes back up into the second lorry.

A storage and distribution center. Men with Kalashnikovs and Uzi sub machine guns patrolled around. Whatever those trucks carried, they had to be valuable.

Dan looked up. Only the iron roof with skylights on them. Steel girders crossed the roof space. Kim would not be on the ground floor. Unless she was tied up in one corner, but that would make her a witness to their operation.

He looked around and saw another office similar to his, directly opposite. The door opened, and a man came out. He looked different from the Burmese. He had a scar going from his left eye to his left cheek. Dan recognized the Chinese man he had seen before. Dan closed the door shut, retreating. He heard footsteps coming in his direction.

He tensed his jaws. The weapon was in his hand already. Now, he might not have a choice but to use it. The steps got closer. He crouched down behind the door, waiting. Closer. Less than ten feet away. Five feet. One foot.

Then he heard the steps fading. After ten seconds, he peeked out again. The man was going down a steel staircase two feet away from Dan's hiding place. He breathed in relief.

Dan stole out, and moved like a flitting shadow towards the office opposite. He stayed bent almost double so the men down below couldn't see him easily. He crouched underneath the office window. It was dark inside. He tried the door handle. It was locked. Dan glanced at the office where the gangster was still knocked out. But he would not be unconscious for long.

At the window he whispered, "Kim. Kim! It's Dan. Can you hear me?" He repeated himself twice before he heard a voice. A strangled whisper.

It was Kim's voice. "Yes. Dan, that you?"

"Yes. Can you get to the door?"

"My hands are tied behind my back. The door's locked. But wait." There was a sound of fumbling. Kim's voice was closer now. She said, "I might be able to open the window."

Dan waited. More sounds of scuffling, then the window opened a fraction. Dan could see Kim's back. She was sitting on a table and using her fingers to open the window.

There was a click, and the window opened. Dan prised his fingers inside. They touched hers. Dan gripped Kim's fingers and said, "It's ok. Let's get you out of here."

He opened the window wider. Kim got off the table and turned around. Her blonde hair was plastered over her face. Black grime masked her forehead, and her right cheek was swollen with a bruise that was turning purple.

Dan waved to her. "Come to the window, turn around and I can cut the ropes."

Kim moved quickly. When her hands were free, she put her hands on the window ledge and lifted herself. Dan lifted her up under the shoulders and she was out. Together, they crouched under the window. Kim had a look of relief on her face, and a fire in her eyes. With a determined look, she nodded at Dan. He pointed towards the office opposite. Kim nodded. She went first, and Dan followed with his gun.

They had almost reached the office when there was a shout from downstairs. All other sounds ceased abruptly. The ear shattering explosion of a gun suddenly rattled the warehouse. Rounds flew off the railings of the walkway.

"Inside, now," Dan yelled.

CHAPTER 19

Kim dived inside, flinging the door open. Bullets streaked the air around them. One of them burned a hole in Dan's lower pant as he launched himself in the air. He slammed against the doorframe, and felt Kim's hands land on his shirt collar, pulling him inside.

He had to give it to her – she had been through hell, but she was a tough cookie. Remarkably composed, and strong as well. She fell back on the floor, and Dan landed by her feet.

"Thanks…" Dan said, but the words died in his mouth. Behind Kim, the gangster he had just knocked out, was getting up. He had a gun in his hand, which he must have concealed. The small snub nosed compact gun was now lifting itself up, lining up on Kim's back.

Dan acted without thinking. He lifted himself up and threw himself at the man. The guy saw him coming, and made a mistake. He tried to adjust his aim to shoot Dan, instead of shooting Kim in the back.

Those two brief seconds' delay was all the time Dan needed. Dan had trained in the highest altitudes of the world for many years. In low oxygen atmospheres of the Himalayas, not far from Mount Everest. He had reflexes most human beings did not possess.

Two hundred and twenty pounds of hurtling muscle knocked the man against the wall. He fired the gun, but the shot went into the ceiling, ricocheting against the blades of the fan. Dan was up first. He kicked the gun away. He drew his own weapon. Without hesitation, he shot the man between the eyes. The 9mm round tore into the forehead, slamming the head down on the floor.

The sound of gunfire was getting louder. Kim was up already, and she knew the score. She had climbed on a chair, and was grappling on the window ledge.

"Can you make it to the fire escape?" Dan shouted.

"You bet," she shouted back. She went out the window, got her feet on the ledge at the bottom, then jumped for the railing of the fire escape. Dan watched her grab the railings, then swing. She lifted herself up, grunting, then climbed over the fire escape. She looked back.

"Keep going," Dan said. He wanted her to get a head start. Kim looked undecided, but then realized it made sense. She clambered down the fire escape.

Dan looked around the room. It was an office, but in one corner he found something interesting. Tin cans of gasoline. Three in total, each carrying a gallon. He had found a pack of cigarettes and a lighter when he had searched the dead man before. He picked up the lighter now. The sound of gunfire outside was getting louder. Dan opened the door a fraction. Bullets smashed into the doorway. Dan opened all the gasoline cans by the doorway, and tilted them towards the floor.

He withdrew, cocked his weapon, and returned fire. Heavy rounds were prising chunks of wood out of the door. There was not a great deal Dan could do with his handgun. He fired till he was out of ammo. Now he only had one magazine left, and he had feeling he would need that later.

The gasoline was now pouring out the door into the walkway and dripping to the floor below. Dan lit the lighter, and threw it outside the door. A blaze of yellow flames erupted, heat blasting up to the steel girders in the ceiling.

Shouts and screams filled the air outside. Dan ran back to the window, and levered himself up. He heard a crash inside, and the heat from the gasoline flames seared his fingertips as he hung onto the thin ledge. He bent his knees, and jumped. His fingers curled around the railing of the fire escape. He hauled himself over.

Fire and black smoke was rushing out the warehouse window. Two onlookers had stopped. One of them pointed at Dan. He flew down the stairs. Kim had gone straight on, following the path behind the warehouse that led into the shanty town. Dan sprinted in the same direction.

The huts were close to the street. Children played on the dirt, and women squatted, washing utensils by the drains. They looked up as Dan ran past. Then they pointed towards the burning warehouse. Dan did not look back.

He needed to find Kim. He came to a crossing. There was a shop advertising Wi-Fi and broadband, and a few more selling food. Dan looked left and right. Which way had Kim gone?

Dan heard a shrill whistle, then a shout behind him. A khaki policeman, gun in hand, was charging towards him. The cop was not alone. There was a whole horde of them. Behind them Dan could see yellow flames curling up into the sky, smearing the horizon with black smoke.

"Welcome to the party," Dan muttered. He ran straight on, this time shouting Kim's name.

*****

Kim was exhausted. She had run till she could run no more. Her hands were at her waist, squeezing. She was bent double, sucking great breaths of air into her lungs. She coughed, and a trail of mucus dripped form her mouth. She wiped her mouth and stood up. Behind her, she heard an explosion. The warehouse was burning.

Briefly, she thought about Dan. She wanted to go back and help him. But he had told her to run. Maybe because he wanted to create a diversion. She didn't know for sure, but her gut told her to follow Dan's advice.

She came to a crossing. She looked left and right, then carried on straight. She had no idea where she was going. People were coming out of the shanty huts to look at the burning warehouse. Many of them stared at her. Kim paid them no attention. She kept running till ahead of her, she saw a car turn in and stop. Kim skidded to a halt herself.

It was a red police jeep. Four policemen piled out. They had not seen her as yet. But all they had to do was look. Kim glanced around wildly. This place must be crawling with cops, she realized. Next to her was the door of a hut. It was open.

Kim swallowed. She had no other choice. She composed herself, then stepped inside. There was a small opening like a cubby hole to her right. To her left, a small dark living room. A sofa and a bed on the floor. She glanced at the cubby hole. A TV was on, and on a bunk bed, there sat a little girl, watching TV. About ten years old. She had a floral dress, and bright red flowers in her hair.

She turned and looked at Kim with large eyes as she walked in. Her mouth opened wide. Kim put her finger to her lips in the universal sign to keep quiet. The girl would not stop staring at her. Then Kim realized why.

It was Maya. The girl gave a small cry and jumped down from the alcove. She came forward.

"It's you!" she said to Kim.

Once again, Kim was stunned, transfixed. This little Burmese girl spoke and acted just like Sarah. It was surreal. Kim swallowed, and wiped the sweat from her face.

"What are you doing here?" she asked Maya.

Maya said, "My friend lives here. I don't have TV where I live, so I came to watch here. My friend has just gone to get water."

Loud voices sounded outside. In an urgent voice, Kim said, "Maya, can you help me? Dan and I are in trouble. The police are out looking for us."

Maya hooked her eyebrows up. She dropped her voice to a whisper. "What have you done?"

Just like Sarah used to.

Kim blinked and swallowed. "I'll…"

Her words were interrupted by a loud rattling sound outside. Maya's eyes widened. She lifted up a cotton sheet, showing Kim a hole underneath the alcove. A hole large enough for a man to hide in.

Kim understood instantly. She huddled inside the hole, and Maya dropped the cloth. Maya walked to the door quickly. Kim heard voices. A man said something and Maya spoke back in a confident voice. They spoke for a while, then there was silence.

After what seemed like an eternity Maya came back. She lifted the cloth and bent her head.

"It's OK," she said. "The police have gone."

Kim climbed out. "I need to find Dan."

Maya nodded. "Come with me," she said. Maya opened the back door of the hut. There was a swampy land outside, and a wooden walkway across it. Across the swamp there was a brick building and it had two floors with a roof. Clothes were hanging on rails outside. Maya ran to a staircase at the side, and motioned to Kim. She pointed her finger upwards. Kim understood.

She ran to the staircase and climbed upstairs with Maya. The second floor was a roof. A simple brick fence was erected all around it. Kim looked down and realized why Maya had brought her here. She could see all the streets in the shanty town. The entire place was full of ground level hovels. This was one of the few double story buildings around.

Together they searched for Dan. Finally, Kim saw him.

When she did, her blood froze. Dan had come across the crossing to where Kim had been hiding. He had slowed down, and was looking left and right. For her. But Dan had not seen the two figures in a balcony above him. Both had AK-105 rifles in their hand, and they were getting ready to fire on Dan.

"DAN!" Kim screamed as loud as she could.

CHAPTER 20

Dan heard it. He snapped his head to the sound. So did the gangsters. Dan looked towards Kim, and registered the pointed hand. He realized immediately that he was in imminent danger, or Kim would not take the risk of shouting and exposing her own position. He glanced up, and saw the gangsters.

The gangsters had been distracted by Kim's shout. When they looked back down, Dan had disappeared. One of them swore, lifted up his gun, and fired a volley of shots towards Kim and Maya. Kim grabbed Maya in a bear hug and crashed to the floor.

Dan had fallen to the ground, and rolled over. As soon as he was up, he heard the gunfire. It wasn't directed at him. Which only meant…rage boiled and exploded inside him.

The door to the building where the gangsters were hiding was right in front of him. He heard the screams of women after the shots were fired. The police would be on the case soon.

Something told Dan the gangsters would not mind that.

Dan got inside the open door, and closed it silently. He flattened himself against the wall. A cement staircase went up to the second floor in front of him. The door to the ground floor was shut. He released the Browning's safety catch. Like a ghost, Dan crept up the stairs.

He heard a scuffling sound, then the sound of low voices. Then footsteps, coming down the stairs. Dan went low on the stairs, and pointed the Browning up towards the corner of the landing, where the gangsters would appear. He did not have to wait long. They were in a rush to find him. But they did not expect to run into him on the staircase.

The head of the first gangster appeared. Dan could have taken the shot easily. But he waited. The element of surprise was on his side. The second guy was close behind his friend. The first man gave a start when he saw Dan crouching below. He shouted and raised his gun, but by then his friend was on the landing as well. It was too late.

Dan's first bullet ripped out the first gangsters eye socket and exited out the back of the head, splattering his brains over the wall. A splash of red appeared on the wall. Before the bullet had lodged on the wall Dan had moved his aim, and the second guy got a bullet right between the eyebrows. Both bodies clattered to the floor within three seconds. Keeping his gun trained on them, Dan approached. He frisked them quickly. They had similar tattoos on the arm and chests to the gangsters he had seen in the warehouse.

Dan eyed the AK-105's. Tough and durable, they were excellent weapons. But he needed to escape with the minimum of attention. Having a gun over his back didn't sit well with that plan. He did find two handguns on them, one of them a Glock 22 with Chinese letters on the barrel. Magazine full. He was putting the gun in his waist belt when he heard a noise downstairs. He turned around, ready to shoot.

"Don't shoot!" came the scream. It was Kim. Dan sighed in relief. He came quickly down the stairs. The sound of the unsuppressed Browning handgun had been like mini explosions in the enclosed space.

"We need to get out of here, now," Dan said. Then he spotted Maya. "What the..."

Kim explained quickly. Dan looked from Maya to Kim. She read the look on his face.

Kim said, "We need to take her with us."

Before Dan could reply, shouts came from the street. Maya tugged at Kim's shirt. "This way, come on," the girl shouted.

Dan sprinted after Maya and Kim. They crossed the street into the hut where Maya was watching TV. Dan's shoulder caught the flimsy tin door, making the ramshackle hut shake. He had to lower his head as he entered. Maya and Kim almost collided with a woman who was standing in the living room. The woman was Burmese, and had a shocked expression on her face. A girl of Maya's age was clinging to her leg, her eyes large with fear.

Maya spoke quickly to the woman. Kim began to say something as well, but it did not work. The woman panicked.

"Get out of here," she screamed in Burmese. "Get out!"

Dan heard a chorus of voices behind him, getting louder. The woman's shout had been heard by the crowd outside.

Dan said to Maya, "How do we..."

But Maya was already running for the back, pulling Kim with her. They splashed across the duckboards on the small swampland again. Maya led them straight past the back of some single story abodes. Some had cement structures and tin rooves, others were made of sheets of iron entirely. Dan looked behind him, and his worst fears were confirmed. A bunch of khaki police uniforms were chasing them.

"Maya," he shouted as he ran. "We need to get transport. They're behind us, and they're gonna come around the main street to cut us off."

"OK," Maya yelled. "Follow me."

They took a left into the narrowest alley Dan had ever seen in his life. Barely enough space between two brick buildings for him to fit through.

They came out on the other side to the bustle of traffic and a crowd of pedestrians. Shops with bamboo awnings, and short wooden benches occupied the street. The shops sold everything from DVD, posters to women's clothing.

Men in *lyongi*, or sarongs, sat on the benches, sipping green tea and watching satellite TV in the small cafe's. Some of them looked up with curiosity as the three of them rushed past, dodging the shoppers.

They came upon a rack of motorbikes and scooters, the commonest form of streetcars that Dan had seen in the narrow roads of Yangon.

"Stop," Dan shouted. He had spotted a bike whose motor was still running. The owner had gone into a shop to settle a bill. The key was still in the ignition. Dan jumped on it. Kim followed, and Maya was sandwiched between them.

"Hold on!" Dan shouted. He kicked off the support rest, and twisted the handles. The engine revved, the rear wheel skidded, and the bike shot forward into the crowd. People screamed and ran for cover. Dan bleeped the horn, desperate to avoid hitting someone. The path ahead of him cleared. Dan concentrated on the road. His hair was flying into his eyes, and he had to keep shaking his head. Maya's head was jammed against his back, and Kim's fingernails were digging into the sides of his shirt.

They had gone more than two hundred yards, when the red police jeep appeared in front of them. The cops saw him at the same time. The jeep lurched forward, scattering people around it.

From the corner of his eye, Dan saw a road ahead of him on the left. He made a quick calculation. The jeep might get to him before he could take the turning. But he had to go for it.

The only other option was to go straight, which would mean right into the jeep's path.

Dan hooked towards the left and the jeep realized. It accelerated suddenly, setting itself on a collision course with the bike. Dan set his jaws. His fingers tightened around the handles. He heard Kim shout something but he could not make out the words. Her fingernails dug tighter on his shirt.

Dan wrung the handles for all its worth, gunning for the turning.

Pedestrians crossing the road scattered, some diving out of the way. From the left of his vision, Dan could see the red blur of the Jeep rushing at him, about to spear him with its menacing front bumper.

CHAPTER 21

Dan hunched his shoulders close together and gritted his teeth. Wind was blowing into his watering eyes, hazing his vision, but he didn't care. The jeep careened forward, and almost touched the zipping wheels of the bike, missing it by inches.

Dan went into the turning, nearly skidding into the ground. He corrected the wheels at the last minute, and managed to keep his balance. He shot forward, bleeping his horn at the traffic as loudly as he could.

The jeep was not so lucky. The police vehicle was a victim of its own momentum. It missed Dan's bike, and slammed into the front of a shop. Benches and tables were smashed, and the jeep bore right inside the shop, exploding glass and destroying the flat screen TV on the stand. Luckily, the people in the shop had moved out already. The TV fell with a loud smash on The driver's head.

Dan felt Maya lift her head up. Her hands pressed on his back. Dan kept going. They were coming out of the market place. The human traffic was getting thinner, but motor cars were getting more numerous. Dan pulled over.

Kim leaned over and said, "We need to head for the Embassy."

Dan nodded. "Good idea. Anywhere else is not safe."

Maya said, "Head up north, towards the University and Inle Lake. Just go straight, we are still downtown, but you are facing north."

"Roger that."

Dan crossed an intersection, and it looked familiar. He saw the signs. Pyay Road, the same road he had come down chasing Kim's kidnappers. The wide lanes allowed easy flow of traffic. To his far right, the ever present gold tower of the Shwedagon Pagoda gleamed bright in the early evening light, pointing to the darkening sky like a beacon.

Dan dodged around the traffic, speeding as much as he could. Traffic laws in Yangon were lax to say the least, but he did not want another police jeep chasing him. After fifteen minutes, the lights of the palace on the banks of the large Inle lake began to wink at them. Kim directed Dan to the US Embassy on the banks of the lake.

Dan braked to a stop, keeping an eye all around him. Light had faded, and so had visibility. The area around him was brightly lit, but that still presented deep pools of darkness where inquisitive men with cell phones could be hiding.

He did not doubt for a moment that the Embassy was under surveillance by the men chasing after Kim. He figured she had been under their radar right from the day she landed. Along with the rest of her team.

Kim walked back after a lengthy discussion with the MP. A uniformed MP came around and shone a light on Dan, then on Maya. He asked Dan who he was, and Dan spoke the truth – an American on holiday in south Asia.

After some more deliberation, they were finally allowed in. Kim used her creds to get into the lobby.

"Stay here," Kim said to Dan and Maya. The girl was looking around the bright lights of the lobby.

She looked at Kim in silence. Kim knelt down in front of her. "You're going to be OK," she said. "Have a seat here."

Maya and Dan sat down at the large sofas on the side of the lobby. Dan spotted a drinks machine. He used his coins to get a drink for Maya.

Maya took the drink from him and drank in silence. She looked down at her hands. Dan had never looked after a child before. He didn't know what to do, but he felt sorry for her. Emotional closeness was alien to Dan. But he had a protective urge that he could not dismiss easily. Somehow, Maya had grown close to him. For some unknown reason, he cared for her.

He should have known. No one close to him survived for long. They got into danger just by knowing him. He was on holiday, and he had let his guard down. A kid could not harm him, he had decided.

Dan sighed. *Well, shit. Look at her now.*

Gently, Dan put an arm on her shoulder. She was trembling. Dan lowered his head.

"Are you OK?" he asked. Maya did not answer, but her shoulders heaved even more. Dan left his seat and went down on one knee in front of her. Tears were running down Maya's eyes.

"What…what will happen to me?" the girl gasped.

Dan took the drink off her hand and put it on the floor. Then he did something strange. He didn't think about it, nor had he planned it. It just happened.

He leaned forward, and Maya encircled her tiny, skeletal hands around his neck. She hugged his neck, and rested her small head on his massive shoulders.

Dan's hand came up behind her, and stayed in the air for a moment. Then it pressed down gently on her back. He hugged the girl back. He felt the warmth of her tears on his shoulder.

Dan opened his eyes and stared at the well-lit lobby, and the darkness outside. What was he doing? Emotions were alien to him. He knew the way of violence, and the necessity of orders. He thought nothing of looking a dying man in the eye and pulling the trigger.

His heart never came into the equation. His soul was made of stone, and he used its hardness to hurt people. It was the best weapon he possessed.

Yet, what he was doing now came to him naturally. Instinctively. It was almost as if this little girl's tears had the power that no bullet ever possessed – to soften the rock like interior of his being.

That dark, ominous place where even he was afraid to go. When the violence unleashed inside him, he could, and would, do anything. That was how he had always lived.

Until tonight. The first time he had comforted a child.

Well, that's just…weird, Dan thought.

He sat back, and looked at Maya. She was still sniffing. She dried her eyes and looked at Dan.

Dan said, "You'll be fine, don't worry."

Maya shook her head miserably. "I cannot go back. They will hunt me and then send me to…"

"What's going on?" Kim's voice said behind Dan. In a flash Kim was kneeling before Maya. Dan saw a ginger haired woman behind them. He stood up.

Kim was speaking in a low voice to Maya. She held Maya's hands tightly in hers. Dan saw Maya nodding her head as she listened to Kim.

The other woman held her hand out. "Hi, I'm Mary Goldsmith. I work with Kim."

Dan considered Mary for a few seconds, then shook the offered hand briefly. If Mary worked with Kim, that meant she was also a CIA agent. Dan did not like intelligence agencies. They had their own agenda, and pushed men like him to do their dirty work.

Dan suspected everyone who worked inside this building. That included Mary.

Kim stood up. She introduced them.

Kim said, "My other colleague, Estefan, has gone to meet a source who knows about David."

Dan said, "Hope this source will be different from the other two."

Mary gave Dan a look. She said, "This time, Estefan took a government officer with him. He didn't want Kim to go again. He feels bad about what's happened."

Dan said, "Where have they gone?"

"To a public place. At the Shwedagon Pagoda complex."

Kim glanced at her watch. "He left half an hour ago. We should head down to see him."

Dan said, "No. If his asset sees us as well then he might make a run for it. We can go, but need to stay out of sight." He asked Mary, "The pagoda complex is large. Do you know which entrance he has gone to?"

Mary said, "The southern entrance."

Dan nodded. "I know that place." He looked at Kim. "What do you want to do?"

Kim said, "Maya stays here. Mary will look after her. I need to see Estefan."

CHAPTER 22

The Southern Gate of the temple complex that make up the Shwedagon Temple was a marvel in itself. Two huge lion-like statues, called leogryphs, guarded the step leading up to the gate. The lions glistened white, with gold girdles shining in their bodies in intricate patterns.

The man known as Li Yonping watched the man from the American Embassy climb up the steps. He rubbed the scar that stretched from his left eye to the lip. A *banshi* or curved knife injury, during his old Triad days. Before he had found the Communist Party. Or the Party found him, to be more precise. If he had not left the Triad, he might be dead now, Li mused. But then, many Triad members had close connections with the Party. Like himself.

Li took a deep drag from the Classic cigarette, and threw it on the road. It sparked as it hit the asphalt, then continued to smoke. Li walked slowly past the noisy hawkers and shop keepers selling replicas and T shirt for tourists. Li did not like coming to the Southern gates. Too crowded, and too many tourists. But today was different.

He watched as his mark topped the flight of stairs. Li increased his pace. Shop keepers called out to him, hands outstretched. Li couldn't see the man any more. He hurried up. At the top, a flat marble landing led to the numerous temples and shrines inside. Many were made of gold, and the lights overhead had an almost dizzying effect. The bright shine sparkled and lit up the night with an ethereal yellow glow. The main Shwedagon Pagoda with the 99 meter high minaret, made of solid gold, was hidden from Li's view.

But he was not here for the scenery. He looked left and right. He found the man leaning against one of the supports holding up a jade and gold decorated Tibetan roof. He was wearing a white jacket, not uncommon in the heat. But Li also knew it was a signal. For the person he was here to meet. Li watched as the man lit a cigarette, then coughed. Li smiled. Not used to smoking. Another signal.

Li walked backwards, then behind the man, in the darkness where people sat, staring at the brightly lit temple complex before them. He waited for five minutes, sitting very still. Then his patience was rewarded. A Burmese man approached the man from the Embassy. They said something to each other. Must be a password.

Li stiffened. His whole objective was to stop information from changing hands, and probably, that was happening already.

Silently, Li took out the bottle from his jacket pocket. He put on a pair of gloves. He took out a cotton handkerchief, unscrewed the bottle, and very carefully pored a drop onto the handkerchief. Keeping his face averted, and not breathing, he closed the bottle, and folded the handkerchief. He put the bottle back into his jacket pocket, and kept his gloved fingers closed over the handkerchief.

The two men were preparing to leave. Li stood up. In swift steps, he crossed the ten feet of distance separating him from them. The Burmese man was facing him, and saw him coming. His eyes widened. Li cursed himself. He had come up too quickly.

Now, he could only kill one.

The Burmese man turned, and ran into the center of the temple complex, then disappeared from sight in the crowd of worshippers. The man from the Embassy turned quickly, but he was far too late. The man lifted up a hand, fearing an attack, but Li casually struck the hand down, slapping the forearm away with his open palm. His right hand had the handkerchief open, and he thrust it into the man's face, pressing his head back against the support.

Two seconds was more than enough. VX was the most poisonous substance known to man. An liquefied nerve gas that paralysed muscles in the fraction of a second. If inhaled it acted on the lungs even quicker, and the victim stopped breathing within twenty seconds.

Li pressed the handkerchief to the man's face for more than five seconds. Then, just as quickly as he had come, he put the handkerchief back, and walked off.

The man stood still, leaning against the support, looking dazed. Then his knees folded, and his eyes took a faraway, dreamy expression. His eyes remained open, but his chest rose one last time, then he stopped breathing forever.

By that time, Li Yonping was in his car, speeding out of downtown.

*****

Kim and Dan hurried up the stairs of the South Entrance. Dan had never been inside the Shwedagon, and briefly, his eyes took in the majestic, two thousand year old golden glory in front of him.

Then his eyes fell on the crowd gathered underneath a darkened awning facing the temple complex.

"This way," he nudged Kim. They walked over quickly, and pushed their way to the middle.

"Shit," Kim exclaimed as she went down on her knees.

Estefan was lying in a curious position, his fingers crooked as if he was trying to claw the marble floor. His lips were drawn back, like he was in the middle of saying something. His eyes were hollow, vacant. Estefan was dead.

Dan was not looking down. He was looking around.

There was no sign of trauma. It was obvious no one had heard a sound. The assassin could still be around, or his team could be. All assassins moved in teams of at least two. Dan caught a few faces looking at him, but no one suspicious.

No one with the hard glittery eyes of a killer who looked away from him slowly. Dan walked back out towards the steps. He whirled around. He ran to the left of the platform. Nothing. Something told him they had just missed the killer.

He ran back to Kim. She was still kneeling, and her head was down. Her hand was on Estefan's face, closing his eyes. Dan gave her a moment. Then he knelt down beside her. People crowded around them. The cops had not arrived as yet.

Dan touched Kim on the shoulder. "Have you searched?" He asked.

Kim shook her head. Her eyes were like steel, her lips clamped in a tight line.

Dan leaned forward and went through Estefan's jacket and pant pockets. He found a scroll of paper in the left jacket inside pocket. He opened it up. It was a map. He rolled it back. They could examine it later.

He heard a shrill whistle, and a silence fell on the crowd. Police began to push through the crowd.

When the first policeman arrived, Kim introduced herself, and showed them her ID.

"I want this man to be taken to nearest hospital, right now," she said.

CHAPTER 23

Kim looked at the palm fronds moving outside in the breeze. She opened the window of the first floor office, feeling the cool wind flow in. She closed her eyes, but nothing relieved the headache. She looked around her, and her eyes fell on the small, sleeping figure of Maya.

Momentarily, she forgot her troubles. She walked around the large open plan office till she found a shawl draped around the back of a chair. She picked it up, made sure it was clean, then draped it over Maya. The girl slept on the sofa, hand tucked her chin, knees curled up. Gently, Kim touched her hair. Maya's chest rose up and down gently as she breathed, fast asleep.

Kim walked back to her table, dimming the lights around the sofa. Dan was looking at the map. A table lamp shone next to him, spilling light on the table.

Without lifting his head Dan said, "This has coordinates. Do you have any geo spatial software here?"

Kim nodded, and switched on her computer screen. Dan waited for the software to load up, then read her the coordinates. Kim entered them, then watched the screen as the image zoomed to a part of Central Myanmar. The satellite image showed the paler hills on either side, and the deep green of the fertile plains drained by the Irrawaddy river.

Kim said, "A place called Bagan." She looked at Dan. "What else does the map show?"

"A line, marked with crosses. Starts from the coast, near this place called Sittwe." Dan showed her. Sittwe was on the Bay of Bengal, the triangle of the Indian Ocean formed between India, Myanmar and Thailand.

Kim squinted. "Goes all the way across the border into China. What the hell is it?"

Dan shrugged. "Whatever it is, I reckon it leads us closer to David."

Kim pressed her hands on her temples. "Goddamit." Her eyes were closed.

Dan said, "Let it go."

Kim's eyes opened. "What do you mean?"

"I know what you are doing. Estefan's death was not your fault. He was doing his job. It's a shame it happened, but you know it does happen."

Kim stared at Dan for a few seconds. His hair fell over his forehead, and his dark eyes moved stared at her intently. It was like he could hear her think.

Kim caught her breath. Then she said, "Who are you?"

Dan's face did not change. "Is that so important now? I'm on your side, that's all."

Kim felt irritated. "If I find out you are CIA, I swear to God…"

Dan interrupted her. "I'm not CIA. I can promise you that."

"Need to know, huh?"

"Something like that." Dan transferred his attention back to the map. "Bagan is about 8 hours by road from here, or we can take the train. I say we take the road. Gives us more options."

Kim said, "We get there early dawn and then scout out the map locations. Hopefully find some clues about David."

"If not, we follow the map, see where it leads to."

Kim looked at Maya. Dan followed her gaze. He said softly, "You care about her don't you?"

Kim said, "So do you."

Dan looked away and said, "I didn't mean that. I mean the way you look at her, like she means something to you."

Their eyes locked. Neither looked away. Kim said in a low voice, "Guess we all have our secrets, Dan."

Dan said, "Where will she stay?"

"With Mary. The apartments are in the diplomatic enclave, and they are guarded."

"Let's hope they stay that way. Can you trust Mary?"

"As much as I can trust you." Kim stared at Dan for a while, then cracked a smile.

Dan said, "I trust no one but myself."

He got up and walked to the water machine. He came back with two plastic glasses and gave one to Kim.

Dan said, "Let's get moving."

Kim took the glass of water and drained it. She indicated towards Maya. "You take her, and I'll get Mary."

"OK."

Dan knelt at the sofa. Maya was asleep, oblivious to the real world. Dan felt that curious sensation again, like he was staring at something infinitely peaceful. A sleeping child.

He shook his head. He was tired himself, and getting old. Carefully, he slipped his arms under Maya, and lifted her up in his arms. She stirred in her sleep, and said something incoherent.

Dan walked out the office with Maya in his hands. Her head rested against his chest. Kim was standing at the doorway with Mary. They took the elevator down. An MP was waiting for them in the lobby. He took them to a waiting black Mercedes Benz. The MP opened the door, and the two women slipped in. Kim stretched her arms out, and with some effort, Dan transferred the sleeping girl to her lap.

The roads around Inle Lake were empty. The Shwedagon Pagoda glowed in the distance behind them. Houses on the hills around the lake twinkled in the warm night. They arrived at the diplomatic enclosure within ten minutes.

When Maya was asleep in the guest bed, the two women and Dan stood in the living room.

Kim said, "We need a few hours rest. We haul ass tomorrow first light. If we get there in the daytime it give us more time to explore the place."

Dan nodded. "Makes sense. Guess I'll head back to my hotel then."

Kim said, "No way. They now have your place under surveillance for sure." She hesitated and looked at Mary.

Mary said, "No problem. You can take the couch, Dan. Kim can sleep on the sofa bed in the guest room, next to Maya. I have my room."

Kim was relieved. She sneaked a look at Dan, and their eyes met briefly. Kim said, "Good. Let's get some shut eye."

CHAPTER 24

Arlington, Virginia
USA

Solomon Barney let his wife Dorothy fix his tie for him. Married for nigh on twenty years, most of it happily. The bits that were spent in arguing and disagreeing had only made the marriage stronger, for it had led them to respect each other's differing points of view. Solomon took a practical view of these things. Life could have been far worse.

Dorothy pressed a hand on his chest, and they kissed briefly. He pushed back a strand of her coppery hair.

Solomon said, "You know, sometimes I wonder."

"About what?"

"If it is right to do what is necessary."

Dorothy said, "That depends on why it is necessary in the first place."

Solomon smiled. "Because it is the right thing to do."

"That's sounds like a dog trying to catch its own tail. Is that the right answer?"

Solomon shook his head. "I don't think so. I guess what I mean is, it has to be necessary for us."

Dorothy sighed. "Necessary for the country."

"Correct."

Dorothy looked her husband in the eye. "It all depends Sol, if it seems right to you. Don't do anything you don't want to."

"I'll bear that in mind Mrs. Barney."

Solomon walked down to the driveway of their two storey colonial wood brick house. He waved at his neighbour and checked the mailbox. As he got into his Audi A4, he looked at his house. Ever since his two daughters had left for college, most of the rooms of the five bedroom detached house was empty. Someday, Dorothy and he would sell up and move out. Maybe to Florida. He wondered what life would be like then. He might get bored. He needed to occupy his time doing something.

He fired up the Audi, and took off smoothly down the road. It was almost half eight in the morning by the time he got into the office. Spring was coming to Virginia, and he had enjoyed the drive, cheered by the first green leaves appearing on the roadside trees.

He checked his emails, finding nothing of importance. His mind was occupied on something else. After some deliberation, he picked up the phone. He dialled John Hymers' direct line. The Deputy Director of the DO. One down from the Director himself. The Director's name was not made public. Those who knew his identity were on a need to know basis only. It was a long standing tradition of the NCS.

Hymers answered. In five minutes, Solomon was knocking at his door.

"Come in," said Hymers. Solomon walked in to find Hymers on his own. The curtains of the long windows were raised to let in light. Through them, Solomon had a good view of the woods that surrounded the building. Behind the chair there was a photo of the current President, and it was flanked on either side by photos of Hymers standing with other CIA Agents. The office was huge, with a conference desk to the left. On the far left wall, a large flat screen TV was stuck to the wall, used for teleconferencing. Maps of various parts of the world were framed on the walls, between rows of brown bookcases.

"Sit," said Hymers. Solomon did as he was told. "What is it?" Hymers asked.

"This operation on which we just sent Kimberly to Myanmar. I had some questions about it."

"Like what?"

"The Tonkin Protocol. Have you heard about it?"

Hymers face did not change. "Can't say I have," he said. "Why do you ask?"

"The team in Yangon have found several emails sent to and from David Harris' account which have that as their subject. The actual emails are encrypted. They can't get the key as yet. When they do, I think we might find the content has vanished. The programmers have already said the emails looks tamper proof."

Hymers asked, "Any word from Kim?"

"Just what I told you now, and that she has met an ex-military guy called Dan Roy."

Hymers raised his eyebrow. "Met?"

"He saved her life when she was attacked, and later kidnapped. It's bad down there. You got me to send Kim. I'm glad she's getting some help from somewhere, 'cos she sure as hell isn't getting any from us."

They stared at each other for a few seconds. Then Hymers stood up. "Let's go for a walk."

They strolled out into the grounds, and walked for five minutes in silence. Solomon said, "The Tonkin Protocol. Tell me about it."

"Can I be honest with you?"

"Are you asking me to believe you?"

The two men stared at each other. They had been in the same class as rookie agents in Quantico, Virginia. Hymers had always been a skilled negotiator, and not as frank or outspoken as Solomon. It was always the more diplomatic ones who got ranked higher in the CIA. Despite that, the two men had worked together often, and respected each other.

Hymers said, "I just want to be honest with you, Sol."

"That's why we had to come out here."

"I don't know what the Tonkin Protocol is."

Solomon remained silent. When Hymers said nothing, he asked, "You got me out here to tell me that?"

Hymers said slowly, "I know that Harris knew about it. He was sent out there."

Solomon said. "What for?"

"Sol, if I knew, I would tell you."

"So who knows? The Director and DNI?" The Directorate of Operations had close links with the Director of National Intelligence, the President's chief security advisor.

Hymers said, "All I have heard is rumors. It's something top secret."

"Bullshit, John. You know."

Sol thought for a while. "This guy, David Harris, now that he has been caught, he becomes a liability, right? Depending on how much he knows, of course. Maybe there's a circuit breaker. David only knows about a small part of the operation. But still, what's gonna happen if he falls into the wrong hands?"

Hymers was silent. Sol said, "So you sent Kim down for what? Find out where David was and then send a hit squad out to finish them both?"

"No, Sol. We need to get them both back."

"Bullshit. This David is lost in the jungles somewhere. Probably held captive in one of the ethnic conflict zones of Myanmar. You can't send down a hit squad till you know where the hell he is."

Hymers breathed in fresh air, then exhaled. "That was not the purpose of sending Kim, Sol. It was purely to find David."

"And then David meets with an accident, right? Or they both do. Jesus Christ, John, what the fuck you trying to do?"

Hymers had a pained expression on his face. "Sol, come on. Why would I sacrifice one good agent for another?"

Sol looked away and kicked a small stone. It went skittering into the undergrowth.

Hymers said, "John, my orders are to keep Tonkin Protocol alive. Not kill it. Do you understand? I need them both back alive."

"Your order? What, you work for the army now? We work in intelligence, John. Forgive the cliché, but it's our job to know things."

"Sol." Hymers stopped pacing, and the two men looked at each other. There was a frank appraisal in their eyes, but both knew the reality of their jobs. The truth was always convoluted, a grey, obscure landscape that evaded easy capture.

Hymers said, "I'm on your side, Sol. You got that?"

After a pause, Sol said, "Alright. But we need to know more about this Tonkin shit. I stay in contact with Kim, but only if I know she is going to be safe."

Sol had played his card. He knew Hymers had no other way of contacting Kim. She would become suspicious if John Hymers suddenly took over the communication links from Solomon.

Hymers nodded in silence, and the two men walked back towards the massive hulk of the CIA HQ building.

CHAPTER 25

North-eastern Shan State
Mynamar-China Border

Henry Deng slowed the Nissan Cruiser as they drove down the hill. Beneath them the sluggish brown waters of the Pyutaw river meandered over a bend. A convoy of trucks, six in total, stood at the head of the steel girdled road bridge that spanned the river. A military checkpoint stood by the bridge, with the gates lowered. Soldiers in green fatigues stood by the gate, armed with QB-7 sub machine guns.

Deng drove down to the last truck and parked behind it. A cloud of dust followed him down the hill. Li Yonping opened the passenger side door and came out. Together they walked down the road, past the truck.

Three of the drivers were leaning against one of the trucks, smoking. They saw Deng and straightened. Deng was wearing his usual cream colored safari suit, and sunglasses. He stopped in front of the drivers.

"*Ni hao Shangsi,*" one of the drivers said in Mandarin. Hello, Boss.

Deng said, "*Ni hao.* What is the problem?"

"We don't know, *Shangsi,*" The driver said. "We have stopped for the last 6 hours. They wanted to search the truck, but you had forbidden it, so we told them not to."

"Good," Deng said. "Stay here. You will be moving soon."

Deng and Li walked over to the knot of soldiers. One of them had the white chevrons of a Captain on the sleeve of his green combats. He turned as his men indicated Deng approaching. The man feigned nonchalance but Deng knew he was nervous. Deng walked up to him, and stopped very close to the man.

"Captain," Deng said, "Why have my trucks been stopped?"

The man shrugged. "You need to speak to General Sein Tho, Mr. Deng."

The soldiers around them kept a watchful eye. Li stood behind Deng, staring back at the soldiers.

Deng asked, "Where is the General?"

"In the office," the Captain indicated the small hut next to the check post.

Deng moved away without a word. He opened the bamboo door of the hut without knocking. Dappled sunlight fell through the open straw windows on the walls, made of triple thick layers of bamboo shafts. The wooden floor creaked as Deng and Li approached the figure seated at the large desk at the end. A table fan fluttered the lapels of the brown uniform General Sein Tho wore. His shiny, peaked brown cap rested on the table next to him.

Deng walked up to the table and rested his knuckles on the surface.

"S ngya s nyya a bhayya say raw sotae lotenaykya?" He growled in a low voice in Burmese. What the fuck do you think you are doing?

Sein Tho took some time to look up from the paper he was reading. He tossed it aside, and stretched, not looking Deng in the eye. Then he said, "Our agreement was for six trucks a day. Now you are sending twenty every day. The tax goes up."

"You said the tax was for the whole day, not per truck."

"That was before traffic from your truck started blocking up the whole road. You know this road leads to Chiang Mai. And I know how important that is to you."

Chiang Mia, a mountainous region of North East Thailand, was the largest methamphetamine pill distribution centers of Thailand.

Deng said, "How much more?"

Sein Tho said, "I know your business is expanding, *Ko* Deng. Demand is high from the rest of Asia. You are opening new factories every month. But without the *Tatmadaw*'s help, your business would be nothing. The Wa Army does not have the manpower, or the jurisdiction, to manage these border crossings."

Deng said, "You talk without saying anything, General Tho. Do I have to repeat myself?"

Sein Tho took a small breath and relaxed his shoulders. "This does not come from me. Higher figures in the *Tatmadaw* have requested it." He paused, and Deng waited.

"We know you make more than fifty million US dollars per year after your expenses. We want one percent."

Deng smiled. Behind him, Li walked back and shut the door softly. Then he went to the window, and pulled the string that held the straw blind aloft. All of a sudden the room was dark. Deng stayed motionless, his black eyes fixed on the General's face.

Li moved quickly. He had a knife in his hand, and in the blink of an eye, he was standing behind the General. Li put the serrated blade of the six inch knife against the General's neck and pulled his head back. Sein Tho's face was white and drawn. He struggled to breathe, his earlier composure vanished.

Sein Tho stuttered. "You can't…you can't do this. This is an outpost of the *Tatmadaw*. I am a ranking General. You won't make it out of here alive."

Deng walked across the table, and sat down on the edge, close to the General. Casually, he reached out a hand, and slapped him hard across the face.

"Stop sniveling like a bitch. If you had the power, you would have killed me a long time ago. So shut up and listen to me."

Sein Tho opened his mouth to say something, but Deng slapped his again, this time with the back of his hand. A crimson thread of blood dribbled down the side of Tho's face.

"I said, shut up." Deng's voice was low. "I am not here to negotiate." He reached inside his pocket and pulled out a color photo. It had the picture of a woman and two children, taken outside in a shopping center.

Deng said, "This photo was taken two days ago in Yangon. Recognize them?"

Tho's eyes were wide. It was his wife and two sons. He looked up at Deng. "What do you want?"

"Tell the *Tatmadaw* I am willing to pay a tax. But nowhere near one percent. You don't even *know* what one percent means, because you have no idea of the street value of my products."

Li gave a short laugh and Deng smiled, keeping his eyes on Tho. "I will pay you 20 dollars per truck. That's 400 dollars per day. 7 days a week. Every month. 10 months of the year, barring bad monsoon time. And I will replicate that for each one of the 150 check posts on the border. You do the math."

Deng got closer to the General. "But that is only if you do something for me."

"What?"

"Foreigners have been spying on us. Looking at the railway line and other things. The Shan are helping them. We think they are CIA. I need more information on a man and a woman inside the US Embassy. Li will describe them to you. I want you to track them down, and then bring them to me."

General Sein Tho gulped, then said, "OK, no problem."

CHAPTER 26

Deng was asleep by the time the Nissan got to the town of Pangshang in the eastern part of the Wa State.

Pangshang was the unofficial capital of the autonomous Wa state. The town straddled the border of the Yunnan province, in East China. Although within the borders of Myanmar, the Wa state was a Chinese precinct in all but name. The currency was yuan, and the language spoken on the streets was Mandarin.

The car stopped with a jolt, and Deng woke up as his head bumped against the window.

Li said, "We are here, cousin."

Deng blinked his eyes open and yawned. He got out of the car, then stretched. Houses stood on either side of the narrow road built into the mountain. From where Deng stood, he could see twinkling lights dotted around the slopes, and dark smoke rising from chimneys. Light had faded from the sky, only a blue and mauve trace of it remained on the far side of the hills. Den watched for a minute, appreciating the beauty of his homeland.

He walked over to the vermillion colored gate of the *siheyuan,* or courtyard house. He pushed the copper door handles and found it locked. He banged hard on the door. The four homes around the courtyard were well lit, but Deng knew apart from one they were all empty.

"Who is it?" A female voice enquired from within.

"It's me," Deng said.

Bolts slid, and the two doors opened with a creak. Deng smiled at the elderly woman who stood in the doorway. Solar powered courtyard lights gleamed behind her.

"*Ni hao Muqin,*" Deng said, using the tradition Chinese word for mother. Him and Li stepped inside.

"*Ni hao Erzi,*" Biyu Deng said. Hello, son. The r of Erzi was silent, and it had a long drawn out sound.

Biyu shuffled inside the passageway that led to the roughly twelve feet square courtyard. A pair of stone lions guarded the entrance. Terraced apartments with red tiled sloping rooves stood against each other in four corners of the courtyard. Biyu pointed to the one directly in front.

"Get freshened up, then come to my room."

The men did as they were told. When they entered Biyu's room, the smell of incense burning was overpowering. Deng fanned his hand.

"*Muqin*, you need to open the window."

Biyu was sat still in front of an assortment of jade and porcelain figures. Flowers and sweets were placed in front of the figures, in steel plates. The figures had red and black jewel garlands on them. Each of the figures stood for a divinity associated with the elements. Wind, water, earth and fire. The central figure was the tallest, and was called *Muyiji,* or the Father Spirit. The rest of the elements were his children.

Biyu picked up a tray with the incense sticks and rotated it around her, then she stood up. She puffed her cheeks and blew some of the incense smoke towards the two men. Deng leaned back, but Li closed his eyes and inhaled. Both men touched Biyu's feet with their right hand, and bowed.

Deng whispered, "Can we go now? I'm starving."

Biyu said, "Go to the dining room. I'm coming."

Dinner was thick cut homemade noodles, mixed in a spicy meat broth. Deng closed his eyes as he chewed. The aroma of soy sauce, ginger and chilli was heavenly.

"I feel alive again," he said.

Biyu served them green tea and said, "Someone came to see you."

Deng's eyes flew open and Li stopped chewing. "Who?" Deng asked.

"Li Ka Shing."

"The finance minister?"

"Yes. He wants to see you tomorrow." Biyu took some plates away and came back with more of the spicy soup. She ladled some on Li's bowl.

She said, "Everything OK with the business?"

Deng's father had been a commander in the Wa Army, but Biyu came from a Chinese merchant's family in Kunming city. Kunming was the largest city in Yunnan. After his father's death at the hands of the Shan militia, Biyu had raised Deng and his orphan cousin Li as a single mother.

Her rare animals and precious mineral business had given Deng the start in life that he needed. Both businesses were illegal, and both were very lucrative. In China, tiger teeth and skulls, elephant tusks, fetched a large premium. Biyu had made a fortune out of paying poor villagers to kill the animals, and taking them to Kunming to sell them for a profit.

Deng looked at his mother. "Yes, fine. Why should it not be, *Muqin?*"

"Li Ka Shing is a Party member. From Beijing. Remember that."

Deng said, "I will go to see him tomorrow mother, I promise."

Biyu eyed Li. "Go alone, *Erzi*. He wants to speak to you in private. He didn't tell me what it was about."

*****

The sun was blinding as Deng drove the Nissan up the winding road that led from his home to downtown Panghshang. Endless rolling hills, all carpeted with a thick canopy of deep green rainforest, stretched out to the horizon. As he entered Pangshang, he drove past the casino and the nightclub, both of which were his legitimate businesses. Tall buildings were being constructed everywhere, and the town center was a hive of cranes and trucks.

Advertisements in Mandarin hung from large billboards, and the roads were wide and clean. Well stocked department stores lined the glistening shopping boulevards. Pangshang was very different to the rest of impoverished Myanmar.

He stopped outside the four story Wa Municipality Building. The modern building was made of granite and glass. Despite the name, the building was maintained and manned by money and men from the PRC. People's Republic of China.

Deng had to wait for ten minutes before he was shown into Li Ka Shing's office. He stepped into the deep carpet, and admired the view of the lush green hills from the long windows behind the table. Li Ka Shing was in his sixties, with a bald head. The old man cleared his throat.

Deng bowed deeply, holding his position for three seconds before rising up slowly.

"*Zhu* Shing," he said in a reverential voice. Zhu meant master, but was used for senior officials as well.

"Sit down," Li Ka Shing said. Deng obeyed.

Li Ka Shing said, "Myanmar's Interior Minister has died. *Daw* Khyun Sein was useful to us. She had morals, and therefore she was totally ineffective. She had no clout with the *Tatmadaw*. But she was pro-democracy, and her presence helped to silence a lot of critics. Especially in the western biased Myanmar media."

Deng remained silent, watching the older man. He knew what the insinuation was.

After a while he said, "The Party uses me when they want to. You wanted the white woman to be followed as soon as she landed. I did that. I made sure the Shan informers did not pass any messages to her."

Li Ka Shing said, "It is your duty, Deng. That woman is from the CIA. She came here with the purpose of finding out about the man you caught, Mr. Ted."

Again, Deng went silent.

Li Ka Shing said, "Now Mr. Ted has escaped, is that right?"

Deng did not dare ask how he knew. He nodded. LKS sighed and said, "Yet, you never let us know. Party members in Beijing are not happy, Deng."

"I am sorry. This will not happen in the future."

"Some in the Party are saying you are getting too big for your boots. Your money is useful, yes. But we also need to keep the Burmese on our side. The Tatmadaw are complaining about you."

Deng was silent, but his eyes bore into the older man's.

LKS sighed, and rested his hands on the table. "For a while, stop your business across the border." He raised his hand, stopping Deng from speaking.

"I know. This is not weakness on your part, and I know you have enough money stored up. Truth is, Beijing is concerned about this Mr. Ted, and the new woman from the CIA. They are both spies, there is no doubt. We need to investigate what is happening."

Deng said, "Stopping my trucks will not help with that. My business is my own. I built it from scratch when the opium fields closed. It is big now, so you and the Communist Party are interested. But when I had one hut, and two chemists working in it, no one cared."

LKS said in a very quiet voice, "Take this as a warning, Deng. Because I know your mother, I have not shut you down already."

The two men stared at each other in silence for a while. Then LKS said, "Go now. Do as I said."

Deng stood up. "When the Party wants my money, no one complains about my business. I will do what I need to. I do not work for anyone."

LKS' nostrils flared, and he clenched his teeth. He opened his mouth to say something, but Deng had already opened the door and slammed it shut behind him.

CHAPTER 27

A thin film of light stirred at the edge of Dan's somnolence. That brief signal was all his mind needed. Even before he was fully awake, his right hand had dived underneath the pillow, feeling for the butt of the Browning. It was how he had lived most of his life. In his mind, he was operational now. It was not of his own choosing, but the state of mind was his own. And what he was used to.

His legs came off the couch, and he was up, gun in hand. Then he remembered where he was. The apartment was silent. He put the gun away. He checked his wrist – 0530 hours.

The window was next to the couch, and it looked down the hill into the lake. A light mist had gathered near the waters, and he could see two wooden fishing boats moving slowly across the dull silvery expanse. A man stood still at the head of each boat, with a long paddle in his hand, and another stayed seated. As Dan watched, a net was thrown out from one of the boats. It landed without a sound in the water and settled on the ripples, then sank slowly.

He felt a presence behind him. He turned to find Kim standing there.

She said, "A quick breakfast then we leave. Mary has a map, and we can check the coordinates."

"What car we gonna use?" Dan asked.

"The MP's will let us have one of the cars. It should be coming up any minute."

Mary woke up as well, and fixed them coffee and toast. Dan looked at the map, and trailed a finger up the national highway leading up to the middle of the country, near Mandalay.

Dan said, "This more or less follows the Irrawaddy river straight up."

"Myanmar's main river. And this is where we need to be." Kim put her finger on a curve of the river. "Right off the highway, and on the riverbank."

"Where are you going?" a little voice asked.

The three adults turned to find Maya standing by the doorway. Kim went over and knelt in front of her. She brushed Maya's hair back.

"Are you hungry?" Kim asked. Maya nodded silently.

While Maya had her breakfast, the door buzzer sounded. Mary looked at the video display on the door. She called out to Kim, "Your ride just arrived."

Dan got up. "I'll check it out."

Maya had almost finished her cereal. She put her spoon down and said, "Can I come with you?"

Kim reached over and curled her fingers around Maya's hand. "No, honey. It's too dangerous where we're going. You stay here with Mary and we'll come back real soon."

Maya said, "How soon?"

Then she raised her eyebrows. Kim almost gasped. She would not have believed if she had heard about it. Yet, here it was again, right in front of her. Everything this little girl said and did reminded her of Sarah.

It was as if something brought me here, just so I could see this. Kim closed her eyes, and opened them to find Maya frowning at her. She smiled.

"Within two days. Maybe three," Kim said.

Maya said, "That means you don't know."

Mary gave a short laugh as she cleared the plates away. Kim said, "Yes, you are right. I don't know. But I will be back."

"Promise?"

The light was shining on Maya's dark hair, and the red flower pressed against her head was wilting. The girl's eye shone brightly. Something caught at the back of Kim's throat.

"Yes, I promise," she said, letting out a shaky breath. "While I'm gone, Mary will look after you."

Mary came back and sat down with them. "That's right," Mary said to Maya. "You and me, right here. I can work from home for a couple of days."

Kim stood up. "Bye," she said.

She went down the stairs slowly, getting into the right frame of mind. She had a job to do. She checked her cell phone. There was a missed call from Solomon Barney. She got downstairs. Dan was leaning against a Toyota SUV. He saw the phone in her hand.

"You need to put that away," Dan said. "It should be destroyed, but if not, take the battery and sim card off the phone."

Kim nodded. "I was gonna do that anyway. Who's driving?"

Dan looked at the keys in his hand. "Me, I guess", he said. Kim turned her phone on, and send a brief text message to Solomon. Then she powered it down, and took the battery out.

Dan checked the map one last time, and gave it to Kim, who would navigate. Driving through Yangon city would be a challenge, especially with the right hand traffic. Dan stepped on the gas as they left the Inle Lake area behind, moving through the 4 lane traffic of the new highway heading north.

Warehouses appeared on both sides of the road, most of them disused. Women in bamboo hats squatted by makeshift tin huts on the roadside, working on new lanes for the highway.

"Roadworks, Burmese style," Kim said. She watched the women lift buckets of water and pour them into piles of cement mix. One of them she noticed, had a baby on her back, sitting inside a backpack. The baby's head poked out, looking around.

"Poor women," Kim said, shaking her head.

"They have jobs now they would not have in the old days. Myanmar is expanding, and new roads are getting made."

Kim shook her head. "You call this a job? Living by the road with their families and making what, less than a dollar a day? By the way, what's the white stuff on their faces?"

Dan said, "It's called *Thanaka*, a yellow plant extract. It's like a cosmetic that women and girls put on, but it's also good for sun protection."

The urban landscape, in various shades of new and old flowed past them. When they were out in the country, Dan speeded up. He kept an eye out for tails.

Kim said, "We need to take this exit." A sign loomed ahead of them. It bore the legend – Bagan 100 miles. Dan turned. The highway was quieter. A tourist bus went past them, leaving the rest of the highway empty.

After ten minutes Dan said, "We have company."

Kim turned to look. A black SUV was behind them on the empty highway. Even as Kim looked it speeded up, becoming larger by the second. The car changed lanes, and she saw another two similar cars behind it. Dan had seen it already and pressed his foot down on the gas. He took the Browning out from the side and gave it to Kim. She took the magazine out, checked the rounds, and slammed it back in.

Dan put the other Browning in his lap. "I reckon they've been following us since we left."

"Uh-huh" Kim replied. Dan watched the needle climb till he was pushing 120 km/hr. In the rear view he watched the lead black SUV go faster than him. It caught up with them quickly, then changed lanes and drew abreast.

Dan looked. The dark tinted windows remained up. He saw the other two catching up behind him. The lead car accelerated, and overtook Dan. It was a flanking formation. The car behind Dan now drew abreast, while the third car remained close behind.

Dan gave the gas pedal as hard a squeeze as he could. The SUV lurched forward and with a tearing sound hit the front bumper. He jolted, clutching the steering wheel tightly.

"Watch out", Kim shouted. From the corner of his eye, Dan saw the car next to him pull its window down. The snout of an assault rifle appeared. Dan swung the wheel to the left, but the car in front of him had anticipated his move. It had pulled out to the left already, and Dan hit the rear bumper again. The wheels of his car screeched, burning rubber.

"Get down," Kim shouted. Her arm was outstretched, gun pointed out the back window.

Dan had lowered both windows already. Before the rifle could open up, Kim had fired. Her aim was as good as it could be inside a vehicle moving in excess of 120km/hour. She fired twice, the dull roar of the weapon deafening both of them. The rifle withdrew, then appeared again.

Dan gritted his teeth. "Get down," he shouted back to Kim.

He had to do something. If the rifle fired on automatic mode, both Kim and him would be dead. He pressed on the brakes suddenly. At the same time, he ducked his head. Kim was already bent over, covering her head with her hands. The Toyota's rear fender smashed against the car behind, and with an explosion it crumpled. The rifle fired, and bullets shredded the upholstery of the Toyota. Two rounds lodged in the windscreens, and spider webs appeared instantly at the impact points.

Dan's head was pushed against the steering wheel. As soon as he was hit from behind, he ripped the steering wheel a hard left. He was going for the turning that had loomed up ahead. This highway too was deserted, but it would give him a chance of getting away.

The Toyota's wheels fishtailed on the tarmac. The car wobbled, but came out from behind the black SUV in front. It shot across the road, but instead of getting into the turning, the wheels lost grip on the surface.

The rifle chattered again, and bullets shattered the read windscreen. The back of the Toyota swung out, and the car went into a spin on the road. Dan rotated the steering wheel in the direction of the swing. He couldn't see any barriers on the sides of the highway. He gritted his teeth as the Toyota did three circles then came off the road, and into a dirt track.

Kim was sitting up, pointing her gun out the back. The three cars had turned with them and were giving chase. In a cloud of dust Dan fought for control. He pointed the car away from the road finally, and drove straight down the dirt track. To his left, the broad expanse of a river opened up, sun glinting off it.

"A bridge, straight ahead," Kim said.

"Ok," Dan said, and pressed on the gas. The three cars were now close behind, raising a storm cloud under their wheels.

As the bridge became clearer in their view, Dan heard Kim groan. "Oh my god, no."

"What?" Dan asked.

"The damn thing is broken in the middle."

CHAPTER 28

Dan turned his head. By the width of the river, he judged it to be the Irrawaddy. Sandy land banks covered the sides. Thick clumps of reed grew along the banks. Green hills dense with forest rose up on the other side. The suspension bridge looked old and had caved in the middle.

"We got no other choice," Dan shouted. He floored the gas again. Behind him, more shots rang out, whining off the car.

"It's too wide, Dan," Kim screamed. "We are never gonna make it to the other side."

"Don't worry, I have a plan." He felt Kim turn to look at him. He said, "Take off your shoes."

They were almost upon the bridge now. It was an old, deserted, suspension structure, weeds growing all over it. It had a cement roadway on it in the past, but the bridge had broken in the middle. The fall to the river was not more than twenty feet, Dan guessed. The other side of the bridge, that carried on to the far bank, was more than ten feet away. Bent girdles of rusting iron poked out from the broken ends. It looked as if a giant fist had smashed through the bridge, leaving it hollow in the middle.

"Keep the windows down," Dan shouted. He sped up as much as he could. Dirt flew inside the car, and the speeding wheels landed on the cement of the bridge. The sound changed, and they were suddenly moving faster on the cement. Ahead of them, Dan could clearly see the massive break. He felt like he was approaching the end of a waterfall before it plunged down into the depths. More bullets whined behind them, kicking up dirt by the tires.

"Get ready," Dan shouted. He braced himself. Thirty feet away. Then ten feet. Five feet.

Two feet.

Now.

Dan floored the gas so hard the pedal almost went through the floor. With one last ear bending whine, the SUV ran off the road into empty air. Its wheels rotated in empty space.

"Jump, Kim!" Dan shouted. Kim had already opened the door. As the car fell, she jumped and disappeared from view. Dan did not waste any time. He did the same. As he lifted off from the door, he felt the wind slapping against him, blowing into his hair, lifting his shirt from the beltline.

The car, being heavier, fell into the river first. There was a huge *Thwack!* and a muddy mushroom cloud of water spurted high up in the air as the car hit the water. Kim and Dan followed shortly after. Dan plunged feet first, pinching his nostrils as he fell, and taking a large gulp of air. He sliced underneath the dark muddy water, then swam out quickly underneath. With strong arms, he swam to the left, where he had seen Kim fall. Behind him he felt waves move at him as with a huge groan the SUV tipped over hood first and started to sink.

Dan kept his eyes open, but the water was dark , making it almost impossible to see. He felt a movement to his side, and reached out. Human hands. Then he saw Kim's face, up close. They grabbed each other, then swam as hard as they could, staying underneath water.

A fire was burning in Dan's lungs. His vision was growing misty, and a terrible pressure was building up to breaking point in his chest. He could stay underneath water for more than two minutes, but he knew that was not enough to get them away from the gangster leaning over the broken bridge, rifles in hand.

He felt Kim rising up, and he had no choice but to follow her. They broke water, gasping and spluttering. Above him, Dan heard a shout. He pulled Kim and they dived back into the water again. There was an explosion of gunfire above them, and a few bullets streaked into the water, cartwheeling across their swimming bodies. Dan pointed underwater with his arm. Kim nodded.

They could see water reeds. Myanmar was famous for large, hollow water reeds that could grow as strong as bamboo. They could grow tall, and this clump, Dan knew, would reach above water. Dan reached them first, and he left Kim and dived deeper into the river. The bed was sloping up so he did not have to dive far.

All he hoped for now was not to see a crocodile. The Irrawaddy was known to have them.

Dan grabbed hold of one water reed and pulled. The plant was stuck into the soil. His chest and lungs heaving again, Dan scraped out the bottom with his knife. The reed came loose in his hand. He cleaned the base, and put his mouth against it immediately. He sucked. Soil and dirt particles came into his mouth and he had no choice but to swallow.

But then he felt air. Cool, refreshing, air. He felt Kim next to him. He gave her the reed, and she did the same as him. She came off it, cheeks puffed with air, and put her hand on the base immediately. She lifted her thumb up. Dan nodded, and put his mouth on the base again.

In ten seconds, Dan pointed to the river bank. Kim nodded. They could not stay underwater forever. The river had crocs, and other large fish. Above them, the gangsters were leaning over with guns. But the mass of weeds could give them some shelter. Once they were up the bank, they could run for the jungle that grew dense and dark, close to the riverside.

Kim knew exactly what to do. She went first. Cautiously, her head broke water, surrounded by hundreds of waving brown reeds. She went through them slowly, careful not to shake them too much. She stopped frequently, staying under water as long as she could before moving again.

CHAPTER 29

Once she was close to the bank, Kim looked behind. Behind her, on the broken bridge, the gangsters were still keeping watch. She could see the snout of two assault rifles pointing at the water. She felt the reeds move and watched Dan as he came up alongside her. They were waist deep in water now, but crouching to stay below water level in the reeds.

Dan whispered, "They have to look at both sides. Sure they have 2 guns on the other side as well. We don't want all 4 guns firing at us."

Kim said, "But we have to go at the same time. Whoever stays behind, dies."

Dan nodded. "You first."

Dan kept an eye on the bridge as Kim crawled forward. If they were spotted, he knew they were well within firing range of the rifles, which looked like AK-74's. They would not survive. He kept wading backwards, turning his head to see Kim.

She got to the bank, and waited for Dan. He pressed himself against her on the muddy shores, still hidden by the reeds, which had become thicker. Large flies buzzed and flew into their faces. The water was warm, and steam rose off it, and there was a peculiar pungent odor.

"Keep moving", Dan whispered. Kim got to the bank, and hauled herself over. Dan joined her. They lay on the ground for a second, expecting shouts and the sound of gunfire. Dan looked up. The gangster were looking around everywhere, apart from the banks.

Dan lifted himself up on his haunches. "Run!" he whispered.

Kim got up and ran. She was quick on her feet, but the sudden movement did not go unnoticed.

Gunfire rattled above Dan's head. He did not wait, he got up and hurled himself in Kim's direction.

Bullets zipped past his head, then splattered dirt and small stones on the ground. Damn, he thought, they are finding me. He crossed the last twenty feet before the dark green foliage began. He couldn't see Kim anymore which meant she was already under cover.

Just as he was getting to safety Dan heard that deadly sound. So close, he had milliseconds to analyse it. An instinct made him drop to the ground, but even then he was late. A searing pain lanced across his shoulders, and he stumbled. He fell heavily on the ground, and luckily for him, behind a thick tree stump. Bullets thundered around him, thudding into the tree.

"Dan. Over here!" It was Kim's voice. Dan closed his eyes and opened them. Well, he could still hear and see. That was close enough to being alive. He felt a stickiness in his back, and recognized the warmth of blood.

"Dan." The voice was closer now. He could see Kim's outline in the heavy bush.

"Stay away," Dan shouted. Bullets still whined around him. With a superhuman effort, he raised himself up. He ran towards Kim. A massive tree trunk lay felled on the ground. He climbed over, and joined Kim on the other side. He leaned against the brown trunk, sweat pouring down his face.

"You're bleeding," Kim said. "Turn over." Dan did as he was told. Kim ripped open his shirt and pulled the top down.

"Can't be too bad," Dan said. "I'm still here."

Kim pressed on his back. Dan winced in pain. His fists gripped the ground hard, mud squeezing out between his fingers.

Dan shook his head. "Flesh wound, right?"

"Yes," Kim said, sounding relieved. She faced Dan. "But you lost some blood, and unless we stitch that cut, it will bleed more. You got lucky - it just grazed your shoulder."

"Guess I have lady luck with me."

Kim rolled her eyes, but Dan did not miss the smile on her lips as she stood up. He buttoned up his shirt quickly, wincing as the movements caused fresh bleeding. He pointed down the river. "We keep moving. If we follow the river up, and stay under cover of the jungle, we can still make it."

He caught the look on her face. "I'll be fine don't worry."

"I'm not worried, and don't pull the tough guy routine with me, OK? All we need to do is stop the bleeding and you'll be alright."

"Fine, but we need to keep moving. Our friends are already driving around, heading here."

The bullets had stopped for the time being. That meant the gangsters, or whoever they were, had driven off. They started walking. The sun was high in the noon sky, and the sluggish waters of the great river, swollen with water from the surrounding mountains, flowed mightily alongside them. The huge trees gave them respite from the sun. Several times, they crossed trees with roots so thick they were raised three to four feet above ground.

Across the broad sweep of the river, they could see green hills undulating on the other side. Dan heard sounds as he walked. Scurries and slithers in the brush, by their feet. He watched all around and above him as well.

Kim was walking ahead of him. Their clothes steamed in the heat. Kim had her head bent. Dan saw a movement in the trees above Kim's head. He did not waste any time. In three steps, he crossed the gap and hooked an arm around Kim's waist. He pulled her back, and to the side before she could protest. They fell on a heap in the ground.

Kim frowned at him. "What the…?"

Dan pointed with his hand and Kim's eyes followed, then widened. A red and green snake was lowering its long body slowly from the branch above. The body seemed to elongate till it could go no further, then the serpent gently dropped to the ground. Kim stood up hastily, followed by Dan. The snake weaved its way into the undergrowth.

"Jeez," Kim said. "Poisonous?"

"We don't wanna find out, do we?"

They walked on, faster this time. After another mile or so, Dan could feel Kim slowing down. He stopped as she flopped down on a massive trunk root.

Dan said, "You OK?"

Kim was about to say something but Dan caught a movement in the corner of his eyes.

A shape was moving slowly down the river. The waters were gentler here, the flow more sedate. Dan saw the long, pointed stern first, then the rest of the boat came into view. It sat low in the water, and a man stood at the back, manning the currents with a long paddle in his hand, dragging on the river bottom.

The boat was colored vermillion red, and there was a green thatched roof over the middle. Dan could see another person moving under the roof covered section. The boat was long, more than fifty feet, and slender. Front and back curled up with swan neck formations.

In a split second, Dan had jumped over the roots and raced down to the edge of the river.

"Hey," he shouted. "HEY!!"

The man standing at the end turned his head to the sound. Dan waved and shouted. The boat slowed down.

Kim had joined him. "What are you doing?" Kim asked.

"These guys look like fishermen, and we need a ride," Dan said. The two men on the boat conversed with each other. Then they steered the boat towards the bank. Dan and Kim waited on the bank as the boat's long stern came alongside.

The two Burmese men looked down at them with avid curiosity. Dan said "Bagan. Bagan." He pointed with his hand down the river.

One of the men began nodding his head. Dan felt in his pockets, and found some loose money, all wet. He took the wad of notes out carefully, and showed it to the men. The men spoke to each other again, and nodded more vigorously.

One of them reached a hand down. Dan said to Kim, "You first."

"You sure this is a good idea?"

"If you have a better one, I'm all ears."

Kim muttered something under her breath and took the man's hand. She hoisted herself on board, then Dan climbed on. Dan repeated the name of his destination again, and the men nodded.

Kim asked, "Do you speak any English?" The men shrugged, and spoke back in Burmese.

"There's your answer," Dan said.

CHAPTER 30

The men indicated a seat under the cover, giving them shade from the sun. The boat set off, pulled along by the river current. The man came back with two bottles of water. He gave it to them, and smiled with a thumbs up.

Dan said, "I think he means its OK." Dan opened the bottle and drank. The water was cool and fresh and he realized how badly he had needed it. Kim watched him, then did the same. The man had gone behind Dan, and was saying something. He gestured with his hands.

Kim said, "I think he's telling you to take your shirt off." The guy at the back of the boat remained where he was standing, framed against the green riverbank. His friend came back with a small wooden box. He put it at their feet and opened it up. Dan saw an assortment of hooks with string attached to them. The man lifted up the smallest hook, and fitted a fine silk string to the back. Then he looked at them.

Kim said, "He wants to sew up your cut, Dan."

Dan grunted. "I can see that." He turned to Kim. "Can I ask you a favor? Would you mind doing it?"

Kim shrugged. "I done my first aid. Willing to try. Lie down on your chest."

The man lifted his hand, telling them to stop. He reached inside his shirt pocket and took out a piece of folded red paper. He opened it to reveal a black paste. It was sticky, and he pulled a part of it off, rolled it into a ball between his fingers, and held it in front of Dan.

Dan said, "I might have this totally wrong, but I figure he is offering me some opium."

Kim nodded. "Yep, I think so too. They get it from poppy plants that grow naturally around here. He's giving it to you as a pain killer."

Dan said, "I lived with worse pain in my life." He shook his head. The man shrugged and put the black ball back inside the packet.

Dan lay down on his chest. Kim pressed on his back. The man gave Dan a rug, and showed Dan to bite on it. This Dan did accept. He clamped the rug between his teeth as Kim dug the hook inside his skin. Dan gripped the sides of the bench and clenched his teeth tight. He was glad of the rug. Kim sutured his laceration up like she had done it before. Dan writhed and moved under her, and several times Kim had to tell him to stop. She finished, and stretched the stitched wound, making sure it wasn't bleeding any more.

Dan gulped. "Are you done yet?"

Kim moved, and Dan sat up stiffly. He stretched his wide shoulders, wincing. Kim said, "You did well there. I took a field medic course, and I have never seen that done without a local anaesthetic injection."

The fisherman stood behind them. Dan caught him staring. The man looked away, and went to sit down by the bow. A warm breeze struck up downwind, and it cooled Dan's fevered brow. He sat without leaning against anything, watching the green hills flowing by.

The hills began sloping down soon. The river was wide, and they were flowing down the middle. White buildings with golden pagodas appeared through the green foliage. Dan heard gentle sound, like a humming. It grew louder, but remained soft on the ears, like wind rushing through the water reeds. Kim looked at him. She had heard it too.

The fisherman came back and pointed to the bank on the left. On a raised land, there stood a white and red monastery. Red robed monks stood in the large courtyard, chanting their evening prayers. They went past it, and the sound faded, replaced by the lapping of water against the boat's hull.

Kim looked up as the jungle came back to claim the land again. The emerald trees formed a dense space, and as she stared, she could make out white and orange orchids against the greenery.

The day wore on. The noon sun began to lean in the sky. Red, gold and pink suffused the horizon, and the sun grew impossibly large, a round blazing blot that seemed to take over the line where water met the sky. Imperceptibly, as if saying goodbye after a long day, the sun began to dip lower.

Dan heard a cry from the man who was fishing. His friend came over from the rear and knelt beside him. Together, they pulled on the heavy nets till the days catch came on board. One of them got a large fish and pulled out a machete. He put the fish on a board, and held it down with his foot as the fish thrashed around. With the other hand, he steadied the machete, and with a swift movement, sliced off the fish's head.

Dan said, "I hope we get to eat something now." He walked up and went to the men. He pointed to the fish and rubbed his belly. The man smiled. Dan watched as they boiled rice in a pan. The fish was descaled, gutted, then rubbed all over with a red and yellow spice. Then the fish was roasted in a fire. As the sun set, the two fishermen put four bowls out, and indicated to Dan.

Dan said to Kim, "Grub's up."

Kim was standing behind him. "What fish is that?"

"Fish is fish, right? It's from the river, should be OK."

Kim and Dan watched as the fishermen washed their hands carefully, then used their right hand as scoops to break up small pieces of fish and rice. This was made into a soup, and the rice and fish soup was poured into each of the four bowls. Dan realized how ravenous he had been. He finished his plate with relish. The fish was tenderly cooked, and the spicing was just right. They used wooden chopsticks, which the fishermen washed after using and put away.

Kim glanced at him. "Nice, huh?"

"Fuckin A," Dan said. "You like it?"

"Not bad."

Night flowed in across the water like a velvet drape. The blue evening claimed the green jungles on either side, and monkeys hopped from branch to branch as the crickets began to buzz. Dan sat by the hull at the front of the boat. He did not feel the pain in his back any more. Kim came and sat down beside him.

"So Mr. Roy," Kim said, "tell me about yourself."

Dan hesitated, then sighed. She had a right to know, after everything they had been together. With a lot more to come, he surmised.

"I used to work for a Black Ops outfit called Intercept." Dan told her about his early Delta days, and how he had been hired for Intercept.

Dan said, "When I was young my parents lived in Nepal, high up in the mountains near Mount Everest. They worked for the UN. We lived with the Gurkhas, and dad trained me to run up the mountains like they did, carrying weights on their heads called Doko bags. Oxygen was low that high up, and it gave me a level of fitness most Army grunts did not have."

Kim's voice was a whisper in the dark. "I heard about the Gurkhas. Four regiments in the British Army still, right?"

"Five regiments. Great fighters, I rank them with the best guys in Delta and Seals."

The boat jolted in a current, and Kim fell against Dan. She stayed there. Dan felt her warm body resting against his shoulder. He didn't move, and neither did she. Blackness besmirched the rustling waters, and the pinpoints of diamond studs appeared in the dark sky above.

"How about you, Miss Smith?" Dan asked. He heard the snort of her laugh.

"Nobody's called me that since my college exams. So, I went to Amherst, did Political Science and learned Urdu. Worked in India for a while as a journalist. Guess joining the CIA came naturally to me. I was stationed in Baghdad during the second Gulf War. Kind of crazy. You were there, right?"

"Crazy describes it about right. What did you do after?"

Kim shivered suddenly. Dan was about to put his arm around her, but stopped himself. He felt awkward. "You OK?" he asked.

"Yes, I'm fine," Kim said. She was silent for a long time. They sat and listened to the water, and the sounds the boat made. Then Kim said, "My sister died." Haltingly, she told Dan everything. She talked about Sarah in a flat monotone, like she was reading out of a book. Dan listened in silence.

"Jeez," he said. "I'm sorry. No one should have to go through that."

Kim did not reply. Dan turned, and he could see the dark outline of her face. Her expression remained invisible.

Footsteps sounded behind them, with the creaking of the boat. One of the fisherman came forward carrying a lamp. The glass was lit inside by a kerosene wick, and carried on an iron handle. The man squatted next to them, and pointed towards the dark land.

"Bagan," the man said. "Bagan."

"Hey," Dan said, "Looks like we arrived."

Kim peered in the darkness. "Arrived where? I can't see anything."

The boat inched closer to the bank, and they felt a jolt as it hit land. Both the fishermen had lit kerosene lamps now. The light cast long shadows on their faces. Their eyes glinted in the dark as they gazed at Dan and Kim.

Dan said, "Well, thank you." He took out the money from his pocket. All the notes were Kyat, the Burmese currency. He had about fifty dollars' worth in there, or almost fifty thousand Kyat. He put the money in his right hand, and offered it to the men. The two men looked at each other, then at Dan. They both shook their heads.

Dan said, "No. You saved us. We owe you. Please, take it." He thrust the money forward again.

One of the fishermen moved Dan's hand away. He shook his head again. Kim touched Dan's arm. "Leave it," she said, "you might offend them."

The fishermen helped Kim and Dan off the boat. One of them leaned over, and held out a kerosene lamp. Dan shrugged and took it from his hand.

Kim wondered aloud, "Are these guys for real?"

The fishermen stood on the boat, and bowed to them. Dan bowed deeply;

so did Kim. Then he pushed the stern of the boat, till it was free of the mud, and out into the restless waters of the Irrawaddy.

Kim and Dan waved at them, and they waved back. They stood staring at the boat till it got swallowed by the darkness, its only presence the yellow glow from the kerosene lamp.

Kim slipped her hand inside Dan's and gave it a squeeze. "We should get going," she said.

Dan said, "It's a tradition. Burmese do not take money from guests. But I felt bad, and had to offer them something."

"You did the right thing, Dan. Now let's make tracks before the mosquitoes eat us alive."

Dan took the map out from his pocket. He had dried it on the boat. They squatted on the ground and peered at the map in the light of the lamp.

CHAPTER 31

Li Yonping was driving the Nissan Cruiser on the narrow backstreets of Yangon. They passed slowly through a market street, Li honking the horn loudly. They went past the remnant of the warehouse that had burnt down. Deng, in the passenger seat, swore loudly as he saw the burnt ruin.

Li said, "We have been following the Shan informers for a while now. That is what *Zhu* Li Ka Shin told us to do, right?"

"Right. Now the old bastard wants to shut us down. Fucking joke."

Deng ticked things off mentally in his head. Aloud he said, "We stopped the Shan from speaking to the *Baw* woman. We grabbed her, but that man, the American, took her away from the warehouse. How did he even do that?"

"He is *Yaoguai,* an evil spirit. He burnt all our supplies in the warehouse too. More than a million dollar's worth."

Deng clenched his teeth and closed his eyes for a second. Rage boiled inside him. He controlled it with an effort. Getting angry would not help him now. He needed to find a way to get even.

Deng said, "Cousin, we need to get the *Baw* man and woman. They were last seen by the river, right?"

"Yes. How they escaped again, I don't know."

"Where are they headed?"

"The man I killed inside the *Shwedagon* was passed information. He did not live, but I fear he might have something hidden on him that I missed." Li gripped the steering wheel. "*Ta Ma Bi!*" he swore vehemently in Mandarin.

"*Ta Ma Bi*" Deng agreed in a softer voice.

They stopped the car near a cluster of one story houses. Li killed the engine and the two of them got out. Li looked around him, while Deng strode towards one of the houses. One of his men was standing at the doorway holding it open for him. He nodded at Deng who acknowledged.

The owner of the house lay on the floor. He was bound at the hands and feet, and gagged. His eyes widened in fear when he saw Deng. One of Deng's crew bent down and removed the rag gagging the man.

"*Zhu* Deng!" The man on the floor got up on his knees and bent low, his forehead almost touching the ground. "Please spare me and my family."

"Where is the white woman?" Deng asked in a low voice. He flicked a mote of invisible dust off his safari suit. He put one foot on the man's shoulder and kicked him backwards. "Tell me, you *Sha Bi!*"

"The map they were given led to Bagan. That is all I know, *Zhu* Deng."

"And where did they get the map from?"

"Someone came down from Mongwa."

"Wait. Mongwa near the Chinese border? In the jungles?"

"Yes."

Li and Deng looked at each other. They went outside.

"*Cao ni ma.*" Deng said. "That Mr. Ted who escaped. He must be behind this."

Li nodded, "Yes. There is a Shan camp near Mongwa, I know that. Not far from where we hung Mr. Ted in the jungle. We can raze that camp to the ground. But I have a feeling Mr. Ted will not be there."

"No. But the fact that he knew about Bagan..." Deng's voice trailed off. One of his men appeared at the doorway. Deng gestured at him to go back inside.

Deng said, "We find them. The man and woman, and this Mr Ted. Then we kill them very, very slowly."

Li smiled, the scar on his face bending with his cheeks. They went back inside. Li took a silencer out of his pocket and screwed it onto the Browning. The prisoner, a Shan informer, was kneeling on the ground, hands tied. He watched with terrified eyes as Li walked up to his left side and put the muzzle of the silencer against his temple. Deng stood in front of him.

The man stuttered. "Please, *Zhu* Deng. I will do anything, I promise. Spare me."

Deng looked at the man coldly. "Then tell me what else you know."

The man said, "The map was passed down. Who drew it, I don't know. It was meant for delivery that night, where I told you. I did my job."

Stupid man, Deng thought to himself. If he had any brains, he would have kept his mouth shut. Deng said, "Who else knows about the map?"

"The man who gave it to me."

"Tell me their names. Then you will live."

The man blurted out the names as fast as he could. Deng almost smiled to himself. This was useful. One of his men wrote the names down in a pad. Deng now knew of the supply chain that brought information from the Shan State Army to the streets of Yangon.

The man asked, "I have told you everything I know. You promised to let me go if I did."

Deng said, "I lied."

The man gasped as he heard the Browning's safety catch being released. A split second later, Li pulled the trigger.

CHAPTER 32

Kim slapped her cheek softly and said, "Good job I'm not wearing shorts. These damned mosquitoes would have eaten me alive by now." Kim had travelled enough in Asia to know what the dress code was. Her thin, white cotton pants saved her legs from sunburn, and kept the flies at bay.

The dark jungle pressed around them, but they were walking in a clearing. They had travelled from the riverbank in the direction shown by the fishermen. The only word that Dan understood was Bagan. The two men had enthusiastically pointed in the same direction repeatedly.

Dan knew he had no choice but to walk that way. They needed to lie up somewhere, and find their way on the map in daylight. He needed a compass, but that was wishful thinking. Hopefully, the map was detailed enough to take them to their destination.

The night was warm. It was humid too, and a hot, wet breeze blew in from the river. That changed as they walked. Dan walked a mile in fifteen minutes, and after an hour, they stopped to rest. Kim kept pace with him well. They had started to climb up a hill. The path in the middle was wide, and the jungle was fading behind them. The kerosene lamp hung from his hand, providing a small puddle of light by their feet.

The light was good, but it also gave their position away. There was not much Dan could do about that. Kim drank some water from the leather skin bottle the fishermen had given them. They started walking again, feeling the path gently slope upwards. The breeze became stronger on their faces. They were reaching the top of a hill.

Dan stopped. He raised the lamp up. He couldn't see anything but darkness.

"We rest here for the night," he said.

Kim agreed. "We take turns to keep watch, right?"

"Right. You sleep first, and I'll wake you up in three hours."

Kim checked her watch. "It's midnight." She looked around her. "Let's take that spot under the teak tree."

They walked down the slope, to a group of trees growing out of a depression in the ground.

The ground around the roots had been eroded, and it created a cup shaped natural cavity they could hide in.

Dan pulled some fallen branches and piled them up in front. Kim lay down on the ground, folding her elbows underneath her head.

Dan put the lamp by her head, and blew out the light. Then he sat near the entrance to their little lying up point. He raised his head. Visibility was near zero, but after a while, his eyes got used to the dark. He sensed that ahead of him the hill sloped down. The river was behind them, but as the Irrawaddy curved around, he figured it would be ahead as well, in the distance. He pulled out the Browning, and slid the magazine out. The chamber was waterlogged, and the gun was useless. He ejected the rounds.

Periodically, Dan looked around him, and raised his head above the border of their LUP, or lying up point, as he called it from his Army days. He heard no footsteps, and no voices. Animal sounds came from the forest, and flutter of birds wings. Other than that, there was silence.

At 3am he woke up Kim. She took up her watch position. Dan watched her for a while, huddled against the slope, knees drawn up to her chin. He listened carefully, but still heard no sounds apart from the forest at night. The trees creaked in the occasional breeze, and in the distance some birds chirped before falling quiet. It was strangely peaceful. He did not remember when he had fallen asleep.

*****

Kim's head was dropping on her shoulder. She felt something moving on her face, and woke up with a start. She waved the fly away, and blinked her eyes open.

Dawn was breaking, and a clear light was suffusing the forest around her. She looked towards the tree trunk a few feet away. Dan was sprawled on the ground in front of it, lying on his back. His wide, muscular chest rose and fell as he breathed. Kim rose up softly, taking care not to awaken Dan. She climbed out of the small depression they were in. She stretched, and brushed the dirt off her pants and shirt.

She was on the flat top of a hill. The edge was about thirty feet away. Then the land sloped down gently again, this time to a wide expanse of flat land. Pink and gold clouds dominated the horizon and streaked across the face of the rising sun.

Below it, she could see the silver string of the Irrawaddy, its lazy body forming the boundary of the plain the hills sloped down to. Kim thought she could see some spires rising from the plains. Her view was obscured by trees. Intrigued, she walked to the edge of the hill.

The flat land at the bottom became wider, and stretched out endlessly on either side. Straight ahead lay the river. But what she saw below took Kim's breath away.

Tall minarets and pagodas from hundreds of temples dotted the land in front of her. They appeared to be ancient brick structures. Some of the temples were close to each other, and others were spaced wide apart. The larger ones, even from a distance, appeared colossal, with their corn cob like towers rising high up above the trees. The temples stretched out all the way to the river bank, and as far as her eyes could see on either side.

Golden rays of light slanted in between the temples elaborate towers and porticoes, giving the mystical structures magical, other worldly silhouettes. Kim felt unreal, like she had been transported in time to another universe, to a place forgotten in the shrouds of history. She could not see anyone around her, and the view was only hers to see.

Her reverie was broken when she heard a sound behind her. She turned to see Dan walking up to her.

"I couldn't see you," he said. His tone had an edge to it. She guessed he had been anxious when he couldn't see her.

"I was just here," Kim said. "Look."

They stood there, drinking in the magnificent sight before them.

"My God," Dan said after a long silence. "Kinda cool, huh?"

Kim nodded. "Very cool." She knew where she was now. Bagan was famous for these temples. Buddhist kings had built them over a period of 250 years, more than a thousand years ago.

Dan fished inside his shirt pocket, and fished out the map. He squatted on the floor and spread the map out. Kim joined him.

She pointed at the long trail going across the center of the map. The trail was colored black, and it had crosses separated from it, but running in the same direction.

"Some of these crosses must be the big temples," she said.

"Yes. They even have names on them. We should be able to find them easily."

Kim stood up. "We should make our way down now. That big temple," she pointed to the map. "Its name starts with D. If we find that, then we can navigate."

"Sounds like a plan," Dan said.

They set off, with Dan going first. He had picked up a sturdy branch about three and a half feet in length, and he used it to hack away at the undergrowth to make walking down the slope easier. The forest thinned out as they walked down. Kim checked her watch. It was 6AM.

The ground was yellow red and dusty under their feet. The land was flat, and trees sprouted uniformly, but the dense jungles were left far behind. Palm and tamarind trees stood tall around them. As they approached the first temples the light became stronger. They walked past the smaller structures, noting the elaborate lattice pattern of the brickwork, and the ambulatory walkways around the main temples, slowly descending down to the main courtyard.

The temples grew bigger, and so did the height of their tall towers, which rose dizzyingly into the dawn sky. Kim noticed small tin huts around the big temples. They were all shut, but she figured they were for tourists when the peak season started. In April, it was still too hot.

They came up to a huge temple that looked almost Mayan in design. It was so big that it seemed like a castle, with huge portico doors facing in all four directions. The doors, Kim thought, must be a hundred feet tall. From them, a series of smaller doors descended to the front, and two walkways wrapped around the giant complex. The corn cob like temple finial started from a squat base at the top, and then rose up higher.

They stopped and Kim pointed at the map. "Right, this must be the D temple." She squinted at the map.

Dan walked around to a sign hanging from a tree. The sign was comically small, but the name on it was clearly legible.

"*Dhammayangyi,*" Dan said, pronouncing it slowly. "That's the temple's name."

"In which case, we need to head further out to the east," Kim said, looking at the map.

CHAPTER 33

The sun grew stronger, and the shadows slowly shrank from the trees. They still had the place to themselves, but after walking a few hundred feet, Kim saw a horse drawn cart trundle down the road. The villager on the cart turned to look at them.

A short distance from another temple there was a cluster of shacks. The walls were made of bamboo, and the roofs were of thatched palm leaves. One of the tin doors of a shack was open. Kim wiped the sweat off her face. They had been walking from more than an hour. She stopped in front of the shack. Ahead of her she saw Dan slow down. Kim gestured, and Dan turned around.

A Burmese woman sat behind a counter. On the rickety shelves below the glass counter there was a refrigerator, with plastic bottles stacked on it.

The woman stood up when she saw Kim and said something. Kim pointed to the bottles, and got four bottles of water, some chocolate and cookies. Dan paid with the wad of notes that he had, and the woman bowed to them. Kim returned the bow, and drank thirstily. Then they set off on their way again.

After three hours of walking, and resting in between, they had arrived at the red mark on the map. They were far inland now, and had left most of the temples behind. In front of her, Kim could see pagodas rising up between trees, but they were fewer. The small huts had disappeared and the trees were getting denser.

Dan approached her as they stood under the shade of a tamarind tree.

"You OK?" he asked. Kim nodded, and took a swig of water.

"Yep. Let's keep walking. Can't be far now."

After another hour, they had reached their destination. Dan looked around him. Kim shaded her eyes. A dirt path went down ahead of her, curling away into the distance of the hazy blue green hills. On either side stood clumps of trees.

Dan said, "There has to be a landmark. That's what the red mark is for." Kim watched as he put the map in his pocket, and walked up to a tree. He felt for a toe hold, then hoisted himself up. He climbed easily, his forearm muscles rippling as he pulled himself up. He sat on a thick branch and gazed.

"There," he shouted at Kim. "I can see it."

"See what?"

"A temple."

Dan scrambled down, and walked over to her. They walked swiftly, despite the heat, and their increasing tiredness. As they got closer to the temple, Kim realized it was bigger than she had thought. The temple was in ruins mostly, trees growing around and on it. It rose in the similar pyramid shape to the other temple, its corn cob shaped finial mostly eroded to a roundish top. Because of the tree cover, the temple had not been very visible initially.

Dan still had the branch with him, and he used it to clear a pathway to the main walkway that surrounded the temple. Kim brushed flies away from her face. The heat had made her shirt and pants cling to her body. She used her wet sleeve to wipe sweat.

The ambulatory walkway was covered, but the ceiling was high and invisible. She heard squeaks coming from the top, and once saw black wings flash.

Dan said, "Bats."

The walls were made of crumbling bricks, with stucco reliefs and faded paintings. Dan stopped to observe one of the paintings.

He pointed at the map and said, "The same red design as on these maps. Shaped like a pyramid." He showed it to Kim. She nodded.

"This has to be the place," Dan said. They kept walking deeper into the deserted temple. The main chamber lay in the middle of the walkway, but the jungle meant they had to use the walkways.

"You know why the kings built so many of these temples?" she asked Dan.

"Because the more you build, the more good Karma you get in the afterlife."

Dan said, "I could use some good Karma right now. In the form of a juicy burger and fries."

The walkway finally led to an entrance for the main temple. Two large leogryphs, their paws raised and teeth bared, guarded the doorway on either side. Windows inside created shafts of sunlight in the dusty interior. Kim stepped over a pile of fallen bricks as she followed Dan inside.

Once they were inside, the space opened up suddenly. The vast domed ceiling stretched above them. On the far wall, Kim saw two giant, floor to ceiling Buddha statues. They were painted white and gold but the color was fading. They were the largest statues of Buddha Kim had ever seen. Huge rolls of cobwebs covered the ceilings, and bats flew around screeching.

Dan was examining the walls on the far-left side. Similar paintings of red temples and pyramids adorned the far wall. Kim saw him tap the painting with his hand. One of the paintings, the last in a long row, had a hollow sound. Dan looked at her and motioned her to come over.

Dan said, "We need to break this wall."

"How?"

"It's hollow anyway." He gripped the thick branch with both hands. Kim moved back. Dan raised the branch like a baseball bat. He averted his face and slammed it down on the wall. It cracked immediately. After two more blows, the plaster had fallen off, and the branch had broken in half.

Dan knelt down and picked up a piece of plaster. "No way this is a thousand years old. More like a few weeks."

The crumbled wall had exposed a doorway. Dan walked over to it, and pushed it gently. Kim joined him. A staircase went down into the basement. Light wells had been dug, and the stairs spiralled down for a considerable distance. They looked at each other, and Dan nodded.

"I should go on my own," Dan said.

"No," Kim said firmly. "We go together."

Slowly, they descended. They stopped several times to listen. There was absolute silence all around them. The depth of the stairs was more than a hundred feet. At the bottom, there was a circular path surrounding a white building that rose all the way up to ground level.

"You go left, I'll go right," Kim whispered.

This time Dan disagreed. Kim won in the end. She set off, her senses on overdrive. The passage was wide, and unlike the crumbling ruins far above her head, the floor was clean. The white structure in the middle followed the curve.

She could not hear Dan anymore. Sunlight from high above made shapes on the wall. Kim bent low at the waist, and edged forward.

She moved quickly when she sensed something behind her, but she could not deflect the blow fully. Something hit her in the lower legs and she lost her balance. She fell but rolled over in the same movement, and was up on the balls of her feet, facing her attacker.

She saw an Oriental man, and the face was familiar. She recognized the scar on the left side, curving from the eye to the lip. The eyes that were like a dead fish, utterly devoid of feeling. The man smiled. Keeping his eyes focused on her, he advanced. He reached out to grab her, and Kim kicked high, slapping his arm away. She dropped to her knees, and hurled herself to his legs, dropping him to the floor.

The man's knees came up, and caught her on the chin. Pain exploded inside Kim's head as her head was snapped back. She felt fingers clawing at her throat, and she grabbed them, bending her back and pulling her attacker's arms over herself. The move was designed to lift her opponent off the floor, using his own movement. It worked against most men, but not this one. He had expected the move already.

He cannoned into her, wrapping his arms tightly around her midriff. His strength was immense. He squeezed her, and Kim felt her bones crunch, her lungs crumple. He raised his right hand, and delivered a jarring blow to the right of her temple. The shock of pain sent a wave of nausea through Kim's body.

She fought back, but her limbs seemed loose, soft. She kicked down with her foot, but the man stepped out, lifted her off the ground, and hurled her like a rag doll against the wall. Kim's head slammed against the concrete, and a black curtain descended over her eyes.

CHAPTER 34

Dan walked quickly, without making a sound. He did not like this place. It was a hideaway for something, and he figured the sooner he got out of the place the better. He was worried about Kim. He could not stop her. What she said made sense. But they did not have any weapons, apart from the useless Browning.

Dan followed the curve of the passage till he came to a large metal door. He tried the handle. It moved. Dan did not press the handle down fully. He left the door locked, and moved further ahead. After one minute of running silently, he found a similar door. He tried the handle and it was open again. He pushed it down gently, getting ready for the shriek of an alarm.

The handle went down smoothly all the way, and the lock clicked. He opened the door a fraction. Bright lights lit the interior. There was a grill walkway going all the way around, with doors at regular intervals. Stairs from the walkways led to the ground floor.

The floor was a huge, cavernous place. Armed sentries walked around with QB-7 sub machine guns. There was a soft hum of machinery, and occasionally, the sound was broken by a loud crashing boom that seemed to come from deep underneath the floor.

Huge piles of crushed rock lay on the floor. Tractors with carriers came up to scoop the crushed rock and drive it to the other end of the floor. Dan could not see that far away, as the roof sloped down, obscuring his vision. At his end, long conveyor belts emerged from holes in the wall, and brought up the crushed rock and dumped it on the floor.

A door opened on the floor, opposite to where Dan was standing. Two figures emerged, followed by a third. The two men at the front were carrying a body between them. Dan caught his breath, and his heart rate surged as he recognized the body. It was Kim. He could see her face, both sides bruised from being hit. Rage and frustration burned inside him, threatening to explode. He leaned back against the wall, closing his eyes momentarily.

He needed to think. There would be time to vent his rage later. He breathed out, then looked again. The two men carrying Kim, and the man bringing up the rear were crossing the floor. Dan caught the last man's face.

It was the Chinese guy he had seen before, the one with the scarred face. They went inside a door and disappeared.

Dan figured he did not have much time. These men would assume that Kim had come with someone else. And they would be out looking for him. Dan did a quick Sit Rep. He was directly overhead a number of conveyor belts bringing rocks in from underneath the floor. Which meant there was some mining activity going on underneath.

Apart from the tractor drivers, there were not many close by. The armed guards roamed around, but they did not come too close to the piles of crushed rock.

Dan slipped inside the door and onto the walkway. He crouched, and scooted down the stairs swiftly. There was a pile of rocks ahead of him and he ran behind it. He heard the groan of a tractor. The vehicle lumbered past him. It lurched to a stop in front of a pile, and The driver used its claws to pick up a load of rocks from the ground. Dan felt the ground rumble beneath him, like a train was passing below. The rumbling continued for a long time, adding to the sound of the conveyor belts and the tractor.

Dan looked the other way. He could not see any of the guards. The driver was still inside the tractor. Dan looked up and along the walkway. No one. He seized his chance.

Dan stepped out and ran to the tractor. The drivers eyes opened in shock as Dan pulled the door open. He moved for a lever on the machine dashboard, but Dan's arm lashed out, making a dull crunch as he hit the jaw. The man crumpled back, dazed. Dan was on the seat instantly, pushing the man to one side. He checked the levers quickly, bringing them down. He hopped off the tractor, and picked up a handful of the crushed rock. It was dark in color and left a residue when he rubbed it on his hands. He rubbed it on his face, darkening his tanned skin.

He turned the wheel, and the tractor turned around slowly. Dan put the windows up on either side, and raised the collars of his shirt to hide his face. The giant wheels of the tractor turned as Dan drove slowly down the main isle of the floor. Two of the armed guards passed him by. Neither of them looked at the tractor. Dan passed underneath the sloping roof and came to the other side of the warehouse like structure.

The tractors dumped their load here, into a vast vat like cauldron of simmering liquid. Steam rose up from the huge circular structures. They were placed at regular intervals, connected by pipes. Dan parked the tractor behind three others. The drivers were inside. Dan checked the driver he had knocked out. He had no wish to kill the man, and he was still out cold. Dan rummaged around in the tractor cabin, and found a length of nylon rope. He tied the man's hands with it and used a rag to tie around his mouth.

Then he got out of the tractor. He hid behind the giant wheels, almost as tall as him. One of the guards approached. Dan shrank back against the tractor, his heart beating wildly. Had he been spotted?

The guard approached, and walked within five feet of where Dan was hiding. Dan heard the steps come closer, then stop. He clenched his jaws. He could sense the guard moving around like he had seen something.

Maybe a flicker of movement when Dan had jumped from the tractor cabin. Dan waited, his heart pounding in his mouth. Footsteps again, and coming towards him. Desperately, Dan pressed himself into the angled recess between the wheel and tractor's body, trying to make himself as small as possible. If it came to it, he would kill the guard without a moment's hesitation. But the scuffle might cause unwanted attention.

Unless the guard came behind the tractor, and between the wall and the machine where Dan had parked. Dan took out the Browning from his back belt, and held it by the muzzle. He barely breathed. The guard came up to the tractor's wheel, and stopped again. Dan could see the man's feet. Like most men in Burma, he wore open sandals. The guard called something out. Dan waited. He suspected the man was calling the driver.

The guard repeated his question, and stepped inside. As soon as his head was visible, Dan moved like a striking cobra. The butt of the Browning came down with the savage force on the guards head, knocking him to the floor. Dan kicked him in the face as the man went down, then grabbed his collar and dragged him behind the tractor.

Dan waited, his senses on fire. He had been quiet, but he needed to be sure. After one minute, he still heard no sounds. He looked around him. The tractors were still stationary. Dan knelt over the guard's body and frisked the man. He took the QBZ-95 sub machine gun. It had a thirty cartridge magazine. The man had a Glock 22, a light handgun that Dan had used extensively, despite his preference being a Sig Sauer P226. Dan unhooked the two grenades the man had on his chest rig. The man also had a knife, a long black blade with a serrated edge. Nice. Dan checked the rubber scabbard, and put the knife in his back belt.

He crept out, and walked past the huge vats of smoking liquid. He knew the guards were behind him, but he hoped they would mistake him for the guard, with the gun slung on his back. The vats stretched out in a long row, and Dan counted fifteen of them before he got to the end. The circular structures, joined by a pipe, now had hundreds of pipes coming out of them, all flowing into a giant machine that reached high up, more than thirty feet, Dan reckoned. The machine had five tall chimneys, and water dropped from them onto the machine inside.

There was a sign on the side of the machine in large red Chinese letters.

At the base of the machine there was a long grill barricade. Dan walked forward. Through the grill barricade he could see another series of conveyor belts, emerging from the machine. It was a yellow powdery substance. Light caught the yellow powder, and it gleamed as it flowed down the belt, and disappeared into another machine. Pipes from that machine bore into the wall opposite Dan, and disappeared into another room

Dan looked at the walls, and saw the door he had seen the men take Kim into. He pressed the handle. It was open, and he crept inside.

CHAPTER 35

He needed to find Kim. The door opened up into a passage, covered in metal. There was a door on the right side, the left being a solid metallic wall. Dan opened the door and found another smaller passage. He had to duck as he walked. The passage led to another metallic door. Dan opened it and found himself inside a large open space. The vault had high ceilings, and stretched out to a long distance. Dan could see the other end, more than a hundred feet away.

On the floor, standing in rows lit up by floor lights, were hundreds of tubular structures. They were about three feet high, and electric cables fed inside them. Dan stepped closer. Each one had a metallic stand that stabilised them, and were attached to the top, presenting a lock and opening device. The tubes were made of metal themselves and had Chinese letters written on them in red.

There was also a sign on each one of them. A sign that he recognized, because it was global.

A sign that he had been *taught* to recognize, before the start of the first Iraq War.

A recognition that now rooted him to the spot, lightning bolts of fear erupting inside him.

His mouth fell open, and he felt a wave of dizziness overcome him. Now he knew why the sight of that glistening yellow powder had struck a chord somewhere in his memory.

Again, before the first Iraq War, the entire Delta contingent had been shown what that yellow powder was. Because if they found any trace of it in Iraq, the war would be justified.

They had not found any trace of it. But the memory was lodged in his brain. Not the least because of the painful jabs they had to endure in case they came up against CNB weapons. Chemical, Nuclear and Biological.

Enriched Uranium. Radioactive uranium straight up from the ground was of no use inside a nuclear reactor. For the atoms to hit each other at ultrasonic speeds and form fissile material, the uranium had to be enriched. Enriched uranium had a bright yellow color, often called a yellow cake.

Dan's limbs felt cold and numb. The tubular structures in front of him, with the red Nuclear sign on them, could only be one thing.

Gas centrifuges. Rotating cylinders that caused the heavier uranium to collect at the sides, and the lighter molecules to settle in the middle. Which meant the yellow stuff outside was the end product, and these centrifuges were being fed the stuff coming up in the conveyor belts from the mine below.

Dan realized now why the place was such a mass of tubes and pipes. He shook his head. He needed to move, and to find Kim. He could make sense of this clusterfuck later on.

Before he could move a muscle, he heard a shout from the end of hall. He could not see the owner of the voice, but very soon the man burst into view. Dan could not be sure of the features from a distance, but he looked like a Burmese man. The man shouted again. When Dan did not respond, he raised his weapon.

Dan backed off, then ran for the door. A gun fired, and a round smashed above Dan's head into the metallic wall. Before the whine of the ricochet had faded, another round kicked up dust near Dan's feet. Dan opened the door and went through, but he did not run. He waited till the man had run closer. Then he opened the door suddenly, but keeping his body under cover, he fired. The man had expected Dan to have run for his life, and the sudden opening of the door caught him off guard. Before he could get his weapon to bear Dan had fired, the slanted stock of the QBZ-95 rifle firm against his shoulder. The bullets exploded into the man's chest and he crumpled to the floor.

The game was up. The sound of those rounds would cause the other guards to come running. He had to escape. Dan turned, and ran as hard as he could to the end of the passage. An alarm started blaring, deafening him. The sound reverberated in the metallic corridor. Before Dan could get to the end, the door opened and two armed men entered. Their weapons were in their hand but before they could raise them Dan was down on one knee, rifle stabilised at his shoulder. He double tapped them both in the face, almost decapitating them at close quarters. He ran forward, not knowing what to expect. For three seconds, he crouched by the door. The alarm was blaring still.

He could not afford to stay under cover. This place was a death trap now. Men armed to the teeth would be crawling everywhere, hunting for him. Dan stepped out, and immediately saw he had made the wrong move. He was close to the long chamber where the boiling vats pumped their stuff into the chimney like cooling pipes. Where the yellow, enriched uranium came out from a collection of conveyor belts on the wall.

Thirty feet away from him, a five man patrol was approaching, guns at the ready. One of them spotted Dan as he skidded to a stop. Dan almost fell to the floor as he tried to turn around. He managed to twist his body backward and jump for the door of the passageway. Bullets thundered around him. He managed to open the doorway and dive inside. He heard running footsteps behind him. Through a crack on the metal doorway, Dan fired a long burst. He heard screams, and the men chasing him scattered for cover.

Dan caught a flicker of movement inside the passageway. He did not wait for confirmation. He swung the rifle around and fired blindly to the front. Two men had appeared ahead of him, and his first rounds caught the lead guy in the head, making his head erupt into a mass of red blood and bone fragments. The second guy let loose a few rounds, but Dan had been far quicker. His body shook as the rounds from the QB7-95 pumped into him.

There was no time for a breather. Before the second body in front of him had hit the floor, Dan had unhooked one of the grenades, and rolled it out onto the floor outside. Then he slammed back against the wall of the passage. The explosion shook the warehouse, causing Dan's ears to become completely deaf. As the roar faded, he was out with his gun, using the door as cover, but firing indiscriminately.

Smoke poured in from the chamber, making his eyes water, and his lungs itchy. Dan stepped out. A black figure raised itself like a ghost from the smoke ahead of him, then he saw another. Dan fired, and both figures fell. Then he was running for his life, through the smoke, jumping over dead bodies.

A chatter of gunfire came from ahead, just as he got to the large circular vats of liquid. Dan dived to the ground, and crawled behind one of the vats. Bullets slammed into metal, making the large structure vibrate. It was providing him cover for now, but Dan was worried the vat was not bullet proof. And if it was not, he was in trouble. The vats could be full of acid, or some other corrosive liquid used to break the rocks down. If that was the case, he did not want the damn stuff anywhere near him. He leaned out and fired off a few rounds. Then he waited. The enemy made the mistake of being too eager. They thought they had located him, and could pin him down with ease.

They came forward. Dan was on the floor, spread-eagled. Five men, running out of formation. Helter skelter, no discipline. No cover. Dan fired at their heads, aiming carefully. He needed to preserve his ammo. Five bullets were enough to bring the men down, one by one. They fired back, round pinging off the vat, dangerously close to his face, but Dan's trigger speed was faster than the men firing at him.

More shouts behind him. Men were coming in through the passage. Dan shouldered his weapon, picked up another two rifles from the fallen men, and ran towards the outer section where the tractors were transferring the rocks. He could not see any of the drivers.

He looked around him desperately. He could climb up to the walkway, and use the stairs to go back upstairs. But the staircase was narrow, and cover was scant. He did not relish the thought of getting stuck on it, while getting fired on from above.

The men who had brought Kim down here had used an elevator. That had to be behind the door they came through.

Dan could hear shouts behind him now, and a burst of gunfire. They were firing blindly in panic. Dan found a door to his left and ran for it. He peered inside – it led to a small hallway. At the end of it, to his immense relief, he saw the elevator. He ran to it, and thumbed the button.

After an interminable wait, the door slid open. It was empty inside. Dan jumped in and looked at the controls. He pressed for 1, the highest level. The doors began to slide shut, but Dan had been spotted. He saw men opening the door to the hallway, and raise their gun to fire at him. He shrank back as far as he could, readying his rifle, but the bullets splattered against the metal doors of the elevator as they shut.

Suddenly it was quiet apart from the hum of the machine as it rose up. Dan wiped sweat from his face, then checked his ammo. He was almost out. The two rifles he had picked up had half full mags. He slapped two in, and kept his old mag. Only one grenade left. He also had the knife.

He steadied himself. When the door opened, he would have one helluva welcome party waiting for him.

CHAPTER 36

The bell chimed, and the elevator doors slid open. Dan gripped his weapon. He could hear voices, getting louder. Through the small crack on the ceiling of the elevator, he could see the shapes of men swarming into the elevator. They banged on the sides of the empty elevator, and one of them prodded the ceiling with their rifle muzzle. He counted them.

One, two, three, four...

Now! Dan aimed the best he could through the narrow opening, and fired in a long burst. All four figures shook as their bodies were pumped full of ordnance from above. Dan unhooked the grenade, stuck his arm out, and threw it into the passageway outside the elevator. He heard more shouts outside.

Dan had slid the steel tiles and climbed out of the elevator roof. Now he crouched against the wall of the shaft as the grenade blasted, rocking the elevator, the sound booming against his ears. He waited three seconds for the shrapnel to subside, then jumped down, rifle up, ready to fire. He saw nothing but smoke and the twisted remains of dead bodies.

Dan jumped over them, paying no heed. The passage outside was covered by a brick dome. There was a gate at the end and he rushed to it. It was a black teak door, similar to many he had seen in the temples. But this door was brand new. The dome was made to look like a temple as well, and it cleverly hid the elevator shaft rising up to ground level.

Dan stepped out of the doors and immediately felt the bang and thud of rounds hitting the walls around him. Bullets smashed over his head, chipping dust off the wall, and whined on the floor by his feet. Cursing, Dan jumped back. He ran to the bodies on the floor. He unhooked as many grenades as he could. They were all Type-77 Chinese grenades, built on an old Russian model.

He also found QSZ-92 handguns, each holding a 15-magazine cartridge of 9mm rounds. He put two of the handguns in his back belt. Both were full. He threw away his almost empty QBZ-95 assault rifle, and picked up one that had a full thirty round magazine. He unclipped extra magazines from other rifles.

It was done in a matter of seconds. He ran back to the door and opened it a fraction. Rounds slammed against it again. Dan opened it further, then shrank back against the wall. Rounds poured in, kicking up dust, the smell of ammunition heavy in the air. Dan curled into a corner to avoid the bullets.

It was what he had wanted. A real soldier would have held their fire till they saw him. These men had just given their position away by firing at an open door. Now, Dan knew for sure that the men were clustered about ten o' clock, to his right. Nothing to his front, or left.

If there was, he would come under heavy fire. He needed to take that chance, to get out of here alive. Dan pressed himself to the floor, crawled forward, and threw three of the grenades as hard as he could. He waited for the dull roar of them exploding, almost knocking the heavy door off its hinges. He fell backwards from the impact of the grenades, but was up in an instant. He charged out the door, lips drawn in mad fury, squeezing the trigger of his rifle. To his right, about fifty feet away, the survivors of the grenade attack were stumbling to their feet. Dan mowed them down, then threw himself to the floor. No bullets came to hit him from the front. He looked up and saw a green line of dense jungle, leading up to a hill.

Behind him, he heard the roar of a motor engine, squealing to a stop, and the scream of multiple voices. Reinforcements had arrived. Time to take cover.

Dan got up and ran as hard as he could, heading for the trees.

*****

Henry Deng leaned against the wall and watched his mother.

Biyu Deng sat in her worship room, surrounded by jade, porcelain and terracotta figures. The greatest of them all, the originator, was the large central figure of *Muyiji*.

Muyiji had started the great cosmic dance many millennium ago that caused the trees and mountains to exist. When He was happy, men earned a living from the forest, and trade across the border flowed. When He was angry, ethnic conflict flared up, bombs blasted deep in the jungle, and business dried up.

Biyu had her eyes closed, and the heady smell of burning incense sticks coated the air around her. Deng knew his mother was praying.

His mind went back to the sacrifices she had made to get where she was.

This was the center of her universe. From where she had built up her animal trading business. When she was starving, raising two little boys on her own, no one had cared for her. After her husband died, her family in Kunming had told her to stay in Pangshang. Deng had heard the story from his elderly aunt who had now died.

When the boys were in school, Biyu had gone far into the jungles, to make the villagers kill animals for her. They ate the animals too, as they had no other food. Horse and elephant meat.

Her first elephant tusk had got her ten thousand kyat. That opened her eyes. She broke her back every week lugging the heavy backpack with bones across the hilly borders. The border guards stopped her, even though she was a woman on her own. On more than one occasion she had to pay them…favors.

One night, she got stuck in the monsoon rains, and her bag fell open. She lost all her precious bones down a mountain ravine. She could not look for them, because the boys were alone at home. She wept all the way back to the little shack where they lived. Deng remembered waking up as his mother came in later at night. Those awful days, he knew, had hardened her heart even more.

Later, when she had money, she bought herself a beat up second hand Russian Lada. She was the first woman in Pangshang to drive a car. The small town folk gaped at her as she drove around, honking her horn.

When Li and Deng were teenagers, they started helping her. Biyu had stopped them, she wanted them to finish school. Deng remembered with a smile how they had refused. For the business, that had been the turning point. Within months, they were trading more than she had done in the last five years.

Deng watched as his mother opened her eyes. They focused on the opulent jade figure of *Muyiji*. She murmured a small prayer, and pinched a grain of rhinoceros horn and elephant tusk powder from a porcelain bowl. She threw the grain of powder at Muyiji as she whispered under her breath.

Deng's phone beeped inside his pocket. He looked at the screen, feeling his mother's head turn to look at him. Deng stepped outside. It was Li.

Li's voice was strained. Deng listened, his chest starting to heave with fury. When Li finished, Deng closed his eyes. He controlled his breathing with an effort.

Deng asked, "Where is the *Baw* woman?"

"We got her," Li said.

"Good. Keep her safe. And find this *Yaoguai*, this evil spirit, and kill him once and for all. Pump the *sha bi* full of lead for me."

Li whispered, "Cousin, I will see to it myself."

Deng put the phone away and paced the courtyard. He stopped when he saw his mother. Biyu's face was calm, reflecting the storm on his countenance.

"Who is your enemy, *Erzi*?" Biyu asked.

"This *Baw* man and woman. I have got the woman now, but the man is proving to be difficult." Deng told her how Dan had escaped.

Biyu came closer. "I felt this man. He is a spirit from over the hills, across the seas. Something comes with him. A storm perhaps. I want you to be more careful son. Did you listen to what Li Ka Shing had to say?"

Deng looked to the ground. "I have donated millions to the Party, mother. I built the casino and nightclubs which bring tax dollars to Pangshang. Why should I let the Party dictate terms to me now?"

"Because you are now playing for higher stakes, *Erzi*. You have to be more careful. You need friends. You can get rid of them later, when they are no use to you. But if you surround yourself with enemies, you will not last long."

"*Muqin*, I want to finish the dream you started. I want to make the Deng family name resonate all over China. Our family in Kunming will know who they are dealing with. They will come here, to pay their respect at your feet."

"They respect me already, Henry. If you want to make the Deng family famous, you need to have a wife and children." A smile flickered on the old woman's face.

"I would endure all the hardship I have in life, all over again, just to see the faces of grandchildren. One day, they will carry your name, just like you carry your father's today."

Biyu stepped forward and touched her son's cheek. Deng shrugged, looking embarrassed. He would not meet his mother's eyes.

Biyu's eyes hardened. "Remember what I said, *Erzi*. Be careful of the storm that is coming."

CHAPTER 37

CIA HQ
NCS OFFICE
LANGLEY, VIRGINIA

Solomon Barney leaned over the analyst's screen. The office lights were dimmed, and multiple blue screens in desks around them showed satellite images from various drone feeds at different global locations.

Solomon stabbed at the slate grey line in the middle of the screen. "That's a river, right?"

The analyst cleared his throat and bobbed his head. "Yes sir. The Irrawaddy river. The longest river in Myanmar, coming down from the northern mountains…"

"I know what the Irrawaddy river is," Solomon snapped. "Is that where the signal is coming from?"

"Yes sir. From this location, specifically. Which is roughly 75 miles southeast of a town called Mandalay."

Solomon squinted at the image. Kimberly Smith's cell phone had a PINS or Precision Inertial Navigation System microchip fitted to it. GPS signals were prone to jamming by enemy radio waves, and did not work well inside buildings or underwater. But PINS did, and it was now becoming the standard device inside the cell phones of every CIA NCS agent. It worked even when the phone was damaged, or separated from its battery.

Solomon murmured to himself, "What the hell is that phone doing under that river?"

The answer was not a palatable one. He straightened. "Alright. Do me a report on the exact locations, and send it as an email to the DDO, John Hymers."

"Yes sir," the analyst said.

Solomon placed his palm on the digital pad on the door and the door opened. He walked out into the long hallway, April sunlight streaming in through the long windows on the sides. Head bent in thought, he walked slowly. He climbed three floors, and knocked on John Hymers office.

"Come in," said Hymers. His face changed when he saw Solomon. Solomon walked over to the glass wall facing the forest beyond, and rested against a table.

"We don't know where she is. We have a situation now. Estefan Fernandez is dead. Poisoned with VX liquid, one of the most poisonous gases known to man. A few drops can be fatal. Kim has vanished, with that man called Dan Roy."

Hymers stared at Solomon. "Jesus Christ."

Solomon set his jaw in grim line. "There's reports in Yangon local media about a big crystal meth factory burned down. A white woman and man escaped. Myanmar, as you know, is one of the largest methamphetamine pill producers in the world."

"I didn't know that."

"Well, they are. They supply the whole of Asia. Think billions of dollars in trade, similar to the cocaine drug cartels in Peru and Ecuador."

"And Kim got mixed up with them? Why?"

"Developing some assets, I'm sure. Most of the drug labs and smuggling is done by the Wa State Army who answer to China. If they had an informer, Kim would be chasing him."

Sol stopped and looked at Hymers. "Somehow, this is all mixed up with the Tonkin Protocol."

Hymers frowned and slowly shook his head, holding eye contact with Sol. He knew what that meant. Not here, and not now.

Hymers said, "So we have one agent missing, one agent dead, and one agent chasing some drug dealers, location unknown?"

"That's about right. And she has this man with her."

"You mentioned him last time. Someone called Dan Roy."

"Right. I don't know who he is, but Kim seems to trust him. She reckons he's ex-military."

Sol reached inside his jacket and pulled out a USB drive. He showed it to his boss and raised his eyebrows. Hymers tapped some button on his keyboard and moved back from his desk. Sol stepped up and inserted the drive. Some photos came up on the screen. They both peered at the screen. The screen showed Kim, Dan and Maya running down a market street in Yangon.

Hymers said, "Who's the kid?"

"The kid helped them to escape. They got back to the Embassy. They have a map which Kim thinks might lead them to David Harris."

"And that's the last you heard?"

Sol didn't answer. He fixed his gaze on Hymers, who returned his unblinking stare.

Hymers said, "What do you want, Sol?"

"This thing is blowing up in our faces, right? A total of three agents missing or dead. A foreign national in protection of our Government…"

Hymers stepped forward, frowning. "Whoa, whoa. What foreign national?"

"That kid. She's living inside the diplomatic enclave apartments with one of our agents, Mary."

Hymers looked stricken. "Sol, you know she can't be there. Anything happens to her, it's our goddamn fault. Plus, she's a juvenile. Where's her parents?"

Sol said, "This is Myanmar, John. Kids work on the streets. Harsh, but that's the way it is. Anyway, you're gonna send her back when she's been helping us? I can just see the headlines now – US Government Embassy in Myanmar refuses to help child who supplied them information." Solomon leaned forward on the desk. "A whole new can of worms, John."

Hymers paced with his hands on his hips. "We are in a pile of shit regardless. But best to send her back where she came from. It's the only way, right?"

Sol faced his boss, who stopped pacing. "John, tell me about the Tonkin Protocol. Read me in if you have to. Tell me who I have to see to get clearance. But damn it, if this thing's gonna blow up, you *got to* have me in the fucking loop."

Hymers closed his eyes and ran his hand through his hair. He put his coat on and gestured with his eyes. Sol left the office, followed by Hymers.

Outside, their footsteps crunched gravel as they walked down a dirt trail. Tall trees loomed around them. Solomon took a breath of the nascent Spring air. It didn't seem so fresh to him anymore.

Hymers said, "The Tonkin Protocol is a plan to put pressure on the Chinese about their activities in the South China Sea."

"How? Through the Seventh Pacific Fleet based in Okinawa?"

"No, that's too obvious. You know how China gets all its oil, right?"

"Remind me."

"The majority comes through the Malacca Straits south of Singapore. It's a narrow channel of five hundred miles, and shallow in places. It's like a choke point. But there is no other way to connect the Indian Ocean to the South China Sea. China bound oil tankers have to go through the Malacca Straits."

Light was beginning to dawn in Solomon's eyes. "This is about that oil tanker from Iran that got blown up south of Singapore, in this Strait. Right?"

"Not blown up. Fire in the engine." They looked at each other, and Solomon instantly knew it was more than a fire in the engine. He breathed out.

"I see. So we cut off China's oil supply by closing off Malacca Strait. They sure as hell ain't gonna be happy about that John."

"No, that would be an act of war. That is precisely the reason we always have a US Navy Destroyer within 100 miles of Singapore. To keep an eye on Malacca Strait, and on the South China Sea."

"Get to the point, John. What does this have to do with the Tonkin Protocol?"

"Right. China knows about this, so they have built an oil pipeline that goes from the west coast of Myanmar, right across to the Yunnan Province in the east of China. To reduce their reliance on the Malacca Straits, and the South China Sea."

"Carry on."

Hymers took a deep breath. "So we put pressure on the Chinese. That oil tanker was a warning shot."

"A warning shot to say we could sabotage their oil pipeline in Myanmar?"

The two men stopped walking. Solomon said, "To make them aware we know what's going on. Myanmar has a lot of oil in its coastal water, Sol. Billions of barrels. That country could become key to Chinese oil security, say 20 years from now."

Solomon smiled despite himself. "Myanmar becomes the Chinese Saudi Arabia?"

Hymers did not smile. "The Protocol planned to blow up some of the stations around the Myanmar oil pipeline, and the railway tracks. We worked with the Shan State Army. We gave them weapons, they took the blame."

Solomon nodded. "Then we negotiate with the Burmese Army not to attack the Shan State. Politics as usual, right?"

"Right. We put pressure on the Chinese via Myanmar, they stop claiming islands in the South China Sea, and harassing Taiwan."

"Sounds like a bargain to me."

"It would be, but then David Harris got caught. Now the boot's on the other foot." Hymers looked towards the sky. "Find them, Sol. It doesn't matter what it takes. Just find them."

CHAPTER 38

David Harris was waist deep in the river water. The water was clear, and he could see all the way to the bottom. Small fish nibbled at his feet. A black water snake curled around a rock, then untangled itself and darted away. David relaxed. Maung Thin had taught him that river snakes were harmless.

David was naked from the waist up, but he had a rifle in his hands. He lofted the AK-47 above his head, elbows straight. The river was narrow, and they had come down from the heavily wooded banks sloping down to it, heading for the huts on the other side. Further upstream, the river had been dammed up using felled logs, so the flow here was gentle. David got to the other side, and a strong pair of hands helped to lift him up.

"Thank you," David said to the naked chested man who had helped him up. A few more had come out of the cluster of huts to stare at him. They were all men. This was an outpost of the Shan State Army, the SSA. About fifty men who patrolled the long and uneasy border between the Shan area and Mandalay.

David heard Maung Thin splash on to the bank behind him. The young Burmese walked forward and spoke rapidly to the men. They nodded, sneaking looks at David.

David sat down on the bank of the river, leaning against a rock. The jungle rose up thick and heavy on both sides, the river cutting a silver thread through it. It was a tributary of the Irrawaddy, Maung had told him. They had walked for 3 days, eating fruits and river water. Maung had managed to kill an animal that was called a *chetal,* which seemed like a small deer to David. They had roasted the meat over a fire, and carried the rest with them.

They had followed the river till they got to the camp. David heard voices raised behind him, and he turned to look. Maung finished speaking to them, and walked to David.

"They are not happy," Maung said. "They say you bring trouble to us. They will hunt for you and come here."

David looked at the sparkling waters and said, "At this point, I guess they're right, Maung Thin. I need to get back to Yangon, ASAP."

Maung nodded in silence. He opened his mouth to speak. The word never left his tongue. His head exploded in a geyser of red blood and bone. His arms came up, like he was trying to stop himself from falling backwards. In slow motion, it seemed, he collapsed, slamming down on the river bank.

David was paralysed for a second, but then he moved quickly. He grabbed Maung's legs and pulled him behind the rock. From the far bank there was a chatter of machine gun fire. Men around him shouted and ran for cover. Bullets sparked off the rock David was hiding behind. David forgot the chaos around him, and looked down at the face of the man who had saved his life.

Maung Thin's head had literally been blown open. There wasn't much distinguishable about his face anymore. David screamed in frustration. Men lay dead and dying around him. He lifted himself up, and using the rock as cover, fired back. He could see the flash of machine gun fire, shredding the huts around him to ribbons. It was aided by small arms fire from the trees.

David fired at will, but noticed after a while there wasn't much return fire from his side. The men had fled into the jungle, their only chance of survival. David lowered his rifle and turned around, but he was too late.

A rifle butt smashed down on his face. The men had crept up on him while he had been firing. David fell to the ground, dazed. Before he could lift himself up, a heavy boot kicked him in the abdomen, knocking air out of his lungs. The AK-47 was ripped from his hands. Through a wave of nausea, he looked up, and saw a ring of men with assault rifles surrounding him. A pain exploded at the back of his head, and his eyes went black.

*****

The burlap sack around her head was chafing Kim. Her face felt puffy and painful. She opened her mouth to breathe, and the fabric of the sack made her cough. The light outside was a dim haze. The floor beneath her rattled and shook, and the smell of dust was strong in the air. She realized she was on the back of a vehicle.

Thirst consumed her. Her lips were dry and cracked, and sweat caked her head. Even a drop of water would be heaven sent. But all she could taste was her own dry tongue. After a long, long time, the vehicle shuddered to a stop. She heard doors slam, and then voices speaking in what she recognized as both Mandarin and Burmese.

She felt rough hands grab her, then lift her to her feet. She stood up, stumbling. Her hands were tied in front and she was pulled forward. She could smell the sweat of a man as he stood near her. She was led down a dirt trail, kicking small stones as she walked. She could smell the jungle now. Wet earth, trees and a trace of fresh air. Birds called out in the distance and nearby, answering each other.

She heard more voices, and detected a change in the light around her. She could see hazily ahead, and it seemed like a clearing with small buildings around. Kim heard the sound of a door being opened, and then a hand on her back pushed her into darkness. She stumbled again, and this time, tripped on something and fell over. The darkness remained, and the door slammed shut behind her.

Kim grunted and moved. She had scraped her knees when she fell, and her bruised wrists had taken the brunt of the fall. Her arms hurt like hell. The sack around her head was driving her mad.

Her legs touched something, and she recoiled. Hastily, she dug her heels on the ground and moved away. Her back was to the wall. Then she heard a moan from ahead, where her legs had made contact. The moan came again, and it was louder.

The moan became a voice, and it swore loudly in English. A man's voice. The accent sounded American. Kim's heart raced.

Kim cleared her throat, and raised her voice. "Hey, who's there?"

The man's voice stopped immediately. Kim's eyes had not got used to the dark yet. Even if they did, she guessed she wouldn't see much in the dimness.

Kim repeated her question. She felt something shift in front of her, and a shadow raised itself from the floor. Kim shrank back against the wall.

She heard a man's hoarse voice. "Who is that?"

Kim thought she had nothing to lose. "My name is Kim Smith. I am an American. Who are you?"

The voice said, "My name is David Harris. What are you doing here, Kim Smith?"

Kim groaned inside. She had just fulfilled one part of her mission. To find David Harris. In the worst possible place imaginable.

"David, please tell me you don't work for the NCS, and you were not sent here about the Tonkin Protocol."

The silence she was rewarded with spoke volumes to Kim. "David", she sighed, "I was sent here to locate you. Solomon Barney and John Hymers of the DO sent me down here. Do you copy?"

There was an audible sigh, then the voice said, "Yes, I copy. How did you end up here?"

"David, can you get this thing off my head?"

David coughed. "My hands are tied, but I can try. Wait." Kim felt David stand over her, facing the other way. She tried to help him the best she could. Eventually, the sack came off her head. Kim breathed deeply. David flopped back down in front of her. Kim could see him now. It was a shocking sight. His face was mangled like it had been chewed by a predator. Dried blood caked his head. The effort to take the sack off her head had clearly exhausted him.

Kim told him her story. When she finished, David said, "So this guy, Dan Roy, where is he now?"

Kim closed her eyes and opened them. But when she spoke, her voice was stronger.

"He's looking for us, David. He's somewhere out there."

CHAPTER 39

Guns chattered behind Dan, which meant he had been spotted. Bullets whined overhead. He ran faster, carrying the two rifles and extra ammo he had picked up. The jungles loomed up ahead, a thick, impenetrable emerald shroud. Panting, Dan reached the tree line and plunged into the undergrowth.

Dry twigs cracked under his feet, sticky vines fell in front of his face. Dan brushed them away with his hands. He jumped over fallen tree trunks, and kept moving. The hot, sticky jungle grew denser around him. The canopy of trees overhead made the jungle dappled with shade, but also more humid. The leaves and branches pressed upon him from all sides, reducing his field of vision, suffocating him. Sweat poured down his face and body like taps had turned on inside his skin. He was dying for a drink.

Keep moving. Stop and you die.

In the stillness of the jungle, Dan heard voices behind him. Men, moving in fast. There would be many of them, and they would know this terrain well. More than ever, Dan needed a compass. That would make life easier. He knew he had to head down south to get to Yangon. But he did not know where Kim had been taken. That place would be his first port of call.

A bullet splattered against a tree trunk behind him. The shouts increased. He had been spotted. Dan ran faster, but the jungle held him back. His hands bled from the thorny vines hanging from the trees. He used one of the rifles to hack away at the growth, wishing he had his long kukri knife with him. He did have a knife, but it was only 8 inches, not long enough to cut through this undergrowth.

Dan huddled under a large tree trunk to catch his breath. He listened. Birds tweeted high above, along with the swish of branches moving. Far behind him, he could hear the voices of the men, calling out to each other. They made noise as they moved. Hunters, looking for the hunted.

How many? Dan didn't know. He had to put distance between them and himself, but they would have reinforcements. He could keep running, but the jungle was slowing him down. They could catch up with him, and he might be exhausted by then. He needed water, and there would be a river or stream up ahead, he was sure.

But he had to get there first, and he sure as hell didn't want the enemy following him there.

Time to make a stand.

Dan rubbed mud from the jungle floor over his face and arms. He smeared mud on the rifle muzzle as well, in case a ray of sunlight fell on it. It would cover moonshine as well. The ground was soft beneath his feet, so he stepped toe first now, to minimise sound.

Camouflaged, and on his tip toes, Dan ran like a hare. The jungle covered him in its sticky claustrophobic embrace, and he submitted to it – a black, shadowy figure running for his life.

Then he spotted something that made him stop.

The land had a gentle upwards slope, and to his right, he could see craggy black rock formations jutting out of the jungle floor. He saw the yawning dark mouth of a large cave. Dan moved towards the caves. He saw a human shape in front of the cave and dropped to the floor, rifle trained in his hands. Then he lowered the rifle.

It wasn't a figure. It was a Buddha statue, neglected and weather beaten, with thick yellow root vines growing around it. Dan raised himself and rushed forward. Behind the statue, the cave loomed huge and dark. The roof of the cave was easily twenty feet above him. He could see a few feet inside, and heard the trickle of water.

Dan took the magazine out of one rifle. He lifted the rifle up and smashed it down as hard as he could against the stone floor of the cave. The sound was like an explosion in the stillness of the jungle. Dan raised the rifle up and smashed it down again. Then he left the empty rifle on the floor, and ran towards the rocks at the side of the cave. They were about thirty feet away. He got there in the blink of an eye, and vaulted over the top. He looked back, and the cave was now ahead of him. He pointed his gun and waited.

The men appeared slowly. Bent at the waist, they moved in formation. Dan was perched about ten feet high, and he watched them move. One darted ahead, while the others covered him. The leader raised his hand, and then the rest moved from the back. They repeated this movement till they were crouched in a ring, about twenty feet away from the Buddha statue.

Not good. These men were trained in tactical movement.

Dan waited patiently. He counted ten of them in total. Once they had cleared the area, the men relaxed. Most of them joined the leader at the mouth of the cave. One of them bent down and picked up the rifle. Others looked inside the cave.

Now.

Dan took the pin out and threw the grenade – flat and fast. It exploded by the feet of one man, ripping his legs from his waist, and sending a yellow orange fireball raging to the sky. Dan ducked as the shrapnel fell, but then he was up, the QBZ-95 set to automatic mode, shaking in his hand, deafening his ears as round after round erupted from its flaming muzzle.

Ahead of him the surviving soldiers wilted and fell to the ground. Screams filled the air. Dan stopped firing. As the smoke cleared, but his ears still ringing from the gun, he counted eight dead bodies in the ground, not moving. He fired a quick blast at the mouth of the cave, then jumped down from the rock. Rifle at the shoulder, scanning for movement, he crept towards the mouth of the cave.

A flicker caught his eye at the floor of the cave, and he fired instantly, without waiting for his brain to tell him what it was. A scream rewarded his effort, but Dan had already dived for the floor, and rolled behind the Buddha statue. He got up and fired again at the prostate figure. The man was wounded, and trying to lift his gun. Dan fired and the rounds smashed into the man's body, jerking till it stopped moving.

More bullets came from the cave, from the last survivor. Dan moved to the other side. He picked up a branch near his feet, and threw it. Bullets followed the branch, giving away the shooters location. Dan moved out from behind the statue and fired a long burst. A scream came from the dark mouth of the cave, then a figure lurched out. He was still holding the rifle in his right arm, but the left was hanging useless. Several bullets had shredded the left shoulder. With another scream the man lifted his rifle up, but Dan's bullet smashed into his face and he toppled head first into the ground.

Ten down. It was still all of a sudden. A deathly quiet. The birds had stopped twittering, and the wind in the trees was silent. Dan moved forward. His rifle was steaming in his hands, the muzzle too hot to touch. Good to go still, but he would need to check the gas soon.

From one of the dead bodies, he found a heavier QCW-05 5.8mm sub machine gun. He had seen these weapons once in the PLA garrison of Hong Kong. The weapon had the same bullpup configuration as the QBZ-95, but had a longer firing range, and this weapon was even fitted with a silencer. Chinese serial numbers were engraved on the side.

Dan found a QSZ-92 hand pistol as well, 15 round magazine loaded with 9mm rounds. He got extra ammo, and some more hand grenades. He found a metallic bow with explosive tipped arrows, compass and a map. But no water, the one thing he needed badly. Within one minute, he had restocked himself. He got up, and melted into the forest behind him.

CHAPTER 40

The sub machine gun was heavier than the assault rifle – and he now had one of each strapped to his back. About nine pounds altogether, he figured. He kept moving, as quietly as possible.

The jungle began to slope down. He was near the crest of a hill, and he stopped when he heard a sound he had been waiting for – running water. He moved forwards, and found a river at the bottom of a valley. He allowed himself a second to look around him. He listened hard for sounds.

The carnage he had left behind would be found, and they would return twice as strong.

Swirling mists covered the distant wooded green peaks, undulating into the far horizon. On the crest of one far mountain peak, sunlight glinted off the yellow walls of a monastery. Windows in the mist offered a magical view of luminous paddy fields reflecting the sky, bordered by crystal clear blue lakes.

He looked down at the river far below. Its waters were muddy and brown, and it curved round the hills in an S shape before disappearing from view. Dan knew if he followed the river for long enough he would find human habitation.

He began his descent. He used a machete he had found on one of the soldiers, hacking away at the vines to clear a path for himself. He felt a sudden sting in his left arm and looked down to a find a soft black shape attached to his skin. It was about four inches long. Dan reached for the knife, and hooked it under the organism. It was a leech. The leech came off his forearm with a sucking sound. A trickle of blood poured out and Dan covered it with his hand. He squashed the leech with his foot, and it erupted in a small ball of blood.

After almost an hour, Dan had reached within a hundred feet of the river bank. The waters were swollen by mountain streams, and the current was strong. Dan wiped his forehead. He needed to get to the river to taste the water. But then he saw the long white stream that was falling from the green hills. It was to his left, in a clearing on the river bank.

The waterfall fell on black rocks, and then gurgled away in a slipstream to join the river. Panting, Dan approached the clearing. It was a relief to walk in the open air, and he rushed to the waterfall. He turned his back to the river, and crouched by the waterfall, facing the hills he had just descended.

Like a man supplicating himself in prayer, Dan reached out his cupped palms and drank the water thirstily. He took four gulps and splashed water on his face.

When he opened his eyes he saw a man crouching at the edge of the clearing. His rifle was ready at the shoulder, aimed at Dan.

Before Dan could move the gun had fired, and the round streaked past his ear, singeing his hairs. Dan dived for the floor, pulling out the handgun tucked at his front belt line as he did so. He fired twice, and the man fell back, gun falling useless from his hands. Bullets came at him thick and fast. They zinged off the rocks, whined past his face. This time, they were staying under cover. Dan looked for a rock, but the clearing was bare. A muddy surface that went straight down to the water.

He had no time to think. He fired back rapidly, emptying the magazine. Then he leaped up and ran as hard as he could. He dived into the water, sinking down into the muddy, murky depths. He lost the submachine gun and the rifles. The handgun would be waterlogged as well, he knew.

No use to me if I don't live to fire them.

Dan had taken a deep breath before he had jumped in the water. He could stay under water for two minutes, and sometimes longer. He swam fast underwater, not being able to see anything. His lungs began to burn and his vision dimmed. A dizziness spread across his head. He had to surface. He lifted his mouth up to the surface, then his head. Even before he could focus, he heard the sound of a motor engine. Dan took a deep breath and dived back in the water.

The droning sound of the boat grew louder, then it faded as it got closer to him. The engine cut out just as it approached Dan. He treaded water, seeing the black shape above him. They couldn't see him, but he could see them. He knew what he had to do.

Dan thrust upwards with his legs. The knife was out, in his hand. He wanted to use the machete, but in close quarters the knife would be easier. He saw the snout of a rifle aimed at the water, and a black shape behind it – the man holding the rifle.

They had not expected what Dan did next. They expected him to hide, or to have drowned by now.

Dan burst out of the water, grabbing the trigger finger of the man holding the gun, pulling him into the water. Before his shocked friends could understand, Dan had buried the knife to the hilt in the man's neck. Even as blood spurted in a high crimson arc, Dan had ripped the rifle from the man's hand. One of the men fired, but Dan had pulled the dying man in front of him as cover, while he held the rifle with his right hand.

Dan squeezed the trigger and bullets erupted from the muzzle. The figures in the boat shook and jerked as the rounds hit them almost point blank. Several rounds were fired towards Dan, but he had the dead body shielding him, and half his body was under water.

Then he heard the drone of another boat behind him. Dan grabbed the knife, pulled it out of the man's neck and clambered aboard the boat. He chucked the three dead bodies overboard, leaving their weapons. The fifth man was still alive, and Dan shot him in the face, then chucked him overboard as well.

He sparked the engine and it came to life, just as another speed boat came hurtling around the river bend, its bow raised, sprouting a head of white foam. Dan gunned the engine and the boat took off at high speed. Wind whipped around his face, pushing his dark hair back. He heard a sharp crack and ducked. A bullet whined inches past his face. Dan turned the boat to the left, away from his chaser, then right again, zigzagging.

He knew he could not keep this up. He headed for the banks. The river had widened up now. Dense woods still climbed high on both sides. Dan gunned for a clearing. He picked up a rifle. The boat came off the water at almost full speed. It hit the landing of the mud bank and lifted clear into space. Before it crashed back down, Dan had jumped already, landing on the soft mud and rolling over.

He was up with the rifle chattering in his hands, seeking cover behind the overturned motorboat. Three figures with guns aimed at him shuddered and shook as his bullets found them. But the boat was larger than his, and it was full of men. They had ducked for cover.

Dan turned and ran for the green trees behind him. He climbed quickly, glad for the cover the thick jungle provided. But then he stopped and looked down. The boat had grounded, and men had spilled out into the clearing of the bank. Dan stayed under cover and fired, the rifle set to manual so he could conserve ammo. He saw four figures fall before the rest took cover.

Dan heard a swishing sound, like something big was moving through the air. He turned to the side, but he was a fraction late. The iron club missed his head by inches, but glanced across his neck. It was a heavy weapon, and the blow dazed him. Dan tried to stand up, but fell to his knees. This time the club did not miss. Like a wrecking ball, it crashed down on his shoulder. Pain jarred his arm, and his gun fell useless to the side. He looked up and saw a man standing in front of him.

A face he had seen before. A scar that ran from the left eye to the lips, disfiguring the face. The lips twitched into a smile.

Dan grimaced and reached for the handgun he had picked up on the boat. Something heavy hit him like a sledgehammer from behind. A shockwave of pain blinded his eyeballs white. Pain seared across his head, followed by a wave of nausea.

He could not see anymore.

But he was Dan Roy. He stood up, a silent scream forming on his lips. He felt warm blood ooze down his forehead. He said something that he could not decipher himself. His words were a roar in his ears. He reached for the handgun again.

The blow came again, heavier this time. Pain blasted across his head like an imploding supernova, and then he was falling, deep, deep into an amniotic abyss.

CHAPTER 41

Dan's eyes flickered open. There was a buzzing in his ears, and a dull ache that clouded his vision. He felt light, like he was suspended mid-air, and floating in space. He could see a pair of boots in front of him. They seemed large, till his eyes refocused. They were not large, he was just close to them. He could not see the body to which the boots belonged.

He shook his head. Then he tried to move his hands. They were stuck. He looked at them. His arms were spread apart, and his hands were tied to a cross with rope. Dan looked up. His vision was still hazy, but he could make out a figure above him. With an effort, he realized the figure was the same one wearing the shoes.

He felt that strange floating sensation again and looked down. He was in a swamp. Muddy water came up to his upper chest. He watched with a detached sensation as a black leech crawled out of the swamp and worked its way up his chest and began to feed on his shoulder. He felt the sting of pain and shuddered.

"Lift him up," the voice above him ordered.

Dan heard creaking and groaning sounds. He felt a shift in the air around him. Water drained off his body and he blinked as harsh sunlight hit his eyes. The creaking stopped and he felt himself jolt forward. Then back. He pulled on his arms and leaned back against the cross. His feet and arms were tied to the wooden structure, but the rest of his body was hanging.

Dan blinked till his eyes focused. A man was standing on the bank, observing him curiously, like he was some sort of scientific experiment. Dan recognized the scarred face. The man smiled again. He spoke in English.

"Ah, finally. You decided to come back to us. Have to say, not many survive as long as you did in the swamp. It's nice not to pull out a dead body."

Dan stared at the man. He tried to speak but his throat was bone dry. He coughed and said, "Who are you?"

"My name is Li Yonping. What's yours?"

Dan did not answer. He could feel leeches crawling all over his legs now. His mouth was craving water.

Li Yonping gestured to one of his men. A man came over with an earthen jug of water, and tipped the edge on Dan's mouth. Dan opened his lips and drank thirstily. Abruptly, the jug was moved from his lips. Dan's head lolled forward on his chest.

Li said, "The way you die depends on you. A quick bullet to the head, or a long session in the torture chamber."

Behind Li, Dan could see a cluster of bamboo huts with thatched palm leaf rooves. The compound was not large. A tall bamboo fence went around the perimeter. The jungle hung dense and foreboding behind it.

Dan said, "Where is the woman?"

Li said, "Ah, the woman. She has been taken to another place. Don't worry about her. My men will have fun with her, once she has told us what she knows."

"If you touch her, I'll kill you."

Li threw his head back and laughed. "You? You will be dead soon. But if you don't tell us what you know, death will be so slow you will beg me to kill you."

Li spoke to one of his men again. Dan felt himself being moved towards the ground. Once the cross had moved from the swamp, Dan's hands were untied, then tied again behind his back. His feet were freed and he could stand. He fell to his knees, then felt arms pulling him up.

A rifle muzzle prodded him from behind and Dan started to walk. He bumped into a hard structure, then walked straight. He was guided to a chair. He sat down heavily.

Shafts of sunlight pierced the dimness inside the room. Spliced bamboo shafts acted as grills on the two windows. Behind it, Dan could see the fence. There was a broken mirror on the wall. Next to it, red and yellow Chinese calendars with pictures of different deities. In the far corner he saw a gurney, with a cabinet next to it. The floor underneath the gurney was stained with blood. There was a machine with dials on it on a table, with what looked like headphones attached to it.

Li Yonping was sat opposite Dan on the table. Next to him sat another man with similar Oriental features. This man wore a cream safari suit, and had sunglasses that were hooked back on his grease slicked hair. He was smooth shaven and smelled of aftershave.

The man said in English, "My name is Henry Deng. Do you know who I am?"

Dan said, "Should I?"

A man came in with a sheet of silver aluminium foil. He put it on the table in front of Li and Deng. He opened the foil up to reveal a small brown object on the foil. Li took a lighter from his pocket, lifted up the foil carefully, and heated the bottom. The brown object melted instantly, becoming a liquid, and giving off a pungent steam. Li leaned forward and inhaled sharply, then passed the foil to Deng. Deng used his hands to move more of the smoke towards him, inhaling all the while.

Dan watched them without any expression on his face. Deng inhaled the smoke again, and when the liquid dried up into a crust, he crumpled the foil and threw it away. Li looked at Dan and smiled. His eyes were red rimmed, but there was a new alertness in them. His nostrils flared. He opened his mouth and shut it, then gave Dan that dead smile again.

Dan said, "Crystal meth, right?"

Deng answered. "Only the best from our labs. We get top dollar because we make the best product. Just like any normal business."

"You guys are ruining this country. Opium farming's been cut down, but the amphetamine market is booming."

Deng said, "Take off your privileged glasses and look around you, *sha bi*. You see Uncle Sam coming around here with Aid money? Even if he did, it would end up in the pockets of our corrupt politicians."

"So, that makes what you do right?"

Deng said, "We give jobs to our young men. Put food on their plates. And soon enough, I shall do a lot more. Everyone will know the name of Henry Deng."

Dan said, "Anything to do with the enriched uranium I saw down there?"

Both men went very still. Deng's chest heaved up and down. Dan knew the crystal meth was starting to work. Both men would now be up for hours with little need for sleep. Their self-confidence would be high, with a higher tolerance to physical pain.

Deng breathed out and said, "You are CIA."

"No."

Deng raised his arm and brought the palm of his hand down with a smash on the table top. A pen went skittering off the table, on the floor. Dan did not blink.

"You are a spy!" Deng shouted. Dan sat quietly, unmoved.

Deng leaned forward. "Admit it. You and those two bastards we have in Pangshang. You're all in it together."

Li said something in Deng's ear. Deng stood up suddenly. He pulled out a pistol. Dan recognized it as a QSZ-92 handgun. Deng pushed the muzzle into Dan's left ear, bending his head till Dan's head was leaning to the floor.

"You want to see that bitch suffer, *ta ma bi*? You want to see my men take turns with her? They haven't had a woman for months. I'll let them. And I'll make you watch. *Cao ni ma*!"

Dan's head was leaning so far forward he was almost falling off the chair. Deng got his face closer to Dan and whispered, "Tell me about the Tonkin Protocol."

Dan eyes dilated and a blackness spread inside him. He kept his face impassive. The muzzle grinded into his ear even more.

"Tell me," Deng hissed. "Oh yeah, I know. That's why we found that white man by the rail tracks. Tell me, or the bitch suffers, with the white guy. So do you."

Deng raised the pistol and hit Dan hard above the ear. Dan grunted as the pain exploded in his head. Somehow, he kept from falling over. With a huge effort, he straightened up in his chair. His breath came in gasps. As soon as his head was straight, Deng hit him again, harder than before. This time Dan shouted. The pain was terrible, like a red raw deluge of blood smearing across his senses. His head fell back down, mucus trailing from his lips. His knuckles went white and he gritted his teeth.

Deng grabbed his hair and pulled his head back. "Tell me," he repeated.

Dan mumbled something. Deng got his ear closer to Dan's lips.

"Speak up," Deng said. "I can't hear you."

Dan sucked in air. "I said…Go fuck yourself, asshole."

Deng hit Dan again, then let go of his head. It fell back on his chest. Li rose up and said something to Deng.

Deng said, "Goodbye, *ta ma bi*. We will have fun with the bitch. When she's half dead, we'll bring her back and you can die together."

CHAPTER 42

Dan heard the door open behind him. A man came and stood in front of him. The man was broad chested and thick around the shoulders. He dwarfed the two Chinese men. Six two, two hundred pounds, Dan guessed. His features were European, skin tanned brown.

Li said, "Meet Dr Yuri, our pain specialist." Yuri grinned. His teeth were stained yellow, and old scars pockmarked his face. He was wearing a dirty vest that was torn at the top.

Deng said, "The good doctor is ex-*Spetznaz*. I am sure you two will get on well. If you are still alive when I get back, you won't be for long."

Li and Deng left the room. Yuri shut the door, then went over to the gurney. He checked the drawers of the cabinet.

Then he plugged the machine with round, white dials on into a plug socket. Lights came on the machine. Yuri came back to Dan. The door opened and a man with a rifle stepped in. He kept the muzzle aimed at Dan while Yuri wheeled the machine around. Dan could now see the Russian letters on the white dials. Yuri took the headphone, and clamped them on Dan's ears. He cranked up a round black knob on the machine, and there was a buzz of static.

At first Dan did not know what it was. Then it hit him. Electro convulsive therapy. Charging electric current through the brain. A treatment used in epilepsy and mental illness when all other treatments have failed. If the current was high enough, it could also fry the brain.

Dan clamped down on his jaws. He caught Yuri's eyes. They danced with mirth. Yuri bared his yellow teeth.

"Now we play, *da*, pretty boy?"

Yuri turned the black knob further. Dan felt a sudden, sharp high pitched sound in his ears. The sound went louder till it shrieked inside his ears like a psychotic, banshee wail. The pain was like a white hot skewer between his ears, ripping his skull apart. Dan screamed, but he was not aware of it. His legs came off the ground, and his body twisted, trying to be free from the chair.

Slowly, the sound faded. The knife stuck between his ears dissolved, then disappeared. Dan gasped, and opened his eyes. Yuri and the other guy were standing, watching him. Something winked on the floor. The fallen shards of glass from the mirror.

Then without warning, it started again. Dan yelled, and thrashed in his chair. Then he felt himself topple over, and crash onto the floor. Darkness fell over his eyes.

"Look, he's broken the damned chair. And what has he done to my sensors?" It was Yuri's voice. "Go get a new chair. I need to pee."

Dan's cheek lay against the cold wooden floor. Through a mist of pain, he saw the two pairs of shoes step over him and leave the room. He breathed heavily, unable to move. Strength had drained from his body. Dehydration, loss of blood and the torture had taken its toll. He tried to lift his head. Pain lanced through him, and with a groan his head fell back with a thud.

He opened his eyes again. Sunlight glinted on something. The shards of glass. Dan opened his eyes wider. He was a survivor. This was his only chance.

He bared his lips, mucus trailing from them. His hands and feet were tied, so he could only move by wriggling his torso. Somehow, he managed to move. His whole body was wracked in agony. He shifted backwards till he could feel the broken glass with his fingers. Grunting with the effort, he managed to sit up with his back against the bamboo shafts on the wall. Curling his right fingers, he was able to grab a sharp piece of glass and saw at the rope on his left wrist. The rope was thick, and it was slow going.

Then he heard voices. Yuri and the guard were coming back. Dan heard the wood creak, and shadows arrived at the door. The men stopped, speaking in low voices. Dan did not have any time left. He lowered himself back on the floor, and shuffled across the floor to the broken chair.

The door opened. Yuri was in first. Dan heard the sound of furniture being dragged in. Then he heard the door being closed. He opened his eyelids slightly. The guard was picking up the remnants of the broken chair and putting it away. His rifle was on his back, out of reach. He would need a few seconds to free his hands, unhook the rifle and aim. That was all the time Dan needed. He could see Yuri's feet in front of him. Dan opened his eyes. He lifted up his face, an expression of pain written all over it.

"I will talk," Dan whispered, "But I need water."

Yuri leaned over him, bringing his face closer. "What did you say?"

Dan's voice faded even more.

"What?" Yuri asked. He kneeled on the floor, bringing his ears close to Dan's face.

Dan said, "You're a dead man."

He had sawed through the rope, and his hands were free. On the right hand, he clutched the jagged piece of glass.

Yuri began to lift his head, but Dan's right arm shot upwards with lightning speed. The sharp tip of the glass thrust into Yuri's neck, embedding itself deep inside. The carotid artery was severed instantly, and blood gushed out. Yuri screamed, and jerked his head back, but Dan's left hand was clutching his shirt, dragging him down. He pushed the long piece of glass till it almost disappeared inside the neck, smashing into the soft sinus bones of the skull base. Yuri fought back. He lifted his fist and punched, but Dan ducked and the blow hit his shoulder. Yuri's eyes began to glass over.

Dan heard a movement behind him. He dropped his right hand to Yuri's belt line, leaving the glass inside Yuri's neck. With his right hand on Yuri's shirt front, he heaved the two hundred pound weight till the body rose in his hands like a shield. The guard came to hit Dan with his rifle, but Dan was quicker.

His feet were still tied, and he pressed them against the floor and rotated Yuri around, cannoning into the guard as he came up to deliver his blow. All three bodies tumbled on the floor. The guard had not fired for fear of hitting Yuri, and now the gun was trapped under his body.

Dan's left arm rose high up and punched the guard in the face, destroying his nose and jerking the head back. His eyes rolled up, but he clawed for his rifle. His mouth opened to scream, but before he could make a sound, Dan had pulled out the shard of glass from Yuri's neck, and stabbed the guard at the base of the neck. With his other hand, Dan clamped the guard's mouth, and fell on top of him. The shard went deep inside the man's neck with a squelching sound. His legs thrashed twice, then he was still.

Dan was up in a flash. He found a knife in Yuri's belt line, and quickly cut through the rope tying his feet. All four limbs free, he stood up.

The door was still shut, and apart from the sound of the bodies falling, there was silence. Dan picked up the guard's QBZ-95 rifle. He frisked Yuri quickly. He looked around the room and found a squat military flask. There was water inside. He took a long gulp, then hung it around his shoulder. He armed himself with another QSZ-92 handgun from Yuri's belt. He went up to the door and listened. Jungle sounds, and wood creaking in the distance, but no voices.

He looked through the cracks of the bamboo shafts. A courtyard with a swamp to the left, where he had been submerged. To his right, three huts clustered around the courtyard. Excluding his. Beyond the courtyard he could see a tall bamboo and wood reinforced gate. About ten feet high, with spikes at the top. There was a sentry box above the gate, but it was empty. The gate looked shut, but from here he could not be sure.

The entire complex was dozing in the afternoon heat. There was no movement. Dan opened the door a crack, bending down low. He was about to run out when he saw movement from the hut directly opposite.

Two men wearing dark green combat vest and pants came out, with rifles. The wood walkway creaked as the boots headed in his direction. Dan shut the window and retreated inside the hut.

There was no escape.

When he was hung out side, he had counted five men altogether, apart from Deng and Li. He had killed two. Three remaining. There could always be more. But he had to take that chance. He took out the knife and waited.

Boots arrived at the door. A voice asked something loudly in Burmese. The question was asked again.

Then they made a mistake. Instead of going away, and getting more men to surround the hut, they opened the door. Dan was waiting behind it. He grabbed the first man by the collar and dragged him in, pushing the knife into his neck in the same movement. He sliced the knife off, cutting the trachea, and threw the man against his friend behind him.

The man shouted, and tried to free the muzzle of the rifle from his friends falling body. But Dan's handgun was faster. It jumped in his hands, the 9mm rounds thudding into the man's face. Before the body had hit the floor, Dan had jumped out of the hut, rifle out and aimed forward. A barrage of bullets greeted him, splattering against the walls.

Dan dived for the ground, and rolled from the wooden walkway onto the mud of the courtyard. He fired as he rolled onto his chest, aiming for the direction of bullets aimed at him. He saw a gun poking out of the hut the two men had come out of.

On automatic mode, Dan squeezed the trigger of the QBZ-95, and he saw a flash of red and a scream as his rounds hit home. But the firing did not stop. It opened up from the hut next to it. Bullets thudded into the mud near Dan. The overhanging lip of the wooden walkway was the only cover he had. Under heavy fire, keeping his head down, Dan commando crawled forward. Fragments of wood chipped off and burst into fragments above his head. When he was closer, Dan raised himself up a fraction more.

His attacker would have to re aim, and that gave Dan two, maybe three precious seconds. It all came down to hand-eye coordination and the speed of reflex. Dan saw the muzzle of the sub machine gun poking out of the hut. He raised himself into view, and the muzzle moved in his direction. Dan fired fast, and his 5.8mm rounds made a mess of the window from which the gun was firing. He saw the gunman topple back before he could press the trigger. Dan jumped on the walkway and ran up to the hut. He fired in through the window, then looked. Two dead bodies lay on the ground. Dan fired at their heads, making sure of the kill.

Something moved in the extreme left of his vision, and he had dropped to the floor before he knew what it was. A bullet shrieked into the wood where his head had just been. Dan saw a wounded man lurch out of the first hut. The green combats were dark with seeping blood. It stained his right shoulder and soaked the chest. With an oath, the man raised the handgun again.

Dan had his rifle at his shoulder. Calmly, he aimed and shot the man's gun hand. The man screamed, there was a flash of blood, and the gun dropped. Dan scurried forward and kicked the gun away. He put his knee on the man's chest and aimed the muzzle of the rifle at his neck.

The man was lying on his back and panting, his chest heaving for air.

Dan said, "Where have they gone?" The man said something in return. Dan pressed the muzzle of his rifle against the man's neck.

"Name. I just want the name. Is it Pangshang? Pangshang?" Dan repeated. It was the name that Deng had mentioned when he was high on the crystal meth. The man's face cleared, and Dan had the answer he needed. The man swore, and tried to spit in Dan's face. Dan stood up. He felt no remorse. It could easily have been him lying there, soaked in blood, looking up at the muzzle of a rifle.

If it was him, he would have wanted a swift end. A soldier's death. Dan had no fight with these people. This was not his war. But they had unleashed hell. Now they would have to deal with the demons.

Dan pressed the trigger and the body jerked as lead filled the chest.

He walked into the hut. He collected several rounds of ammo, some grenades and another machete. There was a bookshelf on the wall, and he found a detailed map of the region. With the compass he had collected, Dan checked his direction. When he had escaped from the underground site, he had headed east, roughly.

Pangshang lay on the border with China's Yunnan Province. It was going to be a long trek, and he would have to avoid the main highways. Dan put his ammo and weapons into a duffel bag he found. Then he stepped out of the camp.

CHAPTER 43

Thick jungle covered the camp on either side. With the machete, Dan could now cut a trail for himself. He did it carefully, if a tracker came after him, he would be easy to find. After an hour, he found a gravel path leading into the rolling hills.

The ground turned red and stony. Red dust settled on his clothes as he walked as fast as his heavy bag would allow. The jungle had thinned, but the slopes around him were heavy with trees. Dan realized he was on a wood cutter's trail. That made him cautious. He did not want to meet people unless he had to.

From the map, he guessed he was more than a hundred miles away from Pangshang. If he walked for 6-8 hours a day, he would get there in 4-5 days. He knew that was too long. He needed transport, eventually. Right now, he needed distance between himself and the camp.

The path sloped down, the green woods descending to a river fed by gurgling streams. Dan crossed the streams, balancing on the rocks. The sky was blue, and a large yellow butterfly flipped its wings in front of his face, almost making him fall in the water. He knelt down to fill his water flask. The water was clear here, and he could see the stones in the river bed below. A white and red fish swam up to edge of the water, feeding from the rocks. Dan drank his water, watching more fish join the feeding. Then they turned, a blur of red and white against the brown rocks, and sped away into the depths of the river.

Dan took a swig of water and took out his compass. He was heading East still. He got up and started trekking again. The boulders became smaller, and he splashed across the river bed and climbed onto the bank. The trail he was following now went up into the hills.

Light was fading from the sky when he stopped to rest. He dropped the duffel bag, his shoulders weary. His stomach rumbled with hunger. He checked the barrel and decocker of the handgun, making sure there was a round in the chamber. The QSZ-92 was similar to the Sig Sauer P226, it did not have a safety catch. Dan liked that, the P226 was his handgun of choice.

The knife was in his front waist belt, and the machete strapped to the side of his leg.

He got up in five minutes and followed the trail again. It was now sloping down, and he could heard the sound of water again. Abruptly, he stopped.

A shadow seemed to have passed in the trees ahead. Dan dropped to the floor quietly, pulling out his handgun.

He saw something move again. Then he relaxed. It was an animal. The creature emerged from the bushes. It was a goat. The animal looked at Dan, then turned and ran back.

Dan cursed. That goat could have been his dinner. He got up and ran towards it. He stopped again. There was a whole herd of goats heading his way. In the front, there was a boy, no more than ten or twelve years old. They saw each other at the same time. The boy looked at Dan in astonishment. His mouth fell open.

Dan put the gun back in his waist belt. He held his hands up. He tried to smile, not knowing what else to do. He needed food, or he would not survive. This goatherder boy might be his best chance of having dinner tonight.

Dan took a step forward. The boy stood his ground. As Dan came within six feet, the boy suddenly turned and ran. He was quick on his feet, and the goats stopped Dan from getting to him. Dan did not want the boy to get back to his village. He would spread the word, and within minutes they could be after him.

Damn it. All I wanted was a goat, kid.

Dan grabbed a fat goat nearest to him. He had survived in the jungles of Belize and Borneo. Living off the land came naturally to him. He would have to make a fire, it could not be helped. Roast goat meat, with wild berries and river water was on the menu. He would make camp by the river, and sleep there too. But first, he needed to haul ass. He couldn't afford gunmen from the village catching up with him.

Dan took out his knife, and killed the goat quickly. The other animals bleated and ran away. Dan lifted the animal on his back, and turned to leave. He heard a rustle behind him, then the breaking of a twig. Dan ran three steps to get behind a tree trunk. He unhooked his rifle, breathing heavily.

No one had fired as yet. That was odd. Dan leaned back and sneaked a glance. A figure with a rifle separated itself from the trees. Their eyes met, and the figure jumped back, and fired. The round chipped bark off the trees, shattering the silence of the forest. Dan fired quickly, then picked up his belongings and plunged into the jungle.

He came to a halt when three more figures rose up from the bush in front of him. Two of them were bare chested, holding AK-47's. One wore green combats. All three pointed their weapons at Dan. Behind him he heard more sounds. Three more figures emerged behind him. He was surrounded.

Dan waited. In a firefight, he would be shredded to ribbons.

The men waited too. Dan glanced around him. The rifle was at his shoulder still, and he scanned them, going round in a circle. Suddenly, he heard a shout. The three men at the back stood aside. A taller, older man in a brown khaki uniform emerged, holding a rifle. He looked at Dan with curiosity. Then he lifted up his hand. On his silent command, the rifles were lowered.

Dan did not lower his rifle. He kept his finger on the trigger, rifle set to automatic mode. The leader stepped forward. He said something that Dan did not understand. He came forward again. Dan still had his rifle raised.

The man said in heavily accented English, "It's getting dark for a firefight, don't you think?"

His face was craggy and weather beaten, tanned brown in the sun. He had to be in his fifties, Dan guessed. Dan eased on the trigger.

"Who are you?"

"You come into my territory, yet you ask for my identity?" The man said. "I should be asking for yours."

Dan said, "I am looking for a friend who has been kidnapped. By a man called Henry Deng and Li Yonping. My friend has been taken to Pangshang. I need help to get there."

The man took a deep breath and gazed at Dan. "Those men are Wa. They belong to the Wa State Army. They kidnapped your friend?"

"Yes." Dan noticed the men around him had grouped behind their leader.

The man said. "Lower your weapon. You are in Shan country now. We are enemies of the Wa."

Dan did not lower his weapon. "How do I know you are speaking the truth?"

"If you knew our ways, you could tell by the lack of tattoos on our bodies, and the way we look. But you are a *baw*, so you don't. You have to take my word for it."

Dan lowered his weapon slowly. The duffel bag was on his shoulder and he had left the dead goat by the tree trunk.

"My name is Gyi Noe. Call me Noe." He paused. "You are hungry, yes?" Dan nodded.

"Then come with me," Noe said.

CHAPTER 44

Dan followed the six men and Noe through the jungle track. Monkeys chattered in the trees above him, and several times he looked up to see the long, thin, hairy arms of the primates lope around a branch and swing leisurely from one tree to the other. The monkeys were a darkened yellow color with a dash of white between their eyes. A deep blue colored bird with a heavy tail skipped on the ground alongside him.

Deep tracks were dug in the red earth and down the hill side. They looked like marks left by landslides. A hundred metres below, Dan could see the river curling between the hills like a silvery snake. White clouds with dark, low bellies had moved against the verdant green of the hills in the horizon. Light was fading fast. Dan noticed the men were walking quickly. It made sense. No one wanted to be in the jungle at night.

After half an hour, they had reached the riverside again. Three boats awaited them. Engines were fired up and the boats took off, cutting through the water in an arc. These boats were different from the speedboats that had chased Dan earlier. They were basic skiffs, with an outboard motor at the back.

The light vehicles went quickly in the water, borne by the currents. Darkness fell. Invisible, the jungles were like a thick, dense presence around them. The boats ran to ground, and someone lit a lamp. That solitary lamp guided their way up a dirt track into the hills.

The jungle had been cleared here, and they walked into a mud road with huts on either side. Yellow lights shone brightly in the darkness. The huts were raised on teak poles, and all of them had thatched roofs.

Women and children came out of the huts, watching them with curiosity. Dan could not help noticing the stares were directed at him. Gyi Noe and his men stopped in front of a wide, squat hut on the ground. All the men took off their shoes. Dan did the same. A woman came out, holding a large earthen jug. She was dressed in a dark vest up to her neck, and a sarong like piece of clothing down to her ankles. The men held their hands out and she poured water. They cleaned their hands and splashed water on their faces. The woman came around to Dan. She glanced at him and then looked down quickly. She had a small nose, full lips and long black hair that shone in the lamp lights. She was very beautiful.

Dan kept his eyes on her as he washed his hands. She looked up, met his eyes, and almost dropped the vase from her hands. She bowed to him, and retreated hurriedly, keeping her head lowered.

Inside, the men were sitting down in a canteen like space. Kerosene lamps flickered on the walls, and at regular intervals on the table. Women brought out food from a kitchen adjacent. The men ate with their right hand, never using their left. Dan followed their example.

Steel plates were laid out on the table. Dinner was boiled white rice, dumplings filled with a spicy, fishy mix, and a meaty broth of goatmeat. Dan watched the men mix the broth with the rice using their fingers. They rolled the rice into a ball, then flicked it inside their mouth. Fingertips separated meat from bones, and did likewise.

Dan closed his eyes as he chewed. Food had never tasted so good. After dinner, he followed Noe outside. They walked down the road to a hut raised on stilts like the other. Noe gave him a lamp.

Dan said, "Thank you."

Noe said, "They will follow your tracks. You cannot stay here long."

"I know. I need to reach Pangshang as soon as I can."

Noe stepped forward. "I can sense death around you. You have killed many men. It is your way of life. Am I correct?"

Dan said, "It used to be. I am trying to change."

Fireflies glowed in the dark around them. Noe said, "Sometimes, trying to change is like a tree trying to live without its shadow." He paused. "Better to be who you are."

"Unless you don't like who you are."

"Be careful of who you change into. Perhaps you are not as bad as you think you are."

The lamp lit Noe's face from below, giving it a ghostly glow. Dan thought of Maya's small arms on his shoulders that night at the US Embassy. The frightened look in her eyes. The raw need he had felt to protect her, somehow, anyhow.

He thought of Kim's face as they sailed down the Irrawaddy on the fisherman's boat. Something had changed inside him, he could feel it. He didn't know what it was. Maybe he didn't need to. Some things were best left alone.

Maybe he wasn't as bad as he thought he was.

Noe said, "Most of these villagers used to hide deep in the forest. Only recently the fighting has stopped, hence they have moved closer to the river. I, too, have seen a lot of deaths. I don't wish to see any more."

Dan said, "I understand. I will leave tomorrow at first light."

Noe left and Dan climbed up the stairs of the hut. He stashed his gear, and fell gratefully on the wooden bed on the floor. He listened to the insects chirping outside. He did not know when he had fallen into an inky, dreamless sleep.

*****

He awoke before the sun's rays hit his eyes. His eyes opened, and his fingers curled around the butt of the handgun under his pillow. He listened to the voices outside. Mostly women and children. Little feet running around. He sat up in the bed, releasing the weapon. Sturdy bamboo walls surrounded him. His bag was in one corner. Dan stretched, feeling refreshed after the sleep.

Dan's mind went back to the day before. What he had seen in that factory. Enriched uranium. He shook his head. It seemed like a bad dream, but it was reality. He thought about Deng, and what he had said. Deng knew about the Tonkin Protocol.

Henry Deng was more than a drug smuggler. He had contacts, and inside information, that only people with the highest security clearance possessed.

Dan knew of the games the CIA loved to play. Going circular, like a dog trying to catch its own tail. Such a game was going on now, and the stakes were high. Kim and David Harris had just been pawns in this game. Dan didn't know who had drawn the map he had followed to Bagan. But David had been on the trail of something. That map could have led to it.

The map was now lost, taken from him when he was captured and tortured. Dan figured someone would want that map, pretty bad.

Personally, he didn't give a shit. He wanted to get Kim out of there. His jaws hardened. That was his mission objective - right there. He would not fail, come hell or high water.

Images of Kim resurfaced in his mind. Her hair pulled back in a ponytail, her high cheekbones, the light glittering in her eyes. Dan stood up. He had work to do. Idle thoughts could wait.

Dan got ready, and came down the stairs. He walked down the road, attracting looks of open wonder. He knew why. These parts of Myanmar were the Black Zones, the regions of ethnic conflict, where even ordinary Burmese were not allowed. To see a foreigner like him was a rare event.

Hell, it was rare for him to be here, too.

Dan heard someone say his name. It was Noe. He was wearing his green combat uniform, and also a green cap that said *SSA* on the side. He wore a belt with gun holster. Noe bowed, and Dan did the same.

"Have you had breakfast?"

Dan shook his head. They went back into the canteen, and had Mohinga, the rice noodle and fish soup that seemed to be the traditional breakfast in Burma. Tea leaves, floating on boiling water in white porcelain cups was brought out to them.

After breakfast, he joined Noe and a group of heavily armed men. They set off into the jungle. As they climbed down a slope, Dan noticed one side of the hill had been deforested. Bare red earth covered the hill, looking strange in the canopy of green around it. He looked closer.

They were about three hundred feet away. He could make out two black lines coming down the hill into a valley. The black lines carried on in the low ground then raised up into another similarly denuded hill, disappearing around the bend.

Dan stopped and patted Noe on the shoulder. "What's that?"

Noe frowned. "Oil pipelines. Taking oil from the deep sea wells outside Sittwe and the big tankers that dock there in the Bay of Bengal. All the way to China."

Dan digested that. He knew the oil tanker routes. It made sense to cut the tanker route short by putting oil pipelines from here to China. He thought of David Harris, and the unknown reason he had been sent here. Something was gnawing at the back of his mind.

Dan asked, "Does the pipeline have any security? I mean, if someone wants to sabotage it, can they do it?"

Noe raised his eyebrows. "That sort of talk can get you killed, my friend. The Chinese are very touchy about this pipeline. It brings them a lot of oil, on a much shorter route. They get to avoid the Malacca Straits."

"You didn't answer my question."

Noe dug his heels into the hill slope. "When the government built this damn thing, they never asked our permission. Trouble flare up. We wanted compensation. We got it in the end, but in return we have to keep this damned pipeline safe."

Dan stared at it. "Ugly thing, right?"

Noe swore in his dialect. "Damn right. They destroy our forests, and act like they're doing us a favor. They sent the Wu to do their dirty work, but we beat them off. That's why they still have that camp there."

Dan nodded. The camp where he was held. It made sense now.

Noe said, "We don't want that thing here. But not much we can do. The money we get paid for its upkeep isn't much. The Government makes millions out of it. Do you see any schools and hospitals nearby? We have nothing."

They trekked for two hours in the forest till they came to a road. A truck was waiting, its back filled with felled teak trunks.

Noe said, "This truck will take you to Pangshang. It's going across the border into China, but don't wait that long. You can trust the driver. He knows what you have to do."

"Thank you," Dan said. "I mean it."

"The names you mentioned are well known," Noe said. "Henry Deng is the largest methamphetamine smuggler in the whole of Myanmar. He is Wu, and ethnic Han, so he is Chinese, really. But his loyalties lie only with himself. A cruel, evil man. His cousin Li Yonping is similar."

Dan nodded. "I got that impression too."

"Is your friend a woman?"

Dan stared at him for a while before nodding. Noe nodded, a smile on his face. "I knew that. Its written all over your face."

Noe's expression became serious. "One of our spies has informed us that there is a lot of security around Deng's hotel. It's the main hotel in town. Trucks arrived in the middle of night, and at least two prisoners were unloaded. They were taken inside the hotel. Deng would not do that unless these prisoners were important. They must be your friends."

Dan nodded. "I have a plan. Thank you for the information."

Noe said, "Pangshang is the effective capital of the Wu State. Trouble there could lead to trouble with China. You might need help."

Dan said, "I work alone. But I might need an extraction. Do you have any helicopters?"

Noe nodded. "We do, yes. But I need to get clearance to use it." He took out a cell phone and gave it to Dan. "Take this. Only call if you need to. If the helicopter is confirmed I will call. But I cannot promise."

Dan nodded. He threw his duffel bag at the back of the truck and climbed aboard. The Shan men waved at him, Noe at their head. Dan waved back. The truck set off down the winding mountain road in a cloud of dust.

CHAPTER 45

CIA HQ
NCS
Langley, Virginia

Solomon Barney cradled the telephone receiver in his hand. He stared at the white dials on the red phone as thoughts appeared like bubbles in his mind. Then he sighed and put the receiver down. He got up and walked up the stairs to Hymers' office. He was not in. Solomon asked his secretary, who informed him he was in a meeting.

Solomon went down to the canteen and got himself a coffee. He was heading for the elevator when his cell phone beeped. It was Hymers.

In my office, the text message read. Solomon headed back up. Hymers opened the door before he had a chance to knock.

"Come in Sol," Hymers headed back to his chair. "Just had a meeting with the boss. He wanted an update. Said I would speak to you."

Solomon sat down on the chair, taking a sip from his coffee. He thought about what he was going to say.

"We have no information as yet. Believe me, we have been trying. That little girl is still living with Mary. Questioning her has thrown some light. She used to work in a street side restaurant run by a drug smuggler. She met this guy, Dan Roy there. Saw Kim with him." Solomon related Maya's story.

Hymers said, "So Kim had some trouble with these drug smugglers."

"Yes, and if you remember, Kim was last seen escaping from a warehouse owned by drug dealers. So, we tracked down the owner of this warehouse. Name's Henry Deng. Big kahuna in the methamphetamine world. DEA have a thick file on him. Long story short, he has a series of companies, whose HQ is in Beijing."

Hymers remained impassive, but Solomon could see the sudden light that came into his eyes. "Beijing?"

"Yes. No other names have come up as yet. But you know where this is leading to, now."

Hymers sighed, and stood up. He went to the window. The first vestiges of green were arriving on the bare branches that stretched out for acres below. A welcome reprieve from the iron embrace of the ice and sleet. Not that it made any difference to the plates spinning in both men's minds.

"What do you suggest?" Hymers asked, without turning around.

"We juice our assets in Beijing. I have been through the list already. The Governor of Yunnan Province, which is closest to Myanmar, is an ex-senior member of the MSS." The Ministry of State Security was China's version of the CIA.

"Do we know him?"

"Yes. Li Ka Shing. But before we go any further, I need to know who else will know about this."

Hymers walked back to his chair. "We keep this to ourselves, Sol. If I tell the boss, we need to show results. It gets messy."

"You sure about that?"

Solomon held his senior colleague's eyes. "Yes," Hymers said quietly. "I'm sure about that."

The Chief of the DO was in direct contact with the Director of National Intelligence. Most operations of the NCS were sanctioned by him. But men like John Hymers, one step below the Chief, sometimes took decisions that were kept secret, even from the men responsible for national security. For some operations, the less people knew, the better.

Hymers said, "Ok. Talk to this guy. But what will you give him?"

"That's what I was gonna ask you," Solomon said.

Hymers thought for a while. "Tell him we sent someone down there to speak to the Shan State Army. Only for surveillance purposes. No weapons exchange actually took place, did it?"

Solomon shook his head slowly. "No. Nothing to identify us."

"Then it's OK. Tell Li Ka Shing we lost this guy, and we need his help. That should show him we are being honest, and essentially, we are giving him up. But everything else remains top secret."

"Fine. We lose some pride, but nothing else. But I need to head down there myself."

Hymers looked up, surprised. "Really?"

Solomon said, "John, one of my best agents is down there. God knows what's happening to her as we speak. Probably being tortured for information. You know how that makes me feel?"

"Sol, if anything happens to you, we just can't deny it. You are my deputy for heaven's sake. It's gonna cause a diplomatic row."

"There is no other way. If I am on the ground, Li Ka Shing will be forced to pay attention."

Hymers appeared lost in thought. Then he said, "OK, on one condition. You cannot leave the embassy. You go into the jungles, and get lost, we have a serious international incident on our hands. A fight with the Burmese Army. If the Chinese get even a sniff of the Tonkin Protocol, it means curtains on a lot of bilateral deals. You got that?"

"Yes, I got that."

After Solomon had left, Hymers tapped keys on his laptop. He turned on the sound diffuser, the low volume waves that masked any sound his voice made. It muted any invisible listening devices. He got a phone number he needed, and rang it. He waited for the beep of encryption before he spoke.

He said, "Do we have a sniper squad of the SAD in South East Asia?" SAD - Special Activities Division was the paramilitary arm of the CIA.

Hymers listened carefully then said, "Copy that. Prepare to engage targets in Myanmar China border. Commence drone surveillance. I will provide coordinates."

CHAPTER 46

The truck lurched and weaved its way across the green mountains. Dan sat on the piles of teak timber, and watched a yellow river curl like a snake through the valleys far down below.

After three hours, the truck pulled over into a side road, and drove into a small clearing surrounded by a bamboo thicket. Dan got off the truck, fully armed, with a large sixty pound backpack he had borrowed from Noe. The pack was mostly empty.

"What's your name?" Dan asked the driver.

"The driver Kyaw," the man said, and bowed slightly. "*Mingalaba.*"

Dan bowed back too. "*Mingalaba.* My name is Dan Roy."

The driver pointed, and they started walking. At the highway, they waited till all the cars had passed. Then they crossed, and scrambled up the hill quickly. Dan could hear the machinery long before the sight greeted his eyes.

Between a cluster of mountains, land had been dynamited and levelled. Bare brown earth stood in stark contrast to the emerald forests around, and the blue sky above. Huge tractors dotted the landscape for miles, some moving up and down slopes. On hills of brown rubble, whole armies of men were on their hands and knees, sifting through the dirt to find stones that would make their day worthwhile.

Dan and the driver lay spread-eagled over a hill that provided a bird's eye view of the mine down below. The driver said, "Jade mine. Big business."

Dan nodded. He knew Myanmar was one of the largest jade suppliers in the world. There was a lot of demand for it in China.

He looked around till he saw what he was looking for. Security. Armed men were patrolling the perimeter. One of them turned to look towards them and Dan ducked, pushing the driver's head down in the grass.

The driver pointed to his chest. "My land. Army take jade money. My family work there." He pointed to the brown rubble filled hills where men hammered and clawed with bare hands. The driver spat on the ground. He patted his belly. "No food for family." His eyes flashed with anger. He indicated the soldiers. He swore in Burmese.

Dan said, "Where is TNT?"

"Come, come," The driver said.

They circled the wire fenced perimeter. Dan could see lights and electric cabling. There were signs on the barbed wire that said *220 Volts, Danger*. After ten minutes walking, they went to ground again, and crawled to the edge of the hill.

"There," The driver pointed. A brick hut with a tin roof stood next to a sentry box, about two hundred yards in from the barbed wire fence. The driver showed Dan a door in the fence.

"Open," he said.

Dan watched as a labourer, no more than sixteen years of age, came out through the door. He chalked up his chances. This was his best chance of getting high grade explosives. If the door to the brick hut was shut, his plan was up in smokes. But it was worth a try. The guards were the problem. They were heavily armed, with fingers on triggers, and watchful eyes. Primed to shoot anyone trying to escape with precious jade stones. Dan knew ex-military men when he saw them.

"Go and wait in the truck," Dan said to the driver. The man stared at him for a while, then nodded. Dan waited till he had gone. He timed the rounds the security guards did. One of them was inside the sentry box, placed as security for the explosives shack.

Dan waited till the guards had crossed from both directions. He took the suppressed QBZ-95 rifle and slithered down the hill. The door in the fence was open. He slipped in, and went flat on the ground. Dust went into his nose and eyes. He swivelled his head left and right. Villagers working to his far right. Straight ahead, more than five hundred yards away, tractors groaned on dirt tracks, carrying rubble up from the quarry. The hut was two hundred yards. He could make that distance in a few seconds. The guard was sat upright in his box, looking around.

Silently, Dan flipped up the rear sight of the rifle. He located the guard's head in his cross hairs. He gave himself five seconds for his eyes to adjust to the light, and for his breathing to even out. His finger caressed the trigger.

With the sound of air escaping from a bicycle tire, the 5.62mm round left his weapon. It hit the guard half a second later between the eyes. Brain and blood splattered on the wall of the sentry box as the man went down. Dan waited three seconds. No one had spotted him.

He ran for the hut. The tin roof sloped down on both sides providing some shade from the sun. Dan looked in through the glass. Stacks of explosives arranged from floor to ceiling. He turned to the door. Locked, as he had imagined.

The twin padlocks were no match to two shots from the suppressed QSZ-92 handgun. They smashed the padlocks, but also the wood, making a sharper crack than Dan had hoped. He looked around him. In the distance, he could see two guards slowly walking in his direction. No shouts as yet, and no fire.

Dan went inside quickly. He found large amounts of short sticks, bound together with rope. He picked them up. These were made of gelignite, and were widely used in mining. They were basic, but highly effective. He picked up detonators for them, stuffing his back pack full. He was about to close the backpack when he heard the voice outside.

It was a loud voice, designed to awaken anyone nearby. Dan did not hesitate. He slung the backpack on his shoulder, taking the rifle in his hand.

He crouched, and uttered the one Burmese phrase he had picked up. "*Na keung de la*? How are you doing?"

Hearing the voice, the man walked in. Dan saw the green uniform, then the guard was upon him. His weapon was in his hand, and his mouth fell open when he saw Dan. He opened his mouth to scream, and his fingers went for the trigger, but they were the two last movements he made. Two rounds from Dan's gun smashed into his forehead and neck. A clean double tap. The man fell back like he had been kicked by a horse, the weapon clattering to the ground.

Dan leaped over the body, and emerged into the harsh glare of the sunlight. He saw movement to his left, 9 o' clock. He fired from instinct as soon as he saw the snout of the weapon being raised towards him. To his right, he detected something as well, but did not have time to turn and aim. He dived for the ground, rolling over. The window glass above him smashed, showering him with shards. He brushed them off, and aimed at his attacker.

There was more than one. Bullets now thudded into the woodwork around him.

A group of three men were crouched about a hundred yards away. Dan remained calm. He fired once, watching one of the men stumble and fall, a puff of dust rising from his chest. Then he scrambled backwards, and went around the corner of the hut. He used the cover to fire again, twice, and got both men with quick shots. The firing stopped.

His relief was short lived. The window next to his head blew up into fragments of glass, exploding into his face. Luckily, he had his face averted. But he still felt painful burns as small bits of glass went into this face. In the same instant, bullets pinged at him around the corner, where he had just killed the three.

He was getting attacked from front and back. Enough.

Dan unhooked a grenade, and lobbed towards the source of fire directly behind him. He slammed down on the dust and covered his head. The cluster of men were not close, which was just as well. He had no intention of damaging the several thousand pounds of explosives right behind him. The grenade explosion shook the ground, expelling a cloud of dust from the ground.

Dan waited for the shrapnel to fall, then he rose and turned backward. The QBZ-95 chattered its death rattle, now set to automatic. Through the dust and smoke, at least three figures emerged, but they were halted by the hail of lead pouring towards them. Their bodies shook and jerked before they fell dead.

Dan turned, and ran for the door at the fence. His senses were on fire. Just as he got to the gate he saw a man appear, rifle ready at the shoulder. Dan had spotted him a fraction late, and he fired before Dan could. The bullet grazed Dan's shoulder, and he felt the burn of metal. He dived to the ground, making himself a smaller target, but fired at the same time. The flurry of bullets shredded the man's body. Dan rose and ran as hard as he could, jumping over the body.

Behind him, he could hear the tractors nearby had stopped. A new sound hit his ears, the roar of jeeps.

Dan went through the gate just as a blizzard of ordnance poured towards him. The wooden door exploded in the onslaught, showering him with timber dust. Dan recognized the gunfire. This was a jeep mounted machine gun, a fifty cal. It laid down suppressive fire, killing anyone within eight hundred metres.

If he got hit by that his life was over.

Dan scrambled over the slope and flung himself down the hill. He tripped and fell, rolling down the slope. He hit a tree, and it knocked the breath out of his chest. His head hurt. He got up and started to run like a madman. That fifty cal machine gun could be unhooked from the jeep, and a two man crew could lift it to the brow of the hill.

He needed to make himself scarce before that happened. Dan slipped and ran down the last slope, getting to the highway just as a bus roared down. Dan missed it narrowly, and the bus swerved, honking loudly.

Sorry dude.

He got to the side road, and to his relief found the driver had turned the truck around, and was waiting with the engine running. Dan hopped on the back, screaming for him to move. The driver got the drift. With a clash of gears, the leviathan set off down the road, joining the highway.

CHAPTER 47

Henry Deng roared down the main street of Pangshang in his black Range Rover.

The tall neon lights were not lit as yet, but this being a Saturday, crowds had already gathered by the numerous shops that thronged the sides. At the end of the road, lay a major junction with roads branching off to smaller sections of the town. To the left of this junction lay the large Casino building. With its triple decked opening gate, and interior a façade of the main building of Beijing's Forbidden City, the 7 Dragons Casino was by far the centerpiece of the town.

And owned by Henry Deng. He cast the building an appraising look as he drove past. There was a small motel attached to the casino, ostensibly for guests to stay the night, but which functioned as a brothel. Business was booming with gamblers who came from the cities of Yunnan, and rich Thai businessmen. Now that Myanmar was open, a handful of western tourists came too.

The hotels were also full, and construction of new buildings was going on full tilt, thanks to Chinese investment. Many of the condo apartment blocks being built were under Deng's control. All of which, he thought with a sigh, should be putting a smile on his face.

But Pangshang was small fry. It was a backwater of Yunnan, its only importance lay in how China used it to operate its influence on Myanmar. Especially now that the oil pipeline was built. Deng gripped the steering wheel harder.

Oil pipeline? He would show them. When the enriched uranium came to the attention of the Americans, Myanmar would have hell to pay. China would be scrambling for a foothold. And he, Henry Deng, would fulfil his destiny as the most powerful man in Myanmar.

But these CIA agents were pouring cold water on his dreams. It was too soon. Somehow the Americans had got to know. Now they were here, trying to disrupt things.

He braked as the only five-star hotel in Pangshang loomed over his windscreen. Naturally, a hotel he owned. He did not turn in. Armed security stood everywhere, as did two trucks full of Wa State Army soldiers. At the back of each truck there was a machine gun on a tripod. Two more trucks were parked behind the hotel. The place was surrounded.

Deng nodded at the security guards as they saluted and opened the gates for him. The marbled lobby was empty bar the armed guards. Deng took the elevator to the top floor where more armed men lined the hallway. One of them bowed to him and opened the door to a room.

Deng walked in, curling his nose up at the smell of sweat and fear. The woman was strapped to a chair. She was sitting up, but her head was rolling forward. She had been injected with scopolamine, the truth drug.

It hadn't worked. The bitch was still refusing to talk. Deng looked towards the floor. The other man was lying there. He had given up his name, and the fact he worked for the CIA. Two of the fingers on each hand been broken for that information, with regular beatings to the head and face. The man looked half dead.

Deng was about to say something when he heard his cell phone beep. He picked it up, saw the name on the screen and stepped out of the room.

He walked to the window, away from the guards.

"Li," he said, "what is it?"

Li's voice was strained. Deng listened, his hand balling into a fist. He clenched his teeth.

"Yuri is dead?"

"All of them. He took their guns and ammo as well. This man is a *Youguai*, an evil spirit, cousin."

"Stop that talk," Deng said sharply. "He bleeds like the rest of us. A bullet to the head will finish this nonsense. Where is he now?"

Li said, "Nobody knows. There is a Shan camp here, and I think he got refuge from them."

"He's coming here," Deng said softly. "Chase him up here, Li. Call me when you arrive, and if he's still not dead."

"He will be, cousin," Li said. "I will kill him, and then set fire to his heart, to make sure the spirit dies."

Deng closed his eyes and breathed deeply. "You do that, cousin. Do it now."

*****

Kim had heard Deng come in the first time, but she had not looked at him.

The second time she heard the door open, she looked up. It was hard to focus. The headache was like a sharp needle in her brain, threatening to poke her eyes out. She blinked and shook her head to refocus. The man in the immaculate cream colored Safari suit, like he just had it pressed, was standing in front of her. Sunlight glinted off the sunglasses he had not taken off. He came forward, and she could smell his aftershave.

"Miss Smith," the man said in his accented English. "Finally, you are awake."

A sensation of nausea filled Kim. She had not had food for more than a day, only sips of water. She heaved and brought up yellow green bile. Her head hung to one side, mucus trailing from her lips. She tried to straighten herself but the exhaustion had paralysed her. She had lost count of the hours she had been roped to the chair. She could just move her toes and fingers. She remained in that position, head bent low, saliva dribbling down her chin.

It would be easy to give up. But Kimberly Smith had not given up on anything in her life. Apart from Sarah....

Her sister's face flashed in front of her eyes. How she looked in her graduation photo. How she helped Sarah dress up for prom. A crushing pain seized her inside, squeezing her heart. A soft moan escaped her lips.

"I'm sorry," Kim whispered. "Sorry..."

She felt her face being seized, and lifted upwards. Bright sunlight stung her eyes. She closed them. A soft cloth dabbed the sides of her lips, wiping the mucus away. The fingers held her face upright.

The male voice asked in a gentler tone, "What are you sorry about?"

Kim's eyes were still closed. "Sarah, I should have protected her..."

The voice was almost a whisper. "Who is Sarah?"

"My sister."

"Where is she?"

"She's..." Kim's eyes fluttered open. She squinted and focused. A man's face, bent lower to face her. The sunglasses had gone. The face was handsome, with sharply chiselled features. His black eyes glittered, and he had short spiky black hair.

"Dead," Kim said in a flat voice. She felt a teardrop course down her cheeks. She couldn't help it. The daily injections in her arm, the lack of food and dehydration had driven her close to insanity.

"I am sorry about your sister." After a pause the man added, "Tell me about the Tonkin Protocol."

Kim whispered, "I don't know what you are talking about."

The face hovered before her for a few seconds, then the man stood up.

"More injections for today. Soon your tongue will waggle. Or your brain will turn to jelly."

From somewhere, Kim found the strength. She shook her head. "No it won't," she sniffed. She raised her head and looked at the man in the cream safari suit. "He will come."

"Who?"

"Dan. He's still alive, isn't he?"

The look on the man's face told Kim everything she wanted to know. He came forward, snarling. He pulled her hair, and slapped her hard with the back of his hand. Kim's head rocked back. She felt the sting of another blow, knocking her face the other way. She tasted blood at the corner of his lips.

The man turned and left the room, closing the door shut behind him.

CHAPTER 48

Dan felt the truck lurch up a slope. While they were taking the hairpin bends on the green hills, he had sat out front with the driver. Several times, as he looked down several hundred feet into nothingness, he wondered how the truck disobeyed gravity and stuck to the road.

The driver whistled as he turned the massive steering wheel with gusto, not batting an eyelid at taking another bend at more than 40mph. The rolling green hills, and the occasional roads meandering down, stretched around them to infinity.

Then the driver stopped. He looked at Dan and gestured past the windscreen. "Checkpoint. Special Zone."

Dan nodded. Myanmar's eastern Shan State was under the control of the powerful Wa State Army. All drivers needed papers to gain entrance. He went to the back, and clambered aboard the felled timber. He squeezed himself between two solid trunks.

The truck roared on, and then he felt it decelerate. He sensed other vehicles around them. Through a slit in his hiding hole, Dan saw a green uniformed soldier jump aboard the back of a truck. He reached down and felt for the handgun. The suppressor was still screwed on. His duffel bag was nearby. If he had to shoot and run, so be it.

The truck came to a standstill. Dan heard voices. Then he heard the driver's door open. Boots came around to the back. Dan took the handgun out, finger on trigger. He lay very still. He could not see the rear of the truck. But it would take him a few seconds to sit up and fire if need be.

He heard the tailgate being lowered. The truck was open topped, and the timber pieces were racked up high, held together with rope. Dan saw the flash of green uniform. He could fire between the slats of timber. He didn't move a muscle, but got ready to burst into action.

The driver was speaking to the guards. Dan couldn't hear what they were saying, but he knew some sort of transaction was happening. Money often changed hands at the check points.

A few more minutes passed. Then he heard the tail gate fixed back into place. The boots faded, and the driver went back up to his cabin. Dan breathed out, and relaxed.

The truck rolled past the check point. Dan lifted up his head. They were on the open road again. The green hills had gone. It felt like a giant hand had depressed the land into flatness. All around him lay red brown earth from denuded hills. Tractors moved around, and it seemed a multi-track highway was being constructed. Traffic was thicker, and the smell of dust and pollution was heavy in the air. Huge lorries drove past them, some carrying building aggregate, others with metal barrels, oil leaking from the rusty seals. The names on the lorries were all Chinese with names like Sinopec and LiuGong. The road signs were in Chinese alphabets.

They turned a corner, and a large, stylish casino appeared. Its gate was a three tiered pagoda-like structure. The name, 7 Dragons, was written across the top in English and Chinese. Next to it, a golf course stretched out for miles. Arranged next to the casino were internet cafes, gambling houses, and all you can eat buffets with Chinese signs. Dan couldn't see the Burmese language anywhere. Cranes moved across the horizon, and the sound of intermittent drilling punctured the pop music blaring from shops.

All of a sudden, Myanmar looked very different.

The driver pulled into a parking lot for heavy vehicles. Dan waited till the driver came around and banged on the tail gate. He picked up his duffel bag, kept a hand on the handgun at his waist, and stood up. Dan clambered over the timber logs and jumped down.

The driver patted his stomach and said, "Food?"

"Hell yeah," Dan said. They walked out of the parking lot into a market square. Several street side stalls were open, selling dead animal products. The signs were mostly in Chinese, but one stall had English subtitles. Dan stopped to look at the shrivelled remains of tiger penis, bear paws, pangolin hides and elephant tusks, cut into small pieces. The shopkeeper came forward, bowed, and said something to Dan.

The driver nudged Dan and said, "He's asking if you want to see python teeth." The driver bared his teeth. "It gives you longer erection."

Dan shrugged. "I'll stick to what I have, thanks."

They moved on, Dan keeping a sharp eye around him. He could not see any uniformed guards anywhere, but he knew the Wa had spies everywhere.

He had seen a few western tourists, but mostly Chinese, Burmese and Thai. The market square was large, with shops selling everything from barbecued food on roadside grills, to gambling shops with electronic *mahjong* tables. Beyond the cluster of huts Dan could see tall hotel buildings that gleamed in the sun, with signs in Chinese.

Further beyond he could see the flow of green hills they had descended from. Golden pagodas of monasteries were nestled in the hills. That was the last sign of Myanmar, Dan thought. For all intents and purposes, he felt like he was in a third rate Chinese industrial city that doubled up as the local Las Vegas.

They walked into the shack like structure of a restaurant, and sat down. Dan had a hat on, shading him from the sun, but also keeping his face hidden. Two Tsingtao beers arrived. It had been a while since he had a beer, and the journey had been hot. Gratefully, he lifted the bottle to his lips.

Roasted meat arrived, and the smell of soy sauce and spices was mouth-watering. There was rice and a noddle soup to go with it. Dan tucked in, using chopsticks. After he finished, he leaned back.

"Enjoy food?" The driver asked with a grin. He tapped the beer bottle. "Drink." Then his face became serious. He cast a look around the restaurant, which was mostly empty.

"We go quick. Danger," The driver said.

"Show me Deng's hotel. Then you go," Dan said.

The driver nodded, and drained his beer.

They paid and prepared to leave. Dan hooked the bag on his shoulders and followed the driver outside. They walked through the rest of the sprawling marketplace, and emerged onto a road busy with traffic. Hotels stood on either side of the road. After ten minutes, they stopped and went down a side road. The road curled around, and the driver stopped before they came out to the main avenue. He pointed to the tallest building around, a fifteen floor granite and black glass structure.

"Deng's hotel," the driver said. Dan could see the two trucks parked outside the main gates. As he watched a soldier hopped out of one, stretched, then lit a smoke. More armed guards stood near the gates. Two roads went down either side of the hotel. At the back he could see a similar truck. From its back, the barrel of what seemed like a fifty cal machine gun poked out. Guards patrolled around the back gates and sides. Dan's eyes travelled up the hotel all the way to the top. The roof was flat and wide. Enough space for a bird to land.

He turned to the driver. "Thank you for bringing me here."

The driver said, "Deng own the city. You be careful. You do this for the woman?"

"Something like that," Dan said. The driver had risked his own life to bring him this far. The man wore a torn shirt, and rolled up pants that had seen better days. He was obviously poor.

Dan felt in his pockets, and pulled out some dollar bills he had picked up from the hut where he had been tortured. He held them out.

"This is my way of saying thank you," Dan said.

The driver shook his head firmly and pushed his hand away. "No" he said. "You are guest. Guest never pay."

Dan said, "Do you have kids? Children?"

The driver's face changed as he studied Dan. Then he nodded. "Why you ask?"

"Buy them something from me. A present. Please." Dan held out the notes again. Indecision was written all over the driver's face. Dan couldn't help but consider the man's sense of honor. He probably lived on less than a dollar a day, struggling to put a roof over his head. But yet he would not take his money.

Dan grabbed the driver's right hand, and pushed the stack of bills into it. "For the children," Dan said. "Buy them sweets."

The driver looked down at the hundreds of dollars in his palm, then looked up at Dan. Slowly he nodded. "Ok. For the children. I buy food for all children in my village, right? Say it's from you."

"Yes."

As soon as he said that, Dan remembered Maya's face. His insides turned to ice.

He glanced back at the building. Kim was in there, with David Harris. He clenched his jaws. He had a job to do now. He turned to say goodbye to the driver. The Burmese man stepped forward and did something curious. He lifted his right hand, and touched it to Dan's forehead. He closed his eyes and murmured something. Then he opened his eyes.

The driver said, "I pray for you. Tibetan prayer for the living. You are good man. Kind spirit."

Dan nodded and said, "Go now. Get out of Pangshang, and stay out. There will be trouble here tonight."

The driver stepped back and bowed. Dan bowed back. "See you again, friend," The driver said. Then he turned and left. Dan watched him disappear from sight. He walked into the main avenue, and went quickly past Deng's hotel across the street. The name was written in Chinese, he could not read it.

He walked for a block, then stepped into a side road. The road was smaller, but shops thronged the sidewalk on both sides. People browsed at the merchandise on offer, bargaining with the stall owners. Dan heard quick steps behind him, and he turned briefly. He froze.

Looking straight at him was the man with the scar. Li Yonping.

CHAPTER 49

Dan turned, and ran straight ahead. He pushed tourists out of his way. A fat man bumped into him and went sprawling on the floor, screaming. Dan heard shouts behind him, and the sound of boots on the ground. People scattered before him.

Dan hooked a sharp right, and headed for one of the stalls on the street. Slabs of meat were cooking on the grill, and pieces of goat, chicken and other animals hung from skewers. A piece of meat slapped Dan in the face. He pushed it aside, along with the shopkeeper who tried to stop him.

The guests moved away rapidly. Dan moved deeper into the darkness of the shop. He smelt something dense and cloying – opium. Men sat semi reclined on the back of the shop floor. Cushions had been arranged, and men lay smoking opium pipes. Dan only had a second to register it.

He heard a scream from the back, and the sound of tables turning, cutlery smashing on the floor. He got to the back door and kicked it savagely. The thick door smashed open at the padlock and flew open under the force of his onslaught. Dan turned and jumped through the door. He was in an alley, and at the end he could see the cars moving in the main avenue ahead. He was at the mouth of the alley when he heard the gun fire behind him. He dived straight for the ground, and the bullet hit the side wall of the alley.

Dan was up in an instant, his eyes scanning the road. A combination of Chinese and Japanese cars, with a smattering of old Mercedes trickled down the road. He saw a motorbike slowing in front of him, and he sprang into action.

The man did not have a chance to realise what was happening. Dan grabbed him by the collar, lifting the man clean up with one hand. The motorbike went sliding down the road, wheels whining. Cars honked and slowed down around them. Dan let the man go, and ran to the bike. He straightened it and jumped on the seat. Wheels screeching on the tarmack, Dan roared the bike down the road in a cloud of dust.

He didn't know where he was going. But he knew his plan was shot to shreds. He needed to get away now. Despite the wind whipping at his face, he heard the growl of engines behind him. In the side view mirror he saw two jeeps. As he watched, a figure stood up from the passenger seat and aimed a rifle at him. Dan ducked, and the bullet hit the side view mirror. Glass exploded, and Dan flinched, even as he pumped the handles to go faster.

He opened his eyes and looked at the opposite lane. Traffic was flowing sedately in the other direction. He looked behind him. Three jeeps now. He was open in the bike, and could be hit by a round any time. The jeeps would catch up soon. Then he was a dead man.

The two lanes were separated by a white and black painted cement culvert. But there were roadworks going on up ahead. A truck was laying down molten pitch for the tarmac. A wooden plank was laid from the road to the truck, on an incline, for a wheelbarrow to move up and down.

Desperate times called for desperate measures.

Dan cranked the bars to accelerate, and bent low, heading for the road works enclosure. The bike couldn't go any faster. Rushing air made his eyes blurry. Workers shouted and jumped for cover as Dan hit the bollards hard. They went flying in the air. Smashing through the rickety fence that served as the enclosure, Dan was upon the truck laying the pitch down. The bike roared onto the wooden plank and shot almost vertically up in the air.

Dan clenched his teeth tight as the bike soared up, airborne over the cars honking and moving underneath him in the opposite lane.

He screamed as the bike came to ground, narrowly missing a Toyota pickup truck. He wobbled on the seat as the rear wheel, then the front, hit the road. By a miracle, he managed to keep his balance. The bike shuddered underneath him, the shock absorbing springs creaked under the strain, but it still moved. Dan weaved his way in and out through the traffic. The cars thinned out eventually, and he sped down the road. He turned his head, and almost missed the three jeeps that came out of the side road. His eyes moved forward, and caught the jeeps moving up alongside him.

Damn. Damn.

Dan picked up the QSZ-92 handgun from his beltline and fired to the right. The man standing up on the nearest jeep caught the round with his head and it exploded like a watermelon.

Another two were standing up in this jeep, and with fear Dan recognized the installed weapon on the jeep. Another fifty cal, general purpose machine gun or GPMG.

Driving the bike with one hand, he straightened his right elbow, and fired twice again, taking the bike closer to the jeep. He saw a splash of red and one figure fell, followed by the other. Only the driver was left now. He looked at

Dan and their eyes met for one brief, fear crazed second.

Dan drove the bike alongside the jeep. With both vehicles racing alongside each other, Dan let go of the motorbike and grabbed the railing running across the roof of the jeep. He swung his legs off and the bike went veering off, smashing into one of the jeeps running close behind. The jeep trampled over it, bending its wheels. Dan was hanging now, but he pulled himself on the jeep quickly. Before the driver had a chance to react, Dan had positioned himself behind the GPMG.

He aimed at the two jeeps running close, and fired. He aimed for the wheels first, then at the men in the jeep. The windscreens folded as cobwebs spread across them, and bright bursts of red colored the fractured screens.

The driver had realized, and pulled over to the roadside. Normal traffic had stopped a way back, and they were alone on this stretch of the road. But pedestrians had gathered by the side, watching.

The driver flew at Dan with an oath. He had a handgun in his hand. Dan moved quickly, grabbing the gun arm and bending it. The man screamed, and the shot fired into the road surface. Dan hit him under the chin with his right fist, and followed it up with an elbow upper cut. The body sagged to the floor. Dan lifted him up and threw the man on the road. He jumped on the seat, and gunned the jeep down the road.

The shops and buildings by the roadside got thinner, and soon he was out in the open again. The green hills appeared, rising up on both sides A muddy river ran to his left, bending with the road. Dan turned a corner, wrenching the jeep's steering wheel as he pressed on the gas. The wheels whine on the road, and the jeep straightened. Ahead, Dan saw a check post. The river had intersected the road, and there was a bridge going across. A red and white traffic bar was lowered across the entrance to the bridge, and soldiers with rifles were patrolling it.

They looked up as the speeding jeep approached them. Dan looked up at the sign above their heads. It was mostly in Chinese, but he read the English letters below it. His heart sank.

"China-Myanmar Border. Welcome to China."

He heard a sound in the sky. He craned his neck and saw what he had expected to, a helicopter. It looked like a Russian make. The bird banked and swept down low, the sound of its rotors becoming louder.

It's seen me.

Dan pressed on the gas. He hurtled towards the check point. He could see the guards more clearly now. They were soldiers, dressed in green uniform.

But they wore helmets with red insignias on them. Soldiers of the Chinese People's Liberation Army. PLA.

The soldiers raised their arms and shouted, but Dan was not in a stopping mood. He rushed on at breakneck speed. He saw two of the soldiers bend down on one knee and raise rifles to their shoulders. Dan ducked underneath the dashboard. He heard the sharp retort of the weapons, and the bullets whined over his head. He glanced up to see a spider web spreading across the windscreen. Another bullet hit the windscreen, and it obliterated, showering glass fragments on him.

Dan raised his head a fraction, and saw he was almost upon the check point. The bar was still lowered. Dan kept the wheel straight and ducked again as he saw rifles aimed at him. His main worry was the bird hovering above his head. They were holding their fire right now because they did not want to hit the soldiers. But when Dan was across...

Dan was thrust around and jerked as the front of the jeep smashed against the barrier. The red and white barrier snapped like a twig and flew up in the air in two pieces. Dan kept his head down, bullets following the jeep as he raced forward.

The road bent, and curled up into the mountains. The rotor blades of the bird thundered above him. He was out on the open road now, and the machine gun on the bird was free to fire at him.

Dan heard the loud whine of the 50 cal bullets hitting the road behind him. He bared his teeth, and flattened the gas pedal, heading for the hills.

CHAPTER 50

Dan knew he wouldn't make it. The jeep presented an obvious target, and the winding road did not have any turnings. The swish of the rotor blades was deafening now, heading down towards him.

The heavy gun opened up again. Dan gunned for the first bend up the hill. He went around it, and screeched to a stop. The bird would have to fly out laterally to see him now. That gave him a few important seconds.

Dan reached for his duffel bag and heaved it on his back. Then he was at the rear seat, behind the machine gun. He flipped up the view finder, and tracked the bird as it came into view around the hill's green edge.

He let off a volley of shots, the large weapon shaking in his hands as the spent rounds flew out of the breech. The bird swooped up, then down. Its weapon was mounted on its right gate. It would have to swing round to be able to fire on Dan, who was to its left. The bird did precisely that manoeuvre.

Dan could see the pilot, and the soldiers on board. Two of them crouched by the gate facing Dan's jeep, and began to fire. Dan fired back, hitting both of them. Then he aimed for the fuel tank at the rear of the bird. He missed at first as the bird banked and turned, but he hit it dead straight at the second attempt.

There was an explosion as the fuselage burst open, black petrol spilling out into the air. Dan fired again, and a giant yellow and red fireball erupted with a cataclysmic soundwave as the bird blew up in mid-air. Dan threw himself to the floor of the jeep as shards of shrapnel came flying at him.

He heard the whine of the engines as the wreckage flew down to meet the trees far below. There was another explosion, muted this time, as the wreck hit the forest floor.

Dan jumped off the jeep. He had no wish to drive further into China, and encounter the PLA Special Forces. He ran down the to the bend and looked out. There was activity at the check point, about 400 yards away. In the mid distance, he could see a convoy of jeeps winding their way down the hill road. The soldiers at the check point loaded themselves up onto a jeep, and it careened out on the road, heading straight for him.

Not good news, but it could have been far worse.

He was still alive, and he had a mission to accomplish. Pushing the jeep down the slope would have helped, but now he did not have time.

Dan got his rifle in his hands, and checked his waistline for grenades, handgun and extra ammo. He patted the knife in its scabbard. It was not his usual kukri knife, but it would have to do. He turned, and melted into the green forest above him.

Dan climbed quickly, heading up into the hill. He was held back by the heavy duffel bag on his shoulder but he still made good progress. Dan had trained, and then done operations in tropical jungles. He knew guerrilla warfare, and how to use the jungle to his advantage.

He climbed without stopping for more than half an hour. Panting, he looked down as he crested the top of a boulder jutting out form the hillside. Visibility was poor given the thickness of the trees, but the quietness of the surrounding hills amplified the sounds the men made, trampling through the undergrowth. He guessed about fifteen, twenty men. The check point guards were joined by the soldiers who had come down in the trucks.

Dan took two long swigs from his bottle, taking care to conserve water for later. He got up and started to climb again. The gentle slope carried on upwards. His strong thigh muscles were burning with the effort, but he was in combat mode now, and fighting for survival. If a grizzly landed in front of him, he would fight it with his bare hands if need be.

He topped the hill, and ran forward. He burst through a screen of trees, and stopped.

He had come into a clearing. A large one, more than two football stadiums length. The sight in front of him was entrancing. Hundreds, if not thousands, of Buddha statues were arranged in neat rows and columns. Beyond the field of statues, a craggy wall of rock rose high up in the air. At the very top there was a golden pagoda, with the white walls of a monastery just below it. From the base of the monastery, a white waterfall fell like a silvery ribbon, splashing against the rocks.

Dan shook his head, and kept moving. He needed to get down to Pangshang, as quickly as possible. Light was fading from the skies. He figured it would be dark in an hour. Darkness was good, it gave him cover. Dan came to the last row of statues. He looked back at the solemn, silent figures one last time. The Buddha's all faced in the same direction, rain and wind beaten faces without expression. Briefly, he wondered who made them.

Then he was in the jungle, enveloped in the sweaty, sticky embrace of the thick leaves and vines. He turned left and started to veer down. It was getting difficult to see now, but he stopped and took his bearings.

Ahead of him Pangshang sprawled out for a good few miles. Lights were coming on, and the long neon signs were flickering to life. The town was nestled in a valley with green, grey and blue hills all around him, stretching out to the horizon. Roads were few, and airports non-existent. A beautiful, but difficult landscape to escape from. No wonder the Wa had such a strong grip on the region.

Dan heard dog barks behind him. He listened. Sniffer dogs would pick up his trail easily. Judging by the sound, they weren't far behind. Dan unzipped the duffel bag and took out two sticks of gelignite.

Working with the knife, he cut off the fibre casing, and carefully eased out the jelly like chemical inside. Gelignite was highly explosive but it was more stable than dynamite. It would not blow up in his hands. Dan laid out a row of gelignite across the trees then faded into the trees again. The dogs would come across the line, their paws would not trigger the charge. Neither would the first group of men. But repeated pressure on the chemical would cause it to explode.

Dan descended down the hill. The darkness was complete now. His eyes were used to it, and he could pick his way between the trees. The vegetation loomed with shapes like claws. He heard the dogs barking again. Dan pressed himself on the ground behind a tree trunk and waited, rifle in hand.

The night was lit up in a sudden explosion. It sounded like firecrackers going off, right next to his ears. It culminated in an almighty deep booming sound that made the ground shake behind him. Dan got up, then ran down, bent at the waist.

Running down a hill was harder than going up. It was easier to get injured. If someone had eyes on him, it was easier to fire from above as well. Dan flitted between the shadows of the trees. Finally, he came close to the road again. The drop from the grass verge on to the road was steep. He dropped his duffel bag first, then jumped. He felt a glancing pain in his ankles, but stood up and hobbled away from the road. The check point was dark, as he had expected. But he needed a ride. Pangshang was too far to walk.

Dan got to the check point and had a quick look around. It was empty. No cars that he could hot wire. As if on cue, he saw the flash of headlights. It looked like a brown Army truck. Dan thought quickly. If he tried to flag it down, they might just open fire. He hid the rifle in the crook of his arm, and lay down on the road. He turned his back to the oncoming vehicle, so the headlights would only see a man lying on his side.

He heard the ground shake beneath him as the truck approached. If it came too close he would have to make a run for it. The curb wasn't too far away – he needed to judge the time to do it.

The truck came closer, then shuddered to a stop. The road and the check point was lit up by the headlight glow. Dan heard a door open and shut. Boots clattered on the tarmac. Then he heard footsteps approaching.

He wanted them to come close, but not too close.

Four, three, two, one…

Dan uncoiled himself and turned around, gun pointing at the man approaching. He had a gun pointing at Dan, and his eyes widened. He didn't stand a chance as Dan fired before his startled brain even registered what he was seeing. Dan double tapped him on the face, then turned his fire towards the driver before the body had hit the ground.

The windshield cracked into a thousand pieces, and the driver fell back in his seat, blood oozing from his forehead. Dan ran towards the driver's cabin. He hauled himself up, rifle ready to fire. The truck was empty, bar the two men he had just killed. Dan pushed the dead driver to the road, then got behind the wheel. He revved the engine, it was working. He got down and grabbed his duffel bag, then set off towards Pangshang.

CHAPTER 51

Dan was roaring up the hillside when he noticed a set of headlights behind him. Closing in fast. He stepped on the gas. The incline was steep and he had set the manual gearbox to first in order to get traction up the hill. Speed was suffering as a result. The vehicle loomed behind him, headlights blinding.

The distance decreased further. Dan lifted his hands to shield his eyes. It was another truck, and without a doubt, it was coming to ram him. In the split second before collision, Dan recognized the man in the passenger seat. The man with dead eyes, and the scar disfiguring his face.

Li Yonping.

The trucks rammed together with a twisting, shearing sound. The engine grill of the truck came off with a moaning bend of metal, stuck to the rear bumper of Dan's truck. Dan felt the wheels skid underneath him. He rotated the massive steering wheel, but the truck fishtailed, moving out towards the edge of the road. Towards the dark abyss of the forests below.

Dan braked lightly and steered in the direction of the skid, preparing himself to jump before the truck ran out of road. But it fishtailed again, out of control, and smashed into a rock face on the hillside. Dan had crouched behind the dashboard as he saw the hill rushing up to meet the windscreen. He braked but it was of no use. Jagged rocks splintered the windscreen. The truck came to a stop, stuck to the rocky hillside. Dan tried to lift himself, feeling dazed. His head was swimming.

He caught the headlights of the truck behind him. It roared to a stop alongside, and he saw the snout of a rifle emerge from the window.

Dan crawled on the cabin floor as bullets flew in, glass exploding form the remnants of the windscreen. Dan shook his head, trying to clear the pain inside. He managed to open the passenger side door. He did not drop to the floor. He slung the rifle on his back, and climbed to the roof. Just as he had expected, a few of the men on the truck was on the road, shooting below the truck. The others were firing inside the cabin. Dan knew some would be around the back, looking inside the tarpaulin covered rear.

Dan had survived this long doing what was unexpected. He flattened himself on the driver's cabin, and looked at the men standing on the road.

Four of them in total. None of them looked up to see the shadow holding a rifle over them. They didn't stand a chance. The bodies shook and gyrated as ordnance pumped into them from a ten feet distance.

Dan rolled off the roof, and holding on to the metallic lip of the windscreen, dropped to the ground, light as a cat. He used the corner of the truck as cover, and peered out. Movement straight down, near the rear of the truck. Dan fired instantly, and a man fell back with a cry, weapon clattering to the road.

Suddenly, there was silence. Dan advanced, his senses on a razor edge. Every sound was magnified in his ears. He stepped over the dead bodies on the road, rifle at his shoulder. He bent down and scanned underneath the truck. Clear.

He heard something creaking inside the truck. He turned to look and caught a black shadow hurtling at him from the sky.

Dan averted his face and twisted his body out of the way, but the body caught his midriff, depressing his ribs and squeezing air out of his lungs. Dan tumbled on the ground, the shadow pressing down on him. The rifle had fallen from Dan's hand. He felt a sickening, jarring blow to the side of his head, and pain mushroomed inside his skull. He grunted, and tried to move, but the shadow was sitting astride him now. The thighs were pressing his lungs again. The man was immensely strong. Dan couldn't breathe, and his eyes grew dark.

Dimly, Dan saw the right hand raise itself, then rushing down to hit him. A knockout punch. The problem with a knockout punch is the commitment required. The attacker has to throw all their strength behind the punch, and it makes them off balance, even when sitting on top of the opponent, like this man was now.

Dan moved his head at the last minute. When he moved, it wasn't just his head, he flung his whole body to the left, as fast and hard as he could. The man missed, and his right fist slammed into the tarmac. Dan saw the hideous scar, and he knew it was Li Yonping.

Li screamed in mortal agony as his right fist and shoulder jarred from the blow.

Dan put both hands on Li's chest and pushed back, hard. Li fell down, clutching his right arm. Dan stood up and whirled around to see him reach inside his coat pocket. Dan jumped and slammed into Li. Li grunted in pain, but his left hand was already gripping something. Dan held Li's left hand inside the pocket. He drew his head back and headbutted him on the face.

His nose exploded with a dull thwack and he screamed, his head falling backward. The trigger finger contracted and a round fired, slamming into Li's left leg.

It was Dan's turn to punch. He hit Li with everything he had, hard like a sledgehammer, but light from the shoulders like a short arm jab. Li staggered back, and Dan closed in, turned, and flew up in the air to do a roundhouse kick that smashed into the side of Li's face.

Li lay motionless on the tarmac, and Dan bent over him. He moved the left hand out from the jacket, it was holding a QSZ-92 handgun. The fingers were loose and Dan ripped the gun from his hand and threw it over the edge into the darkness. Li's eye lids fluttered. He turned to look at Dan, and his lips moved.

Dan said, "Where is Deng holding them?" Li stared at Dan, murmuring something inaudible.

"Tell me!" Dan shouted. Li shook his head, a smile appearing on his lips.

"I don't wanna do this. But you're not leaving me with much choice," Dan said.

Dan took out the knife from its scabbard. He grabbed Li's right hand and slapped it down on the tarmac, palm down. He pushed the knife tip between two fingers, and pressed down hard, cutting the flesh. Then he pulled the knife down, cutting the finger webbing. Li's eyes bulged, and he screamed, thrashing with his feet.

Dan let go, and lifted Li up by the jacket. He walked him to the edge of the cliff. He dangled Li over the edge, and lowered him down slowly, bending his own knees. Li's feet were hanging out in empty space, his only support Dan's hands around his throat.

Dan spat out the words. "I'm done playing, asshole. Tell me now or you die." Li shook his head, his eyes wide. Dan shook him. "Tell me! Are they in the hotel? Or somewhere else?"

Li whispered, "*Yaoguai!*"

"What?"

"*Yaoguai!*"

"What the hell are you saying?"

Suddenly, Li's devilish, pale face twisted into a sick smile. For a nauseating moment, Dan thought there was someone behind him, but a quick look assured him that was not the case.

Li screamed, "*Yaoguai!*" and laughed a maniacal, derisive laugh. The sound echoed off the walls, eerie and forlorn. Then he raised himself somehow, and sank his teeth into Dan's hand.

Dan shouted, and moved his hands from Li's neck. Li had no other support. He flew backwards, and within seconds, his body was lost in the blackness of the night, crashing to the earth far below.

Dan stood up, panting. "Crazy," he whispered.

He turned and did a Sit Rep. All tangos dead, weapons on the ground. Dan was picking up extra ammo, when he heard a phone ring. It was a cell phone. It lay where Li had fallen, and it had to be his. Dan looked at the caller ID, it was in Chinese. He pressed green and lifted the phone to his ear.

The voice was familiar. Henry Deng. But the words were in Chinese, and he couldn't understand them.

Dan waited a beat. Then he said softly, "Li is dead, Deng. Now I'm coming after you."

After a pause, Deng spoke, his voice low and menacing. "*Ta ma bi*. You are lying."

"Get ready to die, Deng."

Dan hung up and put the phone in his pocket.

CHAPTER 52

Deng held the cell phone tightly, his knuckles bone white. He was high up in the penthouse apartment of the hotel, and the light of Pangshang lay twinkling below him. Very slowly, he lowered the phone, his chest heaving up and down. A geyser of red hot rage was shooting inside him.

"*Cao ni ma*!," he screamed, and threw the phone at the wall opposite.

It hit the wall and shattered into pieces. He was standing near the floor to ceiling windows, and there was an armchair next to him. He kicked the chair and it overturned. Balling his fists, he stormed out of the room. A group of his most trusted men were gathered in the corridor outside. They turned as the door to Deng's office flung open and he rushed out.

Deng's eyes were wild with hate. "Brothers, Li Yonping is dead. That *sha bi* has killed him. I want revenge! This man needs to be shown who he is dealing with!" Deng walked towards his men, and they surrounded him in a circle. Deng lifted his balled fists upwards and uttered each word between clenched teeth.

"Find him. Keep him alive so I can torture him. But if you have to kill him, then bring me his head. Now!"

Deng shouted the last word, his voice like a whiplash. The men murmured consent, and checked their weapons.

Deng called out to one of them. "Leung Kim." The man turned and walked back. Leung was one of Deng's most trusted lieutenants. He was the son of Biyu Deng's best friend. He used to be a senior Triad member in Kunming, before he had joined Deng's team.

"*Zhu* Deng."

Deng spoke rapidly. "Keep some men here. If he comes up here, we make sure he dies. Put men near the elevators, at every stair case landing in every floor. I want all the exits covered. Where are the trucks with the Wa soldiers?"

"Two of them went up to the check point, *Zhu* Deng. Two are still here."

"Get them out, and form a perimeter outside. No one comes in or out of this building. Do it!"

"Yes, Zhu." Leung bowed and left.

Four men remained guarding the exits of the corridor. Deng walked down to the room at the end and entered. He turned the handle of the steel door and walked in. There was an armed guard at the door who stepped aside. A yellow bulb lit the room in a hazy glow. The woman was still tied to the chair. Her face was haggard and pale, hair falling all over it. The man was still on the floor, tied up. She didn't even look up as Deng entered. Deng watched them for a few seconds, his chest heaving, lips bared in fury.

He took out a knife and walked over to the woman. With his right hand, he pulled the woman's hair till her head was pointing upwards.

"What is this man's name?" Kim opened her eyes slowly. Deng pulled on her hair harder, and thrust the sharp tip of the knife close to her neck. He repeated the question.

Kim opened her cracked, dry lips. "Tell me!" Deng bellowed in her face. "Or I'll slit your neck right now."

Kim swallowed. "Roy...Dan Roy." Deng stared at her for a few seconds, then let go of her hair. Kim's head dropped back on her chest. Deng cut through her ropes. Kim moaned as her hands came free. Deng walked around to the front and slapped her hard across the face. Then he motioned to the guard, who came and tied Kim's hands behind her back again. Deng pulled on her hair and made her stand up.

"You will be my security," he hissed. "If he comes anywhere near me, you die first."

Kim looked at him. She managed a small smile. "He's here, isn't he?"

"Yes, he is here. But not for long. You will have the satisfaction of watching him die soon."

There was a sound from the floor. Deng turned to look. David Harris was staring at them with a vacant look in his eyes.

"Let her go," Harris said. "She knows nothing. It's me you want."

"It's too late for that," Deng snarled. "Now all of you will die."

He signalled to the guard who stepped up with his rifle drawn. "Kill him," Deng said, pointing to Harris.

Kim turned her fearful eyes to Deng. "No. Please don't. Please..."

Her words were lost as gunfire rang out loudly, reverberating against the four walls.

*****

Dan could see the lights of Pangshang in the distance. He was coming down the hill, and had slowed down as he approached. Tin roof one story shacks lined the side of the road. Homes of the men and women who worked in the gambling parlors of Pangshang.

Dan raced past them, getting closer to the main drag of the city. To his left, towering above the other buildings he could see the blazing blue lights of Deng's hotel. Opposite lay the brightly lit 7 Dragons Casino and brothel. Dan slowed down and pulled over. The road was dark and empty on both lanes. He had less than a mile to get to the town center.

Dan went to the back of the truck and got his duffel bag. He put it on his back, and checked a new QMB-95 rifle. He chugged on water, and chewed on some bars of chocolate he had found in the dashboard drawers of the truck. He also found a jar of red pills. Under the torch, the inscription WaY 99 was clearly visible. Methamphetamine pills, used by the soldiers. Dan threw the jar away.

He started running along the side of the road, staying behind the screen of bamboo trees so he couldn't be easily spotted. He saw the first patrol 500 yards from the town center.

Three jeeps had closed down the road. Pedestrians were not visible. At least a dozen men were standing near the vehicles, spanning across the road. Dan had no way across. Steep hills went up from the sides. It was likely they had men at the top of the hill as well. Perfect place for an ambush.

He crept out of the bamboo trees and flattened himself on the ground. He looked at the tops of the hill on either side, and saw the glow of a cigarette. Dan aimed with his suppressed weapon. The cigarette burned bright, and Dan fired, aiming for just below the mark. There was a soft grunt, and the glow disappeared. He unhooked two grenades from his belt.

He threw the first one as far as he could, to the other end of the road, where four soldiers were clustered, smoking and talking. He ducked as the ground shook under the explosion. He lifted his head, pointing his gun upwards. Sure enough, the man on the hill closest to him was standing, rifle raised and shouting. An amateur mistake for a sniper. Dan took him down with a headshot, and the body fell almost vertically to the road below.

Bullets zipped around him, thudding into the bamboo shoots. The soldiers were firing, panicked. Dan counted eight, spreading out slowly, firing at random at anything that moved. Dan aimed at the one closest to him, caressing the trigger.

He had to be careful. One of them was already speaking on his cell phone, calling for back up. When Dan fired, he would give his position away, so he had to be quick. He flicked the gun to full automatic.

He pressed the trigger and the two men closest to him, a mere twenty feet away, shook and jerked as a wall of ordnance hit them from the right. He got return fire from the remainder, but he was concealed below the dip on the roadside. They did not stand a chance. The suppressed weapon's butt jerked against his shoulder as he fired in short bursts. The men fell like a stack of dominoes.

The cacophony of the gunfire ceased, and there was a sudden quiet. Dan got up and ran, scanning with his raised weapon. All clear. He put down the duffel bag took out four sticks of gelignite. He fit them into the jeeps, and set the detonator to a time fuse of one minute. The less vehicles the enemy had to chase him, the better. Then he started running again.

He was nearing the hotel and casino when the jeeps behind him ignited. The ground shook as the gas in the jeep's petrol tank erupted into a massive red and yellow fireball. The noise rattled the trees and echoed around the hills. Ahead of him, Dan saw uniformed men forming a blockade around the hotel. Pedestrians and tourists mingled in front of the casino.

Everyone looked up in shock at the explosion.

Way to make an entrance, Dan thought to himself.

CHAPTER 53

Dan considered his options. Orders rang out in the soldiers ranks, and some of them began to ran towards the burning jeeps. Dan watched them crouch and flatten on the road, rifles aimed at anyone coming through. Only the spectre of hungry flames lapping the burning vehicles greeted them.

The diversion had worked. Dan unhooked three grenades from his belt line. He could see tourists starting to come out of the casino. The soldiers blocked his view, but they were congregated around the hotel on the opposite side. The grenades would not hurt the tourists. And once they exploded, everyone would haul ass.

Two trucks stood behind the row of soldiers, beyond that he could see the steps leading up to the hotel's main entrance. He looked up at the hotel. Lights were on in some floors, but the topmost floor had all its lights on, blazing like a lighthouse. Deng had to be in there, and he would keep his prisoners with him.

Behind Deng's hotel, other tall buildings were being constructed. Dan saw the red lights of a tall hydraulic crane, several hundred feet high. From the long central column, a long arm jib protruded sideways into the skyline. The crane was now still, and Dan could just make out the operator's cabin, halfway up the main column.

Dan lobbed two of the grenades towards the trucks. He was almost a hundred yards away, and he hoped the grenades would roll under the trucks, igniting the fuel tank. He didn't wait for them to explode. He threw the third grenade towards the soldiers.

All three exploded at almost the same time, and the shock of the blast threw Dan off his feet. The trucks erupted into gasoline volcanos, lifting up in the air with a cataclysmic sound before coming to rest in burning wrecks on the road.

Dan got up and ran across the wide avenue. Panicked bystanders were now pouring out of the casino, screaming. It was a stampede. There were some western tourists as well. Dan wiped the mud from his face and body, and put the duffel bag in his hand. Then he joined the confused melee of human bodies rushing to get out of the nightmare on the street opposite.

From the corner of his eyes, Dan could make out the survivors getting to their feet, shock and disbelief on their faces. Hoarse voices barked and shouted. The entire front façade of the hotel was destroyed in the explosions, littering the sidewalk with glass fragments. More soldiers and men poured out of the hotel, rifles aloft.

Ahead of him, a continuous stream of people was running out of the market square. Dan slipped into a side alley. He saw soldiers and men with guns run into the market and set up positions on the road. They did not fire, but scanned the crowd, speaking urgently into radios.

Dan slipped out again, and used the confusion to run into the market square. The square was on the same side as the hotel. Shopkeepers had turned lights off, and the once busy square was emptying rapidly. Dan scurried from one darkened awning to another till he reached the edge of the square.

Across another street, he could see the building zone where the crane was located. The zone was protected by a makeshift timber wall about ten feet high. The back of the hotel was in front of him now. The construction site with the cranes was directly behind the hotel, as Dan had expected.

As Dan watched, a group of armed men came out of the back entrance. They filed out the door and stepped across the road, getting close to where Dan was hiding in the market square, behind the tin doors of a gambling den.

The men stayed in position, guarding the rear of the building. If Dan was to get to the crane, he had to get through them. He had no other option. His grenades were all finished. The duffel bag still contained several gelignite sticks. The last of the soldiers stepped on the pavement, less than twenty feet from where Dan was hiding.

Dan unzipped the bag, and took out four sticks, and put one on the ground next to him. He left the bag where it was, and put extra ammo for the rifle and handgun into his belt. He worked very slowly. The soldier ahead of him just had to turn sideways and he would see Dan.

Dan set the detonator to 45 seconds. He reckoned that was enough time to run across the street and climb up the timber wall. He crept out of the shadow and scooted down the road, bent at the waist. He had to cross the street. The soldiers had formed a line, and were looking around. He would be seen, without a doubt. He heard a shout, and a second later, a flurry of rounds kicked up near his feet.

Dan lifted the rifle, and fired. The blur of rounds caught the men unawares. Dan got most of them, but the last two fired back. Dan was exposed now, and time was running out.

He had to get over the wall before the sticks exploded. Dan got up and fired, aiming at the remaining men. Head shots got them both, and Dan ran as he fired, crossing the street. As he got to the other end, the gates opened and more men poured out.

Dan reached the wall at a fast run. A piece of wood was jutting out, and he stepped on it with his right foot, and levered himself to the top. He heard a shout, he had been spotted. Bullets rang out, smashing against the woodwork just as he went over. He went into a blind fall on the other side, and dropped into a pile of rubble. He scrambled out, raising his rifle to the top of the wall. No one had come through as yet, but he could hear them on the other side.

Dan checked his watch. Ten seconds left. In front, the red lights of the cranes gleamed, more than a hundred yards away. The construction site was large, he could not see the ends of it in the darkness. The light of Deng's hotel rose high up to his left. Dan sprinted for the cranes.

The explosion behind him ignited the night into daylight again, the sound louder this time as it was contained by the buildings. The deafening soundwave drummed against Dan's ears, leaving a ringing sound afterwards. He knew half the market square was destroyed.

Dan jumped inside the crane's control room. He flashed a torchlight inside. It took him a few seconds to find the ignition switch. The dashboard lights shone brightly. Two levers stuck up from the dashboard, and he could move both in 360 degrees.

Dan sat down, and moved one of the levers. There was huge clashing sound above him. He looked up to the lights on the column and protruding, long jib arm. The jib was moving from side to side. The tip of the jib narrowed to a hook. Dan moved the lever on the left, and with a groan of metal, the jib lurched to the left.

Dan moved the lever till the jib arm was close to Deng's hotel. It reached close to the well-lit penthouse floor at the top, stopping at the floor below.

The tip of the arm was near a window, the hook hanging below it. That would have to do. Dan exited the control cabin and jumped on the metal struts that constructed the central column. Metal rungs ran all the way to the top, where it connected to the jib arm. Dan climbed quickly. The wind grew stronger, whipping around his face, pushing his dark hair back.

He got to the connector, a large steel structure welding the jib arm to the column. He went across it, and stepped on the jib. This thinner, long structure formed the bridge to Deng's hotel. He knew he would face far greater resistance if he had tried to fight his way in.

Now he had to fight gravity, hoping he won the battle.

Dan looked down, and saw pinpoint, tiny lights, some of them moving. He looked forward, at the black strip of metal stretching into the darkness to the blue lights of the hotel, and steeled himself.

He stepped on it, then withdrew rapidly. He noticed the jib arm was a double storied structure. There was a sliding rail on the bottom, used to retract the massive, dangling hook at the far end. The space between the sliding rail and the top, where he was standing, was long enough to fit a man.

Dan grabbed for what he could on the metal struts, and lowered himself to the side of the jib. He was hanging in open air, till his feet found some purchase on the railings of the sliding rail below. Gently, he lowered himself, and got inside the sliding rail. The structure was almost like a miniature railway bridge with two levels. He had to hold on to the sides, and make sure his feet did not fall into one of the regular spaced gaps on the metal work.

He moved fast, and the lights of the hotel began to loom larger in his eyes. Soon he could see highest floor. He faced the back of it, and it was lit at the front. He got to the end of the jib arm, facing the darkened window. He had not got the jib flush with the window.

There was a space of four to five feet, he guessed. A space of empty air. Dan stood at the tip of the structure, wind rattling around him, feeling he was standing at the brink of a precipice.

He lifted his weapon, and fired a long burst at the window. The glass fragmented, then broke. He fired again and the window yawned open, showing a black space behind. Dan hoped and prayed no one lay in wait for him. The gunfire would be heard in the hotel corridor.

He took off his shirt and used the knife to make two strips. He wrapped the strips around his palms. Then he bent his knee, and jumped from the end of the jib arm into empty space.

He soared in the air, having powered his legs to thrust as hard as he could. He flew, and slammed into the space were the window had been. His palms fell on the exposed window sill. He winced in pain as some of the glass shards dug into his hands. But the sill held his weight. He heaved himself, and topped over the side into the dark room.

He fell into broken glass that lacerated his arms and body, but he breathed a long sigh of relief. Naked from the waist up now, he unhooked his rifle, and slapped in a new 30 cartridge magazine. He checked the handgun and his knife, and the last two sticks of gelignite.

All set.

Then he heard a woman scream from inside.

CHAPTER 54

Kim was tied to a chair in Deng's sumptuous penthouse office. There was a long conference desk to one side, and a personal mahogany desk closer to the window. Deng sat there, reclining in his chair. He pulled out a silver foil from the top drawer and spread it on the table. He opened a jar and dropped a small square object on the foil. Then he lit the foil from beneath with a lighter, and inhaled the fumes. A pungent smell filled the room.

Kim crinkled her nose. Deng took several lung fulls of the smoke, then approached her chair. He took out his gun and put it against Kim's head. He took out a cell phone and thumbed a number into it. A man came into the room, and he took the phone from Deng's hand and put it against Kim's right ear.

"Speak to him," Deng said. Kim shook her head. Deng pushed the gun against the side of her head till she was leaning out the chair.

"Now. Speak," Deng ordered.

"No."

Kim's hands were tied to the back of the chair. Her legs were free. She could stand up, but she wanted to bide her time. From the explosions around the hotel, she knew Dan was close. Very close.

Deng lowered his voice, and got his face close to hers. She felt that pungent smell again, and it made her gag. "Well, if you don't obey me, then no point in keeping you alive."

"Goodbye, Kim Smith. We will deliver your body to the Embassy."

Kim heard the safety catch being released. Her heart pounded. This man was crazy enough to do this. A black weight was pressing down in her chest.

She felt the trigger being squeezed and she screamed, bracing herself for the impact. The trigger clicked softly in a hollow chamber. Deng laughed.

"See, everyone is scared of dying." He reached into his pocket and loaded rounds into the chamber. Kim's face had fallen to her chest. Her breath came in gasps. Anger filled every pore in her body. Through a shadow of pain and exhaustion, she lifted her head.

"Why don't you untie me, asshole, and we'll see who's scared of dying. You're using *me* as a shield to protect yourself. What sort of a man are you?"

Deng said, "The sort of man who gets what he wants." He opened his mouth to speak again but the sound of gunfire drowned his words. Deng looked around him like a wild animal. He turned to the man standing next to Kim.

"Get down there," Deng shouted. The man nodded, and ran out of the room.

*****

Dan moved out of the room hurriedly. The scream had come from Kim's voice, and from upstairs. Outside the room, he was in a small hallway. The furniture around him was expensive, and he realized he was in a suite. Only the penthouse lay above him.

Den opened the front door a crack and looked outside. Three guards at the elevator, and three more near the stairwell door. There was no time for hesitation. Dan pushed the barrel of the gun out, and fired at the three men nearest to him. He dropped down to the floor right after, hearing bullets rain down on the doorframe above him.

He edged forward, crawling on his elbows. The guards rushed towards the open door of the suite. They saw the figure on the ground way too late. Dan fired a long burst, and all three fell, dead before they hit the floor.

Dan took out a gelignite stick. He had not wanted to use it. The heavy explosive would take the whole floor out, and he could injure himself. But he had no choice. He heard footsteps running down the stairs. Dan ran back inside the suite, flicking on the light switch of the hallway. Inside one of the bedrooms he found what he was looking for. A dresser. He climbed to the top, and waited. He had an angled view of the well lit hallway.

The men came in crouched low, weapons trained. They moved in formation, one scouting up front, the others behind him. Dan waited till they filtered in. Three of them moved inside the bedroom. A light switch came on, and Dan fired immediately. The three inside the room fell instantly. Dan got another in the hallway, but he knew there would be more.

And the one thing he could not afford was to get boxed inside.

He topped off the top onto the bed, and fired from the hip into the hallway. He heard a scream, and then he was outside, crawling flat on the ground. Two shadows loomed out of a doorway and he dropped them both. He was heading for the front door, when he heard something slid across the ground, and drop a few feet away from him.

He glanced, and knew immediately what the oblong black object was. A flashbang. A stun grenade.

Dan ran for the door and dived through it, bullets pockmarking the wall behind him. He landed in the corridor just as the flashbang exploded. Dense clouds of acrid smoke blew out of the suite. Tears streamed down Dan's eyes. He saw the black snout of gas masks emerge from the white smoke. He fired immediately. Both men fell, and Dan crawled over. His lungs were heaving and he could not see anything. He ripped off a gas mask from a dead man's head and put it on.

He coughed, feeling sick. He shook his head and stumbled to his feet. He needed to keep moving. He lurched into the stairwell, rifle ready to fire. Which was just as well. Two men were waiting at the landing, but their eyes were compromised by the thick smoke. They saw Dan a few seconds late, and it was all the advantage Dan needed.

Dan fired, and ran as the bodies fell. More men now came down the stairs. Dan fired, but the return fire was too heavy. He shrank back against the wall, hiding against railings of the floor below. The men came down. None of them glanced down the staircase. Dan counted twelve. In formation, they moved down the landing, through the door, and into the hallway of the lounge suite.

Dan waited. Only one man remained on the landing, weapon scanning around. It would not take them long to find out he was not there. Dan took out the gelignite stick. He cut off the fuse, and took out his lighter. He would have less than ten seconds before this erupted. Maybe enough time to get up the stairs, and into the penthouse.

Maybe not.

Only one way to find out.

Dan fired at the man crouching by the door, killing him instantly. As the man sagged down the red stain on the white doorway, Dan lit the fuse and chucked the explosive stick into the hallway. Then he turned, and ran up the staircase. A gun emerged above him, followed by a figure. Dan pressed the trigger hard and kept firing as he bounded up the steps.

Two more figures emerged and they shook uncontrollably as bullets pumped into their bodies. Then Dan heard shouts from below. The men were coming out, and up the stairs. With a sinking heart, he realized the gelignite stick had failed to ignite. He knew he could not hold back all of them. He would be hemmed in, from behind, and from top.

He was a dead man.

He was wrong.

The gelignite blasted on the floor below, throwing Dan forward into the landing of the penthouse suit. The bone jarring explosion blew out the entire floor with awesome power. The windows exploded, throwing out fire flames into the air. The concrete posts were reduced to rubble, and the heavy metal shafts of the building bent with a sepulchral, other worldly moan. The staircase dissolved below Dan's feet. Dan was on the floor of the landing, and he was dazed. The air was filled with dust and smoke. His eyes swam, unable to focus. A headache was spreading across his forehead. He tried to stand up, but lurched and fell on his knees.

Dan kneeled, panting. He shook his head, trying to get his vision back. Behind him, where the staircase had been, there was a huge gaping hole. The explosion had formed a crater, and gone through the ceiling of the floor below. Metal pipes stuck out from the walls, bent at insane angles.

Dan transferred his attention to the front. He wiped his forehead, it came away sticky with blood. He saw a figure step out of a doorway, wobbling. Dan fired, and he fell. He ran forward, and fired as two more gunmen stepped out. An alarm bell was ringing loudly. The men were barely visible in the smoke, but Dan dropped them both with prolonged bursts. He was either out of ammo, or would be soon. He didn't check, he slid the mag out and slapped a new one in.

There was a heavy oak door in front of him with Chinese letters inscribed on it. Dan held his weapon up with one hand, and turned the handle with the other.

He couldn't see much inside. He scanned, dropped to his knees, and entered. He could see a dim shape ahead of him. A fresh breeze blew in from an open window. The shape became more distinct.

A man, standing over a woman tied to a chair. He had a gun to her head. Dan recognized Kim's face. The smoke cleared more, and he recognized the man as well. Henry Deng.

"Welcome," Deng said. "Now put down your weapon, Dan Roy, or the woman dies."

CHAPTER 55

Kim stared at Dan's bleeding and scarred body. He was naked from the waist up, and lacerations crisscrossed the bulging muscles of his chest and arms, like he had been cut with a knife. Sticky blood matted his long dark hair, and his eyes were wide, wild. He moved his head from side to side, taking in the room.

"Put your weapon down!" Deng screamed suddenly. Kim did not wince as she felt the handgun bore into her temple. She clenched her jaw tight. This time, she knew Deng wasn't messing around. The gun was loaded. If it fired, she would die.

Dan said, "You're dead if you kill her Deng, and dead if you don't. So I'll give you a choice. Let her go and I'll put a bullet in your head. If she dies, you're coming with me to the jungle. I'll feed you to the animals."

Deng smiled. "I don't think you are calling the shots any more, Dan."

Kim saw a shadow appear outside the door. The man called Leung Kim had stayed behind, and he had a rifle aimed straight at Dan.

"Dan!" Kim screamed. Dan fell to the floor, moving faster than anyone Kim had seen. He drew the handgun from his belt and fired while he was on the floor, cheek pressed against the ground. Leung Kim fired too, but it went high above Dan's head.

Kim did not wait to see the result. Just as Dan fired, she placed her feet flat on the ground, and heaved upwards with every remaining ounce of strength in her body.

She stiffened the muscles of her neck as her head smashed into Deng's chin. He grunted, and stumbled backwards, surprised at the sudden movement. His gun jerked forward, away from Kim. She moved backwards, slamming the chair into Deng's body, and they tumbled on the floor in a heap.

Deng was pressed underneath the chair. He was strong, and he threw the chair back, scrambling to his feet. Kim was on the floor, unable to free her arms. Deng stood above her, gun pointed to her head.

"Should have killed you earlier."

Kim strained to look towards Dan. Her head had hit the floor when Deng pushed her back, and her eyes were blurred. She heard a bopping sound, and looked up to see Deng's head explode into fragments of blood and brain matter. There was another sound, and Deng fell backwards, his body falling to the floor in a heap.

Kim heard footsteps, and then felt the cold metal of a knife on her hands. She felt her hands come loose. Then arms strong as steel helped her to sit up right.

"You OK?" It was Dan. She reached out and passed a hand over his face. It came away with bits of dirt and curdled blood.

"Yes," Kim whispered. She stared at him for a while. His dark eyes bore into her face intensely. When she spoke, her voice caught. "I knew you would come."

"I had to," he said simply. Kim reached out again, and placed her palm against his cheek. His skin was warm. Dan held her hand briefly, then lowered it from his face. He glanced towards the door.

"Let's get out of here."

*****

Dan took out the cell phone that Gyi Noe had given him. He pressed the contact number. After three rings, Noe picked up.

Dan said, "Henry Deng is dead. I could really use a bird to evacuate us." He told Noe the story quickly.

Noe listened then said, "We heard a helicopter was destroyed by gunfire near Pangshang. Was that you?"

"Yes."

After a pause Noe said, "I can get one down there for you."

Dan said, "How long?"

"15, maybe 20 minutes."

"Hurry, before this building collapses under us."

All the while Dan spoke, Kim had been staring at the door. She held Dan's handgun in her hand. Dan hung up.

"Where's David Harris?"

Kim told him. Dan led the way, weapon raised at his shoulder. They stepped over the dead bodies. In the prison room, Dan bent over Harris' prone figure. He felt for the internal carotid artery pulsation, then shook his head.

"Gone," he said quietly. He put his rifle away, and lifted Harris on his back. Kim lead now, holding Dan's rifle. The way she held it, Dan knew she would use it well if needed.

They found the staircase going up to the roof. Chunks of masonry fell from the crater in the floors beneath. Sirens were sounding, and hearing the clang of bells, Dan could tell some fire engines had arrived. Police as well, and the rest of the Wa State Army. It was the latter that bothered Dan.

As they went up the stairs, there was a huge, tearing sound and the building seemed to shake. The stairs moved under their feet. The walls shuddered, and Kim fell backwards. Dan reached out a hand to steady her. Kim rebounded. She got to the top of the staircase, and fired a burst at the locked door.

It swung open. A crash came from below them as another large chunk of the building fell away inside. Dan heard the booming sound far below. This building would collapse soon. It was held together by metal structures in four corners. The gelignite had bent some of them, and the rest of the concrete and steel was now giving way.

Heart pounding, Dan ran to the top, bursting out into the rooftop with Kim. The building shook and wobbled underneath them. They both fell as another booming noise reverberated around the block, emanating from the dark depths of the hotel.

Kim got up, panting. "Your friend better come soon." A wide H sign marked the helipad in the middle of the large roof. They stood to one side with Harris's body.

Dan was going to say something when he felt a cell phone buzz. It was Li Yonping's phone he had kept in his pocket. Dan didn't recognize the number but he answered it.

"Who is this?" he asked.

A man's voice said, "I know you, Dan Roy, but you don't know me." The accent was American.

"Do I need to?"

"Yes, you do. But before I tell you, there is someone you need to speak to." There was a scuffle, and a scream. Then Dan heard a voice that made his blood run cold.

"Maya?" he said. Kim turned around, paying attention.

Maya's voice was scared. "Dan...this man...he has a gun...says he'll kill me. He wants Kim and you to come here, quick."

"Where are you, Maya? I..."

The phone was snatched off Maya's hands. The male voice came on again. "I know where you are. Get back to Yangon within the next 3 hours. If you don't, I torture the girl before she dies."

"Who are you?"

"Is Kim Smith there?"

Dan grit his teeth. "Who wants to know?"

"Just give her the damn phone."

Dan waited a beat, then held the phone out to Kim. "For you," he said. "This asshole has Maya. He wants us there, or she dies."

Kim snatched the phone off Dan's hand. As she listened her face lost all color. Dan watched as Kim stumbled back, then sank down to her knees. He went over to her.

Slowly, Kim removed the phone from her ear. She looked up at Dan with a shocked, disbelieving face.

"That was my boss. Solomon Barney."

Dan heard the sound rotor blades splicing the night air above him. He felt the building shudder again, and looked up as the helicopter hovered directly above them, preparing to land.

CHAPTER 56

The almost 22,000 gold bars that make the surface of the gigantic Shwedagon Pagoda emits a blazing yellow glow when lit by the sun, and from surrounding lights in the evening. A glow that can be seen from the lower reaches of the atmosphere, and easily visible to any plane approaching the Yangon International Airport.

The tip of the pagoda, too high to be visible to the human eye, is encrusted with 5448 diamonds. Kim watched the lights winking off it, impossibly bright even at the midnight hour.

As the cab approached the Eastern Gate of the 2,500 year old temple complex, Kim turned her head to look at Dan. He stared out the window, his face calm as the surface of a pond without ripples.

Kim was feeling anything but calm. Once the bird had touched down at the helipad of the US Embassy, they had received further bad news.

Mary was dead. An intruder had broken into her apartment and kidnapped Maya. It was likely the same intruder shot Mary. They received the news in stony silence. David Harris' body was taken to a mortuary. He would receive the hero's burial he deserved when his body was flown back home.

Right now, they had a job to do. They could not tell Military Police anything. Solomon had been precise in his instructions. Come alone. Or the girl dies.

The whirlwind of thoughts ran amuck in Kim's mind, but more than anything else, she could not stifle the dreaded curse of a memory. It reached its claws deep inside her heart, raking out old wounds that had never fully healed.

Losing Sarah.

Kim did not understand why Maya reminded her of Sarah *so* much. It was beyond weird that a little girl halfway around the world would have the same mannerisms as her sister. But Maya did. Even thinking about her face moved Kim deeply inside, and her mind was colored with images of her own sister as a little girl.

And she knew she would rather die than let anything happen to her.

Kim lowered her head, touching her temples. She felt Dan's hand on her shoulder.

"It's gonna be alright," he said softly.

Kim did not reply. She stared straight ahead as the cab rushed through the well-lit streets of downtown Yangon.

They circled around the Shwedagon, a few tourists and street hawkers jostling around even at this late hour. They went past the eastern gate of the temple complex and entered a wide street called Bahan Road.

Colonial English buildings lined the sidewalk. The road became darker as they moved along to their destination. Trees grew on either side of the road soon, and all they could heard was the sound of crickets, and water rustling.

The driver stopped in front of a dark gate. "Kandawgyi Park," he said, without turning around.

They did not pay the driver. He waited, engine purring. Kim looked at the entrance, a sense of foreboding filling her. Dan checked his weapons, then nodded to her.

"Time to finish this," he said quietly

*****

Dan walked with a light step, his eyes doing 180 sweeps. He turned around a couple of times. All was still in the overgrown parkland. Dense clumps of jacaranda and bamboo trees grew all around them. Dan felt Kim's hand slip into his. He gave it a squeeze.

As they walked deeper into the park, Dan lit the way with his torch. The cry of a bird rose harsh and clear in the silent night air.

"The blue-tailed jay bird," Dan said.

Kim frowned. "What?"

"That's the cry of the blue-tailed jay bird," Dan said.

They came to the central square of the park. The darkness was pitch black now. Dan flashed his torch. Kandawgyi Park lay on the banks of a lake with the same name. The park was large, over 110 acres.

But they were told to come to a specific spot. The Karaweik was a concrete replica of a Royal Burmese barge, built in 1972. Two huge flying dragons adorned the head of the barge, which was moored in the lake. Lights shone upon its golden surface.

"Well, we are here," he said.

Almost in reply the headlights of a car came on, directly in front of them. The light was bright enough to dazzle in the darkness. Dan held his hands in front of his eyes. Behind them, another set of vehicle lights came on.

Dan saw a figure step out from the car in front. As the man was illuminated in the headlights, Dan felt Kim stiffen. He came and stood opposite them, clasping his hands behind his back. He wore a freshly pressed business suit.

"Where is Maya?" Kim said.

"She's in the car." Solomon Barney said.

"I want to see her," Kim said. Solomon looked back and nodded at someone. The passenger door opened and a man stepped out. Behind him, the small figure of Maya was visible.

"Happy now?" Solomon said.

Kim stepped forward. Her voice was like ice. "You fed information about the Tonkin Protocol to Henry Deng."

Solomon said nothing. Kim continued. "You told them about David Harris meeting the Shan Army elders. That's how David got caught."

Dan said, "I bet you helped Deng make the uranium enrichment facility as well, right?"

Solomon shrugged. "When we knew, there was uranium in these hills, there was no point in waiting. Yes, I helped Deng make contact with a North Korean nuclear scientist, who was eager to sell information for money."

Kim said, "You're a double agent. Who do you work for?"

Solomon gave a small laugh. "Who for? The client varies, my dear Kim. I work for myself."

"You take money to sell state secrets."

"In a word, yes. But it's more than that. Myanmar has real potential, you see. Lots of oil here, and very close to China. I wanted a toe hold here, to leverage later. Henry Deng was the perfect partner. But the Tonkin Protocol had the power to change all of that. I knew about it long before John Hymers told me about it. But I still made him spill the beans."

"Who else is in this with you? You have contacts back home, right?"

Solomon smiled. "That would be telling, Kim."

Dan said, "The game is up now, Solomon. You are finished. Deng is dead, and the uranium lab will be seized by the Burmese Army. The Chinese are also aware of your games now. Give us the girl, and we'll let you go."

Solomon transferred his attention to Dan. "Aha, the elusive Dan Roy. Turns out you have quite a reputation. Well, it's a shame it has to end this way."

Solomon raised his hand. Lights from cars turned on in the darkness all around them. Dan glanced around.

Solomon said, "You are surrounded. There is no escape."

A group of men walked up, rifles aimed at them. They frisked Dan, and took his weapons. Dan felt the muzzle of a gun prod him in the back. Next to him, Kim had the same treatment. Together, they walked towards Solomon Barney, and the waiting car.

A stout, wide chest man was holding Maya with both hands on her shoulders. To their left, Solomon stood very still, a Glock 22 in his right hand. The men formed a semi- circle behind them, guns pointing straight at Kim and Dan. The harsh cry of a bird rose up again, echoing in the dense, dark screen of the surrounding trees.

Solomon said, "Goodbye, Kim. You were my protégé. We could have done greater things, but it's not to be." He lifted his gun and pointed it at Kim's head.

Dan said, "It's the cry of the blue-tailed jay bird."

Solomon frowned at him, "What?"

In a blur of movement, Dan grabbed Kim, and smashed into the man who was holding Maya. Solomon fired, and Dan felt the bullet graze the side of his body. Pain lanced through him, but he hoped it was a flesh wound. Enter and exit, not embedded inside. Even as their bodies hit the wet grass, a volley of gunfire rang out around them. Sporadic yellow gunfire blazed in the trees in the trees, lighting up the night.

Kim rolled out from under them, grabbing Maya. The stout man tried to hold on to her, but Dan punched him in the neck, aiming for the trachea. The man gagged, but tried to hit Dan back. An uppercut to his chin snapped his head back like a rag doll, and the man was still.

A massive firefight was erupting all around them. The park was illuminated with gunfire. Glass smashed above them, showering them with shards. Dan crawled over and covered Maya and Kim with his body. Bullets hit a car's gas tank and it exploded, sending a fireball into the sky. Bodies twitched and jerked in the grass around them, then became still as more bullets pumped into them.

The gunfire became less, and then stopped. All of a sudden, the silence flowed back. Footsteps trampled in the grass towards them. Dan sat up, looking around him. Solomon lay on his front, blood darkening the grass around him. Dan walked over and turned him around. Several bullets had pierced his chest, and one had decimated his face.

Solomon Barney was dead. His secrets had died with him.

An older man walked over, flanked by soldiers in green combat dress. They spread out, looking for survivors.

Dan stood up. "Gyi Noe."

Noe extended his hand, and Dan shook it. "Thank you," Dan said.

Noe said, "The blue jay bird has a very distinctive cry."

Dan smiled. "Perfect as a signal." They had arranged it while Dan was flying back from Pangshang. Noe and a group of his soldiers were near Yangon for the night.

Kim came over, holding Maya's hand. She touched Dan's back. "You are bleeding," she said. "Let me see."

Dan sat down on the grass while Kim inspected him under the torchlight. "A laceration. Didn't go any deeper. You were lucky."

Dan said, "Guess I had lady luck with me."

"You said that last time."

They held each other's eyes, aware of something that passed between them.

Noe said, "I have to go, Dan. The *Tatmadaw* and us are not the best of friends."

Kim turned to him. "But you are our friend. And I will see you again, to pick up where David Harris left off."

Gyi Noe bowed, and both of them bowed back.

"*Thwa doe meh naw*," Noe said. Till we meet again.

"Goodbye," Dan said. Noe called out to his men, and they gathered back around. They trailed back towards the trees, and were soon lost in the darkness.

Kim took out her cell phone, and called the US Embassy. Dan knelt on the grass and looked at Maya. Her face was streaked with tears.

"That man was bad," said Maya.

"Don't worry," Dan said, feeling that peculiar emotion flutter in his chest. Without realizing, he reached out a hand, and patted Maya on the head. "He won't come near you again."

*****

Dan leaned his hands on the window sill of Kim's apartment. He could see the circle of extra guards at the door. The light on Inle Lake gleamed in the distance. Maya was asleep in the spare room, and he had the couch in the lounge.

A shower had done him the world of good. A few bowls of hot curry and rice had made all of them feel human again. Dan pressed his head against the glass. He needed to sleep.

He heard a sound behind him, and turned to find Kim. She had come out of the shower, and was wearing a bathrobe. She came and stood next to him. She smelled fresh, fragrant. Together, they looked out at the view before them.

"Nice and quiet," Kim said. Dan nodded.

Then he felt her finger tracing down his cheek.

"How's your back?" she whispered.

Dan turned to her. "Don't know," he said, trying to keep his voice steady.

"Can I have a look?" Kim asked. She started to unbutton his shirt. Dan pulled her closer to him, and he felt her warmth. The bathrobe fell away, and he slipped a hand around her naked waist. Their lips met gently, then they kissed in a frenzy. Dan picked her up in his arms, and they headed for the bedroom.

Kim nuzzled his neck, then bit his shoulder softly.

"You got sharp teeth," Dan said.

"Mmm. What have you got?"

"Only one way to find out." He went inside the bedroom, and kicked the door shut with his heel.

EPILOGUE

2 weeks later

Sunlight flooded in through the tall windows of Yangon National Airport. Dan watched the long queue for the JFK flight forming. Maya sat next to him, wearing a pink floral dress with a red flower in her hair. Kim sat next to Maya, holding her backpack. As the flight was called, they stood up.

Kim reached her hand to Dan's neck. He lowered his face, and their lips met in a lingering kiss. Dan felt the warmth of her hand on his face, and his hand snaked around her back. She broke off, and hugged him.

"I'm going to miss you," she said in a husky voice.

Dan looked at her. Her eyes were red rimmed, and he reached up a finger and wiped her tears away. He struggled with his own emotions. Kim, and Maya, had reached into a corner of his soul he did not know existed. Maybe it had always been there, and like a blind man he had stumbled around looking for it.

It seemed insane that he had to say goodbye, to the very person who had helped him find himself. He knew, deep inside, he would never find anyone like her. Kim was going back to her life in the CIA. Something told Dan their paths might cross again. How, and when, he did not know. Life was like that. But he knew that he would treasure her, and the moments they had shared, for the rest of his life.

"What will you do, now?" Kim asked, her head resting against his chest.

"Maybe head up into the forest, and go south into Thailand. See where my two eyes take me."

Kim raised her head, and they kissed again. "You have my number, right?"

Dan did not carry a cell phone. He tapped his head. "In there. Forever." He smiled.

The flight was called again. Dan kneeled and faced Maya. She smiled. Dan tickled her ear, then smiled back. They hugged, and as Dan felt the tiny, thin arms around his neck, that strange, uplifting sensation reared up inside him, lightening his heart, taking him to another place.

"You'll be going to school now, right?"

Maya said, "What if they don't like me?"

Dan said, "They will, don't worry."

Kim draped a protective arm around Maya. "You are easy to like, honey. Trust me."

Dan stood up, and embraced Kim one last time. He watched them go, Kim holding Maya's small hand tightly, like she was afraid to let go.

He watched till they disappeared around the bend of the gates, and he couldn't see them anymore.

A heavy weight had formed at the back of his throat, and he found it hard to swallow.

He rubbed his eyes, put his sunglasses on, and walked out, a solitary, lonely figure in the crowd of the airport.

THE END

EXCLUSIVE OFFER

I would love to hear from you, so please feel free to visit my FB author page
- https://www.facebook.com/WriterMickBose

My website - https://www.mickbose.com

or write to me at mick@mickbose.com.

If you want advance notice of a new title and other offers, then Join the readers' group. It's spam free and I will only contact you when I have a new release.

Join here - https://www.subscribepage.com/p6f4a1

Made in the USA
Lexington, KY
03 May 2019